MW01165508

MAN ON THE
EDGE

A Novel by
BARRY WOOD

Associate Editors:
Kenneth Wood, Grace Lindblom,

Cover by: Janet Sierzant. Thanks for her constant efforts with the cover and formatting.

La Maison Publishing, Inc.
Vero Beach, Florida
www.lamaisonpublishing.com

It matters not how strait the gate,
How charged with punishments the scroll, I am the
master of my fate
I am the captain of my soul.

Excerpt from W. E. Henley's Invictus

Notes from the Author

At times, pages in this novel will read as a primer for the actual events leading up to, and into, the Second World War. This was imperative to convey a feeling for the era and for the characters emotions, reactions, and terrors in those frightening years.

Looking at a map you will find the cities and locations given are actual. Yet BergFalke, the castle, minor locals, and Ravensmoor are composites and therefore must be fictional.

Most, if not all, European maps of the era were measured in kilometers. As the United States has never accepted this form of measurement, I have converted them to miles. The same holds for English weights and measures. If I wrote a person weighed 13.6 stone, and was 1.9 meters tall, most Americans would not know the person's weight was around 190 pounds with a height of just under six foot three inches. The same difficulty holds true for the European Temperature Celsius; I stayed with Fahrenheit and also changed most of the English monetary system of pounds and shillings to dollars. Again as to actual UK English spelling versus US English, such as kerb for curb, monetary cheque for check, colour for color and then lorry for truck, I have kept most of them Americanized. I hope you understand and agree with all this.

I would like to thank Robert D. Colburn, Research Coordinator, IEEE History Center, Rutgers University, who supplied invaluable insight into wireless J-E transceivers/ transmitters, and clandestine aircraft in WWII.

The Joan-Eleanor (J-E) High Frequency Radio System referred to in the book is an actual wireless system developed for the US Office of Strategic Services (OSS) by Mr. Al Gross, IEEE Fellow, Mr. DeWitt R. Goddard, and Lt. Cmdr. S. H. Simpson. The J-E system was classified Top Secret until 1976. I have used it a bit ahead of its time, as with the British de Havilland Mosquito warplane.

With the exception of Mr. Colburn, I have been my own researcher. I trust people with more expertise in historical events will forgive any errors.

Special thanks to Peter Haase, whose advice and support were quite helpful. Peter is the author of six books including *The Gang of Seven*.

Appreciation also to good friend and Author Gene Hull for far more than can be listed.

Endless thanks and love to my wife, Christina for many reasons including the review of 600 pages in first manuscript form to refine points from a reader's perspective.

Barry Wood

April, 2015

Prologue

North by West of Kufstein, Northern Austria, August 1940.

A CURSE BURST worthlessly into the night. "Damn it! Why did I allow them to lure me here again?"

His fingers rubbed across the black star sapphire ring. He quieted…remembering something else. In sorrow he whispered.

"You tried to help me, Daphne…yet I drove you away."

Alone, gasping, deep in the shadows, he stood on the narrow ledge, attached to a climber's line, fastened off to pitons driven into a shallow crevice.

He shivered from exhaustion and the raw wind as it snatched at his uniform and seemed to clutch about his throat.

Once again he realized his surroundings and gazed into the night and face the terror of his undertaking. Bile came to his throat. He vomited.

Waning moonlight signaled the coming of dawn. He glanced at the wall of stone that loomed above and disappeared into the night sky. The wall continued down past him to fall away three hundred feet into the trees. He'd been here before. Two years before. A lifetime had passed before this moment.

A castle was below him, off to the right. Interior lights flickered within. A Strauss waltz faintly emanated from the castle while shadows shimmered as phantoms behind the drapes. It was strange he thought, there were no blackout curtains, then remembered the castle was far from a city…and the bombers.

Other than his own harsh breathing, the sounds of the waltz were all that intruded on the night.

As he moved to ease the ache of his cramped position, his forehead caught the eyesight of his weapon. He gritted his teeth and wiped away the blood that dripped along the scar down his face. The cold night air would soon ease. The east sun would bring some warmth, yet with it, the beginning, and the end, of his undertaking.

VOLUME ONE

PRELUDE TO WAR

Chapter 1

BERGFALKE (Mountain Falcon) Spa, Northwest of Kufstein, Northern Austria.

September 1938. Two years earlier.
"Jim...Hello there!"
The melancholy of his thoughts dissolved as James Royce turned toward the woman who called out his name and now strode toward him. He hunted through his mind and found her there, there in a niche he hoped forgotten.

For the past few days, Royce spent most of his time on the sundeck of a spa tucked away in the Austrian foothills, a spa known primarily to experienced climbers. He needed time to convalesce, gather himself. The four Nazi youth persistently pervading his mind were not about to depart. Yet still, he struggled to grasp his anger back then, and the ensuing tragedy.

Royce had reached the point where there was no one he wanted to meet. No one. He had expected to continue this way, yet now, damn it, he saw that wasn't to be.

Royce remembered her. She hadn't been forgotten. She was the exception—a breathtaking exception.

He rose to meet her, murmuring. "Hello, Daphne."

"That's all? Hello?" She really wasn't surprised.

His mind raced over the two years since he had seen Daphne Elliot. She was hard to decipher. How she could even look at him, or why she liked him back then, he still failed to fathom. The forceps the doctor used to help his mother birth him, had gripped his head and crushed, atrophied and finally killed tissue and blood vessels.

Although the indentation in the back of his head was unseen under hair, his face remained marred by a white depression. A crease, which ran down the right side of his temple and cheek, then continued past the edge of his lip and across his chin. No matter how deeply he tanned in the thin mountain air and sun, the white disfigurement remained. He knew he wasn't attractive.

He was kept conscious of that fact since childhood. From his father's coldness, to the cruel jests of his classmates at Harrow and University, he was always reminded. As if he needed reminders. The fights that followed found him with a distinct lack of friends, male or female, as he grew to manhood.

He never explained the scar. People who had to associate with him at his father's factory assumed he'd been struck by lightning. That, they felt, would help explain his mood swings and perpetual endeavors to be alone. He let them think what they wished. They didn't know, nor did he ever give any reason behind his brusque manner.

And so, he became a recluse, further inhibiting his persona with only his older brother, David, David's wife, Mary, and one or two others who could look directly at him without flinching.

Royce met Daphne Elliot during a climb. He above her, alone, she below with friends who struggled up a moderate pitch. As he rested on a shelf glancing down, it became obvious her friends were struggling, not her. This woman, he immediately saw, was no novice. She picked her steps, glanced ahead, and found the unseen track. She caught his eye for a moment, a quick smile before looking on. He smiled only inwardly. God, how her green eyes sparkled.

When the group reached the shelf, they sagged down laughing, thoroughly exhausted. Yet the woman did not sit, nor was she tired. She searched for the man she'd seen and found him off to the side, his head turned away, ignoring them.

"Excuse me." An unusual, American accent, yet shaded with South England.

Without thought, he looked up, yet not saying a word.

The green eyes blinked seeing his face, although she didn't miss a beat. "I watched you climb. You're incredibly skilled."

He nodded, lowering his head again to dismiss her, yet thinking how beautiful she was, those green eyes, her auburn hair glowing in the light.

She wouldn't be put off. "My name's Daphne. Yours?"

She held out her hand. He couldn't help but see it. Ignoring the hand, he stood and looked her straight in the face to be sure she fully saw the scar. Then he picked up his gear to leave.

She didn't budge. He was confused. Why did she speak to him, or stay after seeing his face? Was it fun for her? Amusing her friends? That must be it. He started to walk off.

"Mister whatever your name is, could I climb with you?"

Her words stopped him. He was captivated. Not able to take another step. This American woman was certainly brazen, wouldn't simply leave well enough alone, let him leave.

"Why?" His word a challenge, more than a question.

"Why? Quite clear really. Because I want to learn from you and you really shouldn't climb alone."

"My climbing alone isn't your concern."

"True. So then let's just say I want to learn from you."

"I'm not an instructor. Go find some pretty, blond boy down in Kufstein. I'm *sure* he could help you."

She showed no affront, simply stood, brash, and waited. He was at a loss for what more to say, and blurted out.

"Some other time."

"That's a put off and you know it. You're not being honest. Climb with me now and I promise not to say another word, other than to ask your name again."

He had never met anyone so annoying. "You've your friends to help down."

"Off to the east there's a simple hiking trail, I'll bet you know that."

He was trapped. "Tell your friends where the trail is. My name is Royce."

He would take her for a climb, he thought, a little tougher area, wear her out. Then with not so much as wave goodbye, he'd be gone. That would be the best way to get rid of her type.

She never quit in their climb. Wearied to the point of exhaustion, she wouldn't give up. He'd been quick to find her a good climber. But now, tiring, she would go on until a misstep…and that would be wrong of him. He stopped. Not a word spoken to this point. Daphne stared at the back of his head sucking in deep, painful breaths in the thin air.

"Well? What are we stopping for...*Royce*? Or whatever your damn name is."

He turned and looked at her unsteady stance. She was an exhausted, defiant mess. Yet by God, he couldn't deny it, she was one beautiful, defiant mess.

As she blinked away the sweat, he started to smile, then to laugh. She became incensed. "You...BASTARD! You... you damn BASTARD!"

He couldn't stop his laugher...not knowing why.

In some bizarre way, despite, or due to her near collapse, she found his laughter went from maddening to infectious. Through her tears, she began to see the absurdity of it all, and somehow started laughing with him.

At last, when he could speak. "Miss, that's the first time I've ever been called that to my face. At least by a woman!"

"I find that very difficult...no, *extremely* difficult to believe, because...because, well...you *really* are!"

They sat on the ground and laughed themselves hoarse.

* * *

Royce should have guessed that Daphne was his true opposite. Naturally striking looks, loose auburn hair, lithe climber's body, assured, confident in her own skin. She was outgoing and outspoken for a woman in the 1930s. Still, it was those radiant green eyes, as she gazed his way...eyes that mesmerized him.

Nevertheless, from the moment she spoke he was on guard. Why would any woman, much less a woman this beautiful, be friendly to a man with his face? He knew it certainly wasn't his personality. There was something else uncommon as well. Women didn't take climbing seriously; at least seriously enough to come anywhere near her expertise. Women usually walked about with their long, pretty skirts and expensive hiking poles. Yet this woman wore woolen pants, thin leather gloves, and boots, well-worn climber's boots. There definitely must be something eccentric about her. It would probably be true that climbing was all they held in common. He had nothing else to offer, other than money, and he doubted that mattered to her. Upper crust, he thought, American or not.

Her speech pattern gave that away. Boston he supposed.

Otherwise, nothing gave a hint of her background.

Eventually, after their initial hostility faded, she told more of herself. Her mother English, hence her English name. Her father American. They once lived between London and Boston, although they had stayed in the States for four years, until close to the end of the Great War in 1918.

When she was eight, the family returned to England to see her brother who suffered a severe wound in the war. Afterward, her father returned to Boston, the parents divorced and Daphne elected to stay with her mother in England. She told Royce she had no other secrets. She had always been single and at twenty-eight, traveled the continent often, loving the Austrian Tyrol.

* * *

At the spa, Royce thought of their bygone days as he held the chair for Daphne. For a few moments, they kept to their private feelings—she could tell he was recalling their time together.

Slowly he filled out his memory and smiled, remembering their angry first encounter. After that, their companionship, morning hikes through the mists, evening strolls over moon washed trails. The silence they shared, no need for words to express their pleasure. How they enjoyed their nights of lovemaking, their warmth…

She broke into his thoughts. "It's been two years, Jim."

"Yes, now that you mention it. I came to Austria in '35, met you in '36. Now it's '38. Two years."

He looked worn, she felt, yet did not ask why. "What have you been up to?"

He was still climbing around the Tyrol, he said. No, he hadn't been back to England, perhaps he would. Yes, did keep in touch with his brother, David, by telephone, wire, or letter when he got the chance, or remembered to, which wasn't often.

He asked her what she'd been doing. Well, she pondered, mostly climbing, that and back to England to visit her mother and friends in Belgravia, London. She and Mum had gone to the lakes district to see her brother, and then she came back to the Tyrol. Her mother wasn't well, she commented, yet said nothing further regarding her. The conversation labored into the trivial, then the awkward. He wanted to say so much. Yet couldn't. She waited for some word, a sign—which never came.

"Daphne, I really must leave for a spa further into the mountains. I'll need the remaining daylight to get there."

Devastated, she watched as he picked up his pack and an old bamboo ski pole. "Just like that, Jim…same as before?"

He said nothing.

Daphne stared at him bravely. "This will be the last time we meet. I'm returning to England, probably for a very long time."

He turned and nodded. "Then I truly wish you well, Daphne …God speed."

Half a mile away he stopped, turning to look down at the spa. He could see she still sat there. What to do? What should he do? If he let himself think about her, he knew he cared deeply. What difference did that make? She only thought of the present. If they became too serious, always together, he thought that in a few weeks from now she'd wake one day, look at his face, and wonder what she had done. Wasted her life and friends for this?

He shook his head to free himself from the thought. Was this fear an excuse? Did he need her? Maybe that's what he should ask. His only real needs, before her, were to get away from England and the shock of what happened there. Find contentment in the mountains, away from people. He had always been that way, from his youth into manhood. The mountains. Find solace. Away from people, deep in Cumbria or the Highlands of Scotland. And now, it was Austria. Yet a different and worse hell had found him, even here.

At times, the love of mountains saved his sanity. Their majesty, their treasured hush. To lose himself, to wander along valley paths or summits for endless days was the only real pleasure he knew. Away from meeting people. He would never have given thought to explain this need to survive. It was, subconsciously, simply his way to endure.

He shuddered. An insidious murmur from deep within grated on his nerves to whisper he no longer belonged. At first, the voices were so alien he refused to listen.

He knew one reason. He was letting them—those four German brats—haunt him. To forget, he tried to force his thoughts away from them and drive his body and mind to exhaustion. He had tried to regain his former strength along passes and ledges. Yet in the end, he came to grasp that doctor was right. By his refusal to face the inescapable truth, he had dropped once again into a state of lethargy and allowed the inner demons their argument.

* * *

It had been into these reflections Daphne Elliot had imposed, however innocently. Still, she had come, unbidden and unexpected. God, he thought, how nice it was to see her. The feeling when she'd say his name. Her distressed look as he left. Christ, how that cut him to the bone. Should he go back and speak to her about…about what?

Right now, he couldn't tell her what had happened. Yet is that the only excuse not to return?

"The devil take it." He muttered, and started back.

Daphne met him half way. "I saw you stop and turn. I willed you to come back."

"Then you've beguiled me, I fear."

"You've nothing to fear from me, Jim."

"I guess we'll have to see, won't we?"

She took his arm as they walked back to the sundeck, shaded now by the mountain. The air chilled, the patrons gone inside. Royce and Daphne put on wool jackets, and remained alone on the deck.

"Is it by accident you found me here, Daphne?'

"Being too honest, Jim, no. I was in Garmisch. A friend of remembered seeing us together in Innsbruck and recognized you even with your new beard. She saw the scar and told me you were around here. I guessed BergFalke, and lo and behold, here you are."

He said nothing, noncommittal, so she asked. "If you're not pleased I'm here, why didn't you just keep walking? I would have let you, you know. I did before. Why did you come back?"

Typical, Daphne, he smiled. Get to the point. It must be the American blood in her.

"You probably know that answer better than I."

"Yes, I probably do, and perhaps someday it will dawn on you as well. Until then, I'll wait."

"Why? That's what I don't understand."

"Because even though you try to hide it, you're really a damn nice bloke."

"Bloke? You're becoming more Anglicized every day. And aside from that, being a nice bloke as you say doesn't get me past my face."

"You know, Jim, I've given that a lot of thought, probably too much actually, still I've come to work something out. Now this is about as deep as I can get, so try to understand me. Your face doesn't bother you as much as it troubles you that other people have to look at it. In other words, I think you're more upset for the person who has to look at you than for yourself."

She was fumbling, "Damn it, this sounded simple in my mind until I try to put it into words. You feel bad that the other person has to look at you. There! That's the best I can do. And, I might as well add, it's why you hide in these mountains."

He had never heard this before—no one ever cared— and didn't know how to respond, yet he tried to keep it lighthearted.

"Really, Daphne, you've been over thinking the situation. How can you look at my face—now be truthful about this—and say I'm not an ugly man?"

"I've seen worse, I've seen far worse."

It was a flat statement, no sentiment. He didn't know how to respond. Then he saw she was about to cry. He put his hand on her shoulder, "What is it? What do you want to tell me?"

"I don't *want* to tell you anything, but I've got to, for you, for us. I've thought of this long and hard and it will to be hell for me."

He waited, watched her get control of her emotions.

"Before the Great War, Jim, my family travelled back and forth between Belgravia in London and States. When the war started, we were living in Boston. My brother Robert, who, believe me, was handsome, couldn't wait to get into the war. He was only twenty, at Harvard, when he and two friends left to join the army. In three months they became officers and went to France, assigned to the American Expeditionary Force, the AEF. At first he sent back great letters about the exciting time the three Harvard men were having.

I was only seven or eight and I can remember my parents

reading them aloud repeatedly. Then, the letters stopped. We heard the AEF was putting a big push on against the Germans in the Meuse Argonne, so we thought that to be the reason. However, no more letters came and my parents were worried."

Daphne's eyes began to water. She blew her nose, laughed nervously, then took a breath and continued. "Even with my father's contacts, we couldn't find out anything, the fog of war and all that blather, you know. Eventually Dad received a telegram that stated Robby was wounded and in England. My parents cried, they were so relieved he'd only been wounded. Dad beat on the War Department to get information when Robby would come home, but he couldn't get any answers. We finally received a letter from the Addington Palace Hospital, near Croydon in South London, stating Robert had decided not to return to the States. Right then my parents knew something was terribly wrong and they became desperate."

Daphne stopped, wiped her eyes, and then rushed her words. "It was brutal getting to England with U Boats still out there and we were frantic by the time we got to Southampton. From there we hurried by train to London.

We got to the Center and were treated courteously, although my folks could see we weren't welcome. They kept us in the visitor's room while a doctor agreed to ask my brother to see us, despite Rob already stating flatly he wouldn't. I was standing off to the side and I saw where the doctor went down the corridor and through a door. When the doctor came back, he didn't see me and I heard him tell Dad that it was no use. That wasn't good enough for me so before anyone could catch me up, I ran down the corridor and pushed open that door.

My brother turned from a window, certainly not expecting me. I went into shock...Jim. The whole right side of his face was gone. His eye, his ear, his cheek were gone...gone. God, there was only bone and ragged flesh. That sight was flashed into my memory forever. My poor brother's handsome face, destroyed. I...I fainted."

"Daphne, why don't you stop?"

"No, damn it! I've gone this far, damn it, I've got to finish. I was unconscious and Rob relented after seeing me fall. The doctors bandaged his wounds so my parents would not react as I did. To see their son alive was all that mattered.

"Over the next few days, the Center molded a mask of rubber and leather. It was his seeing us there and that we still loved him, that helped Rob come out of his hell. Dad remembered a cottage we all enjoyed once in the Lakes District, just outside the little village of Bow-on-Windermere. He bought a lovely place on the lake and we took Rob there. He's still there. He paints and walks, has no real friends. That's why I go back to England twice every year for a month or two to see my mother and we go visit him. We drive him crazy. He loves to have us come and he's not too sad to see us go. He's thirty-seven now...a loner because of his face. Strange, a loner like you—now as I think of it."

"I don't know what to say, Daphne. I feel terrible for you and ashamed of myself."

"I didn't tell you this to make you feel ashamed. I told you so you wouldn't ever ask me again how I can look at you."

Daphne deliberately omitted portions of the story. Even at eight, her psyche had been scarred. Only after being under psychiatric care for two years, did she come to accept what happened, and once again truly love her brother. She also failed to mention that her father, Roger Elliot, had always doted on his one son. He planned on his son assuming Elliot Corporation's brokerage business and never got past Robert's wounds. Roger Elliot stayed on at the cottage for a month. Then said he had to get back to the states and handle his business affairs. This was true. He said he would be back, which wasn't. They knew he wouldn't return. And so later, the divorce.

* * *

After Daphne's revelation about her brother, she and Royce came to an unspoken accord. Neither quite knew what that meant, although one thing was sure, they would continue to see each other, however erratically. Despite this, she still sensed something was amiss. She couldn't put a finger on it; he was different from before. Aged, weaker, not strong willed as she remembered.

Something ate at him. He had changed too much in the past two years for her not to notice. What happened, he wouldn't talk about, and she thought that was him, only now even more so. He had grown a beard since she'd seen him and now it was sun bleached, streaked with gray. She thought the gray odd, as he was only thirty-three. Nonetheless, the beard looked good, helped hide the scar, if only a trace. Was that the reason for it, she wondered, or was it hard for him to shave, knowing the way he lived in the mountains for days on end.

They spent two days together and enjoyed the time. He did seem fragile, yet Daphne could see him begin to unwind.

BergFalke was built beneath the escarpment of seven inspiring peaks. As they moved over the narrow plateau above the escarp and further on toward the mountains, he taught her how to study the formation's track, the seam as he called it, the hand and footholds needed. Remember to reach only as far as she could grasp and hold as long as needed, he reminded. Visualize everything they climbed past, as they must descend, as well.

They sat eating sandwiches, quiet, absorbed by the snowcapped slopes, the fir trees distinct in their green on the snow. BergFalke was below them and after that, nothing but meadows down to the valley of the Inn River. Below the snow line, miniature colorful chalets were dotted now and then on either side a meandering dusty road.

He continued to teach her, she improved. She learned more in five hours than five months in the past. Finally tired, they started walking the remaining way to the spa, watching the sun lay a golden patina on the mountains.

"Be careful of stepping across those rocks, Daphne, they're covered with lichen, don't slip."

She stopped and turned, resting her hands and chin on her climbing pole. "Now, Jim, thanks for the advice, but I began climbing when I was eight. Started on a little mountain called Mount Washington in New Hampshire. I may not have your ability and technique, *yet,* but at least I know whether I'm stepping on moss or lichen. I guess you're apprehensive because of some clumsy women you've climbed with in the two years since I've been gone."

"Fine, Daphne, I'm only trying to save you from the embarrassment of a sitzmark."

He touched her cheek. "And, I've never taken another woman for a climb, or even a hike—before or since, you."

When they reached the plateau, he put his arm around her as they continued walking. She slipped her hand in his back pocket. She smiled; no need to wonder if there were other women in his life.

After two days, their enjoyment came to an end. She had to leave. She told him on the sundeck after a hike while they snapped pictures with his Leica and sipped Uzo.

"Jim, I've got to go to London. I should have left before now, but I wanted to see you."

Was there a fleeting look of relief in his eyes? She tried to ignore it. "Mother's not well. She lives in London. I should start for home on the morrow."

"I'm sorry about your mother. I hope it isn't too serious."

"I think it may be very serious."

"Then I'll avoid the subject, so as not to upset you more."

"You don't seem bothered that I have to leave."

"To be truthful, I'm not." He saw her try to hide the hurt, and quickly added. "I might be leaving shortly also."

"Really, to where?"

When he said England, she was delighted. "Why might you leave? I thought here was your world."

"It was, but…a number of reasons. Look around, haven't you noticed people have changed since the Nazi's annexed Austria and the troops paraded in? I was in Vienna in March when they came, the conquering heroes. People waved those little swastikas, yet a lot more cried. Since then, I hear over fifty thousand people have been removed. These are not good times, Daphne, and they will get worse, I fear."

"You can't be talking war? It's only been what, not twenty years since one ended? How on this earth could our leaders let this happen?"

"I won't go as far as to say war, yet things I saw in Vienna and even just east of us in Salzburg aren't good. I also overheard talk from other climbers that the Germans have taken over everything, police, all the banks, businesses, you name it. They've deported thousands of people, more specifically, Jews."

"To where?"

24

"To what they call relocation camps, and that can't be good because there are rumors that as they do, they confiscate everything the Jews had."

"You know rumors are always around, Jim. When I was in France, people felt it's only Germany taking back land that was taken from them after the war. And right or wrong, I understood the Austrian people asked them to come."

"Those of German blood, yes. They don't know what they're in for. Yet it shouldn't matter what the German people say. Austria was an independent country. Look, Daphne, I admit I never gave much thought to this, being tucked away here. I assumed nothing would bother me. Then something happened that opened my eyes to what these people are like. Don't ask me about it because I can't even explain it to myself yet. My opinion is Europe's going to change for the worse with that possessed dictator in Germany."

"You don't think he's just another pompous ass, like that Mussolini braggart in Italy?

"Not at all. Il Duce threw his army and air force at a bunch of Ethiopian tribesmen and then had to rush in more men and all his air force to beat them. He's too full of himself and his dreams of a new Roman Empire. Hitler's different, he's a schemer. No one lifted a finger when he took over France's Saar Basin and the demilitarized Rhineland. Not even France said a word, so that simply made him go for more. Do you mind a history lesson?"

"No, however you've now made me nervous."

"I want you to be nervous and that's why I'm glad you have to leave. Really, it's for the best."

"Tell me then, what do you think will happen with Hitler."

"I only look at his record. He came up as a fraud, spent time in prison and from what I hear, he wrote a book, stating what he intends to do and everyone dismisses him as barmy. Next thing you know he has a following of unemployed soldiers and brutes. Puts them back in uniform—Germans are like the Brits in that way you know—love uniforms, and began bullying everybody. People started to believe he'd bring back glory and respect, or perhaps fear is a better word. Well, so far he's doing it. Look at the record. Along the way he received the second highest vote tally after Hindenburg who, I might add, wasn't well and couldn't withstand Hitler's intensity. Then, I think it was in '33, Hitler was made Chancellor of Germany! A blatant anti-Semite, a fanatic, is Chancellor! Can you fathom that?"

"I know some of this from when I was in England a while back, Jim. Still, most people over there don't seem to care. What's the matter with them? Don't they see it?"

"It's they don't want to see it or face the future. But the future is coming. Look at Hitler now."

"I heard he pushed through something called the Enabling Act, didn't he, Jim? And that enabled him to become Dictator, and Germany's no longer a voting Republic."

"That's correct. But then his problem was his old friend, a thug named Ernst Röhm, had his own little army. Röhm helped put Hitler where he is and he wanted a share of the pie. So what did Hitler do? If you haven't one iota of morality, it was simple. He had the militant arm under his control slaughter hundreds of Röhm's men in one night! Good friend Röhm included.

"I'll try to shorten this up, Daphne. Hindenburg dies. Hitler becomes Supreme Commander of the armed forces. It's true the army was not much at the time due to the Treaty of Versailles in '18 after the war. However, he has sure changed that. His glider club is now an air force, the Luftwaffe, and he's building the army up to over divisions. This is strictly against the Treaty and no one does a thing about it. At the time he did it, England and France, working together, could have finished him right there and then. Yet our Prime Minister, Baldwin, ignored what Hitler was doing, so France ignored it too. Nothing has been done to stop him. And Chamberlain taking over last year as England's Prime Minister has made things worse."

"Why didn't France stop him? I recall when Hitler took the Saar Basin from them."

"Yes, that was in '35, Daphne, when Hitler took back the Saar. They let him do it without so much as a whimper. So as I said, he remilitarized the Rhineland as well. Now, Hitler's consolidating, except in April he started trying out his new Condor Legion. That's part of his new air force and they're bombing the hell out of Guernica and other cities in Spain to help Franco win their Civil War against the Communists."

They reached the spa, climbed to the deck and rested on the chairs. Royce stopped talking, staring intensely across the veil of snow. What he saw, she didn't know.

"How do you know all this, Jim? You don't talk to people; you hardly listen to the radio."

"Most is from my brother, David. He has contacts throughout the Ministry and Military in England, a lot of hush-hush stuff. He was furious with former PM Baldwin, and now it's Chamberlain who David feels is easily deceived. Yet other countries are doing nothing to stop Hitler either. Your country, America, is strictly hands off. Until two months ago, David would send me newspapers wrapped up tightly. In them were his memos on all this and I would send him news I found here, like the Nazi's in Vienna. No one inspected newspapers in those days. Now the Germans have control of the mails, so David only wrote me not to send info and come home, Father's not well."

"Oh, I'm sorry."

"Don't be. Our Father died in '34. It's David's way of saying I could get in trouble as a spy if I send any info. Also, get out of Europe."

"When did he write that?"

"About two months ago. I know, don't shake your head—yes, I should have left. But like everyone else, I ignored the signs, felt David was exaggerating. Now I'm sure he isn't."

"Why not, Mister Unintentional Spy?"

He laughed at that. "Daphne, you have a lot of questions."

"Yes, questions you're not answering. You've had a run in with them, haven't you? Tell me!"

"Another question. Subject's closed."

She was stung, again. That was he. He saw the indignation.

"I'm sorry, Daphne. There are some things I can't talk to you about right now. Someday when I know…then…"

He fumbled for words. Somehow, she understood. "Let's let it slide, Jim, but someday, you've got to tell me."

He nodded, saying nothing.

She would have to pack; the bus for Salzburg was leaving early in the morning. "Jim, why don't you come with me now? There's nothing to keep you here."

He sat back, hands behind his head. "To be dramatic, I have

a feeling I'll never come here again. So if not, I want one last hike, to clear my mind." He stared into those green eyes. "Then look forward to seeing you in England."

She felt something was hidden. "I could put my trip off a day and climb with you tomorrow."

"One day, Daphne, we will talk. But it's more than just a climb I must do, and for that, I need to be by myself."

It was not said sharply, yet she wasn't allowed in. "Jim, you know it could be dangerous if you stay any longer."

He laughed. "Daphne, you've seen me climb. Danger's in my breakfast food."

She rose, walked past him, cuffing the top of his head with her hand. "At times, Jim, you can be a pain in the arse."

He laughed, watched her move up the stairs. "English accent of sorts, but still wonderfully American."

Later that night he handed her a letter to mail as soon as she reached England. It was to his brother he said, to let him know he'd be home, probably within two weeks.

She finally believed he was going home and couldn't have been happier. She looked at the address.

Sir David Walker Royce,

Ravensmoor, Burton Green, Coventry, West Midlands, Warwickshire, England. No return address.

She looked, questioning Royce, 'Sir'?"

"Yes. My father won a Knighthood. David is first son, so he took it." He paused. "That's rather crass of me. I don't know why I would say it like that. David is doing great service for the Crown in his own right."

He was embarrassed. She wondered if he had expressed his true feelings.

Chapter 2

ROYCE SAW DAPHNE off in the morning, not wanting her to go, yet knowing it was for the best, best for him as well. He needed time alone. He decided on a half day tune up on one of the cliffs not far from the spa, although the sun was not in the position to shade the rock and make the climb more difficult, which he wanted. Until then, he whiled away the time packing for his longer two or three day hike, planning to leave the heavy climbing gear in his room. He was not going into the high approaches; simply stay above the tree line. Packing enough canned food for two days, he added one set of warm clothes plus three pairs of socks. Also crampons, for traction, in case he hit ice or crusted snow, steel spike pitons, with clipping holes and a dozen carabineers, locking metal loops which snap into the pitons. The pitons and carabineers were tossed in from habit. The same held true for the coil of line added to the backpack, he had no plans on using that either. A short climbing ice axe was strapped to the outside of the pack over a poncho. He threw in a few other odd items, a toothbrush and soap. Soap was not a priority item as was only going to be gone for two days, still, he threw in a used bar. He finished by strapping a down sleeping bag to the top of the pack. He left his backcountry skis as there was not enough snow in the passes and the spa's wireless set forecast none.

Finishing his packing, he saw the early afternoon sun was past its zenith and now fell on the area he had chosen for the climb. He estimated that same area would be in shadow in two hours, making the descent more difficult. For this exercise, he wanted five strenuous hours free climbing.

The cliff he'd chosen was a mile from the spa and no one would be about. The last guests left on Daphne's bus as the weather had cooled and vacations at an end. Royce studied the face on his approach and picked his line and working up the cliff to the first ledge did not appear difficult. There were crevices for his fingers and foot holds. He started up with deceptive ease, never looking where he was, only to his next position. He continued this way until he reached the ledge, pleased at a good half hour of exercise. To reach the next ledge was more complicated, not for his ability, but simply due to the scree, loose rock, leading up to the cliff itself. When he had moved over to the cliff face, he found it coated with a thin sheet of ice. Verglas, the locals called it, and it was melting in the sun. Interesting, he thought, this would keep his attention. As it turned out, the face wasn't vertical and fell away seven or eight degrees. He could build a friction with his body even though the wall was wet. He started upward before seeing a fissure, two or more feet deep, three to four feet wide. He smiled, not having chimney climbed in a long time. Putting his back on one side of the fissure and feet the other, he pushed up with his legs, then braced with his back and hands while bringing each leg up, to push up again. Monkey climbing they called it. By the end of the fissure, his aching legs were giving him notice. It had taken him an hour to go a hundred and fifty feet holding that position. Every muscle quivered.

He rested, looking at the next level. Uninspiring. There was a small col, a saddle, between two peaks, not in the least challenging. Instead of continuing, he sat back, munching on a sandwich. Admiring the view down the valley, he waited for the sun to shadow his descent; shadows would make it more deceptive.

Daphne, he reflected. His way of life was ending so she was to blame. She came to him; he didn't seek her out. He admitted he loved her. What if she found someone else? Or something terrible happened on her way back to England. He shivered with the thought. He never had this feeling about someone and couldn't say he liked it in any way.

Clouds hid the sun. Should he have gone with her? He couldn't. This had to be alone. Alone, where no one would see him try to shake off the demons crouching in his mind. God, he loved her. He wanted to be whole when he saw her again.

Holding himself together the last two days had been difficult. He managed to hold on...for her. She could see something wasn't right, knew him better than he realized. Now she's left and, starting tomorrow, he would walk into a mind numbing state. Time to think of what he had done to the four of them.

But that would be for tomorrow's journey; put his mind on today. Starting his descent, his mind cleared. No feelings troubled him. Moving with surefooted grace, he flowed with the pattern of the mountain's face. Not a handhold missed, a foot placed incorrectly, he never stopped. He knew he was a remarkable climber and where he wanted to be. Except now he wanted her to be here as well.

He returned to the spa, the sun's glow gone from the valley. He planned to eat early, check his packing, and get a good night's sleep before the next day's hike. But first, a nightcap. The spa's pub was empty. After waiting, Royce put money on the bar, poured out a scotch with a splash of water. He settled into an old leather wingback chair in front of a waning fire, half awake, comfortable.

The barman returned, saw Royce, the drink, the money, and lumbered over.

"You English?"

"Yes."

"You friend, she is gone to English?"

"Yes."

"She smart. You be smart too, to go. Austria no longer good for you, anyone."

Royce looked up at the man, knowing he was the owner, climbing and skiing instructor as well as barman. He was also big and overweight, yet still obviously strong.

He sat down unbidden, pointing at Royce's face. "Blitz?"

"Yes." Knowing the German word for lightning, and to say yes would save further conversation about his face.

The man dropped the subject. "I watch you climb."

Royce was surprised, "I didn't see you."

"That because I on deck with telescope. It sees lot more better than you."

Tortured English or not, it struck Royce funny, his first laugh of the day. "My name is James Royce, call me Royce."

"Ernst Becker, you call me Beck. You relation to Rolls Royce wagens?"

Royce shook his head. "No, they're upper crust cars.

Beck didn't follow the comment, got up and, ignoring Royce's minor protest got him another scotch, no charge, and himself a stein of beer. Royce felt there was no choice but to stay. The man was pleasant; no reason to be rude.

"You great Bergsteiger, mountaineer, Royce. I watch you. You have the technik."

Royce nodded modestly.

"You got it. I was good, good. Not now, before this."

He rubbed his stomach.

Beck jumped up again, asking Royce to wait. Returning, he spread a series of colored cards. "Carte postale."

The cards predated The Great War.

"I climb or ski all." Pride filled Beck's voice.

Royce leaned forward, staring at the cards in wonderment mixed with a bit of jealousy. He read the titles. St. Moritz. Gesamtansicht…Der Jungfrau Gipfel, 4166 meters…Chamonix, Chalet et le Mountebank…das Wetterhorn…Wengeralp. Eiger und Monch…das Matterhorns 4482 meters…Grindelwald,

Card after card spread along a table. Royce dropped back in his chair staring at them. Although the cards weren't in English, he could understand the meters enough—one meter equaling a little over three feet—to be impressed. Beck, sat there proudly.

"I envy you. You've climbed all these, over how long?"

"Climbed all, skied with other men's. All over Alps I work, before buy here. Much years I do it. You could, you better."

Royce smiled, simply shaking his head slowly. This large man, well before The Great War—one card, postal marked 1906; thirty-two years ago—stood on the peak of all these mountains and surveyed the world around him. And, he did it with antique gear, nothing like being used in this day. Royce felt deflated. Beck saw it and told him that even in only the three hours he could watch Royce move on the cliff, he had a technique in free climbing that was superior to any Beck had seen in his lifetime.

"You as good climbing werkzeugs, tools?"

"I think so."

"Then no problem, just weather."

They both laughed. Weather, always the ultimate problem.

At the end of four scotches and seven steins of beer, they were passing friends, each telling stories into the night. At last, Royce managed to stand and say he would be back in a day or two.

"You should go England…instead."

"I will, after the climb."

"You should now go, Royce. I hear there be peoples, SS peoples—look for someone…with scar."

Royce was startled. "Where are they now?"

"Telefunken say Badgastein. Come west. Look in spas. All spa, hotel, all places. They know man is good climber…you?"

"More than likely."

"They bad people. They after you. I study you, you not be bad. Go England, now."

"I've got to do what I've planned. There's a reason—I should be back and gone before they get here. Still, just in case, will you hide the rest of my gear and skis?"

Beck nodded. "Get back quick, my new friend Royce."

It took longer in the morning to get started; he wasn't accustomed to drinking so much. It was after an hour on the trail, moving one hundred and thirty steps a minute over uneven terrain that he at last felt the hangover burn off. He thought of the searchers, it had to be the SS. Royce knew there were scores of spas and hotels for them to check between Badgastein and BergFalke Spa. It would take days to get here, if they even found this place, tucked as it was so far into the mountains.

He rid the SS from his mind by thinking about Daphne. He missed her already. When he got home to England, he would take her to meet his brother, David and his wife, Mary. Then the two of them would vacation in Scotland. He had two favorite mountains there, Glamaig and Marso in the Red Cullins. On the way to Marso, there was a wonderful old stone bridge to stop by and see across to the mountain. The Cullins would seem small to him now. Scottish mountains were older than the Alps; more worn and rounded, but he loved them still. It would be even more enjoyable with Daphne, wandering around the hills he had experienced when younger…and alone. He would have loved to have her listen to Ernst Becker's stories, too.

He smiled, Beck had not been around when he left, perhaps ten steins of strong Austrian beer kept him in bed. He liked him, then again, what true climber wouldn't? Being able to talk with the man, who must be close, or in, his seventies, about his experiences on those mountains was incredible, a once in a lifetime experience. Royce hoped when he returned to the spa he could learn more about climbing techniques before nineteen fourteen, before the Great War. Then Royce returned to the news Becker had given him of people looking for him. That was to be expected. The Nazi annexation had completely taken over Austria. What happened to those four Hitler Youth brats won't be forgotten. One of them even bragged he was the son of an SS Adolf Hitler Division Sturmbannführer, a Major.

Royce deliberated over the SS. The German word was Schutz Staffel. In English, Protective Squadron. He did think of another association for the letters SS, an automobile called the SS, Super Swallow, manufactured by Swallow Sidecar Ltd.* in his home city of Coventry. They'll get rid of that name, or at least the SS letters, he thought.

He glanced about, coming out of his musings. He'd held a north by westerly course for no reason other than he hadn't traversed the area. Since dusk had crept through the valleys he decided to camp under a protective overhang. This will be the time to face his demons, get them into the open, and let them bring on their dreads in the dark. Then face them and rid him of them. The staff in the sanatorium impressed on him this must be the process. Accept what he had done. Realize, everyone has rage within. Yet constrain it, not act upon it blindly. He had decided to reach deep into the why of his rage just before Daphne intruded. Now, at last, there was no one here, no one to interrupt. No excuse, alone to think about the people who were after him, or rather, the reason they were after him.

The demons began to stir.

*Renamed Jaguar Cars, Ltd.

Chapter 3

THE TRAGEDY BEGAN two months before Daphne found him at the spa. She had sensed he had a run-in with someone and she was only too right. Sitting under the overhang, he shuddered even now, at the thought of the four blond, young men. They had done considerable climbing and running in one of the numerous Hitler Jugend, the youth groups. For their excellence, they were given a holiday in Austria, a country recently overrun by their Führer, Adolf Hitler, and his SS. Their obnoxious manner created animosity in the Salzburg hotel pub where Royce was staying. The people resented them, which didn't bother the youths in the least. They were Germans and their attitude was they owned Austria, united with the Motherland. Hitler renamed it Ostmark, Eastern March. Why should anyone be unhappy, other than the Jews? The four young men laughed. The Jews, they said, were going to be extremely unhappy. Apart from their comments, and as infuriating, were the boasts of their durability. They said their blood was pure Aryan. Of course no explanation of what Aryan meant, yet no one dared question.

Royce had returned from a climb and, as he opened the door to the pub, an elderly couple was hurriedly leaving. They bumped him, apologized and then said, "If you are Jewish, don't go in there."

He went in, troubled by their remark, and saw the four youth laughing. By the look of the patrons, the Germans were the only ones having a good time and Royce understood at once what occurred. The Hitler Cult was now in Austria despite there being only a short time since the Anschluss, the takeover.

Royce ignored them, went to a corner of the bar, and ordered a scotch. They saw he was a climber by his gear and wandered over. When he looked to them, they pulled back in shock. The largest of the four shouted "Blitz" and fell to the floor as though struck by lightning. Royce ignored the rude fools. The four had their laugh yet still hung about him.

Since Royce had ordered in English, they knew he must be an Englishman, and verbally assailed him with their scientific proofs of German endurance, ability, desire. Everything German was superior to impure English blood. They kept hounding him to hike with them. Royce thought for a moment about the Jewish couple forced to leave and stood, trying to check an unexpected temper. He started to the stairs leading up to his room in the hotel; they followed, laughing stupidly. He smiled at the taunting youths, and spoke with forced calm.

"We'll hike. Six tomorrow morning, backpacks. Let's see if your endurance matches your mouths." He left, they giggled.

He lay awake sipping the warm scotch he'd taken with him and cursed himself for being trapped into this folly. He'd given them just what they were after, a contest. They would love to carry him back exhausted, and dump him on the floor of the pub. He foolishly challenged four superbly conditioned young men to an endurance contest. A hike! He should have said a climbing contest. There, he was sure he would be superior. Too late to change. He had no doubts of his ability; nevertheless, he was thirty-three. Whereas, this might not be considered old under normal standards, he was going to be hard pressed sustaining his strength against these sixteen or seventeen year olds. Another thing bothered him as well. Where did accepting challenge spring from? Why had he done it? He recognized he couldn't walk away or fight them physically, even though he had fights at Harrow, behind the buildings. He doubted that would help him here. Had there been no other way out? The best of a bad situation? He decided that must have been his reason. Except, it was not a simple challenge. He saw it in their eyes. They were easily angered and their faces, behind the sniggers, showed hate, even before a foot stepped on stone.

Determined not to be carried back, he set to a scheme to beat them. He had said backpacks without thinking. Past hikes helped him recall German climbers carried everything, save for their mother's picture and a chamber pot, in their backpacks.

Royce carried only essentials, the weight difference would

help. In addition to this, he must assume the lead. It was important to set the pace and the ground conditions. He couldn't let them go over ground where they could almost run. It had to get difficult, quickly.

Get above the timberline onto loose, rubble strewn ground, into rough country. Disrupt their running muscles and developed rhythm. He wanted them irritated, moving over unsure footing, growing tense, constantly alert. Get them angry, incautious, and careless. That was his plan. Yet, his prime hopes? They would continue drinking in the pub and forget the whole challenge.

* * *

Under his overhang, Royce could feel the rain. Slipping into his poncho, nervousness crept through him as, once more, the youth edged into his awareness. It was five-thirty the next morning when their shouting and hooting sharply awakened him.

"Come on English! You sleep to noon? Don't want to give up now. We will help drag you back!"

Royce grunted, his first hope gone, they were here and ready. He opened the window, "I told you six! So shut up! You're waking everyone."

"We want to wake everyone! We want them to see how you look when you leave and the dead dog you will be when we drag you back!"

He closed the window. The weather had turned colder. He could feel it, and the four Germans' were in shorts. At least that was good.

Dressing, he finished packing his light backpack and got a bite to eat downstairs. A few early risers, fearful for him, wished him luck. He walked outside to the Germans' ridicule of his long woolen pants. He walked past them to assume the lead. That was imperative. He glanced at their gear. First rate, in perfect repair, nothing forgotten or ill packed. It also appeared they truly had brought everything other than their mother's picture and pot, as Royce hoped.

The tallest of the group stepped in front of Royce, "My father is a Fallschirmjäger, and SS Major, Dieter Schmid. Staff Officer, Leibstandarte Adolf Hitler."

"What the devil is that?"

"Leibstandarte? In English it mean bodyguard."

"So your father is a bodyguard. What is that supposed to mean to me? Because I'm not impressed,"

"It means, English, I will lead."

Royce chanced it. "No. I made the challenge and I'll lead, starting now."

He walked off to the northwest, wondering what the Germans would do.

They soon fell in behind, they deeply wanted this show. Royce braced now, steeling himself. Do not stop…a long day lay ahead.

Across the foothills was undemanding, although Royce had all he could do to contain himself from constant jibes and insults in German. Yet after a half hour, they stopped their ridicule, soon discerning it was not provoking him and they weren't setting their breathing to the pace, which they found to be unexpectedly hurried, though not a problem.

Silence enveloped them, foothills fell behind, and scrub pine they pushed through, stood as grotesque spectators.

Above the timberline for two hours, the sky became a milky gray, giving little warmth. The breeze stiffened, blustery cold air swept across the barren stone. One of the Germans was speaking. Glancing back, Royce saw him point to his legs. Major Dieter Schmid's son shook his head. There would be no changing into long pants. Leg muscles would tighten with the cold. Tendons and ligaments not pliable lose their feeling. Royce loved their arrogance.

"That's it, please keep up your bloody pride." he whispered. He felt the change in his opponents self-confidence; their curse when shale gave way beneath a foot, a sudden gasp when a stride was broken. His plan might just work. He moved steadily across the range holding to a westerly course two hundred yards above the tree line. With his body now in hiking rhythm, his mind wandered. It wasn't in his nature to be goaded into such a contest. Yet with each step his control was, in some odd way, turning to anger. How did it happen? And why was he continuing to let it? Whatever the reason, it had the better of him. Admit it. "Beat them…or drop in your tracks."

* * *

Royce abruptly sat up, soaked with sweat. Rain blowing past the overhang didn't bother him. To this day, despite what happened, they were still his enemies. It would always be. They weren't four harmlessly bragging schoolboys. He had seen it in the pub. Sitting under the overhang stone, he remembered their eyes and the hate. He felt his tension rise. The doctor told him to relive what happened and control it as a frightening memory. He must free his mind of the animosity he still has for them; work through it, learn not to act on impulse. Think of what he had done, accept it, and then go on from there. Royce's eyes glazed over as their images came back, one at a time. And still, he hated them.

* * *

Changing direction, to again disrupt his opponents, he had angled upward from the tree line, chose an irregular course, rougher than before and stepped up the tempo. He heard their cursing and smiled. He had the passion now, the drive. Nothing would stop him from walking them—no *grinding them*—into the ground.

At noon, the first German went down. They had been moving without stop for six hours. The scream caused Royce to spin around to see the youth roll onto his side clutching his knee, blood streaming between his fingers. He had lost his balance and driven his knee into a ragged edge of stone. Looking at the German's red legs, Royce knew the cold made them numb, causing the fall. Smiling, he retraced his steps. The bleeding was slowed with a cloth. By the sight of the crescent gash, the youth would not be continuing. He would, however, carry a visible reminder of this day the rest of his life. Through his pain, the German glared hatefully as Royce stood over him and uttered a single word.

"One."

It was said without conscious thought and walking away impatiently he waited for the Germans to decide which of them would help their injured friend down the mountain. Then two of them would be gone. Knowing movement would increase the blood flow, they applied a tourniquet, and then to Royce's surprise, they left the crippled youth to find his way down. The shock of that decision strengthened Royce. No matter what happened, he would not give an iota of solace to them. They were the enemy.

Resuming the pace, he stopped thinking of the Germans as humans. They were only objects, nothing other than machines; wear them down and break them. Despite the haze drifting across his mind he never forgot there were still three moving parts and that thought kept compelling him on.

The afternoon sun broke through the overcast and beat upon them harshly in the thin, cold air. They squinted in its glare through tinted goggles. Sweated clothes hung limp. Backpacks bent them over, yet failed to hide trembling bodies. Each step was painful. Each step caused muscles to cry out to stop this folly. Beyond reasoning, it was no longer win or lose. It was life or death, no other choice.

They labored on. Above eight thousand feet, their lungs rasped painfully, fighting to find oxygen. Royce sipped water and munched a chocolate bar, aware his strength had seeped away. Stomach and thigh muscles torn inside, hand barely able to hold his hiking pole.

Then, concentration gone, he halted. Why did he stop, was he beaten? He turned uncomprehending. Finally, through the pain, he recognized another German was finished. The youth dropped his pack and simply stood. Slowly, he knelt, and then fell face down. His chest heaved in great racking sighs, blood trickled from his nose. Royce couldn't make the distance dividing them. He somehow grasped that the first German to go down had slipped, but this heap on the ground had no such excuse, he was beaten, beaten! The Major's son kicked at the youth, ordering him to get up. There was no response.

"Two."

The contest worsened into ponderous slog, no one giving thought to anything other than sliding one foot after the other. Dusk settled upon them. Barely seeing through tear bleared eyes, Royce stood waiting for the last two Germans to catch up, fearing they would keep going and pass him. They staggered up and stopped, dropping on their knees, retching. At first, the youths thought an unspoken truce had settled between them. Then they saw that every few minutes Royce, though utterly drained, would slowly move, from leaning to flexing and then ramble about erratically.

Major Dieter Schmid's son stared at him and slowly comprehended. The Englishman was keeping his muscles from stiffening, contracting. He planned to continue. This wasn't a draw. Not the end. Dread filled the mind of the Major's son. His adversary intended to plunge on…on into the dark. To go on was horrifying. To do so in the dark was insanity. Yet, the German's pride and hate prevailed. If this was what the damned English wanted, this he would get.

Failing to rouse his comrade, the Major's son stumbled to his feet and began emulating Royce's efforts. After periods of moving and rest, Royce motioned for them to pick up their backpacks; the next leg of their journey was to begin. The German again bent over to raise his exhausted friend. Finding it useless to rouse him, he cursed the boy's weakness. The youth's ligaments, his whole body, had contracted his legs up to his chest, his fingers being twisted into petrified talons.

"Three." Royce barely managed a whispered rasp.

Mindless, the two blundered on into the night. A half-moon gave barely enough glimmer for the absurd final act to play out. They groped along insensible, ignorant of their surroundings. Royce braced himself against a stone wall. Blood dripped from his nose, staining his beard, tasting it in his mouth. Unable to find his way for a few moments as clouds passed over the moon, he tried to listen. There were sounds behind him. The Major's son was trying to find the way. The youth was delirious, crying incoherently for his Führer to please help him, give him the strength to continue.

Now! Royce's brain screamed. One final attempt! Now is the time. One more effort. Keep going, keep going. Increase to assent. "Finish him now. You've got to or you'll lose!"

He tried. He couldn't move. There was nothing left. He was finished, beaten. He had lost.

No sound disturbed the night. Not even a murmur of wind.

Sinking to his knees, Royce sobbed quietly and waited for the German. Where was he? Why didn't he come and gloat?

A gunshot! He felt his body, nothing. It had to be a gunshot. The sound reverberated around the ledges, fading off into the valley. Had he been shot, yet felt nothing through his pain?

Nothing more happened. The quiet returned. Was the Major's son lost, did he have a pistol and fired a shot for help? Royce fought to think, then became angry. He wasn't going to let the bastard be lost and get away. Crawling back along rock-strewn passages, he screamed through collapsing lungs, "Four! Number four! Where the Christ are you? You bloody Nazi bastard! Here I am!" His cries…incoherent. His hunt…painful lurches…then shrieking silence.

* * *

Royce shivered. Soaked from sweat and rain, his breathing went from sporadic gasps to slow exhaling after reliving the end of the contest. He did as the doctor asked. He lived it again, but the question remained. Would it be enough? Would he accept that in his pride, and anger, he caused the death of two people with two others injured mentally, as well as physically?

Following the challenge to its end, Royce never knew how long he continued to rave, or how he got below the timberline. He had no idea at what point his physical and mental systems ceased.

He didn't remember collapsing beside a seldom used pathway. There, a physician on his way to his analysis and psychiatric clinic, found him.

The staff put him in bed, medicating to the doctor's instructions. His symptoms were a clear case of exhaustion, which did not make sense. There were no signs of bodily injuries other than scrapes, there was food and water in his knapsack, and he wasn't malnourished. It was nothing other than sheer exhaustion. Why? Why would anyone physically destroy himself? The doctor's curiosity kept Royce at the clinic, rather than sending him to a hospital. That bit of inquisitiveness saved Royce's life.

With their patient under sedation, the staff began work-up procedures. His backpack gave little information. A passport, a considerable amount of English money, uneaten food, a room key with a Salzburg hotel tag, and a letter with a Coventry, England return address and signed, David. Nothing more. They started with Royce's name on the English passport.

As the days passed, rumors became fact. Four obnoxious youths, taunts at an Englishman, a challenge, five climbers leaving. Then a blank in the story. No one returned to the hotel and no one knew what happened.

Some evidences were revealed as one of the youths was found crawling back down, five miles from where they started. He had a severe gash in his leg and wouldn't say what had occurred. Seven miles west from there, they found another youth, talking deliriously about a lunatic with a scarred face, tormenting them. Five days on, a search party of climbers found a third German, a body terribly contracted, dead from exposure.

This was seventeen miles west of the start. No one knew about the fourth climber, or the Englishman.

The doctor saw every stage moved westward, toward his clinic. The facts were becoming frightening. Their patient, as well the clinic's staff, could be heading into a grave dilemma. If the new German police became involved, they would be vulnerable.

The staff massaged and exercised his legs and arms virtually around the clock. He woke from the induced coma as the doctor reduced the medication. Royce glanced about, puzzled.

"Don't question things right now, Mister Royce. Your memory about what happened should slowly come back."

Royce began to remember. The doctor watched it happen and interrupted. "My name is Wilhelm Arnheimer, Professor Arnheimer. I found you on the side of a path in a terrible state and brought you to my clinic."

Royce nodded and with scratched voice. "Thank you."

"You seem dizzy."

"Yes, I think I am."

"Could we get you into a chair for a while?"

"I can try, with a little help."

"Mister Royce, to remind you, my name is Doctor Arnheimer. We have been hearing rumors that point to you as the person who was climbing with four Germans. I imagine you will remember, slowly of course. It seems they apparently infuriated you and you reacted with a challenge, which has turned tragic. There will surely be voids in your memory, but this is what we think we know, or surmise. The patrons from the Salzburg Hotel where you stayed said you challenged four obnoxious German climbers to a, ah…hiking contest. Some patrons told the local authorities that you went north, some said south and others, east. We know, and I suppose the authorities also know by now, you went west as you are here and the trail of broken bodies leads this way."

Royce winced at the broken bodies comment.

"Mister Royce, I imagine you could not know that of the four Hitler Youths, one was severely injured and as no one helped him down he may lose his leg. Another is mentally ill, screaming you are a lunatic. The third youth is not saying anything as he was dead of exposure and the fourth youth has disappeared. Do you recall having anything to do with his disappearance?"

"The hike had something to do with it…I don't know what happened…to him." Royce hesitated, searching his memory. "I do remember hearing a gunshot."

"A gunshot? Was he shooting at you?"

"I don't think so."

His patient was conscious and alert. Whether the proper time or not, Doctor Arnheimer had to express his concerns.
"Mister Royce we have to discuss a subject which will be distasteful to us both. Nevertheless it must be broached. Everyone in my clinic and true Austrians everywhere are trying to survive the Nazi occupation. To be truthful, we applaud the fact there are three or four less occupiers to harass us, but as long as you are here, you present a grave risk. A number of our Jewish friends and most government members have been arrested and deported. I am a Jew and I will accept the risk you pose. However, my staff is here out of loyalty to our country and me. I do not have the right to risk their lives any further than

they have to help you.

"We are a private clinic, isolated from the mainstream, yet I fear the investigation into those deaths will find its way eventually. We have learned the missing youth is, or was, the son of a SS Staff Officer, a Major I believe. If he comes on the scene, he will not accept lame responses from witnesses. It has already leaked out the challenger was English with a serious facial scar. What I am trying to say, Mr. Royce, is there is no specific trail that leads you here, only a general direction. If they come, you cannot be here. I am embarrassed to say this, but you must get back in condition as soon as possible. Unfortunately, we do not have a network set up to help you escape. Yet, we can give you food, equipment, and maps for the best route to get out of here and into Switzerland."

Royce stared to rise, but fell back with searing pain.

"Don't!" The doctor ordered. "You will only make things worse. Let us rehabilitate you our way, or you'll never recover your strength. One item privately, you have quite a serious indentation at the back of your head. It is not new."

"Ignore it doctor. It's been there for years. Please don't mention it again."

So began Royce's efforts to regain his flexibility and, in three days, Doctor Arnheimer was surprised at the physical response. Diet, vitamins, fluids, and correct exercise procedures were doing the trick and they knew a well-trained body was there to start with. His muscles and tendons needed only stretching and reconditioning. With that, the rest of the body would rebound. The mind, they felt, was another matter.

Royce wanted to leave. Doctor Arnheimer took him aside and told him that although he was nearly well physically, there was a long way to go to rationalize what he did. He must learn that inside his psyche, there was anger. An anger ready to lash out as it did with the Germans. Royce didn't accept the observation. Doctor Arnheimer told him he should find a process to bring it out for it will surely rear up again. Try to face it and rid the anger within. Royce again chose to ignore it. He wanted to bury it, and the frightening hike. The doctor said he would have been keen on working with him, but afraid for his staff, he must send him away to an uncertain fate.

The parting was tearful, the staff hopeful Royce would get to Switzerland. He was thankful to all. They knew not enough was done to help in the too short time, and could only wish him the best. There was little new information. Rumors were rife about a German SS officer asking more questions regarding an English climber with whom they wished to speak. Nothing ominous, simply that the Major would like to contact the Englishman.

He had a full backpack. The clinic's staff had given him all he needed with nothing to link them to the supplies. He slipped through the lowlands with no problem, then worked his way to the higher approaches and turned east—backtracking above the same ground he had taken the Germans. His thought process was basic. If people were searching west, he would go against the flow, except scores of yards higher. Then, as soon as he got past Salzburg, he would head south, then move more freely west towards the Swiss border. His hope was to be behind the backs of his pursuers.

It took him three days to cover the same ground he had traveled with the Germans. True, he had climbed higher and it was more difficult, but he was far from being back in climbing condition. He also had to be more careful, watching for search parties, so bypassed well above Salzburg and his hotel, having to abandon the rest of his climbing gear in his room. East of Salzburg he turned south, chancing being picked up by a produce trucker heading south to Bischofshofen. Getting off twenty miles before the town, and finally swinging back west toward Switzerland, he now had one hundred-fifty intimidating miles to the border.

On a second ride by a lorry driver heading for Switzerland, he recalled BergFalke Spa where, years past, he once stayed. It was west of Kufstein, isolated, well into the Alps escarpment and out of his way. Still, he needed time to rest, think, and plan.

Dropping off at Innsbruck, he bought some light hiking gear and started south. Once out of anyone's sight, he swung around and headed north, hoping all the direction changes would shake off pursuers. A twenty-five mile hike through mostly heavy pines brought him to BergFalke Spa. And there, a week later, Daphne would find him after not seeing him for two years.

* * *

Well before Royce's stay on the mountain reliving the horrifying hike with the four Germans, Major Dieter Schmid, Staff Officer, SS Adolf Hitler Division arrived in Salzburg, his search party followed behind, ordered to find his son.

With the Major's arrival, the questions and actions took a sinister turn, people holding any possible knowledge of the circumstances were roughed up and forcibly brought in. In one fashion or another, their stories were the same. All they knew was that four youths were in the pub that night and went off for a hike with someone the next day.

The Major listened; the answers ran in a pattern. He'd let them be confident for a day, and then challenge them again. It was a simple matter of breaking the weakest person and he or she, would talk. It wouldn't be difficult. Then he would let that person go, but a good number of storytellers would pay for their lying, he would see to that. Send them with the Jews and political misfits his men were picking up, to Dachau, a few miles above Munich.

In two days, a description evolved: a severe facial scar and the name James Royce. The story unraveled. The person was English, had stayed at the Salzburg Hotel, and challenged the young men to a hike after they mocked him. The SS ransacked the room, finding little more than a few articles of clothing and mountain climbing gear.

Three days later a search party discovered the Major's son. A pistol shot to the temple, the pistol still in his hand, obviously self-inflicted. The Major ordered the finding expunged. The official story was his son had been waylaid, shot and killed by a man named James Royce. The SS were after him. If found alive, he would be tried for murder.

But Schmid had to *know* if Royce was alive. If he was, he must know what happened and that a chase would be on. The search party hunted fruitlessly for signs of him. Schmid knew if his man were alive, he was getting further away each hour because these stupid peasants kept quiet to protect the Englishman. They'd be severely taught who was in charge, and they wouldn't forget it.

Fifty-four Gentiles, Jews, and Gypsies were shipped to Dachau, solely from Schmid's anger. Then, in the chance Royce was alive; Schmid ordered the search expanded by bringing in more SS and police. They were to comb every spa, hotel and camp from the Austrian, German border to the west as far as the eastern borders of...

Major Schmid stopped in mid-thought. An engineering student before joining Hitler's attempted Munich Beer Hall Putsch back in 1923, he methodically studied routes from the Salzburg region. Just because the Englishman took the youths west, would he continue that way? He wondered. It would make sense. Then again, this Royce person must know a search would be on because people said Schmid's son bragged of his father being an SS Major.

The question then became, which way would his prey attempt to escape? East would take him farther into Austria, which would be foolish. North was the German border. South was Italy and no safety there. If his man was alive, and Schmid felt in his gut he was, he must be heading for Switzerland. But, he would do it roundabout, going east was the wrong direction. There was nothing sensible about that, other than the unexpected. It would put his prey *behind* the searchers. Schmid changed his plan. He felt Royce would go east first, drop south, then west to Switzerland. It would take him time. Still, he had a head start due to these Austrian peasants.

The Major phoned his superior in Berlin, asked for and received authorization for an all-encompassing search. First, alert the border posts between Austria, Switzerland and Liechtenstein. The scar would give the fugitive away. Next, from Salzburg, the SS were to hunt south, down to Badgastein and Lienz. Then, they were to move west, checking every possible place a man with a noticeable facial scar and possibly injured, could hide. With his planners, Schmid decided to have flying squads of five men each, with zones covering every spa, hotel, and hospital to the west.

Concurrent with the flying squads, they developed a deeper combing of the same area with additional troops. The troops would be slower, yet could dig deeper into homes and businesses. Their orders stated the murderer was the primary goal. Nevertheless, when they found Jews, gypsies or any other undesirables such as problem priests or Masons, have them imprisoned prior to shipment to Dachau. In addition, his troops would impress upon the Austrian police that, if any of the prisoners escaped, the police would take their place in the shipments to the camps.

Major Schmid ordered an increase of SS officers to oversee the number of German soldiers along the roughly two hundred miles of Austria's mountainous border with Switzerland. Hundreds of people were trying to escape the German occupation and the SS were to stop them all of course, but not miss any chance to get the murderer. Another order sent a Hitler Youth cadre of experienced climbers to patrol the passes. It was of absolute importance to instill in them that the Englishman had shot and killed one of their own. It was their sworn duty to track down the scum like a rabid dog, this enemy of the Fatherland.

Finally, he ordered Storch aircraft to blanket the border from dawn to dusk, from the foothills to the aircraft's maximum altitude. Now, all his flying squads had to do was to catch the man, or funnel him toward the border crossings. The question then became which crossing?

* * *

Ignorant of the power Major Schmid had and the plans now put into action, Royce climbed from under the overhanging cliff feeling exhausted. The rain had stopped; stones glistened as the morning sun touched on them. He had spent most of the night sleepless, and although tired, he was calmed after reliving the harrowing confrontation with the four Germans. Now, to try and live again, disregard the fears. Hope the doctor was right, that he should face the incident, not let it rule his life. He thought of Daphne and England as he gathered his gear.

He felt better, and looked about, deciding on a few more hours heading west. This would be his last small hike before the swing back to BergFalke to collect the rest of his climbing gear. Until then, an easy trek, with a clear mind and build his strength for the challenge of reaching the border with Switzerland.

With the valley floor a few hundred feet below, he walked

along the upper rim of a col. His thoughts of England and Daphne were somehow interrupted. Something was not in keeping with the surroundings. Looking about, nothing seemed odd. Below, a sea of massive pines, perhaps the trace of a road winding through them. Then he saw the glint of the midmorning sun off a building of some sort. He reached for his monocular and scanned along the foot of the mountain to where it soared upward as a sheer cliff.

"Well, I'll be damned, a castle." he muttered, shaking his head, confounded.

Intrigued that a castle was constructed this deep into the Austrian Alps, he dropped his pack and walked to the edge of the cliff. The castle was remote, far from the mainstream, although close to the German border. Sweeping his monocular the length of the valley for some clue, some reason for the castle's existence, he found nothing other than reflections off a few roofs far down the valley. Not a thing held his eye. The castle did not guard a main roadway or river. It didn't block the valley from invaders. It was simply there. Some monarch's hideaway from the past, he supposed, a toy to spend his subject's money on. Royce eased closer to the edge of the shelf for a better view, but the castle became blocked by a curve in the mountain. To his left, he could see a narrow, flat ledge fifty feet beneath where he was standing. The ledge traveled the length of the shelf where it became lost from sight behind the convex bow in the mountain's wall. How to get a better look? He could rappel down without a problem, but doubted he had rebuilt enough strength to haul himself back up. Over to his left, he could see the ledge continued until it disappeared under tons of cascaded rock.

He walked seventy feet to the rubble. The land this side of the castle rose up in a high berm and the rubble and boulders continued down at least a hundred feet to where it all spread out around the top of the berm. While on the shelf, he estimated a descent of around fifty feet to the ledge and, although awkward to traverse, he managed with little trouble. He liked what he saw when he reached the ledge. It looked eight inches to a foot wide along the hundred and fifty feet or so to the curve of the mountain. The cliff wall itself was not vertical, sloping away from the ledge making it possible to lean inward, away from the edge. He studied the ledge. The equipment in his backpack was adequate for the traverse. This would be his remembrance of his last climb in the Austrian Alps.

Removing some of his pitons and carabineers from the pack, he put them in convenient pockets, and kept his ice axe and line handy. Although the ledge narrowed in sections, inching along it was little trouble except for the dampness from the morning mist. Rather than take chances, he drove pitons in the many fissures with the hammer end of his pick. He snapped in a carabineer, and then looped in his climbing line, keeping it slack around him. He shuffled along, repeating these steps until six pitons were driven home and the last carabineer snapped in as he reached the bend. Now he could look around. He saw diagonally down and across to the castle. He smiled. He was considerably nearer, the balustrades discernable to the naked eye. The monocular sharpened his vision, showing the mist creeping around the foot of the walls to the rear. The sun's rays reflected multifaceted gems off the red slate tiles on the watchtower, giving a mystical aura to the entire scene.

As he scanned the area, it became clear the location was as fascinating as the castle. Cliffs ringed and stepped down from three sides of the castle's foundation. At the rear, the mountain rose in a massive granite wall like a great stone curtain hung there by the gods. Viewing it through his lens he marveled at the sheer façade, which, with the exceptions of a minor bulge or two, was otherwise unblemished. Even this ledge no longer existed around the bend.

With a practiced eye, he saw no one man and probably no party of men ever scaled its awesome face. He took out his Leica, set the exposure setting, and snapped a few photographs of the area, primarily of the castle. He was sure Daphne would like it. The camera put away, he paused for a moment, and recalled something had caught his eye through the telephoto lens. A black something...he looked again through the monocular. There it was, a motorcar, no, two motorcars, parked in the front. There could be more but the castle partially blocked his view.

The autos were imposing. Where had he seen that type?

Vienna? Yes, that was where. Mercedes Benz motorcars, Nazis in them as they drove in, taking Austria.

What were they doing here? He watched, fascinated. Then, a door opened onto the rear terrace and five men filed out, looking about. Two of the men with long black leather coats, SS officers. He slipped back behind the mountain's bend, his heart racing. One damn thing after another, he thought. Could they have seen him? A quick check to see. They hadn't seemed to notice, they weren't looking up.

His first fright was they were after him, yet surely, that was ridiculous. Still, he'd seen enough, nothing mattered but to flee, get away—as Fast and as far as possible.

Unaware he was tiring, he anxiously turned to retrace his steps, his mind on the Germans, not the movement. His foot scraped off the ledge's damp edge. He grabbed for the line and caught it, yet as he did so, his other foot slipped off. The slack line around his waist cinched up, jerking him to a halt. With the sheering force, the pitons held. He was sure they would, yet he was hanging over the ledge at chest level, and if the people on the terrace looked up, they could be able to see him. He froze, fearing any movement would catch their attention. The two SS officers sauntered along the low wall at the edge of the terrace, then turned and with the others, left. Royce hung there, cold, sweating. Then, at last, the vehicles were gone, four in all.

As there was no chance of his feet finding purchase in the smooth stone, he should pull himself up with his arms, as any good climber would be able to. In fact, his arms were not in the shape he would need. He relaxed his hold on the line, allowing it to absorb the weight and let his arms rest, as well as his mind. His next moves were obvious. Making slack line into a foot loop, he tied it off to the line coming from a piton. He brought one leg up near his chest and inserted his foot in the loop then pulled up on the line with both arms and shoulders until his leg could add its strength. The extra energy pushed him up so his other foot could find purchasc on the ledge. He was safe. Still on the ledge, yet safe. He had fallen before of course, yet this slip was carelessness, plain and simple, and it shook him. He badly wanted to get off this ledge. Still, some*thing* deep within made him want to push away from the lip and float to the valley floor. He could feel it beckoning him. Each time he leaned out, muscles tensed and his bleeding fingers gripped the line and carabineer tightly. Carefully, he moved back across the ledge, leaving the pitons where they were. Sorry to leave scars, he thought, but I'm was in no condition to remove them. At last, he stumbled blindly onto the rubble and staggered on a few more feet, exhausted, weakening with each step.

Too much was happening, piling on top of him. Making him spiral out of control. Sitting on a boulder, he wiped the stinging sweat from his eyes and blood from his hands. The pounding of his chest and agony of his arms slowly receded. He lay back, numb to the stone pressing on his head. Then, slipping past the point of terror's hold on him, he passed out. Hidden spirits were liberated. He thought he had forced them deep within his mind, but it was not so. Four apparitions picked him up, pushing him off the ledge time and again. Grotesques of stone and gnarled pines snatched at him, dangling his helpless body over a black, eternal gorge.

The sun crouched upon, and then fell behind the mountain. He did not wake. Dawn, and in a blinding streak of light the nightmare burst apart. The demons scurried about and, finding no response, skittered away, yet ensuring to be back.

He had lain throughout the night on the stone and could barely move. The memories of his dreams evaporated, except for a wisp of awareness they'd return. Then even the wisp vanished. He moved stiffly and stumbled toward BergFalke.

In a daze, his mind erratically thought of the ledge and its formation. It had formed eons past when the range was settling down for the ages. Countless tons of stone, outwardly immovable, built enormous pressure on a fault. The tectonic plate or an earthquake shifted this mountain until its base fractured, then forced outward a few inches and formed the ledge. It remained unnoticed for incalculable eons, until fate linked it to Royce. A grim smile. The amusement of discovery ran through his mind. This ledge quite possibly had never been seen, or at least, not been traversed. His smile turned to laughter as he spoke the thought. "My ledge, Royce's Ledge. They'll have to make an annotation on the maps with an arrow pointing it out. Traverse at your own risk!" An echo mocked him.

Clouds, seeking a pass through the mountains, drifted across his path. He moved among their grayness and felt, rather than saw an absence of color, a ghostly pallor lying across the mountain. Leaving the clouds to their futile search, he stayed above the tree line, following along the verge of a mountain stream until it broadened into a chilly pool.

There he bathed his face, then shivered on the bank, studying his reflection. He was looking at another person. How old he looked. Thirty-three and his beard streaked with the grays of age. His face gave mute testimony to the power of the wind and sun. The twisting white scar marred the deep bronze of his skin. The dullness of his eyes now distressed him.

"You know you may be on the brink." His voice startled him, more by the anguish than the words. Finally spoken. The subject Doctor Arnheimer obliquely hinted at in the clinic. The time of convalescence there after the Nazi youths. The doctor tried to tell him what he had done on the mountain was wrong and Royce mostly agreed. At first he had mistakenly treated the four as brash youth who really needed only to be taught a lesson. The lesson degenerated into a struggle of death and the doctor tried to explain to Royce he should have had more sense. Should have known where his challenge would lead. However, there wasn't time to work through his thought process and get to the bottom of his anger. As long as he stayed at the clinic, there would be fear in the eyes of everyone there. Although he hadn't fully recovered, he left to protect them.

After he dwelled on the fourth youth, number four, the one he couldn't find, Royce brought his mind to the previous day: the incident on the ledge. An accident and fall is one thing. However, to put oneself in that predicament, knowing he was not in condition to handle the unexpected was inexcusable. Still, there was nothing to be gained finding excuses once more. Something was driving him to self-destruction. What? Too much solitude? Too long in the Alps? More than likely. And now...there was Daphne.

Why was he losing control? Too long in the Alps—or too long in the Alps—alone? More than likely. Did he dislike himself, wandering devoid of any focus? Perhaps.

Without guile or knowing, Daphne brought that possibility out into the open.

He glanced one last time into the pool. The ripples distorted his face, mirroring his state of mind. He wasn't quite right in the head. So, did this mean he knew he was going off the deep end, yet was unable to avoid it? Or, is there a chance, however slim, that he could reach deep within and prevent the slide?

Too many questions. He needed Daphne, she would help answer them.

An awareness of what must happen evolved. It truly was time to leave. He never believed this time would come.

Chapter 4

"WHERE YOU BEEN? They was here!"

Becker hurried up the path, grabbing Royce in a bear hug, agitated.

"Something happened on the hike that delayed me, Beck. What's wrong?"

"You lucky Royce. You here yesterday, they get you!"

"What happened? Are you all right?"

"Ja. But not if you here back then."

"Damn it! Tell me."

Becker took a deep breath, trying to get his English correct. "I see them come. Up road comes big Benz tour car. Three get out. Big. Black coat. Look for you. I hide gear before. I know nothing. They search chalet and spa. We lucky all guests gone. They would talk. Nazi find nothing. They very tired, say hunting man with scar. We talk, I talk old German army. I afraid they stay, then they leave, after ask me report if I see you."

Royce was a day late. At least some good came from the ledge. "Thank, God, nobody was here, Beck. You're sure you're all right?"

"Ja. I show them Prussian medals. Even though stink SS, they salute, leave."

"I don't understand, what medals?"

"I tell you later. Now we get over border with my idea."

Over drinks, Royce listened intently as Becker laid out the story he heard from the Germans about Royce killing a SS Major's son, and the traps being set to ensnare him.

"You shoot Major's son, my friend?"

"It's too long a story, Beck. I was in a hiking challenge with four Nazi youth. It went too far. It was bad. Three of them dropped out and I lost sight of that Major's son. I do remember hearing a loud sound, like a shot, but I couldn't see anything in the dark."

Royce knew he shouldn't have mentioned the dark.

Becker rubbed his earlobe. "You hike in dark?"

"Not at first, but in the end...yes."

"No one should climb with you in contest in daylight. In dark, never, Major son stupid."

"Unfortunately, it happened."

"For him, unfortunate."

"For me also."

"I think I know. I see how you look when you come here this time. Only this woman friend helps you."

"I afraid you're right. Anyway, it's time for me to get my gear and try for the border."

"Royce, you know border over hundred forty miles? Nazis tell me all. Stop trains, cars, have Gebirsjäger, mountain troops, aero planes. Everything blocked. They catch all try to escape. Hundreds Jews caught, deport. Is bad, Royce, still we do it."

Royce was disheartened, then surprised. "We do what?"

"I get you out."

"How?"

Becker got up, went to a drawer. He returned with a velvet board laid out with fourteen medals.

"Not worry, Royce, only show three."

"My name, von Becker. I stop von, not good after war. Lose all, no longer nobility. I not Austrian at first. I Prussian, Hohenzollern. More size than Germany once. I from Saxony, Count Bismarck too. I in 1st Garde Regiment, Oberleutant in war. At end, Colonel. Fight in Italy Alps. Win Eiserne Kreuz, win others there."

Royce was confused by Becker rushing his words and switching back and forth between German and fractured English.

"Slow down Beck, I'm quite baffled."

"I slow. I win medals in Austria and Italy border. Not shoot English, Russian, French. Only Italy soldier we fight. Italy army try to get over Isonzo River. Six time battles they try, fail. Then I sent to Gorizia, town on Bainsizza Plateau. They try cross river five time more. We lose small ground, only small. Lot of shell come. Men die, my men, First time I wonder why we do this."

"But you seem to have made it out all right."

Becker concurred, then laughed, "I get these."

He pointed to eight silver badges, "Wounds."

"You were wounded eight times?"

"Some scratches some leave mark, like your face, only not show, not see."

Royce shook his head, "You were certainly in the wrong place at the wrong time a lot."

"Three years go over Italy side, come back, go to Italy side, come back."

"I'm not following you."

"We sneak. Ski in Italy side, then blow up train, trucks, supplies. Shoot officers. Climb out quick."

"So your group infiltrated the Italian lines and among other things you were snipers?"

Becker shrugged his shoulders, not understanding the word.

"We shoot Italy soldiers you mean? Ja. I show you fine German rifle I hide."

"No, Beck, that's okay. Tell me about the rest of these medals first."

"This Eiserne Kreuz. You say Iron Cross."

"Yes, I know it, only not by the German name. What is this one? It's beautiful."

"That Odren Hans Orden. I stop supply train with no one."

"Alone?"

"Ja. Aero plane spot troop train fifty miles away and below to us. I say I get it. Ski down blow up. I gone thirty days, hides from enemy."

If Royce hadn't known the man, he wouldn't have believed the story. Becker sat upright and smiled. "This is the Order of the Red Eagle with Cross Swords. Only forty-three ever. I catch Italy General, get him over froze Isonzo River. We shot five times by Italy soldiers. Two where you friend say you are."

Mystified, Royce asked "What are you talking about?"

"You woman friend. I hear she say you pain in ass. That where I am shot twice."

Royce remembered Daphne's comment and burst out laughing. Becker joined in. They needed the laugh.

Wiping his eyes, Royce tried to continue. "All right Beck, you, and the Italian General are going across the ice and you get shot in the arse. What next?"

"It night, we slip all over, then flare light all. General and me, what you English call sitting duck. We slide, soldiers shoot us, then my Austrians shoot at Italy soldier. Hell, all hell. General shot two wounds, me three. But he tell us all plan for Italy to cross river, attack us. They stupid. Know we got General, Yet still they attack same plan, not believe he talk. They die, too stupid. Big victory for Austria. Order Red Eagle, Crossed Swords for Becker."

Staring at Royce, Becker unbuttoned his shirt and exposed his chest. There, above his left breast, was tattooed a Red Eagle with crossed swords below it, and the Roman numerals XXII. Royce shook his head in admiration while Becker re-buttoned his shirt.

He fingered the Eagle's wings on the medal. "We lose war, Royce. Probably for best. All stupid. Each side do what General say. Many soldier die, All general live."

He was quiet for a moment before continuing. "This medal is twenty-two of forty-three ever gave to officers and first gave to Oberleutant. Me. All before I Colonel. This medal get us past border."

"I don't understand."

"Listen then, I tell you. Ten years I go over border to Chur in Switzerland for spa many time, get skis, poles, boots, clothes. Things like that, climb gear, crampons, axes. They know me at border, know Red Eagle too. They envy, stand and salute. Good treatment. That why even SS when they here, salute. They know I do big honor to Fatherland. Not know I do for Prussia, not damn German. Now border most closed. Not to me. I will tell them now have no patrons for they closing border, so I take back all things to Switzerland. I get through."

"I still don't follow you, Beck. You get through, how does that help me?"

Becker led Royce out to a barn behind the spa's rooms and opened a large door.

"When you gone I think to go work. This my auto, made by American company, General Motors Germany. Not fine, like

Mercedes or Horch. Good for here."

A dirty white 1936, four door Opel, more than a little worn from two years of rough roads and little care, appeared to crouch forlornly in a corner. As Royce moved closer, he noticed the worn interior, except that the front and rear passenger's seats were packed tightly with boxes. Included were snowshoes, skis and other equipment Becker kept on hand to sell or rent. The trunk though, was open and empty. More boxes and equipment were lying around on the floor. Royce caught on quickly, and was doubtful.

"You're going to put me in the trunk and dump boxes on me. Do you think they're not going to move a box or two?"

"They maybe do. Not find you."

Reaching into the forward wall of the trunk, he detached what was once a fixed panel behind the rear seat. With the panel out of the way, Royce saw Becker had removed all the rear seat supports and springs so the entire seat was hollow underneath. With its own weight and the boxes piled on, it was barely kept from collapsing by wooden supports at each end. Royce could also see the rear panel stops had been moved toward the rear to give slightly more space. With the panel in place, the minor variance wouldn't be noticed and would make available four more inches of room.

Skeptical, Royce squeezed in. knowing Becker would replace the rear panel and pile in boxes and gear. It could work.

"I thank you for doing this Beck, but I cannot let you take the chance of being caught."

"I not be caught, you not caught."

"I can't have you take the chance. Just drive me as close to the border as you dare and I will climb into the high country and go from there."

"I check Switzerland. Telefunken say blizzard coming soon. You die there."

"You telling me the truth?"

"Ja." With that, Becker placed his hand on the Order of the Red Eagle.

There were too many forces arrayed against him, and a blizzard in the Alps he knew would kill him, no matter how good he was. He did not want to die. He had a reason. He dearly wanted to get to England and see Daphne.

"Two questions, Beck. How long must I be in there and how will I breathe?"

Becker smiled. "You make right..." He couldn't think of the English word 'decision', so instead clapped Royce on the back, "You not worry. Maybe be hour, maybe be little more. Get in, I show you to breathe."

It was awkward, extremely awkward, a near fetal position. Other than that, he fit.

"I know you get in. Not big, like me. Move head. You see tube? If air go bad use tube, go to under auto. You can easy breathe it."

Royce tried it. The air tasted like old rubber soaked in gasoline. He felt he could tolerate it and would never think of mentioning this minor problem after what Becker was doing to help him escape.

"Royce my friend, you dress warm. No heat there. Lay on blanket, many socks, mittens, hat over ears. You think tight now, wait you got more clothes."

They poured over a map for the best route. Becker wanted to go due west, better roads, enter the small country of Liechtenstein, then a short trip for Royce to reach a rail line and into Switzerland. After studying the map further, Royce decided on a different route.

"Beck, the main routes from Austria go through the Feldkirch border post into Switzerland, or the Vaduz crossing into Liechtenstein. To me, those are where the Nazis will concentrate their efforts. We should swing more to the south. It shows a crossing point southwest where I can get over to Davos, in Switzerland. There's a rail line. One problem would be if there's a snowstorm, the map shows a narrow road. You're serious about a blizzard?"

"Nein."

"What do you mean, nein? You swore on the Red Eagle Medal."

"Medal not religion."

They laughed, more to relieve the stress. Yet, blizzard or not, he was now committed to the plan. Becker had two negative points. "That long way Royce. Don't know guards there. That important to me."

"I know. But I think it will be safer."

"Then we go that way."

"When?"

"When day come."

Chapter 5

"RAVENSMOOR, the Sir David Royce residence. Good morning. Albert speaking."

Daphne thought the person answering quite condescending, "Is David Royce there, please?"

"Sir David? Whom shall I say is calling?"

"My name is Daphne Elliot. I'm a good friend of David's brother, Jim."

"James's friend?" The head servant sounding startled.

Daphne didn't answer. She was immediately lost patience with this Albert, whoever the damn fool was.

"One moment," Albert inhaled, "I'll see if Sir David is about."

God! She thought. What a crock of …

"David Royce, speaking."

A masculine voice, cultured, but masculine. Thank goodness. "Dave, sorry if I'm bothering you. I told Albert my name is Daphne Elliot and I have a letter here from your brother, addressed to you. I've only now arrived back in England from being with him, and he asked me to mail it as soon as I arrived. Then I thought that as the mail is frightfully slow, you may be down to London in the next couple of days and I could give it to you then."

What is this? he mused. This woman has an acquired speech pattern. Not artificial, just acquired after being here awhile. Probably American. However, a lovely, deep woman's voice.

"You have the advantage of me, my dear. From where do you know James?"

She mulled this over. This is hard to believe it's Jim's brother. Sir David? James? What the hell happened to Jim and Dave? Do they even know each other? Whatever, she'd be damned if she would call him Sir David. "I know him from the Austrian Tyrol. We climbed together a number times, he taught me a few climbing methods and we got to know each other quite well after a while."

"I must say I'm surprised. I was under the impression James climbed alone, didn't care for people. At least that was the way he always was. At least, as I say, here."

"Well Dave, now you've learned Jim isn't always alone. Look, I don't want to take up any more of your valuable time. Do you want to pick up the letter or have me mail it?"

The cheek of the woman, he thought. Had to be American, calling me Dave. However, before he told her to mail it he asked. "Are you pretty?"

She burst out laughing, "You're exactly like your brother! Coming out with the damndest comments at times! However, to answer your question, I'm a ravishing beauty."

It was David's turn to laugh. "I'll settle for pretty. So, yes, I would like to meet the pretty woman who knows my brother and I will pick up the letter. I'm to be in London tomorrow, at the Admiralty, late morning. Could we meet, say around two at Laddys? It's in Covent Garden, if you don't know."

Oh, the Admiralty, I'm impressed, she grinned to herself.

"I know where Laddy's is. See you there at two. Cheerio, Dave."

The line went dead. David was at a loss. Calling me Dave indeed, he thought, then caught the eye of his wife, Mary, as she came down the hall.

"Who was that, David?"

"I'm not quite sure I know. This woman, a bit of a twit I should think, said she was a friend of James. Has a letter for us from him and wanted to know whether to mail it or would I pick it up."

"That is strange. Still, it would be nice if James had a woman friend for once."

"Mary, let us not kid ourselves. The type of woman that would even look at him, apart from you that is, would not be the type of person we would want around."

"Then why did you say you would meet her, David? Why not simply tell her to mail it?"

"I thought of doing that, but the letter may be of importance. So I decided to pick it up. I do admit to being curious about her, and I'm going to be in London tomorrow for meetings anyway."

For Daphne the phone conversation was a revelation. What a dandy this Dave is, she thought. It's hard to believe he and Jim are brothers. Well, she wanted to find out more about Jim, and called with the pretext about the letter. My fault, she admitted. So, just learn more about Jim, when she meets his brother, David, then get it over with.

* * *

Daphne arrived at Laddy's a little after two o'clock. David Royce was not there, nor did she expect him to be. Society arriving late and all that rot, she thought. She told the maître'd she was awaiting David Royce and was immediately escorted to "Sir David's booth." At two fifteen, she was getting restless and irritated until she caught the eye of, as she recalled later, one of the most handsome creatures she had ever seen. So, this was the Sir David Royce, in person. Elegant, impeccably dressed. She stared, fascinated. He nodded to her as he was stopped three times by restaurant patrons. Each time, as he bent over to whisper a word or two, a wave of blond hair fell loose across his brow. Daphne couldn't help smile in admiration as David Royce made a grand progress towards her with people staring at the tall Englishman. Probably six-foot two she thought. Good Lord, he is something, she kept musing, with his blond hair and blond mustache, tailored suit and all the rest.

Finally at her table, he reached out and took her hand, looking deep into her eyes, and frankly, her body. "Sorry I'm late, Miss Elliot. I was subject to the Admiralty's whim."

She commented effortlessly, "I understand completely, Mister Royce. I find the Admiralty always runs terribly behind schedule."

David Royce did not so much as blink. My word, he is good, she smiled.

"Miss Elliot, you were quite accurate when you said you were a ravishing beauty."

"Did I really say that? I'm embarrassed. But thank you, Dave."

He had never been called Dave in his life and it grated, yet he knew she was baiting him, "And I want to thank you for not calling me Sir David. I get so tired of that."

He smiled as he said it, watching her intently. She knew he was her equal for satire and was gracious with her response, "I'll remember that, and I'll never call you Dave again either, if you'll not call me Daffy, my nickname at grammar school."

"I admit that was being saved if I needed another repartee."

There was a quiet laugh between them. They had sized each other up. He enjoyed her spirit, and her laugh, a laugh that came from some innate depth within.

She found his attention disconcerting and felt this man, so handsome, so sure of himself, would outstare anyone until they had to look away, unsettled. She would have none of that, and without taking her eyes off his, handed him the letter, which brought him back to the reason for the meeting.

"Of course, thank you for delivering it. But first a Sherry for you and I'll have Port."

He had the audacity to order for her without asking. She'd let it pass this once since she liked Sherry, but not if he did that again.

David took the letter, carefully checking the handwriting. "James's hand seems a little shaky."

"Yes, I know. Something happened he won't tell me about." David nodded and proceeded to read. Finished, he folded it neatly, looking to her.

Damn, she cursed inwardly. That blasted stare, why is it so bothersome?

"James wrote he is coming home to stay. I find that difficult to believe. Did you have anything to do with it?"

"I really can't say, although I hope so. But you don't seem particularly happy about his returning."

"Ah, I am most pleased, Daphne. If true. I need him very much. Royce Bearings Limited needs him very much. He will be invaluable to us if he can be himself again."

"What do you mean? Would you tell me a bit about him, David? Why he is, who he is?"

David glanced down, rubbing his forehead. "That would be personal, quite personal. So before I would do that I must ask who you are and what you and James mean to each other."

"Fair enough, David."

She wanted to sound friendly, so briefly led him through her early year's right up to the present, just as she had with Jim. However, whereas Jim had no questions, David peppered her with inquiries over whether there was any scandal attached to her parent's divorce, had she been married, friends, education and so forth. When Daphne inadvertently mentioned her brother's ruined face, David immediately understood how she could accept James's disfigurement. He admired her for her fortitude.

When David started on another question, she finally had enough. "I'm tired of answering your questions David, what's this all about?"

"Please forgive me if may I seem, shall we say, curious, Daphne. These questions were to be sure you were not interested in James for his wealth and…"

"Wealth? What on earth are you talking about? My father is certainly no pauper. I would rather imagine I have a touch more wealth than Jim!"

"There you would be quite wrong, Daphne, believe me. Please, let me finish. I do not believe you are after James for his money. However, and this will sound conceited, I have a duty to protect the reputation of my family and company. I do not intend to be in the House of Lords the rest of my life, and I intend to have Royce Bearings expand and acquire other companies as it does. Let me say this immodestly, I fully expect to become a Member of Parliament before too long and if I am able to get some fools bumped aside then…"

David stopped in mid-sentence, then continued. "Let me just say it is pertinent I ask you such questions as it is important to our family's future."

Daphne nodded. Did he think she was going to be so impressed, she'd swoon? She picked up the thread of his conversation.

"…cannot allow any hint of scandal become attached to any of us. As you quite well know, Daphne, you called out of the blue, and I knew nothing of you other than what you just told me. James does not mention you in this letter so would you please enlighten me as to your, and I choose the word carefully, what your association is with my brother?"

"David, I honestly don't know what it is. I know he likes me and I very much want to see him again. If your next question is do I sleep with him, the answer is yes."

David was flustered. He had never met any woman so forthright, and stumbled out his next comment. "Well, if you feel that way about him, and I do not doubt you, then it is more than I have ever known him to be close to anyone, myself included."

She could see a crack in his demeanor. "What do you have against him, David?"

The question caught him off guard again. She was too direct. "Why do you say that?"

"Once you said, 'myself included', it became plain. Tell me about you and him."

"I'll have a difficult time knowing where to start. God knows I've worked it over in my mind endlessly. However, I've never spoken of it, not even to my wife."

"Then how about starting with me? How about his scar?"

"Daphne, that would be at the beginning, his birth."

Shocked, she kept her composure. "Then that's a good place to start. I've the time."

"Daphne, of course James knows this, but obviously didn't mention it to you. He was a difficult birth. The doctor used a forceps to help in the birthing. However, the forceps…well…it crushed the part of the baby's head and killed more of the nerves where it pressed. This is the man, and the scar, you see today."

She put her head down. Tears filled her eyes, "People think he was struck by lightning. He lets them believe that."

He gave her his handkerchief. "James always left them to think that. Anyway, our father hounded the doctor out of the country. He would have him killed if he thought he could get away with it. The disfigurement, from what Father told me, for I was too young to know, broke mother's heart and health. She died four years later. I was seven, James four. I admit I blamed James for mother's death and barely spoke to him for years, and our Father had little interest in him. I was around fifteen when I came back from Eton to learn Father's business and met a man by the name of Clive Henderson.

"Clive was, still is in fact, Chief Engineer at Royce Bearing. He found I cared very little for James and he took me to an orphanage and made me stay there for two hours with deformed children, children abandoned by their parents because they couldn't stand the sight of them."

Daphne blanched. In essence, her own father had abandoned her brother. David was too engrossed in his story to notice.

"Then Clive took me home, and this is the truth, Daphne, he dragged me to Father, slapped me in the face, turned to Father, said shame on both of you, and left.

Unfortunately, it did not change Father. However, I reacted quite the contrary. The word shame, more than the slap, was an epiphany for me. Nevertheless, it took months for the two of us to break the ice. Who could blame him? James was used to silence from me; I was not to be trusted in the world he lived in. By the time he was fourteen and came back from Harrow, I from Eton, we got along better each time we were together for holiday. We learned to accept each other although, I hastily will say, it was relative compared to other brothers. James was never what one could say, a true friend. When I was twenty, I found he couldn't stand the tormenting, the fights at Harrow. Father didn't give a damn although he let me teach him at home when I was around, and tutors when I was at Eton. The breakthrough with James happened when it became clear he had Father's genes for applied geometry. It just poured out of him."

David stopped, as he saw a person he wanted to speak with, and excused himself. Daphne needed the break. In five minutes, she had learned more of Jim's past than she would ever have gotten out of him. Now, it began to make sense. It wasn't her. It was his personality, developed and deep-rooted over thirty-three years of hurt and, she would bet, thirty-three years of pent up resentment.

David returned, apologized, and immediately picked up where he left off. "He's an engineering genius, Daphne. He visualizes components of multiple shapes and their interaction. A quick example, when I was a management student under

Father's tutelage at Royce Bearing, Clive Henderson, our Engineering Chief, the one I told you about, had a problem with creating a single yet complex roller bearing configuration. The design configuration had to perform on variable surfaces but on one driveshaft, as well as function under severe loads. No one could work it out for three weeks, so we decided to develop two bearings, which would require changes to the case molds and recasting, a considerable loss in time and cost.

"I showed the problem to James because he looked interested. He walked off with the drawing and in thirty minutes sketched out a design. You probably don't know he's an excellent mechanical illustrator. He said give it to Engineering. I couldn't make heads or tails of it and I was embarrassed when I gave it to Clive. What if James had made a fool of himself? Clive stared at it for an hour before he comprehended the concept and that it would work. At the end all he said was, he wanted James. That was it. James blossomed under Henderson. Without formal training, he's a brilliant, conceptual engineer. Quite better than Henderson. By the way, it's obvious father didn't fire him for slapping me."

David took a sip of wine. "I could stop now, if you wish, Daphne."

"No, don't stop, David. I want you to bring me up to date."

"Very well, and I'm dragging out this story because it's why I need James back so badly. I cannot find an equal for Royce Bearings. Our Father started the company, and as far as Father went, he was a good engineer. He was a Raj in India constructing bridges so the British Army could maintain supply lines along the border with Afghanistan and after that he was ordered to Fort Abdul Rahman in the Kahibar Pass. He won a knighthood while commanding his engineering regiment when they held the fort against overwhelming odds for over a month, until relieved. I don't know what else he got up to over there, but old friends of his said he came back with more money than a Major could earn in a lifetime. We were never told of that, nevertheless, the fact remained he knew engineering processes. Although it turned out he was better at organization. That was his forte. He had an instinct for getting the best people for what he needed done. Father resigned his commission, bought a struggling ball bearing company up in Coventry, changed the name to Royce Bearing Limited, and grew it to a somewhat successful operation."

Daphne leaned forward, and took a sip of her Sherry. It was obvious David enjoyed his own voice and she, because of her interest, was the perfect listener. Still, as she already disliked their father, her patience was running thin as David rambled on.

"Royce Bearings became a mainstay in Coventry because of the number of automobile and bicycle manufacturers located there. It wasn't that the people he hired liked him, they mostly didn't. It was because they knew he was good at what he did and believed in the vision he created to succeed and, of course, he paid well. I've grown the company even more since Father died, because I have his knack for bringing the best people together. I inherited his genes, and had the foresight to use them. James has his genius for engineering development and it is far above the ability of anyone I could buy or even know. I had expected James and me to become sort of a team; I would run the company and he manage the Design and Engineering. It wasn't to be.

Daphne, I know some, or perhaps none of this is of much interest. Still, it is necessary, that is if you want to know what happened, what shaped James. And why he left it all…"

David stopped, leaning back, looking at memories years long past, yet understandably not forgotten.

"All of it is interesting, David. It gives me insight to Jim, and you also I might add."

"I'm not sure I like that, Daphne. Would you like another Sherry?"

"Thank you, no. I rather have scotch, splash of water. I'll even hit you up for single malt."

"Excellent, Daphne. I'll join you. Walter, Glenfiddich, Ancient, two, side waters."

The drinks came and he asked her if she would mind his having a cigarette.

"Not at all, David, if I can join you."

Surprised a mountain climber would smoke, he opened a new pack of Craven As, tossed away the small sports card inside, and offered her a cigarette.

"Oh dear God, no, David. They make your lungs rasp. Here,

try one of my Camels."

"American. Pretty pack, with that dromedary and pyramid."

"That's the only reason I buy them, for the picture." She smiled sweetly.

They relaxed, watching the smoke curl about the booth.

"What else did Jim write in the letter?"

"That was it. He would be back in two weeks and to stay. That's him, no frills."

"Good he's returning. For some reason he wouldn't come back with me. Had to have one more climb he said. Still, I know there was more to it than that. Something else, I could see it in his face. I was bothered that he wouldn't tell me."

"James was never too forthcoming."

"You can say that again, David, but please, don't."

The drink warmed her. Laddy's had yet to turn on the heat even though it was the middle of a chilly September.

"Tell me the rest please."

"Where did I leave off?"

"Telling me how great Jim was in design."

"I sincerely hope it's not *was*. But anyway, as you must know, James likes to be alone. And I imagine he's been that way since the torments and fights at Harrow. Added to that was Father's distaste for him, other than his ability, and of course, the way I was. Father, was not subtle, he let it be known through the years he blamed James for Mother's death. When I finally tried to make things up with him, I think we did quite well, although, to my mind, he retained every slight and insult from everyone. Perhaps unwillingly, nevertheless, it did make him antisocial. Then of course, employees at work avoided him, not only for how he looked, but also his attitude of ignoring them whenever he could. He simply immersed into his work and that was that. When he worked out a design he would drop it on the desk of the appropriate person and walk off. There was no need to review what he drew. Every design was immaculate, every description, explanation, bill of materials, perfect. People would not believe it was all there in his head, yet, other than Clive Henderson and me, no one said a word to commend him."

"How terrible for him."

"It must have been. Although remember, he did not help

things by the way he slighted everyone. And, when he comes back, he'll probably be that way again."

"I can relate to that part. I hope that perhaps I could bring him out of it."

David raised a questioning eyebrow. Daphne did not respond. "Well, whatever, Daphne, there was a terrible event that triggered his flight. In the mid-thirties I was traveling constantly between Europe and the United States generating business and not paying attention until it was too late."

"Too late?"

"Walter, another Glenfiddich please. Would you like another, Daphne?"

"No thank you, I'm still sipping this one."

The waiter brought the drink. David stared into it. She waited, knowing he would continue eventually. He at last looked up, glancing at her. She could see his mind locked in the past—an unpleasant past.

"What made it too late, Daphne, was father's death. Or rather, the way he died."

Again, David stopped, took a sip of scotch, and put words to his thoughts. "I was in the US when it happened, June 4th, 1934. From what I pieced together, James had ordered a Tensiometer. For our application, it's equipment used in testing the tensile strength, or strain on metal. In other words, what stress will make a specific structure rupture. We needed it as we were bidding on an aircraft mainframe. Henderson said he heard James explicitly tell Father not to connect the device as he did not approve of the construction of the mainframe. James thought he might have to rework the manufacturer's design even though it came from Mannheim in Germany. It was a Saturday, James was going to Cumbria for Sunday and would review the equipment Monday morning. Now I will say this about Father, no matter his feelings about James, he always listened to him. However, I think that, as James did not say the equipment was definitely defective, Father ignored him. Either that, or he wanted to show my brother up by assembling it on Sunday."

David hesitated. Then leaned over the table between them and stirred his drink. The present was gone again. His voice became harsh, strained.

"Monday morning Henderson said he came into work at six-thirty and Father was already there working on the machine. He was also shouting at the top of his lungs about where in hell everyone was. I understand he castigated each worker as they came into the research department at seven. As I look back on it, my belief is Father was trying to demonstrate he could get the machine up and running and didn't have to wait for James. Whatever reason, when James walked in before seven he must have heard Father shouting and ignored it, as we often tried to. James got a cup of tea and started walking down the corridor to the research department. He caught up with Henderson who told him Father was testing the apparatus. James became angry, and hurried down the corridor. They heard a high-pitched whine getting louder, and then a screeching sound. Both knew what happened. Other employees told me later that Father had the machine stressing some sort of reinforced aluminum alloy, and a stud on the flange immobilizer sheered. They said for a moment they had no idea what happened; one instant Father was cursing, then the screech and Father went silent. They saw him clutch his collar, blood spurting everywhere. It seemed that under stress, a stud head sheered, flew off and ripped into Father's throat."

David looked at Daphne oddly.

"My, God, Daphne. Damn. I've never told this story. I can't believe how it's distressing me even at this late date. Let me get my wits about me."

"I can understand, David, it was your Father. Take a moment, have a sip."

Another cigarette, another sip, his words unsteady.

"They grabbed him and laid him down. There was nothing anyone could do. One of the men said Father was wide-eyed...and died. When Clive and James got to Father, there were already five or six other employees around him. I was told that James must have heard someone mutter it served the bloody tyrant right, but Clive told me James never said a word. He just looked at the Tensiometer, then the printout, which registered some God awful level of stress and he turned around and walked off. Walked out of our lives actually."

Daphne, pent up, forgot she was in the quiet of Laddy's. "For Christ's sake, David! After all this, you wonder why he's the way he is?"

David stiffened, patrons turned at the vehemence in Daphne's voice.

"Please, Daphne, calm down. Let me finish and you can have another drink, or leave."

"Get me another scotch now, and I'll be discreet."

The waiter heard her and brought it quickly. David ambled on. "It was Clive who wired me, not James, about Father's death. I managed to take get a train to Miami, Florida, board an Imperial flying boat out of there the next day and take the southern air route home. James was gone. Nowhere to be found. He had packed, turned his bank account into a letter of credit and left. I had no idea where. My wife, Mary, whom James idolized, knew nothing. We buried Father without James present; there was nothing else to do. It wasn't until ten days later that he sent a wire from Metz, in France. He said he had decided to head for Austria and he would contact me sometime. Nothing else. That was June of '35."

"I met him in March of '36. It was quite contentious at first, and then we got along famously. Then he left without a word, just like you said he did after his Father's death, I suppose. I didn't see him again for two years. Not until this August."

Daphne didn't know what else to say. All of David's revelations were sinking deeper in to her brain, blending with the scotch. She fidgeted with her hands.

"Think you should have never have let yourself get involved with him in the first place?"

"As they say, David, hindsight is always twenty-twenty."

"Yes. It would help with people and countries."

Daphne looked up, thinking the remark odd. David had a detached look about him.

"Other things on your mind, David?"

"Yes, and I really should be getting back to another evening meeting."

"Jim said you fear for England's future and have insider information that makes you that way. Are things that bad?"

"Daphne, obviously both of you weren't up to date over there, because this is common knowledge here. We let Hitler take Austria, and two days ago, Hitler demanded Germany absorb the Sudetenland, which is part of Czechoslovakia. People with any brains at all know it's the whole country he's really after and the Skoda works. The Czechs have refused, which is the honorable thing to do. I'm sure they will mobilize their army and then who knows what will happen? We must uphold our honor if Germany attacks the Czechs. The problem is we have an irrational, and I might add ill, Prime Minister in Chamberlain, and he's flying to see Hitler with hat in hand, tomorrow. I fear what he will give away to that brute.

Daphne, I have a reason for what I am going to tell you now, which I will explain shortly. Endless meetings go on all the time and tonight's is with an influential group of concerned individuals who can see a future that is not pretty. There are many of us like that. Anthony Eden, who resigned as Foreign Secretary last February in disgust over the PM's appeasement of Hitler, will attend. Also at the meeting are the First Sea Lord, representatives of the other services, and two industrialists, myself being one. Most everyone in the know is aware of these meeting, although we try to be sotto voce. We meet, not to replace Chamberlain, but solely to prepare for the consequences of his actions. We are continuing to organize our plan for war as far as we are able. Hitler calls us warmongers. Typical pot calling the kettle black sort of thing. War will come and, with God's help, we might be ready.

"Tonight, I'm acquiring production estimates to be sure Royce Bearings can conjoin Ministry requirements to our research and production capacities quickly enough."

With the word 'war', Daphne blocked out the rest of his conversation, looking concerned, but doubtful. "I can't believe that, David. Haven't we learned anything since the last one?"

"Honestly? Not in the least. This is why I'm telling you now—you should take your mother and brother and go back to the States, Daphne. Tell anyone who will listen, that the old Mother Country will be calling on them once again for help. It's no secret that in June we already ordered four hundred Curtis P40s from the US. They're not the best. Still, we'll need hundreds more."

David's mind was wandering onto different subjects. "Of course it would help our cause if your Charles Lindbergh would stop visiting Germany trying out German war planes and getting medals. He must be of German descent to be…"

Daphne didn't hear and interrupted. "We won't leave. Mother was born here. I know she wouldn't begin to entertain the thought. My brother and I have adopted England. We're expats. No matter what, we will stay."

"I felt just from talking with you that would be your answer. However, I'm sure James will tell you the same thing."

"He can damn well tell me what to do all he wants. He can't make me."

David smiled. "Well Daphne, I tried. Now I must be off. Pleasant meeting you. Please give me your telephone number and I'll ring you up if James is late arriving."

He walked her to the curb, offering to drop her off at her home. She said it was a short taxi ride and did not want to make him late for his meeting. They shook hands as the taxi came. He helped her in and walked away. Her taxi took a few moments to enter the traffic stream, and she turned back in time to see a two-tone green Bentley pull to the side of the pavement. David hopped in.

She turned to the front smiling. "He's really something." She then laughed outright. "I don't know what, but he really is."

At nine that evening her phone rang. It was David Royce.

"Hello, Daphne, I've given your association with my brother some thought and frankly, there's one thing more I should tell you about James. Can we meet?"

She thought the call suspicious and had a quick response to his question. "We can meet here, my mother is recovering from an operation, but she won't bother us."

"That would be fine then, give me your address."

She was relieved, suspicions groundless. Although the thought carried interest for a moment. She told her mother a male friend was going to stop in for a few minutes and for her not to read anything into it. "He's happily married."

Daphne's mother immediately recognized David Royce, from the cinema newsreels, she said. He was charming and delightful, her mother thought, thrilled to have met him and insisted on referring to him as Sir David. He smiled when Daphne rolled her eyes at him over the word, Sir. At the same time, she couldn't help wondering how her mother would react when, and if, she met his brother, and how he looked. When Mrs. Elliot was finally convinced she needed to rest she left regretfully, wondering what on earth her daughter was up to.

"You look worn, David."

"I'm weary from the meetings and what they expect from my manufacturing capacity. We've got to expand exponentially and thankfully James will be available to take some of the development load off me."

"I think you might want to go a little easy on Jim, at first."

He said nothing. She could see something else came to his mind. Probably the one more thing he wanted to tell her about Jim. Daphne waited.

"I've gone over this, Daphne. I never dreamed I would ever have to tell anyone. Yet now, you've popped up and your feelings about James have forced the issue. I hope you will not hate me afterward."

He walked a few paces away, and then turned to face her. She could see distress in his face and couldn't imagine what on earth was so terrible.

"For God's sake David, what is so dreadful? Get it out!"

"You see, the back of James's head, under his hair has an indentation deeper than the front."

"I've never noticed it. His hair must hide it well. And what does it matter anyhow?"

"Yes, well, when James was eight, two Doctors said that part of the cranium is pressing on his brain."

Not fully comprehending the impact of the statement, Daphne was puzzled. "What does that mean?"

"We don't really know. The doctor's said it could possibly press on the Cortex and they believe that sector of the Cortex controls the thinking processes."

Her eyes betrayed confusion. "What was their prognosis?"

"I don't recall."

"I think you do." One thing after another, she thought.

"Daphne, this was in 1913. James was diagnosed in 1913. "The prognosis was inconclusive and they've made amazing strides since then. James always refused to have tests as he grew up and I seriously doubt he's done anything about it over there. And that's been another three years. In all frankness, I wish you every amount of success if you try to get him to do anything about it now. Still, please remember one thing. If you mention you have the slightest inkling about this, James will understand I was the one who told you. And believe me, that will be the finish of any hope of his coming back to work for the company."

Daphne sank back into the chair as her shoulders slumped. "Then what can I do? What will Jim do in life?"

"James doesn't have to do anything, or simply do what he is doing. He can live very securely with the income he receives off Royce Bearing, or he can go climb somewhere else. Forever, if he wants. But I think he would be a wastrel at this troubled time for our country."

She was not following David's comments and he could see that. "Look Daphne, I see you're not a gold digger so I will tell you this in rounded figures. Our company is privately held. When Father owned sixty-eight percent of Royce Bearing, James and I each held sixteen percent. When father died, his will left sixty-five percent ownership of the company, including Ravensmoor, our home, to me. The will moved James ownership up from sixteen to thirty-five percent of Royce Bearing, its holdings and all future acquisitions. Remember, the will had been legalized before James left. To give you some idea of the scope of the company, we now fabricate bearings for all models of the Rolls Royce Merlin and the new Griffon engines. I'll give credit to James for his bearing designs and concepts on the Merlin engines. They go into the Supermarine Spitfire, the Avro Lancaster four-engine bombers, the Hawker Hurricane and more. I was recently over to Ontario, Canada, as they're going to make some Hurricanes there eventually, and we will supply bearings and other equipment for them as well. In addition to this, the First Lord of the Admiralty wants us to supply bearings for the next refits of the Carrier *Ark Royal* and all the *King George* Class battleships, plus other ships. The list goes on. These are tremendous, costly undertakings and are critical projects for England and again, another of the reasons James is needed quite desperately."

David became intense. "What I'm taking a long time getting

at Daphne, is James still receives a fixed percentage from the company's profits since he left. I wired twenty percent of this income to Vienna each quarter for three years and deposited the remainder to his bank here. You can imagine after what I've just told you, what that income is and might grow to. Suffice to say he has no financial concerns. So now, I'll be straightforward with you, I believe it's time for James to have concern for his country's peril and earn his inheritance for once."

Daphne accepted David's comments; they did sound reasonable. Nevertheless, he was imperious, unused to being challenged and she had been holding herself in check all evening.

"Tell me, David, now that you've had your say, let me ask you a question."

Her voice carried an assertiveness he didn't care for. He became guarded. "What is it you would like to know?"

"Let's just suppose I did not meet your lordship's lofty standards? What would you have done?"

He was mystified, thrown off balance. "What do you mean, what would I have done?"

"Come off it, David, you can do better than that. Would you have refused to allow me to see Jim? Would you have told Jim I was not acceptable by your standards and he wasn't to see me? Tell me—what would you have done?"

Disoriented, he remained cautious. "I'm not quite sure I understand your attitude, Daphne."

"Then let me make my *attitude* perfectly clear, Sir David. What if you don't meet *my* standards for what I want in Jim's brother. Did you ever think of that? Of course you haven't, it would never enter your conceited, handsome head. If Jim wants to see me, we will see each other. Get that straight. So come down off your high horse, your Lordship, I'm not here to get along with you. So face up to it. You and I start off on an equal footing, or we don't start off at all, period."

With that, Daphne courteously escorted David to the door.

Chapter 6

11 Sept. 1938

THE GM OPEL WHINED AND CREAKED as Becker struggled the auto up to speed under the additional weight of the equipment and Royce. A balky clutch fought each gear change and blowing snow drifting onto the roadway made the car slew from side to side on its worn snow tires.

Becker felt Royce would not survive in the trunk for what would now be a hundred and sixty miles and they had pushed skis aside so he could sit in front. There, due to a rusted heater core, only wisps of heat was shared between them. Each time a vehicle went by going the other way or, when one lorry actually caught up and passed, Royce would duck as far as possible under the dashboard as passengers in the other vehicles stared hard at Becker.

Royce and he discussed how to get in touch with each other in the future. Mail and telephone were out of the question, with the Germans in total control of both. Becker got most of his information from his Telefunken wireless set. Transmissions could not reach England due to weather conditions and, of course, the mountains. The same conditions may not prevail for receiving, he emphasized. Messages to him by wireless would be open so there had to be a code, and a code name.

"My receiving must be brief." Becker said. "I use pieces from war code words. I write code for things—names, time and dates, after we cross border, you safe in Switzerland."

Their conversation, and Royce's often ducking under the dashboard, went on for over four hours until Becker judged them ten miles from the border. Pulling onto a side path and checking there was no traffic, they removed the boxes and trunk panel. Royce, smothered in a coat, hat, mittens, three pairs of socks and a blanket, squeezed into the cramped space. Becker refitted the panel and boxes, and threw a few boxes into the passenger's front seat. The Opel lurched and they headed for the Austrian-Swiss border.

Vehicles and soldiers of several military branches blocked the border crossing to Davos, Switzerland. Becker stopped, staring at the confusion. Three-ton GM Opel and German Ford Wagens, Personenkraftwagens (personnel carriers), Wehrmacht (regular German army soldiers), Gerbirgsjäeger (Mountain troops) and, worst of all, Waffen SS (Military arm of the SS, above any law, other than their own.)

For a moment, Becker thought to turn around, which he quickly knew would be fatal—they would pounce on him like hawks. Best to brazen it out. With that resolve he pulled out of line and drove west on the east bound lane. Cargo Lorries, crammed with civilians, their drivers cursing him, squeezed past. Three Wehrmacht troopers pointing Mauser machine pistols stopped him near the guardhouse. Becker got out of the Opel, indignant. As a former German Officer, he knew how to demand respect.

"What in hell is going on here?"

The soldiers were caught off guard by the authority in the voice. "Who are you?"

"I am retired Colonel von Becker. Who's in charge here?"

Two Wehrmacht Captains came up, questioningly him angrily. Becker introduced himself and turned up the collar of his jacket, showing the Red Eagle. The two officers came to attention, saluting. This in turn hastily caused the three other troopers to do the same. Courtesies then offered, they asked what they could do for him.

"I am not going to wait in this Goddamned line. What's going on here?"

"Sorry Colonel, the Waffen SS is arresting Jews trying to get over the border."

Becker feigned being perplexed. "I thought Germany was deporting them, so why don't they just shove them over the border and wash their hands of them?"

"Because in Vienna, Sir, SS Colonel Eichmann ordered them to leave months ago, and they didn't. Now he says he is teaching them a lesson for not doing as they were told. We're sorry Colonel, we have no choice in this. The Waffen SS is now in charge of the Wehrmacht."

Becker could see the officer's dismay. They needed permission to let him through the crossing, and they asked him into the guardhouse to meet the Waffen SS Major in charge. To his surprise, the officer recognized him.

"Colonel von Becker!"

Becker didn't know the officer coming up. "Colonel, I'm Reinhardt Dietrich! I don't expect you to recognize me. I was a fresh Oberleutant in the 1st Gard when you were made Colonel. That was in 1917, '18. You were my hero!"

Becker was embarrassed as they shook hands, although he thanked God someone knew him here. Given a cup of burnt coffee, he suffered through Major Dietrich's stories of Colonel von Becker's heroics. Everyone gathered around, saluted him and the Red Eagle, and listened to the tales. Everyone, he noticed, except an officer at the far end of the room. Becker stayed calm and smiled to all, yet he couldn't forget Royce was jammed into the trunk with the temperature steadily below freezing. After a half hour of stories, facts mingled with false memories, he said he would like to be getting on so he could make Davos before dark.

They wished him well, walked him to the Opel, and called the gate to order it lifted. He was stopped as he got to the vehicle, and introduced to Fallschirmäjger Dieter Schmid, SS Staff Officer, and Adolf Hitler Division. Becker guessed there was something about the lone officer in the gatehouse and managed to keep his composure. "Hello Major, long way from Berlin aren't you?"

The Major did not salute, was not interested in the question, nor impressed by the Red Eagle. "Yes, my starry-eyed staff omitted telling you there is another mission for all the military arrayed here. We are looking for the murderer of my son. I am personally at this forsaken post because I feel the killer would try to get through this crossing rather than the more obvious ones at Feldkirch or Lichtenstein."

"Makes good sense to me, Major."

"Tell me Colonel Becker, What brings you to this gate?"

"The equipment supplier for my spa is in Chur and I'm returning the goods I bought as my clientele is dwindling due to the union with Germany. Many people are leaving."

"Do you question decisions of our Führer?"

A barbed question, which Becker saw could lead to a wrong answer, Red Eagle or not. Yet, he wasn't about to be cowed, staring at the SS Major. "Only as far as it affects my business, Major."

Unspeaking, Major Schmid walked around the Opel. With barely a glance through the windows, he opened a rear door. Then looked at Becker.

"Open the trunk."

"It's unlocked." Becker didn't move. He was not going to be ordered. Major Schmid stood there. A Captain ran forward and lifted the trunk lid. Two boxes fell out.

Ernst Becker did not so much as blink. Major Schmid gave him a fixed look and, without a glance at the trunk, started to walk off. He turned. "You should remember one thing, *former* Colonel Becker. Red Eagle or not, you Prussians lost that war. We will not lose the next one and suffer the same humiliation as your military."

As he drove the fifty yards to the crossing gate, Becker could have wept. Countless trunks, suitcases, and winter clothes were piled on the ground haphazardly. Scores of vehicles were scattered in a field. Worst of all, people huddled together in small groups, trying to withstand the twenty-degree temperature. He watched as a German Ford truck pulled up and people forced into it until it was tightly packed. No tarpaulin protected them from the wind as the truck drove off.

It was all Becker could do not to lash out at the injustice of the moment. He was no fool, and had heard the all too true rumors.

An SS Captain walked beside his car to the Austrian gate. As Becker produced his passport, he commented to the Captain the truckload of people would not last a long trip.

The Captain smiled. "They're not going far. Just over that hill, there's a ravine. If the wind is right, there are times we hear the singing of the machineguns even from here. It's like the Americans said about Indians. Dead Indians are good Indians.

And dead Jews are good Jews."

It was almost more than he could endure. If he had been out of the Opel, he would have strangled the Captain, yet he had to remember the reason he was there. A man freezing in the trunk. The gate opened and he drove through to the Swiss side and their border guards. Passport, a few needless questions, and Becker drove the auto around the building, out of sight from the German side. Three Swiss border guards came up to him as he threw open the trunk and started throwing out boxes, calling to Royce. When there wasn't an answer, the guards were quick to understand and helped remove the inert body from its hiding place. Royce was a ghost, barely breathing. One of the guards ran off and brought a Swiss Army van, they carried Royce to it and, with Becker in pursuit, the van raced to a medical dispensary two miles away. From a distance, Major Schmid saw the van and Opel race off. He wondered, and then began to curse and curse...

Swiss doctors see countless cases of frostbite and know how to bring the body circulation back slowly. This time they felt something more was wrong, the breathing too erratic, shallow. They put Royce on pure oxygen. Becker had a speaking knowledge of Schwyzerdutsch, the Swiss-German dialect of eastern Switzerland and he easily understood when they asked how he was hidden. Becker walked one of the doctors out to see the trunk. The doctor knew many had tried this hiding place and been caught. Of more interest was how the patient had been able to breathe. Becker showed him the breathing tube, finding it plugged with a mitten. Why would Royce do such a thing? The doctor, putting his head closer, caught a lingering whiff.

"Carbon Monoxide, Mister Becker. Do you have a leak in your exhaust pipe?"

Becker bent his head down. That had to be it. He had almost killed Royce trying to save him. "Will he be all right?"

"I think so. We will test his motor skills when he regains his senses, then a few cognitive tests. He'll be moved to a rehabilitation facility if they're positive. May I ask if you know what happened to his face?"

"He was struck by lightning."

The doctor was skeptical. "I would seriously doubt that, sir.

In the back of this head under the hair is a severe indentation."

"I didn't know that doctor, what does that mean?"

"Does he function normally under ordinary conditions?"

"Yes, as far as I've seen."

"I'm surprised." The doctor said no more.

Royce regained full consciousness after two days, but was ill at ease; with aching, stinging fingers and toes. His throat was sore also, but thankfully, the little speaking he did confirmed he understood what had happened, and eased everyone's concern over any impairment of the brain.

Two days later, he was moved to the Davos Infirmary to repeat processes similar to those performed while at Doctor Arnheimer's Clinic in Austria. He asked Becker to send a telegram to David Royce stating he was in Switzerland and safe, although delayed two weeks. He did not give a reason. The message stated he could be contacted, care of the telegraph office in Davos.

While Royce recovered, Becker took a day trip to Chur and his supplier, who refused to take back the equipment. Of course knowing he could not return through the border with a full automobile, he sold them to the supplier well below cost.

It was after dark when he returned to Davos and instead of going straight to his hotel, he stopped in to see Royce. The door to his room was slightly open, dim light filtered in. Becker was quiet, not wanting to wake Royce, then saw he wasn't asleep in the half dark and watched him staring, unseeing at the wall. Now and then Royce would lower his head, slowly nod, then lift it again. He never blinked. He was somewhere else, lost in memories. Becker read the sorrow there. To enter this world would not be welcome.

* * *

12 September 1938

Hitler demanded the Sudetenland region of Czechoslovakia be 'returned' to Germany. The Czechs said they would not give in, despite attempts by Chamberlain and Daladier of France to force them to relinquish their land. Chamberlain then flew to confer with Hitler on the 18th and again on the 22nd. Most diplomats knew what the negotiations were about and, the British cabinet to their honor if not the Prime Minister's, refused to accept the partition of Czech land.

21 September 1938
Czechoslovakia, without aid from the West, was forced to cede the Sudetenland to Germany. The next day, the Great Powers of Europe met in Munich. The Czech's were excluded.

On 30 Sept. Prime Minister Chamberlain went to Hitler and asked for a peace treaty between the United Kingdom and Germany. Hitler laughingly agreed. On that same day, Chamberlain returned to Britain, delivering his infamous 'Peace in our time' speech. The shameful peace would be short lived.

David Royce sat at his desk contemplating Prime Minister Neville Chamberlain's speech at the airport on his return to England. David leaned forward and unlocked his diary.

September 30, 1938:
Chamberlain (the ill fool) and the French PM (as big a fool) have flown to Munich and been completely hoodwinked by Mussolini (idiot and oaf) and Hitler (lunatic) and signed a Treaty allowing partition of Sudeten without informing the Czechs! Another blot on our history has been committed!

The Prime Minister (should be sacked) is back and waving a paper claiming 'peace in our time'. This disgrace will haunt us to our grave. He has sold out the Czechs who have a good army. Whom will he give to that sick man next? We must get rid of the PM and replace him. With whom? Hopefully Churchill.

Must step up our rearmament program. RB growing incredibly. Be sure to listen to Kaltenborn and E Morrow tonight and hear their comments about our appeasement.

David sat back, and put down his pen as Albert handed him the telegram from his brother. Reading it, he wondered what was going on. His wandering brother was out of Austria at least, yet now, another delay. Why? Climbing a few more mountains in Switzerland before returning? This was annoying with so much ahead to be done. He went back to his diary.

Received another message from James-another delay. No reason, no telephone call. Just telegram. Tired of his actions and paying him for nothing. Would like to buy him out and let him go his way-need the brain. Get him back, make him useful to RB and my future.

David tossed the pen down in disgust.

* * *

"I'm serious, Beck. Why don't you come to England? There's nothing here for you until Hitler pulls back, or gets what he deserves."

"My friend, Royce. You English, go to England, you home. I Prussian, Austria become my home, I not fit in England."

"But your country has been taken over by Nazis, by the SS. It will not be the same."

"Still home. I...what word, stubborn? I *stubborn.* Won't leave. Maybe be help."

Royce knew it wouldn't happen, so stopped asking. He was surprised when Becker gave him back his Leica camera, passport, and money. He had forgotten that when he was in the Opel, he had stuffed them in his coat. He was still a touch unsteady on his feet and annoyed by intermittent headaches although he felt ready to continue his journey.

On 1 October, David sent a message to Royce via the telegraph office in Davos: **contact me date you will arrive either Zurich Bern Geneva will send plane David**

"What on earth is this about flying, Beck?"

"Brother has money to order special plane?"

With Royce's nod, Becker went on, "You fly before?"

"No."

"I fly 1918. Fokker three wing, one motor. Scare. I not want to go up now."

"You scared? Someone with all your medals?"

"Hero on ground, scared in air."

They both laughed. "Well Beck, I can imagine they've improved somewhat over twenty years."

"Last May, German bomber, two motor, crash in Stubai Glacier near Innsbruck. All dead. You not know?"

"No, I didn't. But I really want to thank you for that bit of information, Beck."

It took Becker a moment to translate British irony into German, and then he burst out laughing. "You are welcome, Herr Royce."

They scanned a map for the best airport and transportation. Royce couldn't help notice there were few straight lines for railroad tracks and Becker reminded him there were countless mountains in Switzerland as well, and mountains everywhere required many detours to get around. Distances measured as the crow flies didn't mean a thing here, Becker commented, even crows have to go around. They decided on Zurich's Kolten Aerodrome, as the closest from Chur by train. Estimating the trip would take most of the day, Royce telegraphed David on 2 October: **Kolten Aerodrome Zurich there 3 October Monday remain for your instructions James**

David was quick to reply: **meet brit attaché at train Zurich get going David**

"Your brother quick."

"He's all right, Beck, a little impressed with himself that's all. He'll get over it."

"How old?"

"He's about thirty-five."

"Late for get over it."

"Maybe, hope you're wrong, Beck."

"You can hope, Royce, not me."

They bantered on for a while longer until the train was leaving. It was time to part. Royce tried to give him money. Becker wouldn't hear of it. They hugged, saying they would meet again—doubting, but wanting—to believe. Becker had put the Opel's rear seat and trunk back together in case Major Schmid was still prowling the border crossing and decided this time to check the entire car. He was going back through the border crossing to his home in a country under Nazi occupation, a country, which would no longer respect the Order of the Red Eagle. Royce, going back to a world he once escaped.

They shook hands, "Take this, Royce." A folded paper. "My code, Royce. We keep touch."

The steam locomotive hurried along its silver rails, swaying into the dawn. Once the sun cleared the peaks of the mountains, Royce moved from the east side of the train the west, to stop the glare in his eyes that had given him a headache. The train swept northwest past the border of Lichtenstein. As the sun rose higher, he moved back to the right side and stared into the eastern distance, toward the white-capped peaks of the Raetikon Range, far off to the east. Royce knew the range was not as high as his Alps, but still wished he were climbing there now. He thought how he always loved to sit on an upland plateau to watch a mountain's mood change as the sun slipped beneath the peaks and fingers of shadows crept into the valleys. Pinpoints of light would start to randomly appear and a town he didn't even discern was there would shine out of the dark, long into the evening.

"All this will not miss me, but, God, I will miss it." He whispered. Yet now he was tired and weak, somehow still feeling the cold from the Opel's trunk. His fingers pained as he stretched and gripped them alternately. His head ached. He fell into welcome asleep.

Eventually passing the spur rail lines to Glarus and Zug, the locomotive then took the Northeasterly sweep around Lake Zurich, the last leg to the city itself.

Chapter 7

ENVELOPED IN BILLOWING STEAM, the engine hissed to a stop. Royce eased slowly down the steps looking about for someone to recognize him. A young man in a commerce suit approached. "Mister James Royce?"

"Yes, how did you know?"

The man was embarrassed. "Well sir, you do rather stand out among people."

Royce smiled. "Quite diplomatic, my man. And you are?"

"Michael Cameron, Sir. British attaché here in Zurich. Your brother, Sir David, asked that you be escorted to the airport."

"That's very good of you, thank you."

"Is your luggage here, sir?"

"I don't have luggage, just this sack. In fact, there's a kiosk, I would like to pick up some toiletries."

Cameron thought no luggage strange, yet it was not for him to question. Royce collected the items he needed and a kit to store them. After freshening up in the airport's guest room, he was guided to the attaché's Armstrong-Siddeley Saloon for the short ride to Zurich's Kolten Aerodrome.

"I've called ahead, Sir. They're waiting for you, ready to go as soon as we arrive."

"Fine, Michael."

Royce wasn't rude, but not in the mood to talk. David said a plane would be there, so one was waiting. Of more pressing concern was the fact he had never flown and Becker's comments about flying were on his mind. Then again, he felt if other people could do it, he probably could to.

The Saloon drove directly onto the concrete runway and down the far end, stopping beside what Royce thought to be a very large aircraft.

"What is this, Michael, quite a size isn't it?"

"It's a Royal Air Force Armstrong Whitworth AW 38 bomber, Sir. It's called a Whitley and, I rather imagine, a few other names as well. Only twin engines, so she's not too large. The fuselage has been converted from a bomber configuration to carrying toffs around the countryside. Sorry Sir, I mean getting important people to where they're needed."

"No offence taken, Michael, I'm riding on my brother's reputation."

"Whatever you say, Sir."

The clatter of twin unmuffled Rolls Royce Merlin engines hammered on Royce's headache as he climbed the ladder and assisted into the aircraft. Comparatively quiet inside, he could at least hear himself think. The person who helped him was the co-pilot and involuntarily paused when he looked at Royce's face. Royce simply said. "Lightening."

The co-pilot nodded and asked if there were any luggage. When told there was none he asked another question, "Me name's Jock, Sir. You look nervous, first flight?"

"Yes, it is and I'm quite tired…and Jock, I admit to a bit of nervousness also."

"You'll find no need for concern, Sir. We just had new R-R Merlin's mounted, and we've a superb pilot. So other than a bit of noise and a few bumps, you can just take a little snooze and we'll have you back in Old Blighty before you know it. Strap yourself in like this and we'll be off on our way, Sir."

Royce sat back, managing to relax slightly, and then heard the pilots shouting over the clatter of the engines.

"Are you sure you don't want to add more petrol, Colin?"

"Of course I want to add more bloody petrol! You know it makes us too bloody heavy to takeoff on this short bloody runway. We'll be bloody lucky to clear those bloody trees at the end and even if we do clear them we'll be lucky if they don't rip off our bloody landing gear. But as I think of it, Jock, if we run out of bloody petrol we can drop in on Frenchie in Rouen."

"Whatever you say, Colin."

"How's our most important bloody person, in the rear?"

"If he's heard you I don't think the gov feels too good."

Colin let out a shrill laugh, and then was quiet as he studied each gauge and lever.

"All right now, Jock, you keep those bloody brakes on tight while I wind up these bloody engines and hope we don't blow the bloody top off a piston. When I give the word, let them bloody go."

The wheel chocks were pulled as the RPMs started winding up, the unmuffled engines high-pitched roar soon increased. Simultaneously, the aircraft shuddered and vibrated so badly Royce though it was going to shake itself apart. The engines' twin superchargers kicked in. The plane, still on the ground, rattled even worse, and Royce felt panic coming to the surface.

"Now, Jocko me boy! Let her go!"

The brakes released, the Whitley's tail skewed from side to side as Colin fought the controls to keep the aircraft aligned while it gathered momentum.

Royce, damp with sweat, shut his eyes. Colin threw the Whitley down the runway with engines roaring and every rivet in the fuselage straining to hold the metal skin together. To Royce, it was an introduction to hell.

The bumping stopped. Royce took a breath, but was thrown back and sideways onto his left shoulder, the harness girded tightly on his body. The aircraft swerved sharply, angling steeply upward. He gritted his teeth, unable to understand the shouting in the cockpit over the roaring of the engines. He was close to throwing up when the aircraft leveled and the engines backed down from their excessive revolutions.

"See Jock! I told you, piece of bloody cake!"

"Aye, Colin, other than you forgot how close that flaming mountain was at the end."

"Well, matters bloody little anyway, we cheated the devil again. Go back and check the bloody condition of our guest. See if he's peed his pants, or worse."

"Mister Royce, Sir. Please excuse Colin's language; it was a wee touch close. Would you like to use the…ah, lavatory?"

"Thank you no, Jock. I've still got all my bodily fluids, but only barely."

"Well then, if you'll excuse me, sir, you weren't up there, I'll use it."

Colin set a course due west, avoiding any possibility of crossing German territory. When they cleared Delemont in northwest Switzerland, Royce heard Jock contacting French airspace for RAF flight RAFB511 with their flight plan—northwest over Dijon, then Paris and leave French airspace at Le Havre.

Compared to takeoff the flight was relatively smooth, although up and downdrafts were a concern for Royce. The pilots kept talking nonchalantly ignoring it all and Royce, therefore, decided the vibration may be of no matter. Engines could cause vibration. Colin and Jock were the ones to watch. If they were calm, he would be—if they got upset, he would panic.

Flight sergeant and co-pilot, Jock came back to talk. "Mister Royce, Sir, we were told you've been in Austria for some time and might be out of touch, so we brought some papers along to help you catch up."

"Kind of you Sergeant, I'll be sure to read them. How's our flight going?"

"Bang on, sir. Colin's having a bit of bother trying to synchronize the Merlin's, that's why we're sensing a touch more rattle than normal. But he'll get it sorted out sometime before we land. When you're finished reading why don't you pop on forward?"

"I would very much like to, thank you again."

Jock then began a recitation for Royce to bring him up to date from the   previous twelfth of September, when Hitler had demanded Czechoslovakia's Sudetenland territory. How PM Chamberlain flew to see Hitler and France and then England asked the Czech's to give up the Sudeten. The Czechs refused, Jock said, and that Chamberlain flew again to see Hitler.

Finally, Jock told how the Czech army mobilized and Chamberlain and Daladier flew to Munich twice again without the Czech Government present, both Daladier and Chamberlain reneged on their agreements and Czechoslovakia was left to suffer the same fate as Austria.

After Jock's recital brought Royce up to date, he settled back disgusted at the information and turned to the papers. They were dated 1 October through the 3rd, the previous day. He started with the earliest. The Daily Mail reported the Prime Minister returned home with "Peace in Our Time. The PM met with The House of Commons today and expects the House to endorse the Treaty." Manchester Guardian "...King thanks Nation...PM states, Peace in Our Time is Hope, not Pledge." The Times..." First Lord of the Admiralty Churchill, condemns Treaty...Hitler can have what he wants now...Churchillian's too weak to stop Treaty approval."

Between Jock's knowledge and the papers, Royce knew enough to follow peace would be tenuous at best. He was about to set the paper aside when another name caught his eye.

"Industrialist, Sir David Royce said today, 'England is dishonored, another courageous little country has been thrown to the wolf. A wolf which will chew up the Treaty and spit it in England's face.'"

Royce smiled. So David's making the papers now, although on the second page. He wondered how long it would be until his brother made the first. He leaned forward and called into the cockpit. "Who is this Churchill fellow?"

Jock came aft. "You'll remember him, Sir. He was a back bencher at Commons. The First Lord of the Admiralty in the war. When the army and navy mucked it up in Gallipoli, he got the sack. Only other things I recall is he was on King Edward's side when he abdicated in '36 over that American Simpson woman. And of course his articles warning of what's to come."

"You a wee Geordie, Jock?"

"Aye sir. Newcastle on Tyne. Both me and me mate, Bloody, Colin Dennison, the pilot, Sir, His nickname's Bloody. "

"I can't imagine why." Royce laughed. "And what is your surname?"

"MacDonald, but Jock's fine, sir. There's one other thing I could kick meself for forgetting, Sir. Your brother's quite taken by Mister Churchill."

Two thoughts caught Royce's mind at once. Jock knew David and David's comment on Churchill. "How do you know my brother?"

"Why me and Bloody fly Sir David everywhere he wants to go. His factories make bearings for us, you know."

"Yes, I'm aware of that."

"Well then, he asks for us special. We fly all over England and the Continent. He's a good friend of the RAF he is, so we fly him wherever he wants. He takes the controls now and then, don't tell anyone, and he tells us bits of things like his ideas on the government, which me mind tells me, should be kept tight to meself and Bloody."

Royce stared out the window at the ocean. We've cleared Le Havre, he thought, only one more leg and a new life. What's going to happen? He felt odd, neutral to thoughts on the future. Let the preceding years go. That's the thing to do. Put a proper face on coming home. It's quite possible this will work out. Especially when he saw Daphne.

"Mister Royce, Sir, we'll be coming up on the coast soon, over Brighton. If you would like to take the copilot seat, you'll have a cocker view."

He met Colin, the pilot, and found himself dazzled by the array of dials, switches, handles, knobs, levers and lights. He sat, amused by working out each control's function.

"There she is, Sir."

Whitley Mark IVs fly marginally nose down, so Royce had a perfect view of the dome on Brighton's Royal Pavilion, the coast and the city. Then, unfolding before him, the green, rolling countryside. A chill coursed through his body. Jock and Bloody sensed his emotion and kept quiet, waiting for him to control his feelings. Royce thought of Harrow and excerpts from Shakespeare…This Royal throne of kings…this sceptered isle…this seat of Mars…this precious stone set in a silver sea… this blessed plot, this earth, this realm—this England.

He couldn't believe how the sight and thought choked him up. His eyes watered and he fought to control his feelings. Without looking at either pilot, and to change his emotion he asked why he could sense vibration on the seat of his pants. Surprised by the question, Colin explained he couldn't get the motors synced despite their equalized rpms and petrol metering. And, he was emphatic, neither motor was misfiring.

"They're going like the clappers, sir."

Royce partially stood, looking sideway to the port engine and then to starboard. "I worked on the bearings for the early Merlin's years ago, Colin and I think you're right, it's not an engine. They're brilliant, don't have a weakness other than not being petrol injected."

Struck that Royce had anything to do with engineering, all they could say was to ask what he thought wasn't right.

"I think you'll find it's the port engine nacelle or rather the engine mount. You're getting transferred vibration from there, right to the seat of your pants, and with that violent maneuver at full throttle at the end of the runway we've quite possibly fractured a mount or strut. You know you generated tremendous torque on the downside engine with the aircraft's pitch. So, my guess is it's the port side, consequently the vibration, which seems to be a bit worse as I sit here. Understand one thing, if the vibration starts there and transfers to here, it will return to the engine by a greater magnitude each time it transfers. By that I mean it will fluctuate back and forth, until the engine falls off."

The two men looked at each other, shrugged their shoulders until Colin spoke. "Sounds bang on to me, sir. I'll throttle back and we'll just coast home, wouldn't want to lose one of His Majesty's bloody motors over Buckingham."

"Colin, I suggest you shut that one down if this plane will fly and land on one engine."

"Sir, if you'd like to watch, I could fly it and land it backwards with only one engine."

There was relieved laughter as Bloody shut the engine down.

"By the way you two, where's home?"

Jock blinked his eyes. "Why, Sir, if we make it, we're delivering you to RAF Badminton. That's almost on top of Ravensmoor."

Too sudden he was home. Too difficult to believe. "There's an airport at Coventry?"

"An RAF one now, just outside, Sir. Far as we know your brother will be picking you up. We probably should have thought to mention it. Colin will wake Operations at the field in a bit."

Colin performed the landing and run out smoothly, brought the Whitly around and stopped beside two Hawker Hurricane fighters.

Ground crew chocked the wheels after the starboard engine was silenced. The three flyers dropped down from the hatch, walking to the port engine.

Jock was the first to spot the metal fracture. The tear curled for a good twelve inches around the offside of the fairing, where the nacelle was riveted.

At this point, David Royce's Bentley ghosted to a stop. David got out and stood quietly. The pilots and Royce, engrossed, had their backs to him.

"You were right Mister Royce, it's the port nacelle."

Royce was inspecting the tear in the aircraft's metal skin. "How old is the aircraft itself?"

"Around two years, Sir, and we picked it up with new engines at RAF Manston only a fortnight ago."

"All right then, we can rule out metal fatigue. Either the vibration was caused by the fit between the leading edge of the wing and the fairing being too snug, or it's a broken engine mount. My money's on the mount, and I'll give you odds."

Jock pulled up the edge of the loose metal of the nacelle and peered inside. "No bet with me, Sir. There it is, pretty as you please, left front mount cracked and almost split wide open."

"Colin, I know we had an extremely hard maneuver leaving Zurich, so tell your Squadron Leader what you've found and recommend he write up a report suggesting to add a strut, gusset or whatever on the mounting frame to absorb excessive force on the mounts, or someone may very well drop a King's engine."

"Glad you were aboard, Sir."

They turned together and saw David standing there. He nodded to the pilots and shook his brother's hand. Colin and Jock were told to jump in front with Albert, the driver, as David and Royce climbed in the rear. David ordered Albert to drop the pilots off at Operations, and then rolled up the divider window to the rear. At Ops, David got out and spoke to the pilots. He was told that "Mister Royce diagnosed the problem correctly. So, he's either a great guesser or a genius."

David smiled at them "Which do you think?"

"Bloody genius." They said in unison.

David sat back in the Rolls. "You certainly amazed them."

"I suppose. Although theoretically, it was fairly simple. Merlin engines don't go out of sync unless Colin clipped a prop and he would have known that, so it was a simple process of elimination. They would have worked out the reason for the vibration sooner or later. And I do admit it was a guess as to which engine mount had failed."

David smiled at the modesty and looked closely at Royce. "You look like something the cat dragged home, James."

"I always looked like that David. However, you look overstressed, in a way you never did."

"Nice to see you, James."

"And nice to see you again."

"Seriously James, you look as if you had some problems in Austria."

"I did, both in Austria and getting out."

"You should have left when I told you to."

"Yes, yes, I know. Though there's more to it than that. I'll tell you some of it when I relax with a few scotches in me."

"Fair enough. By the by, I met with Daphne."

Royce turned his head so quickly it could have snapped.

"What's that you said?"

"Merely that your Daphne called. If you're surprised then I suppose she found Ravensmoor's number on her own and rang us up."

"Why did she call?"

"Well, she said she had a letter from you for me, and if I was going to be in London, which I was, then she could deliver it to me in person. Save a few days in the post, she said. However, I think she really wanted to find out more about you. Did you mention me to her, James?"

"Yes, though little."

"Well, I mentioned a lot about you, so I wanted you to be prepared when you see your beautiful, ah…friend."

"Are you trying to annoy me, *Sir* David?"

"It always takes little trying with you James, and I see you haven't changed. However, try to pick yourself up a touch, will you? Mary sees you like this and she'll want to mother hen you all over again."

They sat back, neither saying a word, enclosed in their own thoughts. Royce pondered that, whereas he had no choice other than getting out of Austria, he didn't have to return to Coventry. He could have gone to London instead, and seen Daphne. Then again, the RAF pilots wouldn't have given him the option. In addition, he supposed, after reading the headlines in the papers when he was in the aircraft, it perhaps was best to find out the seriousness of the tension where England was concerned. He was, after all was said and done, British. He found that to be true when he took in the '...this precious stone set in a silver sea'.

David Royce, on the other hand, analyzed the situation methodically. He was going about this altogether incorrectly. Number one, he needed his brother's brains whether he liked it or not. Number two, creating tension was not the way to approach James. He should have known better than to let his own irritation show. And a third point, he should change his attitude. James is a decent person, fouled up in life, left when he was needed, yet now, he's needed even more. Remember that, no matter how it may stick in the craw.

David resumed the conversation first. "Forgive me James. There is just so much on my plate right now with Royce Bearing expanding into other segments of industry, we're stretched thin. The government is not going to cut back on rearmaments, thanks be to God, and that means the volume clauses in our contracts will increase two-fold at least. That is nice to have, for us as well as England's survival, although with it comes the trials and tribulations of handling the growth. The Munitions Board is pre-paying fifty percent of order *cost* only, so that means it's not paying for construction expenditures involving the new assembly buildings. My concerns are the people we need and the fact I can't do it all myself; that is why I need you to...we're almost home James. We'll talk later. Again, I'm sorry, and let's start on a new footing."

Toward the end of David's comments Royce was only half listening. From the rise of a hill, the massive limestone walls of Ravensmoor imposed upon the forested landscape. It came back to Royce how much he disliked that cold block of gray. It epitomized his father's arrogance and David's indifference as he grew up. Well, his father was gone, and David did try to improve their relationship. Now, if ever, was the time to bury the hard feelings and start with a clean slate. At least give it a go, damn it.

Chapter 8

THEIR FATHER HAD RAVENSMOOR BUILT in 1919, from war profits. Constructed of white-gray Portland limestone from the Isle of Portland in Dorset, Father never missed telling every guest his manor's limestone came from the very quarry that supplied stone for Saint Paul's Cathedral and Buckingham Palace.

Originally, the building was a plain three story, thirty-two room rectangle, with one long side facing the drive. In the fading sunset, Royce noticed that in the three years he'd been gone, David had added a wide, centered portico and frontward facing two story wings on each side of the original building now made an inverted **U**. Scottish slate topped the roofs and nine eyebrow dormers, in groups of three, ran along the full length of the original three story building. Evergreens of various types, presently tinted with snow, formed within the three inner sides of the structure, and then continued half way around the cul-de-sac. The distance from the main roadway to the manor was a curved mile and a half drive, lined on both sides by sentinels of oaks, bereft of their leaves for winter.

A stag, with five doe moved casually through the trees and across the road.

"What's with the deer?"

"I bought up land to the south, some of the Ghosly estate. The deer came with it and I sort of think it adds a country touch."

"Yes, it sort of does. How much land did Ghosly sell you?"

"I bought eight hundred acres with a stocked pond from them. That makes Ravensmoor eighteen hundred acres now, giving us a little more breathing room."

"Sounds good. What's that glass building on the right wing?"

"It's called an atrium. Mary wanted one for her plants, so I had it built. It makes a wonderful palm court, similar to one I saw in America. Unfortunately it creates an asymmetrical view from the road, so I may have to put one on the other side also."

"Might as well. Looks like Royce Bearing is doing well."

"Yes, it is, you should know by the income you receive each yearly quarter."

"In truth, David, I don't notice. I never draw it all down and when I closed the Vienna account like you asked, I had it transferred to Credit Suisse BA in Zurich."

"I see. Anyway, James, as far as RB doing well, that's true. Although we're a bit tight right now due to all the construction and renovating we're doing to keep up with Kingsley Wood's orders, he's now Secretary of State for Air."

"Perhaps I've got enough to tide you over. Who's my bank here and how much is in there? We could work something out."

"I structured your account with Rothschild and Sons in London three years ago after you left. I don't know the total amount you've got there, although I should think well over a million, five-hundred, in dollars."

Royce blinked in disbelief. "Are you serious?"

"James, don't you ever look at the account statements I send? You must have had more than three hundred thousand dollars in your former Vienna account alone. I wrote you at least six months ago asking if you wanted me to wire it from Vienna to Rothschild's London. You didn't answer, but at least you moved it to Zurich, away from the Nazis."

"I'll try to keep more involved in the future and make money available if you need it."

"Thank you for that, James. We'll see how things go."

The Bentley swung around the cul-de-sac and stopped at the front entrance. David's wife, Mary, was waiting in the cold at the bottom of the stairs.

Without a word, they wrapped their arms around each other. She then jokingly commented how he was her favorite, despite being her only, brother-in-law.

"What on earth have you been doing to yourself, James? You look to be in need of some attention."

"I probably do, you darling little thing. You're just as beautiful as ever."

"All right dear, although I do thank you. Now what on earth have you been up to, getting yourself in this condition?"

Royce laughed. "It's a long story and part of it has to do with being quite cold, so why don't we move on in to some warmth."

The antechamber was not large, only enough to hold guests to remove their outer coats or wraps before entering the great room. From there, the manor went on to sitting and congregating rooms. They went into one of the more intimate drawing rooms where a fireplace warmed and glowed throughout the space. Royce settled into an overstuffed wingback chair.

"First," Mary said, "the children. You'll remember Elizabeth. She's eight now, as extroverted as ever."

Beth ran to Royce, kissed him and ran a finger down the scar.

"You're the same uncle I knew, even with the beard." She snuggled on his lap, took his arms, and put them around her.

"And this," Mary smiled, "is Victor, he was only two when you...Victor!"

Victor took one look at Royce and started crying.

David was angry, Mary embarrassed. "For God's sake, Victor! We told you about it! Now stop, for goodness sake!"

Beth, sitting in Royce's lap called Victor a big baby and jumped down, took her weeping brother's arm and dragged him up to Royce. "See." Beth said, still holding her brother's arm to prevent him from running. She showed him how she ran her little finger down the length of the scar and into the beard.

"Uncle's not going to bite my finger off."

Nevertheless, Victor looked on wide-eyed waiting to see it happen. When the finger did not disappear, everyone could see Victor's surprise turn to disappointment.

Then Beth closed her hand so that no fingers showed and screeched. "My fingers are gone!"

Victor screamed even louder than Beth, and ran away as fast as he could. His father picked him up and scolded Beth who laughed as hard as she'd ever, while the adults struggled to keep straight faces.

Mary tried desperately to control herself. "Beth, that's a terrible thing to do to your little brother, now show Victor your fingers."

Beth held up only three fingers, grinning wickedly. Victor counted them, and the outcry started again. Royce loved every bit of it and finally, as it sorted out, everyone laughed, even Victor, though rather timidly.

Royce felt badly not having had time to pick up gifts for the children; there really had not been an opportunity. He would make it up as soon as he could.

Eventually the children were packed off to their bedrooms and the adults sat back to chat aimlessly over their slowly warming drinks. Royce kept nodding off. It had been a long day and a long way from Austria. They walked him to his bedroom, and closed the door behind him.

Mary and David sat, with troubled expressions, pondering the situation. "So, Mary, what do you think of him?"

"I don't know what to think. He's just...I don't know, older, worn. A shell from when he left. Something dreadful must have happened there. What could have caused him to get in this state?"

"He said he'd tell me, except of course he didn't say when. Daphne said he wouldn't tell her either, so I guess we will just have to wait him out. My problem is we don't have the luxury of time. Chamberlain's September peace only gives us breathing space and we must try to make the most of it. Do you know Supermarine has produced just 300 Supermarine Spitfires for the RAF? It's insane how naked England is. I need James. He's got to help and I want you to remember one thing; he chose to come back to us. I didn't ask him back even though he was sorely missed and I was tempted. And now, the more I give it thought, it appears the only choice left open to him was to come back."

"I understand, David. We thought his return would give the company the skills it needed. Still, I don't see how you can push right now, look at him. Give him a couple of weeks to recuperate. Perhaps that's all he needs."

"Mary, just the way he keeps rubbing his fingers gives me doubt, although at the aerodrome, he did help the pilots with a problem they couldn't solve."

"Well then, you see dear, give him a little time. Wait! I've an idea; let's ask this Daphne woman up here, she may be the key.

From what you told me she likes him, so let's ask him if he's interested in having her visit."

"I don't know. I mentioned her to him, but he wasn't forthcoming on her or anything, at least at first."

"Well, I'll ask him. That is if you're sure she's not after his money. You're certain?"

"Yes. She's quite unique, Mary. Intelligent, educated, beautiful and I must say blunt, bit too blunt to my liking. I did have her parents checked out. Family's divorced, as she mentioned. Father's wealthy and he supports his ex-wife, son, and daughter in a comfortable lifestyle. Their home's in Belgravia, near Chamberlain's by the way, and if that's any indication, I'd say it's a very comfortable lifestyle indeed."

Mary looked questioningly at David. "Oh? You've been to her home?"

"Don't question me, dear. I didn't mention it because I was afraid you would read something into it that wasn't there. Her mother was at the home and I wanted to tell Daphne one more thing that I thought she should know about James before things went too far."

"And what was that?"

"About the indentation in the back of his head."

"Really? You thought that was necessary?"

"Yes, I did. It would give her a reason to back out before it went too far."

"And do you think you stopped anything?"

"Not in the least."

"Very well then, it's settled. I'll ask James in the morning."

Chapter 9

5 October, 1938

SS Major Dieter Schmid was furious. His Führer had ordered him back to Berlin without giving a reason, even though Schmid hadn't found the Englishman yet. He ordered the troops continue the search for another week and report immediately if they found him. Then, whether they did or not, return to their Commands. He wired for a ski equipped Fokker tri-motor to pick him up in a field at the border crossing. On the way to the aircraft, he could see a ravine where Jews were being herded into another ditch. He glanced absentmindedly at them and, after boarding the Fokker, he never gave them a second thought.

The meeting with Hitler was short, pointed. "Overall Schmid, Colonel Eichmann is doing an excellent job in Austria to rid the country of the Jew. Unfortunately, he does not know how to dig deeper, he only knows how to get the visible, the surface Jew. He does not know how to get down into the trenches. I was in the trenches in the Great War. I won the Iron Cross, Second and First Class. A hero. I was wounded and blinded by mustard gas. That's called getting down in the trenches. Eichmann has no idea how to do that. I heard about your orders to find your son's killer. Your soldiers found hundreds of Jews and other agitators in the villages throughout central and western Austria. That was good work."

Hitler stopped, staring out the Führer Kanzlei windows at the military traffic heading east. He turned back to Schmid.

"Now that I have the Sudetenland, my plan is to take Czechoslovakia next. I'll give the whole country to Heydrich. He is very efficient, yet a dreamer. He thinks everyone loves him when in fact they all hate him. Fear, that is better than being loved. If I were loved, Germany would still be on her knees. You mark my words. Heydrich will be attacked someday no matter how he is protected. Someday he is going to be off to ski or drive somewhere and there'll be a fanatic hidden in the trees to shoot him. The things I have to worry about. I should stop him before he becomes too stupid in his activities.

Now, I'm off my subject. Eichmann and Himmler said there were only a handful of Jews left in Austria. You proved that wasn't true, you proved them wrong and Eichmann doesn't like you for that. Too bad. Even though Goring ordered all Jews to leave, only some of the young left. My opinion is there are still hundreds, thousands of young and older Jews still there, still claiming Austria is their home. No longer is Austria their home! I want them rooted out in eastern Austria too! Every last one of them, in camps in two months! I will tell Himmler those are your orders. He will not like it, but he will give you all the troops you need, Waffen SS. He will also find a way to take the credit. Don't worry, I will be watching you. You can expect to become a Standartenführer, Colonel, by the end of the operation."

Hitler took a breath. "When did you join the Party?"

"In 1929, my Fuhrer."

"Why did you join?"

"I was a junior engineer. No work, going nowhere. I heard you speak and joined."

"Good! An engineer? What kind?"

"Physics, the study of Electromagnetism. Those disciplines."

Hitler thought a moment, handing Schmid a card.

"You have done well in my SS division and I did not know your educational background. It is nice to have someone with an education instead of these oafs around me. Fill out this card with your information. In the future I may have use of someone in that field. An engineer and organizer. With good work, you will be rewarded. I will inform Eichmann of your orders."

Leaving, SS Major Schmid resolved to do well. He'd also make damn sure he got the credit. Not Eichmann, not Himmler.

* * *

"Well, what do you think? Would you like me to call her?"
Mary brought the subject up. It had been noontime before

James had woken, dressed and come down to breakfast, and now she was eager to know.

"It sounds all right, although it may be too much total immersion for her in this group all at once. I was going to call her and then borrow a vehicle to drive down, but you and David sound so keen on the idea I think it will be all right. Except I'll call her myself."

Mary was pleased. "That will be fine, James. Let me speak to her afterwards for sort of a formal phone invitation to replace the written one a person would normally expect."

Daphne's conversation with both Royce and Mary went well. Daphne was happy to hear from Royce, and learn he had at length gotten out of Austria and called her.

She had also enjoyed the formal phone invitation and surprisingly, had a long conversation with Mary, unheard by the men. The invitation, at Royce's request was not until the 9th, Sunday. He wanted the four days to rest and be a bit more himself before he saw Daphne.

Mary was pleased. "She sounds wonderful, James. You must tell me how you met."

Royce smiled. "Well, it was quite romantic. We were climbing and she called me a, and I'm only quoting her, a *bastard*. Twice. Before I even got to say two words."

David chimed in laughing. "I'm not surprised."

Mary was taken aback. "What on earth would cause a woman to say such a thing?"

"It will wait until she's here to defend herself."

They chatted for the next hour over Daphne and planned the activities when she arrived. Royce then felt well enough for a walk. The children heard and had to go with him. Two Springer Spaniels, and a twelve year old black Scotty understood the word 'out', and were at the door.

The weather was mild, in the low forties Fahrenheit, yet Mary dressed the children in heavy coats. Royce suggested she layer their clothes, a sweater over flannel shirt then a light jacket, wool hat and mittens. This way, he said, if they get too hot they could shed a layer and still not be cold. One of the Spaniels was Milton, the other Shakespeare, called Shaky as he shook when excited. David told Royce that if the dogs took off after a deer, or rabbit, to shout come, and they'll return. And not to worry about Scotty. He wasn't going to run after anything and would probably have to be carried home.

Mary and David watched from a window. Royce, stoop-shouldered, sort of shuffled along, as the two children laughed and pulled on his hands to speed him up. The two dogs ran madly back and forth while Scotty brought up the rear, staying in their footsteps, away from the dusting of snow melting in the sun.

They were gone for an hour. Royce returned more upright. The children straggled along behind as Royce carried their coats. The Spaniels' heads were down, and soaked, tongues hanging loose. But old Scotty was dry and warm, dozing as he lay on the children's coats, comfortable in Royce's arms.

The rest of the week mirrored the walk with the children with few exceptions. After Royce tired the children out and sent them back to their tutor, and Scotty found a warm sunlit window, Royce and the two Spaniels would be off for another walk. The dogs stayed within shouting distance when the walks went for another hour; then as Royce extended them up to two, they would come home panting long before him. To the dogs, Royce was not their master, didn't feed them, and when they were tired from all the play, they felt they shouldn't have to continue.

Another exception to the week was the arrival of one George Farber, Esquire, who had driven up from Henry Poole and Company's London office to fit Royce for sets of clothing for country and daily suits, tweed sport coats, Cardigan sweaters, Raglan jackets, shoes, boots and accessories. David insisted on Royce acquiring an informal dinner jacket with black waistcoat and tie. The man from Poole's said six weeks and David said three. It was settled at three.

Next, was the question of a motorcar. David had five. He and Royce walked down to the carriage house, which had the front converted for automobiles while the rear of it, facing away from the manor, contained a four horse stable and paddock. David showed the vehicles; a 1937 Aston Martin Sports, 1934 Riley Saloon, which Mary used, David's personal green Bentley Saloon, a modest Humber Estate Wagon for the staff and then another Bentley. This vehicle was a 1930, 6.5 liter Speed Six, two seat, open tourer. Royce was more or less indifferent to vehicles, nevertheless, this caught his eye, asking if David was going to race it, or why else would he have it? No, David didn't expect to race it, but a similar one had won at Le Mans in 1929 and 1930, and he simply had to have one. Royce noted the supercharger mounted on the front and when told the Bentley could sustain speeds of over one hundred-twenty-five miles an hour, he quietly and definitely declared. "Not while I was in it."

After David mentioned the Bentley Company had gone bankrupt and was acquired by Rolls Royce, what little interest there was ended. Royce would have settled on the Humber but as it was for staff, David decided Royce would share Mary's Riley, or if she was using it, the Aston Martin. Royce could then decide on what, if any, vehicle he wanted to buy.

They walked around the other side of the carriage house and entered the stable. The groom, Marco Herrera, showed Royce the two Chestnut English Hunters owned by the family. David was quick to state he and Mary only used them for casual canters around the countryside, and Royce was welcome to avail himself of them whenever he wished.

After exiting the carriage house, David had to leave. Royce stood on the terrace looking over his brother's estate, an estate worthy of a Lord. Eighteen hundred acres and a manor house few others would match in the Midlands. Motorcars, horses, a wonderful wife, children, successful company. And not to forget his apparent elevated standing with government leaders.

"And here I am." There wasn't much else to say. Yet perplexed, he couldn't help asking himself if this was the world he wanted. Daphne would help answer that question.

At one o'clock the hairdresser came. Shocked as expected, he then settled down to transform Royce's unkempt beard into a controlled appearance. He trimmed his sandy hair—streaked with gray as much as his beard—to a more manageable length, but kept long enough to cover the indentation in the back of his head.

Now, he thought, except for my face, I'm ready to meet the public. A poor attempt at humor and he smiled with the thought that Daphne would have cuffed him on the side of his head and called him an arse. Neither David nor Mary knew why he was smiling. He wasn't about to tell them.

* * *

They decided Royce would take the Bentley to London and pick up Daphne. He didn't want Albert to drive, as the trip back would give them a chance to renew their time together. It was approximately ninety-five miles one way, and David gave rather vague directions, as he seldom drove himself. Albert wrote down the instructions, which were more easily followed.

"Did you find the town house all right, Jim?"

They had turned onto the motorway from London's Belgravia section, heading for Coventry in Mary's Riley Saloon. Royce felt better using it, rather than the pretentious Bentley.

"No problem at all. Directions were good, although I was a bit rusty driving. I think I got the shift pattern and clutch worked out driving down here."

She smiled. "Very good. I've only heard the gears grind two or three times since we left. Do you have a license?"

He was lighthearted. "Of course, from '35, when I left."

Daphne went along. "Well I can't see why they wouldn't find that perfectly acceptable for a man of your standing."

A quiet moment, Royce pensive. "Your mother seems a very pleasant person, Daphne. What's wrong with her?"

"You're too keen; I was hoping you wouldn't notice. David didn't. Just goes to show how different you two are. Well, I wasn't going to bring it up until towards the end of the trip. I guess I have to now. It's the same reason I left you in Austria."

Royce had a sinking feeling. "What is it?"

Daphne stayed strong. "Mother has cancer."

"I thought that. In Austria they have sanatoriums for…"

He wished he hadn't said it. "I meant for serious cases."

"Mother's is serious. As I said, I wanted to leave this to a later time, Jim. I'm taking her to the States the end of the month."

"Why there? We have excellent hospitals for cancer right here in London."

"Father has everything set up with his contacts at Boston's Mass General. Despite their being divorced, there's still a close bond. It was Robert's war wound that caused them to part. Mother wants to be at our Boston house…and with her husband

111

at a time like this."

Royce paid attention to his driving. "When were you planning to be leaving?"

"Dad made reservations for us on the Liner *Aquitania*. It leaves Southampton on the 28th of this month, that's a Friday."

The liner *Aquitania* was old, built before the Great War. One of her sister ships, the *Lusitania*—torpedoed at the start of that war—took over twelve-hundred lives down with her. A Cunard Line ship, the *Aquitania*, had served the Atlantic run from Southampton to New York before relegated to the Mediterranean as a cruise vessel. At present, she was back in the Atlantic until the new *Queen Mary* joined her sister ship the *Queen Elizabeth* on the Atlantic run. When the second *Queen* was ready, the *Aquitania* was condemned to the breakers for demolition.

"Why not the *Queen Liz*? *Aquitania*'s an old ship."

"She's the liner we travelled on between Boston and Southampton before the Great War. We must have taken her four or five times. In fact, we were on her maiden voyage in 1911. She's luckier than her sister the *Lusitania* as you know. Dad thought Mom would like to have the memories of all of us on it. Rob and I were just little kids then."

"I hope I'll see you a few times before you leave."

She glanced at him sideways. "Jim, you're so addled-headed at times I don't know how you get by. Didn't you think the amount of my luggage was a bit much for two days?"

Royce was puzzled. "Well now, I truly don't know how many clothes women bring."

"For God's sake, I'll spell it out for you. Mary and I connived—behind your back, obviously—for me to stay three or four nights at Ravensmoor, and then you and I are off to my brother Robert's home in the Lake District. He's going down to see my Mother before she leaves, so we'll have the home to ourselves for a few days before I have to leave."

"You and Mary concocted this all up on the telephone?"

Daphne gave him a smirk. "Well it would be hopeless to think you could work it out."

"You're a very brazen woman, Daphne. Mary must have been scandalized."

"You knew I was brazen when we met. And no, Mary wasn't scandalized. In fact, she helped me set it up."

"Women," Royce looked at her, shaking his head over the two them, "little wonder you'll rule the world someday." Then he thought a moment, and changed the subject, "I don't know, Daphne, that's a long time for me to be with anyone."

"Well don't think it's going to be a walk in St. James' for me either. What with you and your idiosyncrasies. But you know we've got to find out where we're going, if anywhere."

"Whatever do you see in me, Daphne?"

"As I said to you before, Jim, you're a good bloke. Other than that, I haven't the foggiest. But please don't ask me again, I might get to questioning it more myself."

Nearing Ravensmoor, Royce drove around Broadgate's shopping area, then past Swanswell Gate, showing Daphne a bit of center Coventry, before heading for Burton Green, the people and the life at Ravensmoor.

* * *

In five minutes, Mary and Daphne were fast friends, whispering together, thick as thieves. After the first introductions and conversations, David and Royce sat back, observing the two of them. Without question, they were simply beautiful. Daphne, tall, auburn hair, high cheekbones, green eyes that flashed as she laughed, then softened when concentrating.

Mary, slightly shorter and as slender. Ebony hair with deep blue eyes, magnets to anyone, and a personality to match.

The staff at Ravensmoor were enchanted seeing them walking arm in arm through the home. The principal housekeeper curtsied. Every week she and five other housekeepers and maids went through the mansion, cleaning. She slipped away again to be sure Daphne's bedroom was remained perfect. David's valet, Alfred's composure slipped when introduced. The children, tutor, and nanny were spellbound, and all four were hard to dispense with, as the tour continued. Amanda, the chef nodded, murmuring she would do something special for dinner. When they met with Marco Herrera, the groom, he and Daphne conversed in Spanish over her years as a dressage equestrian and his fervent hope that he and the two women could ride together at least one time before Daphne left the estate.

Time with the family flowed, Daphne accepted by the family, although David somewhat reserved. Royce was uneasy, that was his way. What if something negative happened between them? He didn't even have his feet on the ground yet, how could he take someone with him, when he didn't know where he was going in the first place. He felt carried forward without a say. As he delved more into his psyche, he found he loved it.

One evening, before dark, the flock went for a stroll. Royce, Daphne, Mary, and the children set off, followed by Alfred and Marco. The lead taken by two barking Spaniels, while trailing behind trotted one slow Scotty. David watched them go and turned away. There were calls and business decisions to be made that must keep the company halfway solvent and rushing forward headlong.

* * *

Royce's story unfolded on the third night. For the previous two days he and Daphne along with Mary and, when he could spare an hour or two, David, toured the countryside, explored Coventry's Cathedral, wandered the shops and hiked the many walking trails.

During one walk, they asked Royce when he was going to tell what happened in Austria. He agreed to tell them that evening.

They sat back by the fire and relaxed with scotch, gin, brandy, and wandering conversations. Scotty settled on Royce's lap. They waited expectantly. It took Royce three Dewar's before he could begin. Little did they dream of the story that evolved.

"When I think of what happened it's still difficult to accept. I knew I have a temper and have mostly kept it under control. I try to only get mad at inanimate objects like an ice axe, a bent piton, or a frayed piece of line. Little things like that, things which don't matter and don't hurt anyone. The exception

114

was one night I got mad at a person, actually four people to be exact. I was going into a pub in Salzburg where, as it turned out, they had driven a Jewish couple from the pub. They were frightened and that lit a fuse in me. It turned out there were Hitler Youth inside the pub and they started in on me by saying that Germans were superior to us Brits in every way. I simply got angry. I admit it. They got under my skin, so I challenged them to a hike the next day. It became dreadful. We walked from six in the morning until sometime after dark…"

Daphne, interrupted. "How on earth could you go that long, yet still climb after dark?"

"I know, it can't be done, but we did, and there was some moonlight. Three of them dropped out. I'll admit it was a bad time. There was this one youth, I think about eighteen. He kept bragging his father was Major Schmid, the SS Division Hitler.

I was done in, but this kid wouldn't quit. I was a bit ahead and lost him in the dark. I was shouting for him, then the next thing was a gunshot."

"He shot at you?"

"No. I found out later he must have shot himself, there was no one else around."

"Why would he do such a thing?"

"It was very stressful, horribly stressful. He must have gone off the deep end. The *goddamned* Nazi couldn't take being beaten by an old Brit!"

His audience was startled at the intensity. "Sorry. But anyway, I wasn't in good shape after that and spent a week or two in a hospital. While I was there the staff found out the youth's father, this Major Schmid, reported I had shot his son and he was directing soldiers to track me down. Anyone found hiding me would be put in prison. And believe me, from what I've heard, anyone sent to one of their prisons never comes back. The hospital staff knew this; still they helped to get me back on my feet. I could understand they wanted me out of there, so as soon as I could I went back into the mountains. As the climb with the four went to the west I doubled back thinking that was where this Major would hunt. I hiked east past Salzburg then got a ride to the south and then another lorry west to Innsbruck. From there I climbed north to a spa called Mountain Falcon, BergFalke, to rest and think over what to do…"

Daphne almost shouted at him. "Jim! You had gone through all that just before I met you again?"

"Yes."

"And you kept it from me?"

"Yes."

"Why?"

"Because I wanted to think it out by myself, come to grips with what happened that day."

"So I interrupted."

"Sorry, but again, yes. That's why I tried to leave. You'll remember I came back to the spa because of you, but I still had to get my head sorted out. It was why I couldn't go back to England with you. I know, you don't have to tell me there was no logic to my actions. But I just had to get it out of my system. Alone."

"If I'd only known, Jim."

David spoke up. "Were you able to? Sort out your thoughts I mean."

"I'm fairly sure I have. Going for that hike I told Daphne I needed, helped me."

Everyone was pensive. It was an intensive narrative, which left them needing another drink.

Daphne deduced there was more. "That's not the end of the story, is it?"

"No. Except, it could hold for another time."

"No, you won't tell it another time. You'll tell us now."

They waited, David shaking his head at her audacity to speak so forcefully to his brother.

And so, Royce continued. "Ernst Becker, the Owner of that spa, is a Prussian. Believe it or not, he and I became friends because he was once a climber. He hates Nazis and let me know they were looking for me. They were fifty miles away in Badgastein on twisty old roads, so I wasn't concerned. There were literally scores of spas, hotels, and small villages for them to check out, so another day wouldn't make any difference. At least that's what I thought. I hiked and then stayed overnight on the mountain working things out. By the next morning, my head was clear and I felt good enough to continue along for a few more hours before turning back to the spa."

Daphne glared at him. "Despite the fact you knew the German's were after you."

"Yes."

"All you can say to that is…yes?"

"If you weren't so blasted impatient, I'd get to the story!"

The mood quickly cooled. Daphne did not accept being spoken to sharply. She held her tongue; the people here she very much wanted to like her. She glared at Royce, not speaking.

Royce disregarded her scowl and resumed. "Now where the devil was I?"

She couldn't contain herself longer and smiled sweetly. "Why dear, you were saying you were traipsing around a mountain, happy in your own daft little world, while all the time the German's were hunting you down…*like the dog you are.*"

David Royce burst out laughing along with Mary. Tension eased, the black moods dissolved. Royce smiled sheepishly. Daphne had made the point she wasn't to be easily dismissed.

Mary spoke up. "Daphne, for a minute there I was ready to help you pack up and head back to London."

More grins, everyone relaxed, another round of drinks ordered. Royce suggested they call it a night, it was ten o'clock. But again, though tired, no one felt he would tell the rest of the story another time. They insisted he continue.

"Well as it was so tacitly put, I was traipsing around the mountain like some daft chap, when I saw something gleaming below me in the forest and I was damned if it wasn't a castle. It stuck out in the middle of nowhere and behind it was this massive mountain wall, quite like a curtain. You should have seen it, Daphne. The trouble was I couldn't get near it. If I rappelled down, I knew I didn't have the strength to climb back up. Then I saw a horizontal ledge about a foot wide running the entire length of my part of the mountain, or at least to the curve. It started at a mass of stone rubble that had avalanched. All it took was a few minutes to get over that debris and there was the ledge. From there I needed only six pitons for about fifty yards and I was at a bulge in the cliff. That was where the mountain curved away behind the castle. I glanced around the corner and there was this incredible sight. I guessed the castle was a hundred or fewer yards away. Looking through the monocular it was beautiful. The sun just burst on it, the slate tiles on the roofs were sparkling. The tower and battlements were perfect. It was something to see. There was nothing else around, just a small dirt road leading away down into the valley, but as I took a couple of snaps of it, I was shocked. Parked out front were at least two black Mercedes touring vehicles. I scanned the castle again and out on to the rear terrace came five black-shirt Nazis. Two of them, wearing those blasted black leather trench coats. I slipped back behind the bend where I couldn't see them and they couldn't see me. I was shaken. Even though I didn't believe they were after me, I admit to being nervous, so when I turned I got clumsy and both feet slipped off the edge."

David and Mary gasped. Daphne didn't blink. "Your line was coupled off to the pitons."

"Quite right. I let the line absorb my body weight, rested for a while, and then leg looped my way back up."

She looked directly at him. "That's the way you taught me, but I'll bet you were shaken."

"Again, you're quite correct. I was still weak and it shook me. Can't deny it."

"So you scooted back along the shelf and got the devil out of there, not feeling well."

"Daphne, I admit to really being in that daft little world you mentioned. I was meandering, unsure of who or where I was."

"But you got back to the spa and this Becker person. You've had two close calls. The four Hitler Youth and the castle where you fell off the ledge. You know, being around you could be dangerous."

David was thoughtful. "Yet despite all this, you were still in Austria. Are we to believe there's yet a third fright? Is that why you were late?"

"Yes, getting across the border. Although I'll do my best to keep that story short."

David commented that James must admit the plots were becoming a bit incredible.

Daphne smiled. "Jim you've kept us spellbound with your stories, rather like our American movies of the Perils of Pauline. One heart wrenching peril after another. Seriously though, I wish you had come out with me when I asked you."

Royce asked her. "Did you have any trouble at the border?"

"A little. It seemed they were looking for someone...My God! Was it you?"

"Possibly, although I believe this Major Schmid was just getting started at that time. They were probably looking for Jews. And not to make you nervous, if I had been with you there's a good chance we'd both be in a Nazi prison right now."

Mary was now spellbound, asking. "God, Jimmy, when you think of it, it's frightening. Tell us, how did you get out?"

"That was my third Peril of Pauline, as Daphne so aptly put it. The owner of the spa, Ernst Becker, was a Great War hero, for the German side. The Order of The Red Eagle was one of his medals. It carries a lot of weight in German military. Now, as I said, Ernst hated Nazis, and liked me. Because of that, he hollowed out below the rear seat of his Opel and he moved the trunk panel back a bit to give me a little more room. I got in, wrapped in heavy clothes, then he filled the vehicle and the trunk with boxes of sports gear."

David hadn't heard Mary call James, Jimmy.

"And you and this Becker chap thought this would work?"

"*I* didn't have a choice. Ernst said he'd tell the Nazis he had to return the equipment to his supplier in Switzerland. He had put a tube through the floorboard so I could breathe and that's where things went wrong. There was a leak in his exhaust pipe and I started breathing fumes. When I realized what was happening. I stuck a mitten down the rubber tube but I was too late, and lost consciousness. Ernst told me later I was in the trunk nearly two hours before he could get through the border. Nazis everywhere he said, even the devil himself, SS Major Schmid, the Nazi who claimed I killed his son. He actually guessed where I would try to cross. Ernst said Schmid even glanced in the Opel before walking off! Thankfully, the Red Eagle medal got us through. Ernst got me into a clinic and then to a hospital in Switzerland where they put me on oxygen and thawed me out. That's where I woke up, in a stupor, although I knew enough that Ernst saved me. Almost killed me, he said, but saved me. He stayed until I was well enough to get on the train to Zurich, then he went back to Austria. It's his home so he wanted to do what he could against the Nazis."

They sat mesmerized. It was a story of terror. No one spoke as they visualized his tale. Royce freezing in the cold, the carbon monoxide fumes, trapped in the trunk, Nazis everywhere. One slip up and his family and Daphne would have never seen him again. No one wanted to think of what would have happened to him.

They could tell Royce was half-drunk. If he weren't, he would never have been so candid. He closed his eyes in thought, and then began to nod off. They quietly turned him on the sofa, put a pillow under his head, and placed a blanket over him. Scotty hopped up on the couch and settled down beside him.

Daphne lay awake that night wondering how Royce kept from going over the edge. What could she do to help him? More than that, why is she pursuing him so blatantly? There's something in him she couldn't see and couldn't fathom if it was good or bad. When she got inside his shell, even just a bit, she'd found a wonderful person. Still, she'd known a lot of nice guys. Why did this one affect her so much more? Was there something about his scar that drew her because of her brother's ruined face? She loved her brother. Was this transference of that love? What did they really have in common? The mountains, true, what else? What else? God, if there's nothing else, how frightening. She just knew there had to be more.

Mary and David sat up for a while in their room.

"David, I know it's worrisome, but look what's happened to him. He needs time to heal, get the past behind him. I feel just his talking it out, getting it out, will help."

"Can't you understand, Mary? I don't have time to coddle him. We have contracts to fill and dates to fulfill them. We have engineering problems at the plants in Birmingham and Manchester as well as here. I'm not saying James can solve them all, but damn it, he can help keep the programs going."

David stretched, got up, and went to his writing desk, jotting some notes. Mary waited for him to finish.

"All right, Mary, this is what I've decided to do. I'll have James tour our Coventry plants with Clive Henderson, and have Clive ready to talk to James about a few things just to get a feel for his response. Clive will show James one or two of our secret programs. If anything will get him fired up like the old days that should do it. Then he and Daphne are going to the Lakes where they'll have time to themselves. When they get back, I'll lay it out for him, either he gets himself together, or he's out, for good."

"David! How can you do such a thing?"

"I'll tell you how. I've told you before there is going to be a war and we're going to be fighting for our lives. Everyone must help. If my brother can't or won't, whether he's too lazy or unbalanced doesn't matter…"

"You believe James is unbalanced?"

"If he isn't, he puts on a good show of it."

"Why do you say that?"

"Because I've always believed it. Father did also. Look, Mary, I'm not saying he's irrational, he's just, shall I say, not quite right. You knew how he was before father's death. I told you his actions in the engineering department, only came out of his office to give instructions then withdrawing into his shell. Then there was his always running up to Cumbria, even Scotland at times, for the mountains. If it weren't for Clive Henderson, all hell would have broken out at the plant. Father caused enough trouble without James adding to it."

"I know he's an introvert, David, yet…"

"Put the adjective severe in front of introvert, Mary."

"Please, David, hear me out. I feel he wants to be alone because of his face. You know he didn't cause major trouble at the plant. It was your Father! Look how James was with the children. He was fine and they loved him. You saw Beth when she saw him again, she didn't forget. James' problem was everyone was jealous of him. Yet Clive understood him. He understood James was a genius and helped him cope. Other than Clive, there was no one else who could follow his thought process. That should have been their problem, not his."

"Mary, I'll tell you straight out, I don't have a good feeling about his future here with the Company, and especially with Daphne. I can't imagine what she sees in him."

"You're just jealous because she's prettier than me."

David disregarded the remark. Mary would have preferred he deny it.

"I'm willing to give him the benefit of the doubt until they come back from the Lakes District. If he's not going to work out, I'll have to go to America and acquire two or three top engineers.

It will cost us, yet there's no other choice. But I'll wait."

On Wednesday morning Royce and Daphne purchased clothes for him in Coventry. Poole and Sons in London couldn't deliver attire in time for the Lakes trip. After lunch, they motored back to Ravensmoor. Daphne stayed with Mary and the children while Royce went off with David to the main Royce Bearing office.

The company owned six factories in Coventry, and two each in Birmingham and Manchester. Clive Henderson, in charge of engineering, met them at the gate and David excused himself for a meeting. It was apparent to Royce that, as Ravensmoor had changed so had major alterations occurred in the size of the factories. The visual layout of the complex had been revised and expanded. Old machine shops and tin roofed workshops were gone, replaced by concrete and brick two and three story buildings. Additional structures were lined in rows, each one with signage indicating their function. Another change, the entire fifty acre complex was now enclosed by ten foot high chain link fencing topped with barbed wire. At set intervals, high intensity light posts, and guards patrolled the restricted area. All the sites were now like this, Clive mentioned.

At the gate, guards nodded to Clive, glanced at his tag, then issued Royce a yellow visitor pass for most areas. Royce was amazed David had the authority to issue Secret clearance and Clive offhandedly mentioned that David, "Does as he pleases."

The different building functions were pointed out. Planning/Scheduling, Fabrication, Milling, Boring, Preassembly, Assembly, Engineering, and Royce's old area, Design Engineering, now three times the size. There were greatly enlarged shipping docks with over a dozen lorries under load. Buildings denoting Compliance and Execution were new signage for Royce, although he understood them. Clive went on about concepts David was instituting after a tour of American companies. He explained methods of technology and newer concepts of initiating vertical integration for all Royce Bearings plants. Royce followed it all, impressed and interested.

Clive then drove Royce to a secluded, wooded hill at the far end of the site. They stopped at a steel access door mounted to a concrete frame imbedded in the hill.

"This is David's latest project, a massive one," Clive stressed, "and very Top Secret."

Royce mentioned he did not have clearance for Top Secret and Clive simply said. "David told me to show it to you."

Although he only shrugged, Royce's beliefs about security was stretched.

They entered and proceeded down twenty steps under the hill where he was amazed to find a massive underground chamber.

"Eight acres." Clive informed him. "The complete area incased within three-foot thick walls and ceiling."

Inside the concrete cocoon, laced with loadbearing columns, were replicates of Spitfire and Hurricane fighter structural components for wing assemblies, cockpit layouts, and a mockup of assembly lines for Rolls Royce Merlin V12 aircraft engines. Engineer's and workers studied at each area, fine tuning each assembly process.

"I assume you excavated the area, constructed this chamber, and then used the excavated earth to build a hill over the whole thing, and grassed and treed it."

"Quite right, James. It's being done for Military Procurement in a few other places in the country, especially by Rover Motorcar. However, ours will be the most up to date. We've fitted fully independent power generators, heat and air filtration systems. We are setting this up as a Shadow Factory for the Air Ministry."

"Shadow Factory?"

"Yes, the government is already doing them at Alcock Green. It means we'll be setting up the same machinery as the original aero engine and framing manufacturers themselves and duplicate their equipment under license from them. They call us a Shadow Factory as it's all done as quietly as possible with Government help. The Government promised we'll be supplying bearings for the Lancaster, Spitfire, Bristol, Hurricane aircraft and more. They're all using various models of Rolls Royce Merlin and Griffon engines and of course, all those and others will use our bearings. We're also getting into the fabrication of structural components for those aircraft, and de Havilland is in talks with us about a new plane they're developing. If you can imagine, the thing's made out of plywood and spruce. In this age that's hard to believe. The Air Ministry turned them down so they've prototyped it at their expense. They think it will go like a bat out of blue blazes. David believes in them, so we'll just have to see."

"When you think of it, Clive, that material can be readily shaped and could be extremely durable. Need a hell of a lot of glue though, and that could make it flammable. But changing the subject, what impresses me more than anything is the tiger David has by the tail."

"A good analogy, James, and a very expensive tiger it is."

"I don't follow."

"Simply put, all you see around you, all the new buildings in this complex, plus the additional two companies David bought up in Birmingham and Manchester, puts the company on quite a financial hook."

"You mean the Government's not helping?"

"Oh, in a way, by the back door that is, with help from some of the back bench Members. They've put in some initial capital. Nevertheless, David has mortgaged the company on the prospect of there being a war. If there isn't one, it's more than likely there won't be a company. David wanted me to tell you of that possibility."

"Really? And he told you to tell me. Strange, am I supposed to be upset knowing that?"

Clive was taken aback. "Well, you are the only other owner of the company. If it goes down, what will you do?"

"I haven't given the slightest thought to it. Let me work this through. If there's a war, it appears obvious the company will acquire tremendous growth and profit. Therefore, David and I will be even richer. However, if there isn't a war, then we'll be poor souls. Then again, if there's not a war, thousands of people will not die. You remember the Battle of the Somme in the Great War. Forty thousand of our boys, the cream of our youth, a generation, gone in just one day alone. Then look at the rest of the war. Verdun and the other slaughters. Am I supposed to hope there's a war? For God's sake, how could any of us? How could you? You were a Lewis gunner in the Black Watch at Verdun."

"Of course I'm not hoping there's a war, James. Then again, what I hope doesn't matter. However, if there is a war we've got to be ready. David's not hoping for a war but we've put every effort into it…"

Royce interrupted. "From what you're saying, Clive, he's ignoring or eliminating our long standing clients, leaving them without our bearings. If memory serves, that's called burning ones bridges behind them."

"True, except you've got to remember, we're not just a bearing company anymore. Our scope has expanded into multiple disciplines, which, I admit, we're not well schooled in. That's one of the reasons he needs you to come back. I don't argue your points about the direction your brother is taking the company. Even though I trust you, James, I have to beg off from the subject. David's the Chief."

"Fair enough, although I wouldn't believe I'd hear that from you in a million years."

Clive was embarrassed and fell silent while exiting the underground plant. He could not speak freely to his old friend. Royce had only one thought, far different. Of course David hopes for war, that's plain and simple. He must have one to survive.

They went to the office, noticing a black Rolls Royce Saloon parked beside David's Bentley. The secretary told them they were to go right into the conference room. As they entered, David Royce was pointing to a graph and speaking about vertical integration, dates for factories to come on line, production output schedules, cost projections…At that moment he looked back, acknowledging Clive and Royce to the four men in front of him.

"Gentlemen, I would like to introduce Clive Henderson, and my brother, James."

The four men turned, saying hello, trying to ignore the scar. David did not introduce the men, all dressed in suits.

He continued the introductions. "Clive Henderson, starting next month, will be the Superintendent of Military Production Facilities, which, as we've just discussed, is now all our factories, one way or the other. My brother, James, has recently returned from occupied Austria where he had a harrowing escape from the Nazis after some trumped up charges. He's still recovering from that incident, although I expect that within two weeks he will be able to return to the company. He will be Vice President and Superintendent of Design Theory, Concept and Application. That will be for all military programs. Thank you, Clive and James for stopping in."

David turned his back to them, they were dismissed. Royce was angry and as they walked outside, he asked. "You knew about this, Clive?"

"I knew about my position, James, but I didn't have permission to divulge it. I hadn't an inkling of his plans for you. If you knew nothing either, then he obviously kept it to himself. Although I will say this in his defense, you are eminently qualified."

"Thank you for your vote of confidence. Nevertheless, I'm not ready, and even if I were, I do not want the responsibility."

"Then what are you going to do?"

"I don't have the foggiest, other than David and I are definitely going to have a talk."

* * *

The men in the conference room were quiet, as they mulled over David's and Royce Bearings continuous problem, cash flow to continue growth.

"David, you've stated your fiscal problems and now you must grasp ours. We, and by that I mean the four of us here, and other Members of Parliament, are the Minority in the Government. The peace at any price MPs are deluding themselves, yet unfortunately, at present they are in the Majority, which, I don't have to tell you, means in control of the Exchequer. They control Treasury assets. Its true Westminster has increased spending for defense although not nearly enough. Quite simply put, most have no sense of urgency."

The gentleman hesitated, speaking as a conspirator. "As you know we, and the others, have funded you by means of the diversion of funds from ancillary programs. Programs, which have little attention paid to them. However, we must be careful. If these diversions see the light of day, we'd be censured and our efforts exposed. I know you are concerned after having dropped all your non-military, commercial accounts and their income flow. Nevertheless, believe me, when it appears the war will start, or even before, we'll see to it the Government will give those clients who stuck with us, orders for aircraft components and equipment of all types. When this happens, they will be coming to you for bearings. They have to. You know we've set specifications that only Royce Bearing can meet. That will be of tremendous benefit to only you. Until then, you must hang on. We can send you a few thousand pounds more each week to help carry on. Can't you also add to the company mortgage for a few more months longer? We h a v e Anthony Eden and Churchill speaking up for us to mock and discomfort those MPs who refuse to see the storm coming."

Another of the gentlemen spoke up. "One point, Sir David. You're a Member of the House of Lords so you could use your voice in Chambers to help. We need all we can get."

The men stopped talking. They had made their points.

David rose. "To answer your last comment first. I am too busy juggling a dozen balls to spend my time in Sessions. It is your job to move Westminster to a greater war effort. If it becomes necessary, I will be there. Now, I do not say the position of Royce Bearing is dire. I am saying that it will become dire if, *if* I am to keep investing as you expect without more assistance. Our initial success came about by developing unique and quality bearings, which are the standard of the world. I've also hired the best engineers I wanted and you yourselves requested. It is that simple. Despite this decade long world depression we continue to suffer through, RB has remained profitable. Most every surviving producer of quality machinery and manufacturer of aircraft engines have continued with us. That is why the four of you came to me in the first place with this offer from certain minority members. I agreed to work with you to prepare for war. At that time, you told me there would be no problem for you to raise funding. Due to that, I went ahead and did what you asked, and more. Now you ask me to hang on, and your best advice is for me to increase the mortgage on RB. My response is, RB and my home, are now mortgaged to eighty percent of value and RB, not the government, is paying the interest. If Lloyds finds the cash flow from my long-term clients is gone, I will be lucky if they do not call the notes. If that happened, I would be hard-pressed to find alternate financing with every bank in Europe and the States hoarding their assets due to this worldwide financial crisis and the European situation.

"I employ five thousand, six hundred people. If it comes to

the point where we can't pay them or buy materials, I will lay this failure in your collective laps. Of course I do not want to. However, if you bankrupt me, I will have no choice."

"Most of what you say is true I admit, David. Nevertheless, you must acknowledge you have exceeded our initial concept. Buying those additional companies in Birmingham and Manchester, although strategic, was not anticipated. Added to this is your initiating on your own, to build the Shadow Factory. This expenditure, I might add, is for an underground factory that we consider too close to your main facility for safety. This is another example of an unexpected investment. We never said, and you should not have expected, us to have available a bottomless fund. At the very least, you should have informed us of your plans and given us time to find additional funds. We are not questioning the value of acquiring the companies or the Shadow work. It simply comes down to the fact you did not inform us beforehand. If we push too far, to fast, it could jeopardize our whole program. If that happens, we will be blackballed and you will be placed on the Not Approved list. Therefore, in essence we are asking that you not commit to any further investments until we can digest what has been committed to already."

David was not a trifle concerned about the Not Approved listing. He felt he knew enough A list personages to squash any possibility of that happening. His main efforts with the four men in front of him, and the other Ministers they fronted for, were to keep as much income flowing to afford the opportunities available to him. It was they who were in a bind. Exposure would ruin them, not him. His company, scandal or not, was indispensable. At least, he thought that.

What he did not mention to these men was his agreements with the Admiralty to Priority Service their ships in Royce Bearing's sphere of expertise. This Priority agreement brought with it a prepayment for a significant amount of income each month. The first of these payments had now begun and were for prioritizing only. The actual servicing would be cost plus.

David's mind reverted to the men. He looked thoughtful.

"As far as your concern for the Shadow Factory being too close to buildings which can be seen from the air, I intend to place all my factories underground as soon as possible. Then I will dismantle the buildings here and grass the area over or designate them all as a hospital complex. I'm confident our Government will approve and finance this operation.

"I also understand your concern over the difficulties in financing my other efforts. You must forgive me for being perhaps being too explicit, but my interest is to rush forward as fast as possible. That should be in your interest as well and your singular concern. These projects, and others, should and must be completed. By doing this we will buttress our beloved country from the menace we will surely confront.

England is in her time of need, and the obligation of each man is to answer her need, especially we few who have knowledge and ability. We, you and I, must do what is required and the rest be damned. I will pledge myself to go forward and do more than I can financially afford. All I ask of you is to dedicate yourselves to the limit of your capabilities, to aid, do what must be done, and sustain my efforts for our country."

Standing, they shook his hand, feeling invigorated, noble. They left vowing to renew their efforts to keep RB financed. It was difficult for David to suppress a smile as he walked them to their vehicle.

Clive and Royce eventually returned from the interrupted tour. They had stopped at a Triumph dealer where Royce bought a used, although pristine, 1936 Alvis 3.5 Liter Sports Coupe. Once Clive confirmed who Royce was, the owner, though surprised he would buy a used vehicle, promised it would be delivered that evening to Ravensmoor, in first order, complete with topped off petrol. The bill would be sent to Royce's attention at the company.

To a degree, Clive had mollified Royce. Actually, Clive was unaware of the actual reason Royce had returned. Because of this lack of understanding, he went blindly on the assumption Royce must have come back to help the company. Why else would he have come home? He convinced Royce to look carefully at the complete picture.

Many people, Clive reasoned, don't think they're capable to take on positions until they have to. James should accept the possibility. Clive also reconfirmed David's position was precarious. He was overworked, yet still had to get more work done. Granted, he had brought it on himself, and granted again, James was only a cog in the wheel, but an essential one. Without him, the wheel may seize, vital time would be lost trying to replace him, and time was of critical essence for the country.

Royce accepted all this to be true and though calmed, still balked. They finally hit upon a possible compromise. Clive would ask David for James to become the needed Assistant Supervisor under Clive with the rest of James' time spent as Supervisor of Design. It could work as Royce was already expected to oversee all designs, all factories. It could work, as long as Clive interceded between Royce's lack of patience with senior engineers who could not follow his thought processes or creativity for problem solving.

They both recognized Royce would be not able to quietly discuss this possible compromise with David, so it was left up to Clive to do the presentation. Royce would stay out of the negotiations altogether. He was, however, adamant. Either David agreed to their offer, or Royce would leave, perhaps, to the States with Daphne.

Clive dropped Royce off at Ravensmoor where they found David's Bentley left near the front door. No one was in sight as he walked through the manor and Royce continued straight on until he reached the gardens at the rear. He noticed Mary's automobile was gone from the carriage house and assumed she, Daphne, and the children had gone out. He was about to return inside, wondering where David was when he heard voices, faint, further into the garden where taller shrubbery blocked the view. As he came closer to the voices, it was obvious one of the speakers was Daphne. The other, undoubtedly, David.

"I don't understand why you're so obstinate, David."

"I have to be, and you should be helping me on this. Look Daphne, admit it, James could not last anywhere else with his scar and attitude."

"I don't know that at all."

"Well I do. It's almost as if you've never looked him in the face. What on earth do you see in him?"

"I can't say in words what I see in him, David. But whatever it is, you don't have it."

"We'll see about that someday."

The voices became louder, closer. Royce darted behind a row of poplars and slipped back into the house by a side door. He was embarrassed at overhearing their conversation, although he did try to decipher it.

David was obviously telling Daphne his plans for him. Daphne not agreeing, good.

So, my looks and attitude. Well I cannot help my looks. I'll try to improve my attitude. David implying how ugly I am. Why state the obvious? Why bring up what she could see with her own eyes? It's not necessary for David to remind her, or is it? What's his reason?

Daphne said she didn't know why she liked me, however she did, and told David straight out that whatever it was, and he didn't have it. Nice to hear.

Then David said we'll see about that someday. What in hell did that mean?

They came through the French doors chilled and brought up short, self-conscious, seeing Royce in the study. David spoke first. "Didn't know you were back, James. I was just showing Daphne the maze."

"You didn't get confused in there, did you?"

Neither party knew how to answer. Daphne saw Royce's eyes, and read into his words.

David ignored it all. "Want to speak with me, James? I mean about that office meeting and how I've restructured the operation and strategies to encompass your expertise?"

"No, I don't wish to talk about it. Clive will talk to you tomorrow. And while I think of it, Daphne and I will be leaving for the Lake District first thing in the morning."

Chapter 10

THE ALVIS CRUISED through the cool, sunny morning. They chatted over her stay at Ravensmoor and this trip they're taking to the Windermere cottage.

Royce was relaxed, enjoyed Daphne, the drive, and looked forward to the adventure. For no reason, his mind wandered to Ernst Becker. Royce wished him well, wondered how he was, and yet knew if Ernst had come to England when Royce asked, it wouldn't have worked out.

Daphne's thoughts were on her last phone call to her mother who said she was not feeling too poorly, the drugs kept her mostly without pain. She also considered her brother Robert. How would he accept Jim? Would they get along? She had seldom brought a boyfriend home. That was funny. Calling Jim her boyfriend. Would Robert wonder why she liked a person with a damaged face, though not as damaged as his?

Slipped between chats with Royce, her thoughts somehow drifted to David. It was inane even to let him enter her mind. A conceited, egotistic excuse for a man she thought. He had seen her out in the garden when he arrived home, and knew Mary was gone with the children. Daphne had not given him the slightest come on, yet he suggested a get together when she went back to London. She felt her hand move to slap him and stopped, an awareness such a move would finish her at Ravensmoor. Her ice-cold look made him ease off, he said he only wanted to talk more about James. Talk more about James my foot, she thought. David had already talked too much about Jim, to her liking.

Still, David did have magnetism. Can't understand why. Is it just because he's tall, handsome, aristocratic, polished, rich and whatever else. She laughed silently to herself.

Jim wasn't upset when David and she came in from the garden, yet she knew he must have overheard. But how much of the conversation did he hear?

She had to know. "You overheard our conversation in the garden, didn't you?"

"Yes, though not all of it."

"Where did you come in?"

"You were asking him why he was so obstinate. I assume he was talking about his plans for me."

Daphne breathed easier. Royce hadn't heard the beginning of the conversation. "That's correct. How are you going to respond?"

"Clive and I worked out what we feel is a good compromise and we agreed *he* should present it. He doesn't need me there. David takes it, or he doesn't."

"Want to tell me?"

"I don't mean to shut you out, I just want to get him and Royce Bearing out of my mind for this trip. If no call comes through while we're at Windermere, remind me to tell you what I worked out with Clive. But not until we're nearing Coventry on the way home. I'll tell you then. But not now, please."

"I'll go along with that." Well, she thought, he's getting better. Not completely shutting me out.

Royce looked over, "What did David mean by…we'll see about that someday?"

So, he heard that part. She stayed calm. "I've thought about that a once or twice. I simply don't know what he meant."

Royce only nodded. She's thought about that a few times, he mused. His next question startled her. The subject of David had evaporated. "Tell me Daphne, do you think I'm selfish?"

She laughed at him. "Of course not. Why would you ask?"

"When I talked to Clive Henderson the feeling came to me he thought I was self-indulgent. You know, because I left and now I'm back, still causing David difficulties. I'm asking you again, do you think I'm selfish?"

"No, I don't think you're selfish. Although at times you appear that way. But I know you, and as I said to you in Austria, you allow your face control your emotions and personality. That makes you look selfish. What I do think is there's something *inside* you, driving you. I don't know what it is, and I don't think you do either, yet it's there. Good or not too good? I still don't know."

She didn't dare bring up David's conversation with her in London, when he told her about the indentation in the back of Royce's head. She wanted to broach the subject and find if he would have the area re-examined, but she was afraid to ask. And that wasn't the way it should be.

"However, there's another point I'd like to bring up, Jim. Don't worry about David. He's a different breed of cat. He knows how to get inside your head—and you let him. Yet I also see he's under a lot of pressure. That's obvious, but he's a chameleon. He changes personalities to fit whom he's speaking with. I watch him with the staff, Mary, and especially with you. When I met him in London, he was charming and open, acting as if I was his closest confidant, telling me his plans to be *the* man in government someday. What rot. I couldn't believe how he was trying to impress me with his…"

"You think David plans on being Prime Minister?"

"That's what he implied. Please don't bring it up to him. Damn it! Now I'm concerned David might be upset."

"So…he plans on being PM…I can see that happening, Daphne, I really can."

Royce drove on, still thinking of David's plan as he subconsciously watched the road as it curled around each knoll. So, that was David's intention, not just be rich, but powerful. Of course! What else could be driving him?

The road passed west of Birmingham and Manchester; then swept along the coast, heading north. He stayed alert, knowing this coastal road was a favorite area for cyclist groups, even in winter, and they were not shy of taking wide turns on narrow curves.

The light fog that had hugged the coast dissipated by the time Stoke-on-Trent, Lancaster, and Cairnforth were behind them. Topping off the petrol in Kendal, they had a rest at Preston for a late breakfast. They took their time, enjoyed the day, involved in themselves, nothing or no one else, and appreciated it.

Over lunch, Daphne asked him to please not comment on her brother's artificial mask, which covered the right half of his face. She frankly mentioned she had already phoned Robert about

Royce's scar so her brother would not look too surprised, or comment. She thought each would except the other.

Back on the High Kingate Pass, they followed it along the east coast of Windermere, the long lake wandering north and south through the Lake District. Passing Storrs and nearing the cottage before reaching Bowness-on-Windermere, they turned toward the lake. Easing down the steep path to the riverbank, they pulled into the parking for the home. The cottage, as she called it, was a stone house, spread along the lake, comprising seventeen rooms as well as three terraces hanging over the lake. Lord such and such had it built in the fifteenth century, Daphne mentioned, and she solemnly asked Royce not to be overly awestruck. Royce answered it was too late, he was already in awe, yet would try to contain it, so as not to embarrass her.

Her brother was out the door of the home before their engine died. He helped Daphne out, and gave her a hug as Royce walked around to meet him.

Robert stared hard at Royce during Daphne's introduction. "My word," Robert commented straightforwardly, "aren't you a fright."

"Said the man with the leather face." Royce retorted.

Daphne went wide-eyed, gasping. Royce and Robert looked so stern. The men saw her dismay and hurriedly burst out laughing. A strong handshake and they knew each other far more than introductions.

"Damn the both of you for putting me on like that!"

The cottage sheltered the cool breeze, the terrace warm in the golden afternoon sun. They sat back and basked into the fading light, their scotch and water not far from their lips, as they smoked Lucky Strike cigarettes that Robert received from the States. The conversations were directionless and enjoyable, with the exception when Robert mentioned he had seen the Hearst 9 October newsreel about the Czech surrender of the Sudetenland to the Nazis. Just another shameless step, Royce said. Although still Americans at heart, Daphne and Robert knew what he meant, and tried to forget, at least for this time together.

Daphne was happy with the two men in her life as they casually discussed Robert's life on the lake, his paintings, and informed views of the outside world.

Royce asked about Robert's wound. Daphne winced. One didn't ask. To her surprise, her brother quietly told of the Argonne attack with the American Expeditionary Forces. After the battle, he said he stood around and discussed it with Harvard friends, friends with whom he had joined the AEF. One moment they were chatting, the next, they heard a shell coming over, no chance to duck. A mass of mud, then nothing. Remembering nothing. He woke in a field hospital. His friends were dead.

He told them when he finally found the mirror that had been kept from him he wished he had died with them. There was more. He left it unsaid.

Daphne's tears welled up. He had never told the story. Yet now, it simply flowed out, emotionless.

Royce looked up the mere. "Not over it yet, Robert?"

"No, never will, never expect to. I can't forget them, or forever hate war with all my heart."

Royce raised his glass. "To absent friends."

Strangely enough, Robert hesitated, then joined in. "Yes, let's say that…to friends."

Robert's hesitation revealed a lot to Royce, there was more to the story. He didn't ask. It was a difficult moment.

Robert turned to Royce. "Think you can cap that story?"

"No, thank God, I can't."

He thought for a moment, looking to Daphne. "My mother had a difficult birth with me. The doctor used forceps, didn't realize he had my head, and he dented it as you see. Killed the nerves."

Robert said it sounded like an AEF doctor he knew. The men laughed bitterly, as if old friends renewing their friendship.

Daphne shook her head, she knew there was a bond between men, or at least these two men, which women could never delve into, much less try to be a part. She was, however, wise enough to recognize it.

Royce turned to her. "You don't seem surprised."

"I'm not. David told me."

Royce pondered the answer. "What else did he tell you?"

"I'd rather not say."

Royce dropped the subject. Another thing, she thought, to be edgy about. As evening set in, the terrace grew cool. They took their drinks inside and continued their conversation while Daphne and Robert made dinner. They told Royce to stay out of the way and he was glad to oblige. He refreshed their drinks, then rekindled the fireplace before dropping into an overstuffed chair.

The men told stories, endless stories. Daphne smiled, she had never seen Royce so animated. At last they became weary, talked out for the night.

Robert decided to retire. "You must be wanting to get your luggage out of the car and as I don't know your sleeping arrangements, I'll just say there are two bedrooms at the far end of the house, the choice is yours."

Like two sinning youngsters, Daphne and Royce went for their luggage.

Robert did not rise until the sun's rays streaked through the windows. It had been one of his exceptionally horrific nights; cruel dreams, pain, and memories. Now day had come once again and he strapped on his mask, ready to face another of the endless mornings. The dreams, he thought, had come because of his conversation about the Argonne with Jim Royce.

He smiled, thoughts of Daphne and her friend. To hell with nightmares. This will be an enjoyable few days with them, even though he would be gone for three to say Godspeed to mother.

As he made tea there was a faint click, then another. A glance to the terrace showed Royce with a camera, as he took photos up the mere, toward the north. The sun had topped the hills, water sparkled a pale blue green under the ice and picked up the flame colored leaves along the banks. Robert grinned. Little wonder so many artists, poets, and tourists came here and, for that matter, the reason he stayed. That, and he had no other home. Someone once wrote you can't go home again, and he knew that all too true. The States were gone from him. His Father couldn't be blamed. Father had dreamed, had planned for him to finish Harvard, then become a partner in the business, eventually taking control. He would have been so proud. Instead, Robert and his friends had left school, gone on a great adventure. They had to go, he insisted, before the war passed them by. Well, they fought in the war and the war charged a fee. It took their youth, made them pay for their exuberance and their foolhardiness.

Now, his former friends sleep endlessly under patches of grass in the Argonne Forest. Earth that France had graciously let them and thousands of others, stay there for helping save the country from the Boche.

Royce called for Robert to come out. He shook off his melancholy, saying he would bring biscuits and tea. "I saw you taking pictures up the mere, Jim. It's hard to believe isn't it… the magnificence?"

"Robert, when we sat outside yesterday, I thought how wonderful it was, but this is simply indescribable. One thing I don't follow though, why do you say mere?"

"My word, you're a Brit and don't know? What a rarified life you must have led. In this region *mere* means lake. You seldom hear the word lake, unless by a tourist. In other words, one does not say Lake Windermere, because mere already means lake. I'll spare you how the word Winder has been misconstrued, you're on holiday, one more lesson would wear you out."

"So very kind of you."

"Not at all."

"Daphne said you paint. I'd like to see your work when you could, although trust me, I'm not a good judge. I wouldn't know one famous artist from another, so a name doesn't mean much to me. I don't fake it, either I like something, or not."

"You mean a landscape by Robert R. Elliot wouldn't thrill you? I'm terribly upset."

"I could possibly make an exception for that signature, still I couldn't be sure. The picture could turn out a poor rendering of a pine tree and look like a palm tree and then I'd be stuck with it."

"Invaluable point, Mister Royce. I'll keep that in mind when I splash on color for a pine, palm. You tasteless, working class clod."

Daphne had overheard their boorish behavior and laughter from the kitchen. She never could understand how men could insult, swear at each other and generally be offensive to one another, then laugh themselves silly. If women spoke like that to each other, they would never speak to each other again.

She leaned through the doorway. "One more comment like that and I'll take your toys and send you to your rooms."

They appeared sheepish, although not contrite. "You know, Jim, I'll bet we could have some fun times if my sister wasn't tagging along all the time."

"Maybe if we go for a hike, we can find a way to lose her."

"Just keep it up and in another minute I'll lose you both off this terrace, you tasteless, working class clods."

They laughed and chatted over poached eggs on toast and tea, after which Robert, now called Rob, displayed his illustrations and oils. The works were all landscapes, no portraits. His only mediums were pen and ink or oils. No watercolors. Portraits and watercolors were beastly to work with, Rob said, and as he couldn't be proficient in them, the devil take them.

What Rob said he was good at was true and impressed Royce. He *was* an accomplished artist. Even though with only one eye, he knew his framing, vanish points, balance, and had complete control of his palette.

"You obviously must sell them, there are so many."

"I do, there's an art shop in Bow, which takes them on consignment. Thankfully, when there are tourists, my work sells fairly well."

Daphne broke in. "The proceeds for every picture Rob sells goes to the Lord Derby War Hospital in Winwick, and he slips in a little extra as well. And he sponsors shows and…"

"Daph, please, enough. I'm sure Jim must already gather I'm nearing sainthood."

"Well nevertheless, you are good to them that way."

Her brother responded. "Jim, before the adulation goes too far, there are Great War wounded at the convalesce hospital, and it is convalescence is in name only. I call them the GLF, the Great Lost and Forgotten. They're stored—that's the correct word, in fact, the only word—in dozens of military homes across the country.

They're crippled, blinded, and gassed, shell-shocked, erratic. All types are ensconced there, and have been for twenty years. And tragically, they'll be there until they die. Can you imagine the stories they could tell? They were the young, full of life, had wives and lovers. Damn it, they once had a future.

Every one of them had a story, but their snuffed out, gone. Just think, what if, a second before they die, there's a moment when they comprehend what had happened to them. Wouldn't that be terrible? Then again, perhaps they simply die, without knowing they lived. I don't know. Yet, if you allow yourself to think of it too long, it's enough to make you scream for them. What I do can never compensate for what's been done to them."

Rob leaned against the terrace wall, stared along the mere, and shaded his eyes from the sun's rays reflecting off the ice. For a moment, he was in the Argonne—then it was gone. He turned as if he hadn't stopped talking. "The nurses and aides do what they can on miniscule budgets, so I do my bit. Giving my sales money is no hardship, believe me. Dad bought this cottage and shifted my trust over to Lloyd's, so I live quite comfortably. If I can get them some entertainment now and then, it helps brighten a day or two. Daphne and I've managed to have Noel Coward and Leslie Howard come up here to entertain and they're wonderful. When we offer payment, they refuse. Said they'd be ashamed to take it. They've been back many times, and often bring burlesque and cabaret shows with them. Gives the forever wounded something to think about other than how to kill themselves."

Robert stared at the floor. "God, I hate war."

Unexpectedly, he walked off into the parlor.

Royce had only listened. Daphne turned to him in tears.

"Christ, Jim, I've never seen him like this. He never said these things to mother or me. It's as if he kept himself bottled up, and all it took was you to uncork the bottle."

"Let him have his say, Daphne. He could have rolled up in a ball, ignored reality and been one of them. Yet, in spite of what happened, he made a life. A paradise to live in, his paintings to express there's still beauty, and he's found pleasure in helping others. Still, I wonder, why do you think he's lived here alone for twenty years? He must wonder what his life would have been like. Home, wife, children. Despite his outgoing nature, he doesn't allow anyone other than you and your mother to be close. There's more to his reason for staying here than the mask. He's only told us part of what happened. Have you noticed there's not a trace of his army years here? There's more to his story."

They packed a lunch, took Rob's Hillman wagon, and followed the narrow country roads south along the Windermere, then reversed direction, following up the west side of the mere until Rob pulled over. A short, rising hike brought them to an old, wind and rain worn, stone building. Rob told them that the government, to promote tourism, even back in the 1700s, had a number of these buildings erected as viewing areas. The one they were at was called Calife Station. Royce and Daphne sat in the frame of a long gone window, marveling at the scenery north and south along the mere even in winter. Jim touched her hand.

She was surprised. "Mister Royce! You're being quite presumptive don't you think?"

"Sorry, Miss Elliot," he laughed. "I lost my head."

They laughed. Robert Elliot turned away, thoughts of Harvard…Harvard and the girls engulfed him...

They hiked along the bank. Trees were bare, the air cold and crisp in a cobalt sky.

Rob enlightened them. "Spring, summer and fall are the seasons the tourists pour into the area. Trains, steamboats on the mere, automobiles and even seaplanes. They soot the air, and people crowd the trails. It does get a bit suffocating, although I don't mind. That's life as I see it, and there's always a spot without distractions to set up my easel. And, you know, that world fades away and beauty reigns supreme."

Daphne asked Jim if he wanted to rent climbing gear. He said probably not, he'd be satisfied simply doing a little free climbing along the way and let it go at that. She sensed a subtle change settling over him. Whether it was simply the passing diversions, she couldn't fathom. Ever since he and Rob talked, Jim was evolving. Embryonic, yes. Yet she could look at his past, and it was always Jim's self-awareness and the protective veneer behind which he kept people at arm's length. Without knowing, Rob had brought Jim out from behind that barrier. He was almost relaxed with Rob. No, not true, he was relaxed. From the moment Rob said what a fright Royce looked, she began to see a change. It must have been her brother's disfigurement brought empathy that quickly turned to friendship. She recalled Jim's edginess towards her in Austria. That, and the uneasy atmosphere between the brothers at Ravensmoor was really the only way she knew him. When he took her hand at the viewing station, she could have fallen out the window. She grinned at the thought of it. A man so diffident, held her hand. She giggled at it like a schoolgirl.

"What's so funny, sis? Telling yourself jokes?"

"No, I can't help laugh at the two of you, chatting on like two magpies. Doesn't give a girl a chance to think."

Then Rob, she mused, gazing at the back of their heads. What is he feeling? From all outward appearance, he has no friends. Despite meeting people who want his paintings, and his jokes with the maimed at the Centers, it was as if a moat surrounded the cottage. No one was allowed in, except my mother and me, and now Jim. And that was only because of me. Yet just to hear them talk as they walked along, it seemed Rob is changing as much as Jim. It's what they have in common she thought. Still, both came to their disfigurements in particularly different ways. Jim, from birth, never knew another face, and hasn't learned to live with it. Never tried, she'd bet, to get on with a life that could have been quite pleasant.

Rob's fate was different. He'd been handsome, unassumingly handsome. The type, as they once kidded, who charmed the girls into his arms. Football hero in high school, grades which gave him a pass to any ivy college. It was Harvard, the Crimson, football, and girls and beer and a charmed future for the taking. Father was so proud. But damn it, it wasn't to be. Rob and his two best friends were off to an adventure more testing than football could ever be. Now his friends are dead, his Father brokenhearted, feeling his son had thrown his future away. Father still loved him, simply wasn't able to look at him without tears.

What does Rob think when he's alone? She never dared ask. And honestly, she didn't want to know. His beautiful face, torn apart. Worse, he must wonder what his friends could have made of themselves. Lives gone before they became men and able to look back and laugh at how young and foolish they once were. Did he feel he was the cause of their deaths and endless sadness of their families? How could he not?

Jim's comments about Rob hiding something came back to her. Was he? Rob didn't want people around, yet he helped others. He created beauty with his paintings and sold them and that made the owner happy. Then he gave away the proceeds to bring a little comfort to men scarred by the war and also add part of his trust income to them as well. Simplistic? Perhaps, but subconsciously, that may be the only path he found to survive.

A covey of quail skittered across their path. The men stopped to watch. She came up on their left, glancing at their profiles, the undamaged sides, and stopped. Both men were so handsome in profile, tears sprung to her eyes. She couldn't accept what had been done to them. How on earth could they?

Previously, she had an easy life, going where she pleased, whenever she pleased. A boyfriend here, a boyfriend there, with few cares to concern her. Her only continuing cause for distress had been Robert and his lonely life. That was enough. Then she intentionally forced herself on Royce, and after the beastly first meeting, she liked him more each time she was with him. What is it, she wondered, that draws you to a person? How would she explain the magnetism? He wasn't just another male friend. Now, she worried about him. Added to the two men there was the anxiety over her mother. "Well, damn it. She mumbled, "If they can take the life fate has thrown at them, I sure as hell can handle my pitiful problems."

She couldn't *begin* to imagine what fate was contriving—for each of them.

On the drive back to the cottage, Rob listened intently as Royce gave his thoughts on the war scare. "Well, it isn't like we should be surprised. We gave Czech land to Hitler at Munich. Now they're doing what they do best, taking over and sending their undesirables to a place called Dachau. That's where they send people from Austria when I was trying to get out of there."

Rob was surprised. "You were there when that was going on? How'd you get out?"

"With great difficulty, believe me."

"I should think so, those Nazis seem tough. I've been reading up on all this, and Hitler started out hating communists and you'll agree that's not a bad thing. Hitler's hate for the Jews is only a ruse to blame someone for Germany's failure in the war. The problem for the European mainland is the German's are also basing their actions on their version of history. The reparations we demanded after the war were devastating for the Weimar Republic, that's how Hitler got to where he is now. You know, before 1918 there was no Czechoslovakia. The western powers carved it out of the old Austro-Hungarian Empire to satisfy ethnic races. Now the Germans have taken the Sudetenland from the Czechs by claiming the German population there demanded it, and I imagine Germany will shortly lay claim to the rest of Czechoslovakia. They say this land is their right from as far back as 1866, if I recall the date correctly."

"Robert, they don't need a reason, they're going to take it back. They simply go by the maxim might make right. The Sudetenland Mountains were the Czech's best line of defense. Now, thanks to the French and us, they don't have that defense line any longer and as a further insult, everyone knows we're not honoring our commitment to them. We've left them naked, so it's natural for the Nazis to grab it. The point I was trying to make is our Government and the Majority of the Ministers think they have chosen Peace with Honor. But, as a rabbi in the United States said, it will be dishonor without peace. Our leaders have made a deceitful agreement and lulled the people into a false security. The French and our government have no will. Hitler sees that. He blames the communists and the Jews for fomenting dissension and making the Deutschemark worthless. He's going to destroy them and the people of the other countries. Should we let him? We have little choice. You can only negotiate with the devil with a hammer. And we don't have one. Another thing. Hitler's got to use his army, if not, Germany will go bankrupt in a year."

Daphne made a conscious effort to follow Royce. "Damn, Jim, you're jumping all over the place. I think you've had one too many. Maybe Rob can make more sense, even though I'm afraid to ask the question. What do you think is going to happen? Jim and his brother, David, said there'll be war."

Rob ran a hand through his hair in frustration. "Sis, the man who invented the machine gun stated it would outlaw wars, because his invention was too devastating. We all know the outcome of that. Then, it was said the Great War was The War to End All Wars. Only twenty years ago that statement was made, twenty pitiful years. Now, here we are again, waiting. I shudder to think it so, but we don't have the fortitude to stop war before it's too late. Though even now, it probably is too late."

Robert shivered, gripping the steering wheel, and continued. "We can't let this go on, yet I see no way out. Most, not all, but most of our alleged leaders are blind to the truth. It doesn't take a crystal ball to see what we did to Germany after the war. Reparations destroyed them. Yes, the Kaiser was stupid for starting it, but we forced those people into an unjust peace. Like Jim said, Hitler's the result. He promises a rebirth of Germany, why wouldn't they flock to him. If he could just see what another war would do, perhaps he would stop. The Treaty ending the war left Germany powerless, so he builds up and we counter, and so it goes. No one steps up to say, *stop and think*! What are we doing? So yes, Daph, there will be war. We didn't have the brains to find a just peace in the past and we'll pay for that. All those soldiers we left buried in French soil, all those in our Convalescence Centers, will have suffered and bled and died for nothing. Not a damn blasted thing! Each one of us must find a way to stop this."

When they reached the cottage, Rob was still troubled. He remained courteous, but upset. He had a few more words with them, then went to his room to pack. Royce followed him. Neither man spoke of the war clouds.

At last, Royce spoke. "Rob, you've got to take it easy. There's nothing we can do to stop it."

"Each of us must to do something, Jim. Something! Otherwise there *will* be war. We build up, Germany builds up. It's a tennis match, back and forth it goes until the ball explodes."

Royce felt it best to change the subject. "Do you drive nonstop to London?"

"No, I stop by the Lord Derby Hospital in Winwick, Northhants, then to Birmingham to drop off some paintings. An artist colony there carries my work when the tourists leave. After that I get a Bed and Breakfast for the night, then a real early start to reach London by the early afternoon."

Royce didn't answer for so long Rob turned to see if he was still there. He wasn't, so Rob continued to pack until Royce came back holding his camera.

"Rob, I'd like to commission you to do a painting, or an ink drawing, whatever you think best. It's from a photograph."

"Of course I'll do it. Where's the photo?"

"In here."

"The camera? I'll need something more than that."

"I know, but I was thinking. If you could have the film

developed on the way down, and pick it up when you return, I could give you the photo I'd like."

"That's fine. There's a Kodak photographic store beside the artist's shop, so no bother. What's the picture of?"

"A castle."

Daphne overheard and came into the room. "You sure you want a painting of that? I should think you wouldn't want to see it ever again."

"I want *you* to see it, Daphne, it's beautiful. I'm sure I'm over the fall now."

Royce asked another favor. "Instead of staying at a B&B, you'd do me a good turn if you'd stay at our family home, Ravensmoor, tomorrow night."

"Jim, are you joking? You want me to barge into your brother's home and say I'm sleeping there? Don't be foolish."

"No, no. Not like that. Of course, I'd call first. I have to call David about the business. I'll tell them about you. I need to find something out, Rob. So please, listen to me. I want you, as an outsider, to meet my brother. I'd respect your opinion on him. I just want to know if it's me who's wrong about...I don't know what. Do this for me, it would mean a lot."

Rob glanced to his sister for help, she nodded.

"All right, Jim, against my better judgment, but I will. You call them now; find out whatever it is you need to know. If it's what you want, you tell them about me, everything about me."

Royce got Mary on the phone and she immediately handed him off to David.

"Hello, James, I hope you're having a pleasant time resting up there."

"Yes, a great time. You should come up here with Mary sometime. Did you speak with Clive about our thoughts on my position with the company?"

"Yes, we spoke. The position is acceptable to me."

Royce's hadn't expected that answer, and he was of two minds, though overall he felt relieved. At least he had direction. Even when David continued and mentioned he wanted Royce to start Monday, the 24th, it was acceptable. Daphne was leaving that day for the States with her mother and they had planned to say goodbye on the 22nd, so she would have time to pack.

David's voice came back. "Are you there? I said is this the only reason for your call?"

"That was one reason. The other is Daphne's brother, Robert, is going to London and I would like him to stay at Ravensmoor, going down to London and back up here."

"What on earth for?"

"He's a unique person. Wonderful artist. Was in the Great War, with the AEF, seriously wounded, lost his best friends and hates war, although he's reconciled we must have another."

"Interesting, hates war, yet wants one."

"No, I didn't say he wants one, only that he feels there is no honorable or realistic way out of this blasted mess the Government's put us in."

"I could use that attitude in Commons. You said he was wounded. Not a cripple, or without legs I hope."

"No, it's just that he has only half a face." Royce was intentionally crude to upset David, simply to get his reaction.

"Good Lord, you can't be serious to send him here. Think of the children."

"David, don't get your knickers in a twist. Robert has a leather and rubber mask on one side of his face. You may not believe me, but it's not a put off, like mine. I wouldn't send anyone there who would frighten the children or Mary—or you, for that matter."

"Daphne is, or was, American, so I assume he's American."

"Yes, an expat."

"Interesting, we need Americans who see the case for war."

"So you're all right with it?"

"Half a mo, I'll check with Mary. Oh, never mind, she's off somewhere. It would be a weekday night and I don't have many appointments."

"I would imagine he'd be there around the middle or late afternoon, tomorrow."

Given David's telephone number and address, Robert agreed to stay at Ravensmoor without further grousing other than telling Royce he was in debt to him. They had dinner, an evening libation, and he retired for an early morning departure.

Later that evening, Royce had second thoughts and in the morning, he got up to have tea with Rob before he left.

"You seem troubled, Jim."

"Perhaps I am. That's why I got up. I've asked you to spy on my brother and it's not sitting quite right with me."

"I follow what you're saying. Still, I think you're wondering if you've wronged him and want my opinion. And really, I have no problem with giving you my opinion. You haven't asked me to pry into his desk or get him to reveal some dark secret with which to blackmail him. There I'd possibly draw the line. So don't give it the time of day. I'll have a pleasant chat with him and tell you my thoughts, simple as that."

"Good, thank you. One other thing. Today I'll tell Daphne what my conversation on the phone was about. Now, I want to tell you, so you won't go into Ravensmoor without knowing my arrangement with my brother. I will be Assistant Supervisor to a great Supervisor named Clive Henderson. Clive was my mentor before I left the company and he's overseen the incredible strides Royce Bearing has made in the last three years. I have no doubt David is struggling to get this growth under control, both with the three new companies he's acquired, and financially. I won't get deep into any of this, as David may confide in you, and I'd rather have him inform you rather than my muddying the waters. From what little I know, he has done a brilliant job. As far as my new position, I have no design or engineering degrees, or even background other than RB. Strangely, I'm able to put things together mechanically. On the other hand, I'm able to know why someone else's designs will or won't, work. I simply don't understand why a degreed engineer can't conceptualize in three dimensions and see that the damn thing has flaws. In retrospect, I was never too tactful in conveying why a design wouldn't work and explain the flaws calmly."

Rob laughed, "So you think you weren't too tactful. I'll bet that's a first for you."

Royce laughed in return. "My word, you're right. Turning over a new leaf. This must be your fault."

"I don't know that it's a fault or not, Jim, it's probably the air up here that's done it, very catching."

"Well, whatever, I'm holding you up. Have a safe trip and stay in touch with Daphne on your mother's condition."

"I will. If you have a chance drive over to Skiddaw Massif up by Keswick, there's some excellent climbing there."

"I climbed up there four or five years ago, it is good climbing."

"Then just rest up. Get ready for your new position."

Royce went back into the kitchen, decided to have a cup of tea, and brought a cup to Daphne. "I just saw Rob off."

"I heard the car leave and you weren't here. I thought that's what you were doing."

"Yes, I wanted to have a few words about David before he left about the situation at Ravensmoor."

"You wanted to be sure he didn't query David too deeply on your behalf."

"Something like that. How did you know?"

"You've become a wee transparent."

"You just guessed, Daphne."

"Maybe, maybe not. We'll have to wait and see, won't we?"

The day progressed amiably. They drove to the north end of Windermere for a strenuous hike, afterwards stopping for a bite at one of the few tea rooms still open this time of year. They spoke of Rob and his life, yet tried not to dig deeper into his mind. Daphne hoped, that even after all the years, he could someday become more outgoing. Royce, although just as withdrawn, agreed, yet only if Rob was not happy in the life he lived. Why on earth change him, if he's actually content?

Royce then sat back and told Daphne the offer he and Clive Henderson had worked out and Clive had presented to David, and the positive response.

Daphne was pleased. "Now I understand why you hadn't told me the plan. I think you going back to RB is for the best, but do you think it's simply change for change's sake? We've discussed Rob's life, so now are you sure you wouldn't prefer to do something else—instead?"

"No, the decisions made. Like you said, it's for the best."

Royce broke into a smile. "Wait until you return from Boston. You'll see a new, outgoing, loveable person. Possibly, I'll get a mask like Rob's and he and I will make the ladies swoon as we strut along London's Strand."

"Good Lord, Jim, how will I keep you down in Coventry,

after you've seen the Strand?"

"The song goes, how do you keep them down on the farm, after they've seen Parrie."

"I know that, but it fit here."

They finished another low mountain hike and then drove back down the east side of the mere, stopping at Bow-on-Windermere for varied items and picked up the Manchester Guardian.

Daphne drove, Royce scanned the headlines and read to her. "…Polish troops move into Teschen, Czechoslovakia… Hungary claims some Czech territory."

"Well, Daphne, aren't those tin-pot little countries something? Germany's little scavengers, taking parts of the Sudetenland from the Czechs. They're stupid not to know they're probably next on the menu of the biggest vulture, and a vulture always starves last."

He continued reading aloud. "According to our sources, the infamous SS, along with Wehrmacht troops who occupied Czechoslovakia's Sudetenland at the beginning of October, were reportedly rounding up all former Sudeten officials. Those officials, who England tragically ignored by not giving diplomatic protection, had resigned in protest to the Nazi takeover. They, as well as all other undesirable elements, are being deported. We have it on authority that they will be sent to the Dachau concentration camp."

"Damn, Daphne! The Czech diplomats resign in protest, and we don't give them diplomatic protection. What a bunch of spineless weaklings we have in Government."

Royce looked hard at the next paragraph before speaking. "And listen to this rubbish. Cosmo Lang, Archbishop of Canterbury, spoke on BBC one night. 'As a sign of recovered sanity', he said, 'once and for all the use of bombing aircraft shall cease.'" This is more rubbish, Daphne, England's awash with idiots. That Pact's not worth wiping my arse with."

"We've got to hope they're right, Jim. And bye the bye, horrid language, you crude Limey."

"Me? You've been known to utter a few dubious idioms yourself in the past, my dear."

"Why you nasty man! How can you even *think* such a thing?

150

I'm the epitome of proper behavior. In fact, for your information, I was voted the embodiment of scrupulous comportment four years in a row at grammar school."

"That was a long, *long* time ago. A lot of behavior and comportment gone over the dam since then."

"Mister Royce…you are a beast! I was right when I called you a *bastard* when we met, and it obviously holds true to this very moment. You continue to be one!"

The Alvis pulled into the drive. She jumped out, giving Royce the evil eye, then flounced off toward the house. Her show of indignation brought Royce to laughter.

Daphne turned. "You cretin! It's your fault I swear, you bring out the worst in me! You'll rue this day; you wait and see."

By now, she couldn't hold back a smile. She returned as Royce got out of the car. "I mean it Jim. Someday you'll be sorry for those callous remarks."

With their arms around each other they laughed all the way to the house. She poured two drinks, as Royce continued reading. "I see we've got some Arab terrorists in Palestine raising hell for our troops and we have to send reinforcements. Christ. There's always something. Hello, what's this?"

'…Winston S. Churchill attacks the Munich Agreement when in House of Commons…Quote: "The utmost Prime Minister Chamberlain has been able to secure, has been to insure the German dictator, instead of snatching his victuals from the table, will now be content to have them served to him course by course." And Lady Gladstone called the Pact "vivisection without anesthetic." Duff Cooper, formerly First Sea Lord, having previously resigned because of Munich, said…"So, finally people are speaking out. Let us hope there are more than these few.'"

In the evening, after dinner, they sat bundled up in front of the fireplace. The cottage, built in 1825, was only meant as a summer retreat; therefore no allowance was made for heat other than four fireplaces. Robert had installed two kerosene heaters, which helped to take the chill off, although the rooms were drafty. Drafty rooms, cold air, the world going to hell…

They shut it all out. They were alone.

Chapter 11

DAVID WELCOMED Robert to Ravensmoor, and told Albert to take the small valise and place it in the third bedroom in the west wing. Robert was straightaway put off, thinking that information could have been passed to Albert before his arrival. Perhaps, he thought, David wanted him to appreciate the fact the west wing has at least three bedrooms.

Mary and the children were introduced. They had been briefed concerning Robert's mask and were not upset. After a short welcome, they walked toward the study, David explaining that two military officers had stopped by unexpectedly and he would be pleased for Robert to meet them. Two Royal Air Force officers stood as they entered.

David began to introduce them but Robert stopped him. "I already know General Sir Miles Alcott, and his aide, Colonel Tommy Tomlinson, quite well."

"Of course, Rob." The General already grasping the outstretched hand. "We know each other very well, David. Rob here helps tremendously at Lord Derby's War Hospital for the wounded in Winwick. I don't know what they'd do without him."

"I'm sure they would find some other way, Miles."

Sir Miles Alcott, whom David Royce addressed as General, was called simply Miles by Robert. Interesting, David thought.

No harm in having Robert as a new friend. Robert turned to the General's aide. "Hello, Tommy how are you?"

"Very well thank you, Rob. Good to see you again so soon."

General Alcott broke in. "Tommy should be feeling well, makes Brigadier next month."

Robert broke into a smile. "Well, that's wonderful news! Congratulations. Are we going to lose you?"

"Yes, and the General as well."

"Will we see you again? Where will you be stationed?"

Colonel Tomlinson turned to the General, who nodded it was all right to speak.

"We're both going to the Dover area, in charge of finalizing the construction of the new RDF system. After that we've another assignment."

"I have no idea what you're talking about. RDF?"

"Sorry, actually, it's Top Secret."

General Alcott spoke up. "Well, Tommy, the reason we're here is to further enlighten David about Chain Home, and I'm sure Rob's not a spy. So, I'll give him special clearance for the evening."

"Very good, Sir." Tomlinson knew Top Secret had a loose connotation in peacetime.

"I'll try to be clear and brief. Back in '34, a report circulated in Government circles, which laid out facts that showed if an enemy attacked us by air, their bombers would get through to our manufacturing hubs and cities. This was because ground spotting, even with listening horns, would be too late to warn our population centers and fighter bases. Bombers are now too fast. The RAF had been performing flyovers since 1934 to test response times and every analysis proved without question, many enemy bombers would get through. We had RAF Squadron Leaders as observers in Spain and what Nazi bombers did to their cities such as Guernica was a terrible shock to us, so it spurred the Air Ministry to—unobtrusively, mind you—form a committee with a mandate to find some sort of air defense."

Tomlinson looked to the General for permission before continuing. The General nodded.

"We foolishly started," Tomlinson went on, "with a 'death ray', which had but the merest chance of success and quickly proved of no value. During that time however, we were contacted by a physicist, a Scot, name of Robert Watson-Watt. He said, straight out, he knew this death ray we tested to bring down a plane wasn't feasible. However, he did say radio beams could be developed to sort of bounce off a plane and return to receiving equipment. He thought that could be a valuable start. Do you follow what I've said? There might be a system to know the enemy was approaching long before he knew we knew."

Robert and David weren't sure they understood, neither had heard of such a thing. It sounded like witchcraft to them.

Albert entered and refreshed their drinks. With the door closed behind the butler, Colonel Tomlinson went on. "Now here is where it becomes quite exciting. The Air Ministry commissioned a demonstration using a BBC tower to test a Radio Echo Detection System and damned if we weren't *stunned*. It tracked a bomber from east of the channel! Hugh Dowding, the Air Marshal, was keen on the idea, got financing approved, and we were off to the races. We started building five stations in 1935 and the towers, which are three hundred and fifty feet high, became known as Chain Home."

Tomlinson took a breath and a sip of his drink. "To explain the words, Chain means the towers are linked together by telegraph wires, underground. And Home means the base station. While we were building the physical units, our friend, Watson-Watt put together a group of electronic engineers at Bawdly Manor in Suffolk, and we now have a system to track an enemy's azimuth and altitude as well as the approximate number, speed and direction. It's simply brilliant!

"We became operable the first of September, and other than our citizen's complaints about all the towers ruining their view along the coast, we are Go."

General Alcott broke in. "Let me give you a breather, Tommy. You were quite clear. Not brief, but clear."

Everyone laughed and General Alcott continued with the story. "The RAF has finally taken over the complete system, and will quickly work out the minor problems left in our Fighter Control Network. Nevertheless, even now, we've achieved more than eighty percent detection, and seem to improve every day. Understand the full import of what I've said, gentlemen. We can now detect bombers and fighters coming from the continent well before they get here. We will know the position, direction, altitude, and rough numbers. Our pilots will no longer have to spend wasted minutes searching. We are able to scramble fighters and vector them directly to enemy bombers, actually *directly above* enemy bombers. This is a spectacular advantage for the RAF. And here's the wonderfully strange part. The concept has been around for years! Germany, France, even the hopeless

Russians, have primitive systems. However, they, in fact no one seems to understand its importance. Our agents in Europe say they've heard nothing about what we're up to, nothing!"

Robert looked up. "Agents? You mean we have spies in Germany sending us information?"

Colonel Tomlinson smiled, "Of course. This is not some gentleman's cricket match, although some Parliamentarians seem to think so. We have agents up in Nazi offices. Have for years. Just as they have lurking in our country. They're called Moles."

"Be that as it may." General Alcott continued. "If the Boche attacks us, and we have enough fighters, they will soon find out the value of our system. Privately, David, for your information only, the system is code named RDF. Radio Direction Finding. It's term for other applications, so we use it for misdirection.

Now, to change the subject and the reason for this background information, David. Number one. You must put major efforts with Rolls Royce to assist them in their production of Merlin engines with the model numbers for the Supermarine Spitfires and Hawker Hurricane fighters. I know you're helping RR on bomber engines also, but the primary importance, until I tell you otherwise, is fighters. General Harris, Bomber Command, won't like this, but there's simply no other way. No matter how we feel about Chamberlain's infamous peace pact, the sad fact is, the RAF had only 300 operational Spitfires when he signed that Pact. So at least it gives us a little more time."

David spoke up in an effort to sound knowledgeable. "General, if I might make one comment. That engine is brilliant, but it's carbureted. The German Messerschmitt 109 has fuel injection. My brother feels that if a Spitfire goes into a steep dive the aircraft could experience fuel starvation and, of course, lose power, whereas the 109 would not."

"Your brother? I didn't know you had one. Anyway, is your brother a fighter pilot?"

"No, no type of pilot. Actually he's rather a pseudo engineer. By that, I mean he has no degree. Nevertheless, in the past he had worked out bearing configurations for the Merlin engine. I believe the carburetor problem was worked out in his head."

"When did he tell you this?"

"It must be about three years ago."

The General glanced at Colonel Tomlinson, then back to David. "We know of the problem. However, it is not common knowledge. I'd like to talk to your brother. See how a non-pilot came to the idea, especially in his head."

Robert chimed in. "He's staying at my cottage at the Lakes right now, Miles. I believe he is starting back with Royce Bearing sometime in the next week. Isn't that right, David?"

David was annoyed with himself. He hadn't meant to say 'brother'. He simply intended to let the General think he had inside information. Instead, James was getting the attention and this was getting out of hand. Now it was difficult to get off the subject. "Why yes, Robert, quite true. He is coming back."

General Alcott was curious. "What position is he coming back at? Pseudo guesser? "

David was distressed. "No Sir, he will be Assistant to Clive Henderson for Plant Supervision."

The General was serious. "For all the plants? Isn't that a rather lofty starting position? Any nepotism here, David?"

David was trapped. "Not at all, General. My brother worked for the company in the past where he was second to Henderson in Design Engineering. Henderson stated he wanted my brother to have the new position, and I agreed."

General Alcott was searching his mind. "Royce, Royce." He mumbled, then asked. "How long had your brother been gone, and where?"

David told him about two years, mainly in Austria. The General held up his hand for silence. Taking a sip of Brandy, he quietly asked. "Your brother's name is James Royce?"

"Why, yes, Sir."

"And he is recently back from Austria. Is that correct?"

"Yes, General. How did you know he recently returned?"

"I don't believe this! Do you know what happened over there? Do you know he killed an SS Major's son? And not just any Major, but a Hitler Division, Major?"

Robert and Colonel Tomlinson came forward in their seats, wide-eyed. David was embarrassed. "I didn't know about that until a few days ago, Sir."

"A few days ago? And when were you going to inform me?"

"Sir, I confess to confusion. It never entered my mind this

could be of importance. James told me the accusation was false, he said he thinks the youth took his own life. I believe him. I've heard nothing further. I thought that was the end of it."

"Well, blast it, it's not the end of it, not by a blasted long shot. I don't fathom how you can't see the importance of this—so let me enlighten you. Yesterday, the Foreign Office received a formal demand that a James Royce be extradited to Germany. He will be tried for murder. I assume the Foreign Office is all aflutter wondering what this is all about, and who this James Royce chap is. I'll now inform them of the *whom* to their problem, and they can decide how to muddle through the rest."

"General, again, reporting the incident never for one moment entered my mind."

"Understand something, David. I don't give a tinker's dam whether your brother killed an SS Major's son or not. All I care about is protecting secrets. We must know about even the smallest incident, and this is far from small. Don't worry that your brother may be extradited, it won't happen. We're not in the mood to do anything the Nazis want.

"Nevertheless, if your brother knows elements that are not common knowledge, or if he is of value to our war effort, then we'll have to hear his side of the situation. Then *we* decide on his security clearance, not Royce Bearing. So get your brother back down here on the quick, and contact me. I'll set up a meeting with MI5 and the Foreign Office. End of subject."

David was uneasy. General Alcott was acting like a General, and David had never seen him this way. Robert hid a smile.

"And now David, to another subject." The General, still irritated, began once more. "The company you purchased in Manchester is, I'm sure you know, a precision small equipment manufacturer. You're to set up an immediate meeting between them and Metropolitan Vickers. Vickers makes the vacuum tubes for the RDF units and we need equipment to assure the integrity of tube vacuum. Metro Vick will explain. Get your people on it."

The meeting was over, but one point bothered Robert. "Tommy, or Miles, you made one comment about spies. You said we have them in Germany in high places. Are they safe if a war should start?"

General Alcott was devious. "Yes it's true, we do have them

there, and this is strictly private. Are they safe if there's a war? God only knows, I surely don't."

"And Tommy, you said the Nazis have spies over here? Why don't we arrest them?"

Tom laughed, the general smiled. "Because we know who they are, twenty at least, and if we arrested them the enemy would replace them with spies we don't know. They don't find anything special, such as the value of Chain Home, so we let them bumble along. It's that simple."

* * *

Generals Alcott and Tomlinson were gone. David and Robert relaxed and sat back with brandies. "Welcome, Robert, to the world of madcap happenings. And, while speaking of madcap happenings, how are my brother and your sister getting along?"

Robert grinned. "Like peas in a pod, sir, peas in a pod."

"Then do me a favor, will you?"

"Of course. I assume you want me to ring up my cottage and tell Jim he must come back here as soon as possible to face the powers that be."

"You read my mind, Robert."

Robert dialed up his number while David poured them another brandy. He left the room to where Mary was reading in the library. He gave her an overview of the meeting, the news of his brother's new troubles and his need to return immediately.

"That could be a bit of a problem, David."

"Well, I hope Robert makes it clear that if James won't come down, they will go up, with security personnel. Then there'll be a row. Wait...I heard Robert hang up. Come with me and hear what happened."

Without preamble, Robert gave a synopsis of the phone conversation. He said how he got his sister Daphne first and explained the problem. She expressed disappointment, but understood. Then there was a minute or two of silence, obviously Daphne was explaining the difficulty to Royce, after which he came on the line.

Robert said Jim seemed calm, so apparently Daphne had an effect on him. He was bothered by this turn of events. Still, toward the end of the conversation, he agreed to leave the next day, although he wouldn't say what time.

Mary went back to the library and the men stayed in the study to finish their brandies. David was angry with himself and his brother, wondering how this new circumstance would pan out for his plans for James, and the association with the General.

Robert recalled the whole conversation with the officers, amazed at what had been said. "Sir David, I'd like to broach something that has come to my mind. If I may?"

"Of course. Go right ahead."

"I've not thought this out too well I'm afraid, but here goes. After all the talk of war here, I find I'm...I'm not sure of the word I should use...but, I find I'm *avoiding* it. Sort of hiding up in my cottage, while all this is going on around me."

"I shouldn't be surprised you want to shut it out. Look what it's done to you."

"I know, although there are others far worse. Nevertheless, they do what they can. What I'm getting to is, I want to help. I don't know how, and then I thought...perhaps I could help you as an assistant. Be your liaison with General Alcott, Tommy Tomlinson and a few other officers I've met at Windermere, and at the Lancaster Center. Just a thought, Sir."

It took David only a few moments to appreciate Robert had an excellent idea. A perfect contact with what would soon be two Generals, maybe more. A wounded man with half a face, not ugly like James, could acquire a number of contacts. Who would refuse a war hero? The officers he would deal with were all from the Great War and so was Robert. Excellent tie in for RB.

"I think it's a good suggestion, Robert. I'll put some ideas together and get back to you, and it should be soon."

Robert went to his room; David retired to his office and opened his diary.

Oct. 18, '38

General Alcott, Tomlinson & Robert Elliot (Daphne's brother). I blundered. Did not report James escape to authorities. Alcott irritated but all right now. Elliot helpful. Make him offer after further discussion. James still causes problems. Is he worth it?

Believe yes. He had better be. We'll see shortly or he'll be gone.

* * *

Robert lay awake for hours in the third bedroom in the west wing. He had to decide a course. These men tonight hoped for a war. A war would allow them to try out their new apparatus their new toy. David can't wait for the orders and the money to come in. Why? So he can build a south wing or buy a larger manor? David was probably more of a warmonger than the officers. Of course he would be, he'd never been to war. God, this is terrible. Who's to stop them? What could he do?

There must be some way to stop this militaristic spiral.

One idea came to mind. He still had an old phone number tucked away. A number he had never called.

Early next morning, as Robert was about to leave for London, David confirmed his initial thoughts and assured him there would be a position offered after he returned from his mother's home.

Driving found Robert full of ideas for the position, traveling everywhere, hobnobbing with the key players. He'd find ways to help stop another war, another waste of boys being shot up and stacked like so much cordwood. That would happen again should war break out. He had to do his part to stop it. He thought of his war and the loss of his men. It still hurt. Moreover, it would come again, sure as hell, and worse. The idea he formulated through the night, had to be initiated, it was his obligation.

He could see the pain in her eyes. Mother was hurting and he ached for her, wishing he could take on her burden, her anguish. They had to get her to Boston; Father would help her. He comforted her until she slept from the drugs, then put on his coat.

From a phone booth, fumbling with a piece of paper, he made a call and then an appointment to meet outside a pub in Soho, on Rupert Street at ten o'clock that night.

There, he was met by a man and woman whom he did not know. The man called him Phillip, taken aback by the half mask. The woman, stood off, and said nothing.

"Well, well, Phillip, it's been a long time. We wondered if we were ever going to hear from you, much less perhaps with something of importance."

The voice was Irish, Sean, he said. Probably more a British hater than a Nazi sympathizer.

Robert was hesitant. "As I said on the phone, you must not have been followed."

"No problem, mate, I've slipped Bobbies for years. Never been caught yet, I hasn't."

"This is different, Goddamn it! It's Brit Intelligence I'm concerned about, not some sleepy street policeman."

"Just give me what you have, Mister Phillip and I'm gone."

"I'll give you nothing. I want someone with authority. I won't pass information to a lout such as you. I want someone else here in one hour, or I'll never be heard from again."

"Keep talking like that, mate, and you'll get your wish never to be heard from again."

Robert looked around. No one else in sight. He brought an Enfield revolver from his coat and pointed it directly at Sean's face. "You frighten me terribly, Sean. One hour."

Robert retraced his erratic path back to the car on Berwick Street. After fifteen minutes, he returned to Rupert Street, to stand in the shadows further up from the pub. A person he assumed to be his contact arrived just prior to eleven o'clock. Robert waited another fifteen minutes, long enough for the person to get restless and start to walk away. This convinced him no one else hung about. He left the shadows and moved towards the person. The nearer he got brought a surprise. It wasn't a man, but a woman in long pants and hooded jacket. The same woman who had accompanied Sean.

"Hello again, Mister Phillip."

The voice, South European, Spanish, Robert guessed. "Hello to you, Miss…?"

"Names don't matter, whatever I tell you would be a lie, same as you, Phillip. Shall we go inside? It was freezing out here waiting for you to come out of the shadows. Do you think I didn't know?"

As they sat in a booth, Robert was blushing. "Sorry you got cold, I'm new at this."

"I gathered that as soon as you pushed the gun in Sean's face. A dangerous thing to do. I believe you've seen too many movies, Mister Phillip."

They ordered two glasses of Merlot. Robert became a bit unsteady and put it down to waiting in the cold. The woman was calm and handsome; she had been through meetings such as this. They stared at each other at first, sipping the wine. Robert relaxed, telling her he couldn't possibly pass his information along to a stranger. He must know her name.

She whispered. "If that is a requirement, how about Madame Tosca? I'm sorry I only have a hood, not a slouch hat to cover my face, or perhaps long blond hair over one eye, like one of your actresses."

"One of my actresses? How do you know I'm not English, rather than American?"

"Well your accent is almost Anglicized, but you'll never get rid of your Boston enunciation, Robert."

He froze. She knew his name. "How did you..."

She stopped him. "Don't you think we know who you are? Did you think I would meet with a stranger and expose myself? Please, Robert, give us more credit."

The cat was toying with the mouse, the mouse bewildered.

"Let me explain to you, Robert. Up until 1938, we had an agent in that war hospital in Lancaster. You'd be surprised how Generals and other officers talk so openly about military matters to the patients. Our agent also heard you talking in the early '30s, about your hatred of Bolsheviks, and praising Hitler in his efforts to rid Germany of them. You also spoke, later on, still speaking at the time as an American, of how the War allies, England and France, had humbled Germany into submission, and you could understand how Germany wanted her rightful place in Europe back. Your main hatred was war itself, you were very outspoken against it, back then at least."

The door opened, Robert tensed as Sean stood and glowered at them. Madame Tosca rose. Robert could see her anger. She approached Sean, said something Robert couldn't hear then took Sean's arm, and shoved him away. Submissive, head down, Sean stumbled out the door.

Tosca returned and sat on Robert's side of the booth. "Sean is very possessive, jealous."

"I can see why, Madame Tosca."

"Why thank you for the complement."

162

Robert blushed. Men, Tosca thought. How easy.

"Now, as I was saying, you were very outspoken back then, Robert, so one of our agents put a telephone number in your communication box at the Center, which said if you wanted to help drive out the Reds and stop war, contact us. It was a long time ago, nevertheless you kept our number, and here we are. We know your father lives in the United States and we think that's where you get your money, aside from your paintings, which are very good by the way. We know you have a sister who lives with your mother, off and on, in Belgravia, although I admit, we don't know where she is at present. All this information came from your speaking to one person or another at the Center. Amazing what a person can overhear. Isn't it?"

Robert *was* amazed. He didn't know how to respond other than to be defensive. "I do hate war, but after what Hitler's been doing, we may need one to stop him."

"Tell me Robert, just what has Hitler been doing? Think. He has lifted up a country, which was beaten into the ground after the war. And remember, he didn't start it, that ass the Kaiser did. Hitler was wounded, gassed and an Iron Cross hero in that war. He hates war too, but he wants the land Germany once had, and it's only right. Look at all the people cheering when he brings them back into the Fatherland. You're trying to tell me that is wrong? It's the reason England and France didn't step in. They know the vast majority of the people in those countries want him."

"What about all the people he's deporting? Anyone who opposes him, and Jews?"

Her eyes wandered the room; she was exasperated, having to justify Hitler again.

"Fine, let's discuss them. First, you didn't mention the Bolsheviks, who we now call Communists. They were the gang you wanted out. He's done that, deported them, and eliminated them. The very thing you were complaining about. England, France, and America should do the same thing. You'd better hope it happens someday. As far as his opposition, most of them were Communists, and the ones who weren't, were leaches, corrupt, or wanted to keep the country the way it was, so they could steal its wealth again. England has corrupt politicians as well, and you know it."

Her voice lowered, he could feel her passion. "And now, about the Jews. They were the ones who financed the war you hate so much, and gave you that face. Hitler doesn't want them around, so asked them to leave. Some do leave, some don't. But, do you know that since '34 to now, Jewish immigration has slowed? So how bad can it be for them? When you hear all this talk of mass deportations, don't believe it. Judeo lovers exaggerate the stories. Of course the Nazis deported some communists and corrupt Jews, but these tall stories are ridiculous. When communists are deported, nobody complains. But remember, the papers are owned by Jews, and when the Germans deport ten Jews, they say a thousand, when a hundred, they scream ten thousand. Be realistic. How could this happen? Where Germany could put them? Eden, Churchill, Cooper and other warmongers claiming Germany is doing this is all nonsense. It's so ridiculous no person with a brain would believe it."

This woman made sense to him. She was right; almost everything he believed was from the newspapers, which she said are owned by Jews. The communists? Who wouldn't want to get rid of them? She captivated fascinated him. Articulate, intelligent, handsome, and made sense. What more could any man want?

Madame Tosca read it in his eyes. God, she thought, these American and English men are so simple, so pliable. Still, this one has guts. To stick a gun in Sean's face took nerve, or maybe stupidity. As soon as Robert turned his back, Sean's knife was out before she grabbed his arm. And, Robert didn't know a damn thing about it. Dumb. First thing she was taught, you pull a gun, pull the trigger. Everyone knew that. Robert was in the war? Not for long, she guessed. But still, he was intriguing, his face, so handsome on one side, apparently so disfigured on the other. Then again, perhaps it was in his money she found the fascination. She must find out.

"All right, Robert, what do you have for me?"

Because he was entranced, for a moment the reason they met was forgotten.

"What? Oh, of course. Sorry, my mind was wandering for a moment there."

I'll bet it was, she smiled behind her hand.

"Well, Madame Tosca, Britain has…"

"Wait a minute, Robert. You don't have this written down?"

"No, that would be foolish of me, don't you think?"

Smarter than she thought. She fished for a pen and paper.

"All right, Mister Phillip, proceed."

"Well, British Intelligence has spies in German Intelligence and the German Army and..."

Robert stopped in mid-sentence. Even though he was an expat, not a British citizen, he was becoming a traitor to his adopted country. He was crossing the Rubicon, there would be no turning back. Madame Tosca could see the fight within himself. She knew this moment was a challenging time for a traitor to get past, if they had any ethics. She reached over, touched his hand, and could feel a chill run through him. She knew he wouldn't be difficult.

"Robert, I know your feelings. But, neither England nor America is at war with Germany, and perhaps some of your information will help prevent a war from happening."

She stared at him intently. She knew how traitors fell in with that line to justify their actions. "So make up your mind right now, because what you've said so far isn't even near secret. We know there are British spies in Germany. So what? Every country has spies in everyone else's country. You've got to do better than this."

Robert felt challenged. "They know you have spies in England."

"Let me make this clear, Robert. I don't have spies anywhere. Germany has spies in England, I don't. I am not German. I will tell you my given name. It's Donnatta, Donna in English. I am Italian-Spanish. Germany hired me, that is all. I sell my ability. If the Brits wanted me, I would work for them.

Robert, believe me, my only loyalty is to peace. My husband died at the hands of the communists in the beginning of the civil war in Spain. If anything, I hate any war and the stink of communism more than you. But, Hitler is fighting them, and doing it the only way that scum understands, with guns, clubs, and deportation. The only other country doing that is Spain. So I defend his actions, even if some of them are questionable, I defend them and work for him. Now, I've been honest with you. So speak, or leave. One thing more first, if the Brits know Germany has spies here, why don't they arrest them?"

"The officers said the German agents aren't doing any harm, so why arrest them and have Germany send in spies they don't know. The officers said spies will be arrested if war started and then, I guess, Germany would be left with next to no agents here."

Tosca felt anxious. What if she were known. She hid her concern. "Now that is interesting, Robert. Interesting the way Brits think. They say how many Germany had here?"

"Probably twenty, at least."

She mulled this information over. Most agents, or moles, operated through cells making it easier to catch one member and then roll up the rest. That was why she worked alone; using just one or two other people and only if needed. Even Sean did not know who she was. She received information and questions straight from Berlin. The phone number Robert had was Sean's. Then Sean called her. That was the weak link, but she would know if something happened to him, they had set times to contact each other and a key word. Sean did what she needed and she paid. Simple, clean. Still, she felt a shiver.

"I don't think that's of much value, Robert, what's else?"

"The RAF has a warning system to detect airplanes, bombers."

"Robert, again, that's old news."

"They say they can detect bombers when they're still over the continent, Tell how high, speed, bearing and approximate number. They used the word azimuth. I don't know what it means."

"I don't believe they can do that."

"Well, I was with a General and another officer who's soon to be a Brigadier, and they are now in charge of a new system. It operates towers along the coast and ties in signals with Fighter Command. And they are quite serious; anyone who attacks here is going to get a very unwelcome surprise. They call it RF …something…RF Chain Home."

"Maybe so, still, I've heard it's fake, but I'll pass this along. Chain Home. Where were you to hear this? Lancaster?"

"No, I was in a manor called Ravensmoor, in Coventry. It's owned by a man named David Royce. He and his brother own Royce Bearing and a few other companies. The company is really priming for war. The General told him to concentrate solely on assisting Rolls Royce with their Merlin engines for the Spitfire and Hurricane fighters only."

"See, Robert, this is what bothers me. If they continue to talk and build for war, it will happen. It's self-fulfilling. Same thing about this Chain, whatever that is. Who's around to attack them? Switzerland? Belgium? Germany? Some Arab country? Don't be stupid. Hitler's not going to attack west. You can see with your own eyes, he's headed east. He's already said he wants peace with Britain. His only complaint is with the warmongers in the British Government. But tell me, Robert, how you came to be at this Royce's home?"

"I'm a friend of James Royce, David's brother. It may interest you to know, I may also become David's liaison with his other companies and the military."

"A very interesting position, Robert."

"I thought you might think that...Donnatta. But, there may be a hitch, because David's brother might not get clearance to work on military projects. From what I could follow, Jim Royce, the brother, escaped from Austria after he was accused of killing some SS Major's son. Jim said the Major's son must have killed himself, although the German authorities want him extradited. The General said it won't happen, still, without military clearance, I don't know what position Jim or I will have at the company."

Donnatta was silent and Robert thought, too late, he was saying too much. "I want this clear. I'm doing this for peace. Not for money."

She wanted to tell him he was an idiot, but instead ended the conversation. She had to digest all this and get it in code and report to her contact immediately. This was a good contact, notably so if Robert worked for a military contractor. It could also mean a bonus, particularly with the information Robert thoughtlessly gave her as to where his friend Jim Royce could be found. She knew the reach of the Gestapo and SS. If the German Government couldn't get him legally, the Gestapo would snatch him with little problem. She told Robert she would like to see him again, simply for something to say, and took his hand knowing he was captivated.

* * *

Once more at his Mother's house, he was torn by two extremely discouraging emotions. He had become a traitor. Still, he justified his actions with the knowledge the countries were not at war and he had spoken nobly in the name of decency and peace. He must believe that. Nevertheless, he will be thought a traitor. If he did his part to stop a war before it started, it was worth it. The other

167

emotion, he was infatuated with a spy. A spy for the highest bidder. Seemingly no ethics whatsoever. Perhaps he could find how much she received and match it. Would she be interested? How stupid, he thought...nevertheless.

He found his Mother still sleeping. He crept into bed and remained awake most of the night, thinking of Donnatta. Whatever the confusion of Robert's thoughts, he still had the sense of mind not tell her of the possible carburetor problems with the Merlin's engine. He also omitted naming the company making vacuum tubes for the Chain Home System. These omissions would assure he could see her again. If he had thought less about her, and more of what he had done, that apart from the damaging military information, he would comprehend he may have placed his friend Jim Royce in mortal danger.

* * *

Royce and Daphne took the same leisurely drive back to Coventry. They had agreed, after his speaking on the phone with Robert, he would meet them at Ravensmoor. Daphne would continue down to her mother's home, as it was determined her mother would benefit more from Daphne's attention rather than Robert's.

They stopped before proceeding to the manor and spent the last few minutes they'd have to themselves. It would be their last time together for a prolonged period, until he met her at Southampton on her return from America. How many weeks or months, they didn't want to think. As they started toward the manor, she put her hand on his as he shifted through the gears. She couldn't have said more with a thousand words.

It was evening when they brought the Alvis to a stop behind Robert's Hillman. Albert led them inside where everyone gathered near the fireplace. The children sat on the divan, quite somber, picking up on the mood of the adults. When Mary asked, Daphne agreed to have a bite of food before Albert drove her to London. There was an unspoken affinity between the two women aside from being the same age. However, their upbringings were so different, it was hard to explain.

168

* * *

Mary was the creation of old wealth and English private schooling. Her whole life was controlled until allowed, with a chaperone, to entertain. Luckily, or unluckily, according to ones point of view, she met David Andrews Royce. Her parents felt she would marry beneath her station and argued the association, but they had another daughter to pass off. Although David Royce hadn't the preferred pedigree in their eyes, he would be able to maintain Mary's standard of living. Due to this, they allowed the marriage. Not approved it, just allowed it. If the incomes of the two families were compared, David Royce was superior to his in-laws. Nevertheless, status was based on family heritage, and David's name, even with a *Sir*, was not in the running on that score. They referred to him as nouveau riche. It galled David, and although he added to his estate until it well surpassed her parents, he could never overcome their coolness.

Mary enjoyed her life, with reservation. When single, she had her secret fling. That was over. Now she lived for her children. In her own way, she loved her husband, aside from never really trusting him. He was too fine, too driven, too involved with self. She was the pretty wife with a title, who would never cause a scene over what she imagined happened in London. She never felt trapped or stifled, yet when she gave it thought, she wished David were more like James in some ways. She often tried to dismiss the thought.

Daphne was nearly Mary's inverse. A father and mother completely open about what she did with her life. Despite their money, she attended public grammar and high schools and they shaped her personality. She was willful, not obnoxious, and would often go her own way rather than join a group. She searched for different paths, went with different boys. She was egalitarian in her thinking and very straightforward in driving down any person who put on airs when referring to 'those' people. She never gave it a second thought if her frankness often caused her to lose companions, other than reasoning the devil take them. This happened often, especially in college. Despite being an honor student in her major, Languages, she left college in her senior year to tour the continent for a semester. She never went back to school.

169

Her only emotional bonds were to her mother, father, and older brother Robert, more so, due to his injury. Her only constant enjoyment was mountains. The solitary majesty, the sensation she knew when climbing was enough for her to know it was where she planned to build a chalet someday. However, she knew something was missing. That indefinable something, which kept her wandering, at times with others or, more likely than not, alone.

It was the time she climbed with friends, tired of their chatter, that she spotted someone climbing above her. He was alone. She stared at the person above, so skilled, graceful, sure of his free climbing ability. It sent a chill through her. Somehow, she knew the individual felt as she. It was inexpressible. She childishly understood him, what he felt. She had to meet him. When they met face to face, she was caught up for a moment, yet not deterred, her brother's face was worse. The man's attitude was not expected. Still, she forced him to like her, feeling his challenging manner was pretense. Then he left her, simply walked off. No goodbye, no explanation. She never forgot him, searched, and found him again. He was what she sought. She wanted him to share her chalet.

* * *

It was time for Albert to take her to her Mother's home. Robert, David, Mary and the children left her at the door. Royce walked her to the Bentley. Public displays of affection was not to their liking. A hug, brief kiss, and she was gone.

Back in the study, David spoke first. "James, you will not know anything of this, but I've decided to hire Robert here, as my assistant with the military."

Royce, startled, did not appear to be disturbed by the news.

David continued. "I don't have a complete grasp of his official position as yet, but I foresee Robert being my liaison with our military, and working together with you. So many projects need straightening out. Dozens of glitches continue to pop up every damn time we turn around. We must be able to get programs running and moving forward. Robert will be answerable to you, Clive, and of course, me. Robert, since General Alcott gave you somewhat of an approval the other night it should be a simple matter to get you confirmed tomorrow. We'll let you know. Hold any questions you have until you start with us, hopefully in two weeks. As an afterthought, I'm sure there will be some surprise when our employees see the two of your strange faces together."

David settled into the couch, facing Robert and Royce. "Now James, for tomorrow's meeting. Other than General Miles Alcott, I'm in the dark as to whom else will be there or the questions asked. So listen to what is being said, and do not over answer a question, which may lead then to another question and so forth. In other words, James, don't volunteer you were climbing with the Nazi youths in the dark."

Royce nodded agreement, Robert surprised by the comment. David told Robert it would be incorrect for him to be at the meeting without proper clearance, so he should overnight and leave for home in the morning.

David started to leave, then stopped. "Oh, one other thing while I think of it. As we are no longer just a bearing company, I am changing our name to D. W. Royce Industries, Limited."

Royce and Robert sat by the fire with scotch and sodas. "What are your thoughts, Jim?"

"You mean his changing the company name? Doesn't matter to me, it's his call. Actually I'm quite all right with it. It is his company. We were born to it, yet David built from what Father left. Another thought leads to you, Rob, and the position you're going to assume. I'm pleased, very pleased, you and I are going to associate. Nevertheless, I was surprised. To leave the life you have and come to this, does make me wonder about your priorities, or should I say your sanity."

Robert laughed. "I felt if you could do it, I should also help in the coming troubles. Perhaps in some small way I might be useful in preventing war."

Quizzically, Royce looked seriously at him. "Now I truly am questioning your sanity."

Glasses touched. "To sanity. May we both find it someday."

Chapter 12

THE MEETING WAS HELD at 12:00 noon, in a private residence to the north of the Imperial Science College in Westminster. Royce had only heard of General Alcott and Colonel Tomlinson and knew none of the other men present. David knew most of them, although there were only nods, no introductions.

The seating in a drawing room, though appearing casual, was explicit. David and James Royce sat on one side of the room, four men in business suits sat on the other. The General and Colonel Tomlinson placed to the side of both parties.

Colonel Tomlinson initiated. "For the record, let it be known to all present, this meeting is being held at a private home at 17 Aytron Road, Westminster, on 10.20.38. All parties present are subject to the War Powers Act of 1917, amended 1933. This meeting is held in camera."

He turned to David and James. "In other words, the findings here are to stay within these walls and not be disclosed under the risk of imprisonment. The purpose of this meeting is to discuss and resolve the official request by the Nazi—sorry, change that to German Government—to extradite and surrender one, James A. Royce, British Citizen, to German authorities."

With that clear, the Colonel continued. "Present are senior representatives of MI6, The Foreign Office, Scotland Yard and His Majesty's Government, as of this date. Also present, General Miles C. Alcott, David W. Royce, James A. Royce, Angus Coleman, with MI5, myself, Colonel Thomas G. Tomlinson, and the Recorder, Sergeant Sara Bertram, MI5.

"The charge, as stated by the German Government, is murder, by gunshot, of one Fritz H. Schmid, aged eighteen,

German subject, while on vacation somewhere in the vicinity of Salzburg, Austria."

The names of the Government representatives were not stated and all, along with the General Alcott and Colonel Tomlinson, tried to keep their eyes off Royce's face.

Colonel Tomlinson continued. "Mister James Royce, will you please give us your response to the allegations of the German Government?"

As everyone was seated, Royce did not rise. He had not rehearsed his story and it did not flow smoothly, yet it had the ring of truth. He led them through the tale of the four Nazi youth bragging and obnoxious behavior in a pub filled with people who recently had their country taken over by the Nazis. How the youths were challenging him with their taunts of superiority over the English. His throwing down the gauntlet, which lead to a hike. Royce did not gloss over the stress of the climb and the failure, one after the other, of each German, until only he and the SS Major's son remained. Royce openly admitted he was near total collapse, unthinking, only wanting to make the last German finally cave. He couldn't find him, he stated. Then, he heard the gunshot, and his erratic search for the German went on until he lost consciousness, and found himself somehow off the mountain, in a clinic, saved by the clinic's owner, a Doctor Arnheimer.

Royce stopped talking. He had relived the time once again, and was perspiring. The representatives, General, and Colonel were silent, looking from one to the other. They could tell the story was true simply from the discomfort of the speaker. True, and dreadful. Yet what was left out?

One of the unnamed representatives asked. "Mister Royce, I'm a trifle confused. Who is this SS Major of whom you speak?"

"The boy I couldn't find said two or three times he was the son an SS Major in the SS Adolf Hitler. So I'm assuming Fritz Schmid is the father of the boy who was shot."

"So, Mister Royce, could we assume it could be this Nazi Major is after you, and perhaps not the German Government? Never mind, you couldn't know."

Another representative asked. "You say you heard a shot.

Was there anyone else who might have possibly been in the area at that very time?"

Royce nearly said that it was too dark to tell, but caught himself. "There was no one that I saw anywhere around."

Not a lie. He heard David take a deep breath.

"Did you see the youth carrying a gun?"

"No, although they did have backpacks. One could have been in there."

"Are you convinced, Mister Royce, the youth shot himself?"

"It's the only way it could have happened in my mind, unless of course, he slipped and accidentally shot himself."

The man smiled. "Doubtful. Tell me, how old are you?"

"Thirty-three."

"And the Germans, going by the age of the Major's son, were around seventeen, eighteen. Yet you, at thirty-three, walked them into the ground. I admire you, sir."

"Thank you. Except in truth, I'm not proud of it. I was older, and should have had more sense than they."

"From what I hear, Mister Royce, Hitler youth never will have sense. Then again, how could we expect them to, they've been so brainwashed by the Hitler cult."

The last representative spoke carefully, intently. "So, you never saw a gun?"

"That is correct."

"You never saw one, touched one, or fired one. Accidentally or otherwise."

"That is correct."

"So there is no way your fingerprints could be found anywhere on a weapon?"

"That is correct. They may have my fingerprints on climbing gear if they found my room, but not on any weapon."

"Thank you."

The speaker then left no doubt who was in charge. Turning to one of the representatives, he ordered, "John, instruct the German Embassy to supply a set of fingerprints found on the weapon. If they are Mister Royce's we will consider extradition. If they state the prints were smudged, or Royce must have been wearing gloves—any of that poppycock—send them a 'His Majesty regrets', and so forth. I'll speak to the King."

He turned to the Recorder. "Thank you, Sergeant. As this meeting is now over your services are no longer required. Gentlemen, let us retire to the drawing room for cocktails."

When they settled in, relaxing with drinks and small talk, the lead representative, who gave his first name as Edmund, started speaking again, "Mister Royce, I'll now call you James. All this is off the record. I finally can put a face on the dispatches, which crossed my desk about a certain fugitive the Nazi's were chasing across Austria. All our reports had to go on indicated he was English, and had a notable facial scar. As soon as you walked through the door, you were obviously that person. Congratulations. Please enlighten all of us how you escaped."

"Sir, if I may call you, Edmund, it's another long story."

"You may certainly call me, Edmund, and if your story is as interesting as the last, I'm sure we will bear with you."

Royce thought where to begin. "There is an Austrian, a former Prussian officer in the Great War, former climber, who owns the BergFalke Spa in the mountains west of Kufstein in Austria. His name is Ernst Becker. I stayed at his spa when I was recovering from the hike with the four Germans. Ernst is in his seventies, and we became passing friends. He learned through his wireless contacts of a search going on for me. At the time, I had inkling there would be a search for me, although I had no idea of the intensity until Ernst told me. My plan was to get to the Swiss border, into the high country, then hike and ski out. But storms were coming in, so Ernst got me to hide in his vehicle to get across the border. As it turned out, that Major, the father of the boy who died, had read my mind as to which border crossing I would pick."

Royce physically shuddered. The strain from telling the tale again was apparent. He took a breath and continued. "From what I learned later, there were SS and Wehrmacht at the crossing. I won't go into all the problems Ernst went through, but it was very brave of him. He hates the Nazis. He told me later that if he wasn't the holder of the German Red Eagle medal, and one of the officers recognized him, we wouldn't have made it. I knew nothing of this at the time. I was under the hollowed out rear seat, boxes piled in the trunk. The main problem for me was, even though bundled up, it was freezing. The other problem was the breathing tube Ernst had put in the floor pan. Carbon monoxide entered my hiding place. I managed to get it plugged, but I inhaled too much of the fumes and lost consciousness.

Once we got past the Swiss border, Ernst said a Swiss ambulance got me to a clinic and he stayed with me until I was well enough to take a train to Zurich. My brother had sent a plane, and here I am."

Another story they were amazed by. Edmund turned to one of the men. "Sounds like something you would get up to Charley. James, meet Charles Kendal Wentworth the Third—or at least that's' one of the names he goes by—foreign agent extraordinaire. C W has known a tight spot or two as well. Only difference is, he does it on purpose."

They shook hands. To Royce, C W Wentworth seemed a modest, reserved man of middle age. Nothing about him indicated his life would be anything more than a good book beside a fireplace. "Don't listen to Edmund, Mister Royce. He often spins tales of daring about me when I'm rarely doing little other than having a walk in the park."

"Don't listen to me? James, Charley's walk in the park would more than likely be a dark alley in Berlin or Moscow. In fact, I'll bet a shilling to a pound C W is already thinking of some way to use your Ernst Becker in some nefarious scheme against the Nazis in Austria."

Royce looked at C W. "I wouldn't like that. Ernst is too old to be involved in any of your games."

C W stared back at Royce, unblinking and nodded once, noncommittal.

Edmund broke the moment. "All right then. General Alcott, you have something else?"

"Yes, Edmund. There's an American expat, Great War veteran, our side. His name is Robert Elliot. Colonel Tomlinson and I can vouch for him. We know him well from his past work in the Soldier's Home over in Lancaster. We need Secret classification identity passes for him and James, so they can work with David Royce at his plants."

Edmund looked at James, then to David sitting beside him.

"Of course! I feel like a damn fool, wasn't thinking. David's your brother."

"Yes, Sir."

"I'm damned again. All right, Miles, if you vouch for this Elliot fellow and David wants him, we'll issue it. Do you want Secret or Top Secret classification?"

"I think Secret will suffice for Elliot. If we need higher in the future I'll get back to you, Sir. I do request Top Secret classification for James. From what I understand, David feels he's an engineering genius and, he is also going to be Royce Bearing's Assistant Superintendent for all plants."

Edmund gave Royce a momentary look from above his glasses. "Another surprise about you, James. Glad we didn't lose you. With that recommendation, I'll see to it. You will be informed about the main differences between various Secret classifications."

"Thank you, Sir."

"Does anyone have anything further to discuss? If not, I believe the proper etiquette is to have a bit of a chat while we finish our drinks, then, as has been written, we shall fold our tents like the Arabs and as silently steal away. One at a time, gentlemen, one or two at a time. C W and Angus, please stay for a moment."

When the others had departed, Edmund, C W and Angus were silent while another round of drinks poured. Edmund asked for a few comments on Royce, then made a few of his own. First they were surprised how anyone could survive the harrowing hike, and then amazed at the story of the escape from the Nazis into Switzerland.

"Well," Edmund commented, "quite the stories. Perhaps we could have him fill us in on more of his Austrian, shall we say, mêlées, in the future. C W, we have an agent there, I hope?"

"Yes, Sir, two, maybe three, if they're still operational. The Nazis are really bearing down. Also, Sir—and I didn't want to bring this up in front of this Royce chap—but that Major Schmid he mentioned caught a significant number of 'undesirables' when he was hunting for Royce. Because of this, Schmid has been put in charge of clearing all remaining Jews out of Austria. A lot of people are being deported due to Royce's little hike."

Edmund thought for a moment. "Well, C W, the law of unintended consequences applies here. Keep this close to your vest. I think one more event could be difficult for Mister Royce to absorb."

"Yes sir. About this Becker fellow, is he off limits?"

"No. Although I would tread lightly if I were you. It didn't appear you particularly endeared yourself to our new friend."

One side of C W's mouth twitched slightly. "That really bothers me, Sir. I'm sure you know that."

"All right C W, you heard what I said. Now to matters that are more pressing. As you all know, in February of last year, Hugh Christie met with Hermann Göring, Hitler's toady. As Christie's Top Secret memo reported at that time, Göring stated Hitler wanted Austria, which he took in March of this year, and Hitler intends to take Czechoslovakia. Now, he has the Czech's Sudetenland, and as we've told him England is hands off Czechoslovakia, it suggests, as I'm sure you see, that country will soon be gone. Göring also stated, straight out mind you, they want a free hand to the east. So I assume that means not only the Czechs but Poland and, quite possibly, he intends to go on and declaw the Russian bear. Yet whatever happens, that would mean the destruction of Poland in the short term and strengthen Germany. At present, we here know what the Czechs are going to face is terrible, and it's useless dwelling on it. As our leader's shillyshally, we prepare."

General Alcott broke in. "There's to be no options at all, sir? Chamberlain's adamant?"

Edmund rose, pacing the room. "Absolutely adamant. The part that galls me even more is one of my agents in Berlin has high military contacts and he confirmed that if England and France had signed a military pact with the Czechs, German generals would have tried to oust Hitler. Of course, with Chamberlain as PM, and Halifax as Foreign Secretary you know that information will wind up in the trash. So, until there is someone with power who can see where we are heading, and personally I hope it's Churchill, here's what I want done. Angus, MI5 Intelligence informs us the Germans are increasing their agents' activities in the Midlands, industrial areas, and with slightly more effort along the Dover coast and the RF towers. I'll have MI5 intensify B division's counterespionage efforts, but only if it appears the agents are on to something. I don't want our boys charging in there, raising hell with anyone and help them realize they actually *are* on to something. I want to keep their agent cells dumb until it comes time to draw the net. However, there is one part of this, which is causing us sleepless nights. An agent in Europe informed us there are also a small number of sleeper spies here. Not working within a cell's network makes them hard to track. But my main concern at present is over one agent. Before I came here this morning, SIS informed me there was an exceptional amount of coded wireless traffic sent from five areas, starting at Salisbury, then east, on over to Kent."

Turning to face the men in the room, Edmund stressed his points. "The signature of the key was unique, and the same each time, ergo the same person. The duration of the traffic indicates something important being transmitted, and that, of course, indicates the agent is on to something, or some things. They're not calling home just for a chat. On this same subject, because the key signature's known, this same operator transmitted off and on from Ireland about a year ago, It was and still is, very dicey to track anyone over there, and it's disingenuous to think the Irish wouldn't make a pact with Hitler, or the devil, to get us out of Ireland. My points are these. One, there is nothing we can do about the political situation. Until it changes, we'll have to live with it. Two, an agent, perhaps an emerging mole, formerly in Ireland, has moved his or her operation to southern England; at least that's where the last transmissions emanated. Three, the wireless set being used must be portable, Telefunken or better. However, they may be transmitting only as far as France, then have it sent on from there. Four, they're going to be a bitch to find. And five, that's what we get paid for, so hop to it. Get some answers. For a while I'm not going to use Y section to deliver coded information. So Angus, hand deliver this file to Admiral Sinclair at Code and Cipher. Did you know he's bought that architect's hallucination, Bletchley Park over in Buckinghamshire? I couldn't believe it. But anyway, he's in the process of moving all ULTRA decipher activities over there no later than the start of next year. A Polish mathematician has given us a lead on how to decipher Hitler's Enigma encryptions and that, with luck, could lead us to decipher their Naval Lorenz Company code as well. I know Admiral

Sinclair can't give us top priority because of Enigma, but still, he may have a second or third tier code breaker who's just sitting around learning how to twiddle his thumbs."

Edmund was ready to end the get-together, and then remembered one more item. "Bye the bye, can't forget this. Speaking of our friend, Hitler, I want you to hear an excerpt from Admiral Sinclair's brief. Again, remember, this is Top Secret. Background for this is the Admiral was asked by our beloved colleagues at the Foreign Office to compile a dossier on Hitler. He sent his review over to me for comments before it's sent on to the PM and Halifax. Miles, please give me that file."

General Alcott unlocked his briefcase and handed over the file to Edmund. "Gentlemen, I'll read page five, last paragraph only, the Admiral's description of Hitler."

'...as possessing characteristics of... fanaticism, mysticism, ruthlessness, cunning, vanity, moods of exaltation and depression, fits of bitter and self-righteous resentment, and what can only be termed a streak of madness. But with all, there is a great tenacity of purpose, which has been combined with extraordinary clarity of vision.'

Angus shook his head. CW, mouth open. "Good Lord, what are we dealing with here? Chamberlain's made a pact with the devil, sold the Czech's out, and then afterward, had the gall to say at the aerodrome his peace was 'a hope, not a pledge.'"

"Gentlemen. Remember, you've not seen this. Still, it's necessary you fully understand the kind of person the PM, and Foreign Secretary have trusted with our future."

At the time of this meeting, while these men debated what to do about one foreign spy, Hitler, partially described by Admiral Hugh Sinclair as '...what can only be termed a streak of madness..' had decided the horrific fate of millions.

* * *

"Look, James, if you want your own place, not that I blame you, why don't you buy the Gostly house next door? I hear it's going for sale."

Royce laughed at David's comment. "Next door? It must be a mile away."

"Well yes, except it abuts Ravensmoor's property and I think they have about five or six hundred acres left, which would be perfect for both of us."

Mary chimed in, pleased at the thought of having Royce near. "It's a charming little place, James. It's only about sixteen rooms, but it is sunny and well kept. It was built sometime in the sixteenth century, but it's been updated since then. You know; piped in heat, electricity, even indoor plumbing."

They all laughed, Royce acting shocked. "My word, even indoor plumbing? How could I say no? I'll run right over there now and buy it."

And he did.

The Gostlys, it became quite clear, believed there would be a war and wanted to vacate immediately, leaving most of the furniture there. So Royce, with their permission, moved in before possession was finalized. Royce had spoken with Robert, telling him that when he came down from Windermere with most of his luggage and personal effects, he would stay with Royce.

"As long," Royce specified, "as you don't get underfoot."

Royce called Daphne three times in the next three days. The first call was to let her know he'd bought a house, been cleared of wrongdoing, and was being approved for his position at the now renamed D. W. Royce Industries. The second call was just to talk, and she gave him her mailing address on Beacon Hill, Boston. The longest call was a long goodbye and his hope she had a safe trip.

Along with his other possessions, Robert had brought his art supplies and the photographs he had developed for Royce. The photos were few. A mountain or two, a valley Royce couldn't recall where, two photographs of Daphne and Royce at BergFalke. He lingered on them and, when seeing Ernst in the background of one of the photos, he paused a few more moments. The only others were of the castle. He physically shuddered. Robert saw it, but said nothing. Royce exhaled and appeared to clear his mind. "There's not much choice, Rob, I couldn't move around much to get a different angle."

"I know you couldn't, although look at this one. While the rear is in a very light mist, it's cleared toward the front, and look at the tower. It absolutely radiates with a reddish tint from the moisture. Strange though, there appears to be two cars out front."

"There were, Nazi SS staff cars. They didn't see me. Don't put them in."

Robert gave a grunt. "Let me write that down—Don't Put In SS Cars—got you! Anyway, you dullard, that's the picture you want. I'll do it in oils. An ink etching wouldn't do it justice."

"You're not going to charge me an arm and a leg, are you? I mean you're not in a top gallery. In fact, I don't even know if you're in *any* gallery."

"Tell you what, have your maid do my room, and I'll call us all square."

"I'll wait until I see the painting."

"Jim, you are truly a thunderous bore."

"Thank you, I work hard at it."

"I don't believe that, I'll bet it comes natural."

"You know, Rob—I think that could very well be true."

"Well, as long as you realize it, I'll try to cover for you."

"All right, now to continue my being a bore, until we receive our clearance and can actually enter the plants, let's review the structure of D W Royce's plant locations, operations at each plant, and the managers. You'll need a general knowledge of what we do so when you speak with the lord high military mucky mucks you'll be able to make some sort of sense, if that's possible for you."

"Will I be able to go into the plants with just Secret clearance, Mister high and mighty?"

"Most of them I should think. We'll clear which with Clive. He'll know even more than David on that. When we both receive clearance, Clive will give us an overview, then I'll go in depth with him, and you'll get an education from David."

"Jim, I may speak out of line? All this war talk that's going about, do you think David is sort of a warmonger like they say of Churchill?"

"That's an odd remark." Royce pondered a response. "Hold on, I think you need some schooling, Rob. You were living in a vacuum up at your cottage, just as I was in Austria. I had a rude awaking, it's time you did. First, Churchill is not a warmonger. He's only asserting the obvious. Aggressively, yes. But our government has blinders on, and we are going to pay dearly for that. As far as David is concerned, I wouldn't say he's helping generate a war but, one is being forced on us. I'll admit Royce Industries needs one, and when it comes, as it surely will, David is bound to make money—*if we win.* Call it avarice or being astute. But whatever it's called, people make money out of war and we'll be thanking the David Royce's of this country."

The screams started at 2:00 in the morning. Royce, not fully awake, grabbed a bookend, ran to the central room, and threw on a light. Now alert, he darted to Robert's bedroom and pushed the door open. In the dim light, he could see his friend, twisted in a blanket, writhing on the floor. Royce snapped on a lamp, and then pulled back involuntarily. Robert had taken his mask off for the night. Royce saw the red, torn and twisted scars stretched over bone, the sealed socket where once an eye, the closure where an ear had been.

Royce muttered. "You poor bastard." Then started to shake his friend.

The strange part was, although Robert was in deep sleep, his eye was wide open. He appeared in deep shock, constantly murmuring. "I'm sorry I cursed you, I'm sorry, I'm sorry."

He woke, frightened. "Christ, Jim? What did I say? What?"

"You were saying 'I'm sorry I cursed you', over and over."

"Nothing else?"

"No."

"Good."

Robert rose, went over to sit in a chair, and covered his face with his hands, embarrassed. "Will you turn out the light, or give me my mask. I apologize you had to see my face, no one has since the hospital."

Royce handed him the mask and sat on the edge of the bed. "All right, Rob, open up."

"What? I told you what happened at the cottage."

"You told us a part. There's more, isn't there?"

Robert was desolated. Royce was about to leave before Robert faced him. "Yes…there is more. If you'll just hear me out and then just leave, I'll tell you."

"I'll hear you out, I might not go."

Robert nodded, fatalistic, and began the story he'd never told. "I had two close friends at Harvard. We hung out together, dated together, like guys do. We were football heroes. Sorry, I learned the word hero should be for doing something heroic. Let's just say we were football *stars*. But to me it was obvious the bigger game was Europe. That's where the real excitement was. I thought what if I came back wounded? Compared to football, wouldn't that outshine anything? I'd be a *hero* to my father and everyone, not just a star. I wanted that, I admit it."

Robert was lost, thinking of his Father for a moment. "Anyway, Jim, I talked my two best friends into joining the army. If I hadn't asked them, they probably would never have done it. The three of us went to Officer Training School, suffered through boot camp, and of course we were the best in everything we did. From intelligence tests, running, target practice, you name it, we excelled. We were cocky. War loves cocky people. After six months, we were getting afraid the war would be over before we got into it. When we got to France, the 14th of September 1918, we were happy the war was still going full blast. We were now shave tail Second Lieutenants, Infantry, 1st Army, II Corps, 35th Division. With General 'Black Jack' Pershing leading us. And we were ready for a fight."

Robert readjusted one of the straps on his mask, thinking aloud. "My God, when I say it right out, I can't believe how plain stupid we were. We hung around for days and trained even more, then finally, finally, on the 25th, we went up to the front trenches before the Hindenburg Line. Our objective was the railroad hub at Sedan. We were somewhere around Sedan or Verdun, I don't remember now, but I do remember the veteran Australian troops beside us. They were worn out from three years of fighting. But not us, we were full of piss and vinegar, full of fight. When we heard our Corps was going to be a part of the spearhead to end the war, we shouted at the top of our lungs. The Aussies said they were that way once, and looked at us as knlowing we were damn fools. And Damn fools we turned out."

Robert saw it all again. Royce could sense the feeling, the pain, but could offer no comfort.

"If you don't get it out, I can't help you, Rob."

Robert nodded, picked up where he left off. "Even now, Jim,

as I think of it, we weren't as bad off as the poor bastards who fought at the Somme or Verdun. Cannon fodder for officers, thrown at the Germans and mowed down with machineguns by the thousands. At the time none of that mattered, the three of us made a bet on who would get to Sedan first. But none of us got there. Our side opened with unbelievable shelling that started right after midnight. It went on for five hours. We went deaf and actually pitied the Germans. We couldn't imagine how anyone could live through it. At 0530 the whistle blew and we scrambled out of our trenches, yelling like crazy and charged ahead. Barbed wire was everywhere, although there were gaps from the bombardment. We got to the first of the German trenches and there weren't many left not wounded, but we shot them all anyway. I remember thinking as we charged, 'We're killing people, and we're actually killing people, human beings'. I threw up, but my men kept me going forward."

Rob stopped, memories never spoken welled up. He didn't want to continue the story and lay back on the bed, facing away from Royce.

"Come on Rob, you've gone this far, now get it out of your system, once and for good."

Dreamlike, he continued recounting. "Sure, I will. Our three Companies raced ahead capturing Baulny and Charpentry. We rolled the Germans up. Then, God damn it all to hell, we were stopped dead in our tracks. We got blasted on the left and the right flanks by German soldiers with what they called maschinegewehrs-machine guns, a lot like British Maxims. And I don't mean just any soldiers or guns. They were the best, we weren't. It was brutal. Jim, they destroyed us, they decimated us.

I did what I could to hold my sector, but my men were taking heavy fire, being ripped to shreds from the front and both sides. I looked for my friends' companies. They had the only Vickers guns and were there to cover my flanks…"

Robert stopped again, grim. It took no time for Royce to grasp what took place, or rather, what didn't take place. He walked to the window, staring into the dark.

"They weren't there, were they?"

Silence. Then a whispered. "No."

"Your *friends* retreated, left you and your men there, alone."

"Yes."

"Your *best* friends."

"You don't have to remind me, I remind myself every day."

"So what happened?"

"At that point, I lost at least twenty of my men and told the rest to retreat as fast as they could. Five of us held a rearguard action. It was insane. I ran out of bullets for my revolver and used a dead soldier's rifle. We got to an enemy bunker, which gave us some protection. I lost two more men, yet we had agreed never to be captured, so we fought on.

"Then we heard cannon fire, and the Krauts stopped firing at us. It turned out two Mark 4 tanks, Brits, with one of our Machinegun Battalions and even an Engineer Company had counterattacked to help us. Luckily the Krauts were afraid of tanks and I guess they didn't have any of their new antitank guns, so it was their time to run and saved our asses."

"Your friends weren't with the soldiers who saved you."

"That's correct, but I tracked them down."

"And?"

"And they had no excuse. I lost twenty-two boys. Twenty-two boys that would never see home again, never see their families, or laugh again. I swore at my friends, I was only twenty-three at the time and I yelled that they killed my boys, that they should be dead instead. I cursed them until the air was blue. If I had bullets left in my weapon, I swear I would have shot them for the cowards they were. The men I had left cursed them, refused to salute as they walked past, and I let them. They earned that right. I started to walk off, still swearing at them, and then there was the scream of an incoming shell. God had sent it for us, Jim, I knew that. Everything happened in slow motion. I turned to face the two of them, refused to get down, and they just stood there, frozen, frightened of me. My last image was a puff of sand and I woke days later with half my face gone."

He stopped, looked up at Royce as he turned from the window. "You know, Robert, through this whole story, you never mentioned their names."

"That's because I never want to hear, or say their names again. Never, never, never!"

"So now, you grimace and cringe in your sleep. You cursed

them and they died."

"What do you mean, Jim? That I *regret* I cursed them? That's not true. I curse them every time I think of them. They were cowards. They killed my boys. My former friends and the war *killed my boys*! That's why I hate both! The only good from the two of them being killed was that their parents and Harvard never knew their shame. God damn them!"

"Rob, take it easy. It's been twenty years. You can't carry this with you the rest of your life. They were afraid and ran. I've known fear, fear does that, it happens. Let them rest in peace."

"I can't, we were all afraid, but we didn't run out on our buddies. That wasn't heroic, it was duty. My men stayed. We would have died for each other. Do you want to know the truth, Jim? War showed my two best friends to be cowards. None of us would have ever known. If there hadn't been a war we would have always been friends."

"True, they weren't brave. Yet remember, you were the one who took them to war. So who's to blame here?"

"Yes, I made a mistake, and I take the blame for that. But I didn't make them cowards. They did that to themselves."

Robert couldn't admit the major guilt. He rolled over on the bed and turned off the light. "Good night, Jim."

As they went about cooking breakfast, neither person was untroubled. Royce now knew what to say, yet held his tongue. The bond between them strained to the breaking point. Last night, Royce thought he could have helped, instead he had caused Robert to say more than he wanted. Their companionship was slipping away.

"You know, Jim, I think I should get another place to stay."

"That's probably best. But I gave this a lot of thought through the night, and I've got to get this out. This hate you've been holding against your friends for twenty years is misdirected. It's yourself you hate, and you don't know it. You hate yourself because you talked them into going to war. You hate yourself for exposing they were only football stars, not heroes. All this time you've blamed them. Look in a mirror. What happened is past. Not forgotten, that's apparent, but past. But even if it was your fault, you can't take the blame forever.

"You try to shake blame by your art and helping others. That's a façade, penitence, for the guilt you feel. Look Rob, I'm not a doctor, but after hearing your story, it's obvious what's wrong here, so all I can say is get a grip on yourself. Then see a doctor who can put your head on straight."

Royce was about to leave the room. "One other thing while I can get this out. Wars happen no matter how we hope against them or try to stop them. And yes, people die. There's no good answer. We all hate war, but you're excessive. I'm surprised you're not parading around Trafalgar Square carrying down with war signs like the rest of that peace at any price souls. You know the ones who praise Chamberlain, and the rest of the blind dreamers. You've got it in your head that just because we don't go around and shout against war and while military men prepare, it means we're somehow responsible. You're going to speak with men whose business is war. If you start rants about how bad war is, then you'll last about one minute in this business. They know wars are bad. They've lost men in battle. You think you're the only one who hurts? Get it into your head, if there's a war, Hitler's on the bad side, not us, and like it or not, it's the military and the David's of our country who will save our necks."

Robert remained silent as he absorbed Royce's comments. Could it be? Could he have hated the wrong people, his past friends, for twenty years? If it was true and he was wrong, what had he done? Wasted his life? No, no, no! He wouldn't accept the thought. It might destroy him. He nodded to Royce, as though he would think it over.

"Look Rob, there's no hurry for you to leave. Stay here as long as you want. Take your time. Look around. We'll be doing a lot of work together, so we'll be in constant contact. Let's work things out. On the other subject, if you want, I'll find a doctor out of town, there'll be no talk."

As he sat at his desk getting ready for the work ahead, Royce couldn't help wonder if he had a trace of Robert's problem. He still thought of how unnecessary the German youth's death had been. However, he thought of it only now and then. Robert, however, was still hung up over something that happened twenty years past.

Royce forced his mind to engineering concepts, while Robert, in his room, pretended to study the presentation concepts supplied by David. What Royce said about war and Hitler didn't jell with Donnatta's statements. She knew what was going on. She'd been in Spain. True, Royce had been in Austria and saw what was happened there. Did that mean anything? Doubtful. Then again, what if she was wrong? What would he do? He was a traitor. Whether for peace or not. Traitor. Think. She gave him nothing in return. This was one sided. What did she supply him to help England offset the information he gave her? Nothing.

He had to see her. The problem was he had to give her information so she'd see him. He needed reinforcement, assurances he was doing the right thing. Donnatta had to give him German intelligence in return. Yet, what could he do with it? How could he say he received it?

Chapter 13

29 Oct. 1938

NEWLY COMMISSIONED Oberst, Dieter Schmid, had two reasons to be in high spirits. Hitler had promoted him to Colonel for his work in ridding Austria of the Jew. For the Colonel's organizing skills, Hitler said he would soon award him with another project, which would move him further up in rank. That is, of course, if he performed as expected. Schmid's other pleasure was, that even though the Nazi government would not demand the return of James Royce, they had nothing against Schmid taking matters into his own hands. His own hands as long as he understood whatever happened must not trace back to the government. To help Schmid out further, Hitler's aide found a contact that may be able to help him. Madam Tosca.

* * *

"Phillip wants to see you."

Madame Tosca wasn't in the least surprised to receive the call from Sean. Sean only knew Robert as Phillip, just as Sean did not know Madam Tosca's true identity. Donnatta confided in only one other man in England, yet for some reason she couldn't fathom, she had told Robert her given name. Actually, she could only be tracked down by that name in Spain. Still, the brief slip in telling him annoyed her and at some point must be remedied.

* * *

Her name was Donnatta Maria Azenar y Mira. She was born the beautiful daughter of street vendor's living on the fringe of the Castilla slums around Madrid, Spain. She referred to her younger years as los tiempos vergonzosos-*the mean times*. She meant the struggle through her youth, to try and earn or steal enough money to make life bearable. Her looks and how she learned to use them saved her.

As time passed, she was the mistress of a number of men, never in love with any, using them as they used her.

Yet, it was in 1935,that she did find love, and lived in northern Morocco with Lieutenant Colonel Simon Garcia-Lorca, heir of a wealthy Spanish landholder. The life and love she had strived for all her thirty-seven years was hers.

Events, however, unfolded across the Strait of Gibraltar, in Spain, the mother country, which would destroy that life forever.

Spain, was a cauldron of strife. A dozen belligerent factions were fighting to grasp the upper hand, either to control the government, or if that failed, destroy it. Communists, Fascists, Republicans, Monarchists, Basques, Spanish Loyalists, Nationalists, and more splinter groups fought for power. Assassinations happened day and night until, aided by Russia and Mexico, it appeared the Second Republic Communists would gain control over the democratically elected government. This fear fractured the country into open insurrection. At this key moment, adding to the intrigue, a new troop of right-wing Army officers became intent on the overthrow the lawfully elected government. In Morocco, a prominent Spanish General, Francisco Paulino Franco, now assumed a primary role in the Army's plans of armed rebellion.

The Spanish Navy, remaining loyal to the government, refused General Franco's request for ships to move his Foreign Legion troops across the Mediterranean Sea. To overcome this severe disruption of his plans, the General solicited and received the air transports of Fascist Dictators, Benito Mussolini of Italy, and Germany's Adolf Hitler.

Altogether, by air and sea transport, over ten thousand troops moved from Tangier, across the Strait of Gibraltar and into southern Spain. Assembling his Moroccan troops in Sevilla, Franco's forces, now labeled as Nationalists, began a series of early victories, which included the Alcazar fortress at Toledo. These actions, and the death of the overall commander of the Nationalists, paved the way for Franco to become the General in charge of the Army. The Army's rebellion divided Spain and led to a vicious, unfettered Civil War.

Franco's Nationalists were determined to destroy both the Second Republic and the Communists, and replace them with an authoritarian government. Border towns still under control of Republic forces were shelled and captured. Only the fortified border city of Badajoz, the last source of supplies from Portugal, remained in control of the Republic. Franco sent Colonel Juan Yague, to Badajoz with orders to take the city. Yague, with Donnatta's lover, Lt. Colonel Garcia-Lorca, assembled Spanish Legionnaires and Moroccan troops to begin the preliminary assault. On 11 August, 1936, Simon Garcia-Lorca, was given the honor of commanding the Legionnaires for the initial attack. With his Moroccan Legion beaten back time and again, Garcia-Lorca, amassed the remnants of his Legion, and heroically led a charge that forced a breach in the walls. Though severely wounded, he fought on with his men. At noon, Lt. Colonel Garcia-Lorca died.

The aftermath of the battle was horrific. The fury of his remaining Legionnaires finally overwhelmed the defenses and began unrestrained days of horror and slaughter in revenge for their Colonel.

Donnatta Aznar y Mira, in Morocco, learned of her Colonel's death from General Franco. Her grief was profound, yet kept within her. While previously she had been indifferent to Communism, her heart now clenched with revulsion and hate as only a Castilian woman could. In her school years, history classes taught her to detest the Moors. Now, with her Colonel gone, she turned with vengeance toward Communists. She stayed alone, inside her home, seeing no one, incensed with anger. She only showed herself in public when Colonel Yague accompanied Lt. Colonel Garcia-Lorca's body home for military burial with honors to Ceuta, Morocco.

A shocking insult to her honor followed the service When one of Colonel Yague's aide's offered to take her in as *his* mistress, her hand slashed out. The aide, his cheek, cruelly knifed, fled the room. Later, he was demoted by Colonel Yague.

Donnatta's final distress came when Colonel Simon Garcia-

Lorca's parents, appalled that Donnatta had lived with their son without the blessing of the Holy Church, evicted her from his estate. As the Colonel had failed to write her into his will, she had no recourse. The Garcia-Lorca family held the power.

Donnatta left Morocco and was received by General Franco. She offered her services as an agent for the Nationalists, and became the perfect spy. She slipped across the border to the Republican stronghold at Madrid and met other agents with contacts within the Communist leadership. Her charm and guile opened doors to many secrets which filtered back to the Nationalist forces. Madrid was her previous home for many years when she was younger, and after a year spent to gather and pass information, her past knowledge of the back alleys and secret paths would save her life.

A deceitful friend who, with all the foolishness imaginable, stated blatantly to her face he had betrayed her to the Republicans. He was, he laughed, going to hold her until they arrived and thereby make a great deal of money. He giggled up to the moment her blade entered his throat and Donnatta escaped into the alleys and pathways of her youth.

General Franco told her she was now too well known and it would be perilous for her to continue as a spy. Even with his protection, he said, an assassin could stalk her. Franco mentioned the Germans would be only too ready to hire her services for England. The British, he commented, lived in a dream world, numb to Europe and Hitler's plans. Donnatta, with her light skin, could easily blend in to continue her work.

An agreement with German officials, beneficial to both parties agreed upon and in early 1937 Donnatta took a steamer from La Coruna, to Belfast, Ireland, the gateway to England.

* * *

In Spain, the southern and northern Nationalist armies eventually united after the fall of Badajoz, and the vicious Civil War went on with nonstop destruction, bombardment, pillage, and massacres for three more years. Despite the intrusion and deaths of thousands of foreign volunteers, such as the far leftist

American Lincoln and British Brigades to aid the Republic's cause, the war ended in victory for Franco, the Nationalists and their allies, Italy and Germany. On 1 April 1939, Francisco Paulino Franco, became Generalissimo of the Army and el Caudillo, the Leader, of the Spanish State. Then began the purges, trials and the extinction of all Bolshevists. The exception being those few who escaped to South America.

* * *

Robert drove down to his mother's home in London under the pretext he had to pick up some forgotten belongings. After he contacted Donnatta through Sean, they met at a crowded cafe off Trafalgar Square. Donnatta had other things on her mind, so was put off by Robert and his questions. She had little patience hearing about his and Royce's discussion over who actually was at fault for the possibility of war.

"Look, Robert, we went over this before. I can't keep being your preceptor each time we meet and made to reinforce your beliefs."

Robert was apologetic. What a damn simpleton, she thought, obviously infatuated, and wants to believe me. It's the people he talks to who mess him up. "Robert, tell me this. Do you believe in God?"

"Of course I do."

"That's good. Do you see God?"

"No, but I believe he's there."

"And why? Because you have faith. You can't see Him, can't hear Him, yet still you believe. Now perish the thought that I'm comparing myself to God, however you can see me, you can hear me. You've got to have faith in me as well. You don't listen to people who talk down God, yet you continue to listen to people who blame Hitler for all the world's troubles."

"I guess, but..."

"You guess, but? You've got to do more than guess. There was a civil war in Spain. I was there. I've seen what the communists do to people. They are of one mind. If you protest their actions, you are dead and that means anyone and everyone who disagrees. There were scores, hundreds, of stupid people

194

here in England, America and other countries people going over to fight for the damnable communists. Where are their brains? What's the matter with yours?"

Donnatta stopped. She knew she had said enough. Robert would conform. She changed the subject. "So tell me, what's going on up in Coventry?"

Robert was glad to get away from her berating. "I'll get my clearance for Secret, and Jim Royce will receive Top Secret clearance. We'll both be working for Royce Bearing, I mean D W Royce Industries, Limited. Sir David has renamed the company after himself."

"How does this Jim Royce feel, slighted like that? Is he angry about it?"

"He said he doesn't feel slighted in the least. It doesn't seem to bother him."

A dead end, she thought. "Why do you only get Secret and this Royce person Top Secret?"

"I don't know, probably because he works directly in development on the design and development of the newest RAF equipment. There are certain buildings I will not be rated to enter."

Donnatta mulled over the possibilities. She had a spy in the British war industry that couldn't enter Top Secret areas. This wasn't good, she thought. Where else could he be useful?

"What will you be doing? Do you still think you'll be liaison with the military?"

"I have yet to find out from Sir David. I would think so, yes." Donnatta would have to wait and see, so she changed the subject once more. "Tell me about this Jim, who doesn't mind his brother taking over the company."

"Jim? It seems funny to hear someone else call him, Jim. Only Daphne and I call him that, his family calls him James."

"Elitist, are they?"

"Well, David is. His wife Mary has the title although she and the children aren't stuffy, and Jim certainly isn't. Very down to earth, no airs about him. He goes with my sister, Daphne."

"Does he? Is she in Coventry?"

"No. Our mother is not well. Cancer, I'm afraid. Daphne has taken her to Boston, the U S Boston. Father has it set up for mother to go into Massachusetts General."

"I'm sorry to hear about your mother, I wish her well, Robert."

Donnatta was pleased. Robert now talked and acted like a friend. "So, Jim goes with your sister, is it serious?"

"Well, I know they're very, shall we say, taken with each other. Jim is closed mouthed about it. He's an introvert."

"Like you."

"No, he's worse than me. Even with this face, I do get to meet people, whereas he shies away from them. It's his scar I guess."

"A scar?"

"Yes, I have my mask to hide behind. With him, there was an accident at birth, and he has a white depression all the way down the side of his face into his beard. I must say it's not attractive. My sister accepts it. Probably because she once saw my face, and his is not as bad as mine."

"You're a handsome man, Robert, I feel sorry for you."

"Please don't, Donnatta. I'll ask you to like me, not to feel sorry for me."

They were quiet. Robert believed what a wonderful woman she was. Donnatta amused. A scar made Royce easily recognized. She had made an offer to Colonel Schmid to have Royce eliminated, for a considerable price, of course. Unfortunately, the Colonel wanted Royce alive and on a boat to Germany. She refused; it would be too dangerous for her. She let Schmid know she was the only one who knew where Royce was. To make Schmid nervous, fear his quarry may slip away, Donnatta misinformed him that Royce had planned to change his name and take a Clipper to the United States for plastic surgery.

She asked for fifty thousand American dollars, up front, deposited to her Swiss bank account. She knew if she did not get the money before the assassination, she would not see it afterwards. Schmid was furious. At present, she awaited his response. Donnatta opened the subject of Royce once more to keep Robert in line. "Strange, don't you think, Robert? Your sister likes a man with a scar, and so do I."

Robert's emotion revealed itself. She didn't give him time to enjoy her remark. "Now that your sister is away, does Jim live alone, like you did in Windermere?"

"Not right now, I'm living with him for a while before I find my own place."

"So where is that? Maybe I'll stop in sometime. That is, if I'm invited."

Robert's heart soared. But how he would explain her to anyone? It didn't matter for the moment, it was just the thought she might come to see him.

He fumbled with the answer. "Jim has bought a home next to Ravensmoor, I mean it's probably a mile or more, but they own the land in between, so they call it next door."

When Donnatta said nothing, Robert resumed. "If you would like to visit sometime, perhaps it would be better if you came up to my cottage at Windermere."

"I understand what you aren't saying Robert, and you're right, best not to visit Coventry. Tell me, does this mean you've invited me to your home for a weekend?"

Robert flushed and answered firmly. "Yes."

"Fine. I'll see when I can make it. But right now, what information do you have?"

Back to business, the spell was broken.

"It seems one of David's companies in Birmingham makes equipment for testing to assure the vacuum in the RF tubes for the Chain Home system and the new Merlin engine superchargers…"

Donnatta jotted down Robert's information, and then wrote out a number. She stared at him and pondered. She needed to be confident he was devoted to her permanently.

"Robert, this is my telephone number. Only you, Sean and one other person, has it. This shows how much I trust you. Please memorize it and dispose of the paper."

He was captivated. She had given him her trust. He would never betray it. He didn't ask who, beside Sean, had her number.

"Finish your wine and pay the check, Robert. Come, walk with me."

They left the café and walked northwest from Trafalgar Square, then right onto Craven Street. She stopped in front of a series of row houses. Robert was baffled. He could see she was thinking, in conflict with herself, before she spoke again.

"Robert, this will be our little secret, I don't live here,

although I keep a flat here. The telephone number I gave you is not for this place. I don't have a phone here. This is where I come when I want to be alone. No one knows about this place, not even Sean. You must never tell anyone. Is that understood?"

"I will never tell anyone, Donnatta."

"Would you like to see inside?"

"Yes, I would."

She looked around as they walked up the two stairs and unlocked the door. The rooms were neat and clean and she showed him around the parlor and kitchen.

"This leads to my bedroom."

Taking his hand, she knew techniques to seal his devotion.

Chapter 14

THE CLOSE OF OCTOBER, 1938 slid into November. The weather quickly became colder and sooner than expected. Royce and Robert had done the 'loop' as Clive Henderson called it, visiting the forty-seven buildings and plants, which comprised D W Royce Industries. The company owned, or was in debt for seventy-three percent of the plants, and the British Government sponsored, at present, the rest as Shadow factories, yet under the control of Royce Industries.

There were four buildings specified as units. Robert, with only Secret clearance, could not enter those units, which were astutely designated one through four and clearly marked Top Secret. They had no windows, one entrance, and each guarded day and night by two guards. One of these units housed research on the Spitfire wing to improve laminar flow—an effort, an attempt to improve perfection—of the wing contour to enhance performance. Royce thought it a waste of time and stated it. Another unit held initial designs and pre-castings for petrol injection for the RR Merlin engine. New bearing designs, through the nose 20 MM cannon concepts, developed by the Germans, and numerous other projects comprised the other two units.

The secured section of the underground complex was explicit and committed solely to RF System development for continued augmentation of Chain Home and its sites. In the same underground complex, again secured and separately guarded, was an enclosure designated 'No Admittance: No One Ever. No Matter Who the Hell You Are.' This was a self-contained area solely for turbine blade design, development, and manufacture for the super-secret E28.39 turbo jet engine. To enter this area, even James Royce had to have his Most Secret rating upgraded. The last Top Secret building, actually two units, was strictly for the development of four, Vee Twelve-cylinder, Rolls Royce, Merlin engines. These specific engines were under development for one of two prototype twin-engine de Havilland Mosquito aircraft. Despite the Air Ministry's previous rejection of de Havilland's proposal for a laminated plywood aircraft, the company felt that with Rolls Royce engines, they could create an exceptionally fast fighter-bomber. When de Havilland presented their remarkable concept to the Royce brothers, David, with James' nod, offered to assume all initial costs associated with the RR engines. David's one proviso was that James, as well as responsibility for engine configuration, would supervise the design for the mounts and engine installation. This was agreeable to de Havilland and they, with David, came to a cost plus program for Royce Industries, only *if* the aircraft went into full production. The agreement was accepted after being sent to Hawker-Siddeley, de Havilland's parent company. It would prove a beneficial contract for all parties, including the RAF. James Royce's only reservation was he, and Rolls Royce, would not have time to finalize the designs to cast and fit a petrol injection system to replace the carburetor, or develop a Pressure Carburetor System.

* * *

By the first week of November, Royce was settling into a regimen. He called Daphne in Boston every three days. They were sad about the diagnosis of her mother. There was not much that could be done to help her condition, other than keep her comfortable with drugs. Mrs. Elliot was moved to a private clinic in Salem, where she could see the harbor, and manage a smile each time her husband or Daphne came through the door.

The doctors were candid. Mrs. Elliot would linger. How long, they didn't know. When she was cogent and the drugs balanced in her system, she spoke of going back to Beacon Hill and staying with her husband. She wanted Daphne to bring Robert over so they could all be together again. She couldn't comprehend why they weren't, and her eyes would tear and she would lose herself in memories. Then the pain would course through her system and she'd shiver as Daphne held her.

Roger Elliot was desolate, jeopardizing his own health as he spent day after day to sit by his wife's side, hold her hand, and speak of days irreplaceable. All the guilt he had harbored inside surfaced. He spoke of his son, the dreams for him, his future planned out.

Then the war, and like all young fools, Robert just had to be in it. It was his wound and the handsome face destroyed along with a brilliant future and that Roger Elliot couldn't bear to look at his son without tears. He left them in Windermere, returned to Boston, and even when his fortunes waned in the early years of the great depression, he kept his wife and children secure. Neither Daphne nor Robert had trusts back then. Their father had lied about that. He sold the house on Beacon Hill to keep them comfortable. It made him happy. Only when his fortunes returned through his health destroying efforts during the early Nineteen-Thirties, was he able to buy the house back and return to the affluent life. Yet it was not the life he once had, when his family was around him. Only the memories remained to trouble him.

His wife was dying. His son would never return, and he couldn't face him if he did. His daughter Daphne, once American through and through, elected to stay with her mother in England when the divorce had been finalized. Who could blame her? Her mother and brother needed help. He knew Daphne would leave him again, once his wife died. When his daughter left, he would revert to a recluse. Until then, he would stay with his wife. When she was lucid, they endlessly spoke of when they were young, courting, and a family.

Daphne was worried for her father, and struggled with him to go home with her from the clinic each day. He wanted to stay, get a room beside his wife. His health was failing right before her eyes. The doctors checked him out but found nothing more than a tired old man. They gave Daphne sleeping pills for her father. These helped, and eased her concern.

She was lonely, pouring her heart out to Royce on the phone. She missed him, missed the climbs and sitting with him in front of the fireplace. Royce felt the same, on the phone when he heard her voice, the stress, and loneliness came through. He hurt for her. For years, he had been alone, and lived the life he thought he wanted. As he looked back on it now, it would obviously have consumed him. Then she came into his life, and now he didn't want to be lonely ever again, just alone with her. He came to understand that love was not easy. He hurt when she hurt.

His outlet was the diversion of work, into which he fully immersed. He arrived at the main office in Coventry each morning at six and read his mail and messages from the other plants. Then he worked on various projects until David or Clive needed his attention. After their requests, he traveled between Coventry, Manchester and Birmingham, working out solutions to glitches. If there wasn't a rational solution, he told them to stop. They were not to beat their heads against the wall, attack the problem from another angle, or end the project. This was the reason David needed him. A problem solver not programmed by engineering schools; not constrained by formal thought, not trying to prove himself. Those who remembered him from the past whispered among themselves how he had changed. Naturally not his looks, but his personality. Although he was not overly friendly even now, he worked with them, helped them follow a routine of questions, stare a problem down, look at it from different directions, ask their peers. Royce had formulated a program of integrated design, development, and manufacture. Team leaders in each city met the start of each workday to thrash out problems no matter how long it took. Senior and junior engineers functioned together, it was the best way for both to learn and help the company progress. There was only one goal for all divisions. Success of every project they took on. Absolutely nothing else was allowed to interfere.

Additional ideas Royce had were laid out for David and Clive's input each Sunday. David told him he had carte blanche as David didn't follow many of the concepts anyway. Clive came alive, enthused at the prospect even though he, in essence, had been demoted. He was glad it was settled. Royce had complete management jurisdiction over the company, subject to David, of course.

Royce felt strange. He had shied away from responsibility as long as he could remember. Now and suddenly, he had unintentionally talked his way into it, and he felt all right with it. Was it Daphne's doing? Had she given him the strength or was it his duty to Britain? He sensed unease in the atmosphere, his people were anxious to finish an assignment and get on to the next project. He would feed off that. The main thing to remember, it was his job to control it. Find a comfortable peak for his people to work at, and then manage it.

Royce was in discussion with Clive when David interrupted.

"James, no argument. I've ordered a Bentley Saloon for you, like mine, only in garnet. We can't have the second in command at D W Royce, and also my brother, puttering around in a used Alvis. It would not keep our image. Give that car to Robert so he can dump his Morris on some poor soul. Next, of more importance, and extremely private to the three of us, is what I'm now going to explain. I don't recall if I've said much to you concerning a shadow government, so understand what I'm up to. I, the former Foreign Secretary Anthony Eden, Duff Cooper, who quit as First Lord of the Admiralty because of Chamberlain, Winston Churchill and Harold Nicolson, Labor MP, have privately discussed the problem of our present leaders. Their attitude towards Mr. Hitler's intent confounds us. We, and others of like minds, have established a Shadow Cabinet of loyal opposition. We are informing newspapers and the radio outlets of what we see ahead and get the truth out to the people."

David stopped and looked about, assured no other engineers were listening. "I'll give you one example. The real reason Hitler wanted the Sudetenland from Czechoslovakia was not to protect people of German ancestry. It's a lead in to get hold of the Skoda factories. You know the name from their automobiles, but Skoda is one of the largest arms manufacturers in the world. They are a self-contained industry. They have mines, forge machinery, steel foundries and milling systems. These allow them to produce everything from gun barrel turnings, to the complete weapon. Skoda builds tanks, thousands of field guns, howitzers, rifles, as well as motorized vehicles for their army and to ship around the world. So don't doubt our Hitler is going after all of Czechoslovakia eventually and use this production to his own advantage. So, next question, what is he going to do with all this armament? He's based his whole economy on the military and rearmament so he's got to do something with it."

David paused, obviously with something more on his mind.

"I wasn't going to mention this until I was quite sure of the outcome, however I think it's best to bring it up now. The French Government under Daladier is in shambles. Strikes are hampering all their industries including aircraft and military production. To counteract this problem, England will need even more war material. I will be gone next week from the 6th to probably the 12th. I'll be meeting together with the principals of Vickers-Armstrong and ICI Industries. Both these companies are at least five times the size of D W Royce. But, we will discuss a Government concept called Division of Production. We do this now in a rather small way and simply put, it means to disperse the load. Our friends in Government have set this up whereby we will supply the major portion of the ancillary equipment these companies require, under a cost plus contract. I've been working on this program for months and it is finally coming to fruition. I won't go over the details until they're firmed up, but I want you to grasp the ramifications of a possible two-fold increase in our workforce over the next three to five months. In other words, don't fine tune your programs until I get back."

Royce and Clive looked at each other, then back to David.

"Financing, David?

"This is the actual Government now, not my private sources. Money will come as the projects develop, and that includes prepayments for new factory space, additional personnel, and equipment. This is where both of you come into the picture. You have your plates full right now, but despite that, I want some front work done before I get back. Work together on this as best you can. Scout out another one hundred thousand square feet of manufacturing space in the Coventry, Manchester, Birmingham area. I don't want to take the time to build if we don't have to. If push comes to shove we'll buy out some small companies to get space. Get me costs and try to keep it to as few buildings as possible. I'll bring back Vickers and ICI's manuals for the components we'll produce, employee training, ethics, employee obligation, secrecy, and whatever else you can use. Fabrication and assembly manuals are supplied with each product and I'll try to get you those manuals beforehand as well. Keep them under lock and key, I don't want their names getting out."

David left that same evening. Royce and Clive reviewed the dozen and one things needing attention. Royce then returned to his home, now dubbed, in a feeble attempt at humor, Blackbird Cottage, to distinguish it from Ravensmoor. He thought Daphne and Robert would find it amusing.

Robert was there ahead of him. "Good Lord, Jim, what's that stack all about?"

"It's fabrication instructions labeled Top Secret which I'm supposed to review, edit and approve, so keep your nose out of them—you, with only a lowly Secret clearance." Royce kidded him. "I thought they could be read in front of a fire with a scotch just as well as not."

"You supposed to take that stuff home with you?"

"Christ! Now that you mention it, I really don't know. That brings up an interesting question. Who's responsible for all this Top Secret stuff? Henderson? I'll get answers in the morning."

"By the sound of it, you'd better, can't have self-important employees taking information home any bloody time they feel like it."

"Blast it! Never gave it a thought. Where are my brains? I'll set up a program first thing."

"You? When did you become sole propriétaire?"

Royce laughed. "I became Lord High Poo Bah the sixth of November. Remember that date; we'll see how long I last."

"You'll do all right. I've got faith in you. Here's your scotch, I'll touch glasses to your future. How are Daph and my mother doing?"

"To be frank, it's not going well over there, Rob, Daphne's worried about both your Mother and now your Father. As you know, your mother's prognosis isn't good, and now Daphne's worried about your Father beginning to fail."

"Christ, I'm sorry to hear that. I would like to see him again, Jim, because I think he feels I've wasted these years. Guess it's my fault. Unfortunately, the folly of youth can't be reversed. He can't face me, or the way I ruined my life."

"Do you think you ruined it?"

"Most certainly, and maybe I'm still doing it."

205

"A queer remark, Mister Elliot."

"Yes, I suppose it is, don't know where it came from."

"Oh, before I forget, David's ordered me a Bentley from Crewe, says my little Alvis is unbecoming to my new position at Royce Industries."

"Well I should think it is unbecoming. Every Grand Poo Bah should have a Bentley."

"But, for you, one of my lowly employees, I've been told you get my beautiful little Alvis."

Royce read and scribbled notes across his papers while in the background, Robert listened to the radio playing a recording of America's Benny Goodman's orchestra as they beat out his 1938 recording of Sing, Sing, Sing. Then came the opposite; soft sounds from Frankie Carle and Alvino Ray.

At 10:00 pm, Royce said good night, packed up his forms, and wandered off to bed with them. Just another fourteen hour day and he was only just getting warmed up.

* * *

7 November Monday, 1938.

French radio announced the shooting of a German Embassy official in Paris by a seventeen-year old Polish Jew. The boy, the radio reporter stated, said he was despondent over his parent's deportation from Berlin.

"What do you make of that, Clive?"

"James, any Jew who shoots a German will light the fuse Germany wanted. Do you remember, back at the end of October, when the Nazis deported thousands of Polish Jews living in Germany? That's probably the real reason for the kid's revenge."

"Well, all we can do is wait and see what happens."

"I'll wager we don't have long to wait."

"You're likely right, Clive. One thing after another I guess. Anyway. right now we've got to set up meetings with all the senior and junior managers in each city. You and I will meet with them over the next few days to get them prepared, without mentioning names, before David gets back with his news. If we're to more than double our size over the next few months, our top managers must be made aware and get prepared."

"You know, James, I've given that some thought. It's one thing to hire people if they're available, but where will we get them? This military increase doesn't only involve Royce Industries, there's lots of companies who'll begin to compete for skilled employees, we could be in trouble especially if conscription phases in."

"I worried over that very subject last night when I dozed off on my paperwork. We'll bring employees in by train in the morning; send them home the same way at night. No charge. We can do the same thing and lease buses, or buy our own. There's a lot of people just to the south of us. Let Manchester and Birmingham find people north. Might be an extra hour or so more travel for them, but it sure beats sitting home and twiddle their thumbs with not a shilling in their pocket."

"You've begun to think like a real leader of industry, my good man."

"Please, Clive—spare me."

"Why don't we get Robert onto transport estimates from Sheffield and British Leyland, and then work with London Midland for rail service?"

"Good idea, but I think Rob heads down to Gloster Aircraft at Gloustershire tomorrow and then he's over to the Royal Naval College in Portsea."

"The naval base? What's he up to there?"

"It seems David's acquired contracts and Robert's to meet with some upper naval types to show the Royce flag and ask what we can do for them, not that he knows."

* * *

Donnatta was as specific as Sean could follow. She didn't want any slip-ups. "The man I want you to find is named James Royce. He lives in Coventry. There's an estate there called Ravensmoor, which you'll have to find on your own. About a mile from there is a smaller stone estate, no houses in between. I don't know the name or even if it has a name. I want you to go up there and look around. Unless you make a spectacle of yourself, you won't be known because Phillip is down in

Gloustershire and he's the only one likely to recognize you. Now, listen and understand. You're going to kill this man, but not now. I'm making a deal with the Nazis for his death, so understand; the money is not in my bank. If you killed him now, it might get back to Germany because this man's brother is well known in London. If that happens, the deal will fall through and you, Sean, will be out five thousand American dollars. Have I made myself clear?"

"For five thousand dollars American, I will follow what you say to the letter. You want me to get the lay of the land, find the best place to ambush the gov, and when you say the word, put him down."

"Very good. Now, from what I've been told, he's about six feet and slim. However, the best way to recognize him is he has a scar that runs down the right side of his face. All the way down supposedly."

"You make it too easy for me, Tosca. Do you want me to shiv some other Brits at the same time, no extra charge?"

"No, nothing stupid like that, and be sure you don't take this fellow down right now either. So get up there and check it out."

Donnatta watched the little man swagger off. If her deal, finalized at twenty thousand American dollars, worked out, she would have to do something about him and, as she recognized a while back, something about Robert as well. Sean's a liability in general and Robert knew her given name, which could be used to trace her if a person passed her name around Spain. There was one other person she had worked with intermittently, but he would never be a problem, they were more lovers than spies.

She thought of Robert again. What an flaming fool. For him to think she could love a man with half a face is absurdity. True, he was a decent person, but, after they made love and he offered to buy her contract from the Germans and take her off to Windermere, she could have gagged.

"Good thing, she said aloud, "I was skillful enough to keep a straight face." She had done enough to keep Robert pacified.

She smiled. Ah, love is wonderful. It keeps one from using their brain, to see holes in her stories. She dialed her Swiss bank to find if a rather large deposit had been made. There had not, she was impatient and cursed.

9 November, Wednesday 1938.
In retaliation for the shooting of the Paris embassy official, the Nazis initiated the horror, which became known as Kristallnacht, Night of Broken Glass. A pogrom, wherein scores of synagogues were burned with the collusion of the government. Rioters looted Jewish businesses and houses by the thousands, leaving them plundered. In the aftermath of two days and nights of destruction, over thirty thousand Jews were shipped to concentration camps. The final insult? One billion marks for damages to non-Jews were charged to the Jewish community.

Robert put down his paper. "God, Jim, have you read what the Nazis did to the Jews the last two nights?"

"I heard it from David. It's worse than we think. I don't see how our government can look the other way much longer."

"What is it about the Jews that make Hitler hate them?"

"Simple. Hitler needs a scapegoat, someone Germany can blame for losing the war in '18. The Jews stay together, don't have a country and get by, even in Germany's hard times. That's why they're vulnerable. Yet to me, the *main* thing is they don't have a country. Hitler knows he won't have to have to fight a war over them because it appears no one's going to come to their aid. Where Hitler took a chance was burning down the Reichstag and blaming the Communists. Then the Nazis increased their beatings, killings, and deportation Communists to labor camps. That's got to anger Stalin. Not that he puts any value on life. Then again, Stalin's in no position to do anything. It's been leaked he wiped out his senior officer class almost to a man." *

"But to get back to the point, Rob. As I said, Hitler needs scapegoats to unite the people behind him, and he's got them. What most people don't recognize, it's not just Jews and Communists he deports, but anyone who opposes him. Priests, nuns, politicians, journalists, Masons.

*From 1937 to 1938, it is estimated the megalomaniac, Russia's Losif Dzhugashvili Vissarionovich, self-named Stalin, Man of Steel, purged 1.5 million Army officers, politicians, and Enemies of the State. An estimated 680,000 were executed in this single purge, the rest sent to the Gulags.

"They're all being sent to the camps. If a Nazi accuses anyone, they're gone."

Robert listened intently and tried to find some answers, a possible excuse for Hitler's actions. This couldn't be explained away. It wasn't the Jewish newspapers who made this up. There were newsreels that showed thousands of people taken off in trucks, pushed into cattle cars, and gone. Nothing, not even a letter was heard from them again.

Donnatta couldn't begin to justify this inhumanity. Robert knew she was wrong in her rationalization. Did she know what the Nazis were doing? Of course. Perhaps she doesn't know everything, but enough. And he had believed her. Had she turned a blind eye to this, or used him? He still wanted to believe that he tried only to find a way to peace. What a stupid belief that was. He had played the blind, peace loving fool and now he was a traitor. Why did he do it? She paid attention to him. The first woman since before the war. He loved her. Now, he'll tell her it's over, he's through. What will she do? What if she said she'd report him as a traitor, a spy? She wouldn't do that, she had no reason, she wouldn't. Or would she? Of course she would. Without question, she'd blackmail him.

"Rob! Didn't you hear me? What's your problem?"

"I'm sorry, Jim. My thoughts were on those poor people being deported."

Chapter 15

"WHAT DID YOU find out, Sean?"

"Well, it took me half the day but I eventually tracked down Ravensmoor. Quite an estate, rich British swine. Probably just sit back and live off their Irish landholdings and don't do a thing and let the people starve."

"All right, Sean, enough of that. Believe what you want. Just tell me what you found."

"I found the other place you mentioned. No one was there, at least no vehicles, and the garage doors were open. Just past the place was a path with only two or three inches of frozen snow that I backed my car into. I waited until ten at night, and it was pitch black. A few vehicles went by, then a car turned into the drive and went into the garage and the doors closed. Lights went on in the house so I left, and went back next morning at six thirty. It's still dark at that time but no lights in the house, and the garage doors open, no car. This guy has a hell of a work day, that's all I can say."

"Are you sure it's the right house?"

"If your directions are correct."

"But you've never seen anyone. How do you know it's the right person?"

Sean laughed. "I can check for the scar after I shoot him."

"Funny, but not worth losing the money if you go there and hit the wrong man."

Sean was moody. It wasn't a good setup for one crucial reason. What if the mark knew someone was after him? "Look Tosca, you said he knows the Nazis are after him because they tried to have him extradited, so it only makes sense for him to think they might try to do just what we plan. If he's on guard, then I can't simply wander up to the house, knock on the door, and when he opens it shoot him. What if he's prepared, or has a guard, I'm the one who'll get shot. If I go to the house and it's locked, I've left footprints in the snow. If I go around the house to look for an open window, I've still left footprints."

Sean started to pace, and sweat. He took a sidelong glance at Tosca and saw she had become angry. He had to please her some way. "Look Tosca, this is not as easy as you think. Maybe I could force him off the road and shoot him when he drives back and forth to work. Then again, that would sure as hell as alert him. What if he carries a gun or someone's with him? My best bet is to catch him somewhere and spray him and anyone else, with a machine pistol. To do that, I'd have to go to Ireland to get one. How about I do go back over there and see if Eoin O'Duffy and a few of his blue shirts would be interested, or even Russell?"

"What's that? O'Duffy? He's laid low and anyhow, do you think I want some of his IRA thugs sneaking around England starting a war? And Sean Russell? I had enough of him when I was over there. He's tied in with the Nazis! If he gets wind of who we want taken out, it will get back to Germany, and my deal will be gone! What in hell is wrong with you? You can't take down one man and get away? For Christ's sake, I'll give you two thousand dollars now, but if we don't get this over with, the Nazis will be out for my neck. I've been paid. You understand?"

"All right, God Damn it! When do you want it done?"

"That's better. Now, Phillip has to go to Gloster Aircraft in Cheltenham on the 16th, so he won't be in the way. If he happens to be in Coventry, take him down too. I'll pay you another thousand. But this Jim Royce is the main target, so it's best done the night of the 16th, to save any mix up."

"I hope Phillip is there, I'll do him for nothing. I'll see he regrets sticking a gun in my face."

"Never mind that! Listen to me, blast you! If you hit this him in the house, go through it for valuables, pull open draws, throw stuff around, grab anything worth something, and ditch it in a river later. If you find any papers anywhere, don't touch them other than throwing them around, don't take them…"

Sean interrupted. "Maybe they could be something the Germans would buy."

"No—don't take any papers. The SIS could be drawn in."

212

"SIS? Who's that?"

"Oh my God, Sean, your ignorance is infinite! The SIS is the Secret Intelligence Service. You might know them as MI5. You get them on our backs and we can't run far enough. Now go earn your money, damn it, and leave me alone."

He skulked off, angered at her and his lot in life. This wasn't his type of caper. He much preferred to slip out of a dark alley in London's Soho and cut a mark's throat.

Sean wanted familiar territory, and his switchblade. To go off somewhere strange with a gun wasn't to his liking. Up there he would be in the cold, in a dark he didn't know. He wanted the money and he wanted a mate to help. But then he'd have to cut a mate in. He decided to go it alone. It didn't help his attitude in the least when he forgot to take the cash she offered.

Sean drove past the home and slowed to make sure the garage was open and there were no lights. He backed the car up the path to the east of Royce's house and sat, nervously fingering his revolver. A half-moon laid a pale glow across the crusted snow as he worked his way through the trees and around the rear of the house, then to the far side of the garage. He had planned to duck down inside the garage behind boxes or some other place, but there was nothing there. Then, as he thought to go into the house from the inner entry, he saw lights flash through the trees along the roadway. He darted behind the open garage door, slipped on the ice, and fell to his knees. Gloves and revolver covered in snow, he frantically tried to brush off the weapon. The car lights faded away. It wasn't his mark. Sean shivered as he removed his gloves to dry the weapon on his scarf and decided to wait, hidden behind the open garage door.

It became bitter cold and idiotically, he wore boots with only light socks. His hands were frozen, his gloves of little use.

Sean pulled his woolen cap down harder; and began to tremble from fear as much as the cold. Maybe he should try the next night, maybe that would be better. No, if he left now, there would be footprints across the snow. As he hid behind the door and wondered what to do, more lights shone along the road. A vehicle turned down the drive.

Tires crunched on the crusted snow, headlights illuminated

the interior of the garage, the vehicle rolled inside. Sean heard the door open and grabbed the garage door handle, swung around, slipped, and lost his balance as he fired his revolver wildly at the dark form.

The bullet tore through the car door before Royce understood what happened. Sean fired again; now trying to stand. The bullet rip through the sleeve of Royce's heavy winter coat as he ran to the front of the car. The grill and fender gave no protection. He dashed for the door to the house and crashed through. Another bullet splintered the frame. Sean grabbed onto the car for support and fired two more shots into the door as it was thrown closed.

Royce heard the bullets rip into the wood and ran through the dark of the house, out of breath. He hid where he could see the doorway and reached for the phone, tapping the receiver. Before the operator could say a word, Royce gasped. "Operator, there's an attacker…in my house. I'm James Royce…I live in the house west of Ravensmoor…get the constable here quickly… tell them to be careful…he has a gun!"

He heard movement in the garage, dropped the phone and slipped into Robert's room. He knew Robert had his revolver there and searched hurriedly through the drawers. He found the Enfield in the desk beside the bed. Now, if there was only one person, it was even.

He moved carefully through the parlor toward the garage door, ready for the attacker.

Sean had headed for the door, but stopped. He heard someone whispering. Was there someone else in the house? There must be, but worse, he was scared. He was out of his element, his knee and hip ached, his fingers frozen. He ran out of the garage and struggled across the front of the house toward the trees and his car.

Royce saw him slogging through the snow past the parlor window, then, seeing no one else, rushed out the front door in time to see the man reach the trees.

The figure was a good distance away. Royce leveled the revolver and pulled the trigger. A click. He was furious. What was wrong? He aimed again, hoping for the best. The gun fired, fragments of tree bark hit the figure. Sean screamed; he hadn't been hit, but he had never been on the receiving end of a bullet and knew nothing other than panic. He threw his weapon away and scrambled through the woods. Royce saw the man was frightened. He fired one more shot in the general direction of his target and edged his way carefully among the trees. His attacker stood up and ran and Royce moved more swiftly, letting his natural balance guide him over the snow crust. He wasn't in any hurry; he knew there was nothing where the man was running except trees—and a path. A path, damn! There'll be a car!

Royce ran as fast as possible across the unsure ground. He heard a vehicle start, the grinding of gears. Making out the shadow of an auto, he aimed and fired off two rounds. One, he guessed hit the door on the passenger's side. The wheels spun, not finding purchase on the ice. Then it lurched forward and scraped a tree as it raced away. Royce held the revolver with two hands and fired one more round that shattered the rear window. Squeezing the trigger again there was only a click. The car skidded onto the road and sped off.

Soaked in sweat, exhausted, Royce headed back through the trees. There were sirens in the distance. By the time he reached the house, two police vehicles, followed by Mary and David in his Bentley, slid into the drive. After confirming to the police who Royce was, David, two officers, Royce and Mary went into the house as other officers searched the yard.

As Royce started to explain, David poured a tall scotch for him, and one for himself. Royce shrugged off the officer's brief glance at his face and explained the events that led up to the present, while two officers followed the tracks into the woods.

Chief Constable Rollins remarked. "You were lucky Mister Royce. Although your assailant does sound inept, it was a bit chancy for you to go after him in the dark."

"I suppose, although I admit I was quite infuriated. Tell me something, is it my imagination or did you take quite a while to get here?"

David spoke up. "Yes, well, the way I understand it, the operator could hardly hear you, although she did make out the words attacker, Royce and Ravensmoor, so naturally, Rollins here, raced to my house. When I heard the sirens at the front door and Rollin's explained what the operator said, I realized it was your place, not ours, so here we all are. Better late than never, as is said now and then."

Rollins then asked. "Tell me, sir, is there anyone you could think of who would be involved in this? Because I feel that, although quite inept, this assault does not seem random."

"Anyone involved in this? Not to my knowledge, Constable. I'm at a loss to know why it happened."

Which wasn't quite true. Royce guessed the Gestapo wanted him, but he didn't want to get into that. David let it pass also. The Constable asked a few more questions about size and weight of the individual. Royce couldn't tell about the assailant or the type of vehicle. He only thought it might have two or three holes in it and the rear window would be shot out. Rollins said he would leave two officers for the night and be back in the morning. Royce responded he would be in the office early, if he were needed.

As the Constable and two officers started to leave the house, headlights of another vehicle shown through the doorway. Robert, arriving back from Cheltenham, had come upon the police cars and David's Bentley.

Two police officers approached him. He froze. Guilt coursed through his system. Good God! I'm a traitor! I've been caught! What about Donnatta?

One of the officers opened the door, surprised at the mask. "May I ask who you are, sir?"

Robert couldn't speak, his hands frozen on the wheel.

The officer spoke once more. "Sir, your name and business here, please."

At that moment, David looked out to see who it was and shouted to the sergeant the person was a friend. Robert was nervous while being helped over the icy drive to the house, yet he managed to ask a question or two about what was going on.

While Royce got him a drink, David and the Captain told the story, including Royce using Robert's gun. Color gradually came back to Robert's face, he calmed. He was safe. Now his thoughts turned to Royce.

Who on earth would try such a thing? It could only be the Gestapo, but how could they track Royce to…

One of the officers returned after searching the grounds. "Found this, sir."

He held out dark blue, pullover cap. "Where was it?"

"Snagged on a branch about where Mister Royce chased the

assailant into the woods, Sir."

"This yours, Mister Royce?" Royce shook his head.

"Then it's safe to assume it belongs to the person you were after. Not much of value, common dock worker's cap, no label. Go search for anything else, Corporal."

During that conversation, Robert had glanced over. He was fortunate everyone was intent on the cap. His eyes went wide, his mouth gaped open. He desperately tried to get hold of his wits. The cap was Sean's, no question. Of course there were thousands like it, but this one was dark blue, frayed, worn, and dirty. Impossible to believe it wasn't the one Sean wore the night Robert stuck the revolver in his face. The night he met Donnatta.

He rose unsteady; he had to get out of the room. "Gentlemen, I'm afraid my long drive, the scotch, and this horrid story of Jim nearly being assassinated have taken a toll on me. It's wonderful you're all right, Jim. But if you'll excuse me, I'll retire. We'll talk tomorrow…yes, tomorrow…"

When saying goodnight to Robert, they were concerned at how much the attempt on Royce's life affected him.

The officers were pensive when they eventually left. "Bit of a strong reaction to the cap, don't you think, Constable?"

"Quite, and did you notice he used the word assassinated? Killed, murdered, shot, I could understand, but his use of that word is strange. Nothing specific, Sergeant, but run a background on him and while I think of it, this Royce fellow as well."

Robert lay back on the bed, fully clothed, and filled his mouth with a wad of sheeting to keep from screaming. He pulled the pillow over his head, forced it into his face, in an attempt to smother himself. Failing that, he went to the drawer to get his revolver. It was gone. Of course, Jim used it to chase that Irish bastard, Sean, through the woods. Robert got up and fell into a chair. Sean may have tried to kill Jim, but Donnatta had to be behind it. Robert remembered telling her the story that Jim had been accused in the death of an SS Major's son. She must have made a deal.

All she had persuaded him about unraveled. She was a false hope he created out of an intriguing face and soft words. How could he have been so dense, so utterly, utterly stupid? Every dream of her with him at Windermere, dashed. Despite it all, deep inside he knew he still wanted her. However, he had to face a fact he must be next on her list. It would have been best if she had killed him, he would have never known this pain, this ache that tore him up inside. Put it in perspective, his mind shrieked. She'll try again, you know she will. She'll try for Jim again.

He pulled the blanket over his head. Slowly a plan formulated. Get them both. He had killed in France, he could do it here. He would get them together, shoot Sean, then face her down. Threaten to kill her, then walk away, show how much he loathed her. Let her do what she wanted, it didn't matter anymore.

His mind never wavered. He had to get them together. The key element was to let them think he was unaware of what happened this night. That he wasn't in Coventry.

Late that night, after a check that the police, Mary and David had left and Royce was gone to bed, Robert slipped out and rang up Donnatta's number.

"Sean?"

"No, it's Robert. Hope I'm not calling too late."

His voice was steady. He could sense she was leery.

"No…Robert, not at all, I…I must have dozed off. Where are you?"

Now to start the lie. "I'm in Portsea. An Admiral here wanted to go over some vital papers so I can give them to David Royce. They reference all the new Chain Home locations for the south coast. I won't be able to leave here until sometime tomorrow."

Donnatta was confused. She hadn't heard from Sean and didn't know what, if anything, had transpired. Had he killed Royce or not? Obviously, Robert didn't know anything. Perhaps Sean hadn't done the job yet.

She fumbled for what to say. It was her expectation that if James Royce was killed, Robert would put two and two together and realize she and Sean had everything to do with it. She had enough money to disappear, Sean would go to Ireland. However, to get rid of Robert before he found out about James Royce would be far more convenient and give her more time to plan. Plus she might be able to peddle the new information Robert had on Chain Home. "I'd like to see you, Robert, do they expect you home, do you check in?"

"No, I'm not due back until tomorrow night, and there's no reason to call in. I just show up when I show up."

"Then why don't we meet, say about…about four o'clock tomorrow. At Craven Street, number thirty-seven in case you've forgotten. I'd love to see you."

"I can do that, and I'd love to see you. I'll call if I'll be late."

"I'll wait for you, Robert, no matter how late."

* * *

"You idiot, Sean! What are you telling me? You didn't kill him?"

"Tosca, listen to me! They lay in wait for me! As I went through the woods I saw people move in the house. I began to backtrack and that's when they started after me! There were at least two of them; I was in crossfire…"

"Shut up, Sean! I don't believe you! You cut and ran! I should shoot you right now!"

"I'm not lying! Come and look at my car, it's got a bullet hole in the door and the rear window's shot out! I should be mad at you! You set me up!"

"Don't be stupid! No one set you up. So just shut up!"

Donnatta stopped. Maybe Sean told the truth. She had to think. If there really were bullet holes in his car, it was possible he was right. But how, *how* did this Royce know? Whatever, she was in serious trouble. SS money was in her Swiss bank for a job that hadn't been done. She could return it, but didn't give that a thought. It was her money and she planned to keep it. Whatever happened, she couldn't stay in England. There would be a war, and after seeing the destruction Hitler's Condor Legion aircraft had done to Spanish cities, she wasn't about to wait around for it to happen to London. Her basic plan was to fly to Portugal, take a steamer to Cuba, fly to Mexico, then into the United States. Travel was still lax. Maybe now was the time to go. Money wasn't a problem; it was those two loose ends, Sean and Robert.

Possibly her lover would go with her, but first things first.

"Sean, I'll work out a plan. Go home and I'll call you. I'll get you your money, I guess you tried."

An hour later, her plan was worked out. She called Sean and told him to meet her in front of thirty-seven Craven Street at two

219

o'clock the next day and to be sure to bring his tools. He assured her it was unnecessary to remind him.

Her plan was elegant in simplicity. Sean would knife Robert as he came in, she would back Sean up if something went wrong. Once Robert was dead, she would shoot Sean. With only one person left alive who knew she was in England and who would never turn her in, she could leave when she chose.

The morning after his night call to Donnatta, Robert sat with Royce. "So, are you over the shock of the attack, Jim?"

"I think so, I slept all right. I just wonder if someone from the Gestapo was after me over that Major's son. If it was I'd be surprised, the clod was such a buffoon."

"Did you tell the police the Gestapo might be after you?"

"No, if I did, every damn intelligence agency would come down on me and interfere with my work. David feels the same way, so we'll let it go at that, at least for now."

"Taking a chance aren't you?"

"I don't think so. If it was the Nazis, they know I'm alerted now, and they'll most likely think the police protect me. Still, I do admit I'll get my own weapon, especially after yours misfired."

"My Enfield did what?"

"It misfired the first time I tried to fire it."

Robert gave a wry, embarrassed smile. "Jim, that wasn't a misfire. I keep the first chamber empty. When I was in the AEF, someone dropped their revolver; it discharged and tore open another fellow's leg. Ever since then, I've kept the first chamber empty to prevent that."

"I'll be damned. I might keep that in mind."

"Speaking of my Enfield, where is it?"

"Sorry, Rob, I forgot. Top drawer of my desk. You can get it. I'm off to work or they'll fire me." Royce laughed. "These days, shot at by an assassin isn't a good enough excuse for being late. What are you up to?"

"After the busy week I've had, I think I'll run up to Windermere and check things out. I'll be back by tonight."

"Fine, I'll probably see you then. Why don't you take the Alvis? Give you a break from that rusty can you've been driving. I'll call for a lift. Oh, and you can throw a small piece of tape over the bullet hole in the door."

"You have an appalling sense of humor, Jim."

After Royce left, Robert retrieved the revolver. He reloaded it with six soft nose shells, no empty chamber this time. He glanced at his watch. Plenty of time to drive to London and reach the flat well before Donnatta expected him. As he drove south, Robert knew what he would do, but his plan depended on Sean being with Donnatta. It was a good guess he would be. Donnatta would not miss the chance to get rid of him. If Sean weren't there, Robert felt he could quickly slip away, and give some sort of excuse later.

At one o'clock in the afternoon, he drove along Craven Street, and counted the front doors of the row houses to number thirty-seven. He parked just off Trafalgar, entered the alley behind Craven Street, walked past the rubbish barrels, garages and a whiny cur until he reached the fifth door. The rear to number thirty-seven. Now he had to have luck with him. He figured that as Donnatta did not live here, she would not arrive three hours early for their four o'clock meeting. There was no bell, he knocked. No answer. He knocked again, louder, and waited. Nothing. He tried the door, locked as expected. He looked about, saw no one in sight, and broke the door glass with the butt of his revolver. He reached through, unlocked the latch, and pushed his way in. A mop and bucket blocked the door. That negated any worry that someone may come in the rear. Holding the revolver ready, he moved throughout the flat, checking each room. Satisfied he was alone, he went to the parlor on the street side. He sat in a chair away from the window where he could view the street and front walk through the curtains. Now he needed that last important piece of luck—Sean to be with her.

A quarter to three. He saw Sean park an old BSA motorcycle across the street, then swagger to the front of the flat, looking about. Robert tensed, his plan would work, Sean was here. Now, wait for Donnatta.

She arrived at three o'clock. As they stood on the street, Donnatta did all the talking. Sean smiled. They started up the walk. Robert quickly went down the corridor to the kitchen and stood behind the pantry door. The front door scraped open and the two of them spoke as they entered. Robert couldn't catch the words.

They came into the kitchen. "...telling you, Tosca, don't worry about a thing this time. I'll stick the cocky bastard like a Christmas goose, quick and permanent."

"After the way you messed up in Coventry, you'd better."

Robert didn't need to hear more. He pushed the door open and stepped into the room. Sean and Donnatta turned, their surprise turning to terror. Robert raised the revolver and fired point blank at Sean's chest. The soft-nosed bullet struck him square, hit his ribs and, as designed, shattered into pieces, shredding his lungs. Sean staggered back and then slowly sagged to his knees, his body's nervous system in shock. He had yet to feel the pain and groped at a pocket, looking more angry than hurt. Robert turned sharply to Donnatta, pointing the gun at her.

"Don't open that purse!"

She shrank back, traumatized, unable to speak. Robert swung back to Sean as he fumbled trying to snap open his switchblade. Another bullet tore into his chest. He tumbled over backward.

Robert turned to Donnatta. He stared, confounded in his emotions. He had thought to threaten her, yet now in her frightened little girl fear, he couldn't.

Donnatta saw it in his eyes and hid a grin. She kept her appearance of fright while her mind rushed through various plots for escape. What had happened? What had he known that incensed him enough to kill Sean, and maybe her? She decided to prolong appearing weak, terrified.

"Give me your purse, Donnatta."

She meekly handed it to him. He opened it, removed a small caliber Beretta semiautomatic, and tossed it on the table.

Trembling, she found her voice. "Why? Why have you done this, Robert? Sean just happened to see me on the street, and I asked him to come in for a moment. Why did you kill him?"

"Because you told him to kill my friend, Jim Royce."

"How could you know...?" She stopped, it was evident.

"Don't bother to deny you knew anything about it, Donnatta, only you knew about Royce and that Nazi Major's kid."

There was no way out, "I'm sorry, Robert, so sorry."

"Not half as much as I am."

"Please don't shoot me. I was wrong. I admit it. I was frightened what you would do to me if you found out I sent Sean to kill your friend...I..."

"You played me for the fool the whole time. If I hadn't known what had happened, that would have been me lying there instead of that scum."

She tried to protest, he stopped her. "Donnatta, leave."

My God! She thought, she had a chance, she was going to live. The stupid fool! She took her purse, desperately trying not to look hurried. She turned, smiled at him.

"Just leave, Donnatta."

She started down the corridor. Tears welled up in his eyes. "Stop!"

She stood, frightened, her back to him.

He loved her. A dreadful love. Yet she would never change. If he asked her to go away with him, she would, then plot to kill him. There was even worse. She would kill him, or Mary, or the children, or some other pathetic person just to get at Jim.

Tears coursed down his cheeks. He raised the .38 caliber revolver, aimed it at the nape of her neck, and squeezed the trigger.

* * *

A month later a neighbor reported the BSA motorcycle still parked across the street, and that she had seen the driver and woman go into the flat next door. The same person also reported that a little while later another man, in an overcoat, went out the rear door of that same flat. She never saw the man or the woman come out, the woman said, and maybe now, she recalled hearing two or three popping sounds. Could the police come over and check? Two days later a policeman rang the bell of the flat in question and, receiving no answer, peered through the front door glass. He could see a large lump of what appeared to look like clothes, crumpled by a steam radiator. He tried the knob. The door opened. The odor was unmistakable.

The police were perplexed. Sometime around a month ago, someone shot these two people. The man had received two mortal wounds to the chest from near point blank range, an unopened switchblade knife in his hand. There was a small .22 caliber Berretta automatic on the table, although it was not the weapon that killed the man or woman. Prints on the gun showed no fingerprint match in England. There were no other prints; the killer must have worn gloves. The woman, shot in the back of the neck, probably tried to escape, they thought. She was identified from a false Spanish Passport as Donnatta Rivera, Spanish citizen. The Spanish Civil War was still raging and no one knew anything over there, so that became a dead end. The motorcycle had an Irish plate and the man's license stated his name was Sean Rourke. The police contacted the English authorities in Belfast, Ireland, for information. The man, it turned out, was also known as Sean O'Leary and Sean Wilson. He had a record of petty theft, muggings, armed robbery and was a known Irish Republican Army sympathizer sought by the British Police.

As it stood now, all the Police had were a dead Spanish woman, and dead IRA thug. Add to them, a mysterious third party who, it was pretty much assured, was the murderer. Police conjectures of all sorts included an arms deal between the Irish and the Spanish Republican forces gone bad, or two lovers caught by an irate husband. Finally, with no third party fingerprints, all the police could do was inform the Belfast Constabulary there was one less IRA hooligan to worry about and dropped the case in the unsolved file. Due to Sean's record with the IRA, the police reported the information to MI5. Although one of their agents hid his emotions, he was utterly distraught.

Chapter 16

November, 1938
IN THE WORLD at this time, Arab and Jewish negotiators met in London to once and for all, settle the Palestine problem between the two antagonists.

There was war in the Far East and it continued as Japan expanded its territory in China. The Japanese, called their murderous aggression "...a new order based on international justice throughout East Asia"

In response to the United States' negative cables over their actions, Japan, in few words, told Washington to mind their own business. This was to be the Japanese sphere of influence.

14 November. The United States, due to the Nazi's pogrom against the Jews, recalled its ambassador from Berlin to '...acquire firsthand information on the event...' Following the ambassador's return to the States, Germany recalled their ambassador from Washington.

Poland and Russia signed a non-aggression pact, which at the time was farcical, even by the low standards of diplomacy.

30 November. Benito Mussolini, El Duce of Italy, demanded France cede its colonies of Tunisia, Nice, Corsica and French Somaliland to Italy.

6 December 1938. France and Germany signed a 'Good Neighbor' pact for '...the preservation of the general peace...'

Delusion, the grand dance of delusion.

* * *

9 December 1938
Margaret Elliot, wife of Roger Elliot, mother of Daphne and Robert, died.

Robert had appeared nervous and despondent for the past

three weeks and Royce, ignorant of the events that occurred in a London flat, easily put Robert's emotions down to the failing health, and then death, of his mother.

In Royce's conversations with Daphne, it was clear she was deeply saddened, yet relieved. Her mother was gone from the pain she suffered despite the increased drugs. Daphne missed Royce and wanted to come home to him. There was, however, another problem. Her father's health had worsened after his wife's death, and Daphne insisted Robert return to the States for their mother's funeral. Robert, she said, was to make his peace with their father, and be ready to help in his decision to sell or liquidate the company.

Surprisingly to all, Robert seemed to be readily agreeable. Recent memories of the murder of Sean and Donnatta haunted him and he felt it best to leave England for a while. When he requested an absence from D W Royce to travel to the States, David agreed and had a resolution at hand. Robert could join a trip planned to depart in five days. The flight would include David, two multiengine rated RAF pilots, and four agents of the British Purchasing Commission, (BPC). The first leg would be by RAF aircraft to the Azores, the southern route to the United States. Typically, scheduled flights to the States would be by Pan American Clipper flying boat from Southampton, England, or Foynes, Ireland, to Botwood, Newfoundland. But for the present, the cold weather and ice in the bays and rivers of both countries had compelled Pan Am and the BPC agents to decide on the southern route via the Azores. From there, the Clipper was to fly to Bermuda and on to Norfolk, Virginia. One purpose of the trip was to evaluate the feasibility of BPC to purchase a Pan American, Boeing, B-314 type, four-engine Clipper seaplane as the Sikorsky S-40 and British Imperial flying boats needed midair refueling. The BPC agents would conference with Pan Am Chief Juan Trippe, on purchasing a Boeing seaplane, while David went on to Washington, DC, for private studies with American power brokers and US military planners.

For the trip, Robert would be David's aide and no one would question him. From Washington, Robert could travel by train or fly to Boston. Royce wanted to go on the trip as well, but David said he needed a person in overall charge to make decisions while he was away, and Royce begrudgingly came to terms with it. David did forget, intentionally or otherwise, to mention the fact he had acquired security services to unobtrusively follow James around.

When advised of the trip, Daphne was delighted. If not Royce, she needed someone with her and Robert was by far the best choice. Robert would be valuable as her Father's son, as well as his university background in finance.

Royce and Mary drove David and Robert to RAF Badinton in Royce's new Bentley. Jock and Bloody waited on the tarmac beside a twin-engine Halifax bomber. They were pleased when they saw Royce walk over to them.

"You two still wrecking his Majesty's aircraft?"

"Doing our best, Mister Royce."

"I see you've got a different aircraft, am I to assume you destroyed the Whitly?"

"Bang on sir, exactly."

You can't be serious."

"Yes sir." Bloody whispered. "We told the Base Commander about the fractured engine mount you found. But instead of the repair here, he said that as we flew all the way from Zurich with her, we could damn well make it over to RAF Manston and repair her there. Well, we didn't like that, but orders is orders. So we taxi out, power up *both* motors and half way down the flaming runway, off comes that bleeding engine, it tears off the port landing gear, down goes that side, off comes the wing, the wing root rips into the fuselage and punctures one of the petrol tanks. We shut down all power of course, but sparks is flying every flaming where, they are. Damn clear what's to happen next, so even before the craft stops me and Jock are out our seats, down the rear, out the hatch and running like flaming burned arse hounds up the runway."

Jock took over. "All the while Bloody's shouting Gore Blimey, Gore Blimey. Never once said bloody, he didn't."

"So what happened?"

"Just what you'd expect, Mister Royce. The Whitly goes up in a blooming fireball, it did. People scuttling everywhere, they was. Fire trucks trying to put out the petrol with water 'cause they had nothing else. A bleeding Chinese fire drill, it was!"

"And Colin never said 'Bloody' once, you say."

"I guess I didn't." Colin jumped in. "All I yelled was Gore Blimey, which, if you knows our slang, Sir, means God blind me, so when Jock told me what I said, I damn well apologized on the quick to God."

Royce smiled at the two of them. Happy go lucky. What happened, happened. Or as Colin would have put it in the past, what bloody happens, bloody happens.

Goodbyes were exchanged all around under the incessant bark of the Halifax's twin Merlins. The party got on board, the chocks removed, and the engine's drone increased as the aircraft turned and lumbered down to the end of the runway.

Royce and Mary walked into Operations to get away from the cold wind and watched through a window as the bomber roared past them, struggled skyward and disappeared.

"You're quiet, James."

"I just though how I would like to have gone with them. And then my thoughts reversed, to how I came back here on an aircraft similar to that from Zurich. Then I thought of Daphne and me over there. And you know how one thought leads to another, the escape from Austria, and that brought me to Ernst Becker. God, I wish him the best."

* * *

The train pulled into Boston's South Station in a coal dust fouled billowing cloud of steam. Robert, alone all the way from New York's Penn Station, had time to think over the past month. He had killed two people. One of them deserved to have his life ended. The other, someone he loved. He still ached when he thought of her, and probably would forever. What happened was for the best, she could never have been trusted. If he had let her go, she would have killed him and Royce, especially Royce, of that he was sure, and if there were others present, she would have killed them as well. Perversely, his mind led him to the fact that now to the best of his knowledge, there was no one left who knew he had given away state secrets. He had, already, mentally avoided the words spy, or traitor. That would demean him. After all, the countries weren't at war, and really, after deliberation, was the information he divulged really that valuable? Donnatta had said the Germans knew about British agents in their military and, for that matter, the Chain Home RF system wasn't news to them either.

When one came right down to it, what harm had he done? It wasn't unreasonable to say his motives were based on honor. He had done it in the name of peace, not because he loved her. Eventually he concluded, he should be practical, and not concern himself about the past. File it away. Forget it. Get on with his life.

His mind shifted to his family. His mother was gone. Daphne had postponed the funeral service until he arrived. He was glad she had done so, it gave him a chance to say farewell to his mother. Now he would see his Father for the first time in twenty years. How would each react? He couldn't blame Father for not being able to look at him without tears. He had thrown his future away; his Father had every right to be angry. But if that was the way he reacted, Robert could bear it he felt; after all, his Father had always supported them all, no matter what. As Robert stepped off the train, he saw Daphne down the platform. His Father wasn't with her. He didn't want to see his son. Accept it, Robert thought.

She met him at the gate with the news—their Father died the previous day.

The single wake and funeral for their parents were not private affairs. Roger Elliot's managers, associates and dozens of east coast friends and associates, made the death one of the winter events for those in the know. People remembered little of his wife and less of the children; nevertheless they overwhelmed Daphne and Robert with kindness and interest in their lives in England. Confidants of their Father assured Robert that once he had time to review the corporation, they would assist in any way they could with concern to legalities or recommend attorneys.

The following week involved the wills. It was no surprise their parents left all belongings, homes, and in Roger Elliot's separate will the business to the children. Even in these lean years of the Great Depression, a quick internal audit estimated the brokerage corporation's worth around fifteen million dollars.

To get away and be by themselves, Daphne and Robert

toured west along Massachusetts's Mohawk Trail. They spoke of their parents and marveled at the damage the past September's hurricane had caused. Yet now, they were more interested in their futures. For Daphne, there was no question of what to do. Her home was England, and with Royce. Robert was unexpectedly ambiguous. Could he, he began to question, with help from his Father's managers, continue the corporation? He felt he wanted to try. It could be rebirth for him.

When they returned to Boston, Robert went to the State Street office of R C Elliot, and sat behind his father's desk, overcome with melancholia. He had made mistakes in his life, which could never be rectified. Twenty years gone, hiding in England from the reality of what he had caused. Now, perhaps not too late, he could live up to his Father's hopes for him. Half a face or not, he vowed to succeed. He brought himself to believe this could be his life. Yet two thoughts ached within him. He wished Donnatta were here to grow old with him and he prayed he would never to run into the parents of the two boys he took to war...and their deaths, so long ago.

Robert had an epiphany; he was in very near the same position as David Royce. He was now master of a successful corporation. David had driven his company forward and bet everything on the prospect of war. Well, why not do the same? Except don't gamble all, that would be the difference. It isn't as if he would be the cause of a war. Still, if there's to be war no matter what, why not make money out of it? In the last war, Wall Street bankers made fortunes on their loans to England, with interest of course, betting she would win. English banks made money on the US stock market and loaned money, with interest of course, to Russia and France. At first, American industry would sell war products to whoever had cash. They didn't worry or have ethics about who was right or wrong. They had their personal profit and stockholders to answer to.

Robert vindicated his thoughts, as most people do, by the knowledge other companies would step in and make money if he didn't. He comprehended it now. If Donnatta hadn't fogged his mind, he would have seen it far earlier. *If* the United States entered the war, it would enter it on the side of England, so why not supply them the needed materials? It would be the right thing to do. Even now, the country seemed to be ramping up. Despite the continuing depression, Elliot Corporation was awash in money. Now would be the time to move his Father's investments into industry, to military production. He would model it after David's actions. Buy up or invest in small or medium sized, military oriented companies, put in the best managers and drive the company forward.

He needed, however, the right contacts in government and military. David knew those people in the States. Robert would work out royalties with D W Royce Industries. It was a shame he couldn't have Jim Royce with him, but Royce would feel loyalty to his country and company. Robert would find other people, the best people, and pay them top salaries just as David. Robert dreamed. He could become a captain of American industry.

When Robert presented his plans to his sister, she was distressed at the absolute change. He completely justified his decision, at least to himself. Daphne was afraid for him, the sudden unmitigated revising of his life. She wanted nothing to do with his decision, although she did not say a word or try to change his mind. To her, it now became obvious, Robert was his father's son. He had only buried himself at Windermere because of his face and his shame to return home. Father's death and Robert's return to America had awakened the internal drive. The genes were there. Robert was an American, always had been. As she thought more on his decision, she became pleased for him. Nevertheless, all she wanted was to go home, and home to her was England. She wanted to leave.

Robert prevailed on her to stay for a few more days while he spoke to the company managers and attorneys. They agreed wholeheartedly with his plans and whereas the company had previously been wholly owned by Roger Elliot, Robert's new share option plan was initiated and snapped up by insiders and friends within a few hours. This allowed Robert to make an offer to Daphne, which she accepted without discussion. Although there were numerous items, the main points being she would receive the Windermere cottage from Robert. One million, five-hundred thousand dollars, converted to English pounds would be deposited in her Barkley's London bank within ten working days. On the first of each year, to commence on 1

January 1940, with a final payment on 1 January 1943, she would receive payments of one million dollars each year. She would retain a seven percent interest in all holdings, now and future, of R Elliot & Partners, Incorporated.

She was now a rich woman, a rich woman ready to go home. Robert resigned his position with D W Royce when he contacted David in Washington on December 16th.

David's business was completed and he wanted to be home before Christmas. He told Daphne if she could get down to Norfolk, Virginia, by the morning of the 18th, she could hitch a ride back on the Clipper to Bermuda and the Azores, then RAF to Badinton.

Daphne agreed to get there. Robert and David continued to have a seemingly endless conversation related to Robert's ideas of the future structure and direction of his company. David agreed with Robert's first moves, added a few suggestions, and said he would discuss other plans at a later date. David also mentioned that to begin, he would get in touch with his contacts at the War Department in Washington for Robert to make appointments. David then suggested he come back to the States in January or February of the New Year, with an objective draft on consolidation, or at least an operational agreement between the two companies.

Daphne was with mixed feelings. Sadness, saying farewell one last time at her parents grave and then cheerio to Robert. Her other feeling was anticipation, thoughts of Royce. She flew Eastern Airlines down the east coast from Boston to Norfolk, and then took a taxi to meet David at the Pan Am seaplane terminal. David was pleased to see her, yet oddly detached. After his condolences over the loss of her parents, he withdrew into his own thoughts and scribble in his note pad until time to board and continued once aboard.

Whether a person had flown on other aircraft or not, the size of the Pan Am Clipper was impressive. Daphne's trips to and from England were always by steamer, and her only flight was in a twelve passenger Eastern Airlines plane from Boston. She was astonished when she entered the Clipper. The sheer dimensions of the seaplane's exterior was impressive and inside, she was taken by the furnishings and comfort afforded the passengers. David showed her around. Thick carpeting, soft couches and tables, and sleeping quarters for forty passengers, and stewardesses, stewards and liquor bars, dining room and lounge areas. All this was contained within the two levels of the craft.

With the doors secured, the four engines were run up one after the other for testing then backed down. She was surprised there were so few passengers.

"Why aren't there more people, David?"

"Pan Am mainly flies long range flights in the Pacific or down into South America. They don't begin fixed schedules for the Atlantic until next year."

"So, what is this flight?

"These European trips are to accommodate high priority people, government agents, and military staff officers from both America and Britain. This aircraft will carry seventy-four, plus crew. Today it only has fifteen, plus crew."

"So, as you're not an officer or agent, I'm to assume you're a high priority person?"

David laughed. "Why of course. Why would you doubt?"

"Then what am I? How do I rate?"

"I told them you were my mistress."

Daphne flinched, and then softly hissed. "I see."

"Look Daphne, you want to get back home. That was the best thing I could think of. Besides, it helps my image. Look around you, what are all these people thinking? Handsome, wealthy, English industrialist, Member of the House of Lords, flying off with a fabulously beautiful, mysterious woman to some secret rendezvous. Think of it. Books are written about this sort of thing. You should appreciate it and act the part."

"David you're a cad."

He laughed now. "A cad? How can you say such a thing?"

She leaned over and whispered in his ear. "I used that word because I didn't want to ruin your precious image in case people heard me call you a son of a bitch."

He stopped smiling. It was quite obvious he'd never been called a son of a bitch before. The fun he'd had at Daphne's discomfort had backfired.

"Look, Daphne, I was just pulling your leg. I told Juan Trippe you were my brother's fiancée and you wanted to return to England after the loss of your parents."

"Then I apologize David, there's a possibility, slim though it may be, that you're not a son of a bitch."

The remark broke the rising friction. As both stared into their scotch glasses, they appeared to contemplate the slight vibration of their ice cubes as the massive seaplane, towed away from the dock, began its move into open water before turning into the wind.

Daphne glanced out the window. "It's hard to believe this thing can fly."

"Sometimes they don't. One disappeared last year in the Pacific, and another this year. I don't believe anyone knows what happened."

"Oh, so nice of you to tell me that, David. What am I supposed to do now? Grab your big, strong arms and ask you to hold me tight?"

"That would be very nice. However, I'd be afraid you'd scream out that I'm a lecherous bounder or some such thing."

"Aha, it's good to know you're on edge too."

"Daphne, actually I'm sorry I mentioned the losses. I only now appreciate this must be your first flight in one of these."

"Yes. And the memory of bouncing all around on the flight to get down here's still with me."

David lit a cigarette for her and kept up talk to ease her fears. "This seaplane is totally different. An American company, Boeing, builds it. They've made hundreds of other types of heavy aircraft before this. There are four Wright, double cyclone engines that develop fifteen hundred horsepower each. It's the largest...."

He chattered on at length, the size, tonnage and so forth, none of which particularly interested her. Still, it kept her distracted and she welcomed it. The enormous seaplane rocked gently while the Captain again ran each engine up and down in turn. Then, the four throttles were eased forward in unison. The whale-shaped fuselage wallowed forward as the Clipper gained momentum across the choppy water, while the roar of the motors limited speech. Their power released the water's grip, the seaplane became airborne, and the city by the sea receded into the mist. The throttles eased back as the seaplane gained altitude, eventually to reach cruising speed.

They finished lunch in the dining salon, complementing the waiter on the quality of the meal and were informed all Pan Am Clipper meals came from one or another of four-star hotels in each port's region. The aircraft's wonders continued for Daphne when their next stop was the lounge to sit at the bar for a drink. Daphne broached another subject that bothered her. "David, you mentioned earlier I was Jim's fiancée. That's not true, you know that, correct?"

"I know it was simply to help get you aboard. Why, does that bother you? Aren't both of you sort of heading that way?"

She took a draw on her cigarette, watching the smoke drift into to a filtering vent. "I don't think of anything such as that right now. Look David, I know most people who fall in love think of marriage and children. I don't follow that mold. I'm not a 'yes dear' kind of woman. Fall in love, get married, have children, and fade into the background like a good, well-behaved wife. That's not me. When I was in the States, I didn't look up any of my sorority sisters because I was afraid that happened to them. It's what they looked and hoped for in college. They fell into the old trap. Get a degree just to show they're smart, and then marry a successful man. Why? Because they're told proper women do that. Then after that, what? They're stifled. For the next twenty years, they speak baby talk and take care of children, look pretty for their husbands and laugh at his boss's lame jokes. And their brains atrophy. I don't buy into that. People say normal women are married at my age. Well, I don't care if I'm abnormal or subnormal. I won't vow to do anything, unless I'm damn good and sure it's what I want."

Daphne took a breath, she was wound up, and David, who had never heard a woman voice such utterly outlandish views, was left speechless.

They sat quietly. She watched the generals and colonels, attachés and bankers, stewardesses' and chefs.

"This is the life you love, isn't it, David?"

"I do, and if you only knew it, you would be fabulous in it."

"Being a woman, even if I were interested, my only part of it would be like you said, as a mistress, and that's not my cup of tea, to be polite about it."

"That's the man's world we live in, Daphne."

"And you don't mind that, do you?"

"Not in the least, why should I?"

"You see, that's what I'm driving at. I can speak and write in six languages, don't know how many idioms, and can converse in three other. Yet, other than as a mistress, the only way a woman with my knowledge could be here would be as an interpreter—for men who don't have my ability."

"Is that what you want?"

"David, will you listen to me? Are you so *dense*? I'm saying women are second-class citizens. Don't deny it. And no, I don't want this world. But I feel bad for the women who do."

The expression on David's face was only bemusement.

"Daphne, I don't follow you. It's not normal for a woman to feel the way you do. A woman's position is in the home. It's natural. To run the household, take care of the children and help her husband. In return, he gives her the children she wants, and supports her comfortably. That's her life and it's important. If she wants to read, or sew or help the Red Cross, perhaps get together with other wives to chat, fine. For God's sake, isn't that enough, isn't that sufficient?"

"Christ, David, you're a Neanderthal, right out of the stone age. Think yourself lucky you're good looking, or you'd still be single despite your money."

"And with your mindset, Daphne, I now know why you're with James. No other man could put up with your attitude."

She had to laugh at the comment. "I admit you may have a point there, David."

He sat back. "One other point. I wouldn't want any women, including Mary, I might add, talking privately with you, you might make them seditious."

"See, David, that's your problem. You look like a man, talk like a man, and act like most men. And, you're right, that's one of the reasons I like Jim, he doesn't follow that mold. I have the freedom I want, when I want. Jim does too. I'll give you an example. Right now, I can't wait to see him, be with him. Nevertheless, I know after a few days, I'm going to go up to Windermere, be by myself and hike and think of my Mother, Father, and Robert. I'll sit, have a few drinks and a few smokes, and wind down for whatever time it takes to be myself. Otherwise I'd be smothered. And don't you for one minute question if I'll be alone. Then I'm back down to Coventry to see Jim again, and he'll understand, because like I said, he's the same as I am."

"James doesn't have time for that kind of nonsense. He'll change, believe me. There won't be time for this 'wind down'. There's too much that must be done at the plant."

"Right, and because he has the company and country at heart, I'll bet you've got him working his arse off."

He was surprised at her choice of words. "Yes I do. And it's going to be that way for the foreseeable future."

"That's where you have me stymied, David. I can't ask him to stop. You've thrown guilt on him because he was away so long. Now he feels he has to make it up to his country, but remember, make it up for the *country*, not you."

She snuffed out her cigarette and knew David was right. Jim wasn't the person she knew, not the person she met and fell in love with. If it goes on endlessly, can she adjust? Stick by him, yes—but she wasn't going to stick to his side. No, she was not going to sit by the fire and wait until he could find time to have a few words with her. She'd find other outlets. Was she selfish? She didn't know. She's in a financial position to do as she wished. First, continue Robert's work at the Lord Derby Hospital when she went up to Windermere, that's where she'd start. Get more entertainment for them. That sort of thing wouldn't enter David's mind. His life is to make money because the power it inevitably collects. That's what he's about. Wish you the best, jocko, she thought, but it's not my goal. Her goal will be decided as she and Jim work it out.

David thought about Daphne. He had never known any woman like her. In love, possibly, but refuses to lose sight of who she is. She was fascinating, there was no other word.

"You seem pensive, Daphne, something I said?"

She smiled amiably. "If it was, I'd never let on. And don't look at me like I'm from another planet. I can't believe you're mystified at what I've said, and makes me uneasy."

David took her hand, kissing it. "The steward will show you to your sleeping quarters and your overnight kit. Goodnight."

The Clipper droned east, over the dark Atlantic, David sat on his bed and opened his diary.

December 19, 1938: Boeing Clipper over Atlantic.

Daphne Elliot, James 'friend' is here-returning from States. Mother, father died, her brother assuming control of father's company. Should become very favorable to D W Royce. Daphne is unfathomable to me. Never met someone like her.

One of the most handsome women I've ever seen, and of all things, she's with James. Beggars the imagination. I suppose she's transferring her love for her brother, and pity for his face, to James. She's blithe, unconcerned about our standards or conventions. I don't believe I've ever met a woman who did not want to get married and have children. Maybe it's just James. Would bet she'd be different if it was me. I know she finds me fascinating-can see it in those green eyes. We'll find what happens when she learns how boring I can make James. She called me a son of a bitch-I don't seem mind in the slightest-Amazing!

The trip was excellent. When my contracts finalize, my company will double in size once again. I'm on the crest of the wave.

He stopped, read the number of comments he had written about her. Yet there was only one sentence on the culmination of the largest contracts he could have ever hoped to close.

"My word," he smiled, "I've a schoolboy crush on her."

* * *

The flight from the States to Bermuda and the Azores by PAN AM and then Halifax bomber to RAF Badinton, outside Coventry, took twenty-six hours. Despite their catnaps across the Atlantic, then north to England by the far less quiet Halifax, Daphne and David were worn out. On a bitter cold night they landed to find Mary and Royce on the taxi strip. Quick hugs, kisses before they hustled into the warmth of the Bentley.

At Ravensmoor, the maid and Alfred served petite sandwiches and drinks. The travelers found it hard to eat, drink, and keep from falling asleep. After half an hour, Royce pitied Daphne's exhaustion. He went out and started his Bentley to warm the interior, then went back inside for a few minutes. He then picked her up bodily, and left for Blackbird Cottage, now so named. She fell asleep again on the one mile trip. He lifted her out of the vehicle, managed to unlock the door, carried her to the bedroom, and placed her on the bed. He couldn't help a smile as he pulled the covers over her.

At three in the morning, she woke him. Just to say hello, at least so she said.

During breakfast, Daphne told Royce the news from the US. He had taken the early part of the day off and quietly listened. She started with the steamer voyage to Bermuda and New York, then by train on to Boston with her mother. Daphne spoke of the hospital, the clinic and the lovely view over Salem Harbor as her mother quietly died.

It was the unexpected death of her father, which brought her to even greater despair. Robert's arrival was her salvation. She spoke of the sea change in Robert's personality, his taking charge, as their father had always dreamed. Finally, Daphne laid out Robert's redirection of the company into manufacturing the products of war. The information was truly puzzling to Royce, knowing Robert's aversion to military conflict. Stranger things had happened, he felt, so kept his thoughts to himself. Daphne continued on about her financial agreement, then on to her seemingly endless flights to Coventry via, the Pan Am Clipper and RAF Halifax bomber.

"Bye the bye, Jim. Jock and Colin were the pilots on the Halifax, and said to be very sure and say hello to you. Collin thinks you're a 'flaming, bleeding genius'."

"That makes me laugh. I can't understand how the devil they stay alive. They take the damndest chances yet walk away without a scratch. David thinks they're so lucky, he insists they fly him. Good luck charms he told me."

"I wouldn't think David thinks the first thing about luck, Jim, Everything he does is so blasted calculating. Anyway, on the RAF plane back to Coventry we couldn't sleep, so he spun tales of his accomplishments in Washington. It was a litany of success, and it wasn't as if he bragged or made it up to impress me, although he was full of himself, as usual."

"So, tell me, what did he accomplish?"

"Well, apparently a company called Lockheed makes a Hudson bomber that England has purchased. They're shipped crated to England and he has a cost plus contract for all assembly as well as all maintenance. He has all sorts of orders for bearings, which, I will give him his due, he gave you credit for developing. I'd guess he has contracts from over five different companies and he also said something about the manufacture of various aircraft components under contract. And remember, Jim, this is all over and above everything you've told me. I'm sure he'll tell you all about it. All right, I'm talked out, except for my admiration of your Christmas tree. You cut this down yourself?"

"Certainly. Went out into the storm, I did. It was cold, bitter cold, but I hacked it down and dragged it back all by myself. Needless to say it fought me every bit of the way."

"My word, mighty woodsman. Dragged all three feet of it back alone, did you? You decorate it too?"

"Not all of it, there the children helped. We might have overdone it."

"Just a touch. One can hardly see the tree. But thanks, it's a nice thought and I can use some nice thoughts right now. So, tell me what you've been up to around here."

"Boring compared to you. I charged into reorganize all the departments from Design, Engineering, and Prototype right through to Production. Thank goodness I had Clive behind me or I'd have botched this whole management thing. Now we've divided our efforts within our spheres of knowledge. I keep up my design responsibilities, along with evaluation of the ability and focus of the engineers. Clive then slots them into the system where they'll do the most good. It's more complicated than that, but you can see the minimalism of the principle. A few grumbles from some of the older engineers who'd resist change to any manufacturing processes no matter what. That's to be expected, and Clive has the personality to present the necessity of change for the company to survive…I see your eyes begin to glaze over, Daphne."

"Sorry Jim. Don't mean to be rude. I'm still tired and what

you've said is going straight over my head. What else have you been up to that are a little less...ah...boring?"

"I warned you my activities were a bore. Maybe this will be of interest. I take time off for an hour at noon three days a week and steal Beth and Victor away from their tutors to go for a walk. Of course, the Spaniels and even the old Scotty join in and its fun telling the children stories of my fantastic life in the mountains. You understand I color it up a bit and leave out other parts, but they seem to love it, they call it their story walk. It's damn cold but they would probably do anything to get away from the tutor."

"Probably, my foot. It's more than simply that, Jim. They like you so much. It does sounds like fun; I'll go with you next time. That is, if I'm invited."

"I'll have to ask the children," he teased her, "but I should think of course, you are. It will mean even more to me. Oh, and Daphne, listen to this. I felt that someone was following me. At first I thought I was paranoid because of the shooting..."

"What! What shooting?"

Royce was struck dumb. What had he blurted out? He had not intended to tell her and, in fact, told Robert not to mention it when he saw her in the States. It was out of the bag now. There was no other recourse other than to tell her.

"Jim, hello? I asked you, what shooting?"

"Well, it seems...I mean David and I think, that that German SS Officer, Schmid, the one whose son died on that hike, sent someone to get even with me and..."

"What are you saying? When did you plan to tell me this

"Well, to tell the truth, I really wasn't planning to."

As Royce spoke, it dawned on him the assassin, inept though he was, may still lurk about, and this could put Daphne in danger.

She looked at him with concern, not fear. "You weren't going to tell me? Well you sure as blazes are going to tell me right now!"

"I'm sorry. I see I've made a mistake. There was an incident while you were in Boston. Someone hid just outside the garage as I came home one night. When I drove in, he took a couple of potshots at me, quite incompetent mind you. I made it into the house, called the operator for help, and then got Robert's gun. I saw the bloke as he ran off, so I chased him through the woods taking a couple of shots at him, but he had a car and raced off. I hit it twice, I think. It wasn't enough to stop him though. That's really all there was to it. Then David, Mary and the police arrived. They searched but couldn't find anything other than a cap. And, as I blundered and tried to not tell you before about the shooting, I found out David now has me under surveillance by a security agency. That's who was following me."

"Let me get this straight. You run off into the woods at night shooting at you don't know who. You don't know if there is someone else there with them, or in the car…What in the devil were you thinking?"

I wasn't thinking. Someone shoots at you, you shoot back."

"That kind of reaction should be left to the police. You, it could get killed. Don't do it!"

Royce laughed. "Daphne, I just told you I acted without giving any thought to it."

"You're beyond redemption, James Royce. Tell me something else, did you tell the police about that SS Major, who may have someone after you?"

"That's very quick of you, Daphne—added two and two together quite quickly."

"Yes, I'm very quick. Now be as quick to answer me, did you tell the police?"

"No, because they would have contacted the military or some intelligence agency and all hell would have broken out, and I would've possibly lost my Top Secret designation."

"I see. So what I get out of all you've told me is there could be one or more gunmen out there somewhere, who would like to shoot you."

"There is that possibility. And now, as you mention it, I'm going to have David's agency protect you as well."

"You mean some twit is going to follow me around? I don't think so."

"Why not? Do you go somewhere you shouldn't?"

"I may, why not, who knows? It's bad enough I know you're shooting up the place. If there's someone else about as well, I certainly don't want to ride around with you."

"Seriously Daphne…"

"Who said I wasn't serious?"

They both started to smile and that lightened up the conversation. "Again, Daphne, seriously. There'll be a person around. You can have him drive you or get the dry goods or greengrocer or whatever, but for a while it's got to be that way."

She glared at him, but said nothing more.

Royce said he was going to run up to his office, check out a few projects, then be back, and after lunch, they would go over to Ravensmoor and take the children and dogs for a walk.

As he left for the office, he drove up to the security agent parked at the side of the road and told him to stay where he was. There was now a woman in the house to protect. The agent didn't like the change in orders. Royce assured him he had a gun under the seat, and was heading for a restricted area. He waved the agent off.

After Royce returned and they had eaten, he walked with Daphne to the garage, and thoughtlessly decided to leave the Bentley and take the Alvis. She saw the square patch of tape on the driver's door.

"What on earth is that?"

Royce fumbled his words and that was enough for her. She tore off tape on the door to expose a ragged hole through the metal.

"That's a God damn bullet hole; and don't try to sell me a different story!"

"Yes. The door was open; I had just gotten out when the bloke took a shot."

She opened the door and saw the neat hole in the leather door panel where the bullet entered and looked again at the metal where it exited.

"So, that bullet went through the leather, whatever else is in the panel, and out through the steel door?"

"The door's not steel; I think its aluminum, much softer alloy."

"And your head is a much softer alloy too! You had better turn this car in for a bulletproof one, looks like we're going to need it. By the way, how's your life insurance? Do you have any? Whose name is it in? Payments up to date?"

She didn't expect answers, walked around to the passenger side, and got in, slamming the door.

The group trudged off through a light snowfall. All of them were bundled well against the cold as Beth held Daphne's hand and Victor gripped Royce's sleeve. As usual, the two Spaniels ran like Norse Berserkers, while Scotty in his fitted wool coat, was ready for a lift any time after the first five minutes.

On this walk, Royce told the children about a mountain man he once knew, called Ernst Becker. Seven foot tall, Royce went on, four hundred pounds of muscle. He could lift up the front of a truck and change a tire while he held it. When Becker bellowed, the snow blew off trees for a hundred yards and bears ran back to their den. But, in truth, he was gentle friend, Royce whispered, a giant who brought him through a terrible storm and bad men and delivered him safe to England, so he could be with his niece and nephew.

The children were enthralled, yet doubtful. How could anyone be that tall or weigh that much? Why would they doubt him, he asked straight-faced, wasn't he here with them? Didn't that prove it? They had to agree he was there with them. So therefore, it followed, the story their uncle told had to be true.

As Royce bent to pick up Scotty, Daphne saw how much he had changed while she was in the States. Comfortable with the children, telling colored-up stories of his past, loving her and, she smiled, Scotty. He was relaxed despite his past tribulations and even his recent encounter with the gunman. Then there was Ernst, a man she only slightly recalled, yet a man Royce missed deeply. Though he knew him for but a few harrowing days, he would never forget him, and never wanted to. She could see that clearly.

* * *

24 December, Saturday 1938.

Prior to Sunday, Christmas morning, it had been hectic for all the family. Mary had ordered garland and lights laid upon all the topiary around the entrance to the manor. A massive twenty foot, decorated tree stood in the far corner of the great room. Lights blazed from every window and the eyebrow dormers along the roof. The massive stone manor looked almost warm.

In the few previous days, David and Royce had visited automotive shops, Daphne the jewelry dealer, and Mary, although having more time only finished buying the last of the gifts for the children the day before. After that, there were gift cards with bonuses for the servants, key company employees, and service personnel. All cards hand signed by her and David. The oak Yule Log would burn intensely for days as the end stuck out from the largest fireplace.

On Christmas Eve, the family relaxed with appropriate drinks, to recall previous Christmases until Beth and Victor, exhausted from the late hour, were carried off to bed. Then most of the gifts were brought out and spread around the tree. In the late eve, as David had requested, church carolers came to the door and sang carols, one of which was Mary's favorite, the hundred-fifty-six year old, *Oh, Come All Ye Faithful*. Asked inside for cinnamon cider and to warm themselves, they gathered by the fire. The mood was cheery, good humored, and as they left, David slipped an envelope to their leader for all to share.

Before Royce and Daphne returned to their home, the four adults remained together by the fire and sipped their drinks either enfolded in their own thoughts, or chatting the late hours away. It was the first and the last Christmas Eve the four would spend together.

On Sunday, December 25th, 1938, at 7:00 in the morning Christmas day, the brass knocker of Blackbird Cottage pounded away. As the door opened, two Springer Spaniels almost knocked Royce over as they raced dementedly past him and throughout the house. They were followed by two eager children bundled to the nose in scarves, winter coats, and mittens.

"Merry Christmas, Uncle James!" Then, as Daphne came in sight, "Merry Christmas, Auntie Daphne!"

"Merry Christmas to you both. Now come in here out of the cold and warm up."

Beth and Victor hustled in, the Spaniels slobbering and sniffing every cranny in every room for only God knew what.

"Where's Scotty, Beth?"

"Oh, he'll be here."

Royce looked out the door and could see Scotty, undaunted as he panted down the path the children had left in the snow. Royce slipped into his coat. The moment Scotty saw him, he sat and waited to be scooped up. Royce warmed the shivering dog inside his coat and Scotty gave him a lick on the cheek for his going to the trouble of going to get him.

While returning to the cottage, he was curious why the children were allowed to walk the mile between the homes unescorted. Looking around, he saw a vehicle coast along. He recognized it as unmarked one from UK Security and gave the driver a thank you wave as the vehicle continued further and stopped at the entrance to Royce's drive. When he returned to the house, Daphne looked at the wet Scotty, and then at Royce's damp shirt. She grabbed a towel to dry the dog.

"You're a nice guy, James Royce." She laughed. "No matter what is said about you."

Royce had no chance to respond. The children, being as overexcited as the Spaniels, told the adults they all had to get to Ravensmoor to open some gifts before going to church, and then get back, to open more.

"So bring a suit and a dress," they said, "and hurry," they shouted, "or there won't be enough time to open some gifts before church."

Royce warmed the Bentley while Daphne got some clothes together. The dogs scrambled into the rear seat with the children while Scotty sat on Daphne's lap, wrapped in a throw. With the clamor from the back seat, Royce thought the distance to Ravensmoor a long way. The UK Security Service followed.

The family sat around the Yule log as it popped and spattered hot sap on the polished granite floor surrounding the fireplace. Wrapped presents yielded to children and adults to disclose ties, silverware, tin soldiers, dolls, scarves, diamond cufflinks, pearl earrings, hunting jackets, leather gloves, children's books, and books for the adults. Opening the presents went on for an hour. Special gifts, mostly secret, were saved for after church services.

* * *

Coventry Cathedral, Church of England, was known as Saint
Michael's. Prior to the cathedral, a Benedictine Monastery
occupied the site, endowed, around the year 1043 AD, by the
largess of Leofric, Earl of Mercia, and his wife, Lady Godiva.

After Leofric's time, building began on Saint Mary's Priory
and Cathedral. This cathedral held influence in Coventry until
becoming a casualty of King Henry the VIII's Dissolution of the
Monasteries decree. While Saint Mary's Priory slowly fell to
ruin, Saint Michael's Church was raised in the 14th and 15th
centuries.

The church became the largest parish church in England,
with a spire the third tallest in the country. The massive walls and
spire dominated the town and surrounding region as one
of the outstanding religious buildings in England for centuries.
In 1918, by the formation of the Coventry Diocese, the church
was elevated to cathedral status.

The cathedral and Coventry had yet to suffer war.

At five minutes to eleven, the family entered Saint Michael's
and proceeded to the Royce family's front pew. It was known
that Sir David, one the major contributors to the church, was also
the largest employer in the region, so his foremost position was
thankfully acknowledged in this time of the Great Depression.

Whispers however, abounded. Who are the beautiful
woman and the man with the most frightful scar? In the pews,
Royce's managers supplied information on the scarred man, yet
the woman was a mystery to them. They had never seen her, they
said, and James Royce never mentioned her. If the ladies in the
congregation knew she lived with Royce at the former Gostly
place, there would have been righteous indignation. If the men
knew, they would have put their heads down, to hide their smiles.

The service was long, Anglican, and Church of England,
and the hall was chill from the severe winter as well as to prevent
people from falling asleep. The children were good, fidgeting as
little as possible. Royce and Daphne attended the service solely
due to Mary, David and the children wanting them to come.
There were coughs, throats cleared, drowsy parishioners, and
the whispers of children. Nevertheless, the Bishop of Coventry,

Mervyn George Haigh, gave them no pity. This was Christ's Day, he boomed, and they were to remember that fact and spend some time with the Lord. To suffer in His name would do them all some good.

The service ended, a relief for many, while others sought comfort in the words of the Bishop and his hopes for the future in these trying times.

At the door, the Bishop's assistant was handed an envelope from Mary, while David spoke to the Bishop.

"The Church and I thank you, Sir David."

"Pleased I can do it, Mervyn. Here, do you remember my brother, James? He recently purchased the old Gostly Place."

The Bishop was amused. "Remember him? Of course I do. Been a long time, James. I often remember how you came through the front door and disappeared out the rear."

Royce was not the least embarrassed. "I never thought you noticed, Reverend."

"Not just I noticed, James. God did also."

"Well, what can I say? I think He's got more to worry about at this time than this one poor sinner."

David ended any further debate by introducing Daphne.

"Very nice to meet you, my dear. You're quite lovely. Are you from around here?"

"Not really, I travel a lot. My main residence is in London."

"Well I'm sure you'll find Coventry a wonderful city, Daphne. Where do you stay while here?"

The question was not meant to pry, asked simply to continue the chat with a pretty woman.

Yet David instinctively knew Daphne was going to say she lived with James at the former Gostly place, and imposed into the conversation before she could speak.

"We've taken up too much of your time, Mervyn, there's a line behind us. We should go along and leave you to the rest of your flock."

Daphne glanced behind her. There were only two or three people approaching. She turned to David with a smile, then back to the Bishop. "Nice to have met you Reverend, too bad we couldn't have spoken longer. It would have been of interest."

As they left, Daphne couldn't help to tease David. "You

knew exactly what I was about to say, didn't you, David? Doesn't that make you nervous?"

"No. It was a guess. I just tried to protect my brother's reputation."

"How funny you sound, David. Your brother's reputation would increase tenfold if people knew where I stayed, at least among the men of this town."

"You're acting shamelessly, Daphne."

She felt irritated, yet didn't show it. "David, you make me laugh. I love Jim, that's why I'm with him."

"Without the sanctity of marriage?"

"Oh come off it, David! Sanctity of marriage? I'll bet if Mary followed you around London at night she'd throw the sanctity of marriage in your face."

Now David was irritated. "Try to keep a civil tongue in your head, Daphne, and for the sake of family peace, I'll say no more."

"I bet you'll say no more. You'd best hope I don't tell Jim you called me shameless, he'd call you out."

"Daphne, you can't imagine your mindlessness with that statement."

She turned to face him, her back to Royce. "What the devil are you talking about?"

"Think, won't you? After what I told you in London, what do you suppose just one blow to his head would do to his brain?"

Her hand went involuntarily to her mouth.

"You'd better get your face on straight, Daphne, dear, before you turn around."

As luck would have it, the children had Mary and Royce walk around the side of the cathedral to see the stained glass windows in the sunlight. James failed to notice Daphne's dismay. This gave her time to breathe and clear her mind from the callousness of David's voice. He smiled dismissively and walked to the Bentley as it pulled to the curb.

By the time Royce, Mary and the children returned, Daphne had recovered, although still shaken.

Royce noticed it and laughed. "Bishop Haigh's sermon fills you with religious emotion?"

"No, you joker. Right now I'd guess it's just the darn cold going right through me to my very bones."

"Then let's get you back to Ravensmoor and stoke up a roaring fire."

She wanted to stoke a fire back at Blackbird Cottage, yet knew the disappointment it would cause Mary and the children.

At the manor, before they all settled back in the study, David caught her alone in a corridor.

"Daphne, I apologize. What I inferred was coarse of me. I don't know why it blurted out. I'm under great pressure. Still, I know that's no excuse. You had every right to retort as you did. Neither of us can unsay what has passed, I just hope we can put the event behind us and go forth in a mutual, shall we say, entente."

She knew he was being false. "Whatever you say, David. The subject bores me to death."

Down the corridor, Mary saw, but did not hear them. She wondered about it, yet said nothing. That was her way, to say nothing.

They sat for Christmas dinner and listened to the King's halting message to the nation as he wished all well in this time of God's peace and hope for the future.

The dinner consisted mainly of turkey, goose, lamb, roast potatoes, gravy, cranberry, and Yorkshire pudding. All of which was thoroughly enjoyed. For desert, a simple treat for the children, strawberries and cream while the family exchanged Christmas cards. It could have been a delightful interval to sit back with a snifter of brandy, but now was the time for the major gifts, and the children could not be expected to contain themselves further.

When they reached the drawing room at the rear of the manor, the children were told to sit and be blindfolded. They shook with excitement as they heard doors open, felt rushes of cold air, doors close, murmurs, then thumping. Their patience at an end, the blindfolds removed, the children blinked, went wide-eyed, and for once struck speechless. Before them, held by Marco Herrera, were two perfectly matched English bred, miniature Shetland Ponies. Raggedy in their shaggy winter coats to be sure, but still, the children were stunned. Beth and Victor found their voices, and their screeching startled the horses and made the adults wince.

They desperately wanted go off for a canter but were reminded they had no saddles that would fit. Their despair was remedied when Herrera brought forth two child sized English saddles, and the tack required. These gifts were from Daphne and Royce and they smiled as the two children traced their names on the etched brass plates on the saddles. Elizabeth E. Royce, Christmas 1938, and Victor T. Royce, Christmas 1938.

The children were proficient riders, schooled at the equestrian stables, and of course, they simply had to ride, no matter the temperature hovered only a touch above freezing. As quickly as the children could, they tacked up the horses and with their endless thanks, were soon seen, and bundled up, in a trot across the grounds with the groom. The Spaniels were off in pursuit, while Scotty decided the afternoon was better spent by the fireplace with people more his age.

Mary and David's gift to Royce was a walking cane embellished at the top with a solid silver knob inlayed with a burnished gold, lion medallion. The lion was rampant, upright on its hind legs with one extended forepaw which wore a gauntlet, closed into a fist. It was their father's design and Royce was surprised David would still adhere to their alleged Coat of Arms in this day and age. Then again, as he thought of it, that was David.

Royce thanked them; it was after all, a thoughtful gift. Daphne's present, from David and Mary, was a striking afternoon dress of multi-layered deep green, silk damask. Mary was shown it in London on her shopping trip and, despite the fact she would have liked it for her own, she knew without doubt, there could never be a more pure color to enhance Daphne's eyes and auburn hair. Daphne couldn't thank them enough.

Royce and Daphne's gifts to David and Mary were Cashmere sport riding jackets. They had never seen the like of them. Royce gave all a laugh as he explained how furtive he had been to find their sizes by asking one of the maids. He had the jackets sent up from Swaine, Adeney's Equestrian Shop on St. James Street in London. The jackets were remarkable-really for show, and David and Mary sat about with them on to express how much they were appreciated.

Mary's gift to David was a Rotherman's of Coventry, rare 1926 gold wristwatch. He fastened the black leather strap, then got up and casually kissed her on the cheek.

When Daphne saw the watch, she could barely believe it, for when Royce opened her gift to him, he found an American, Waltham Watch Company, midi-cushion gold wristwatch. This watch also went on, as Royce gave her a hug. He had been on her mind often while she was in Massachusetts and knew it would be the perfect gift for him at Christmas. This left gifts for the women, yet the men sat back sipped their brandies and looked about nonchalantly until the women started to glare at them.

Finally, Daphne rose. "That's it, Mary! Let's go and find some turkey and let these beasts enjoy humble pie for forgetting to get us Christmas gifts!"

The men jumped up. "No, no wait! All right, we give in. Both of you get your coats on."

As they struggled into their greatcoats, Mary said she hoped it wasn't another sleigh ride in this horrid weather. David told them to be quiet and come along. They walked around to the horse stalls. Daphne and Royce were surprised to see six deer in the paddock along with David and Mary's two horses.

Mary laughed. "The deer would never survive in this winter so we open the gate and they come in for hay and some grain. Once a week Marco makes up a mash for all of them. They get along great with the horses."

The deer, in their hunger, had overcome their natural fear of the groom and although they stayed inside the paddock, they were nervous with the strangers. As the adults went inside, David mentioned that the feed and hay at least stopped the deer from stripping the bark off the trees.

"All right girls, close your eyes."

"Now we're being treated like the children."

"That's right, take our arms, and step over this threshold."

"For God's sake, where are we?"

"Stop here."

They were held a minute as Royce switched on the lights and build apprehension in the women. When it peaked, they opened their eyes. Mary's old Riley Saloon was gone. Before them sparkled two new, identical, Riley Sport Coupes with dark green bodies and black fenders. The autos were burnished from additional lighting placed around the garage. The women were caught completely off guard, but they loved the surprise and hugged the men, enchanted.

"How will we tell them apart?"

"Well, one way to remember is, one will be at Ravensmoor and the other at Blackbird Cottage."

They each gave Royce a sardonic smirk.

"Or, you can see one plate ends in eight and the other, nine. Who wants which?"

The minor question was settled and it was agreed the two vehicles would be stored until the weather cleared in the spring, and then the four of them would be off for a tour through the countryside.

The day came to an end. The children were exhausted and in for naps, the adults tired. Daphne and Royce glad to be alone, at Blackbird Cottage. They enjoyed the day, although between family and later, friends of David and Mary's stopping by, it became tiresome being sociable for two people used to their privacy.

Royce stoked the fire, added a few pieces of kindling, then a split log. While the fire took its time coming back to life, he slumped into his wingback chair. Daphne brought them scotches. She also brought a giftwrapped box.

"What's this? You already gave me this watch."

"This is something personal. I wanted to give you this when people weren't around because I didn't know if you'd like it."

He slowly undid the bow, and then took his time to unwrap the paper without a tear.

"Open it for God's sake, Jim, you're really the most frustrating person I've ever known."

He laughed and opened the lid. A black star sapphire ring glimmered in the box. He sat back, wordless at the ethereal star in the stone.

"I hope you like it, Jim. I hope I'm not being improper. I'm told that only black has a natural star."

"Like it? Daphne, I think it's magnificent. It's the most wonderful gift I've ever had."

"You don't mind I gave you a ring? I certainly don't mean it to imply too much about...I mean us together..."

Royce shook his head. "Of course not and when have you ever been so concerned about being proper? Come here, I love it, and you and being here."

The day after Christmas, Saint Stephan's Boxing Day, is for gift boxes, often money, handed out to the poor, hospitals, British Red Cross and other needy services. David and Royce combined their donations so Mary and Daphne, with the children in tow to teach charity, travelled to houses and institutions with the gifts.

As Boxing Day is a holiday, Royce only worked a half day and came home at one in the afternoon. They decided at mid-afternoon to go to a café near Broadgate. However, Alfred and Amanda, the chef, arrived with two full-course meals.

"Leftovers." They said. "Complements of Ravensmoor."

The two lovers gladly stayed in to enjoy the fire's warmth, the meal, and solitude.

As there was to be a pre-New Year's Eve party at noon on the Saturday before New Year's, Daphne decided to drive up to Windermere for two or three days prior to the party. The main reason for the trip, or so she said, was to pick up the rest of Robert's clothes and other articles he had left there as he never for a moment thought he would leave England for good. Her brother also wanted the rest of his artist's sets from Windermere and Royce's cottage and for her not to forget to enclose the photograph of Royce's castle. As Robert and Daphne had agreed to endow the hospital, she also had to stop there to initiate the paper work.

After a call was made to the caretaker at Windermere to turn on the heat and check for frozen water lines, Daphne asked Royce to buy a steamer trunk to ship Robert's belongings. She was off early the next day in Royce's Alvis. Then Royce, in the Bentley, headed for the main plant, followed by the security guard who could not enter the gate without military clearance. Royce assured him he would not leave the plant premises for at least thirty-six hours so it was up to the guard to do what he wanted.

For a while, Royce listened to various stories of the holidays with various employees, and then held a manager's conference with Clive and the men. After that, he went to his office and drafting table. His first phone call was to tell Maintenance to get a cot from the company infirmary and bring it to his office. He felt whenever Daphne was away he could spend more time at work. Time was his enemy now and it was fighting him.

* * *

Daphne drove north toward Windermere, and stopped at the hospital in Winwick, Lancaster, to sign the endowment paperwork. The Center would then send that information on to Robert's office in Boston. After another stop for foodstuffs and petrol, she was at the cottage. Franklyn, the caretaker, had started two of the fireplaces, checked the kerosene heaters vents, turned the water back on, and gone outside to flush the pipes.

When they moved inside, she was curious. "How did my brother put up with these heaters?"

"I haven't the foggiest, Miss Daphne. Of course, this is one quite cold winter, but no matter, Mr. Robert never complained. Seemed like it was a sort of penance, it did."

"Well, I'm not into expiation. I want proper heat put in here. Can't you build in oil burners, put one or two in the cellar, cut some holes in the floor and put in some grates or whatever you call them? Just to heat the master bedroom kitchen, parlor, and one den would certainly help."

"We can do that, Miss. We can do a bang up job. We can wrap the pipes against the cold too. How long will you stay this here time?"

"Oh, two or three days."

Franklyn was downcast. "I'm sorry Miss. We couldn't possibly get it done that soon."

Daphne laughed. "I didn't mean now, Franklyn. After I leave. This weather's beastly, do it as soon as you're able. I'll give you a payment now and bill me the rest when you finish. I'll leave a check and my address on the table."

He was gone when she made a stiff scotch and settled with a robe into a wingback chair in front of the fireplace. She desperately needed these days to herself. From the time she left for Boston with her mother, she had had no time alone. Endless worry it seemed. Worry about her mother, then mother's death, followed by Father's. Robert coming to the US, the crowds at the wakes and funerals. Next, the shock of Robert deciding to stay and start a new life, the rush to settle the estate, the sad goodbye, the quick trip to reach the Pan Am Terminal. After that, it was David's chatter and innuendo across the ocean and on to Coventry. And the rush continued there. Christmas, the gifts, children, church and people everywhere. It was nonstop and tumultuous. She was grateful that at least Jim had held together.

Yet then again, was that what really bothered her? Granted, the hectic pace had tired her out, but still, what else was it nagging at her? That, she now had time to sort it out. Everything was in flux. The carefree life she had known before Jim, and with him, was at odds with the present. She had accepted that fact at first. Now, however, it seemed to be a tradeoff simply to be with him. Still, it was not only their life together that changed. *He* had changed. Not his feelings for her, granted. But he was not the person she once knew. That person climbed with her, taught her, slept with her, sat on the deck at BergFalke, drove up to Windermere, laughed and hiked with her. That person had faded, transformed into the very person David planned. Did Jim see it? Is this what he wanted, deep inside? Now he had her, a home, and his family around, children, dogs and of all things, a goal.

And that goal mattered more and more. The distant look he had, the mumbles about something not fitting the way it should, irritated over workers' inabilities. Jim was like her brother Robert who suddenly discovered himself. Unfortunately, that wasn't who she fell in love with.

Daphne got up, tossed another log on the fire and made a second stiff scotch.

Am I shallow? She questioned. They say there'll be a war and Jim has thrown himself into his work to do his part. That's wonderful, but what part do I play in this war to be?

She wasn't even married. Thank goodness, she thought ruefully, yet did he expect her to be the happy little housewife, to sit at home and wait for her man to return? Then she could fuss about, make his dinner, and listen keenly to his day at work. That wasn't her, wasn't what she wanted, and would not accept. She desired him and a chalet in the mountains. Definitely not the future she saw rearing its ugly head between them. She loved him, or at least the person he was, and may still be. Nevertheless, she didn't plan to slip into that life she envisioned no matter how much she loved him. He was going to find that out. She was not about to sacrifice her life to his needs if it did not work two ways—that was for damn sure.

Another log went into the fire. Perhaps this was an overreaction. Yet now she became startled by the starkness, the gravity of her disillusionment. Was it the bitter English weather that made her sulky? She'd have to wait and see. Hold your horses, she thought, don't be too hasty, maybe it is just a phase she—and maybe he—will work through. Things could pan out. She would see what happened between now and spring.

She decided to get well into spring and see if her vision of their future changed. But, no matter what, she wasn't going to sit still. If Jim didn't come around, she'd tell him the problem. No, she wouldn't do that. She was sure men are too dense to see beyond their noses at times. If it stayed the status quo, then she could move between Windermere and London. With Coventry sandwiched in between, that could work.

And then at last, her own epiphany. She recognized *she* needed direction, something to wrap her mind around. She started to think about it, and snuggled deeper into the robe. The fire and scotch warmed, but she didn't find an answer.

* * *

For the day before the New Year, David had invited fifty people to a semiformal luncheon. The great room easily accommodated two long tables with a dais at the end for any guests who wished to speak. The guest list was a who's who of first and second tier political and military leaders and those expected to be persons of influence. Only wives, no women friends were included.

As most of the guests traveled ninety miles from the London, Westminster areas, David had them enter the west wing first with its powder rooms, to allow them time to freshen up, before they passed through to the great room. David and Mary greeted each guest with a few words of welcome, then invited them to gather at the far end cocktail tables to chat and served refreshments. Outside, after they left off their passengers, chauffeurs were shown where to park their vehicles and directed to the east wing for hors d'oeuvres, non-alcoholic beverages, and to wait.

By the time most of the guests arrived, the men had already formed into small groups in the library and den. Through a haze of cigar, pipe and cigarette smoke, the talk was all of politics and war. David moved among the groups to listen, sometimes to agree, or with others to discuss points, change minds.

David's proposal was brief and nearly the same with each group. "We are united as the loyal opposition. We do not gather here to bring down the Government. We gather in the name of England. This must be clear and understood."

To the military men present he was equally positive. "Gentlemen, I know you are duty bound to report any nefarious challenge to our present leaders. We only seek to strengthen our beloved England within the framework of the government, current laws, regulations, and circumstances."

With a wink and a nod, it was understood.

The Generals, Admirals and their seconds in command stayed, and often added their concise thoughts to the politicians. Nevertheless, those assembled at Ravensmoor knew the Government, led by Neville Chamberlain, would fall should war come, and they must be ready for what was, at least to them, inevitable.

David was masterful. There were powerful men present. Former Foreign Secretary, Anthony Eden, and Duff Cooper, former First Lord of the Admiralty, both of whom resigned over the Munich Pact. Also Air Vice-Marshal Tedder, Sir Hugh Sinclair, Director of British Intelligence, Harold Nicolson, Labour MP, Harold Kim Philby, another agent with British Intelligence, and SIS Chief Vernon Kell.

Here the personages gathered. Men from Oxford, Eton, Cambridge, and the Military Colleges. Men who would shape the future of the Empire and of course David was right in the thick of it. He reveled in the fact that everyone knew him, or of him. They all had their say, yet in the end, there was agreement.

Everyone must prepare for the future and they all knew their obligations. The individual groups returned to the Great room with a confident air. All that could be done for their country was underway. They thought they were ready. They had no idea of the terror that lay ahead.

David was in an expansive mood. Every move he made, every word he spoke without error. If there was that one fly in the ointment, it happened as Mary handed him an envelope. The note expressed regrets for being unable to attend the luncheon as his wife, Clementine, was not well, and he would not leave her. The writer hoped David and he could have a get together immediately at the turn of New Year or, if his wife was still ill, perhaps David could travel to Chartwell. The missive was signed W S Churchill, Chartwell, Westerham.

David was, of course, disappointed. He wanted Churchill there. He was First Lord of the Admiralty, and the most vocal opponent of appeasement. So much so, Adolf Hitler singled him out as a warmonger. Churchill's supporters, though still in the minority, increased each week.

Although David kept his cards close to his vest, he hoped Churchill would become the next Prime Minister. A note was hurriedly jotted off with the wish Mrs. Churchill would soon improve and that he, David, was available at Mr. Churchill's convenience. The note given to the chauffeur to return to Chartwell. David was proud. Churchill could easily have had an aide simply ring him up with regrets. Instead, he had sent a handwritten note, hand delivered. David was sure to let everyone know W S Churchill was disappointed.

Daphne and Royce arrived. With high heels, her normal height of five feet, eight inches, now neared Royce's six feet. Heads turned.

She knew it, didn't show it, but knew it. The deep green of her dress harmonized with her eyes and set off her auburn hair. Mary had loaned her a diamond choker with a thin diamond bracelet for her wrist. Women and men were startled, the women envious of her looks and manner, the men envious they weren't with her.

Royce wore a semiformal, cream dinner jacket with black tie

and waistcoat. He was handsome in his own right, the guests thought, until he came closer and put off by the scar. Royce didn't mind, he recognized no one there and it saved a need for small talk. He felt bad for Daphne being attached to his arm and to not have the freedom to walk about.

David changed their privacy by his announcement that James Royce was his brother, then mentioned James had a recent harrowing escape from German occupied Austria. David finished with the information Royce had returned to become the superintendent of all D W Royce Industries divisions. "The striking woman with my brother is Daphne Elliot, a dear friend of the family, who will share as hostess with my wife."

Daphne whispered to Royce. "So much for being unseen."

Royce looked at her. "You've got to be joking. You could never dress like that and walk through a crowd unnoticed."

"You're right, but I dressed like this to be a mystery woman. David ruined that."

"How about me? Without you I would have gone unnoticed. Now everyone will have to speak with me solely because I'm David's brother and he's given them a couple of subjects to talk about."

"Jim, you poor thing. All you've got to do is talk, while I'll have to beat men off with a stick. Please, I beseech thee-shield me from the British upper class."

"We both have our crosses to bear; darling and I brought your smelling salts."

They laughed at each other as people approached them.

A few minutes later, as David passed by Daphne, he smiled when one of the men surrounding her, simply to be noticed, asked if his chauffeur would have enough to eat.

Daphne was courteous. "Oh yes, they're each having a large hors d'oeuvres."

"I've never heard of a large hors d'oeuvre."

"It simply means a small meal."

David stopped to listen. The guest continued with his inane chatter. "Then why don't we just say that? What do the French words hors d'oeuvres mean anyway? I know it's a bit of food before dinner, what's the English translation?"

"Basically, it means food prepared outside the main course.

The French actually refer to it as 'amuse bouche', meaning amusement for the mouth."

David questioned her. "What would they call it in Russian, Daphne?"

"Again, loosely translated, or perhaps I should say rendered, it would be zakuski, David."

Other people, standing about, were amused. David tried to trip her up. "How about Greek?"

Daphne became uncomfortable. "That would be mezze, David. Again, loosely rendered."

She wanted to end the subject, yet David still pressed her.

"One more, Daphne, how about Chinese?"

The people around could see he was on the hook and had to stump her. She decided to end the conversation. "Mandarin or Cantonese, David?"

Now, not knowing the difference and discomfited, he mumbled. "Either."

"Dim sum, in Cantonese, David."

As she moved away, she left everyone charmed and David chastised—of course never for long.

Actually, Daphne wasn't sure of the translation and guessed no one there could dispute her. Whatever, she smiled, he'd been put in his place quite well enough.

Mary Royce wore a beaded gold lame dress with a jeweled satin day cap. She was the second most admired woman there and had no trouble accepting that fact. She liked Daphne, and was amused by her putting on the very airs she distained. As Daphne came up to Mary and winked, the two shared smiles.

"My God Daphne, you're honey to the bees. There's a buzz around you."

"I know, Mary, it's terrible. It's enough to give a little American girl like me the vapors here in England."

Mary suppressed a laugh. "Try to keep yourself together, Daphne, all the other American Heiresses over here did. If it becomes too much, I'll have James take you away from this."

"Good Lord, Mary, I haven't had this much attention since college. By the way, I've been so busy trying to fend them off I've lost sight of Jim. Where is he?"

"Over there, with some military people."

261

"Good, it's good he mingles a bit."

Royce was, in fact, trying to control his temper. A circumstance that occurred when he met up with General, Sir Miles Alcott, head of the RDF Program, along with new Brigadier General Thomas Tomlinson. With them, was Charles Wentworth, the British foreign agent who Royce noticed was now in the dress uniform and insignia of a full colonel in the Royal Marines. The conversation began pleasantly enough as Royce, who, recognizing everyone in their group was rated Top Secret, mentioned to General Alcott the upgraded units he required for the 'system' would be ready for shipment by the first of the week.

General Alcott was pleased; they were ahead of schedule. The conversation continued along casually until Charles Wentworth, without concern, mentioned his agents had been in touch with Ernst Becker. Everyone froze. Royce felt his pulse quicken, his fists clench. Wentworth could see it, and grinned taking a step back. General Alcott stepped between them and faced Royce. "I did not expect CW to say that, Mr. Royce."

"You knew?"

"Of course, and approve. Our agents are being hunted down and eliminated thanks to you and your Major Schmid. We have to use whatever means are left to acquire information."

"For Christ's sake, Ernst is stuck up in the mountains, what in hell can he tell you?"

"As a matter of fact, quite a bit. His spa is now popular as a backcountry climbing resort for Nazi officers. He picks up bits of information and then passes it along to Charley's people. Nothing special, yet again, every bit helps fill the puzzle."

"And I suppose Wentworth used my name to get him to help in his spy network?"

"Of course, although Becker didn't need much of a prod. He also said to say to remember him to you. He thinks of you a lot and is glad things have worked out."

"General, if anything happens to Ernst, I'll come after that grinning person with you."

"There's no reason for that kind of talk, Royce. Please stay civil here."

"General, you're not in charge of me."

"That's true. It's simply to protect you. If you went after CW I'm afraid you would wind up in a very painful position."

"I'll give as good as I get, General."

"This has gone far enough. Please be so kind as to leave us, Mr. Royce."

"You don't order me around in my brother's house, General. Although in consideration of my brother, I will leave. Don't forget what I said, Wentworth."

Royce left, his fists still clenched.

General Alcott turned to Charles Wentworth. "You've a big mouth, CW."

"He would have found out sooner or later, I decided on sooner."

"You don't do the deciding around here, Charley. If you think you do, I'll have you disappear for a few years up in the Orkneys where you won't like the accommodations. And there better be a 'Sir' in your next words."

"Yes, Sir."

"Good, now leave, I don't want you to cause any further friction in this home. James and David Royce are more important to our efforts than you at present."

"Yes...Sir."

Alcott knew CW was not in the least bit concerned.

Wentworth left, Brigadier Tomlinson spoke to General Alcott. "You do remember he came with us, Miles."

"Yes. But he's our best agent, I'm sure he'll find his way home in that handsome uniform."

Mary had hired a popular band, formerly owned by British bandmaster, Ray Noble. Noble wanted to go to the States for a larger audience but due to the American musician's union, he couldn't take his English band with him. So, in 1935, he had a US musician, Alton Glenn Miller, put together a group of American musicians for him. Ray Noble went to the US, ending up in the Rainbow Room in New York. His old band stayed behind, and was now at Ravensmoor, playing some of the same swing songs Nobel had written or collaborated on with other composers.

It was the peak time for the big swing bands. They had come into their own in 1938 after Benny Goodman stole the show at

Carnegie Hall with the multiple solos in Sing Sing Sing. And here and now, the military and politicians alike forgot their problems for two hours and danced to the new music of the era. Songs such as "The Very Thought of You," "I Hadn't Anyone Till You," "Paris in the Spring" and "Flying Home" The band played other songs by Tommy Dorsey, "Yours is My Heart Alone," "Fools Rush In," "Take the A Train" and then flowed into other melodies.

It was a time not repeated in peace.

In her duties as a hostess around the tables, Daphne spotted one of her mother's old friends. The woman was saddened when she heard of Daphne's mother's passing and Daphne mentioned she planned to be in London to see people who knew her mother.

The woman, Lady Jane Sommers, was quick to respond. "Let me volunteer to contact your mother's old friends, Daphne. We'll have a memorial service in her memory."

"That's very good of you, Lady Jane. I'll be in touch about the day I'll be down to London. Thank you for thinking of that."

At this point, a handsome young man, dressed to the nines, bent over and kissed Lady Sommers cheek. "I'm back Mother. Sorry to be gone so long."

"Where have you been all this time, Kenneth? I bring you as my escort and find myself left here all by myself."

"By yourself? I would never say I was by myself if I had this striking woman beside me."

"Yes, Kenneth, she is that, isn't she. And unfortunately I suppose I must introduce her. Daphne, this is my only child, Kenneth, the bane of my existence. A womanizer and a wastrel. Need more be said?"

Kenneth gave his mother an exceedingly pained look. Daphne couldn't hide her smile.

"Mother is not my biggest fan, as you may gather from her dreadful remarks."

"Yes, I can see that."

"Your name is Daphne?"

She nodded. "Then Daphne, why don't you take me away from all this and make an honest man of me? It would please Mother, and for that matter, I would rather imagine me as well."

"I'm sorry to disappoint your Mother, or you Kenneth. But unfortunately, at least for you that is, I'm involved."

"What on earth does involved mean?"

"It means there's someone else, and even if there weren't, I'm afraid I'm too old for you."

"My God, I've found my angel at last, and find she's taken and too old for me as well! What have I done to deserve this cruel end to my happiness?"

"Try to muddle through it, Kenneth. It will make you a stronger person." She then laughed at Kenneth's raised eyebrow, which lent him a devilish gaze.

"In that case, dear Daphne, I must go sadly to the arms of—I really don't know who now—to seek solace and try to forget you. Cheerio." With that, and a wink, he left.

"Was I not correct, Daphne? A wonderful, handsome lad, yet a complete rake at twenty-five."

Yet Daphne could see she did have a mother's smile for her wayward son. "It would appear that way, Lady Sommers."

Still, Daphne was amused at his antics.

"It wasn't that way when I was a young girl, Daphne."

"Nothing's the way we were, Lady Jane, or ever will be again, from the way people talk."

"You mean the possibility of another war? If there is, I so worry about Kenneth."

"I shouldn't worry over him, Lady Sommers. If there's conscription, I'm sure he'll work out. Most men do."

"Conscription, Daphne? Oh my dear, no. He's an RAF Squadron Leader, Spitfires."

Daphne sat back, amazed at the statement. "A Squadron Leader? Then how on earth can you call him a rake?"

"Believe me, Daphne, a blue uniform with stripes on the sleeve is a magnet to the girls. He's been on station in India and Palestine, as well as here in England, and my late husband would inform me, discretely and censured mind you, about some of Kenneth's, shall we say, escapades. Things like climbing over a gate in India where no white man should go. My husband was quite proud of him. Of course, my husband was a rake also. Before we met, that is."

Daphne turned and watched Kenneth Sommers as he danced

with a politician's wife. No blue uniform now, he didn't need it. Obviously an accomplished dancer, graceful, fluid in his movements, he held the woman lightly. Whatever she was saying, he gave her his rapt attention—at least until he turned and caught Daphne's eye. He raised an eyebrow and gave thumbs up sign with the hand that held the woman's back.

Daphne shook her head neglecting to prevent a smile. "You're right, Lady Jane, he may be a Squadron Leader, but he is every bit a rake."

"I'm glad you see that Daphne, and please, call me Jane, now that we see eye to eye, I think we'll get along famously."

After Royce had angrily walked off, he went up the stairway and along the balcony to stand by the rail. He looked down at the crowd and picked out the two Generals, Tomlinson, and Alcott while they talked to an Admiral. Royce noticed the agent Wentworth was gone. Good riddance, he thought, and then saw Daphne with an attractive older woman. He recognized Anthony Eden speaking with David and he spotted Duff Cooper to whom Sir Hugh Sinclair had introduced him. Cooper was now attentive to an attractive, apparently unattached woman. Royce glanced about to see Lord and Lady Park-Edwards chatting with Mr. and Mrs. Harold Nicolson. Royce knew from the papers Nicolson was Labour PM. And to top it off, there was the Secretary of State for Air, Sir Kingsley Wood, his wife and attaché.

Royce paused. He hadn't been privy to the private meetings earlier and now he saw clearly who was in attendance and, more importantly, what this party meant. He was surveying the elite of the Government's Minority Party and military leaders, all under one roof. It was quite a feather in his brother's cap. He watched David with a keener eye.

He watched and learned a simple fact. David was a leader in the classical sense of England in the 1930s. It became more evident as he moved about the room. People turned to him as he came up, greeted him, shook his hand, and touched his shoulder. They were serious, or laughed, with each comment he passed. He was in his element. His piercing gray eyes accentuated his clipped Eton speech. Listeners took what he said as gospel. In his own mind, David Walker Royce assumed he had never been wrong and had never given anyone the slightest reason to believe he ever would be. He knew power. He knew its value. It was in his hand, and he was seizing it.

There had been cigars, pipes, cigarettes allowed, and little liquor. Now, just prior to his guests taking their leave, David had champagne filled, fluted glasses distributed to each person. He then asked all to gather around one or the other of two fireplaces.

"I want to thank you all for gracing Ravensmoor with your presence this afternoon. I know that you wish to return to your homes to prepare for your own New Year's Eve festivities. If God wills it, may we all return here next year. Please join with me as I would like to revive and old custom of my Father's in this very manor house."

David held his glass high. "God, king and country!"

Three hurrahs resounded around the granite walls. The glasses were drained and, when David turned and threw his glass into the fireplace, every person followed. Fifty crystal flutes shattered on the stone. All present were silent as the last tinkle of crystal faded. It was the symbolism David wanted them to remember. Even Daphne, caught up in the moment, had added her glass to the fireplace. Then she thought of the waste of fifty crystal flutes. She knew why David had made the grand gesture.

Huge burnished headlamps sprang to life to cast an unnatural yellowish glow over the snow and faces of the guests as they departed. Rolls-Royces, Bentleys and Daimlers crept forward to accept their passengers. Then, the steel monuments to their owner's affluence and influence, glided, silent as ghosts into the unknown shadows of yet to fear nights.

David excused himself to make some notes after reminding the family the party for company managers and supervisors would commence at 9:00 pm. Royce and Daphne could have done without it, but these were Royce's people, at least people he could converse with on an engineering level and not feel stifled.

At 8:45 pm, after changing into more casual sport coats and dresses, they began to greet forty of D W Royce Company's upper echelon managers and their wives. The two large tables from the previous gathering had been replaced by numerous tables for six people each. The food was buffet style, with liquor for those who wished. The same band played the same music, although now with an up-tempo beat, catering to the younger generation.

It was a casual party. Groups from the different divisions intermingled, couples danced, liquor flowed. Managers and their wives unwound from the pressures of projects new to them, and how to meet deadlines and ship product. All of their efforts were directed to the preparation for war. Daphne and Mary spoke with the wives, and of course, their husbands stayed around for a while to be near the two women.

David, Royce, and Clive Henderson met with the engineers. Although it was Royce who most of the men wanted to speak with, David and Clive, were given the deference due. Yet it was Royce's comments to questions, clarifying procedures, future concepts, and giving motivation with his creativeness, that held their attention. Older employees remembered Royce's withdrawn, monastic manner from the past and were baffled by the change. Still, they thanked God for it.

Daphne watched him closely. For all his bravado, she could see the facade. It was a veneer. He forced himself to be there for his men because they needed reinforcement. He gave a feeling of security with all the storm clouds that surrounded and their speed to get quality systems up and function properly. They were stressed. He attempted to ease their burden. Daphne could foresee this effort on his part was going to wear him down as well. He had taken on their anxieties. She was at a loss about it and in a free moment, spoke of her disquiet to Mary.

"I know what you're talking about Daphne. David is stressed many times, although he handles it better than James. James takes every problem personally, as if he was responsible and must worry a difficulty into the ground. David faces a problem and fights his way through it. He thrives on pressure. Then he relaxes for a spell before he attacks the next challenge. He understands stress and power go hand in hand. They give him the impetus to continue—to succeed."

"I can believe that from the little I've seen of him, Mary. But Jim doesn't have the inner drive to get somewhere like David does. I think all he sees before him is people who lean heavily on him and as I saw just now, I can see it's a pretense.

Mary, I'm afraid he'll overstress himself. Some people are just not equipped to handle it. Look what he's been through in the past few months."

"I know and I agree. James has pushed too hard already. I probably shouldn't tell you this, but you should know. Clive told me James had a cot put in his office, so when you're away he can stay overnight and work."

"Damn it, Mary, that's what I mean. I don't think he can handle this. From what David told me, it was the stress of their father dying as he did that caused Jim to escape the country. We can't let that happen again, for Jim or the company."

"Can't you talk to him?"

"I don't know, I was away and didn't fully appreciate how he was until I watched him a little while ago."

"Then talk to James and I'll speak to David, see if he can suggest anything helpful."

"Nothing personal, Mary, but I don't think David's going to suggest anything helpful."

Mary took a few steps to leave then came back and took Daphne's hand. "I know what you're saying, Daphne, and you're one of the few people who see his faults. Yet I'm his wife, I'll always remain loyal to him. And another reason is because his drive will help our country. Having said that, what I don't care for is the way he uses people. You know, the way he glad hands everyone, makes them feel they're one of his best friends, then casts them adrift when he doesn't need them. Of course I won't say anything, that's David, and it's not my place."

"Not your place? My God Mary, you're his wife! Why isn't it your place?"

"I'll confess something, Daphne, something I know you won't take further. When I met David, I was young and thought he was a god, a lesser one to be sure, nevertheless a god. When he asked my parents for my hand, I was ecstatic, even though my parents knew I was marrying below my station…"

"Below your station? What does that mean?"

Mary smiled. "Let's just say I have a lineage that dates quite a bit further back than William the Norman, now known as the Conqueror."

Daphne smiled in return. "I'm not too knowledgeable on

British nobility, but that sounds impressive enough for me, should I curtsy?"

Mary laughed. "Please don't, Daphne. People are watching and I do try to stay humble. Anyway, I'm sure my title is one of the reasons David married me. I don't mean to imply our marriage is not all right, it's just that, with David, his career is paramount. Everything revolves around him and his wants. For some unfathomable reason, he thinks it's his God given right."

"And you go along with that?"

"He's my husband, it's my duty. Don't get me wrong, as you can see, my life is not all that difficult."

"Mary, I won't say anything more, other than if I ever marry, I won't refer to my marriage as not all that difficult."

"That surprises me, Daphne. Look what's happened to you, and you're not even married."

"What are you saying, look what's happened to me?"

"You've just explained how you don't think James can handle the pressure, but think back a few months. You and James climbed together and had a great time in Austria. Now the world has turned upside down for both of you. Even though it's horridly cold, I'll bet Jim hasn't even mentioned about a climb, or even a little hike, has he?"

"No, I'll admit he hasn't. You know, I gave a lot of thought to this very thing when I was up to Windermere. You'll probably think me selfish, but I'm not the type to stand by quietly like a good woman and let Jim drive himself into the ground."

"That's not selfish, you're protective. But what can you do, Daphne? James gets intense. You think you can get him to pace himself? Because I doubt it."

"I don't know, although I'll give it the old college try. So believe me Mary, something or somebody is going to give."

It was near Midnight. The months had trudged their twelve steps to become the old year. It was a year filled with fear, hope, despair, and finally, a fragile peace. As the chimes counted down the seconds, Royce stood beside Daphne to watch the people. The laughter was a bit more raucous, and modestly more liquor consumed than previous New Year's, yet the guests could be forgiven. It was as though they knew blackness; a Danse

Macabre, was on the horizon. They would soon join that dance.

* * *

New Year's Eve, 1938:

The last year of peace Europe would know for seven years. An inferno of terror and death hid in the shadows of the New Year, waiting for the spark to ignite the fire, a fire which would consume empires and dictatorships, the good, the bad…and the innocent.

At the end, generations of warrior and citizen would slumber beneath the geometric patterns of white stones. And after them, the untold millions of the expendables—at rest forever in unmarked graves.

Chapter 17

NEW YEARS DAY, 1939:
David Royce looked over the words he had written in his diary to summarize the year.

Sunday, 1st of January, 1939.

Phenomenal growth the past year. Military contracts driving the company to success. After conversations at my luncheon with General Alcott, Admiral Marling and Trevor Archer in Military Procurement, we'll be one of the top three military contractors this year. We are already the foremost machine tool and bearing company in the country, so most of the manufacturing concerns must come to us or go to the States, which is more costly and time consuming. This must gall them. I have control over every one of their products that need bearings. So by controlling the supply to them it means they must subcontract some of their production orders to me. Their fault. They slept and allowed the specifications to match Royce Bearings only, and there's no way around the specs. They don't know it's a new way of doing business. They don't know who the real key players in the military are and now it's too late for them to find out. I've them in a bind. Five years of listening, kowtowing, and giving product, gifts, and dinners to the powers that be and the military has at last brought success.

James is doing a good job. Finally working hard for a change. Bet Daphne's upset. No carefree squandered life for the two of them now. I'll keep him buried to his ears with work. She'll smarten up someday then we'll really see where I come in. One thing to take care of though-my employees is starting to rally around James. I'll see to it this attitude changes. I put this all together and even the managers James hired are going to understand who owns the company. This is David Walker Royce

Limited, My name, my company! The future is mine. Can't wait for the changes this year.

He locked the hasp, and then slid the diary to the back of the hidden drawer in his desk. It was all going to plan.

Royce went to work on New Year's Day, before Daphne woke and could speak with him about her concerns. Determined to get how she felt out in the open, she made sandwiches and drove to the empty company offices. After a call to Royce, the guard at the gate accompanied her to the main office. She was allowed to remain in the antechamber and the guard stayed with her until Royce arrived.

After the guard left and she opened the sandwiches, Royce still seemed detached, although it didn't take him long to see she had something on her mind.

"You're warm under the collar Daphne, what is it?"

She had points to make, now suddenly gone. "I'm surprised you noticed. So *you* tell me Jim, what's going on?"

"I don't follow you, Daphne, what's wrong?"

"This sounds like a question period with no answers."

He said nothing, waited for her to sort out her thoughts.

"Jim, things have changed from the way we were."

"Things have changed, or you've changed?"

"Christ, another question! How dense can you be, Jim? You're the one who's changed here."

"Me?"

Daphne warmed up. "Yes you, you blockhead. You've got nothing on your mind but work. I can see you when we're at home by the fire, mentally on some problem. You even talk about it in your sleep. This is New Year's Day and still you get up and go to work before I even wake up to wish you a Happy New Year."

"We did that last night."

"You're missing the damn point! Even when you met me here, you had something else on your mind, and of all things, I heard you've a cot in your office so you can work overnight when I'm not at home. You might just as well sleep here even when I am home, for all the company you are."

It definitely was not all she had to say, still, she had

273

his attention. "Daphne, you're right, I admit it. It's not you or me right now, it's just that there's work that must be done."

"I understand that, but if you don't pace yourself you'll burn out on the treadmill people tell me you're on. You've got to have time for yourself, for us. You must know that."

"I know what you're saying, there's simply too much to be done and too little time."

"You're repeating yourself, Jim. They got along just fine when you were gone."

"That's exactly the problem, Daphne. They didn't get along just fine without me. Everything was hit or miss, without method. Other than bearing manufacture, there wasn't a solitary design or quality assurance program that would guarantee components would interface one unit to the next. Almost every part has to be re-milled, filed, or hammered in to fit. Let me explain so you can understand. Let's say we have a transmission gear assembly in the field that fails. We cannot guarantee the part we send as a replacement will fit the base cast as it should."

"So, what do they do if it doesn't?"

"The company sends field technicians with four or five units—that is if we have them—and hope one will work."

"That's crazy."

"Yes it is, Daphne! Crazy, costly and terribly inefficient. In the past, the company made so much profit on the original equipment they could afford it. Not in this day. Speed and cost justification have taken hold."

"So what have you done to correct the problem?"

"Nothing that hasn't been done in other companies. In an American book I read through years ago called *Conformity in Manufacturing Production*, it states the processes, each step required, so that every part, every component, will fit from one unit to the next, anywhere in the system. Conformity is a key word and the American's do it all the time, they started it with rifles as far back as their Civil War. We, and by that I mean most of England and Europe, are far behind the Americans, it's lamentable. I visited an American Company over here and couldn't believe how far ahead they are in mass production. Aside from our handmade Rolls Royce engines, I was humiliated at how outdated our manufacturing and quality base is. And it's the same in Europe. America is a production colossus."

"Of course we are, but look at the size and resources of the United States compared to Britain."

Royce smiled. Daphne, for all her love of England, was still proudly American.

"That's got a lot to do with it, yes, but it's their efficiency and drive that's key. That's what I'm working to implement, but it's got to start from the initial design. It's a fight and terribly wearisome with so many people dragging their feet."

"And the reason for that is…?"

Royce put his head down, staring at the floor. "I guess in a word, it's craftsmen."

"I don't follow."

"It's most difficult to say this, but the company has…too many old world craftsmen as managers. By that I mean they think nothing of the hours spent to finish anything. They have pride in their work and God, it's admirable, but we can't afford the time pride takes, only Rolls Royce can."

"My God, Jim, how you sound like your brother."

He stood. She could see he was upset. "Daphne, I've seen some of the Top Secret reports out of the continent, so I don't care who you think I sound like. There's a job to do, and I'm the only one here who can do it. So if you'll excuse me, I've got to get back to work."

"You're dismissing me? I had enough of that from you in Austria! Who the devil do you think you are?"

"I didn't mean it that way Daphne, it's just that what I accomplish today means the men will be able to start first thing tomorrow."

"Right and tomorrow there'll be something you have to do for the next day, then the day after that. And that's how it's going to be. Isn't it?"

"I don't know. Look, let's talk tonight when I get home."

"When will that be? I really don't feel like a chat at eleven o'clock at night."

"I'll try to get back sooner."

She was as upset as he was, there was a difference however, and she knew where their conversation would lead and tried to head it off.

"Jim, listen to what I'm saying. You'll wear yourself down. This is only the start and already you're burning out. You must pace yourself, you've *got* to pace yourself, or you won't last! Then where will the company be? You're not one of your fancy ball bearings that never wear out, you know."

She saw him smile at the remark and hoped it would ease the mood. After intentionally starting the argument by saying he sounded like David, she now tried to cool things off. Backing down was new to her, having never done it. Then again, she had ever really loved anyone before—was that what love meant? Back down, hold things within? Whatever the reason, she didn't like holding her tongue. It wasn't in her temperament and she wondered how long it would last.

Royce broke the silence. "Tell you what, Daphne, you have a point. If you have two scotches with a little ice, ready at seven, I'll definitely be home."

"Fair enough Jim, I'll cook up a little something too."

"Why don't you stop by Ravensmoor on the way home and ask Chef Amanda who she would recommend as a cook for us and a maid also."

Daphne looked at him with a questioning smile. "You are trying to tell me something about how I cook and dust?"

"No, no, only trying to help you out. But then again, I've never really seen you dust."

Just after seven, she saw the headlights come down the drive and disappear into the garage. Royce came into the house shivering as he took off his coat.

"What's the matter? The Bentley didn't heat the car all the way from the plant?"

"It wasn't that. I stopped at Ravensmoor to see David."

"Ah, this sounds of interest, tell me more."

"Well, I gave what you said some thought, and you're right. I'm not as strong as a ball bearing, and if I do wear out that won't help the company one bit."

"Fine, but you might want to give a little thought to yourself as well as the company. So, tell me, you talked to David about this, how'd that go?"

"Not too well. He felt I've a lot of ground to make up. You

know, all the time I'd been away and now, this is his words, now I've already decided to take it easy again."

"God, he's an obnoxious bastard when he wants to be. In fact, even when he doesn't want to be, he can be an obnoxious bastard. So tell me, was anything settled?"

"For this war emergency mode we're in, I told him I would put in sixty hours a week, Sundays off. He finally gave in, what else could he do? But, and you won't like this, he has two major projects for the RAF. I can't tell you about them, but I agreed to get them designed, prototyped and have Clive get them into production within three weeks."

"Which means what?"

"I'll be using the cot."

"Blast it, Jim! Again, you're too hard on yourself."

"If you knew what it was all about you'd understand."

"My understanding doesn't matter. It's you that matters."

"I'm ready to agree but…"

"Jim, I watched you at the party for the managers. To say the least, you weren't relaxed. You weren't the person I knew, you were edgy. It was noticeable; you still don't want people around you if you can possibly help it."

"You're right in all respects. But I'll just have to work through that."

"Okay Jim, if that's the way it's got to be, let's change the subject. I've decided to go down to the London house tomorrow. At the New Year's luncheon, I met Lady Jane Sommers, who was a friend of mother's, and she had offered to contact some of mothers other friends to set up a sort of get together in her memory. I knew you're always busy so I contacted Lady Jane this afternoon and said I'd be down for a few days if that was fine with her. So you can work your dupa off and not worry about me, although I'll probably worry about you…"

He interrupted, "What's dupa mean?"

"It's an expression I learned from some people I used tohang about with. Figure it out. Just let me mention one other thing, Jim. Not once, since I've been back, or even before I went to the States, have you mentioned climbing again."

"Well, Daphne, you'll have to admit, it's been beastly cold."

"You know what I mean. It won't be that long before the

weather breaks, so you'd better think about it."

"I promise I'll give it thought."

For now, stalemate. Royce could work as much as he wanted while Daphne was in London. She would spend some time with her mother's old friends and worry about him. Not a good trade off, she thought. In fact, not a trade at all.

* * *

Lady Jane Allen-Sommers, now Jane to Daphne, was the perfect hostess. Her chauffeur picked Daphne up in Belgravia and delivered her to The Mount, Lady Jane's winter estate in the London borough of Haverling. The estate encompassed a goodly area of the town of Raynham, with the Tudor style home isolated inside one thousand three hundred acres of forested knolls and valleys. Known for its gardens, Lady Jane allowed tours six days a year for the benefit of Britain's garden clubs and veteran's days. Other than those six social events, few friends found themselves invited through the iron gates since Lord Sommers' death in 1936.

Lady Jane had asked Daphne to stay for three days. The first day to show her around Haverling and plan for the service for Daphne's mother. Then, on the second day, hold the service and meet some of her mother's, and Lady Jane's, friends. The third day would be casual. The two of them would have breakfast together before Daphne would be chauffeured back to Belgravia.

It was at tea with the ladies at The Mount, after her mother's memorial service when Daphne once more caught sight of Lady Jane's son Kenneth.

He came through the French doors at the rear of the estate.

At first, his appearance nearly comical. Still in his flight suit, windblown black hair, crease rings from flying goggles around his eyes, and of course, a white scarf about his neck tucked carelessly into his flying jacket.

Kenneth smiled, surprised, nodding to her, and then went over to kiss his mother. Daphne felt a chill. He wasn't comical she realized, he was debonair. In fact, as she smiled at him, the words smashing, elegant, and handsome fit nicely.

His black eyes sparkled when he came over and took her

hand. "Hello again, Daphne, I'm terribly sorry about your mother's passing. She was a wonderful woman. Meeting you at the New Year's party so stunned me, my mind went blank."

She grinned. "I'll ignore that. But thank you for your kindness. I didn't know you knew her."

"Oh yes, quite well, through my mother of course."

Kenneth said nothing more, and for something more to say, Daphne commented he looked as if he just stepped out of a motion picture film.

His answer startled her. "Out of a movie? God no, I've just stepped out of an airplane, that's why I look so smudged."

"What do you mean? You came from an airfield like this?"

He walked her over to the French doors, and directed her eyes through the glass. There, a few yards away, sat an airplane.

"What on earth…?"

"Well, as you can see, that's a plane. Actually, a Gloster Gladiator biplane. She's the last model of RAF twin wing biplanes. We've switched to monoplanes, that is, single wing design. I use this one to bump around to different RAF stations."

"I don't follow, how did you get it there?"

"Why I flew her in. You didn't hear me because my mother doesn't like the radial engine's exhaust racket when she has guests, so I switch off and glide in. It's really quite simple if you know what you're about."

"There's room to land?"

"Oh yes, and for takeoffs of course. Years ago, Father had some trees removed down the field, over there where the land drops off. There's no problem, even when we have a little crusty snow, such as now, I have no concern."

The ladies were about to gather around and Daphne could see Kenneth was not at ease. He begged off to clean up and become more presentable. The women went back to their tables disappointed.

He returned in black slacks, light blue shirt, and linen dinner jacket. At the collar of the shirt was a dark blue Paisley cravat. He was damn presentable now, Daphne reflected. Just as he was in his flight suit. He motioned her into another room.

"What's up, Kenneth?"

"It's just those women. I'm awkward with them every time I

come here and don't know they're about."

"That's the cross you have to bear. But can you blame them? You being so devilishly attractive."

"Do you feel that way?"

"Of course I do. I'm all aflutter."

"Didn't that Scarlett woman say something along that line in that movie last year?"

"I think you're right. Vivian Leigh must have rubbed off on me. I guess I'm just not original."

"I think you're the most original woman I have ever met. In fact, there's little question they must have thrown away the mold when they made you."

"Please Kenneth, save those stories and use them on the younger women."

"I already have."

That was so unexpected she burst out laughing. Kenneth joined in. She wiped the tears from her eyes and asked if he had much luck with women, using such outdated prose.

"I must say a damn sight more than with you, Daphne."

They laughed together once more, and then she gave him a serious look. "Please understand, Kenneth, I find you most attractive and you do seem a pleasant, articulate chap. However, I'm too old for you, and I'm not available, it's that simple."

"Mother said you were twenty-eight or nine. I'll be twenty-five this year, that's only a three year difference, next to nothing in this day and age."

"True, except women marry older men."

"That's only a fact, not a reason. Now hear me out, Daphne. You know all those women in the next room? Almost all of them are widows. You know why? Because they married older men. So, the solution to fewer widows is obvious, they should marry younger men. I rest my case."

"Very good point and I don't believe I can argue with it. However, I'll bet some of them lost husbands in the war. And another thing, it's not conventional."

"You don't strike me as one to give a fig about convention."

"Well, I often don't. But why do you say that? You don't know me, or is it because when I met you at Ravensmoor I said I'm involved with another man?"

"I believe that stuck in my mind."

"Well, let me be clear. I love, live, cohabitate if you wish, with one man."

"Wonderful! Someone who states her mind without any insincere or discomfiting qualms."

"You don't have trouble with my flouting England's Victorian antiquated mores?"

"Not at all, I love women who love men."

"You're missing the key word, Kenneth. So please make a note of it. I said I love *one* man."

"At present, that may be. But we shall see, Daphne."

"No, Mister Sommers, we shall not see, now let's change the subject. How does a man who is nearly only twenty-five become a Squadron Leader? What rank is that anyway?"

"Answering your second question is easy. Squadron Leader is equal to a Sandhurst Major. On the former question, I'll give you the short version, and omit as much as possible, stories of my heroic escapades."

"Heroic escapades are fine Ken. However, let's just omit your other escapades."

"Difficult, they seem to be tied together, although I'll do my best to stay on the subject."

"See that you do."

"May I start now?"

"Yes, please do."

"I'll begin. In the Great War, Father was a flyer with the 17th Aero Squadron of the Royal Flying Corps, before it was renamed the Royal Air Force. He flew a biplane, a Sopwith Camel, and was a triple Ace, which means he shot down at least fifteen enemy planes.

"At times, he flew with Albert Ball and Mick Mannock. They, and Father, naturally, were my heroes. After the war, Father bought two surplus biplanes. One, his old Camel, patched up everywhere from bullet holes, and the other a Hawker Hart. If you would like to go into the wood with me, I'd be happy to take you to the hanger he had built to store them."

"I'll pass on that, go on."

"As you wish. So, let me see. When I was three, father took me up in the Camel, he said he was a Camel Driver and she would do a hundred miles an hour. I was captivated. I can still remember mother's tirade, I should say tirades, over his doing this because the flights never stopped and I never tired of them. By the time I was ten I had quite good control of the Camel, which was something, because it had malicious right torque from its radial engine and could be quite a piggy little aircraft to handle. When I was twelve, I could fly the Hawker Hart as well and passed the basic Aviation and Navigation tests. My father's money, contacts and his Distinguished Flying Crosses got me into the RAF College, Cranwell, when I was fourteen."

He stopped for a moment, seemingly embarrassed.

Daphne cocked her head. "Surely you're not suffering a modest moment, Kenneth."

"Me, modest? Not in the least. Yet somehow you've made me self-conscious, as if I've over-answered your question."

"No, you haven't. When you get overly windy I'll let you know, don't worry yourself on that point."

"Very well then, I'll be immodest. I was top of my graduating class in aeronautics, and then and now there are only a handful of flyers who could match me even in that Gladiator biplane out there and certainly not in my new Mark I Spitfire.

So, if you're still paying attention, Daphne, the heroics that brought me to my lofty rank include preventing the encirclement of an army company in Mesopotamia and saving the life of a General, Sir Miles Alcott, in Iraq. That was in '35. There are many other incredible adventures. However, perhaps a newly found modesty does prevent me from continuing. I don't want you to be excessively impressed, and like so many other women, throw yourself into my arms."

"Thank you, that saves me from making a fool of myself in front of all these women. But tell me, I still can't believe you acquired your rank just from those piddling little events."

"Piddling? Well, another reason is, the RAF must expand as fast as possible, and experienced pilots, pilots with my expertise, are in short supply. So here I am...we're up to date."

Daphne was unexpectedly serious. "The RAF must expand because they believe there will be a war?"

"Yes."

The pleasure went out of the banter. "Do you think so?"

"Of course, no question."

"How do you feel about that?"

"What do you mean, feel? This is what I've trained for. If it comes, I'm ready."

"Are you ready to get killed?"

"That's not in my cards."

"You might give it some thought."

"There's really no sense in giving it thought now, is there? That would be wasted time. There's nothing I can do about it. Please understand, Daphne. My mother thinks I'm a rake, a womanizer. I admit that's a bit of my life. You can think that too, if you wish. However, I have twenty years flying experience, almost all in fighters. I'm a natural, although I don't depend on simply that. I study everything aeronautical, every government report, every periodical and that includes other countries. As I said before, with the Supermarine Spitfire I got last year, I can outfly, and outthink most anyone. Father taught me aerial combat from the time I was seven. I've studied tactics practically all my life. I developed programs—with my Father and other former Great War pilots of course—for single or battle formation combat the likes of which no one's conceived. Naturally, the Germans have developed similar programs, but what we've devised is better. That will be proven."

"But, Kenneth, I've read Charles Lindbergh has written performance report on the German Messerschmitt and he said it's better than any other fighter aircraft in the world."

"You're quite well read, Daphne, you surprise me."

"Why, because I read more than cinema magazines?"

"Not at all, but I doubt if one person in ten-thousand, excepting RAF and Luftwaffe personnel, know he wrote that. Nevertheless, the canard of his point is that he's never flown a Spitfire."

"I didn't know that part. So, you give me your side. He hasn't flown a Spitfire, have you flown a Messerschmitt?"

"No, and I'll give you that. Yet I've devoured Lindbergh's Performance Report on the ME109Bf, and I've seen some purloined build sheets. Both the Spitfire and ME109 have shortcomings. But I know how to beat the 109. Fighter Command agrees, and I lecture on my theories. So, all I need is to prove them, and that time will come."

She watched his movements as he spoke. He wasn't the impetuous person she met at Ravensmoor. He was sure inside, no longer filled with careless bravado. He defined his version of the truth, which as she listened, could very well be the truth. He was still young, but quite confident, sure of the facts as he saw them. For a moment it took her breath away. If he spoke to other women like this, it was little wonder they fell into his arms. The tragic part? He was young and needed a war to prove his theories…and his worth.

As if reading her thoughts, he held her with his stare. "I guess I got carried away. For some reason you brought it out of me without effort. I wanted you to comprehend how I feel. Please believe I've never spoken of this to any woman—and doubt I will ever again."

"I believe you, Kenneth, and God, I wish you luck."

Daphne could see he seriously pondered something else. She remained quiet.

"Tell me, Daph, have you ever flown?"

She smiled when he called her Daph, only her brother called her that, and then only occasionally.

"Yes, I have."

"Really? When?"

"I came back from the States in a Pan Am Clipper, and an RAF bomber."

"The Clipper's not flying. That's simply a flying guesthouse and a bomber's a bomber. I mean wind in your face flying."

What was he up to? She had to know. "Why do you ask?"

"Well from what mother tells me, you stay here tonight and go home tomorrow. Tomorrow I have to go up to Lincolnshire early. Why don't you go there with me? We can be back in time for you to go home."

"Lincolnshire? That's too long a drive and back."

"You're not following me. We'll fly up and back, little over an hour each way."

"I…I don't think so, Kenneth."

He could see her vacillate. "You'll be home in plenty of time. Anyway, what's the rush to get home? Someone awaits in Belgravia?"

"Prying are we? But no, there isn't anyone there."

"Have a cat that needs to be fed?"

She laughed. "No, I don't."

"Then come with me. I have to give an hour's lecture at the RAF College, up near Sleaford, then pop on over and see a Bomber Command Captain. We'd be home before you know it. You'll love it. This Gladiator has a second seat and we'll get you into a warm flight suit, fleece boots, gauntlets, and you won't even need goggles as the cockpit is enclosed."

"Then why did you have goggles when you flew in?"

"Oh, I slide the canopy back because I like the rush of air past me. What do you say Daph? Will you come?"

She wanted to very much, although it wasn't the thing to do.

"Ok I'll come, but I want goggles too."

"Thank you, dear, Daphne."

"Don't 'dear Daphne' me. Go entertain the ladies before I change my mind."

"Your wish is my command."

"I'll see that you remember that."

Lady Jane was horrified the next morning. She was emphatic that no one should go higher than they're willing to fall. Kenneth was ecstatic. He had the most wonderful, beautiful woman he had ever known ready to fly with him. Daphne was nervous, knew she shouldn't go, but felt it was no more dangerous than a handhold in a cliff, hanging on for dear life.

He had taken a flight suit and boots from the plane and she changed in her room and with them on, waddled back to Ken and his mother. It was difficult for them to suppress their laughter.

"Think this is funny, do you? Kenneth, get me into that airplane before I change my mind."

It was an effort under pressure for Ken. He had never helped a woman into a cockpit before and he struggled to find regions to place his hands to buckle her up without incurring her wrath. The straps, fitted for a much larger person required readjusting and awkward without touching her in challenging locales.

"Careful with those chest straps, Squadron Leader. Your mother told me about you."

"Being as careful as I can, Miss Elliot."

He was however, extremely nervous. Though giving him a stern look, she laughed inwardly. Even in the cold, he was about to perspire. After another severe glance at him, she took pity and feigned impatience. "For God's sake, give me those straps! I'll sort them out a damn sight quicker than you."

She had tied her hair back using a white scarf with green polka dots, so the lightweight Airtex flying helmet, with earphones, fit easily. He plugged in the lead and showed her how to toggle the microphone when she wanted to speak. Although uneasy, she was ready.

As Kenneth walked around for the preflight check, one of Lady Jane's male servants wheeled out an RAF generator and plugged the cable into the engine's power port.

Kenneth climbed onto the wing step and spoke to Daphne. "This aircraft has an electric start, 840 horsepower, Bristol radial engine with no mufflers so when we fire up things will get noisy. When we roll, I'll run us up to the house and come about for takeoff. There will be a racket as I bring up the revs and as we start the takeoff it's going to get a bit bumpy, the ground is frozen, so we'll probably slew about a bit. Don't worry and don't be anxious."

"I wasn't until you brought all that up."

He put on his best confident smile, his hand on her shoulder. "Oh, one more thing. Don't touch those pedals on the floor or the stick, even when they move."

Jumping back to the ground, he finished his preflight, drained water off the petrol, then climbed into his seat for cockpit check while strapping in. Moving the control stick and pedals, he twisted about, checking the controls. Satisfied, he signaled for generator start and in a few moments, he shouted clear and pressed the ignition switch. Turning slowly, the engine then coughed as it ignited. He leaned out the petrol mixture as the engine roared to life, expelling oil laden carbon monoxide.

Daphne closed the canopy to escape the fumes, while feeling the Gladiator vibrate. Damn! She realized this is no Pan Am Clipper and could be one of her bigger mistakes.

Kenneth signaled for generator disconnect and the man moved away with it. The engine's revs increased slightly as Kenneth listened intently. Satisfied with the sound and the instrument readouts, he brought the engine back to idle and signaled again to remove the chocks from in front of the wheels. This done and the man well out of the way, the plane slowly bumped along the crusted snow toward the house. He kicked the rudder over to turn the plane and face the homemade runway. He gave his mother a wave, and saw in Daphne's face in her forward mirror and her wide, green eyes. He fell in love. He clicked the microphone and spoke. She jumped.

"You okay up there?"

Her voice had a slight waver. "More or less, but rather less than more. Shouldn't you be in front?"

"No, we do it this way. Don't worry, Daph, it will get noisy and bumpy, then it's a piece of cake once we're off the ground. There's little wind so we'll have a really smooth flight."

Actually, he knew the takeoff would not to be a piece of cake. He wanted to take off into a prevailing wind, but the problem was there wasn't any. He kept the wheel brakes on as the Bristol IX engine revved as high as he could allow and, with the wheels skidding along the crusted snow, he signaled thumbs up to Daphne. The brakes released, the biplane slithered forward and gathered speed as fast as Kenneth could control it.

Daphne saw the opening in the trees ahead and froze as the bumps and unsteady rush of the aircraft brought the aircraft closer, ever closer to the tree line. She closed her eyes. It flashed across her mind; how would Jim react when he read she was found amidst the wreckage of an RAF biplane? Beside her, the body of a handsome, heroic, fighter pilot. Oh well, as Kenneth said, no sense in worrying over it. She'd be dead.

The racket of engine exhaust was not quite as loud and the jolting had stopped. She opened her eyes and saw only blue sky past the wing struts. She looked in her mirror and saw Kenneth smiling at her. He was on the wireless about a flight plan and estimated arrival.

"How do you feel, Daph?"

"I've still got my breakfast."

"Excellent! See, it wasn't so bad, was it?"

"I'm saving a few choice words for you later."

He laughed. "I don't doubt that. I'm going to drop the wings slightly so you can have a better view. We're at approximately four hundred feet."

The view, she had to admit, was an experience, and although restricted by the biplane's wings struts and wires, the rolling English countryside glistened with a touch of frosted snow. Fences and dividing walls outlined each plot of land, and then fir trees along the ridges, green against the white. He left her to her thoughts until she clicked her mike, "It's very nice, thank you."

Over the roar of the engine, they chatted on aimlessly mentioning people they both knew, places they'd been, what they enjoyed.

"So, you're a climber, where?"

"Some in the French Alps, although mostly in Austria."

"Austria? Recently? Have any trouble getting out? I hear the Nazis are even giving us Brits a hard time now."

"I got out all right, although Jim didn't." She wished she had bitten her tongue. She'd now given Kenneth a name.

"Aha…Jim. And who, may I ask, is this Jim?"

Strange she thought, Kenneth was smiling about it, didn't seem upset at her mention of Jim. "You know who I mean. The person I told you I was involved with."

"Ah yes, Daph, I forgot. The person you're involved with. Such an all-encompassing word. *Involved*. Tell me about your Jim, I'll try to be more like him."

"Oh good Lord, no, you couldn't. The two of you are poles apart." Especially as far as women were concerned, she thought.

"Why do you say that?"

"Well, for one thing, he's a climber, you're not."

"Well, a climber takes chances, right? A pilot takes chances too. So there, point, counterpoint."

"Not really. I'll bet all your chances are calculated. With Jim—other than a wonderful climbing technique—he just reacts too things, and that gets him in trouble."

She thought of his reactions to the four Germans, his attempt to get out of Austria, and then his run through the woods to shoot at an assassin. All reaction, no first thoughts.

"Give me an example, Daph."

"No. I'm sorry I brought him up, let's drop the subject."

"Okay, I'll do some aerobatics instead."

"If you do and I live, you won't."

"Lucky me then, it's too late to do them, we're above the RAF College."

He toggled the transmitter to ground control. A great looping turn, which made her swallow hard, lined them up on the runway. The tires touched once, the biplane coasted, then braked to a stop. He taxied to the apron, spun the biplane 180 degrees, and shut the engine down. As he jotted in his flight book, the ground crew ran to chock the wheels. After a cockpit checkout, he took off his helmet, stood on the aircraft's step, and turned to help Daphne.

"Leave me be, Ken, I'll get out on my own."

He was troubled. "Are you mad at me?"

"Not at all. I'm assuming there's a ladies' powder room somewhere, where I can freshen up?"

"Well, there's kind of an, ah, universal lavatory in Ops, Operations Flight Control."

Off they went, a sight to behold. Squadron Leader K. V. Sommers, whom everyone knew, and some nondescript cadet off to Operations. The cadet in an ill-fitting flight suit, collar turned up, still in boots, flight helmet and small kit. When they walked in, Daphne saw the sign she wanted, checked to see it was empty, walked in, and locked the door.

Five officers, three Flight Sergeants, and seven cadets were in Ops. All of those at hand knew, or heard of, Squadron Leader Sommers. To the Cadets, an aura surrounded him. To his peers and superiors, admiration, respect and, most of all, friendship. They knew, as he had said to Daphne, he could outfly, outthink and, they truly believed, he would outfight every German flyer when war came. On top of all this, there was not one among them who did not in the least doubt he was a womanizer. His reputation preceded him, and at this very moment, was about to be confirmed.

The door to the rest room opened, she let it slam closed. Heads turned. Daphne smiled. Eyes fixated. Jaws went slack.

She wore dark green shoes, light gray slacks, green belt, and a loose white blouse. Her auburn hair pulled back, tied with her white and green polka dot scarf. A small gold pin and gold wristwatch completed her outfit. The men, caught unawares, fell speechless, transfixed. Her eyes smoldered, looking up to

Kenneth. After they caught their breaths, every man there recognized Ken Sommers' reputation was rightfully earned.

Daphne walked up to Kenneth, slipping her hand into his. "Would you please introduce your friends to me, Ken dear?"

As flustered as the rest, Kenneth worked through the introductions. He wondered what in blazes had come over her. She was enchanting everyone. Not in an opaque, hollow-headed way, just delightful, interested in their comments, laughing with their stories. By the time the Cadet lecture was to start, they couldn't apologize enough for her not being allowed to sit in.

"Top Secret, my dear, terribly sorry."

She sat in the lounge, her every wish attended to by ground personnel as she thumbed through the Air Force List book.

"Excuse me, Miss Elliot. I'm Air Commodore Cave's temporary assistant, Group Captain, Godfrey Roxby. I just wanted to stop by and tell you how much your visit here has lifted morale."

"Why thank you, Group Captain, it's my pleasure. Won't you sit down?"

Roxby sat and savored the view, then took the Air Force List from her hands and thumbed through the pages until he handed the book back, opened to one page. There was a picture of six smiling airmen under the caption:

Awarded Air Force Cross: Left to right. RAF Squadron Leaders, Baynes MacDonald, Francis Beamish, Wilfred Freebody, Kenneth Sommers, Ian Grant (RN) & Arthur Loton.

"A feather in Kenneth's cap, Group Captain? What was the reason for this award?"

"Quite so, Miss Elliot, one of many feathers. This one for something he did over there in Spain's civil war. And please call me Maxie, it's short for my middle name."

"Thank you, Maxie, I will. Please call me Daphne. Tell me about him. Without any modesty whatsoever, Kenneth straight out says he's good, yet somehow it doesn't seem conceit, it just comes out openly, naturally."

"It's not conceit. When Ken says he's good, he's actually being modest. He's blessed with his father's genes and incredible talent. Yet at the same time, he doesn't simply settle for that. He does more than fly, he studies as much as any doctor or surgeon would to perfect their craft. He works with Squadron Leader, 'Sailor' Malan, and George Unwin. They're quite brilliant in developing theoretic combat programs, and then prove them under combat conditions with a cadre of the best pilots in the RAF as students."

An orderly arrived to top off her tea. She gave him a devastating smile. The orderly stumbled off.

"You were saying something about the best pilots, Maxie."

"Yes, well then, whether Sailor, Unwin, or Kenneth take the defensive or offensive role, they always win. I flew with Ken's father when we were with the 17th Aero Squadron in France. His father was an exceptional combat pilot, knew when to attack, when to consider withdrawal the better part of valor. As I say, Ken has his father's genes. At least part of them. He knows when to attack. Still, when a situation prudently calls for pulling back, he continues to attack. I admit it's a surprise and unnerves his opponent, but even in mock combat he assumes a calculated risk, so when..."

"Please excuse me, Maxie, but what I mean is what is he like as a person? Does he ever relax? His mother calls him a rake, a womanizer, and yet here he is a Squadron Leader at twenty-five and you speak so highly of him."

"Oh? You've met his mother, Lady Allen Sommers?"

"Maxie lets back up a bit and start over. My mother and I are old friends of Lady Jane. I met Kenneth at a New Year's party he and Lady Jane attended and we had a few words together. I met him again yesterday visiting at Lady Jane's home and, for some reason I've yet to fathom, I let him talk me into a flight up here. I don't know Kenneth other than that, which means I am not one of his women friends. I showed interest in him in front of the air men just to have a bit of fun and keep his image up. Not a thing more. I'm afraid it's my fault if you read more into the situation than is there, and I'm sorry."

Maxie was embarrassed. He had completely misread the situation. "Daphne, I do humbly apologize. I should have immediately gathered that when Ken showed up here with a woman, she must be someone exceptional. He had never brought anyone here before and, I might add, highly against regulations, so I should have known you were special. So please, again, accept my sincerest apology."

"Of course, say no more. I certainly didn't mean to embarrass you. I simply wanted to make myself clear. And please, don't mention this conversation to the Cadets. I don't wish to tarnish the Squadron Leader's reputation, at least with them. Now I have two questions, Maxie. If Kenneth has disregarded regulations, what happens now?"

"I look at it this way, Daphne. Operations will have recorded that a Cadet, in flight suit, with a Squadron Leader, arrived at this base in a Gloster Gladiator. I fully expect to see a Cadet, in flight suit, leave with a Squadron Leader. I imagine I've made myself clear, Miss Elliot?"

She gave him a lighthearted conspiratorial smile that warmed his day.

Maxie chuckled. "My Lord, Daphne. How you must get your way with us men. But now, what is your other question?"

"I admit an interest in knowing more about him. Is he the perfect person he appears, or is there a chink in his armor, something I can kid him over? Isn't that terrible of me to ask?"

Laughing, Maxie then sat back and seriously thought of the question. "I'm afraid you're out of luck. As a person, he's one of the most decent people I know. He has never let on how wealthy he is to anyone, and other than his father getting him into the College at age fourteen, every rank he's gained has been on merit, despite the politics and money that rear their ugly heads in the services. There's none of that with him. I'm proud to call him a friend, as well as a comrade in arms. I don't need to say more on that score.

"Looking at him strictly as a flyer, only a few people I know are his equal. One is Alex Henshaw, the first test pilot for the Spitfire. A wild man and magnificent flyer. However, he's a test pilot. That's how he takes his chances. He doesn't plan to be a fighter pilot such as Kenneth and Mungo-Park, Eric Locke, Doug Bader or George Unwin. Men like them live in rarefied air. Still, to stay with Kenneth, he does have one weakness and unless I miss my guess he'll soon have another."

Maxie had her attention, he hesitated before continuing. Talking privately about a pilot was not his norm. Yet, somehow, he felt it important for her to know. "This is no secret. Ken knows that one weakness is his tactical sequencers are too difficult and evolve too quickly for any other than the best pilots to grasp, much less execute. His reactions are faster than \the normal brain can think. If you follow that. That's a disadvantage when designing fighter curriculum because only pilots like the ones I mentioned can respond that rapidly. He's striving to back down the maneuvers so an average, but good fighter pilot can perform them. To him, doing that is like slow motion, it's difficult for him to change, although he tries."

"That's fascinating, and quite difficult for me to follow. About the other weakness you alluded to, Maxie?"

Maxie vacillated. "Speaking out of turn, I think…think mind you, it going to be…you."

"Me? What in heaven's name are you talking about?"

"Hear me out, Daphne. I've been in many social situations with Ken and I don't mean to imply he's indifferent to the women he's with. However, if they weren't there it wouldn't have bothered him. The difference is, in just the brief time I've seen him with you, he's another person. When you took his hand, his whole demeanor changed. He looks at you and it's almost like he's in awe, and worse, unsure. He's not used to that, and the fact he brought a woman here, so against regs and so unlike him, I don't know what else to think."

"And you consider that a weakness?"

"Of course. Without question."

"I think I know what you're driving at, although I'll still have to ask, why?"

"Frankly, he may have something or someone else on his mind. You can't have this in a fighter pilot. They must be focused on the hunt and the kill, if I may be so dramatic."

"I hope you're wrong in your assumptions, because there's someone else in my life and there really isn't room for another person. I don't expect to see Kenneth after I leave his mother's home later today."

"Then we'll just have to see, won't we."

"Now, that is strange, Kenneth said the same thing."

Back into her flight suit, slip into the Gladiator, run up the engine, roar down the dirt track and airborne. Not really enough time to talk as the ship went up to five hundred feet leveled off for a few minutes then began the descent onto another dirt strip at Pet Wood. Pet Wood, the handsome, rambling, private Tudor home was set among great oaks on the periphery of Lincolnshire and used as a billet for the Officers of 617 Squadron; flying Sterling bombers while they waited for the newer, four engine Avro Lancaster's.*

The Gladiator's wheels were chocked. Kenneth set the brakes and jumped out, the engine idling roughly. An officer walked over and shook Ken's hand before they walked away from the clatter.

With Wing Commander Gibson, of 617 Squadron, Kenneth reviewed a joint training program. This exercise, would use 617 bombers flying from France and Sommers' Spitfires, alerted and guided to intercept by the RF Chain Home System. It was only another of the scores of tests for Group fighter pilots and Chain Home personnel.

Gibson was aware of the plan and made a few revisions from a bomber's perspective. For this exercise, he planned to have his Squadron's flight plan initiate well to the south east with the System off until the last few minutes to landfall without anyone alerted. Including Kenneth Sommers' 11 Group.

*Author's Note: In 1979, while traveling in England on our honeymoon, my wife and I stayed at Pet Wood, presently a hotel called Woodhall Spa. Not knowing its history, I wandered around and into its pub. It was dim, empty. Over the bar, I was surprised to see a tree trunk, which I recall as approximately 6 to 8 inches in diameter and 8 feet long. Further along, I found a plaque with a Wing Commander's picture and the name Guy Gibson. Under it, in bold letters were the words 'THE DAM BUSTERS'.

Their story of heroism in the Second World War: In 1940, nineteen, four-engine Avro Lancaster Bombers of 617 Squadron bombed three dams in the industrial Ruhr Valley, shutting down hydroelectric power to areas of Germany's war machine. Diving low at night across the lakes, the bombers dropped unique cylindrical, 'skipping' bombs, which impacted the top of the dams, sank to the bottom, and then pressure detonated. They destroyed the Moehne and Eder dams and severely damaged the Sorpe dam. Eight Lancaster's were lost, fifty-three men died, three taken prisoner. A movie was made of their exploits and a book on them is well worth reading.

The tree trunk I saw over the bar was impaled in the wing of a low flying, dam busting Lancaster when it returned to England.

The discussion over, a new conversation started with both men glancing over at Daphne. They walked over to the aircraft and, with hand signals, indicated for her to remove the flight helmet. As she opened the canopy, her auburn hair spilled over her flight suit and blew lightly in the prop wash. Guy reached up and shook her hand, nodded to Kenneth and walked away. As Kenneth dropped into the cockpit, he signaled for Daphne to replace her helmet and she spoke into the mike.

"What was that handshake all about?"

"Oh, just that Guy received a call from the RAF College and they said he should take a good look at you. Guy agreed with their estimate, and said to thank you."

"Men," she laughed, "you never change…thank goodness."

It made him laugh as the chocks were removed. The Gladiator bumped down the gravel strip, turned into the wind and roared down the runway. Gibson and Daphne gave parting salutes. Then Wing Commander Gibson turned his mind once more to the bomber vs fighter game.

"So, tell me about this Jim of yours."

"Trapped for an hour am I, until we get to your Mother's?"

"Or longer if you take a while. I can fly around in circles."

"I've already told you about him."

"No, all you've said is he overreacts, or acts without thought. I do the same when flying."

"I don't think it's the same kind of reaction, although the two of you are alike in one way, they say you're both geniuses."

"The nebulous 'they' say that about me, I don't. What is he a genius in?"

"The way I understand it, I guess you'd call it something like conceptual design and engineering."

"Really? To conceive and design something that's needed and functional *is* genius. He works up in Coventry?"

"Yes, at Royce Bearing, but now it's called D W Royce Limited, or something like that."

"David Royce's company? Christ, what a pompous arse. Him and his 'Sir David'. Everyone knows it was his father's title for Christ's sake."

"Don't make me laugh, Ken, although you hit the nail dead smack on the head."

"How does your Jim put up with him? I don't know a person who can stand David. If it wasn't for his company providing us with needed equipment, no one would give him a nod. How on earth does your Jim stand him?"

"Well, it's a unique situation. Jim is David's brother."

There was a slight drift in the biplane as Ken chuckled. "Christ, I hope he's not like David Royce or...hold on, Hold on—your Jim is James Royce. Now I know who you're talking about. He worked on the Merlin engine bearings and the prototype airfoil for the Hawker Hurricane and other things a few years back. Whoever said he was a genius is right. Wonderful designs, easy to manufacture, at least his part is. I'll be damned. Well, it's good to know who my competition is."

"Ken, there is no competition."

"We'll see."

"Again, Kenneth, no we won't."

Daphne had to straighten out the situation. She searched her mind for something more than to just keep saying no to his advances. She finally hit on an idea, which she hoped would put an end Ken's intentions. "I'll make a deal with you, Ken. I'll be your mistress if you stop flying."

He nearly choked on the word 'mistress', then baffled by the rest of the sentence. "What do you mean?"

"What do I mean? I thought you were supposed to be quick witted. I'm quite clear. If you don't fly, I'll be your mistress."

"That's not fair."

"What isn't fair? Flying is your first love. I don't intend to play second fiddle to anyone or any *thing*. That wouldn't be fair to me—you must see that—not fair at all."

He was silent for a moment, then went off on a different approach. "What would I have to give up just for you go out with me?"

She couldn't help her smile. "Nice try, Ken. No options. You fly, no Daphne."

"You knew I couldn't give up flying, didn't you? What if I had said yes?"

"The thought never crossed my mind."

"Then why did you make that kind of offer, or perhaps I should say, bogus offer?"

"To convince you to end the *us* you talk about once we land at your mother's house."

"I see, Daph. But you know, some day, when I'm all alone, and the world is cold, I will feel a glow just thinking of you."*

"Very nice sentiment, Ken. I assume you do know those words are from a song."

"Yes, I do. It's just they were better than anything I could ever make up."

"That's nice of you. Now land this damned plane before I get weepy."

He was the perfect gentleman. No show of emotion and courteous while he brought her suitcase to the car. He didn't ask, or offer, to drive her home to Belgravia. Heading to his plane, he gave her a smile, a quizzical smile she couldn't interpret.

For his part, Ken knew it was only the first round and felt he had done quite well. Daphne had gone flying with him and liked it. Once it sank in, she'd remember the time and understand why he loved to fly and she'd think back on it more with each memory. He was sure he'd see her again. It was his makeup.

He kissed his mother and climbed into the biplane, the engine still clattering roughly. Once again, he gunned the engine and roared down the lawn. He bent the Gladiator into a tight turn and saw Daphne still speaking with his mother by the Bentley. He swung in low and slow. As they waved, he held out Daphne's white and green polka dot scarf, and then brought the plane's nose up, pitched over into a full roll and faded from sight.

Lady Jane eyed Daphne. "Isn't that your scarf?"

"Yes it is and that darn son of yours has stolen it!"

"See Daphne, I told you before—he's up to no good."

"Confidence!" Ken chuckled. "That's all you need with flying and women. That, and skill."

Nevertheless, there is a lot of uncertainty with her.

*From the 1936 song, The Way You Look Tonight. Jerome Kern & Dorothy Fields.

Chapter 18

ENGLAND CONTINUED preparations for war with Germany and the first few days of January 1939 resembled the months preceding the New Year. There was, however, a new anger in the populace and Government against another, closer enemy. Sean Russell, Chief of Staff of the outlawed Irish Republican Army, and the IRA Army Council declared war on England. On 16 January, the IRA commenced a new sabotage campaign by exploding homemade bombs in London, Birmingham, Manchester and Alnwick.

Time magazine named Adolf Hitler, Man of the Year.

* * *

Hitler smiled on reading the news of the IRA bombings. He turned to face his visitor and commented that his agents in Ireland had done good work with the gullible Irish. None of Germany's assistance in Ireland would be traced back. Hitler also savored the fact he was Time's Man of the Year. Time had not shown him frontal, only a line drawing from the rear, playing, what Time called, an organ of hate. "That doesn't matter," he barked, "wait until 1940! Then I'll be on every cover in full color!"

"Well Colonel Schmid, what have you found out?"

Schmid was quite uncomfortable. He wasn't sure how his information would be received or, in fact, if he should lay out everything he had learned. He could be stepping into a mine field. "My Führer, your Directive to me was to research the possibility of a super weapon, specifically the possibility of a bomb made from a process called nuclear fission. Theoretically, this concept holds possibilities. There have been a number of articles written which mix fact, conjecture and fantasy.

Compounding this, even the physicists I have spoken with have opposing views. However, although I admit to limited knowledge on the subject, I believe there is a potential here for the creation of such a weapon. A bomb, such as some envision, would be of tremendous, unbelievable explosive power. That is, if what they call a chain reaction, can be controlled and not blow up the very people who develop it along with the rest of us."

Hitler was pensive and stared out the window of his Reichskanzlei office in Berlin. One of his American agents had reported on an allegedly secret memo Albert Einstein had written to President Franklin Roosevelt about the possibility of an atomic type weapon and recommended—for safety's sake—the United States pursue the hypothesis.

Hitler contemplated the concept, although doubtful. "I don't think we will need something like that. Every nation will crumble around us simply from fear of our Panzers. Nevertheless, if we decide to, how long would it take to be developed?"

"It could be years."

"I don't possess that kind of patience. Why that long?"

"There is a massive amount of theoretical, scientific, technical, and construction work yet to be done and that creates a problem…"

Colonel Schmid hesitated. Hitler saw something was being kept from him and shouted. "What is your damn problem, Colonel?"

Officials in other rooms heard, and pitied Schmid.

"My Führer, it would seem the Gestapo may have been a little too efficient in ridding Germany and Austria of Jews and other undesirables. Some of the best scientists who worked in this discipline are gone. Men like Fermi from Italy, Einstein, Frish, the woman, Lise Meitner from Austria and a number of others have emigrated or escaped. Only one was caught, a chemist named Traube, but unfortunately he was executed by the Gestapo."

Hitler was incensed. "So what are you saying? There are no scientists left in this country that can do this?"

"Not that at all, my Führer. Although the best are gone, we still we still have Fritz Strassmann, who has done work on the bombardment of uranium with neutrons, and there's Otto Hahn.

"This Hahn person created a new scientific field called Applied Radiochemistry, and lectured in the United States. Unfortunately, he resigned from the Institute of Berlin in 1934 to protest the persecution of Jews. Of course, I assure you my Führer, there are other scientists we can track down. I just don't know their value as yet."

"What about this Strassmann?"

"He's little better than Hahn. In 1933 he resigned from the Society of German Chemists when it became controlled by one of our government departments."

The Führer turned to face Schmid, who wisely remained silent. "Remember this, Colonel. I gave you this project because of your organizational skills, not your scientific knowledge. You do this right and you will come into my inner circle, so listen to me carefully. First, we will take away the passports of those two and put them to work in the Kaiser Wilhelm Chemistry Institute in Berlin. That way we keep an eye on those Jew lovers. I will have Himmler's men watch, but not touch them, at least for now. *You* will decide what to do with them. Meanwhile, gather up the best scientists and chemists we have left in this discipline. I want a methodical program put in place to find out if there is some reality in creating a bomb. Money will be arranged. This is to have utmost security. Only me, Göring, Himmler and one or two others will know. You will supervise the program and report directly to me. If you have to hide these people away to keep them quiet, then do so. And while I think of it, I'll see that the Gestapo screen everyone trying to emigrate. We'll get them out of the camps if they have any nuclear or fission knowledge, if that's what you call it and they'll be turned over to you. Dispose of them as you wish. You will be given Führer Top Secret clearance. Take the staff you need and no one will bother you. If they try to, let them know they'll feel my wrath."

Hitler wrote on a note pad, lost in thought before turning back to Schmid. "Take this memo over to 4B4 Gestapo office, that's the Jewish Department, I don't want them to deport any people you may need. I've seen reports from our Bund leader Fritz Kuhn in the United States vis-à-vis that there are some American scientists who support the Communists. Now I see this information you've given me may be just what the Red scum are after. As I say, I don't think we'll need such a weapon, but we can't be too careful. I don't want our enemies to get anything before us."

* * *

19 January, 1939
At a meeting at Ravensmoor with James, David discussed the need to increase security around all the plants. For some unstated reason, David decided James should head up the program. Mary and Daphne were there, paying attention as David went on about his concerns. Royce, only half listening, had other things on his mind; the recent IRA bombings in England, and interjected.

"What on earth are those Irish thinking? Don't they know what Hitler would do to them if he carried out his European domination?"

David stared at him agitated. One of his military plants in Manchester was slightly damaged by one of the bombs and he was in no mood to be interrupted. "For Christ's sake, James, were you living in a vacuum too long in Austria to remember? The Irish hate us. They'd make a pact with the devil if it will get us out of Ireland. We have enough trouble ahead without stabs in the back by a bunch of harpy hooligans. Now we'll probably have to send troops to patrol their beaches to prevent Nazi arms from landing there."

Daphne interjected. "I know Hitler wouldn't give them the time of day if they weren't in England's backyard. But you really can't blame the Irish for their hate of most everything British. They've been kept under the Brit thumb for centuries. I don't see why England doesn't simply give them the island. From what I've seen of it, other than charmingly green, it's rocks and sheep."

David was curt. "Because it's ours, that's why, damn it. It's part of the British Isles and will stay that way. Don't be stupid."

Daphne was ready with an angry reply when James got to his feet. "I suggest you back off, David. You've suffered a little damage to one plant and you're all upset when actually you're the one who's been stupid about protection. As I recall, the War Ministry told you months ago to increase security. That would have saved us the little damage the IRA caused. There are other things as well that you haven't done."

"To hell with what I haven't done! Do you have any idea the amount of war material we're shipping out each week?"

It was off the subject, but Royce responded. "I should, I'm in charge of it."

"Right, you're in charge of getting it out, but by God, *I'm* the one who gets the orders in!"

He glared at Royce, Daphne knew David wasn't used to someone talking back. Although she was proud of Jim, standing up for her as well as standing his own ground, she could see the conversation would deteriorate, and interposed. "Look, David, this is leading us nowhere. What do you want out of this little get-together?"

David, breathed quickly, held his temper. "I'm going to have James take over all security, and that includes the blast berms, underground structure, and everything to do with the plants."

Royce was quick to respond. "Not a snowball's chance in hell will I take over that mess."

David was livid. "What do you mean by that?"

"Figure it out for yourself. At last count, I had between nine and twelve projects aside from the three special projects you gave me. Along with those, I oversee all plant production. I cannot take on anything more and do a creditable job. Clive's going flat out as well. As far as additional underground construction, the ground is frozen deep this year and we don't have the equipment to break through the frost. That is unless you've got it hidden somewhere. So, that's a stalemate until the spring. But let me ask this. I know nothing about security, or building underground, so what's the reason? Why me?"

David rose, ignored the questions, told Royce to forget the whole damn subject and without further argument, stormed out of the room still fuming.

David's unstated reason was lengthy. When he overnighted in London, he no longer stayed at the Lanesborough Hotel. It seemed that a small, twelve room manor house just outside of Hyde Park had caught his eye and, under the name Sir Ashton Hamilton, he had purchased the manor with cash down. It was costly. Thousands of dollars of the company's resources were used to make the down payment. This left that account, which was usually short of funds, now dreadfully short, to the point of barely being able to pay creditors punctually. Added to this problem, the military had insisted he bring his plants into compliance, or they would shift whatever orders they could to different suppliers. Due to these difficulties, he tried to reduce costs. One way would be having his brother help bring the company into compliance by making him responsible for security and construction as David could not afford outside contractors.

David's effort to have James help was, on the face of it, ridiculous, and had failed for had James refused. Now, to David's mind, his next move would be what James deserved. Moreover if done right, his brother would never know.

When James bought Blackbird Cottage, David, with his connections, had done the transaction out of Royce's account. As David always had access to the account, it now became a simple matter to transfer the money he needed out of James's, into Royce Ltd. or David's private account. In this manner, David could continue to pay creditors, start the protection the military wanted done to his factories, and still have enough for furniture at his newly acquired Hyde Park residence.

And, he justified, it would only be a loan, he'd pay it back someday. The sad part was, although James had once offered a loan, David never gave the first thought to ask him. He proceeded to borrow from his brother's account as well as put into play another scheme, which could come to pass quite shortly. If all went as planned he would be able to easily pay off the loans.

* * *

On 23 January, David flew RAF via the southern route to the Azores, then by Imperial Flying Boat, on to the US and up to Boston Airport. There, he was driven by a Lincoln limousine to a high-rise commerce building on India Street, not far from Boston's Customs House Tower. In a spacious penthouse office suite, Daphne's brother Robert Elliot met him. The meeting started cordially, with David's first thought being how different Americans are from the European. Modern, airy offices, quality furniture, an air of affluence and in Robert's case, a view of Boston Harbor. It exuded style, giving the owner and his guest a feeling of confidence. And Robert Elliot certainly had that. He no longer tried to avoid people; if they couldn't accept his new, white plastic mask, they could take their business elsewhere. No one did and the deciding factor was money. Robert, a wealthy, gifted man, had become sure of himself and his personality.

After talk of travel, family, Daphne, Royce and life in general, the conversation slowly turned to the reason for David taking time out of his schedule to make this trip.

"I know you've reviewed the Prospectus, Robert, let's go over it point by point."

"David, as I stated on the phone and in my telexes, I think you should have shared more information, and given far more thought to what the future holds. I've a responsibility to my investors. Elliot Corporation must first look at the aggregate view before we could seriously think of a joint venture, much less combining our two companies."

This was not the way David wanted the subject to be presented. Although he knew from the tone of the transatlantic communications that Robert was not impressed, David hoped that to meet face to face he could use his persuasive talents. He decided not to respond to Robert's comments. Instead, press forward with his discourse.

"Robert, our two companies have the potential to become one of the most successful international industrialized conglomerates in the world if we integrate…"

"Please, David, excuse my interrupting. But we've reviewed this on the phone and any number of messages. Since those communiqués, I handed the process of evaluating your company to my staff in hopes we could find some sort of strategy beneficial to both parties. Unfortunately, you now force me to be blunt. My staff and advisors have come back with an emphatic rejection and stated I should keep your company at arm's length for a number of reasons. The major reason is our international experts predict there will be war. If the German Condor bombings in Spain are any indication of the terrible destruction that can be rained down on a country, then the same thing, multiplied a hundredfold, will more than likely happen to France and England."

David only half-listened. He couldn't entertain the thought that England could succumb to the Germans. "That is where your advisors are dead wrong, Robert. We've a good air force and a secret weapon. We'll stop them."

"You're referring to the Chain Home System. Yes, that will help delay the inevitable, but will not stop the Germans."

That Robert recalled the air defense system left David silent while Robert continued.

"Listen to me, David. Hitler has the whole of Europe to draw from. England has only its tight little island and remote possessions. When the RAF is beaten, your factories and cities will lie in ruin. The Nazis have built a war machine where England, despite her navy, cannot compete. I'm sorry, but this is our considered opinion. My people feel France is in disarray and will crack like a rotten egg. That will leave England naked. President Roosevelt has declared us neutral, although we've heard through our grapevine he is setting up a Lend Lease program for England. That won't be enough. Do you understand, David? England will not survive unless she sues for peace. It pains me to say that, my years there are always on my mind. But she should take Hitler's offer.

"Now, with that said, my company, along with others, is lobbying Congress and the Senate to make them listen. They say we pedal fear, that we simply want to make money by convincing the public there's going to be a war. War mongers they call us, same as in England. Our own Ambassador to England, the ever loveable Joe Kennedy, told the Senate and the President we should stay out, that England doesn't stand a chance in a war. Remember, Kennedy's Irish, has no love for the English, and has Roosevelt's ear. We've got an uphill battle on our hands here. Do you know we let our armed forces wither so much after the war that it's estimated our present army is about the size of Portugal's? We have no Draft, what your country calls Conscription. We'd nearly have to start from scratch and that won't happen right now. We're gambling it will happen ultimately, but it's doubtful in time to save England."

Robert stopped, embarrassed. He remembered the grand American Expeditionary Force of the Great War. "I'm sorry David. Now I'm off the subject. What I must be blunt about is we believe England, and by that I include your company, will not survive the onslaught. I apologize for the speech, but I must state we definitely will not become involved with your company."

David Royce pressed further into the leather chair. He had prepared a presentation that he felt would convince Robert. He had been preempted.

One last possibility. "I would like to speak with your research staff and show them where they're wrong."

"I'm sorry, David, no. It wouldn't be of any value for you to belabor my analysts. I've my stockholders to consider."

David stood. He was not going to lower himself by listening to Robert any longer. He held no further interest in the conversation or his host. "If that's final then, I really should run along, I've other matters to address."

"For Heaven's sake, David, you just got here. I've planned dinner, and for you to stay at my home overnight. Perhaps there are other ways we could assist you."

"I'd prefer not to take up more of your valuable time and the sooner I get to Washington, the sooner my major business over here will be finalized."

"I'm truly sorry you feel that way, David. If I can't change your mind, then there's not much else I can say. But I do have two items I would like you to take back to Coventry. That is if it wouldn't be too much trouble."

Robert retrieved a package and sealed envelope. The package was labeled to 'Jim' and the envelope 'Sister Daphne'.

"I'll see they get them."

"Thank you, David. As I say, I'm sorry we couldn't help in some way. I'll have my chauffeur drive you to South Station so you can catch the night train to Washington."

David hesitated, and then accepted. They shook hands and, without another word, he went down to the waiting limousine.

Driven to South Station, David waited until the chauffeured vehicle disappeared from sight, then hailed a cab and went over to Boston Airport, took a chartered flight back to Norfolk and retraced his journey to Coventry. He had lied to Robert. He did not have business in Washington. An agreement of some sort, any sort, with Robert's company was his sole reason for the flight.

Robert Elliot stood at the window, looking out over the islands of Boston Harbor. It was difficult to be so blunt, yet it was the only way to address David and the proposal he had in mind. In the short time Robert knew him, David would either charm or steamroller people until he attained his goal and that was not about to happen here—not on Robert's home turf.

There were too many problems with D W Royce Limited, not the least of which was the possibility of war. And therein lay the paradox. For his company to survive, David needed a war. If there were war, the enemy destroy his company.

Robert's political and market analysts had researched David Royce's proposition and his company and found it all deficient in many respects. Aside from a war, the worst was its negative financials. Not insurmountable, still, it would take fiscal responsibility to survive and Robert's agents saw no sign that would happen. They saw David as too unnerving in his actions. He committed to orders without enough manufacturing capacity or employees and, most detrimental of all, the dilemma of how to finance the orders. Privately, he bought Bentley's, hundreds of acres of land and gave lavish parties. They knew nothing of David's purchase of the manor house. Yet even without that, Robert's people told him straight out—if it wasn't for Government requirements, most especially for bearings—he would be pushed into receivership.

The intercom rang. "John Mays here, Mr. Elliot. You asked me to call after your meeting."

"Yes, Mays, it's as we expected. It would seem Mr. Royce was basically after a financial bailout and from what I know of David, he would expect to be the Chairman of the combined companies."

"That would certainly have been a good ruse to pull off. A successful company taken over by a sick one."

"Yes. I'm afraid he can't see the forest for the trees, or perhaps it would be more apt to say he can't tell the bombers from the fluffy clouds."

Robert hung up, then recalled David's abrupt, actually rude, departure. When he didn't get the answer he wanted, it was simply to hell with Robert and his company. Robert would have liked to help David, but except for their bearings, the company was an antique. He knew Jim Royce's efforts were to try to bring them up to the present. Still, it would be too long a struggle in too short a time. They make do with machinery from before the past war and the 1920s. Additionally, except for one area, all of the plants were exposed above ground. Even the fact a single IRA saboteur could damage one of David's plants was disconcerting. The Elliot Corporation specialists report closed with the confirmation that Royce Industries had eliminated all production not related to the military. Should any semblance of peace return, those military orders would wither, and David's empire collapse. Either way, war or not, David held a losing hand.

Despite all this evidence, Robert felt a mild sense of guilt. It had been David's contacts in Washington that had started Elliot Corporation on its expansion program. Robert and his advisors had gone on a binge, they acquired small, well run companies that were subcontractors to giant industries. They chose companies working on synthetic rubber development, both neoprene and butyl. Added to this were electronic, hydraulic and equipment supply firms for coal and oil producers.

Robert's corporation physically absorbed those companies and then appointed top managers. Stock purchases in General Motors, Studebaker, Willy's and Ford followed. Their next steps were investments in aircraft companies Boeing and Douglas first, then Bell, along with Lockheed and Vought. Finally, the company moved into shipping with investments in the Bath Iron Works in Maine and Bethlehem Steel's shipbuilding division—mainly in Quincy. Robert had visited that shipyard previously, knew it had built the aircraft carrier Lexington in 1925, and he now saw the carrier Wasp ready for launch. With the battleship Massachusetts under construction along with multiple destroyer contracts, Robert knew Bethlehem Steel was an excellent investment for the long term. His Corporation had diversified, although it would take a war to end the Depression and grow the profits.

The major difference between Elliot Corporation and David's D W Royce was that Robert's company, even after millions spent procuring companies and millions more in investments, was still exceptionally solvent. And as importantly, in America, they were out of harm's way.

* * *

David was in a black mood on returning to Coventry. No one questioned him about the trip. Mary simply accepted his mood, the dogs avoided him, Daphne couldn't have cared less, and Royce was so consumed with work he didn't even notice. After David handed Daphne the two items Robert had sent, and Royce arrived home, they opened the two by three foot package first to find the oil painting of the castle. They stood transfixed. Robert had caught the aura perfectly. The red tower, the sun the moment it broke through the mist, and the massive gray wall as a backdrop. Royce was pleased, yet vaguely bothered. Daphne saw it, but thought it better to say nothing. Let his thoughts run their course.

The envelope of Robert's letter to Daphne was marked Personal & Private, so she retired to their bedroom.

Dearest Daphne,

I'm writing this letter prior to David's arrival as I want to convey some of my thoughts on the world today and my worry for you, as well as Jim- but mainly you.

The world is rapidly changing for the worse, at least from my information. This Hitler fellow is a menace. I didn't see that before and I made some major blunders because of my emotions for another person.

Daphne stopped here, baffled. What was he talking about? She then continued, hoping it would become clear.

That part of my life is forever regretted and forever buried, but it's done. Now I want to speak to you as your brother, a brother who is anxious for your safety.

Daph, mother never made you a British citizen. You are still an American.

My wish is for you to come home. I would like Jim to come also, but he is a British subject and I doubt he would leave. If you do come and he should come with you, be assured I would have any position he wanted made open for him.

I never became a British subject either, and now that I have

309

returned home, I have no regret about that. Without realizing what I was doing, I hid over there from the world. Well, I hid long enough, in fact far too long.

I wish I returned long before, when Father was still alive, perhaps he could have learned to bear the face I was left with. But truly, I feel he would never have been able to look at me, so what happened in the war is just another regret I must put aside.

Daph, I have private information about England. There is a 'Think Tank' here, people with inside knowledge who have been tracking Hitler's activities ever since his jailing in Munich in '23. He's a megalomaniac, and with the German people behind him, no one has dared to stop his rise. No general, no politician, only a few voices crying in the wilderness and even they're being silenced. England and France do nothing. Chamberlain's 'Peace in our Time' will prove a tragic hoax and the people I know say all this did was to allow Hitler to appear even stronger.

Now is the time to leave England, Daph. America will stay neutral, even though they help with supplies. Russia feels safe with Poland between them even though Hitler hates Communists as much as he hates Jews. France's military class is so fractured politically they'll be of little if any help. There is no one else left. I'm afraid England cannot stand alone. Especially when our own Ambassador to the Court of St. James is selling England down the river.

Please, sell your houses while you can and come home. Subject change: When he gets here, I know David intends our two companies to combine. There's not a snowballs chance in hell of that happening for a great number of reasons. So, I don't imagine he'll be in too good a mood by the time you read this. I know that won't bother you, but whatever you do, do not let him know how well off you are and absolutely DO NOT invest with him if he asks. Jim shouldn't either, even though they are brothers. It would be like investing in the Titanic. I'd bet on his company not existing two years from now, with, or

without a war. I'll help where I can, but still, if he gets wind of
just how much I doubt his 'future' I'm sure he would find some
way to hurt you and Jim.

Please do as I ask about returning. There will always be a
place for you and Jim here.

You're loving brother, Rob

PS: I assume you know enough to destroy this letter.

RE

Daphne returned to the room and dropped the letter into the
fireplace.

Royce was curious. "That's an odd thing to do. What did
Rob have to say?"

"He wants us to go to the States."

"What does he mean? For a trip, holiday?"

"No, for good. He thinks the Germans are going to sink this
little island."

"Sink us? Literally or figuratively? Don't make me laugh."

"He didn't exactly say that, only implied…we're doomed,
get out while the getting's possible."

"What will you tell him?"

"I'll say thanks for the concern, brother, no."

Royce smiled. "Well, let's think that a moment. Actually
you're not English. You don't have to *sink* with us."

"I don't like where you're going with that remark. I'm an
American, but as British as you are, so watch what you say next."

Royce felt it wise not to say anything next, and Daphne, still
annoyed, wrote to her brother.

Dear Rob,

Thank you for your letter and we are both well. You
were right in guessing David's mood when he returned-black
as the ace of spades. Poor boy didn't get the box of candy he
wanted from you. Just as well, I suspect, but I am a bit sorry
for him, he does work hard. It's a shame he doesn't work smart,
stop and see what's happening to him, his family and
company.

Jim is doing his best to help- completely preoccupied in work.

Twelve-hour plus days, six and seven day weeks. He said he would slow down after three more projects were finished but then I bet David puts more on him. I worry he will wear out, but he won't listen. It's amazing the change in him- and me for that matter. Not for the best, I'm afraid. And, as I think of it, I guess 'afraid' is the best word. I wouldn't mention this to anyone else Robby, but he is not the person I knew when we met, and since. This drive he now has wasn't apparent in Austria-or maybe his climbing intensity was a way to release it. Whatever it is, 'we' are not on the same wavelength and I can only hope this phase in him passes and passes in me as well.

I go to mum's house in Belgravia and feel her everywhere, I go to your house in Windermere and you're everywhere. Then I go to Jim's house in Coventry and he's not there-no one is. Life has changed so much and I can't seem-or perhaps want - to change with it. I know the thoughts of war permeates the air and everyone I meet seems apprehensive. Perhaps it is the same with me-overreacting.

Anyway, thanks for putting up with whinny little me. We'll see how things shake out.

As you say, subject change: As much as I miss you, I will not be coming back to the States. People here may be worried here, but not fearful. They go about their business, 'stiff upper lip' and all that odd Brit stuff.

Rob, I must be honest, as much as I know it will hurt you, I've tossed my lot in with them no matter what comes. In fact, to the point I'm giving thought to becoming one of His Majesty's Subjects. Please don't tell Jim. If I do, I want to hit him over the head with it the next time he (or you for that matter) starts to question my loyalty to the Crown-
God, listen to me, 'Little Miss Independent American'.

Don't worry yourself over me. I'm just in a bit of a mood-not as bad as David's. Thanks to you. I know things will work out all right-and we expect to see you here again, or we show up over there in Boston.

    I hope so.

Your Loving sister, Daphne

9 January, 1939

The first month of the New Year found Royce still engrossed in his work and David hurtling ahead with his plans to enlarge the company yet again, costs be damned. Mary Royce began work with the Royal Red Cross as they prepared for the possibility of war. Daphne, between helping Mary, also continued her brother's programs for vaudeville entertainers. Just as Robert, before her, she hoped to offset the endless boredom of the forever wounded from the Great War in old Soldier's Homes between Coventry and London.

    She found a valued friend in Lady Jane. The contacts she had in the entertainment industry proved invaluable. Jane knew, as friends or acquaintances, the movie director Alex Korda, Singer Vera Lynn, actors Leslie Howard, Laurence Olivier, Madeleine Carroll, Robert Donat, Merle Oberon and more.

    Added to those, Lady Jane asked for help from people who came from all walks of life in England. Illusionist David Deviant, cricket Captain Doug Jardine and Fred Perry from tennis. Lady Jane asked, they volunteered. The actors and actresses performed in the Homes, often reading Wodehouse's short stories from Blanding's Castle and Agatha Christie's new book, *Death on the Nile*. Perry showed tricks with a tennis ball and told stories of his tournaments, Deviant amazed the bedridden with magic, and the others joined in with their respective talents.

    The fact of Royce being so engrossed in work did not bother Daphne too much. She was away often, going from Soldier's Home to Home, setting up entertainment dates, assembling props and doing whatever needed to help the patients, which included the purchase of supplies on her own. These trips often found her in the Haverling home of Lady Jane.

Jane's son Kenneth was never there and Daphne found herself wishing he would drop by for a hello and a laugh or two. Jane said he was in France up to something with the French Group de Chasse fliers. She also said she had chastised her son for waving Daphne's scarf from the airplane, although Kenneth was just amused and said he'd be seeing her, Daphne that is.

On 30 January, 1939, Hitler made an internationally transmitted speech to the Reichstag.

Daphne and Jane shared a bottle of Port beside a fireplace at the Mount as they listened to Hitler's rant. Daphne translated as Hitler talked on. "He's difficult to follow, especially with his strong Austrian dialect, guttural Rs you know, and he shouts so much he must have a lot of spittle. Basically, he stated something about the Jewish Question, or as he calls it 'Der Ewige Jude', which means The Eternal Jew. There's too much cheering and applause to understand all of it, although you can imagine it's damn negative. I'll tell you in a moment."

She listened intently. Slowly a frown formed, then shock.

"What is it, Daphne?"

Daphne held up her hand. "Just a minute, let him finish."

As the ovations continued, Daphne snapped off the radio and turned to Lady Jane, disgust and fear in her voice. "He's blamed the Jews for all of Germany's troubles and said international Jewry will be at fault if Europe is plunged into another war. But, the terrible part he said is, if there *is* another war it won't be a victory for the Jews, it will be the '...Vernichtung der Jüdischen Rasse in Europa'."

"That's terrible Jane, it means...the annihilation of the Jewish race in Europe."

"My God, Daphne, we've distant relatives in Germany who help their Jewish friends to emigrate. This could mean trouble for them if they're caught."

"It certainly could. If you're in contact with them, warn them. Although with this speech, they must already know. Hitler leaves little to the imagination. At first, I thought he would deport them, and that was appalling enough. But he's hinting at something far more sinister. This seems a lead-in to war."

"Daphne, all this war talk is terrible. You're not old enough

314

to remember the Great War very well, and here we are again. It's the same thing. This constant prediction of war is self-fulfilling. The more we talk of it, the more it becomes likely and then there'll be a spark, something like that stupid Princip boy shooting that pompous, doltish Archduke Ferdinand in Sarajevo in 1914. That's all it took. It seems governments go to war over one ill-advised pact or another."

"Well, I think it was Bismarck who said war is simply an extension of diplomacy."

"Yes, of course he'd say that, as long as he wasn't in the trench. The Prussian fool."

Lady Jane paused, a far-off look. "Daphne, I'm embarrassed to say my husband loved war. He loved the excitement. He said each time he went up in his plane, the eagerness of combat, one machine against the other, one man pitted against another and neither knowing if they would die was, to him, the most exhilarating feeling he ever knew. When the war ended, he didn't have a scratch on him, nothing, and this after he had shot down more than eighteen enemy planes.

You know German flyers didn't wear parachutes, so Amery, my husband's name, wouldn't wear one either. He killed more than fifteen German pilots. And Daphne, I never knew it to bother him. In fact, he was restless when he returned and thought of going to Palestine or Arabia and find another war. I honestly think he would have started one if he had to. That was when I told him if he left, we wouldn't be here when he returned, and I'd take our son and leave."

Lady Jane wondered if she should continue. "I do prattle on Daphne, I hope you don't mind."

"Not in the least, Jane. Although I must be honest, I see your husband in Kenneth."

"Yes, I suppose you would. Anyway, thank God, my threat changed Amery. He told me when he was in combat his only thought was to destroy his opponent. It didn't matter if he lived or not, as long as he didn't burn to death as so many pilots did. That was the only reason he carried a revolver, he said, to kill himself.

Then he told me, that when he was alone in his billet, we were the only reason for him to live. Isn't that strange? Just us, not his homes, his money, or his women, only Kenneth and I.

315

"Thankfully, Amery didn't want to lose us, and we finally had a wonderful life together, except for his indoctrination of Kenneth about flying. He wanted Kenneth to be the best flyer in the world, and of course, there was always his idea of the glory of war should one come again. My word Daphne, you've made me quite a blabbermouth."

To Daphne, there was no longer the slightest mystery why Lady Jane's son turned out the way he had. In the short span Daphne knew him, Kenneth was his Father. With Jim, it was different, his past had to be pried out. Then again, Jim was the product of *his* Father...and brother...and face. Even David admitted that.

Nevertheless, she was curious about Kenneth. "Are you afraid your son will turn out like your husband and love war? Is that your fear? Because I don't think so. Kenneth seems so grounded in honor and duty, not glory."

"No, I don't fear his loving war. I'm afraid what could happen to him in a war. He's my only child, just as Amery was my only husband. I could barely live through it when Amery died and now my concern passes to my son. It frightens me when I'm alone at night and think of what could happen. Can you imagine how many mothers' feel that way?"

"Yes, I think I can. But you should have a doctor give you some pills to help you sleep."

"I've got them and don't you doubt, if anything happened to Kenneth, I'll take a handful of them and don't you ever try and stop me."

Daphne said nothing; simply put her hand on Lady Jane's shoulder. At this moment, both women looked up as Kenneth walked in the room. All three broke into smiles.

"We didn't hear you come in, why didn't Conrad announce you were here?"

"He tried to mother, but I stopped him. I'm tired of being announced in my own home, our home."

"I want you to be announced, Kenneth; I don't want you to slip in without knowing. Like now. Daphne and I were in the middle of girl talk. How much did you hear?"

"I wouldn't do that, mother, I came straight in."

"Why aren't you in France, dear?"

"I had to come back and prepare my squadron for maneuvers with our French counterparts. I did that today and there's a possible chance I'll be back over there late tomorrow."

He turned from his mother to Daphne. "Excuse me, Daphne, I didn't mean to be rude, my mother should be answered first. Don't you look lovely."

"No offence taken, Ken. And don't tell me I look lovely. Your mother and I have been at work right until this evening to try and get our entertainment programs worked out, so we're both a mess. But you look smashing in tie and jacket. Formal blues?"

"Actually it's battle dress," Ken laughed, "for meeting with Air Marshal Dowding. As I say, we may be the first Spitfire squadron going over to France, complete with ground crew and gear. The Air Marshal wants everything to be shipshape and Bristol fashion, using the naval term."

Daphne smiled. "Are you sure you're only a lowly Squadron Leader? There's an awful lot of stripes down your sleeve."

"It only appears that way, Daphne, there's three, two wide, one narrow between them. They're outlined in black that makes it look like there's more."

"Nevertheless, you look marvelous. You're chosen to lead the first squadron into France?

"We're not the first squadron, Daph. Hurricane Squadrons are over there before us."

"Well anyway, yours are the first Spitfires. Can you have a scotch, or are you on duty?"

"At the moment I'm off duty until tomorrow midnight. So if you would be so kind as to make me a double, light water. I'm up to change and back in a jiff, before you've finished pouring."

"Aye, Aye, Captain."

"Good Lord, Daphne, now *you're* into Royal Navy lingo. Just say, Yes, Dear Squadron Leader, Sir."

She smirked, but responded quickly. "Yes, Dear Squadron Leader, Sir."

When he was gone, Lady Jane was thoughtful as she mulled something over.

"Jane, you have something on your mind?"

"Yes, Daphne. You seem to be pleased to see Kenneth again. Am I to believe that?"

"Jane, forgive me, but yes. It's been so long since I've had a chance to sit back, relax and have a drink. And, hopefully have a pleasant conversation with Kenneth, that I…"

"Say no more, Daphne. I know only too well how you feel. I was that way with my husband, and I was tired of talking to women for so long. And now, I think I'll retire."

"Oh, God. Please, Jane, I feel terrible, don't go because of what I said, I'd be devastated."

"Daphne, Let me assure you, the King couldn't say anything that would cause me to leave. I'm leaving because I'm tired and I wish to."

Chapter 19

"MOTHER DECIDED to retire. I met her in the hallway."

"I know. I hope she didn't take offense at my remark."

"Oh? And what remark was that? She didn't say anything about an offensive remark."

"Do I have to tell you? I'd prefer not."

"Then don't."

He took a sip from the drink she handed him and moved to the fireplace. "Perfect drink, Daphne."

"Yes, it takes a distinct talent to make a scotch and light water correctly. You put the water in first, then pour the Scotch on top, slowly. That way the first sip is delightful."

There was a lag in the conversation. She felt strange, jittery.

"Dreadful weather, don't you think, Daphne? Can't seem to get warm. Not good for ground or air personnel."

"It's supposed to warm up through the night, be above freezing by tomorrow morning."

They both were awkward, wished his mother had stayed.

"So tell me Daphne, how have you been? How's everything and everyone in Coventry?"

"Quite fine, I believe. I've not been there much; what with this entertainment program your Mother has been so kind to help me with. What have you been up to, or can't you say?"

He sat on the arm of the couch, at the far end from her, looked down for a moment. She could see he was tired, yet still handsome as he brushed back a boyish shock of black hair that fell across his eyes. She turned away, and then looked back again. It wasn't the lighting or her eyes playing tricks, he had a dust of gray, nearly white hair, along his temples.

She pointed to it. "What's this? I assume you don't bleach your hair."

"No, not as yet." He looked across to her. "It just showed up one morning. Do you think it makes me appear mature, more distinguished?"

"Don't ignore the question. What happened, Ken?"

"Nothing, really. The doctor said at times it happens to younger people."

"Have you been under stress?"

"Really, Daph, it's nothing specific, comes with the job I imagine. Please, let it go and let's just enjoy a talk."

As it happened, there was something. The French Groupe de Chasse officer's attitude. A select cadre of RAF Squadron Leaders, sent to France to report on French preparedness, found the conditions difficult. The stress Kenneth had put on himself to show French pilots proper aerial combat methods, fell on disinterested fliers. Their operational style was élan, a flair, a belief that confidence will win through over any foe. Added to this exasperation, the British pilots were informed that their French ally's air force possessed only seventy-five of the newer Dwointine D.520 fighters. Kenneth had flown the D.520. He thought it a decent fighter, but doubtful of its performance capabilities against the German ME109bf, and knew the aircraft did not match up to Britain's Hurricane or Spitfire.

The French government was in negotiations for American Curtiss Hawk 75A fighters, but they considered the planes too expensive. At this date, only fourteen had been delivered and were still in their crates, unassembled. The RAF officer report to the Air Commandant at RAF Lyneham stated the French had planes of all sorts, bombers and recon planes everywhere, all of doubtful quality. Yet there appeared to be no cohesive plan on how to use them other than to support the army. The RAF officers' main quandary was to mildly point out that no one in British Fighter Command appeared to understand the French Air Force was under the aegis of the 'Armee de l'Air'. The Army controlled the air force, with a heavy dose of politics mixed in.

This could be disastrous, not only for France. Earlier in the day a meeting headed up by Kenneth Sommers, and with more candor than recommended for junior officers, he summarized the Group's assessment. He emphasized the French weren't near ready, were understaffed in ground support as well as pilots and planes and that their confusion, or perhaps indifference, would be the death of them. Even before Sommers report, it had already seeped back to Command that the Junior RAF officers were troubled that their squadrons would be sacrificed due to the boorishness of their French allies command structure.

The upshot of this, and more information circulating from other officers, caused RAF Fighter Command to issue an immediate Brief to Senior RAF Officers on the ground in France. They were to respond to Fighter Command with an immediate, updated estimate of French air capabilities should hostilities commence with the German Luftwaffe. Estimates were to continue on four day increments until rescinded. RAF Command also raised the question over RAF Squadrons being considered— by the French that is—to be under French direct command once over French air space.

On that subject, Air Marshal Dowding would confer with French Air Command, their Army and political parties. But, he was to make it clear. Only British officers were to be in charge of British Squadrons. A negative response to the above would trigger an exit strategy to remove most, if not all, RAF aircraft from France and lead to the dividing of the Allies even before a war.

For the moment, RAF fighter Command informed Squadron Leader Sommers that, after forty-eight hours, unless ordered otherwise, he was to follow existing orders. His entire squadron of Spitfires would transfer to Rouen, France.

Wing Commanders and Squadron Leaders, present at the conference Sommers attended, were informed of the Directive, and returned to their respective Squadrons. As he was about to leave, Kenneth was told to report to the Wing Commander's office. There, Wing Commander Keith Park, in a friendly, but firm manner informed his Squadron Leader that, if he is ordered to France, he is to be there on schedule and await RAF only orders.

Furthermore, he was not to irritate the French with inappropriate remarks. "They are, after all, Kenneth, our allies and, I might add, our only allies. So be a good chap, will you? Don't upset them to the point where they change sides."

Ken thought that might not be a bad idea. Yet, with the admonition fixed in his mind, he left the conference and drove straight to his mother's, and there, thankfully, he found Daphne.

* * *

"Look, if you don't want to talk about it, let's forget it."

He was jolted back from his difficulties. "Please, Daph, it isn't that I don't *want* to talk about it, it's that I *can't* talk about it. Top Secret and all that rot, and I'm sure you appreciate I make it a point not to bring my work home because of Mother's anxieties. I will now flush my mind of anything other than you, for the rest of the evening."

"I don't know if I like that either."

"Nevertheless, let's talk about you. You're an American, with the most odd English speech pattern."

"What do you mean by odd?"

"Where were you from in the States?"

"The Boston area."

"Ah! The fog lifts. I've spoken with some pilots from America, two graduated from Boston University to be specific, and I notice they all speak odd."

"Again, what do you mean by odd?"

"Well I finally figured out they drop the 'r' from the end of words. It's summa, winta, powa and rudda. It's funny."

"And I sound like that?"

"Well, sort of, you know, now and then, although with English idioms. Please, don't get me wrong, I like it, your voice is low to begin with, and the accent gives you a certain mystique which I do love. Still, it's strange you still have Boston in you. How old were you when you came to stay in England?"

"I was eight, although I went back and forth a numba of times," she smiled, "then I went to college in the Bastun area for three years. I returned here after each semesta. Perhaps chats with my sorority sistas and taking Languages as a Maja, confused my speech pattern on how to articulate. It's strange, no one else has eva mentioned it."

She charmed him; he was hardly able to concentrate. "Well, perhaps they noticed and were too…ah, polite to mention it."

"Yes, perhaps they were. But *your* education shows an absolute lack of proper upbringing. I'm surprised not a trace of your mother's refinement rubbed off. And with that clear, to save you further embarrassment, I'll change the subject. How did you come by conversing with some American pilots, you haughty, discourteous, impolite, Brit?"

He tried to get himself together. "Well...let me think a moment...you see it's no secret they've come over here to inquire about the possibilities of joining our air force, but as we tell them, it is best for them to go over their own border to Canada."

"Why there? The RAF is here, last I heard."

"True. However, your American General Arnold and Canada's war hero, Air Marshal Bill Bishop have put together an organization to supply pilots to the RCAF, that's the Royal Canadian Air Force, and our own RAF. They screen scores of American volunteers through the Empire Training Plan in Canada, then send the men they pass over here to a company called British Aviation Limited for further instruction. After that, the RAF picks from a vetted pool."

"Isn't it just as easy to have them come directly here?"

"No, for two reasons. One is. Canada screens out the men who will never meet our criteria and saves us that bother. However, the major reason is that by their going through Canada, it doesn't call into question America's neutrality. That was a problem with Americans over here in the Great War; they became expatriates because they committed their loyalty directly to France. You must have read Hemmingway's *A Farewell to Arms* and how the expats lived, wandering around Europe after the war. We don't want that, so any Americans in our military have to only say they will obey our king, not be his subject."

"Speaking of the subject, you may have gotten off it. Do you have any Americans in your squadron?"

"Yes, I've approved three. That's where I hear your accent."

"Don't get me started again. Anyway, where's your squadron now and how big is a squadron?"

"I have twenty pilots, fifteen Spitfires on line, three replacements, one trainer aircraft, and a complement of seventy personnel. We're about thirty miles from our main base at Biggen Hill but we're being transferred. I assume you're not a spy, correct? Telling the Germans where I am?"

"I haven't decided yet. I'll let you know. But why are you so important? Bit full of yourself, aren't you?"

His face crinkled up. "God, Daphne, but you make me laugh."

"Seriously, Mr. Sommers, please tell me, just why do you think your whereabouts is so terribly important?"

"It's not just *my* whereabouts, it's all Squadron Leaders. Because where we are, that's where you'll find our Squadrons. If a Squadron Leader is in France, or Denmark or Malta, then even a half-witted spy can report where our squadrons are positioned. See, simple."

"Amazing, this spy business. I guess I'll have to work on it. So, to answer your question, I haven't told any Germans anything. At least so far."

"Ok, Daph, good to know. Now, where were we?"

"I was going to ask how my countrymen were doing."

"They're well...they try. Let me first say this, Daphne. The Americans I've got are excellent fliers, they have that instinct, the anticipation required but..."

"But?"

"But they don't have a military history, our background behind them."

"Oh! Now we also decide to be a bit stuffy too, have we?"

"I knew you wouldn't understand and I shouldn't have started this. What I mean is whereas they are excellent fliers, they're not military. They're not from the American Army Air Corps, where they'd have been inculcated in military culture, its customs. They simply don't know, or even care, about the courtesies of the military. The British Aviation Company is not military; they weed out men who won't make it through flight school, that's all. They do not train them to be officers and instill the obligations, the honor, which comes with being a pilot in the RAF or the US Army Air Corp...Blast it! This won't come out right."

"Kenneth, I'll presuppose you're not a snob, so try again. Tell me what you mean."

"I'll try it this way. My Father told me about the American fliers when they came to France in the Great War. Before America entered. Those fliers came on their own, they wanted to fly and fight, they called themselves the Lafayette Escadrille, and their call to arms was 'Lafayette we are here'. That's because Lafayette was a French Aristocrat and he went to our English colonies in America during the revolution to help the rebels fight we English, and unfortunately, we know how that turned out."

"Yes, we *fortunately* do, Kenneth, and don't you forget it. Now try and get to the point."

"The point is that the Americans in that Escadrille were there to find excitement. A challenge they couldn't resist. Fight for glory. It was something they needed to satisfy their psyche. This isn't meant to belittle them, in other times perhaps I'd have done the same thing. They fought well and what they did was heroic, but that was why they fought—to be heroes, not for their country—but for glory. That's the difference between…"

Daphne rose, he stopped. Her brother's rush to join the AEF was to be a hero. Kenneth had unknowingly brought the war and her brother's wound into perspective…and demeaned it. She was physically dismayed.

"What is it Daph?"

"Kenneth, my brother was one of those people. He took two friends into the AEF and they died. He was horribly wounded. They went for the excitement, the glory. That was all, just like you said. He's one of those you're dismissing."

"I'm sorry, Daph, I don't dismiss them, I'm simply telling you the difference. Blast it! I should have kept my thoughts to myself."

"Don't be sorry! I simply don't understand your point, Kenneth. All deaths in war seem to be the same to me, whether for glory or country."

"In the end, yes, I suppose one could say they're just as dead, but it's not the same, Daphne. My three American pilots are as good as my English pilots, and I don't mean to slight them in any way, but they're here for glory, not for country. They saw the Spitfire in the newsreels, or pictures, and fell in love with the most beautiful aircraft in the world. They had to fly one. That's why they're here and in truth, I can understand. But glory is not my reason, or my English pilot's reason to fight. If it comes to a war, we fly for our country, our people. That's different than for personal glory. It makes us proud to serve. All glory does is make you gamble your life for it."

"But, Ken, when we spoke before on this subject you seemed to look forward to a war. At least that's how you sounded. Was it all just your bravado?"

Ken contemplated the question. "I can see my outlook on war has confused you. Do I want war? No. Do I anticipate a war? Yes. And, there is nothing I can do about it either way. Don't ever think I'm a war lover, please. I killed people in Iraq and Abyssinia. I ran, scared out of my wits, from Germany's Legion Condor Stuka bombers in Spain. Now, I worry for my country. If my pilots have to fight, I've instilled in them we're the best, our squadron has the honor to be part of 11 Group, the first line, the wall that protects our country. That is a duty, an *obligation* to our country's people. It's not for personal glory. I tell my pilots that if they're in it for glory, go find another squadron, I don't want them. If some of us die, it will be for a *cause*, not glory. England's leaders have allowed a mad fox to get loose in the hen house, so it's our sworn duty to protect our country and our way of life. If this sounds false or contrived, I'm sorry. And to be honest, Daphne, if you cannot feel a country has a soul, and not understand what I've said, then I'm sorry for you, because you don't have a love for your country. And I won't believe that of you."

Comparing her brother with this man cut her deeply. She stared at him. She had never thought there was any difference between dying for glory, honor, or country. Yet here was a man ready to die for England and yet still disparage men who died for glory. She could see he didn't want to die, but would, solely for the survival of his country. And he felt it was his duty, his honor to serve. Yes, she had once believed he was just a fun loving, talented playboy, who only played with the weapons of war. Between this, and other conversations, she was ashamed. He didn't intend to die simply for glory. The old adage fit here, don't judge a book by its cover. It was solely her fault; she had judged him without thinking to open the book.

This now became more serious. She couldn't stop the tears.

"I do love my countries, both England and America and I apologize. Now I understand you better. But in my defense, you must admit you acted the rogue now and then. "

"Don't apologize, please. I admit I'm a trifle over the top at times. But other times I hold things too dear and get carried away, as I did just now. It's been instilled in me all my life. My father taught me our family has an obligation...Damn, I'm sorry. It

326

distresses me to see you cry. Let me apologize, I've waved the flag too much."

"No, you won't apologize. It was my fault. I feel like a fool."

"Sometimes to feel the fool is helpful, Daph."

"You don't have to be quite so quick to agree, you know."

They used the comment for a welcome relief. The apprehension between them seeped away. She went to make them another drink. He put two more logs on the fire.

As they settled back onto the couch, she gave him a grave stare. "Good Lord, what did I do now, Daphne?"

"I just remembered, I'm quite cross with you."

"What on earth for?"

"You were very brazen the last time I was here. You went into my room, through my luggage—my personal things—and *stole* my scarf."

He made a steeple of his fingers, touched them to his lips, in thought, deciding…deciding.

"Well, Squadron Leader, can't think of anything to say for once in your life?"

"It wasn't me."

"Don't give me that. I distinctly remember I put that scarf in my case. How on earth can you say you didn't take it? Or are you going to tell me the butler did it?"

He gave her a sly smile. "No, not the butler, Daphne—my mother. I asked her to get it for me."

"Your mother? I'm to believe that?"

"I'm telling you, she's the thief, petty thief yes, but still…a substantiated, unmitigated…thief."

"Then please explain this to me. That is, if you can."

"Daphne, work this through. Remember when you were here before, during that get-together in your mother's memory? Do you think it was an accident that I just happened to drop by in an airplane? Or I just happened to drop in tonight by pure chance? Well, it wasn't chance. My Mother told me every time you would be here. I only had to get the time off to show up."

"But why? She thinks you're a terrible womanizer."

"Daphne, she knew you a bit when you would come here with your Mother. Then, when she spoke with you for a while at David Royce's New Year's party, she, well frankly, she fell in love with you. She wanted you for me. I can't explain it. She would almost chase away what few other women I brought home. Something clicked, as they say, and she wants you and me together. She's said that straight out. You've won her over. Believe me, if anyone, anyone else called her Jane, without the Lady preface, she would have given them such a tongue lashing they'd cringe and run."

"I'm astonished about the scarf, I really am. And I'm grateful she likes me, I think of her as a good friend now. But she told me to my face she chastised you for taking it."

"She did chastise me, but only because I waved it from the plane, teasing you, not for taking it."

"I'll be damned. So again, you're not the womanizer, the rake she says you are?"

"Well, certainly not quite as bad as she implies."

The phone rang. He walked over to answer it. "That better not be another woman, Kenneth."

He turned to her, mock panic across his face. "Good Lord, I hope not."

After he hung up, Ken stood and considered the call. When he returned to the couch he was pensive.

"What is it Ken, or can't you say?"

"That was the call I've been waiting for: the Air Marshal's Fighter Command Headquarters at RAF Bentley Priory. Change in orders. They couldn't get the French Groupe de Chasse to agree with a few things we officers brought up. So my squadron's orders to Rouen have been rescinded as well as my two weeks leave, which is fine with me. We're ordered to stand down two days, then report with full squadron complement to Fighter Command, 11 Group, under Wing Commander Keith Park on 2 February. That's fine with me, too. Park's a New Zealander, RFC in the last war, knows his job. He'll more than likely be jumped up to Air Commodore soon. Tell me, Daphne, what the devil does Groupe de Chasse mean anyway?"

"Basically it means Group of Pursuit. In English, clearly Pursuit Group. Didn't you take basic French at University?"

"Not if I could help it, I was quite sick for those classes."

"You've a one track mind and you're hopeless as well, that's a given. So tell me, can you say where you'll be stationed?"

"Yes, if you can follow it. 11 Group Headquarters is in

328

Middlesex. My Sector Station is Biggin Hill in Bromley. My Squadron, along with other squadrons, will be at a satellite field at RAF Gravesend, and from there we'll cover the South East and London. Directly in any enemy's path. That's a feather in my squadron's cap."

"Feather in yours too, I should think."

"I don't need a feather; I've got your scarf."

Before they knew it, it was eleven at night, too late, they both thought, for a nightcap.

"What are you doing tomorrow, Daph?"

"I'm going stay awhile to help your mother some more with entertainment plans. Why are you asking?"

"Something that can't wait until the afternoon?"

She hesitated. It had been a pleasant evening with him despite her discomfiture over his sentiments on war. She was, however, curious, sure he had something up his sleeve and couldn't help but wonder what it was.

"Really Ken. Don't ask me to do anything. I've been honest, there is someone else."

"Daph, I'll be gone after tomorrow. Who knows when I'll be free after this. I really might never see you again. Go for a drive tomorrow morning and have breakfast with me, just this last time. If not, my heart might forget to beat."

"You really do think you can get away with that rubbish, don't you? But, once again and against my better judgment, I guess it will work for me. But only this one more time. However, if the next words out of your mouth are 'should I call you, or nudge you for breakfast', your heart will definitely stop beating."

He was confused, and then smiled. "I've never heard that line, must be American."

"It is one of my female college friends had it used on her. And now as I think of it, she said he could nudge her."

They both broke out laughing. "Well, all I can say, Daph, is that's the furthest thing from my mind."

"Why would I doubt that, dear Squadron Leader, Sir, why indeed? Good night."

"There's an alarm clock up in one of the rooms. Be ready by 0700. Wear slacks, regular shoes, warm shirt, and a coat."

Now what is he up to she wondered, and shook her head,

trying, but failing, miserably, to hide a smile.

Kenneth made two phone calls. One was to his second in command, Ground Personnel, Flight Officer Hastings. Kenneth told him the Rouen mission was scrubbed and the new squadron's reassignment was Sector C, 11 Group, RAF Biggin Hill, Satellite Airfield, Gravesend. The squadron was to land at Biggin Hill first. For now, Hastings was to follow the Procedures Instruction Manual for Non-Combatant Transport and Ken told him whom to be put in charge for the move. After that, FO Hastings was to be sure Kenneth's new Spitfire was clean and buffed. And after that, have the Squadron's Spitfire trainer readied for the morning. He would be there by 0900.

He scribbled out a note to his Mother to say he and Daphne would be out early and gone most of the day. The other call was to a Miss Alice Woodleigh. Sorry for the lateness of the call he said. He couldn't make their date. Duty was calling.

Daphne went to her room and lay in bed and started to weep again. Kenneth had made a person's obligations to honor and duty so clear. He qualified glory. Unintentionally, he had disparaged her brother's dash for glory as a waste. Kenneth was right, damn him. No, she didn't mean to damn him. She didn't know what she meant. Then it came to her, Jim must feel the same as Kenneth. It was only that Ken could articulate how he felt, whereas Jim was hopeless on that score. Now she understood Jim's intensity, his efforts so feverish to finish projects. He was driven by duty as much as Kenneth. He simply didn't know how to say it. Inadvertently, Ken had explained Jim to her and, added to her feeling for him, there was now respect. But where does that leave her and her thoughts of Ken? Damn it! He's doing more than flit through my mind, she thought. He was another man to worry her. An epiphany came, she was a woman and she had an obligation to duty as much as these men. Yet where is it, and how to find it?

Then she thought of breakfast with Ken.

* * *

330

At the end of the bitter cold January, 1939, Hitler had issued Top
    Secret Plan Z: Naval Expansion.

He had also approved, but held the issuance of Top Secret
Action T4: The elimination of all mentally and physically inferior
children. This would be followed by the elimination of all
mentally and physically inferior adults in Germany.

Chapter 20

"ALL RIGHT, KEN, ENOUGH! We've been on the road for over an hour, where on earth are we and where the devil are we headed? This is too much jaunt and not enough breakfast."

"Just a little more patience, Daph."

"Well I'm starting to get just a little bit suspicious. This little dirt path with the 'No Admittance' sign and, I might add, in the middle of God wouldn't know where."

They made another turn, the Humber sedan slowed to a crawl. Two soldiers with side arms appeared out of a gap in the hedgerow. Daphne jumped, they appeared so quickly.

"Good morning Squadron Leader. We saw you from up the road. Flight Officer Hastings said you'd be through."

Daphne ducked under the roof frame to acknowledge them. The men stood taller, pleasantly surprised. Kenneth returned their salutes and asked what was happening at Squadron quarters.

"The FO has everyone running amuck to pack up for the squadron's move to Uxbridge. And before you ask, Sir, all present, even the Yanks."

"Careful Sergeant, I've a Yank beside me."

The sergeant flushed. "Beg your pardon, Miss, you're good people, just a bit tardy at times."

Kenneth laughed. "Well those days are gone, Sergeant. Their training program is over. Tell me, why aren't you down in charge of transport?"

"The FO ordered me up here, Sir."

"Well get yourself down to the field and make sure everyone isn't still running amuck."

"Yes Sir, but the FO ordered me up…"

"Don't 'but' me Sergeant, get cracking. I'll speak to the FO when I get there ."

"Yes Sir!" He was gone at the trot through the hedgerow.

It was a different voice from the Kenneth she knew. "What was that all about, Ken?"

"I'm sure I know what's happened. I'll tell you when I get the whole story."

The vehicle continued further along the path. They stopped on a slight rise.

"Well here we are, Daph."

"Here we are, where? A pasture? You brought me to a snow covered pasture? What's for breakfast, frozen cow and eggs?"

"What a lot of questions. I have the honor to show you the orphan's home of my Squadron. Of which, I might add, I am its beloved Leader."

"Don't you try to put me on; I can see this is a field with an old dilapidated barn and some hay rolls about."

"Ah, but wait. See all the men moving about, and the trucks? And over there by the barn, as you call it, see the wind sock? It's to tell pilots which way the wind is set up."

"For God's sake I know what a windsock is. To me this looks like a place no self-respecting crop duster would fly out of."

"Well look down to your left. What do you see parked under the trees there?"

She squinted. "Goodness, a row of airplanes."

"Very good, Daph. There are sixteen to be exact. And the only reason you see any of them is the camouflage is pulled back while they're being serviced."

"So you're telling me this is an airplane base?"

"This is my Squadron, Spitfires, 11 Group."

"This takes a lot of believing."

"Daphne, think about it. With the windsock down, say you're a German fighter or bomber pilot, you streak along at two hundred miles an hour, at two thousand feet, what do you see?"

"I guess a pasture and a barn and those rolls of hay."

"Righto. Just like a thousand other pastures and barns. Yet you're looking for an airfield with runways and hangers and airplanes. And this is what we want them to see, nothing other than a farm and a narrow dirt path. All our petrol tanks are underground and our service vehicles and planes are tucked under camouflage. We even have more cows in the field when it's a little warmer, messes up the tires a bit, if you know what I mean. "

"So that's why the little dirt road, nothing to catch the eye."

"That's it in a nutshell."

"You're pretty tricky, Squadron Leader."

"Not me, Fighter Command. They have over thirty of these fields all about southeastern England. It's a marvelous idea. We can't concentrate our forces, too vulnerable. We learned that from the Great War. Unfortunately, Biggin Hill is a major air base, so it will be interesting. Although Biggin does have protection of the Chain Home System."

"Chain Home what?"

"Ops, a secret. Well known, still, a secret. If I told you, I couldn't let you out of my sight."

"Please don't tell me then. Just tell me there's a breakfast down in that barn."

As they entered the Mess, those present came to attention, although admittedly, most of the attention centered on Daphne. As an orderly arrived and took their order, Kenneth called to one of the privates and quietly instructed him to tell Flight Officer Hastings the Squadron Leader asks to see him out front in two minutes. After he told the FO, the Private was to have Sergeant Jennings and Corporal Archer out front in five minutes, no more.

"Everything all right, Ken?"

"Just a little question of chain of command, I'll be back in a few minutes."

Daphne could only see him as a shadow through the frosted window and she noticed the men in the barn quieted down, smiling as they sipped their tea. She blew on her teacup to cool it and tried not to stare at the window as another shadow appeared. Two minutes, then back to one shadow. Their meals came and she took her eyes off the window to acknowledge the orderly. Back to the window, she could barely make out three shadows through the frosted pane. She started her meal when the door opened and Ken walked in rubbing his hands.

"Bloody cold." He said to no one as the men went back to their conversations.

He sat down and began his meal. She looked at him questioningly. He murmured softly he would tell her later, and then saw another person he was looking for. "Ho, Mackie! Come over and meet Miss Elliot."

A short, stocky man, obviously older than Ken, ambled over. "Daphne Elliot, meet Flight Lieutenant William MacHalpen.

Mackie to us. This is my wingman and a Scots, so you might not be able to understand him."

"Ello Miss, ow ye mackin ut?" He turned to Sommers, "I dinna thinn she kens me."

Daphne smiled at him. "I be mackin out weal and I de ken ye, or should I say, I'm making out well and I do understand you quite clearly, Mackie."

Kenneth let out with a roar as his Flight Lieutenant near choked on his pipe.

"Now perhaps that will teach you to speak the King's English to an American, Mackie."

"Aye, Kenny, me lessons been taught. But 'twas worth it, Miss, if only to meet ye and hear such a lovely lass speak in me own Scot's tongue."

"Why thank you Mackie, I appreciate that."

Mackie glanced past a nose that had been broken three or four times. "Did you put the FO on the righteous path, Kenny?"

"He's okay now, just a little too…well you know, let's not talk shop right now."

"Righto, Laddy. I know the drill, and I'm sure the FO will let Jennings and Archer run the parade from this point on. We should be ready to have most of the ground crew, techs, engineers, and armourers out of here tomorrow afternoon. That will leave a skeleton crew with the Engineering Officer to leave the day after. You want all pilots ready for fly off for Biggin Hill tomorrow at 0900?"

"That's correct, Mackie, yes. Before we go on to Gravesend. Impress on them that we'll now be entirely under the Wing Commander's direct authority. Their combat training flights are over, from now on they're expected to act like experienced and professional Flight Lieutenants and Sergeants. And by Christ, Mackie let them know if they foul up in any way, any time, I'll come down on them like the wrath of God.

"I want you to do this, I've beat on them long enough, and it will be good practice for you. Before we leave I'll reiterate pretty much the same thing. As much as I'd miss you, you must be up for your own Squadron and you need all the leadership experience you can get. Tomorrow, you lead. Before you get to Group, form in five Battle Vs of three, and pass over the field first in perfect formation, and you know what I mean by perfect. Ops will direct you where to land and taxi."

"Where do you head while we flaunt ourselves shamelessly?"

"I'm up to Group HQ in Middlesex. Something's up. From there I'll go directly to Gravesend and see you there tomorrow night. But first I'll be back tonight for the morning fly off."

"Got you, Ken. To bring up the other issue. I think I see your plan. The trainer's topped off with petrol as you asked. All fluids check out and that includes petrol. I've done the walk around."

"Fine Mackie, have her rolled out. If you've checked her out, I'm safe. Be back in two hours."

"Fine with me, Kenny, I'll leave you to break your fast."

When he left, she couldn't help comment. "He seems like a character out of Dickens."

"He would fit there better than he does in a Spitfire, he's so damn wide. Nevertheless, he's my number one wingman and there's none better. A fast learner."

"Excuse my ignorance, what's a wingman?"

"Basically, if we were in combat, he'd follow me to keep anyone off my tail."

She gave the explanation some thought and stalked it to the obvious question. "And who keeps someone off his tail?"

He spilled his tea laughing. "Hopefully, and if they're lucky, someone on our side."

"Another question, why are you having the trainer rolled out, are you going off to train someone and leave me here alone, with all these wonderful, handsome fliers?"

"No, I'm not leaving you here, that's the last thing I'd do with this group. Especially the Americans. Now think."

It dawned on her. "You're taking me up? In a *Spitfire*?"

"That's the idea."

"But…how can you do that, isn't it a one person fighter? You seriously think I'm going to sit on your lap?"

"As much as I like that, no, you won't sit on my lap, and yes, normally she's a single seat. The Spitfire trainer we have is one of two specially made by Supermarine to help train American flyers in our unique British quirks, although we find they don't need it. You'll have the forward seat. How about it?"

She hesitated for a moment. She wanted to, dearly wanted to. It was crazy. She'd never even seen a Spitfire, but had heard so much about them, that the thought to actually fly in one sent a shiver through her. She nodded yes, afraid of her voice cracking.

"Great, Daph, flying suits are in the next room. This time I'll get you one that fits and that shouldn't be too hard, you're taller than most of my pilots. So, let's get started."

After suiting up and heading for the line of aircraft, MacHalpen joined them to say the trainer was rolled out and the camouflage taken back from Ken's new ship.

They closed on his Spitfire. Daphne looked up and stopped in her tracks. "My God, Kenneth, it's incredible. It's beautiful."

The aircraft was different from any most people had ever seen. A low wing monoplane, she was aerodynamic, with sinuous, flowing lines. She was, without question, the sleekest aircraft in the world. Waves of dark green and tan camouflage, white spinner on the nose, the ship seemed a greyhound straining at the leash. Daphne ran her hand along the red, white, and blue RAF roundel on the fuselage. "This is really striking. Tell me about it."

"Well first, *it* is a she or her, that's how we refer to airplanes and ships, as females."

Daphne rolled her eyes. "All right then, please tell me about *her*. If you can do that without giving her a hug."

"I'll try, and remember, you asked. This is a Mark I Spitfire. She was developed in only two years, '35, and '36 by one of our designers, R J Mitchell. He died of cancer in '37, but, thank goodness, he lived to see her fly. She's thirty feet long, with a thirty-seven foot wingspan. The engine is a Rolls Royce Merlin III, V12, and producing 1,030 horsepower. In the wings are eight Browning machineguns. She has the new variable pitch three-blade airscrew. That's propeller to you. The first seventy or so Mark I's were two-bladed. This three blade is far and away superior. Oh, and another thing, she's the most obedient and docile thing to manage. Quite different from another female I know, although I would never let on whom."

Lieutenant MacHalpen cleared his throat and turned away. Ken cocked his head and smiled sheepishly. Daphne ignored him and walked over to the trainer set away from the rest of the aircraft. She stood by the rear and looked around at all the personnel staring as they worked. She gave them a wave, assuring Ken's reputation.

"Ready, Daph?"

"If you're finished with your clever little bon mots, I am." MacHalpen kept a straight face and smothered a laugh. He would have paid to listen to this exchange. To the best of his knowledge, no woman had ever put Ken in his place like this.

When he could speak, he asked. "Do you have a flight plan, Kenny, me boy?"

"As a matter of fact I do. Mother mentioned Daphne has a home up on Windermere, so when she was changing, I rang up Jimmy Smyth, FO with 12 Group at Watnall. He said it was clear up their way. Leigh-Mallory has his Squadron on stand down for two days, like us. So except for possible civilian flyers, the air should be open. Would you like that Daph, see Windermere from above?"

She couldn't believe it. His clever little remark forgotten.

"I would, Ken, I'd love to go there!"

"I assume you don't want me to help you in."

"That's correct, I'm agile. I'm used to footholds."

"All right. Just a bit of no touch help this time. The cockpit's tight. You'll be in the forward seat where the half hatch is open. So, right foot in the first step, left to the wing root, then grab the sides of the canopy frame, step in with your right leg, then get your other leg over and drop down into the seat. It's awkward, so you'll have to…" She didn't wait and slipped up and into the cockpit with one unbroken, graceful move.

Ken turned to Mackie. "She's a mountain climber."

"I find I'm not surprised to hear that."

They both laughed.

"You RAF pilots having a good time?" She was laughing.

"Daphne, trust me, we never saw anyone glide into a cockpit that easily and we thought to have you teach our more clumsy pilots how to do it."

"Well, into it was easy, but it's snug, even for me. How do you fit Mackie?"

"Well, Miss, when that little bitty hatch is closed, 'tis a wee bit undersized for me shoulders to fit."

"And you're supposed to fight in this thing?"

"Once you're in, she's a part of you; or rather you become a part of her."

Daphne frowned. "Well, we'll see. Kenneth, just sitting in this thing is exciting. Are we ready?"

MacHalpen saluted them both, quietly asking Ken if they should have parachutes. He responded just as quietly the chutes would be of no use; they'd be flying too low for parachutes to open. As he climbed onto the wing root, he leaned forward to explain the transmitter and receiver switches, and smiled, seeing she had quickly worked out the clasps of the harness. He closed her hatch door and told her to close her section of the canopy once they were ready to take off, it would latch automatically.

"Oh, and by the way, Daph, whatever you do, don't press the red button on the spade grip, because the machine guns will fire."

"That's it! I'm out of here."

She started to unbuckle her harness. Ken near panicked, assuring her there was an outer red ring turned to lock, plus there were no armaments aboard.

"For God's, sake, Ken, I knew you were kidding. Not even you would be foolish enough to let me get near a loaded machinegun."

"Okay, you fooled me, no more machinegun fibs. We'll get started. I'll be busy for a few minutes. The helmet is the same as the Gladiator so be sure and connect the transmitter cord. "

He checked again with Mackie, who assured him the aircraft check off was performed and the 87 octane petrol clear of water. Ken dropped into the rear cockpit and buckled in as he started his preflight check. Ignition switch off, undercarriage lever down, green light indicated undercarriage locked. Flaps up and closed wheel brakes on, fuel tanks full. He worked the spade grip and rudder pedals, checked wing ailerons. In the rearview mirror at the top of the windshield frame, he looked to the rudder and elevators for proper function. The mirror also showed two of the ground crew by the tail.

He toggled her. "Daph, the reason those ground crew are there is that the wheels are chocked and if I throttled up the engine without them holding tail down, the aircraft would pivot over the chocks and drive the airscrew into the ground."

She nodded, interested every word. He was pleased she was.

Ken shifted in his seat and reached forward to give Daphne the thumbs up. He then set the mixture control to neutral, the airscrew control to fine pitch, and fully opened the radiator shutter. Now it was time to set both fuel cocks to open. He primed the cylinders with injections of seven shots of petrol. One last check, the airscrew was clear of personnel. With the throttle set at one-half, the fuel mixture now set to rich and the airscrew lever fully back, he shouted 'clear' and pressed the button to activate the Coffman starter.

A whining sound as the airscrew started to tick over, slowly at first until, abruptly, over a thousand horses woke and belched forth blue- black flame. The stink of petrol-rich exhaust fumes discharged along the aircraft's body and Daphne quickly slid her canopy closed. Ken screwed down the priming pump while checking the boost, +9lb/sq. inch, correct. With the RPMs at 2,800, the oil pressure rose to 60lb/sq. inch, correct. The magnetos now tested properly along with the airscrew pitch control. He kept the booster coil pressed until the engine fired evenly, then released it and went through the TMP procedure. Trim tabs set, Mixture rich, Pitch of airscrew fully forward. He clicked the transmitter toggle.

"Ready to go, Daphne?"

A moment's silence. "Ready to go? What are you—new at this? It took you so long I started dozing off."

He put his head down, shaking it from side to side and smiled like a fool and then pulled out her green polka dot scarf and wrapped it around his neck.

She liked it. "Hope it brings you luck."

"It already has, you're here aren't you?"

He signaled to have the wheel chocks removed, and then released the brakes. The crew holding the tail let go. As a Spitfire's nose rides high, he zigzagged to check his direction and the path was clear. The aircraft rocked over bumps and the two inches of light snow. The windsock rippled south, Ken took the aircraft south then swung into the wind and stopped.

Without another word, he throttled up. The engine came up to full boost. The plane lurched forward, bumping over the uneven ground, which didn't bother Daphne as she had been through it with the Gladiator biplane.

Now she felt the acceleration push her back into the seat. The bumps became less. The plane felt lighter, no feel of the ground. They were airborne, five, ten, twenty feet. Assured the wheels would not touch down again, Kenneth maintained level flight and raised the undercarriage. As the landing gear retracted into the wings, the red undercarriage light flashed UP as the aircraft gained velocity. At 140 indicated air speed, Ken throttled back to 2,500 RPMs and checked the oil pressure. He closed the radiator vent, shut the emergency half hatch, and slid his canopy closed against the cold air rushing past.

The Spitfire performed a sweeping arc, rising to the northwest and leveled off at two thousand feet. Satisfied, after using the hand wheel to adjust the elevator trim tab, he switched to call her.

"How are you, Daph? I haven't heard a sound out of you."

"Gosh, Ken…I'm too much in awe, just breathless. This is breathtaking, beyond words. A bit cold, but fantastic."

"Blast it! That's my fault. Up to your right is a knurled knob, it opens a flap to let in warm air. Not the best, better than nothing, sorry."

"No problem. This is so different from the biplane. What an astonishing view. God! I'm running out of adjectives.

"We're around two thousand feet. I'll take her out of trim and lower the port wing, your left side, so you can see better."

"I know it's my left for God's sake, I used to sail with some college hunks. Don't think you're the only one who knows where port is."

She frowned to herself. She really didn't want to keep him on constant guard any more. And he thought Good Lord, can't I say anything right?

The air was cool and dry, no need to use the windshield deicer. Daphne was in awe over the small towns scattered about, thatched roofs, cathedral towers, hills, rivers, ageless churches. She saw something new every few seconds and passed the information along to Kenneth. He let her ramble on. God, how he enjoyed that low, allusive voice.

"Windermere's coming up about two miles to port, if you know where that is, Miss Elliot."

She laughed, then leaned over, enthralled seeing the long lake from the air. "It's fantastic, Ken." Then enthralled. "Look! There's my house. There, all by itself. Can you go lower and slower?"

He eased back on the throttle, kept well above stall, and brought the aircraft down to five hundred feet. "That's a nice little cottage you have there, Daph. What is it? Forty rooms?"

"Thank you and no, it's only seventeen rooms. It was my brother's until he decided to go back and stay in the States, so I acquired it. It's a beautiful spot on the mere and I'm having heat put in so I can enjoy it in the late fall and early spring. For heaven's sake, there's a lorry in the drive, I'll bet that's Franklyn now, probably putting in the heat."

How much he'd love to be there with her, he mused. He wouldn't give a damn about putting in the heat.

"Now I'll show you Windermere from a perspective you haven't seen before, Daph."

He viewed as far as he could see up the length of the frozen lake, no iceboats, or people and held aircraft in a great circle well south. Swinging north again, he increased the fuel mixture to rich and pushed the throttle short of its stop, the nose lowered into a shallow dive. As the speed increased, the pressure pushed her back in the seat. Kenneth checked the area once more and leveled off at twenty feet over the ice. Daphne gasped.

The Spitfire hurtled north up the center of the eleven-mile long mere. Sparkling ice, then a mixed streak of hues flashed past her eyes. Trees, snow, islands—all dissolved into impressions of color, impossible to separate. Her house was there and gone. At three hundred miles an hour, she was stunned into silence, mouth agape, loving the sights.

In seconds, he corrected the aircraft's direction as the lake slipped northwest.

"I'm going to put her into a roll, Daphne. Cinch up."

He brought the yoke back firmly, then shoved it to the left. The spitfire sharply ascended, arced up, and turned a full roll over the mountains.

Daphne found her voice. "Oh my God…oh…my…God!"

Circling southeast and leveling out, he kept the Air Speed Indicator at 275.

"Daphne, you still there?"

"Barely. Actually I'm in another world Ken—your world."

"Welcome to it! Now, hold the yoke lightly."

He trimmed the ship perfectly and took his hands lightly off the yoke. After fifteen seconds, he retook control and told her she could let go.

"What was that all about, Ken?"

"You can now brag you've flown a Spitfire doing 275 miles an hour."

"Are you serious?"

"Cross my heart, my hands were off the yoke."

She was laughing now. "Did a pretty good job, didn't I?"

"Like you were born to it."

"Just like you were born to it. Right…Ken?"

His voice almost failed him. "Yes…just like me, Daphne."

He was still smiling as he leaned out the mixture once more and brought the air speed back to 160. Daphne remained awestruck. She leaned back without a word and watched the sunlight ripple off the wings, the crystalline sky, snow-mantled mountains in the distance and villages appearing as Lilliputian miniatures. There was too much to take in. Her flight in the Gladiator couldn't hold a candle to this. Nothing gave her such a sense of fulfillment. It suddenly struck her. Not even her love of climbing matched it. A new world opened. Her mind rushed through a hundred thoughts. Chills rippled through her. She couldn't stop it, didn't want to stop it.

Ken saw her shiver. "You cold, Daph?"

The spell didn't end, only interrupted. "No, no, Ken, I'm all right. How fast were we going?"

"Along the mere? A touch over 325 MPH. Fast enough for you? We could do it again, slowly, although it looks like a squall's formed on the horizon."

"Don't be silly, let's head back. God, it was incredible, the whole flight has been. Thank you for this. Now I don't wonder how you love what you do. You've a magnificent world I never knew…I, I can't put it into words. Even say I feel a part of the sky doesn't begin to describe the feeling."

"Describe it? Can't be done, Daph. Still, I know how you feel. It's that something that comes to some people and I think it's happened to you. So just sit back and enjoy the ride back. We've been up a little under ninety minutes. I'll leave you to your quiet musings."

Daphne did sit quietly, consumed by those musings. She knew he had done it just for her. Both of them were content.

11 Group's airfield was southeast, so he drifted further south and picked out two landmarks. Then, at two thousand feet, he brought the plane around for the descent onto the field.

The engine sputtered, coughed, and quit.

The airscrew turned slowly, the only sound was the air as it rushed past the cockpit. That, and Kenneth cursing a blue streak under his breath. Daphne didn't hear him and thought nothing of the engine shutdown. She recalled he landed the Gladiator without power onto the lawn at his mother's house. She simply thought he had done the same here. This was different. He hadn't set up for this crisis. She was unmindful of the difference.

He was in a dead stick glide. Nothing he tried brought power back. He reached up and shut off the ignition and fuel cocks. The transmitter was dead; he pulled the forced landing Flare Ring.

Ground personnel saw the flare and rushed to sound the alarm to clear the field. Flight Lieutenant MacHalpen hurried out, saw the height of the plane as it side-slipped into the approach pattern, and guessed at the speed. He knew it was the Squadron Leader returning and told everyone to calm down.

The squall Ken had seen generated bursts of crosswinds ahead of it and he fought to keep the Spitfire steady. He estimated gusts to be over twenty-five miles an hour and at that velocity, the Flight Manual stated, Do Not Land. Even with an engine, a pilot should head to another aerodrome. Very bloody unlikely, he cursed. They were coming in too hot, too high and too out of alignment with the field. He side-slipped again to align and knew he would need to drop the flaps to slow the craft. It became a question of when. Use them too soon and the plane would falter and either come up short, or land too hard. That would drive the undercarriage up through the wings. Lower the flaps too late and the aircraft would overshoot, with the possibility of colliding with the stone wall at the far end of the field.

His dilemma with the flaps was compounded by the fact they would only retract or extend by hand. They were not hydraulic and worse, there was no in-between range.

He extended the flaps to slow the aircraft. When that dropped her perilously close to the trees, he quickly retracted them to glide further. All the while, he fought the crosswinds that lashed on the control surfaces.

MacHalpen became concerned. He now recognized the erratic crosswinds were causing serious problems for Ken in trying to keep the ship level.

He lowered the undercarriage. The green light showed the wheels were down and locked, but the landing gear added even more drag. Mac thought it a mistake. Keep the wheels up he thought, belly in. Far safer.

The Spitfire, with its narrow landing gear platform, required steady, careful handling to balance touchdown on both wheels. Any error, and many were made in the past, often ended in serious injury or worse.

The Spitfire was rocking and wings alternated up, then down from the wind, yet Ken was trying a wheels down, dead engine side-slip through a crosswind, in a ship that handled nose heavy and vicious with a passenger up front. He worked the flaps, trying to slow the aircraft, yet keep the indicated air speed above stall, just over 70 MPH with flaps up, less with them down. He knew a Spitfire judders just before stall, so he held marginally over that speed, intent, confident, secure in his ability. If it could be done, he could do it.

Past the windsock, the ship rocked critically, pitching them side to side from the wind. Instinctively, he knew it was the time to lower the flaps for the last time. At that very moment, the Spitfire began to judder and stall. The plane settled, wheels bounced once, and again, then skated along the ground. He touched the brakes tentatively, then longer and harder as the aircraft skidded along the crusted snow. Finally, the Spitfire slued around well before the wall at the end of the grass field. He simply sat there for a moment. A nervous smile creased his cheeks as he thanked the heavens that his ability saved her life.

Daphne shouted from the front cockpit. "Ha! You didn't scare me, you showoff!"

He removed his harness and opened his canopy and half hatch. Out onto the wing, he slid her section of the canopy back, laughing with relief. She didn't grasp the situation.

"Geez, Ken, you think you'd frightened me? You glided into your mother's lawn in the biplane, so I wasn't…"

She stopped as she saw two Squadron cars and the fire brigade racing towards them over the snow. She turned back to him. "What? What's going on?"

He took her hand. "I wasn't trying to scare you. I wouldn't do that. We lost power."

Daphne's hand went to her mouth. "You're serious? Are you all right?"

"Sure, no problem, don't worry about me. Are *you* all right?" She didn't have time to answer as the vehicles skidded to a stop.

MacHalpen hopped out. "Jesus Bloody Christ! Ken, that was one hell of a bit of flying. For half a mo I thought the plane would be into the wall and plastered all over the next pasture."

"Take it easy Mackie, there's a lady present, don't want to rattle her."

She spoke bravely until the truth sunk in and they saw she was anxious, as would any person in their right mind. Ken, Daphne, and definitely Mackie, were in need of a drink.

Back to the barn for whiskeys and scotches. Even though he was Senior Officer, his pilots and ground crew couldn't help but form around him with backslaps and endless 'Well done, Sir'. Kenneth in turn, reminded them of the Manual. Their bible. Do not try to land in a cross wind over 20 MPH, go to alternate field or belly in if you lose power. That was an order, or else.

MacHalpen sat with Daphne, as they tasted his private stock and watched the men around him.

"What do you think, Daphne?"

"About myself? I guess I'm still a little rattled. About him? I'm so baffled about everything to do with him; I honestly don't know what to think."

Mackie smiled, "I'll bet you one thing right now, when he comes over here, his hand will be just as steady as if he was only back from a walk."

"It really was that close a thing, Mackie?"

"Aye, lass, it really 'twas."

Kenneth finally broke away from his men and came toward her with a serious expression. "Sorry, Daphne, they're my ground

346

and air crews, I couldn't ignore them. How are you doing?"

"Well, to be frank, when we were in the middle of that wild landing, I strangely enjoyed it. Ignorance being bliss. When I found out I wasn't supposed to, it did bother me, but look at this."

She extended her arm, her hand held a full shot glass. "See, not the slightest quiver."

He bowed to her and took a full shot glass from Mackie and held it out to tap hers. Not the slightest quiver.

"We're a formidable couple of pilots." He said. Daphne swelled with pride, tears to her eyes. They swallowed their drinks, made faces, laughed, and openly admired each other.

Ken turned to MacHalpen, "Mackie, before I forget. I'll be back late tonight, there's a sort of going away party with a few friends at the Dorchester in London, so I'll pop in there to wish them Godspeed, then be back. Notify the guard to wake me at 0500 tomorrow."

MacHalpen nodded. Then Ken showed annoyance and called FO Hastings over. "If your crew has to tear that ship apart, find out why in hell I lost most of my electrics and some of the hydraulics. I want a full report in my hand tomorrow morning at 0600 if you have to work all night."

Flight Officer Hastings gave a quick 'yes, Sir' and asked if the Squadron Leader could spare a few moments to sign Squadron Reassignment Procedure forms.

When Ken left, Daphne leaned over to MacHalpen. "Mackie, I've a secret."

"Do ye want to share, lass?"

He expected her to say she was in love with the Squadron Leader. To MacHalpen, it was evident Kenneth was utterly smitten with her.

"Don't tell Ken."

"I won't Daphne."

"I'm going to learn how to be a pilot."

Mackie was completely taken aback. He fumbled for something to say.

Daphne was surprised and hurt. "What's the matter? Don't you think a woman can be a pilot?"

"Of course Miss, it's just I thought you were going to say something about Kenny. You… you caught me off guard."

347

"Oh, I see now. I think I understand your confusion. No, I wasn't about to say anything more about Kenneth than I've already told you. He baffles me, leave it at that."

"Then may I ask you why you don't want to tell him you want to learn to fly?"

"I'm afraid he won't like it."

"And why should that bother you? If all he is to you is bafflement and nothing more, then it shouldn't concern you, right? So it also shouldn't be a problem to tell him, right?"

Mackie confused her. Of course, he was right. Why shouldn't she not tell Ken? She could do what she wanted, right?

MacHalpen got up from the table. "Duty calls, Miss. Most pleasant to have met you."

As she took the offered hand, he bent over and spoke quietly. "You really should look inside yourself, lass. He means a wee bit more to you than simple bafflement."

She watched him walk away, turning over his words. Did she have to admit someone had seen through the façade she'd put up, even if only to fool herself? Kenneth did mean more to her than she was ready to admit. This must and will, stop, she cursed quietly. "He'll drive me to his Mother's, and that's it, thank you very much."

After they changed out of their flight suits, Ken went to warm the car while Daphne chatted up the pilots and crews. They congratulated her on her stressful landing. She told them she had had more traumatic events in the Bernese Alps and on the Jungfrau and Eiger peaks. They were beguiled. Not one of them knew of a woman, never mind a beautiful, articulate woman, who climbed mountains for excitement. Ken stood by the door, watching her fascinate his crews and fighter pilots and have them in the palm of her hand. Then again, he thought, how could he fault them, he was just as beguiled. His mother had excellent taste. He smiled and went to ruin his pilots' good time.

Daphne dozed off as the Humber staff car cruised into the light drizzle. It was fine she slept, for then he could glance over and watch her smile—from dreams of their flight he hoped.
It was only when the vehicle crunched onto the glaze of the road to The Mount that she woke.

"Where are we, Ken?"

"Almost to Mother's. You had a good nap."

"Darn it! I'm sorry I'm such poor company. I wanted to speak to you about something as we drove home."

He stopped the car. "Well, what's wrong with right here? We're cozy, warm…alone."

"Yes, that's all well and good, but now listen to me."

"You have my undivided attention. What is it?"

"I want to learn to fly. There, I said it right out."

He didn't comment, wasn't in the least surprised. She saw an arched eyebrow. His hands supported his chin while he seemed to contemplate the fogged window. The only sound? The rasp of the heater fan. She waited patiently, far more patient than her persona normally allowed.

Without turning his head, he asked. "I have no problem whatsoever with you wanting to learn to fly. I think it would be great for you. But what do you mean, by fly? Private, commercial, military?"

She was at a loss. "Can't I just simply learn to fly? And what do you mean military?"

"It's only a thought that ran through my mind."

"Well, don't stop. Run it through mine."

"Let's go to the house, If you're sure that is what you want to do, then I'll make a phone call. After that, we'll sit and discuss it."

She was sure and while Ken made the phone call, Daphne and Lady Jane chatted about the trip. Daphne spoke of the flight in a Spitfire, not the landing. Jane acted cross with her son until Daphne said she knew all about Lady Jane's covert pretense over her son and that she, Jane, wanted Daphne for Kenneth.

Lady Jane confessed, though not contrite. In fact quite the opposite. She told Daphne that if the two got married she would move out immediately, there wasn't a house built large enough to hold two adult females and one man. Daphne was in too deep and countered by telling her not to be silly, this was Jane's home and she should never be forced to leave for anyone. Lady Jane responded that the home was Kenneth's by inheritance and she wanted nothing more than a small cottage where she could putter about among her roses and leave this wooden lot of sticks to Kenneth, his wife and her grandchildren—three grandchildren.

The conversation had gone far off track, Daphne knew. Time to clear the air. Just as she started to be firm, Kenneth reentered the room after his phone call. Coincidence? Daphne questioned herself as he interrupted all smiles. "Guess where we're headed tonight, Daphne."

"*We're* going nowhere tonight, Ken. *You* might be, not me."

"Ah, but *we* are. We're going to the Dorchester; I, to meet some of my friends and you, to meet Jesus Peron."

"Number one, I'm not going to the Dorchester, and two, who the devil is Jesus Peron and why should I want to meet him?"

"You should want to meet Jesus Peron because he's a flight instructor for British Aviation, the company I told you about. Jesus screens the American pilots prior to going on to the RAF. He's an acquaintance of mine, and he said he would take you on privately for flight lessons. So, are we going to the Dorchester, or was your notion of learning to fly a bored little girl's fancy of the moment?"

"Blast you, Ken! You know I can't say no."

Lady Jane laughed, Ken smiled. Daphne saw she'd not a thing to wear to the Dorchester.

She slipped into a deep green silk blouse, cream trousers, dark brown shoes, and belt. Lady Jane added a silver lace choker and matching watch. Her hair was left to fall over her shoulders and back. It was not appropriate dress, as the men would be in eveningwear and the women in gowns. She had no choice. She was the way she was, the devil take it. When she came down the stairs, Lady Jane felt her a vision, Ken was even more enticed, if that be possible.

He changed clothes and a quick glance showed Daphne he had dressed down, so she wouldn't feel out of place. He wore a white linen dinner jacket, gray slacks and lavender dress shirt with…God! Her green and white polka dot scarf as his cravat!

"Are you out of your mind? Take that scarf off!"

"I will not, if you're committed to go to the Dorchester in that shabby outfit, then I can go like this. And that's final."

She yielded. "Well, I will admit, it does make you look carelessly dashing. Very carelessly."

"Thank you my dear, now let's have a quick bite to eat, I'm famished, as I know you must be and all there will be at the

Dorchester are petit fours and those certainly won't do."

* * *

On the drive to the Dorchester, Ken informed Daphne of a few things to keep in mind with the people she will meet.

"These friends tonight are military, with of course their wives or sweethearts. It's sort of a going away party for them, a quiet going away party. And remember, the women will not be happy."

"Where is everyone going?"

"I'm afraid we've all come to our personal diaspora, our personal scattering. As you know, I'm going to 11 Group Command, then probably on to France as originally planned. Doug and Bertie, whom you've yet to meet, are Captains in the Royal Marines, off to Singapore. Commander Tony Wesley, who is Royal Navy, was ordered to the High Seas Fleet, most likely to Malta. The other three are my peers, Squadron Leaders off to various commands around the Med, and our naval and air base at Gibraltar. I'll save you their names until introductions."

"England is sort of spreading you all around her Empire, isn't she? I guess with the looks of things, she has no choice."

"Quite true. Lord knows when or if we shall ever meet again and that's the pity of it."

"So why will this Jesus Peron chap be there. Just to see me?"

"Not only that. Jesus qualified fourteen of the pilots for the RAF Naval Air Arm and he ingratiated himself and then with the rest of us. He's a damn good bloke. He is, or at least says he is, the bastard…sorry, the *illegitimate* son of Juan Domingo Peron."

"And who, pray tell, is Juan Peron?"

"Peron is a Lieutenant Colonel in the Argentinean Military and pretty much a Nazi sympathizer, if not a behind the scenes backer of them in his own country. Even though he's only a Lieutenant Colonel, Peron's become quite powerful and at present he's touring Germany, Italy and Spain with a military contingent. I'm sure you can see these are all dictatorships, and despite Argentina being a Republic, no one in his country raises a finger to question what he's up to."

"And why would you associate with a person whose father is a Nazi sympathizer?"

351

Ken didn't answer at first. She could see he had something on his mind, so waited him out. "Let me tell you about Jesus Peron first, Daphne, and you'll see where he fits. As Jesus tells it, his mother was one of Peron's women friends…if you follow me, and Jesus said that when his Mother told Peron she was pregnant, Peron shouted Jesu Cristo!"

Daphne gave him a smirk. "And that's how Jesus got his name."

"That's the fish story he stays with."

They both laughed. "Enough of this, Ken, please get on with the story."

"Well, this is where it starts to get interesting. He states he's never talked to his Father and the only time he sees him is in newsreels. However, Jesus lives high on the hog with no visual means of support other than his flight pay. He says he's raced cars in Argentina then over here on the Donington Circuit. And, he supposedly raced gratis for Auto Union after Bernd Rosemeyer was killed on the Autobahn."

"So, you're saying this Peron guy slips him money. For what? To keep him quiet, don't tell who his Father is? If he's being paid for that, his Father's not getting his money's worth, now is he?"

"No, it's not that simple. We think Jesus is being paid for something far more significant."

"That sounds ominous. What, pray tell, is that?"

"Damn, we're here. I'll talk to you about it on the way home. Just remember not to tell him you've been up in a Spitfire."

"I won't. Is it all right to park here, out front like this?"

"Of course. That's my Command Flag on the fender. The staff here knows my squadron number on it. There'll be no problem about it."

She grinned. "I wondered what that was on the fender. I thought maybe you were drying a golf towel."

"Well, aren't you the little wise…ah, guy?"

"You were going to say wiseass, weren't you?"

"I confess the thought did pass through my mind."

"Don't be afraid to say what's on your mind, Ken. I'm not recently from a nunnery, like I imagine some of your younger admirers are."

They exited the vehicle laughing. At last he was learning to love her glibness. Daphne glanced across to Hyde Park and noticed workmen had torn up the frozen lawns, despite the cold.

"What on earth are they up to, digging up the Park in this kind of weather?"

"Air raid shelters."

"What?"

"Air raid shelters. I think that type is called an Anderson shelters. They're all over the southeast country. The next war is going to be an air war, Daphne. Something never seen before, except for what's going on in Spain."

"This seems so surreal. Talk of war, military men taken from their homes, sent all over the world, shelters dug in beautiful Hyde Park. God, I hope all of you prove to be wrong."

"An old English proverb, hope for the best, prepare for the worst and damn the rest—I added the damn the rest part."

"I suppose you must."

"Yes, we must. Come, we're going through to the Promenade Room."

The room wasn't crowded. His friends saw them and waved. At first, their glances were of surprise at his casual dress; then wide-eyed, they looked over to Daphne, as she walked toward the officers and held out her hand as she was introduced. The women, though envious, couldn't help but admire her and her relaxed, no airs manner won them over. Comments were made about Kenneth's haute couture and the polka dot cravat, which he humorously explained his mother had stolen from Daphne's luggage. No remarks were made concerning Daphne's attire; everyone loved it.

She found herself part of a pleasant evening. Short, yet serious conversations on world affairs. A little gossip about Laurence Olivier and Vivien Leigh, sharing the sheets, shall we say, while she was filming *Gone with the Wind* with Clark Gable in Hollywood. Also, Alfred Hitchcock, Director of last year's movie *The Lady Vanishes*, had just left the Dorchester. Was he a little tipsy? Without question, they laughed.

The women were strong, lightly touching their husbands with their hands, not quite hiding a moist eye of worry, yet trying not to let on when their men were near. Two of them told Daphne they were members of the WRN, the Women with the Royal Navy, called Wrens. Other women were with the British Red Cross and Daphne mentioned she often had contacts with the Red Cross when she put on vaudeville shows with Ken's mother, Lady Sommers. Daphne mentioned Ken was only an acquaintance, and she had agreed to come this night because she wanted to learn to fly. They naturally doubted her, glancing from one to the other skeptically, keeping thoughts to themselves. Before Daphne could respond to their expressions, Ken returned from the men.

"Please ladies, I'm leaving too. Let me have a little time with Daphne."

He led her to the bar, where the bartender looked up and smiled. "Squadron Leader Sommers. How nice to see you. Been a while. Now I hear you're leaving us also."

"Yes and hello, Harry, it has been a while. Busy you know. I see you've put in a new bar here."

"Yes, Sir, last year. Though it's not as crowded as then. Mood of the country, I rather suspect."

"Could be, Harry. Daphne, meet Harry Craddock, bartender extraordinaire. Inventor of the Manhattan, Martini, and the White Lady."

"Nice to meet you, Harry. I'm impressed. Which of your drinks would you suggest for a scotch drinker?"

"Pleasant meeting you, Miss Daphne. How about a Martini for a change of pace?"

"Fine I'll start with one of your Martinis."

"Make it two, Harry."

They had a few words with Harry Craddock, then turned and leaned on the bar. "I'm not ladylike, draped on the bar like this."

"I'm surprised that bothers you."

"It doesn't bother *me*. I just don't want to embarrass you in front of your admirers."

"The only one the men and the women here admire is you." He touched her glass with his. "I hope you're having a good time."

"I am. I'm glad you brought me. But where is this Jesus Peron I'm to meet?"

"He must have heard you ask, here he comes now."

Ken shook the offered hand. "Hello, Jesus, good to see you."

"Lider de Escuadron Sommers, que bueno verlo otra vez."

Ken got the first part, Squadron Leader, and, lost with the

rest, turned to Daphne.

"For God's sake, Ken, were you sick when school had Spanish too? He said it was good to see you once more."

Peron, who looked to be in his teens, turned to Daphne, "Ah, usted es una mujer hermosa, y tambien inteligente."

Daphne looked to Ken. "It's clear he's very astute. He said I'm a beautiful woman, and intelligent as well."

She turned back to Peron. "Hola Jesus, encantado de verlo, and to Kenneth, "I told him it was very nice to meet him, you uneducated school skipping Brit."

Jesus Peron started to laugh. Ken turned to her. "He speaks English too, Daphne. You should be careful."

"Me careful, about what? I'm not embarrassed; you're the one who should be self-conscious."

Jesus broke in, in English, "Excuse me, Miss Daphne. You speak with the argots of classical Castilian Spain, the Old World. I am from Moscovi, Northeastern Argentina. I am afraid we have bastardized old world, classical Spanish so much that it is difficult to understand you without translating in my head. Let me speak Latin American English and I will understand your Norte American, Boston English. We should get by."

Daphne *could* speak Spanish with a Moscovi dialect yet didn't mention it. So when Kenneth introduced them with his Southeast England inflections, they all understood each other.

Jesus explained his position as a weeding out of American flyers who wanted to become RAF pilots. There weren't too many who applied at present he said, although the numbers are expected to grow as the threat of war increased. Daphne spoke of her desire to become a pilot and Jesus impolitely—either through a language nuance or not—made the flippant comment that piloting involved more than simply pointing an aircraft where you wanted to go.

Daphne seized the remark as condescending, and wasn't about to let it pass. "Jesus, let's set the ground rules right now. I'm not the addled-headed, flighty little type of bird you may hang around with. It may be difficult, but try to consider me equal to a man in intelligence, and please, keep any attitude to yourself. Just teach me as you would an intelligent person and we'll get along just fine. Otherwise you can go fly a kite in the rain."

Ken burst out laughing. "See what I go through, Jesus?"

Jesus smiled weakly. It was certainly not to his liking, being talked to this way, and by a woman, no less. He bit his tongue, from fear that if he took exception to her comments, he would get the worst of any confrontation. He murmured it was a simple misunderstanding as English was not his first language. A vague apology, which Daphne cordially accepted, and the conversation went on to her background, health, and possible handicaps.

"Tell me, Daphne," Jesus inquired, "do you know Weybridge in Surrey?"

"I've been in that general area."

"When you come for lessons and get near Weybridge, you'll see signs that direct you to Brooklands. It's an airfield and sport racing circuit. I've raced an Alfa Romero there in the past. There are also a number of aircraft manufacturers in the area and I have the use of the Training Centre and airstrip for ground and flight classes. You'll meet me at the Vickers Aircraft office."

Ken was curious. "What do you have for trainers, Jesus?"

"I'll start her on the DH Gipsy Moth biplane. After that, I've got available a 1937 de Havilland 94 monoplane. I don't know if you've seen it, Ken; it's a low wing, two seats. The one I use has the enclosed canopy. She'll do close to 120 MPH."

Daphne started to say something, Ken interrupted. "That's good, exchange phone numbers, and decide on a time, Daphne and I must say goodbye to everyone. I've got to get along."

Daphne said she would be gone for a week in Coventry. They set a time for her first class and Jesus excused himself.

Daphne turned to Kenneth. "What was that all about? You interrupted while I was speaking."

"Sorry, but I didn't want you to say you'd been in a Spitfire."

"I wasn't about to say that, but why shouldn't I?"

"Because it's none of his business. Then again, maybe it is."

"That's very cryptic. What the devil are you talking about?"

"Don't ask anything right now, I'll get to it after we leave."

Puzzled by his manner she looked around, surveying the room, and was stunned.

"What is it, what's the problem, Daph?"

Chapter 21

"THAT'S DAVID ROYCE, KEN."

"Well I'll be damned, so it is. Sir David in the flesh. So? He has a right to be here, doesn't he?"

"I suppose. I'm just shocked. Who's that man with him?"

"Haven't the foggiest, why don't you go over and say hello?"

"Damned if I won't."

With that, she started towards David Royce as the man he was with nodded and left. David was momentarily alone. He turned, saw, and then recognized Daphne. As she neared him, it took no time for her to grasp David was ineptly uncomfortable with her presence.

Daphne smiled, there really wasn't anything wrong with his being there, she thought, yet his expression undeniably revealed there was. He wasn't actually aghast, but close to the brink.

"Hello, David, fancy meeting you here."

"Yes, this is a surprise. I was told you were with some vaudeville troupe out in the hinterlands."

He was unnerved. She became suspicious and determined to find the reason. "I was for a while, David, and then I stayed at Lady Jane Sommers' home to work out more programs. Her son brought me here to meet a flight instructor. What are you doing here? Dining some admiral…"

She stopped in midsentence. A young, perhaps twenty year old girl, with imperfectly applied makeup, came up and pulled on his arm. David froze. The girl, who brazenly evaluated Daphne, turned to David. "Come on Ashton, I'm bored, let's find a party, or go home!"

The blood rushed to David's face. Daphne's amusement turned to anger with the arrival of this blond. "Ashton? Party? Home? What in hell is going on here, David?"

The girl was indignant. "Who are you calling David, lady? This is Sir Ashton Hamilton. You've got the wrong person, so now push off."

Daphne lashed back. "Why you dumb little bimbo! This is David Royce and he has a wife and two children at home! I ought to slap you silly but it's not your fault—It's this bastard's!"

The outburst scandalized the Promenade Room. Daphne, outraged, towered over the blond who, now shocked and frightened, slipped behind a mortified David. Kenneth hurried toward the fray.

He took her arm. "Daphne, really, calm down. You've had your say, there's nothing more to be gained by prolonging this."

Daphne eased off. "Your right, Ken, I know, I know. I apologize to everyone here. I'm sorry about my actions. Nevertheless, this bastard..."

David, always adroit, chanced a response. "And who is this gentleman, Daphne? Is this someone we haven't heard about in Coventry?"

Kenneth instantly suspected trouble. His eyes narrowed, threatening. "I suggest sir; you remain civil and watch your tongue. You should leave now, while you still have the sense."

David took a step back, Daphne moved between them, taking Ken's arm. He was menacing, something she'd never seen in him. This was going too far. She pulled on his arm. "Come on, Ken, let's go back to your friends so I can apologize."

They both cooled down as they walked off. Now Kenneth wanted to keep her that way. "You were just shocked at the situation, Daph, and responded without thought. You got a little hot under the collar, that's all."

"A little hot? He has the greatest wife and children and he pulls this stuff. What is he doing, parading around with a cheap trick? I should have slapped him. And you, you weren't exactly laid back."

Ken's tension had dissipated as quickly as it arose. Now, he kept straight-faced, but silently laughed at her remarks. "All right, let's just stay calm. Nothing's to be done about it."

"Damn, double damn! There's other words I can think of too. Why would he bring that woman here? Where's his thinking?"

"I can't tell you. Perhaps he thinks he's showing off."

"With her? Know what I think of someone who does that?"

"I'm getting a good idea, but don't tell me here, there are people around hanging on your every word. So back off with your temper, Daphne. My word, you'll have me banned from the Dorchester. Mother will die from the shame."

He had her smiling now. "All right, Ken, I'm down to a simmer. Has he left?"

"Yes, with haughty haste I might add and, as you so sweetly described her, the little bimbo sashaying along behind."

Daphne and Kenneth learned more about each other. Kenneth's temper was controlled, menacing. Daphne's was explosive and enduring. She also noted he ordered her to control her temper…and she didn't argue. She thought that curious.

Daphne expressed regret to his friends if she had embarrassed them, although it was so apparent what had happened, everyone told her she was justified in her anger. One of the women went so far as to whisper, "Daphne, you should have scratched his face. Let him explain that to his wife."

The tenor of Ken's friends overall was blasé. Whereas David Royce's apparent affair with the blonde young woman was reprehensible, it at least spiced up their otherwise poignant leave-taking. It also gave them something to whisper about later at home, the officer's club, and the office, especially to one of the women employed by the Government.

Another round of drinks was ordered. Ken declined. "I have to fly tomorrow and we should make our farewells now."

Daphne started to put her second Martini on the table. Ken told her to keep it and walked up to the bar to pay for the glass.

Harry Craddock held up his hand. "No, return it someday. That's an order, Squadron Leader."

"That may be a long time, Harry."

"I know. I can wait," he laughed, "just bring it back clean."

The vehicle warmed as they drove toward The Mount. Daphne sipped the last of her drink. "That was sad, Ken, to have to say goodbye to your best friends. I felt bad for you."

"We all knew it would come to this someday. It's something we had to face."

"Why didn't you agree to have everyone get together for a

reunion? It could be fun, seeing friends after…well…after."

"No. Father told me his friends planned that for after the Great War. Of the twenty friends who were to meet, only he and four others arrived. That five, and two others in convalescence centers—the kind you and mum help support—were the only ones left. Why on earth would anyone want to go to the Dorchester and wait? For what, ghosts of people who would never come?"

She could see he had already thought a reunion could be a tragic affair. "I'm sorry Ken. Guess I still won't believe a war is going to happen."

He changed the subject abruptly. "So you're going to learn to fly, that's great. I want you to keep one thing in mind for the future. We'll need more male pilots for the RAF and you could help. Women aren't allowed to fly combat but, if you're good enough, you could be a ferry pilot and ferry aircraft to different squadrons. That way you'd free up a male pilot for combat."

She brightened; a wide smile glinted in the darkness. "You mean that someday I might fly a Spitfire into your air base?"

"If you're good enough."

"My, God! Of course I'll be good enough. I've already flown a Spitfire, haven't I?"

"I'll be damned if you haven't."

"And you said I was born to it."

She settled back into the seat, the second Martini warmed her as she conjured the scenario of being a pilot for the RAF. "I'll have to join the service, won't I?"

"I'm not sure. The Women's Auxiliary Air Force will be part of the RAF. It's being formed this year, they're called WAAFs. You might be able to fly with them, but I don't think flying's decided yet. You could join the Air Transport Auxiliary; they're civilian flyers for the RAF, although you'd have to have your master pilot's license to be accepted. I don't know how many hours flight time you'd need."

"You make it sound complicated."

"Everyone has to go through it, Daphne, even poor little rich girls like you."

"Well, wise guy, I'm going to go through it starting next week. And as I think of it, what was it you wanted to tell me about Jesus on the way to the Dorchester."

In the glow of the dashboard lights, she could see Kenneth give a conspiratorial smile.

"We're pretty sure he's a Nazi spy."

"You're pulling my leg!"

"No."

"Then why the devil do you let him hang about with your friends?"

"Because we watch what we say, or say things to mislead him. That's why I didn't want you to say you'd flown in a Spitfire, he might just pick up on some little thing that would fit with some other little thing he's heard."

"I'm shaking my head in the dark here, Ken. What could I possibly tell him?"

"I can't tell you what it is, Daph, but in the cockpit is a dial or two, which would mean something to someone with electrical engineering knowledge."

"Then it went right over my head."

"Good, like you said before, ignorance is bliss."

"I beg your pardon!"

"Oh Boy, here we go again."

"No, Ken, we're not. It's been too nice a day and evening and I thank you for a wonderful time. What with the flight, and meeting your pilots, the Dorchester, your friends and getting me set up for flying lessons, what more could a girl ask for? Except for that God damned David Royce!"

"Let's forget him for the rest of our time together, shall we? I'm off for the Squadron soon. Cuss about him after I leave."

"Fair enough, let's get into the house."

"Nightcap, Ken?"

"Love to, but I really must toddle off. Busy day tomorrow, moving the Squadron and I've got to get to Middlesex."

She held out her hand. He took it firmly, then pulled her to him. Before she could blink, his other hand was on the back of her head. He quickly kissed her and then let her go before she could even think to react.

He headed for the door. "Cheerio, Daph! Bye the bye, you're not much of a kisser."

She was dazed, first at the kiss, and now this flippant farewell. She caught up to him at the open door. "Who do you think you are? Damn you! You don't kiss me and strut off! Not much of a kisser am I?" She kissed him and proved him wrong. "And then I push you out the door!"

She slammed it closed and threw the bolt behind him. She headed for her room, not knowing whether to be angry or laugh. She looked up and saw Lady Jane on the balcony.

"Really, Jane. That son of yours!"

"I told you before dear," she beamed, "he's a terrible rake."

The drive back to Squadron gave Kenneth time to think. He had kissed her and she didn't stop him. That was due to surprise. She had come after him and kissed him. That was from being provoked. Nonetheless, she had kissed him, think of it that way. And her pushing him out the door was certainly not from love. Still, it meant...something.

He let his mind go blank, and then refocused well past the windscreen. He had an ability to clear his thoughts and then transfer onto another subject. Now, she was put aside for another time. He did not know when, yet without question, he knew they would meet another time. She must be gone. Father had disciplined him well. For now, there should be nothing on his mind other than country, squadron, men...duty.

Back at 11 Group, he learned the loss of electrics in the Spitfire was due to the lengthening of the plane for the additional seat frame and that frame had crimped the main power conduit and eventually parted a segment of the leads. As the trainer was one of only two produced, the possibility of fault was not in the maintenance manual. Therefore, maintenance personnel could not be criticized. Kenneth thanked his mechanics and ordered his FO to report the problem up the chain of command so they could inform the manufacturer, Supermarine, immediately. After that, he went single-minded to his duties.

* * *

Thinking of the evening, a good part of the night, and the next day through the ninety-five mile drive to Coventry, Daphne was a bundle of conflicting emotions. The wonderful flight in the Spitfire and Kenneth, then Windermere, learn to fly, that damn

David, Ken's kiss, his Mother, what was Jim up to? Keep your mind on the road. She had kissed Ken back, why? The Spitfire, watch where you're going, then again, where was she going? At least she had some direction, wasn't she was going to learn to fly? Her goal was to be the best damn female pilot ever. That will show Ken. Yet, again, why did she have to show Ken?

* * *

Royce paced, then finally stopped and fell once more into the wingback chair in front of the fireplace. He stared pensively into the fire, without a word.

"Jim, say something. What do you think? He's your brother."
"Daphne, I…I simply don't know what else to say. You see him with another woman, or bimbo as you assume, he has no excuse, so apparently he's cheating on Mary. Why on earth did he take that kind of woman there? And where does that leave us? Tell Mary? No. Say something to David? What?"

"As far saying something to Mary, I guess you're right, there's nothing we can do about it. But there's another story in play here. He has another life. She called him Sir Ashton Hamilton and she wanted to go partying or *home*? What's going on here? What if this gets out? You know damn right well it could. The Dorchester wasn't crowded, yet I'll bet there were enough people there who might know him. If it makes the News of the World or the Guardian, what will Mary do? And then what about the company? Bad publicity could hurt the Royce Company. You know the pseudo Victorian elitists in Government. They'll pontificate over the lack of morals in private industry and I'll bet David has enemies that would make hay out of it. He's done a thoughtless, stupid thing, and undoubtedly not the first time."

"Let's not get ahead of ourselves, Daphne. First, is there any way he could injure your reputation over this?"

"Mine? You mean more than our living together?"

"You know what I mean, about this chap you were with."

"Jim, as I said, he's Lady Jane Sommers' son. He's RAF and was at her house. He offered to take me for a flight up to Windermere in a Spitfire trainer, which I'll be frank, I wasn't about to turn down. I loved the flight so much he set it up for me to meet a flight instructor at the Dorchester. I met the chap, we made arrangements for lessons, had a drink with him and then Jane's son Kenneth, drove me back to Lady Jane's. After that, I thanked him and he left to go back to his Squadron. There's nothing David can find to retaliate about."

All of what Daphne said was true and, she felt, there was no sense in mucking up the discussion by being overly truthful. "I'm so blasted irritated, Jim, let's change the subject. Tell me what do you think of my learning to fly? You haven't commented on that since I told you."

"You're right, I haven't. I'm so bothered about the David situation I didn't think to comment. It's good for you Daph, you really should do it. You seem to have become so keen about flying it will give you a goal and a break from all those wounded veterans. If you get the chance, talk to Lady Jane about a woman flyer named Beryl Markham. If memory serves me, I recall Father mentioned her. I think she was also at some affair with Mother.

Markham's English, grew up in Africa as a bush pilot for years. She was the first woman to fly solo to North America a couple of years ago. It was all the news, I even read about her in Austria. She was in some social column a month or two back, so if she's still in the country maybe she could give you some advice."

"Jim, you're a fountain of information when you want. I'll certainly ask Jane. Now to get back to my plan to be a pilot. I hoped you'd be positive about it. This will mean I'll be away a bit more, between work with Lady Jane and flying lessons, but you're so damned busy I guess you'll hardly miss me."

"I'll miss you, although I won't be around either."

"What do you mean?"

"Well, now that you've told your news, here's mine. I'm going to America."

"Really? How come?"

"Two reasons, Rolls Royce has licensed an American firm, Packard Motorcar Company in Detroit, to build specific models of the Merlin engine. I'm going with four RR engineers to review and set up the processes and bearing supply with the Americans. After that, I'm on to Fort William, in Ontario, Canada. Canada Car and Foundry is to build most, if not all, of the Hurricane fighter under license from Hawker."

"Aren't you becoming the world traveler? But what about all the work you've got here? I thought you were indispensable."

Royce laughed. "I thought that too. However, it seems David committed me to go with the engineers. Hands across the sea and all that, I suppose. The Home Office thought it a good idea and David concurred, so off I go. There's probably something in it for him. Right now I do think Henderson can handle most of the problems here, for a while at least. We'll just have to find out."

"When do you leave?"

"Around the first week in March, so I have a week left to clear my desk here. I'll be gone about a month."

"That long? Can you get any time off before then?"

"That would be tight. What do you have in mind?"

"Well, I think the heat will be in at Windermere or, we could go to my place in Belgravia. You know, we could walk around in the cold, like tourists."

"Pick any day, one's as good as the next. As long as we leave in the late afternoon, have the next day together and I'm back to work the following day."

"Ah, Jim, I always said you were an irresponsible romantic."

He smiled, shrugged his shoulders, at a loss what to say.

Thoughts came to her mind and out her mouth involuntarily.

"Jim, do you think we've begun to drift apart?"

His smile faded, embarrassed. "I admit I've given that some thought, Daphne."

She was taken by surprise. "Really? I wouldn't have imagined that. Did you come to an answer?"

"I think…I think the world changed around us when we weren't looking. For you, your parents dying and then Rob staying in the US. Still, you fought your way through that and found an outlet by the help you give others with your charity work. Now, you'd like to be a pilot. Those things will give you direction. Unfortunately, none of it includes me."

"Jim, this doesn't exclude you…"

"Please, it's not something that needs protesting, Daphne. I know I'm not excluded. It's just that right now we're both on other roads, opposite directions. By itself, that doesn't necessarily mean we're drifting apart…I don't know where I want to go with this. I've found direction also, a reason to use my talent to make up for the fact I turned my back on England and the company. You helped me find my way back, whether you realize it or not. I can't explain how, you brought me out of my shell and I'll be forever grateful…"

"You're full of what makes the grass grow green, Jim. You're not out of your shell and you know it. And I don't want you to be forever grateful either. You haven't answered the question."

"I've tried to, Daphne. I want to be precise."

"Spoken like a true engineer. How about from your heart?"

"We're astray here. Let me get back to the subject. I think that your endeavors and my plans to be in America for a month will be good for us. That's when the subject of our drifting apart will be answered…at that time."

She was quiet, a moment. "That's a good answer. Fair enough. However, what does *apart* mean?"

"I don't follow you."

"Does it mean if you meet some woman over there you'll go out with her? I'm asking you, what does apart mean?'

"I haven't given that a thought."

Daphne could have kicked herself. Why on earth had she blurted that out? That damn Kenneth Sommers and his flying machine flitting through her head again. Blast him!

"Well, Jim, what's your answer?"

"What you've asked about works two ways remember. I have no thoughts of something such as that happening, but…I don't know…let's just see how it goes. Listen, Daphne, when all this is over and if there's no war, it will be only you and me. We'll go back to Austria, stay at BergFalke, you'll meet Beck. We'll climb and wonder why we ever questioned ourselves."

She thought it a good way to end the subject. "That's a lot to hope for, Jim, I simply hope for the way we once were."

"All right then, let it go at that. David's away in Sheffield overnight so you won't have to bite your tongue over his dalliance at the Dorchester, or his other identity. We'll go over to Ravensmoor, see Mary, bundle up the kids, get the dogs, and go."

He felt it odd she didn't ask to go to America with him.

They chatted with the children and threw sticks for the dogs. After the children were sent back to their tutor, Mary brought Daphne and Royce tea. It was apparent to both of them that Mary had something on her mind. They were apprehensive, and waited nervously. Had she heard, did she know?

"I've something to tell you both. There's going to be more children in this house."

Daphne looked at Royce in relief, then they were somewhat dazed over the statement.

Mary laughed. "It's not what you're thinking! Let me tell you what's about to happen. That man Hitler has hounded the Jewish people and won't stop until they're driven out, or worse. There is a number of groups who have formed together under an alliance called Kinder Transport. Numerous Jewish groups are involved. Our Christian groups have decided to band together with others and at least try to save the children. We supply money for transportation, homes and education for them to live in England until the crisis is over."

Daphne was fascinated. "You'll bring children here, to Ravensmoor to live?"

"Yes, there will be five to ten children here."

"David agreed to that?"

"I know you're surprised and he didn't at first. Then when I told him the Baron De Rothschild has opened his home, Cedars, David saw the value of a good deed."

"When is this going to happen, Mary?"

"There are some children trickling in now, and there will be about two hundred in from Holland to Harwich next month. After that, we expect thousands from Germany, Austria and right now it looks like Czechoslovakia. The children will be housed at Dovercourt until we find them homes. That's where I'll go to pick them up and bring home."

"Will you have help with them? I mean, who helps you?"

"There's a groundswell of volunteers everywhere. The main thing we need is rooms, we have the people."

"Rooms everywhere?"

"Yes, Daphne. Why do you ask?"

Royce looked at her; he knew what was on her mind. She glanced back, he nodded.

"Mary, you may not know that the home at Windermere is now mine. We won't be there again until God's knows. It will easily hold ten children and their guardians, if that's what you call them. If you say yes, I'll have the workers put additional heat throughout the house and pay all expenses for the children's support."

"Daphne, I don't mean to pry, but you can afford all that?"

Royce had to laugh. "Believe me, Mary, she can afford it."

"Then thank you so much, Daphne. I'll be in touch. It will be in about a month I should think. Oh, and James, before you leave, David called and you're to meet him here at noon tomorrow. He said he wants to go over a number of items before you leave for America."

"All right, if he calls again, tell him I'll be here."

On the way back to Blackbird Cottage, Royce looked to Daphne. "That was a nice thing to do."

"I couldn't do otherwise, Jim, she's such a sweetheart…and he's such a bastard!"

"For God's sake, Please don't go and get all fired up again."

* * *

David was in the den on a long distance call while Royce waited in the library. Mary brought him tea, and then heard the children squabble over some minor nothing. As she went down the corridor, he shouted after her. "Wait until you have ten of them."

She gave him a wave, laughing all the way.

Royce sipped his tea, walked around, looked at the book covers, and wondered how many his brother had actually read. A gold-leaf binding caught his eye. *Castles of the World* and a companion book, *Castles of Europe*. He set his cup down and pulled out *Europe*. In the index, there was Austria. He flipped to those pages until they unexpectedly stopped. It jumped out at him. The castle. He nearly failed to recognize it. The photograph was taken some distance from the front, which he'd never seen, yet the great stone wall and red slate tower roof were there. He caught his breath. The photo affected him more than Robert's painting.

"What the devil's a matter with you, James?"

David had come in, unnoticed.

Royce opened the volume and laid it on David's desk.

"That's the castle."

"Castle? What cas…Oh, where you slipped. I'll be damned. Let's see, pretty little place. And still bothers you, I see."

"More like the ledge and the Gestapo cars out front are what bothers me."

David ignored him. "Well, let's read what it says."

He bent the binding back, flattened the book on his desk and read the caption. "*Stein Vorhang Burg.* (Stone Curtain Castle) 14th century, NW Austria. Private, no tours."

"Well, James, strange name, precious little information. So, where did you fall?"

Royce drew his finger along the wall behind and to the side of the castle. "The ledge would be right along here. And here is where the cliff curves and I fell."

"Christ, you went a long way along that ledge. How wide did you say it was?"

"Less than a foot. If I'd been in good shape it would have been nothing."

"If you say so. Anyway, now you know its name. Whatever that's worth."

Royce put the volume away. "So, David, what do you want to see me about?"

"Your trip. A couple of points. This is your first time in the States, so you'll be shocked by the size of the country and distance between cities. Think of it this way, England, Wales and Scotland comprise approximately 100,000 square miles. The United States is a little under 4,000,000. It's hard to comprehend, I know, but Detroit, where you're going, is in Michigan, and that state alone is almost the size of England. Distances are going to take some getting used to. And the people are quite different from us. They're very open about most everything in life even though they're suffering through the same Depression as we in the UK. Nevertheless, the potential of that country is obvious. We saw what they could do in the Great War and to me that's nothing to what they can accomplish now…*if* they set their mind to it.

This point I want to stress, James. The US is fractured with unrest from unemployment. Because of this, the Bolsheviks and the German Bund have found a modest foothold. Whenever you are asked about the UK's dedication to stop the Nazis or the Reds, be absolutely positive. We're going to need America's help, there's no question of that. We must do all we can to get them on our side so that when war comes, hopefully they will not stay on the sidelines as long as they did before. Follow what I've said?"

"Yes, you're quite clear. I'll do my best."

"Good. James, there's a distasteful subject I wish to discuss."

David walked to the door, closed it, and then returned. "I assume Daphne mentioned she saw me at the Dorchester. What conclusion did you draw from that?"

"I drew the obvious conclusion. You're cheating on Mary."

"It's not necessary to be that blunt, James."

"Blunt? You brought it up, so get it out in the open. You're committing adultery. And Mary doesn't deserve that."

"Listen to me. The girl, or as your friend so quaintly called her, the little bimbo, is the daughter of one of my associates in Commons. As I happened to be staying overnight in London he asked if I would show her the Dorchester, and I obliged."

"And the fact she called you Sir Ashton Hamilton and said lets go party or *home*?"

"That's quite simple. She misspoke my name and actually wanted me to take her home."

Royce got up, headed for the door. "You're full of crap, David."

"Who in hell do you think you're talking too?"

"To you, *Sir* David, you're a horse's arse if you think I'd swallow that rubbish. You're taking chances that could ruin your career and the future of our company by dallying with some trollop. Daphne said there were a number of people there who probably know who you are. You don't think that sort of thing isn't going to start gossip? Why on earth take her there?"

"I'll admit I had too much to drink in Mayfair, she wanted to go to the Dorchester. I...I wasn't thinking. But there wouldn't have been a problem if Daphne hadn't opened her mouth!"

"Oh, I see. So now it's Daphne's fault. You cheat on Mary and it's Daphne's fault you were caught."

"Quiet down, James, for Christ's sake. And let's talk about *Daphne* for a minute! What was she doing there with a man I found out was a RAF pilot."

Royce came back to face David. "What do you mean, you

'found out'? Do you have someone spying on her?"

David became defensive. "No, not at all. Someone in the room told me."

"Daphne said you left quickly, with little what's her name. When did you have a chance to speak with anyone there?"

Royce could see David struggle. "A waiter told me."

"You're lying through your teeth, David. So I'll just say this. If I ever find out you've got someone following her, I won't go to America, I won't be working for the company and…the next time I see you it won't be to talk."

David wasn't intimidated. "Still, you haven't explained how she happened to be there with a handsome man?"

"I'll answer your innuendo once, only once. He is Lady Jane Sommers' son. Daphne works with Lady Jane to entertain the wounded from the War. Daphne told Kenneth—that's her son in the RAF—she wanted to learn to fly. He set her up with a flight instructor and they met at the Dorchester. A slightly different reason than why you were there. So don't you ever, ever raise a question about her again…God damn you!"

There was a knock on the door; both men froze. "Sir David? It was Albert, nervous over the loud voices. "General Alcott is on the line, Sir, said it was urgent."

David needed the break. "Wait here James, I'll be back."

"Don't bother. There's nothing more to talk about."

Before they knew it, they were rushed. The time to leave had come. Daphne left Coventry for she had no intention of being there without Royce, or near David. In addition, she was more than ever committed to become a pilot.

Royce was on his way to the United States. Their separation, filled with uncertainty, was to be an unwelcome test.

The beginning of March, 1939, started the sequence of tragic events leading to war.

VOLUME TWO

WAR

Map of England and the coast of France depicting British radar coverage, RAF group locations, and Luftwaffe bases

Chapter 22

15 MARCH 1939.

NAZI GERMANY'S TROOPS engulfed Czechoslovakia in a bloodless takeover after England and France turned their backs on that nation. Up to the last minute, Winston Spencer Churchill believed the British Government would intervene.

In one single year, Hitler's Third Reich enslaved Austria's six million citizens and Czechoslovakia's fourteen million.

As in Austria, a maelstrom enveloped the Czech people, starting with all government officials who stood against the German demands. Those patriots could have been saved if the British Government had granted them diplomatic immunity. But Britain did not. Those honorable patriots, followed by countless thousands of others, were caught up by Nazi Einsatzgruppen, Special-Operation units, a fallacious designation for death squads. Countless Czechs then perished in the concentration camps at Janowska, Plaszow and Theresienstadt, or the extermination camps at Belzec and Chelmno.

Hitler also got the bonus he was after, the Skoda Armaments Factories. He would use their weapons systems, mainly battle tanks, in the forefront of his next move of conquest.

16 March 1939

Royce met the four engineers from Rolls Royce at RAF's Manston Airfield. On the runway a Short Sterling bomber, reconfigured for extended range transport, would fly them by the Great Circle northern route non-stop, to land in Gander, Newfoundland.

Royce stared at the RAF pilot. "Good Lord, Jock, what are you doing here?"

"Why if it isn't Mr. Royce, Sir! Me and Colin are here to fly some very important people to Canada and up you show out of the blue."

"It's good to see you Jock, where's Bloody?"

"Oh, it's not Bloody anymore, Mr. Royce. It's Colin now. He's made Warrant."

"What does that mean?"

"He's an officer type now, he is. Warrant Officer. And look at me stripes, sir. Three of them, with crown and eagle. I'm a Flight Sergeant, Aircrew. We're cock of the walks, we are."

"Well I'll be damned. Congratulations. I'm so glad you're to be our pilots."

"Thank you, sir. Here's his Lordship now."

Colin walked up and shook Royce's hand. "Hello, Mr. Royce. Didn't expect you, we didn't. You'll be glad to know we haven't wrecked any of his Majesty's aircraft since the last time we saw you."

"Good for you. I've an interest in your record continuing. Congratulations on your new officer rank, Colin I hear you're not called Bloody anymore."

"Well, I'm barely an officer, sir, and believe me, it's been the devil not to say bloody. Improper now, you know."

Royce enjoyed their company. "So Colin, what's the new adjective you use now?"

"Flaming, sir. Used that ever since we blew up the Whitly."

"The three of them had a good laugh. Jock said. "Yes, sir, that's the new word for him. It's the flaming engines, flaming trees, and flaming water in the petrol. You name it, it's flaming."

Royce was glad to have found these two pilots. He had met the four RR engineers and found them stuffy, seemingly unable to get past his scar and onto engineering subjects.

They, in turn, found Royce reserved and were surprised he would enjoy conversation with such a casual manner to lower ranks of the RAF.

Royce looked up at the aircraft. "This is a damn sight larger than the Whitly that looked big in Zurich."

"This sure is, Mr. Royce. The Whitly only had twin flaming engines; this one is called a Short Sterling. That doesn't mean it's short, Mr. Royce." Colin smiled. "She's made by Short

Brothers, so it's called a Short Sterling."

Royce was amused. "All right, Colin, I get the point. What else?"

"Well, she has four RR Goshawk engines as you can see and me and Jock expect them to stay on. They makes a great flaming racket, they do, but they've the range we need."

"So, did I hold you up? We ready?"

"No, sir. That vehicle that just stopped is our second crew. It's a long flaming flight, we spell each other."

"Okay then, I imagine you'll be busy, so I'll see you during the flight."

The flight was noisy, cool, and painfully long. Newfoundland Airfield, at the northeast end of Newfoundland Island, was a welcome sight. The airfield was in a dynamic mode, hundreds of workmen were employed to extend and build new runways on the former outpost of Hattie's Camp, now known as Gander. Gander had become the arrival and jumping off point for the Great Circle air route to and from Europe. The RAF recognized its importance and dispatched a Squadron Leader, named Patterson, along with staff for flight operations as well as to oversee the relatively new inflight refueling for Imperial Airway's flying boats come summer.

A special US Army Air Corp extended range Douglas DC-3 DST waited at Gander and the five tired men from England were soon in the air again, now far more comfortably. The DST in the aircraft's designation stood for Douglas Sleeper Transport and the travelers wasted no time taking advantage of that designation.

With a cruise speed of 150 MPH, it took nearly 10 hours, in headwinds, to travel the 1,300 miles down the east coast, over Halifax, Portland, Boston, and New York to finally land at Washington DC's National Airport. There, identifications were confirmed by Government and Military Officials, and the weary travelers were herded once more aboard the same re-serviced aircraft for the four hundred mile flight to the Wayne Country Airport in Detroit, Michigan.

In Detroit, the DC-3 taxied past the main concourse and, to the traveler's surprise, into a hanger. When they deplaned, an Army Air Corps Major, accompanied by five military Police, escorted them to a Packard limousine. The British engineers looked at each other questioningly. Since they had come under US Army supervision, their treatment had been courteous, yet definitely brusque.

Royce had had enough of the silence. "What's going on here, Major?"

"Sir?"

"Don't Sir me, Major. Since we landed at Gander, we've been treated like lambs being led to the slaughterhouse. What's this all about, are all Americans this rude?"

"Sir, you're Mr. Royce, is that correct?"

Royce knew his scar had preceded him. "Yes. There, that answers your question, now please answer mine."

"Sir, we only follow orders. I'll not say anything further other than to ask you to save any questions for the General."

"And who is the General?"

"I'm sure he'll inform you of that, Sir."

The travelers found barely enough seats in the rear of the Packard limo, an Army Sergeant drove, the Major in front. A Jeep with Military Police led the way and another followed the Packard. No one spoke while the three vehicles snaked their way out of the city. The Rolls Royce engineers, because Royce had spoken up, now looked to him as their leader. Royce could sense it, but said nothing.

They arrived at an estate in Harper Woods on the western edge of Lake Saint Clair. There they were met by a US Air Corps Colonel, who escorted them into the home's den, and then signaled to an orderly to take their drink order. The Colonel asked about their flight, the weather, their family, until Royce spoke up.

"Colonel, what the devil is this all about? We didn't fly all this distance to talk about family and the weather or be kept in the dark. So either cut to the chase or I, for one, am out of here."

"Oh, I don't think you're going anywhere until…"

Royce rose up, angry. "I don't care what you think Colonel, try and stop…"

The door opened, the Colonel and orderly came to attention.

"Good evening, General."

The general nodded at ease and turned to Royce. "Mr. Royce,

did I hear you say you wish to leave? You must be overtired, making you a bit short-tempered."

"Speaking for myself, if I don't get some answers, I'm back to England."

"Mr. Royce, you've no passport, so you won't go anywhere unless the USAAC takes you, so sit yourself down."

The Colonel suggested calling the MPs. The General stopped him, then called him over. "Colonel, please introduce me to this hothead."

"Major General Henry Arnold, Chief of the United States Army Air Corp, this is Mr. James Royce."

"There, Mr. Royce, does that begin to answer one of your questions?"

"General, number one, I'm not a hothead. But I am tired and fed up with all the silence that's surrounded this whole blasted trip. Number two, no, it doesn't answer my question. I fail to see what is so important about our stay that it requires the Chief of the American Air Corps."

"Well, let's start with the basics, Mr. Royce. If war should break out in Europe, what is the posture of the United States?"

"I believe it will remain neutral. But what does that have to do with us and…"

"That is correct, strict neutrality. So what do you think our Senate isolationists would do if they found out what five engineers from the Rolls Royce Merlin Engine Division—engines produced solely for fighters and bombers—were doing over here? Why are they here? Oh, they're only planning for the manufacture of Merlin engines with Packard, that's all. That would raise unholy hell and that's why we don't even say Merlin, it's just the 1650 motor."

"General, I'm not with RR. All I'm responsible for here is to impart processes and bearing information. And this trip is supposed to be secret? To the best of my knowledge, it's not a secret at my company."

General Arnold was displeased. After he queried each of the other four engineers, he found no one considered the use of Packard as a second source of Merlin engines a secret. "Well gentlemen, it's obvious some people don't know what the word secret means but, on this side of the pond, it's Top Secret and that's why you've been isolated and, I'll add, will continue to be."

* * *

The next three weeks were a whirlwind of work, design procedures, conceptual theory, production processes, opposition, and discord. Previously, the Packard engineers received a complete Merlin engine, a disassembled Merlin engine, and comprehensive sets of plans. In the past, from 1931 to the present, Packard made their own twelve cylinder automotive engines, which were classics in their own right, yet weren't meant to be compared to the Merlin. A modified mass production plan for the complex engine held promise, although the time it took to develop the program was painfully long. This was due—not only by Packard engineers' tendency to shortcut wherever possible—but also by the RR engineers' resistance to process changes, no matter how outmoded. Especially contentious was Packard employees' habit that once product, such as a piston rod, was completed it was simply tossed into a parts bin, with the possibility of damage. That, and dozens of other problems from both sides, were agonizingly resolved. But it took time.

Royce was worn out. Even though he had no authority over the RR people, they deferred to him due to his newfound ability to transfigure outmoded British engineering and fabrication processes into America's more advanced production techniques.

General Arnold heard from his group the difficulties to work with the English and entered the conference room to confront the challenges. Royce, unaware the General was behind him, was laying down the law to the RR engineers. The procedures agreed upon were now established. No further debate, end of discussion. There was no dissension. General Arnold listened and then without a word, slipped out and left for Washington.

Royce informed Air Corp personnel he wanted to leave for Fort William and the Canadian Car and Foundry as soon as it could be arranged. When General Arnold received this information, h e ordered his staff to arrange for transport and coordinate a conference date between Royce and the Chief Engineer of CC&F.

General Arnold then flew back to Detroit, verified with the

Packard engineers the Merlin program was underway—with apparent success—and asked Royce into a private office.

"Mr. Royce, I would like to thank you for your efforts to resolve the problems between you Brits and Packard over the V1650 engine. I'll admit your methods to get unanimity were rather unorthodox and your final 'my way or the highway' approach was uncompromising, even by my standards. I do, however, realize the times demand results, not procrastination."

"I never heard the 'my way or' expression before, General, but in England I've learned there's a point where everyone can't be right and every discussion lasts too long."

"True. If you're *sure* you're correct."

Royce didn't answer, the General continued. "Mr. Royce, I assume you're aware of the difficulties in getting along with you, and your only redeemable grace is you're usually right."

"Usually?" Royce laughed. "I think people should not be trusted if they're only 'usually' right, General."

The General smiled. "My, I do believe I left out the word conceited."

Royce waited. He guessed the General hadn't called him in to simply annoy him.

"Mr. Royce, I let you have your head at Packard. I did that to find out what you were made of. I found out. There is, however, one thing I'll now make clear. I can be difficult to get along with as well, and there's no room for two thorny people in the same program. But always remember, the stars are on my collar, and what I say goes."

Royce shrugged. "Then I guess it's time for me to get out of Detroit, General."

"I thought you might feel that way. Nevertheless, before you head to Fort William,* I'd like to make you an offer."

"Now that surprises me."

"Yes, and I'm sure it would be a surprise to everyone who has come in contact with you."

*Since renamed Thunder Bay.

"However, I see something else in you. If you keep in mind what I said about where the stars are, I would like to offer you a faculty position at the Industrial College of the Armed Forces."

Royce was startled. It was a significant honor.

General Arnold continued. "I need decision makers. Of course you know we would have to file off your sharp edges."

"That's been suggested before, but there's really no time for that, General. I thank you for the offer, yet I'll pass. My heart is in England and all I can do to help over there."

"I know I won't convince you of this, Royce, but you can do more to help your country from here, than struggling to bring your brother's firm into today's world—where it won't get to."

"You know D W Royce?"

"I do. When it was Royce Bearings. A few of us toured some military positioned companies in England two years ago to gauge their capacity. I had the dubious pleasure to meet David Royce at that time. If I may be frank, an expression over here is, all smoke and mirrors. Since then, I've also heard what you're valiantly trying to do. However, as you well know, most of your machinery predates the modern era. You can't keep pace. Then again; this isn't anything new to you."

"Yes, I know all that, General. Yet, we do what we must, and devil take the hindmost."

"So, I take that to be a no."

"General, thank you for the offer and I wish you luck. I've got to be on my way."

"Very well then, Mr. Royce, and just to show there's no prejudices on my side vis-à-vis all English engineers, I'll assign you my aircraft and crew until you leave for England."

* * *

The DC-3 crew took their single passenger from Detroit, five hundred miles across the southern tier of Canada to Fort William, Ontario. Royce was tired. He didn't like to fly to begin with, and air travel left him tense. Added to that were the arguments with the RR engineers over the distinction between multiple production of the English and mass production of the

Americans. Royce grasped that disparity from the start. The designers and engineers of Packard were every bit as good as England's. The capstone was his tour of the Packard plant and his realization that American design, manufacturing, equipment and production must be the envy of the world. If it wasn't, he knew it was going to be.

Coercing the RR people to accept that fact had worn on him. Keeping his temper in check wore on him even more. He wanted nothing more than to see the engineers at the Canadian Car and Foundry, answer questions on those segments of the plans for which he had responsibility and leave.

That was Royce's goal. Then get back to England and Daphne. At this point, it was to hell with everything else.

Chapter 23

ONCE AGAIN, he waited. Chief Engineer McGill's secretary at Canadian Car and Foundry had ushered him into an office strewn with plans and sketches covering every table. The secretary brought a cup of coffee, and said the Chief Engineer would be there presently. He was to wait. And wait he did, wait and fume. He decided that if there wasn't a damn good excuse, there'd be a few choice words for this McGill fellow.

Bumping sounds, strange. He heard the door open behind him. As he rose, an attractive woman smiled hello as she came towards him shifting from side to side, supported by two aluminum canes. Royce blinked, ashamed.

"Mr. James Royce, I'm Chief Engineer Elsie McGill. I can see by the look on your face, no one warned you. Sorry for the shock. To answer your unasked question, I had polio when at the University of Michigan, but at least I can still get about. Please, sit down."

Royce couldn't speak. Elsie McGill worked her way around the desk, set the canes aside and with the desk to brace her, eased into her chair. "I'm more fortunate than you, Mr. Royce. I was informed of how difficult you are to work with and your scar, so you were no surprise. And please, don't concern yourself over me, I don't like it."

Royce found his voice. "Miss McGill, I feel a fool, for reasons so small I'm too embarrassed to mention."

"Fine. Then don't mention them. With that said, I'll call you Jim, and I'm Elsie. Let's take it from here and get to work."

Royce found Chief Engineer McGill had done her homework. She followed each process so clearly she could finish his thought process for him.

"You're well versed, Elsie, you pick up on everything I detail. I don't think you even needed me here."

"Ah, that's where you're mistaken, Jim. Everyone needs confirmation. I once designed a biplane trainer for the Canadian

Army and there was no one here to bounce ideas off. That was a mistake. It's hard at times working alone. That's a drawback in engineering too; we get too close to really see. So your being here confirms my ideas on the Hurricane we're to build. If I seem to know where your designs head, it's because they're so logical. Especially on the airfoil concept. Therefore it's great to have your input and confirmation."

"Elsie, it's mutual. After the endless bickering in Detroit, I confess I was edgy. Here, you're a lovely relief."

She gave him a sly look. "You mean because I agree with most everything you've stated?"

Royce fell in with her remark. "Well…in truth, that could very well be the main reason."

They found respect in each other's knowledge. In little time, Royce was able to review his area of expertise and receive her approval. Elsie then surprised him by her plan to add a deicer system for the Hurricane as well as ask him to review her detailed drawings for conversion of the undercarriage from wheels to skis.

More coffee, which Royce began to like, then lunch as they worked on the diagrams and scribbled out fabrication processes. They soon became kindred souls.

"Jim, you must have thought about the Hurricane's fabric cover on the rear fuselage and wings. Can't you speak to Hawker about that? This presents a serious fire problem for the pilot. Haven't they given thought to change to an aluminum alloy? It would allow a lot more speed."

"Hawker's addressing the situation. As I'm sure you're aware, there's the additional rear weight versus stability versus horsepower. Problems that affect how the aircraft's performs. Rumor has it that RR will add horses to the Merlin and that could offset the weight increase. But, there's one value to the use of fabric. We found machinegun shot, and even 20mm shells, may very well go right through with no damage and it's a simple matter to glue on a patch, whereas aluminum is torn and needs replacing."

"Ah, you Brits always find a way for justification of vintage processes."

"Thank you, Elsie. I'll take that as a compliment. Anyhow,

if the change to alloy is approved, your company will be one of the first to get the revision."

"Fine. Now let's take a break and I'll show you around the plant. That is, unless you want to forsake that and get out of here for your trip home."

"I'd like to see the plant and if you're free, why don't we have dinner tonight? I can always leave tomorrow."

"Great. Now, as you can imagine, I'm slow and I don't want to hear any bitching about it or I'll make comments about how your scar frightened my secretary so much she felt compelled to warn me, then flee for her life."

Royce loved her openness. "Okay, if I'm impatient, I'll grouse quietly."

Joined by Works Manager Bill Soulsby, the three toured the plants, met employees and discussed the possibilities of war. A war, which if it happened, would draw in Canada due to her Dominion status with England.

At dinner, Elsie and Royce continued their conversation on war and engineering. Then abruptly, she seemed tongue-tied. Something definitely began to discomfort her.

"You appear to be at a loss for words, Elsie."

"Not at a loss, Jim, I simply don't know if I should butt into your personal life or stay the hell out."

"Well, I can't imagine why you would be curious about my personal life, but I can always stop you if it gets too personal."

"I want to ask you what caused your scar and how long you've lived with it."

Elsie saw him withdraw. She wished she hadn't asked, but felt the need.

"I've had it since childbirth. The doctor used forceps, crushed the nerves."

She grimaced, then continued. "Could we talk about it? "

"I really don't know what more there is to talk about. It's there, what can I say?"

"It's what *I* want to say, if you'll let me."

He nodded reluctantly. "Jim, we both have our physical scars, mental scars too. Yet when you met me your scar was the farthest thing from your mind because you were so concerned for me. When we worked together, again it didn't enter your mind. We just babbled along like we were two normal people. But we're not. Yet when you met Bill Soulsby and the others on the plant tour, you changed. I could see it was on your mind, people had to look at you and you shied away from them."

"I guess that's the way I am."

"No it's not, Jim. It's the way you've let the scar make you."

"I was told something like that by a friend awhile past. She was a bit more wordy than you, but essentially it comes out the same. Well, that's me. Nothing can be done about it."

"I don't think that's true."

"What do you mean, not true?"

"Jim, hear me out. I've tossed this around in my mind since our tour. I have a friend. She's an Inuit. You would think of her as Eskimo, but they're a separate race. She's from Nunavut, which means 'our land' in Inuktitut. Her ancestors were from the unknown lands far past Hudson Bay, beyond the tempests of the forever veiled Sea of Ice."

Royce smiled. "And why the drama?"

"Because I want you to feel she's someone mysterious."

"All right, let's say you've succeeded."

"Good. Her name is Alornerk Aningan, which means Soft Angel in the King's English, and she's an incredible artist. She's known as Aipalovik, a wise woman. Angel is an old now, some say far over a hundred years and she's revered."

"She paints?"

"No, she etches and stains whale and Walrus bone and work similar to tattoo. She draws in ink, weaves cloth and creates all sorts of artistic images. A number of her works are in the Musee Beaux-Arts in Québec."

Royce was clueless. "We were on about my scar, now we're onto frozen artwork. We gone off the subject somewhere here?"

"No, you dense Limey, I'm bang on the subject. I want her to etch and stain your scar."

He fell into disbelief. "I don't see that happening."

Chapter 24

ROYCE SMILED at the woman called Soft Angel. Hunched over from osteoarthritis, she could only look at him sideway. The fingers on the hand she held out to him were gnarled from arthritis and, although she tried to smile through toothless gums, it proved too much an effort for her to bother.

Elsie told Royce that until five years ago, the old woman lived in an igloo during winters and a tent in summers. She was talked into civilized ways and now lived in a one room, shabby cabin on the outskirts of Fort William.

For the better part of his dinner with Elsie, Royce had felt strongly against even meeting Soft Angel. It wasn't until Elsie literally backed him into a corner by asking if he liked the way he looked—because no one else did—that he wilted. And when she made him ultimately admit he did not, he was defeated. Begrudgingly, he said he would listen to the woman.

Angel didn't live up to her name either in looks or gentleness. She pushed him into an antiquated chair and frowned.

"He look like Thomas after Nanuk, polar bear, got him."

Elsie told him that Angel really helped Thomas look better.

Royce saw an out. "Then let me see how he looks now."

Angel did her best to appear sad. "No, Asiavik, killer whale take him off, into dark water."

Royce shook his head in disbelief. "Look, Elsie, again, I really don't think this is a good idea."

They had come this far, Elsie refused to let him off. "Look, Jim, Angel can just do a small section at the top, under the hair line. If you don't like it, it won't show, nothings lost."

Royce pondered a moment. It seemed to mean so much to Elsie and that seemed fair. "All right then, explain that to Angel. Just under the hairline."

Angel grimaced. "I understood good. Nuns teach in Quebec."

"All right then, as long as you understand, don't do any more than that."

"I understood good."

"Good, I just want to be clear about it."

Elsie chimed in. "I'll tell you what, Jim, why don't you draw her a picture?"

"It's okay for you to talk; it's not your face."

"Christ, what have you got to lose?"

"Thanks, Elsie, I needed to hear that."

Angel broke in. "You two finish? I ask. You skin forever fish belly white?"

Elsie fell into a fit of laughter as Royce explained it had been a long winter and that normally he had a good color. Angel was doubtful. Still, with mortar and pestle, she ground pigments of brownish red, white and ocher, blending them into dyes.

She shoved him further into the chair, his head pressed back; her concoction reeking while it heated. She took a needle and pricked it along the scar. The nerves were dead. Royce had no feeling of where the needle touched.

Angel twisted to Elsie. The slimmest smile cracked her lips. Elsie read it, nodded and whispered good luck.

"I tattoo and stain little bit."

"Make sure it's only a little bit under the hair line. I don't want more, Angel."

For thirty-five minutes, she worked intently. Elsie couldn't watch, turned, moved off and simply hoped. Royce's neck cramped from the position until Angel finally pulled back and admired her work. She was satisfied.

Elsie came to look. Royce watched her eyes widen, her mouth turn into a grin.

"What? Elsie, what the devil did she do?"

Angel fetched a mirror. Nothing was said to Royce. He stared at his reflection, held the mirror one-way, then another, at first dazed. He relaxed into a smile. Angel had not merely tattooed and stained under Royce's hairline; she had worked halfway across his temple above his eyebrow. The result astonished him. The stark whiteness of the scar was gone. What remained was a faintly darker shade of Royce's skin and the now barely discernable indentation that would only be seen if a person looked closely.

"Well Jim, your answer?"

Royce eyes were moist as he put his hand lightly on Angel's shoulder. "What can I say other than thank you...and to you, Elsie."

In her halting English, Angel explained she had shaded the pigmentation a tinge darker to compensate for Royce's comment he would have more color when winter passed. She would do another section at present, and the rest through the following day.

Royce shook his head and looked at himself again. Elsie couldn't help josh him. "Jim, I'm serious. Vanity, thy name is man. You'll wear the silver off that mirror."

"But I look great! I'm crazy not to have done this before."

"My good Lord, Angel's fashioned another narcissistic man."

The laughter was gone, the time to leave at hand. "Elsie, these last few days have rejuvenated me. I can't remember when I've been so relaxed. Even when we're in intense design discussions, it seems so easy to communicate with you. I need you in England, but you wouldn't come, would you—no matter how much I offered?"

"No, you've told me too much about your brother."

"Damn, I knew I was being too honest."

"No, it's really not that, I'm a proud Canuck, this is my home. You're a loyal Brit, England's your home."

"I understand, Elsie. So, any loose ends? You're sure the money I wired for Soft Angel is enough to keep her?"

"Enough? Jim, she'll be able to have her whole family together for the first time in her life. She probably still cries in happiness for what you've done. The fact she gave you those vials of her secret concoction in case you're in the sun too long and bleach out. That alone shows how much she appreciates what you did."

Elsie stopped for a moment, and busied herself with some paperwork. "I think we've pretty much finished up, Jim. A couple of my female employees took care of your pilots the last four days, but I think they'll be sober enough to fly you to Boston. I'm surprised General Arnold okayed your change of flight plan and let you keep his precious little DC-3 all this time."

"I'm not surprised, really. We saw eye to eye at the end, and he understood I wanted to see Daphne's brother before I leave and head back to England and her troubles."

"Have you contacted her, Daphne, yet?"

"Not so far. I sent three Telexes's, but never knew where I would be for her to respond. I told her I would be at her brother's tonight. Perhaps she'll contact me there."

"Well, you know what they say; absence makes the heart grow fonder."

"They also say out of sight, out of mind."

"Your face may have changed, Jim, but we should have done more work on your attitude."

"I'm all right, Elsie, really. You've done wonders for me. Whenever I think things are too tough I'll always remember you and love your spirit and personality."

"What a thing to say, Jim, I haven't cried since they told me I'd be in a wheelchair the rest of my life. Well, I showed them, and you'll tough it out too when you have to. Now get out of here before we get too caught up in ourselves."

Elsie McGill held her crutches to the side and Royce hugged her lightly. He kissed her cheek, it was wet.

"Be gone, Mr. Jim Royce, and don't say till we meet again. I'd love to, but we won't."

* * *

Another flight of a thousand miles saw them to Boston Airport. The DC-3 was near the limit of her range although that was no concern due to their lack of cargo. The pilots were ordered to stay at Boston Airport as Westover, the new army air base in Chicopee, Massachusetts was far from completed. They were to refuel and wait for Royce, then to ferry him to Gander, Newfoundland. Royce expected to be in Boston for two days.

Robert was at the gate. Royce laughed, Robert's astonishment at the vanished scar was priceless. After accusing Royce of supreme vanity and other banter, they settled back in Robert's Lincoln limo and Royce spoke of his trip to Detroit's Packard Company and Canada's Elsie McGill. He didn't mention what he was up to at either company and Robert had the sense not to ask.

"Sounds like you were really taken by her, Jim, and she did

you a great favor to find that woman to hide your scar."

"She did. But more, she taught me how to live with an affliction. On top of that, she's one hell of an engineer. And, on the subject of women, have you heard from Daphne?"

"Certainly have, she called last night and wondered where the devil you were. I told her you'd be in tonight and she'll call. She's all excited about something, but wouldn't tell me. She knows I can't keep a secret."

"Great, I'm looking forward to that call. So now, what's new with you?"

"Other than Elliot Corporation's investments performing well, things have quieted down in Europe; at least April has started that way. Anxieties have eased since German troops occupied the rest of Czechoslovakia last month and nothing further happened. Was Chamberlain right...peace?"

"You know better than that, Rob. Hitler's only digesting them. He'll weed out the anti-Nazis and those he considers worthless and send them to the camps, where no one returns."

"Jim, rumor says Hitler has his eye on Poland. What will England do?"

"I'm not privy to what they'll do. I haven't heard from David since I left, so who knows? I can't believe we won't defend Poland. Then again, I thought the same about the Czechs, and look how we turned our backs on them."

"Well remember, no matter what, I'd like you over here."

"Thanks, but you know where I stand."

The phone rang. Robert answered, handed it over to Royce and left the room.

"Jim, let me hear your voice!" Daphne was cheerful. "Blast it, so much to tell you and my mind goes blank."

"Don't worry about it, just to hear you means a lot."

"Anyway, Jim, when are you coming home? Your month has stretched into almost seven weeks."

"I'll be here two days, then a day to get to Newfoundland. I don't know the setup there so I can't say. What are you up to?"

"That's the surprise I wouldn't let on Rob! I'm a licensed civil aviation pilot!"

"You're not serious?"

"Yes! I've flown every day and studied every damn night. I

sooled a week ago. My instructor, Jesus Peron, is fantastic. And he had all the contacts I needed to get my license on the quick. Of course, it's only for daylight hours, but I've already got a hundred twenty-five hours in flight time. He says I'm a natural and he'll work with me to get instrument and night ratings. Then I'll train for multiengine aircraft. It's a lot of classroom and I admit mathematics wasn't my all-time favorite subject, but I'll get through it if it kills me."

Royce laughed. "Make sure it doesn't, I want to see you. But I will say you're a bit excited."

"A bit? I'm over the moon over it! Can't wait to take you up."

"What? You mean you plan to take me for a flight?"

"Of course, why not?"

"Ah…let's talk about it when I see you. Right now, tell me what's going on. Do you know what's up at the plant? I haven't heard from David since I left."

"I'll tell you then. Mary said that plant production has, and she quoted David, gone to hell in a hand basket. It looks like you'll be busy when you get home."

"Just what I don't need, Daphne."

"Just what we both don't need."

"Well, we'll have to see what happens when I get back. Have you spoken to David yourself?"

"No, I manage to avoid him. It's beneath him to answer the phone at Ravensmoor, so I can get Mary without going through him. She asks what I'm up to and I tell her I'm mostly down in Belgravia with Lady Jane or over to Brooklands flying a North American BC-2. That's an American trainer for instrument flying. She seems to accept all this as the reason I'm not around."

"Does she sound all right? You know what I mean."

"I think so, although not sure. Ignorance is bliss you know."

"I suppose. I don't know how David and I will get along. I told you we didn't agree over his, ah…*failings*, when I left."

"I don't give a fig whether you two get along or not. However, I do want to change the subject. Jim, listen to me. Answer my next questions with a plain yes or no, okay?"

"Yes."

"Can Rob hear you?"

"No, he's in another room."

She started to laugh. "You don't follow instructions too closely or too long, do you?"

He returned the laugh. "No."

"That's better. Now, something's not right with Rob. That last letter he sent when you were here somewhat baffled me. He alluded to mistakes he'd made, yet it seemed he referred to a more recent event, not about the war and his friends. And yesterday on the phone he sounded strange. Have you noticed any change since you've been with him? Anything he's said?"

"I can't answer with a plain yes or no. He can't hear me so I'll say I haven't noticed other than he seemed pensive once or twice. Nothing I'd give a second thought to unless it was brought up, like you're doing now."

"Well, keep your eyes open, he might want to talk about something that's bothering him."

"I will, now let's talk about you and me."

After dinner at Robert's home on Beacon Hill, they retired to the smoking room for cigarettes and drinks. Robert dismissed the servants, watched the exterior door close, then returned to the room without saying a word.

"All right, Rob, from the time you picked me up at the airport our conversation has slowly gone to hell. Now you've sent your servants away. What's up?"

Robert started to speak, then stopped. Tears welled up.

"For Christ's sake, Rob! What the devil's wrong with you?"

Robert choked out the words. "I thought I had buried something I had done, but it's come back to haunt me."

"Your friends from the war again?"

"No, listen to me. What I say to you now could mean the end of our friendship."

"Then don't say it."

Robert gave a wan smile, looked away for a moment and then fixed his eyes on his friend. Royce said nothing.

"Jim, I was the one responsible for someone trying to kill you. I stupidly told the wrong person where they could find you."

Royce broke eye contact with Robert to glance into the fireplace, attempting to fathom what was said. After moments of silence, he looked back. "Well? You sure took a long time to tell me this and there must be a hell of a lot more to the story."

"There is. A woman. She used the name Madame Tosca. Her real name, first name is, or was, Donnatta, I never knew her last name. How I met her doesn't matter. She was a spy in the pay of Germany and I knew it. She said if I had some information it could help keep the peace between our…"

"Christ! Don't even start telling me you fell for that crap!"

"At first I did, but what I really fell for was her. She paid attention to me. No women had—since college. I couldn't help it. I was in love. I wanted to believe her."

"What secrets would you know? Stuck up in Windermere."

"I learned some at your brother's house, General Alcott and a Colonel talked about the Chain Home System and the Brit's knew who the German spies were in England and some other stuff like…well other secrets."

"Jesus Christ, Rob! Telling that stuff is treason!"

"I know, I know! I told myself it was for *peace*. That we weren't at war with Germany, so it wasn't wrong! I knew it was, but I made believe."

"Did she pay you?"

"God, no."

"So you fell for a pretty face and a smile and blurted out everything you knew."

"It didn't start out like that, but that's what it turned into."

"And where did I fit into this?"

"It was just some casual conversation I had with her. I told her about you and that you lived in up Coventry and were accused of killing some Nazi Major's son. I thought it was just a friendly conversation. My guess is she made a deal with the Nazis or that Major, and she sent a guy named Sean after you, to kill you."

"That was the person who took pot shots at me? The one I chased through the woods?"

"Yes, I recognized his cap when the policeman held it up."

"So that's why you went off to bed so damn quickly. We were all worried about you."

"I know Jim, I'm sick about it. All I can say is I'm sorry, God, I'm so sorry. I just can't shake off my guilt."

"I don't see how you could. Bloody hell, what a vile mess!

"But the first thing we've got to do is have this Sean and Madame...whatever, arrested by MI5."

"We can't do that, Jim. They...they're dead."

Royce was speechless, confounded. "*Now* what are you telling me?"

"I had to shoot them. If I didn't she'd try again to kill you."

"You *shot* them? Am I going crazy! You said you loved her, then you turn around and shoot her? Are you bonkers?"

"Listen to me, Jim! Christ, listen! If I didn't she'd go after you again, and if Daphne or Mary or the children were there she'd kill them too. I knew she wouldn't stop until she got you. She must have gotten money for your death. Don't you *see*! She could never be trusted. What else could I do?"

"I must be going batty. The only thing I know what to do right now is to have another drink."

They sat with untouched drinks, staring at the dying embers. Dying, like their friendship. Royce was intense, think, think, think. Trying, fighting to control himself.

"Okay, Rob. Is there anyone else who knows about this?"

"No, I'm pretty sure only Donnatta and Sean knew, and they're gone."

"If that's true, and if this woman didn't pass your name or where I was on to the Germans, we should be safe."

"She wouldn't do that, Jim. She'd keep who I was a secret. That would assure no one could bypass her and get information out of me."

"Makes sense. We'll go on that assumption. Here's what we do. I assume you have a typewriter. Put on gloves and use a sheet of plain paper you haven't touched. I want you to type out everything you told her. Whatever you can think of, from the names she went by, where she lived and anything about this Sean. Every damn secret you told her. Put it in an envelope."

"Jim, they might track me down. I'd go to prison, my name and Daphne's would be destroyed. I won't do that."

"Yes you will. Don't sign it. I'll find MI5's address when I get to England and mail it to them without a sender."

"This will make you an accessory after the fact."

"You think I don't know that! From the moment you told me this, I became an accomplice. What the hell else can I do? Turn in

Daphne's brother? That's where you've got me."

"I'm sorry, Jim."

"Stop! Don't ever say that to me again. Why did you tell me in the first place? To make you feel better? Confess to someone who can't do a damn thing about it? If you want forgiveness go to a priest, don't come to me."

"I didn't think of you that way. I thought you'd understand."

"Understand? How in hell did you expect me to understand? You gave intelligence secrets to Germany—damn it! You're a damn traitor to *my* country!"

"We weren't at war."

"That's a lame excuse. Don't even try to rationalize it."

"I should never have told you."

"You're God damn right you shouldn't have. What have you gained? Nothing! Nothing but put a guilt on me to ease your damn conscience. But there's one thing you were right about. This does mean the end of our friendship."

"For Christ's sake, Jim, don't say that. You're my only true friend from England."

Royce exploded. "Are you that blind, are you that absurd, to think we could remain friends after this? Just shut up and go type the letter and put it in an envelope."

Robert returned, his hand shook as he handed the letter to Royce. Without further word, Royce put it in his briefcase.

Walking to the door, he spoke his last to Robert. "Find your driver, tell him to take me to the airport, I'll stay there tonight. And don't be concerned that I will tell your sister of the shameful disservice you've done to a country you once loved."

Robert visibly shriveled, couldn't speak. He understood the depth of Royce's disgust.

* * *

The six hour, nine hundred mile flight to Gander gave Royce time to think. He, with Top Secret clearance, was now shielding a traitor. If he reported Robert, Royce felt that, without question, Daphne would never speak to him again.

She loved her brother, what choice did she have? Did that

mean he doubted the depth of her love? Perhaps he did. Still, he wasn't going to test her love to this extreme. The tragedy of her brother's face compounded by his being a traitor would be too much for her.

How ironic, Royce thought, Robert became a traitor in an ill-conceived desire for peace and then the love of a woman. Now, that same traitor is being protected by Royce, because of his love for a woman. He studied his distorted reflection on the aircraft's window. "Shut it from your mind as much as you can, but you know, nothing good will come from this."

At Newfoundland's Airport he found two familiar faces.

"Colin and Jock. What the devil are you two doing here? Don't tell me you've waited for me all these weeks."

"No Sir, Mr. Royce. We and the other crew flew here a few days ago from RAF Badminton after we dropped off the four Rolls Royce engineers. We were told to get back here and wait for you, whatever time it took. You're a real flaming important person, you are, Mr. Royce. Did you get to see King George and the Queen in Quebec?"

Royce shook his head. He didn't even know British royalty had been in Canada. He smiled to himself as they stared at him, trying not to be too obvious. "If you've wondered what happened to my scar, you probably doubt this. I went by dog sled deep into the northern reaches, past the Arctic Circle, into the mists and met a beautiful ice maiden by the name of Angel who promised she'd rid me of my scar if I stayed with her forever."

The pilot's nodded. "So why didn't the scar return, Sir, and where is this flaming beautiful ice maiden now?"

"Well, I...I told her I had to leave. So I...found an airplane and here I am."

"You just happened to find General Arnold's DC-3 past the Arctic Circle, in the *mist*, Mr. Royce? Very good, Sir. We hear he was at wits end wondering where it might show up."

"You two gentlemen doubt my word?"

Jock quickly jumped in. "Not in the least, Sir. The scar looks to be gone, it does, so it must be true. We just sort of wondered how we might meet this darling little thing and explain why you couldn't stay. Perhaps we'd be a comfort in her sorrow."

"You're so warmhearted Jock, although I will admit, you're far more glib than I. So tell me, have you both had time to hone these skills with the local girls?"

"Local girls me foot, Mr. Royce, there must be five hundred flaming men for every woman here, so put that flaming thought out of your mind...Sir. That's why we were so interested in your ice maiden."

"All right then, on to when do you want to takeoff?"

Colin checked his watch. "If you're ready, Sir, we'll get the other crew, check out the Sterling and be gone."

"I'm ready now but tell me something. Do we have to land at land at Coventry?"

"Yes, Sir. Orders is flaming orders."

* * *

In December, of the past year, 1938, German Physicists Otto Hahn and Fritz Strassmann, after years of work with other Scientists, detected and proved processes that became known as the Dawn of Nuclear Fission. These discoveries unveiled the potential for military application and nuclear energy. Their information was forwarded to the Reich Ministry of Education and then on to the Reich Research Council. From this and other studies, the first Uranverein, the Uranium Club, was formed by German physicists.

At this time, both British and German physicists discovered 'heavy water' could be utilized to make nuclear weapons. The British physicists passed along information to their Government that the German's were studying the potentials of nuclear fission and the British Government informed the United States.

Italy's Mussolini and Hitler signed the Pact of Steel, 22 May '39. After that, Hitler continued the plans for his eastward push.

* * *

In a black mood, which became worse by the second, Hitler's hands tightened behind his back. Colonel Schmid, as he presented his facts on the nuclear fission physicists, did not know Hitler had

399

previously ordered Himmler, chief of the Gestapo, to investigate the physicists.

"Schmid! You better tell me everything. You think I don't know what goes on in my own country? I've had the Gestapo look into every scientist in this field and none of them are to be trusted! That Hahn and Strassmann you mentioned passed information along to that *female* scientist, Lise Meitner *after* she escaped to Sweden. That's right, *after*! Those two are untrustworthy, disloyal, and we have men watching them. Everyone involved is being investigated! Everyone!"

Hitler stopped ranting and took a sheet of paper from his desk, "Do you know physicists named Gerlach, Diebner, Bothe, Esau, Harteck, Clausius and Heisenberg?"

"Most of them, my Führer."

"Most of them? I want you and the Gestapo to find whoever is in that Uranverein Club and put every one of them under strict supervision. Every one of them is disloyal to the Reich! All their documentation will be confiscated and then collected into one area. I have restricted their research and they no longer have access to their records. Let them try to work out their stupid theories blindfolded. The very fact fräulein Meitner knows, means the secret is out of the country. So now I have no choice other than to see where this fusion thing leads. We will leave these men where they are, although I want you to take every principal assistant and the other scientists we've found. Put them together in Himmler's castle in Westphalia. It is very isolated. Himmler has some sort of SS school there for racial purity. He thinks he's the reincarnation of some Norse god. If he is, that must have been one ugly god!"

Schmid didn't refrain from smiling and the little joke about Himmler's countenance soothed Hitler.

"Anyway, Schmid, I'll tell him you are to use part of the castle for research and he is not to interfere. I'll have laboratories, reports, research records, everything they require brought in. If there are any complaints from the physicists we uproot, tell them if they don't like it their next stop will be one of our camps. Restrict their research to this project and give them everything essential. We'll set up a larger laboratory somewhere when you know what they need. I want to know the feasibility of this concept as soon as possible before I commit to the cost of any escalated operation."

Hitler's wrath flared again. "You'd better understand what I want. And I want this immediately!"

Again his anger subsided. "Now, about this heavy water that's required. I don't need an explanation about how to change H_2O into D_2O, all I know is it is necessary in the process. Is that correct?"

"Yes, my Führer, I found there is a company named Norsk Hydro that produces D_2O for biomedical research and other applications."

"Don't bother me about Norsk. At present they don't produce enough and worse, they're in Norway. It will take too long to build our own plant. We will have to do something to offset that without exposing our interest to develop a weapon. I will take care of that."

"Meanwhile," Hitler's mood and displeasure exploded yet again, "do what I ordered! Get those damn people together and get to work on this or I'll see to it you'll wish you had!"

* * *

30 May, 1939

"Come on, Jim, how many times do I have to ask you to fly with me? The weather's warm, sun's up, God's in His heaven. Let's go."

"Look, now that the weather has improved, why don't we start to light climb again?"

"You fraidy cat. You know you won't have spare time to work out before we climb."

"Say what you will, I think you're too inexperienced to take a passenger up. Do you even have a license to take passengers?"

Daphne responded, still teasing him. "Inexperienced? Passenger? Don't give me that tongue in cheek question. You're dodging. I've my instrument and multiengine licenses now. I never dreamed you'd be a nervous Nelly. You used to hang off cliffs without a care in the world."

"That was because I was depending on myself, not on some rickety putt-putt engine. I told you what happened as we landed at Badington. The petrol line separating and the fire."

"I know, I know. You lost an engine again and Colin came in short, clipped the trees and all that. Stuff like that happens, I've landed with one engine dead."

"Sure, most likely in practice when you expected it. You didn't have a fire to contend with."

"Don't you try to kid me. Fire? You didn't contend with any fire. All you had to do was sit there."

"Sit there! Are you daft?"

"All right, all right. It may have been a bit testy but…"

"Testy? Even you, the great aviatrix, would have wet your pants."

"What a thing to say! If anyone wet their pants, it probably was you."

They started to laugh at the same time, touched their glasses and conceded that under those conditions both might possibly have had a crisis with their pants.

"Now what's the smile about, Jim?

"I'm thinking of the look on your face when I got back from the States."

"Well, what did you expect? You come back with a scar barely visible and suddenly turn into a devilishly handsome engineer."

"There are no devilishly handsome engineers. Only devilishly boring engineers."

"I'll agree with you on that. However, perhaps when you straighten out the manufacturing problems once again, we might get some real time together. What's the latest? And you never told me how everyone else handled the scar that isn't."

"As far as reactions, not too much. The children noticed before Mary and they all liked the change, although I think Victor would have preferred I kept it. Turns out I was his private pirate, or so he told his friends. At work, they tried to hide their expressions as much as when I had the scar, so that was funny in itself. I guess the main thing is no one cringes now when I see new people. And Clive was Clive, no expression, no emotion. I would never play cards with him."

"What did David say?"

"He hasn't been around to comment. He's been back and

forth between London and Paris over God knows what."

"Yes, and probably back and forth with his little bimbo in between."

"Careful now, dear, don't let me read something into that."

"Feel free to if you'd like. Anyhow, tell me a bit about all the plant problems."

"Too many to list. The main one at present is the supercharger challenge and that I won't bother you with."

"Is it anything to do with fighter airplanes?"

"Yes, it does in fact."

"Then I'm interested."

"Okay if you want, I'll try to keep it simple."

"Careful how you say that, mister."

"I will, dear. As I said, there's a supercharger performance challenge. We have to know the critical altitude, the 'band', or optimal operational altitude an aircraft is designed for, plus the critical limit. With that information, our company, but mostly Rolls Royce engineers, decide the correct type of supercharger. There's seven basic types, from single stage to multi-turbo. For the Spitfire, Rolls Royce's decision was a two stage, for an engine that now runs on one-hundred octane fuel. First we had problems with the diffuser vanes on the impeller, which we solved. Then…"

Royce gave Daphne a questioning glance. "I'm strictly attentive, Jim. Please continue."

"If you say so. Now the problem any supercharger has is over-boost, which means the gases compress to a dangerous boundary. The only exceptions allowing over-boost are takeoffs and combat conditions, and that limit is a maximum of around ten minutes, although they really will function much longer. Nonetheless, that's a long time and loads the engine to a severe and barely acceptable stress. Now, given there's other variables, not constants, our solution is to approach this with a cut off…"

"Excuse me, Jim, if this is the simple explanation, I think our best solution is for you to build them, I'll fly them."

"That's how I thought you'd feel…my dear."

* * *

While Royce was in the States and Canada, Daphne had thought of little other than flight. If she wasn't at the controls somewhere over England or Ireland, she talked about the science of it. From Kenneth, she learned it wasn't enough to be a natural flier. She studied constantly, absorbed information from Jesus Peron and RAF ferry pilots stationed at Vickers in Brooklands.

With her multiengine license in hand, Jesus Peron helped her apply to the Air Transport Auxiliary, the ATA, to become a ferry pilot. Peron assured her it would take time, which was a good thing—the longer it took, the more hours she logged.

Between flights and classes, she continued the work with Lady Jane and as Kenneth Sommers was never around, Lady Jane kept her informed as to his whereabouts. That is, when she knew, which in truth was seldom.

Though Daphne and Kenneth never spoke, she made sure his mother passed along her progression through flight school up to multiengine, instrument and the Air Transport application. She was unaware that Kenneth knew many of the fliers at Vickers-Armstrong. She didn't know he had contacted them, found Daphne was indeed an excellent pilot, and recommended her to Vickers Management at Brooklands.

He wanted her to be a ferry pilot from aircraft plants at Woolstonor Itchen. Vickers, as well as being the manufacturer of other aircraft, owned Supermarine, the main developer and manufacturer of the Spitfire. Because of this, Kenneth also contacted Supermarine directly at their plant in Southampton, asking that they add Daphne Elliot to their list, especially if any Spitfires had to be ferried to 11 Group.

One evening toward the end of May, while Daphne planned new entertainment at the Mount with Lady Jane, they heard the phone ring. Daphne sensed a chill though her. The maid answered, spoke for a few moments, then entered to tell Lady Jane the call was for her. As Jane went to answer, the maid turned to Daphne with a smile. "It's the Squadron Leader, Miss. He asked you were here and he said he would like to speak with you after he has a few words with his mother."

A few minutes later, Lady Jane called Daphne to the phone, then closed the door behind her.

"Hello…Kenneth?"

"Yes, Daph. Wonderful to hear your voice. How are you?"

"I'm fine. How are you, and where, or can't you say?"

"I really can't say where, but I don't speak the language."

"God, that could be anywhere in the world that doesn't speak the King's English."

"Be kind to me, it's lonely here."

"Oh? Of all your lady friends, none felt the need to comfort you in your lonely hours?"

"Not a one. Oh well, doesn't matter. Do you miss me?"

"What a question to ask."

"What a way to answer."

There was a lag. Daphne felt ridiculous. Why couldn't she answer him honestly? Just not *too* honestly. "Yes, Kenneth, I'll admit to a thought or two of you occasionally, especially when I'm flying and dream of piloting a Spitfire."

"I've heard good things about you and your ability. You'll fly one someday."

"Thanks, put in a good word for me, will you?"

"I already have. Right now, there's one or two other things I want to tell you. One is there's a chance petrol's going to be restricted shortly."

"Don't tell me that."

"It's true. I've told my mother to have our underground petrol tanks filled with 87 octane fuel. That's 2000 gallons…"

"What's this about petrol tanks?"

"Of course, you couldn't know, sorry. Father had petrol tanks installed under the lawn to save visits to aerodromes. If you can't get petrol, fly in to the Mount and load up. The servants know how to refuel, and you'll be all set with the aircraft you're flying now."

"You want me to land at the Mount?"

"You think you can't? That de Havilland Leopard Moth you've flown in the past is a feather. Just cut the engine as you touch and come up firm on the brakes as soon as you can. It's simple, if you can't do that, I'd be disillusioned."

"I can do it."

"That's what I want to hear, Daph. If you don't have boundless confidence, don't fly."

"I guarantee, the next time we speak, I'll have landed and flown off the Mount."

"Just remember, not right after a heavy rain. The lawn could be too soft, and underground tanks sweat when they're not topped off so expect to draw water off the petrol."

"I'll remember."

"When I get back, I'd like to have dinner with you."

"I can't promise you that."

"Is that a no?"

A delay, silence on the telephone, "I won't say no...only that I can't promise."

"I'm all right with that. Now, one more thing. I want you to fly down to Supermarine in Southampton one day this week. Ask for Chauncey Fellows, he heads up Flight Operations. You don't have to ring him up first. He knows you'll be there this week. Look great, as always. Impress him. He'll ask a lot of questions, so study up."

"What's this all about?"

"Chauncey flew with Father in the Great War and we're friends. You impress, and you'll get your dream."

"*Spitfire?*"

"There's another kind of aircraft?"

A shiver went through her. "God, Ken, thanks..."

"Just remember. A Spitfire's the most elegant lady you'll ever handle. Treat her like one."

She knew he was serious. "I'll remember, Ken. I promise."

"I've got to run, Daph, You owe me a dinner for this."

"Now you're unfair. After what you've done, you know I can't say no."

"You couldn't say no before, either. Cheerio."

She heard him laugh as he hung up. She couldn't help but laugh too. God, a Spitfire. Me. Fly a...*Spitfire*...me!

She rejoined Lady Jane. "How did Kenneth sound to you, Daphne?"

"I thought he sounded good, perhaps a little tired."

"You're perceptive, I thought that myself. So, what did you discuss, anything you can tell me? You know that I don't wish to pry, my dear."

"Of course I do. I can tell you some things and I thought

about this when I left the phone. Ken dared me to fly in here and out again, and I plan to do it."

"You plan to land a plane here? You?"

"Yes. And I've decided to take you for a flight. We'll show that son of yours what we women can do!"

"Dear me, Daphne, I've never flown."

"I didn't think you had."

Lady Jane touched her hand to her throat, her voice a whisper. "When?"

"I'm not sure. Ken wants me to fly over to the Supermarine factory in Southampton. I'll do that tomorrow, but I don't know how long I'll be there. I'll call you in a few days."

"Don't call, Daphne, just fly in, put me in shock and off we'll fly off to God knows where."

* * *

Daphne was shown around the Supermarine hangers by Chauncey Fellows. Chauncey, she found, was a person who needed proof, and then convincing.

"All right, Daphne. After Kenny called, I phoned your instructor, Jesus Peron. He supplied your certificate numbers along with an excessive recommendation. He also mentioned you've flown the twin engine Bristol Beaufighter. That's more than I've done. Do you like it's performance?"

"I don't have much to compare it to other than the American Hudson twin engine, but for a heavy plane, I was impressed."

"How Peron gets the aircraft he wants I can't fathom, yet somehow he manages. He gets you twin engine Hudson and Beaufighters, and then you drop in here with one of only five or six, Miles M7 Nighthawks. I'd guess you're the first woman to fly one. He's got to have friends in high places, I'll tell you that."

Daphne shrugged. "I don't have the foggiest either how he does it and I don't ask, Chauncey. I just take what he gives me."

"Well, from what Peron told me about your ability and what I saw when you landed, I won't bother with basic flying skills. Let me look at your flight log, then we'll focus on the Spitfire."

For the next two hours, Daphne sat in a replicated Spitfire cockpit. Two of the dials were blocked out and Fellows told her that, as she had not applied for Secret classification, she was not allowed to access them. 'Not pertinent for this test anyway,' he told her.

When he finished his instruction, Daphne mentioned Kenneth's assurance about the Spitfire.

"Chauncey, one of the things Ken said about the Spitfire was she's an elegant lady, and I was to treat her that way."

Chauncey smiled. "That sounds like something your Squadron Leader would say. He's right, but one thing you've got to remember; and I don't mean any reflection on your ability. But few pilot's handle that lady better than Ken. Not you, not me, not ninety-nine percent of the pilots I know. Keep that in mind. What else did he tell you?"

"A number of things you confirmed, as well as the flaps are not hydraulic and quite stiff, so I'll have to brace myself to move them. And, as you said, wingover to start a dive."

"Good points. The flaps are where she's not a lady and I should have mentioned them. Dive? There should be no need for you to dive, at least at present. All right, Daphne, let's have a go in that Nighthawk of yours. We'll see if you're as good as they say. And I want to warn you, you'll do a number of touch and goes, so it's important how you do them, how they sound that is. Because the Spitfire has a narrow track, which means you've got to be bang on the spot every time."

In the Nighthawk, Fellows put Daphne through a series of sideslips, stalls and touch and goes. On the final approach, he closed his eyes and listened. There was a single chirp as two tires touched down as one. That, and her sum total, convinced him.

"Daphne, you're *better* than the real thing. Hop in that new Mark II over there and go for a jaunt."

She looked to where he pointed. It wasn't expected. "Just like that? Go for a jaunt in a *Spitfire*?"

"What do you want? Fanfare, trumpet, salute? Head south for half an hour, out to sea where we can't see what you're up to. I do recommend you not get lost. While you go through preflight, I'll send out chaps for the chocks and tail."

Chauncey walked off, leaving Daphne with a slight case of anxiety. It happened so abruptly she wasn't near ready. Don't let on, she told herself, everyone is sure to be watching. But she had sat in one before, so she marched to the aircraft and went through her preflight. Finished, she dropped into the cockpit. A flight sergeant leaned over the canopy and smiled. She was grateful.

"Mr. Fellows does this to all neophyte Spitfire pilots, Miss. Some of them stand there frozen in place, it tells a lot about them. You, well, we watched you hitch up your pants—excuse my expression— march right over, do your walk around, then hop in like you've done it all before. And you're beautiful too."

"Thank you for that, Sergeant, I'll readily admit I'm a touch nervous and not sure I've got the cockpit preflight down pat."

"No problem, Miss. They can't see nervousness from the tower—unless you scream, that's a giveaway. Now, here's your cockpit preflight pad, let's go over it while I strap you in."

The cockpit preflight done, the sergeant nodded to her. The area was clear. She couldn't stall any longer.

The starter cartridge exploded, the Merlin's horses retorted, coughing exhaust past the sergeant, as he turned his back to it.

She steadied her nerves, deep slow breaths, as Royce told her to do when a mountain climb looked intimidating.

"Pressure and boost are fine as you can see, Miss. Take her down to the end of the runway, get the feel of the controls on the way. You remember your takeoff and approach speeds?"

"Yes, thank you, Sergeant, any last words of advice?"

"Yes, Miss. You see the way the airscrew is turning? Keep your foot firm on the opposite rudder, or if you don't you'll do a left turn on takeoff. Lot more engine torque than you're used to. Another thing, be sure and remember to bring the undercarriage up, and more importantly, lower it on approach."

That advice, though essential, gave her a needed smile. He jumped down, pulled the lines on the wheel chocks and saluted while men holding the tail down waved her off. The aircraft rolled forward, she tilted her head out of the cockpit, and zigzagged to align the ship parallel to the runway. Increasing the RPMs, she lightly kicked the airfoil a notch to test the effect and began to breathe properly. She knew she was good. It was just another takeoff she reminded herself, except this time she sitting behind an engine with five times the horsepower of any single engine plane she'd ever flown. At the end of the runway, she came about 180 degrees, braked and toggled her transmitter.

"Tower, this Spitfire whatever my number, ready for takeoff."

"Miss Elliot," She recognized Chauncey's voice, "you are cleared for departure. Radar shows clean air, but the Liner *Majestic* is out there so please be careful not to bump into her. Good luck, God speed. See you in an hour or so, unless you decide to keep her. Oh, one more thing, *don't* head for France."

A deep breath, all gauges read true. She pushed the throttle forward. The Spitfire, skittish for a moment, then straightened and bolted down the runway. She felt the tail lift, the plane felt light. This surprised her, the Spitfire intended to fly off on her own. Daphne eased back on the yoke, felt the plane glide into the sky. Amazed at the sheer power in her hands, she brought the undercarriage up, checked gauges and slid the canopy closed. Before she knew it, the airspeed registered 180 MPH. At 225, she throttled back, breathed, and leveled off at a thousand feet.

The land disappeared, only the shimmering silver ocean below. Then, there ahead, was the *Majestic*, her bow carving the waves. Daphne pushed the yoke forward, brought the aircraft's altitude to seventy feet, powered up and hurtled past the jet black hull of the liner. A fleeting, blurred impression of people waving before they and the ocean liner were gone. Her Spitfire bent into a rising arc. She pushed the yoke diagonally to the right, touched the ailerons and the aircraft flowed effortlessly into a full roll.

This was more than her wildest dreams! Her whole body tensed! "My God, I love this…*I was born for this*!"

A shiver surged, then raced through her. She became one with the thundering Spitfire…She was Queen of the Skies.

Chapter 25

HE WAS CLOSE TO SHOUTING. "You did *what* with my Mother?"

"I took her for a flight from the Mount."

"I can't believe it, Daphne! She went? From the Mount? You're serious? What did you use, not that Miles Nighthawk I hope."

"Of course not." She laughed, "Your lawn is too short, you need another fifty acres. I used a DH Hornet Moth. You know it has side by side enclosed seats. We had a grand time."

"I don't understand it. She would never fly with Father or me...never!"

"That's because neither of you were as smooth as I am."

"Smooth at what? Flying, or convincing?"

"Both."

"I can easily believe that. Tell me, did she like it?"

"Well, to be honest, I thought she was having a grand time until I looked over two minutes after takeoff and she still had her eyes closed. Then, I think she finally decided that if she must die, she might as well enjoy the view. We really had a good time, Ken. She loved it when she saw the Mount from the air, except she saw the roof needed to be cleaned on the south side. It was fun until the dead engine landing. She thought we'd wind up through the windows. Gave me a little kiss when we didn't."

"My, God, you've certainly got her wrapped around your little finger."

"It's not only that, I'll bet she's wanted to fly for years, just waited for someone to ask her."

"Ask her? Not true. Mother never took Father or me up on our offers. But back to the Spitfire. I knew you'd love it."

"Ken, really, name a pilot who wouldn't. Thought I'd died

and gone to heaven. She's marvelous, just marvelous."

"No question. Chauncey Fellows called me before I could find time to call you, so I knew you'd flown it. He also said you buzzed the *Majestic* and did a roll for good measure. Said he heard the passengers went wild, loved seeing it."

"My, God! He knew? I wasn't that close, Ken. Chauncey didn't say anything when I landed."

"Probably found out later. He didn't mind, but I don't recommend you do it again. He also said you tested 96 out of a possible 100 on the written exam. 100 means you're God."

"Fat chance to convince anyone of that. But I wanted to be the first to tell you, how did he get in touch with you so fast?"

"There's military communication lines."

"I was disappointed you knew."

"I understand. I'll make it up to you when we have dinner."

"Fair's fair, I guess, Ken. Any idea when?"

"Can't say. This Pact of Steel Hitler formed with Italy's Mussolini has everyone around Command hopping."

"That's a shame you don't know. I'll admit I look forward to dinner. We'll get together somewhere along the way, Ken, I'm sure. Meanwhile, I'm back up to Coventry tomorrow."

"Sorry to hear that, Daph."

* * *

Daphne was surprised to see Clive Henderson's vehicle at Blackbird Cottage. Entering, she saw Royce didn't get up to greet her. "What happened? Are you all right, Jim?"

Clive answered for him. "He won't admit it, Daphne, but he's in pain. Crushed two fingers and fractured his wrist last night at work."

"Christ, Jim, it looks a mess. What happened?"

"Nothing he did, Daphne. We had a cutaway of a RR cylinder wall with a piston set up to run on an electric motor. James was simply babbitting a bearing face when one of our engineers closed the wrong circuit breaker and the piston rod came down and crushed his fingers."

Royce turned away. "Goddamn engineers, they'll be the death of me yet. Four years at an engineering university and they don't know every stupid action creates an equal stupid reaction."

Daphne looked at Clive. "Well, at least he hasn't lost his sense of humor."

Clive was wry. "That's only because he's doped to the gills. It was really quite cruel, what he went through, Daphne. His hand was trapped. To finish the stroke the rod would have to go further down and that would have crushed the fingers more or cut them off. We couldn't get his hand out. He was so bad off I thought he was going to crack his teeth. I got some cloth between them while we clipped the C ring off and pried the wrist pin out of the piston."

She put her arm around him, careful not to move the arm resting in a sling. "Damn, Jim, I'm sorry, let's get you more comfortable. What did the doctor say, Clive? What's the prognosis?"

"He's not sure, he lined up everything, put splints on, and said all we can do is wait and see."

"X-Rays?"

"Yes, although I'm not sure he knows how to read them."

"Christ! Let me think. This is not the place to be. Jim, do you think you could make it to London?"

He didn't answer, numb. Clive spoke up. "I don't think he could, or should, Daphne. The doctor said he'd stop in tomorrow, but Mary just left and she wasn't happy about it either."

"I don't blame her, this isn't good enough."

Her mind raced over options. After they had made Royce as comfortable as possible, Daphne told Clive to stay while she used the telephone.

Ten minutes later, she returned. "I called my Mother's doctor; he'll get in touch with a neurological and orthopedic specialist. I told him that doctor better be up here first thing tomorrow or I'll raise unholy hell. My family endowed that hospital."

"I'm glad you're back, Daphne, things aren't the same with him without you around."

"It's good to be back, Clive, and I don't mean to run off to London as much as I do. Jim understands, and I hope you do. When he works seventy hours plus, a week, I can't simply sit on my hands and do nothing. I go down and help Lady Jane

Sommers with the veteran centers, and I'm a pilot now, so I fly a lot and hope to be a ferry pilot someday."

"I didn't know you were a pilot, Daphne. Jim never mentioned that."

"I'm not surprised. At present, he's got a one track mind."

"Before his father died, James had a two track mind, work and mountains. Now, it looks like it will only be work for a long while."

"I don't know what to say, Clive. He can't keep on like this. *We* can't keep on like this."

"If I may say this, Daphne, you're not cut out to be a hausfrau, and I don't blame you for not wanting that life. I don't doubt you love James, but it's not in you to be tied down to…I'm sorry, I'm an old man who too often speaks his mind."

"You never have to apologize to me, Clive. You mean too much to us. I understand your concern for him, for us. Believe me; I'll never, ever hurt him as long as he wants me. Still, it appears we've become two different people and we're sorely tested right now."

"I follow you, Daphne, and you're right, you surely are two different people—and temperaments."

Dr. Smithfield arrived early the next day. The X-Rays showed the forefinger was set improperly. He reset it, much to Royce's discomfort. Daphne then sat with Smithfield.

"Well, Doctor?"

"The wrist will heal properly if he's careful. He said he's left handed?"

"Yes."

"Then any restriction of his right hand shouldn't be as much of a problem."

"That depends on what you mean by restriction."

"With the few tests I've done and the X-Rays, I would say the nerves are damaged to the point where an operation would be of little value. Which means, he'll be able to move them somewhat, but strength and grip will be quite limited unless there's a great deal of rehabilitation."

Daphne tried to grasp the implications. "Doctor, he's a mountain climber. We look forward to climbing in the future."

"I'm afraid," Dr. Smithfield removed his glasses and rubbed his eyes, "there's no other way to say this, I'm afraid he will only be able to hike. Expert climbing? No."

"I don't accept that, doctor, and if he heard you, he wouldn't accept it either."

"I don't ask you to accept it, my dear. You asked my studied opinion, I told you. If you want, after he begins to heal more, say a month, my staff can set up a program to bring his hand back as much as physically possible."

"We will definitely do that, doctor."

"But please remember, Miss Elliot, the longer you wait, the more difficult it will be for us to rehabilitate it."

* * *

The month of June dragged to a close. Daphne and Royce said good riddance to it. He managed to work, although fewer hours, and not at his best. The work he did, the advice he gave, was correct. The problem was he tired often. Pain shot through his fingers and up his arm each time he tried to use the hand or reduce the drugs.

On the second day of July, the IRA blew up the coatroom in the Coventry Railway Station and slightly injured eight of the staff. As with everyone else in the city, the workers at D W Royce were angry, but Royce and Clive reminded them it could happen anywhere, and that included one or more of the company's plants. Every employee must be diligent; that was to be the new byword.

Into August, Daphne stayed in Coventry yet none of her worries got through to Royce. Clive did all he could, worked himself too hard, for like Royce, he was driven. However, Clive was much older and found it hard to maintain the pace required.

David made only five visits to Royce's office in five weeks, ostensibly to see how he was, yet always followed by a demand to accomplish more.

* * *

415

23 of August, 1939,
The Soviet Union and Germany signed a non-aggression agreement between the two countries. This agreement became known as the Molotov-Ribbentrop Pact after the foreign ministers of the two countries—and shocked Europe. Hitler's persecution of Communists had been unrelenting and for the Soviet Union's Stalin to sign the Pact, baffled most countries.

Unknown at the time, the treaty held a secret protocol, which divided Northern and Eastern Europe into German and Soviet "Territorial and Political Spheres of Influence."

The ramifications of this treaty would initiate in ten days.

Chapter 26

25 AUGUST, FRIDAY, 1939, started out as an exceptionally sunny day. Daphne had talked Royce into an hour off work to have lunch at an in town restaurant. Royce had called to say he'd be tied up until two, and would meet her at Broadgate, Coventry center. She didn't let that bother her and had Marco Herrera, Ravensmoor's groom, get her Christmas present out of the garage. She lowered the windows on the green bodied Riley sports coupe to cool as she drove to Broadgate. She smiled, he was actually waiting in his Bentley as she pulled up behind his Bentley.

He slipped into the Riley. "Here I am. Please note I'm on time. Where do you want to go for lunch?"

"I saw this neat little place on the south end of town; you know the area, Jim, what's the best way to get there?"

"Let me see, this is Broadgate, go down the end and…"

A blinding flash, then a shockwave from an explosion shook the car. They sat horrified as storefronts disintegrated in front of them as shredded debris and smoke confused the scene. Wood, glass and shattered foundation blocks burst through the smoke, becoming deadly missiles that struck down dozens of pedestrians.

With debris still falling, Royce ran from the car followed by Daphne. Injured and dead littered the street. He rushed past tattered awnings and rubble into a smoldering storefront.

"Daphne, I'll get the injured out, you find somewhere for them to rest until ambulances arrive here! Wait, get my car, keys are in it, we can use that!"

By the time she brought the Bentley down, others had rushed to aid the stricken and helped get four of the more seriously wounded into the vehicle. Constables arrived, followed by wardens and the fire brigade. When the ambulances arrived from the Warwickshire Hospital, medical personnel took one of the lesser injured from the front seat of the Bentley and asked Royce to get the others to the hospital. Daphne started for the car and froze. Royce shouted to her, then followed her gaze. Not twenty feet away was the body of a young woman, her face gone.

"Daphne! Don't think! Put it out of your mind, we've got to get these people to the hospital!"

He reached across the seat and pulled her in and drove off, ignoring the pain in his hand.

"All right, all right, Jim. I'm all right, I'm all right. It was just that sudden shock of that poor person made Rob flash across..."

"I know, I know, just stay in the moment, we'll be there shortly."

They were the first to arrive with the wounded. Doctors and nurses hastened to their aid as an ambulance pulled up. Royce moved his vehicle away from the hospital, off the road. They sat, staring out the windscreen, blood smeared, along with the inside of the Bentley.

"You all right, Daphne?"

"I think so. What the devil happened? Was it a coal gas explosion?"

"I doubt that, I think it was a bomb."

"Who...who could do such a hateful thing? Those were innocent women and children there, just walking along. Who would do something like this?"

"I'm sure I know, but I'll hold my tongue until we know for certain. I can't drive this car the way it is, let's walk back to the hospital and see if we can get a ride to Broadgate. We can help some more and get your car."

As they went back to the hospital, a nurse hurried up to them. "You're Mr. James Royce, aren't you, sir?"

When Royce nodded, she continued. "Thank you for all you've done, sir, but could we prevail upon you to give blood? We'll be in terribly short supply."

Royce and Daphne donated blood, while more wounded started to stream in. The blood-soaked staff were to work, without break, long through the night.

Given a lift back to her Riley, they saw there were now hundreds of helpers. Daphne turned her soot-covered auto around and they drove to Blackbird Cottage. After the carnage they witnessed, even Royce found it impossible to concentrate on heading back to the plant.

25 August, 1939
An article in the paper stated: 'A member of the Irish Republican Army rode a bicycle onto Broadgate and parked it on a post in front of Astley's and Burtons, beside Mansfield's business establishments. The carrier basket held a 5-pound bomb and utilized an alarm clock timer.'

Five people, from ages 15 to 82 were killed, 70 wounded, 10 critically, and over 40 businesses destroyed or damaged.

The country was outraged. Tension between the English and Irish communities increased, although surprisingly, no violence occurred.

For the unpardonable murders and destruction, five people were tried. Three were acquitted, two convicted.

7 February 1940
The two convicted men were executed by hanging. They were martyred by the Irish Republican Movement.

The same day as the IRA massacre in Coventry, another, largely ignored, but crucial statute enacted. England signed a pact with Poland, pledging aid in the event of an attack on that country. Fear raised its ugly head.

* * *

Royce had overstressed his hand when aiding the wounded. Daphne couldn't fault him. She was sure anyone would have done the same. In addition, she knew Royce often acted without thought, so his reaction was to be expected. What Daphne would not accept was his disinterest, to the point that he refused to do anything about restorative effort for his fingers. Consequently, the dissention between them on that subject reached to a head.

"Jim, again. All I'm asking is we go down to London once a week and let Doctor Smithfield's staff strengthen your fingers and get them to function better. We can get down and back in the same day, or they could come up here."

"For God's sake, Daphne, stop pestering me!"

She was shocked. "*Pestering you*? Is that how you feel? It's called worry, damn you!"

It came to her. As he grew up, no one had ever shown him the slightest concern. So that now, he didn't know how to accept it. He'd put up a barrier to protect himself from people hurting him. He was doing it still, even with her. She was at a loss, angry. She tried to stay calm and talk to him, but he didn't yield.

"I'm not interested in going down there, or have someone come up here."

"So you're not interested in us climbing again?"

He didn't answer.

One last effort. "You can't even hold the steering wheel properly with that hand when you shift."

He shrugged. "I've got more constructive things to do than argue about this. Why in hell can't you *understand*?"

She held her tongue. He was right, she couldn't understand.

He went to the garage. She fully expected him to return so they would work it out. Instead, he started the car, backed out and drove off. This had never happened. Royce had thrown down a gauntlet. Why? Maybe something at work was on his nerves. But she'd had her fill of that, that—and his silences. Suddenly, she'd had it. Enough was enough. Two can play his game. Had she only clung on for past emotions? He was the one who changed, not she. Perhaps he *wants* to be alone. Maybe he's tired of her protests over his work hours and fingers. Maybe his past is too ingrained for him to adjust. Pestering him, was she? Well, too God damned bad! It's for his own good, If he can't see that, then to hell with it. She was tired of kowtowing. She had her own life to live and intended to live it. Still, there was him and what he once meant...

She stuck a carving knife through a note and into the old horsehair plaster beside the phone.

Damn it, when you want to meet me halfway, call. Otherwise don't.

She signed it:

The woman you used to climb with.

She packed the Riley with more clothes than needed for a week and headed for London.

* * *

After four days, Daphne was troubled Royce hadn't called. She took her mind off the uncertainty when Kenneth called while she was with Lady Jane at The Mount.

They made a dinner date for Wednesday the 30th. Lady Jane smiled. Exactly as she hoped. The pieces were falling into place.

Kenneth arrived at The Mount early Wednesday evening, paid his respects to his Mother, had a few words with Daphne, then retired to change. When he returned, he was dressed in the same outfit he had worn to the Dorchester, including Daphne's polka dot scarf.

"Ken, my outfit is almost the same because I don't have semi-formal wear. You didn't have to dress down again for me."

"I know I didn't have to, I wanted to, and I'm truly more comfortable. This will probably set London style on its head next spring. Then again, probably not." He laughed.

Before they left, they had a light scotch and Daphne asked for more ice, knowing the British kept ice at a minimum. "So, Ken, tell us about your day. Your mother and I have talked so much about the entertainment programs we're setting up for the next few months it's coming out our ears."

"Well, interesting enough, we've been busy fine-tuning our reaction times with our counterparts at Bomber Command. Developing the response time with the RF Chain System has taken quite some work, believe me, but we're spot on now. Even Wing Commander Gibson was shocked how quickly we jumped his bombers. Again, Daphne, this is well known in the RAF, but still a secret to you common people. And, speaking of spies, how's your friend, Jesus Peron?"

"I can't fathom why you think he's a spy. He never asks anything about what I do and only says to say hello to you."

"Does he ask where I am?"

"As I told you before, not at all. Tell me why he should

care? I see you're still a bit full of yourself."

Lady Jane loved it, pleased that Daphne kept her son on the defensive.

Kenneth was amused. "Daph, think back. I told you before, that *if* Jesus were a spy, where I am is where my squadron is. To know Squadron Leaders locals is important to an enemy."

"All right, I recall that now, so I'll give you that point if it helps make believe you're important. But, Jesus hasn't shown the slightest interest in you."

She lowered her voice sinisterly. "However, he did ask about my brother. Is he still in the States? Will he be back here sometime?"

"And you don't think that's strange? Did he know your brother, or he was in the States? Did you tell him?"

"No, I don't recall I did. Damn, Ken, now that you bring it up, I don't really know how he knew Rob. How did he…?"

"Strange again, Daph. Have they even met?"

"Gosh, not to my knowledge…This does become curious."

Lady Jane offered her opinion. "He's probably simply nosy. You know how those Argentineans are."

They both grinned at her. Perhaps, they thought. But still…

They went back to the Dorchester. Daphne felt it would be the last place David would want to be seen. A flower lady at the entrance held out her velvet board. Kenneth took a yellow rose.

"I'll accept it only if you give her a hell of a gratuity."

"Daph, I'll bet no one has ever said you're wildly romantic."

"True, and no one ever said I was easy to live with, either."

"I've no problem believing that."

At the bar, Harry Craddock gave a cheery hello. "Here's your glass back, Harry."

"I'm surprised, Kenneth, didn't think I'd see it for years. And how are you, Miss Daphne?"

"Fine, Harry, nice of you to remember my name." She devastated him with a smile.

"Okay you two, enough flirting with my date, Harry. And Daphne, save that kind of smile for me, if you'd be so kind. We had two Martinis the last time, why don't we try two of Harry's Manhattans this time?"

She nodded as the maître d' told them their room was ready

when they were. After a few minutes more chatter, they left for dinner. Harry said he would have a waiter bring their drinks to their room.

When they were out of Harry's earshot, she stopped, Kenneth, giving him a withering look. "Room? Room? That's twice now I've heard about a *room*. What's this all about, Kenneth?"

"Good Lord, Daph, take it easy, when I called the maître d' for a reservation, I asked for a private dining room. That's all Harry meant."

"Oh? And do you suppose Harry and the maître d' don't know what goes on in *private* dining rooms?"

Ken was exasperated. "Well, all I can say is I doing know what going on in other private dining rooms, but I sure as blazes know what *won't* be going on in our private dining room."

"Fine, let's go to our private room."

Before he could respond, a middle-aged woman approached with a young woman in tow.

"Kenneth, Kenneth, *dear*!"

Ken was the embodiment of decorum. "Why Lady Cunard, how pleasant to see you. Mother was just speaking of you and wondering how you were."

They kissed on the cheeks, and he turned to Daphne. "Lady Emerald Cunard, may I introduce you to Miss Daphne Elliot, of the Boston, Massachusetts, Elliot's."

"My dear, aren't you lovely." Lady Cunard offhandedly remarked while she introduced her companion.

"Miss Kathleen Kennedy, I would like to introduce you to RAF Squadron Leader, Kenneth Sommers and a Miss Elliot. Now, with introductions out of the way, Kenneth, I'm most displeased with you. Miss Kennedy's father is the American Ambassador to the UK and she doesn't get out to see our countryside. I had you in mind to show her around, but I you appear quite taken up by this beautiful creature."

Before Kenneth could respond, Daphne could see Kathleen Kennedy cringe at the words of her hostess. "Yes, Miss Kennedy, I'm afraid Kenneth is quite taken up. However, I'm sure you'll meet a number of other creatures in your travels over here."

The comment flew over Emerald Cunard's head, but behind her, Miss Kennedy's smile revealed she understood quite well.

Then, Daphne had the effrontery to continue. "Nice to have met you, Miss Kennedy, Mrs. Cunard. But I do hope you'll excuse us, our dinner will cool if we linger."

Closing the door their room, Kenneth was delighted. "I don't believe you! First, you implied Emerald was a creature, with an adverse tinge, then you called her Mrs. instead of Lady Cunard. And to cap it off, you tell her our dinner will get cold, which implied our dinner is more important than she. You are unbelievable!"

"Well, she called me 'a creature' first and then a 'thing'. And you made me gag with your 'how nice to see you'. Oh, and the kiss on her cheek was a nice touch. Then you and your 'may I introduce the Boston such and such'. My God, I was about to curtsey. One would have thought she was the Queen."

"She *is* the queen of the social season here in London."

"Oh, and why do those affairs interest you?"

"I take Mother."

"I'd bet that's for cover. No other reason? Such as all the young girls and their coming out affairs? *Affairs* is right. Perhaps I should have left you with that Miss Kennedy."

"Well…the way you're carrying on, maybe she'd be more pleasant."

"Maybe she would, because she doesn't know you. I know what your mother calls you—you lecherous social climber."

"Lecherous social…? God, this isn't going the way I planned at all."

She felt bad for him, "For God's sake, Ken, I'm only teasing you. Is that what you'll say when you meet a German fighter pilot, 'Oh, God, this isn't going the way I planned at all'?"

"If he's as beautiful as you—yes!"

Her deep laugh made him think. "Then again, what did you mean when you said I was quite taken up? Did you mean that, or were you jealous Miss what's her name might interest me?"

"Don't give me that little Miss what's her name fairytale. I'll bet you already have her name in your little black book."

Ready to deny her comment, he instead challenged her. "You didn't answer my question. Am I taken up, were you jealous?"

"I only said you were taken to annoy that Cunard woman. But all right then, I'll admit to perhaps a touch of jealousy."

The Sommelier knocked, then entered with a bottle of Pol Roger Champagne.

"Very nice, Ken, I love Champagne, but I don't know this one at all."

"That MP chap my Mother knows, Churchill, drinks it, so I thought we'd give it a try for a special evening like this."

They tested, and loved it. The Champagne ritual over, the Sommelier left.

Ken held his glass to hers. "May you always be happy."

"That's very nice, Ken but too one way. It should be may we both always be happy." The glasses clinked, they unwound.

"So tell me, Squadron Leader, now that your Mother isn't around, how do things look?"

"Not good, Daphne, we've already been informed the fleet will mobilize tomorrow, and this will bother you, school children will be evacuated from London."

"London? Civilians are to be a target?"

"They were in Spain, I was there, saw it happen, ghastly."

"Then I'll have to call Mary Royce, tell her to place as many children from Kinder Care and London as she can into the cottage at Windermere."

"That's thoughtful, Daph, but if war breaks out, where will you stay?"

"Belgravia, of course."

"Were you listening to me—what did I just tell you? London will be bombed."

She looked distracted. She didn't resist when he took her hand. "Daphne, I have a great favor to ask."

He made her nervous. She waited. "I'd like you to move in with Mother if war comes."

"I don't think…"

"Daphne, wait, hear me out. There are no ties. I'll be away and be her constant worry. I need you to keep her spirits up. She will need your strength and she'll believe you, no matter what you tell her. And you'll be out of London, that will make me feel better. Please, give it some serious thought."

"I'll give it thought, Ken, but I may be in ferry service or possibly up in Coventry to help Mary. I simply can't promise. Still, I will keep what you said in mind and do my best."

"Daph, think. Coventry won't be safe either."

She shook her head, shutting her thoughts to it. Too much champagne, Kenneth thought, and dropped the matter.

The champagne mellowed them as they were served. He ordered another Pol Roger to go with dinner, disregarding her unconvincing protest.

Their room had a couch where they relaxed after the meal. She could tell Kenneth still had something on his mind. "Well, out with your thoughts, Ken."

"It's probably improper of me to ask, but how's everything in Coventry?"

"And why do you suddenly ask?"

"Well, you haven't mentioned your *Jim* yet and, you acquiesced quite pleasantly when I asked you to dinner."

"I could say I promised you, so here I am."

"But you won't say that, will you?"

"No, but I must make a mental note for the future, you're antenna is alert to everything."

He waited, Daphne took a sip. "Things have deteriorated since I saw you, Ken. To a point where I actually used a carving knife to stick a note on the wall. The note said that when he was ready to meet me half way, he could call. It's been seven days and he hasn't called."

Ken couldn't help grin. "Well, I rather imagine a note by knife got his attention. So what do you do now?"

"I actually don't know, Ken. I feel so guilty."

"Guilty? I don't follow."

"The wine is making me far too candid, Ken. You see, *I* chased after him, I really did. It wasn't the other way around. When I was in Austria and saw him climb, he had a technique I couldn't believe. He didn't climb as much as flowed, merged with a mountain. I love climbing and I'm a very good, but he was astonishing. I watched and fell in love. I know, sounds crazy. Anyway, we stayed together for a few days, but he was a loner. One night he just walked off into the mountains. I woke up he was gone. No goodbye, just left me…nothing."

"Then how did the two of you get back together?"

"A friend of mine saw him at a spa near Kufstein, north east Austria, I was in Innsbruck, so I went up there after him. Then, blast him, he started to walk off again! But this time he came back, and here we are. The problem is, he's not the same man I fell in love with. Now he's consumed by work, it seems nothing, or no one else matters. The last straw was his hand being crippled in an accident and he won't have it treated. In other words, we'll never climb together again either."

"And now your problem is you don't know what to do, or where to go."

"That's right, what should I do?" She smirked, "And why on earth am I asking *you*?"

"Well, Daph, if you are, my advice is you should go back and see him. Work it out, or know it's over."

"I didn't expect that answer."

"It's the only answer I can give that makes sense—for us. I look at it this way, Daphne. You chased after him, now you have second thoughts. To me it seems you feel guilty about leaving him because you made him love you in the first place. So you don't know what to do now and that leaves us in limbo.

Look, if you go up there and stay with him, then there won't be a next time for us. If you come back, then I hope you're open to see where it could lead…for us. Fair enough?"

They held each other's eyes. "Yes, Ken, that's fair enough."

The last sips from two bottles of Champagne were gone. Ken pulled a small packet from his pocket, and handed it to her.

She gave him a stern look. "This better not be an enormous diamond engagement ring, Mr. Sommers."

"I'll only do that," he laughed, "after you chase me."

She opened the wrap. A pin, in silver, SPITFIRE PILOT.

For once words failed her, tears replaced them. It was recognition for her hard work and dedication. Kenneth had it made especially for her. She wanted to hug him, but with a bottle of Champagne in each of them, she knew better. He could see how she felt. He put on a fair show of being sober and held her hand.

Leaving the Dorchester, she asked if he was staying at The Mount. "Yes, I've decided to. But I'll be gone by 0400. Why do you ask?"

"I want you to take me to my house. I think I'll stay there tonight…alone."

"Daphne, you can stay at Mother's. I won't…"

427

"I'm probably being too honest again, Mr. Sommers, but it's not what *you* might do. Take me to Belgravia."

He didn't press her, but at her door, he held her tightly.

"In the States we used to say leave room for the Holy Ghost."

"Then how lucky can we be? We're not in the States."

With that, two shadows merged, a warm kiss, felt and shared. With resolve she didn't believe she had, he was pushed away. He managed a wan smile. "Isn't this where you close the door in my face once again?"

"Yes, but this time, a different reason. Goodnight."

He drove off. "God," he spoke aloud, "I'd love to ask her to marry me, although, that could possibly be a touch premature. I won't ask her, and not only because of that damn Jim of hers."

For the first time in his life, he wasn't sure about the unknown future. It wasn't a worry, he wasn't that type. It was a tiny voice that whispered annoyingly in his head. It was never there before Daphne.

On her part, Daphne was angry with herself. "What in the devil am I up to? I might still be living with one man, and I'm falling for another? There must be a nasty word for this."

She couldn't blame it on too much wine. Amused by Kenneth at first, she kept him at arm's length. Then, his bravura became entertaining, his smile infectious, his laugh warm. Yet it was when he became serious about war and his obligation to his country, she felt drawn to him. When at The Mount, she hoped he would call, and when he did, she felt a chill. The final touch was the flight in the Spitfire. It was then she understood him. His whole world, his whole being was revealed…and she cherished the sight.

Then this night, when he told her to go back to Jim and make a decision. That told more about him than words. She wasn't simply a challenge, or a one night stand to him. In his own way he said he loved her. Now she could trust him. Now she was becoming *involved*.

* * *

Back at Blackbird cottage at three the next afternoon, Daphne guessed Royce might stay overnight at his office. She called him there and didn't give a damn at what the secretary thought.

He wasn't there. And yes, the secretary would let Jim know she was at the cottage.

She then called Mary Royce. "Hi, Mary, I'm at the cottage, how are you?"

"I'm good, Daphne, nice to hear your voice. I'm busy with all the children arriving from Austria. And did you know they start to evacuate the children from London today?"

"Yes, I heard that yesterday. Have you used my place at Windermere yet?"

"Not yet. I think we'll start next week. We need all the rooms we can get. Can't thank you enough. How long will you be here?"

"I honestly don't know. I have to talk with Jim. I'd like to see you, but I'm in a mental flux."

"I should think you might be. He's said nothing, but I could see he's hurt. Think you can you work it out?"

"That's why I'm here, to find out. The ball's in his court."

"I understand, Daphne. I won't pry or give advice. I guess we both have our problems."

"I can't respond to you on that, Mary. But if your problems get too much, you have my London number."

"I hope that all I have to do is ring up Blackbird cottage."

"Thanks, we'll see. But I don't give it too much hope."

At nine that night, Royce still hadn't arrived. She started to pack her clothes into the Riley, yet held on to the hope that perhaps he hadn't received the message. She knew that an empty thought.

She finished packing. At nine-fifteen, a car pulled into the drive. The car door closed, the door to the house opened.

"Hello, Daphne."

"Jim. Did you get my message?"

"Yes, I was so damn busy, I couldn't get away."

She couldn't help her retort. "And I suppose the phone lines were cut, so you couldn't call."

She wished her response hadn't been so caustic.

"I'm sorry, Daphne, I got caught up in something with my men and lost track of the time."

"Jim, another few minutes and I would have been gone."

"Daphne, I'm sorry. But, please, I love you. It's my work…"

"I understand, Jim. You love me, it's just that you don't have any time for me a present."

"It looks like that I know, it's just…"

He trailed off helplessly. There was nothing more to say, they both knew it.

There was no sense to drag it out. "Jim, I wish you nothing other than the very best."

"Is there someone else, Daphne?"

That shocked her. Still, she knew how to answer. "Jim, I'd have lived with you happily ever after. It was you who changed, not me. Go look in the mirror. You're worn out, look at the way you hold your damn hand. You won't even try to improve it. I know you think I pester you, but it's called concern, Jim. And you don't want it. So I'll say it again, you're no longer the person I fell in love with, and if I find someone else, it's your fault."

"Daphne, please understand. There's something in me. I can't help what's happened to me. That doesn't mean I don't love you."

"Oh, God, Jim, don't say that."

"Please, Daphne, please stay…stay with me tonight."

She woke before dawn. He was gone. She dressed, took her car keys and glanced about the room, a room she once thought she would never want to leave. Yet at last and in sorrow, she faced a stark fact. He was gone from her.

At the motorway, she turned north to Windermere, where she could be alone and sort her life out. Entering the drive, the rain spattered the windscreen and then a downpour soaked her as she ran to the house. The rooms were as raw and as dark as her mood. She lit some kindling in the fireplace and changed into dry, warmer clothes, then sat in front of the fire to get the chill out.

Guilt, go ahead, say it…she felt guilty. Yet there was no guile in either of them. Or was there? There was nothing left but fading memories of their love and no path to reawaken it. She would not live a lie and conform, then sit like a patient wife, hopeful he would change. She wasn't prepared to wait.

Then, abruptly, she questioned aloud. "Is it possible I wanted this way out because of my feelings for Kenneth? After all is said and done, has it turned out my love for Jim been based on only climbing? Do I have to live with that? Damn me, am I so shallow? And now. Are my feelings for Kenneth only there because we both have a passion for flying? Damn, damn, damn...and damn!"

She couldn't help but smile. Already she thought she loved him. She mixed a scotch and water, absentmindedly glimpsed at the calendar. Jim and I broke up the first of September, she thought, nineteen thirty-nine. She'd remember that date.

Sipping the scotch, beginning to mellow, she switched on the radio to find some music to cheer her up.

"This is BBC Home. At approximately six-thirty this morning, the armed forces of Nazi Germany crossed the border of Poland in a savage attack, led an unknown number of army groups. Polish forces have fallen back..."

Her mind blank, she fell back onto the couch. "My, God, what will this mean for us, for *all* of us?

1 September, 1939
Operation Weiss. The weight of five German army groups smashed into Poland from north to south. The Poles, though brave and fighting with valor, relied on outdated tactics and inferior equipment. They were overwhelmed by the savagery of Stuka dive- bombers, German Panzer and Czech made Skoda tanks spearheading the attack. The German thrust burst through Poland's defensive lines and raced into the heart of the country. It was a mechanized warfare as yet unheard of. The term Blitzkrieg, entered the English language.

Behind the Regular army troops came the SS Death's Head Division. For years, the Polish people, considered subhuman by Hitler, would be used as slave labor or beasts of burden, starved, beaten, eliminated.

On that same date, Hitler activated Aktion T4, the elimination of all handicapped, retarded or chronically ill German children and adults. Sent to Hadamar, they were considered 'Life unworthy of Life' and died under the guises of 'pneumonia', or 'Mercy Killing'.

3 September 1939.
England and France declared war on Germany. World War II began.

Chapter 27

7 September, 1939.

HITLER WAS OVERJOYED. His armies were about to obliterate Poland's existence. At his mountain retreat, the Berghof in Obersalzberg, near the German border with northern Ostmark— formerly the country of Austria—he stared out at the mountain range filling his view. He had done it. He had shown the world and especially his tentative generals, that he was a military genius. He had ridiculed them for their timidity and shown how his audacity won wars. His conquered lands were now larger than Germany.

The only potential problem was England. He didn't worry about the French. England was his vexation. Hitler's plan was to forge deeper east, into Russia. But the damned English honored their pact with Poland—much to his surprise, as they didn't have honor with the Czechs—and this gave him a war he did not want, or at least not want at present. He had to keep in mind England had the largest battle fleet in the world.

First, his peace offer to the English was snubbed, and then they had the effrontery to bomb his naval base at Helgoland. In his mind, Hitler had no choice. He ordered his generals to work up a strike plan across Belgium and Holland, both neutral countries, and into France. Still, he knew winter was a short three months away. He needed to secure his gains in Poland first and bring his eastern armies back to the west. There wouldn't be time to launch an attack before winter.

Closing his mind about the English, Hitler turned to the officer waiting patiently. "So, Schmid, you have found five more scientists well versed in your project, yet you say Himmler has once again stuck his nose where it doesn't belong?"

"That is correct, my Führer. My people are afraid of him."

Hitler laughed. "And well they should be. However, I've good news since the last time you mentioned that problem, I had my Waffen-SS find a place for you, a place the SS had looked at before. Come with me."

They went into an entrance tunnel carved into a mountain and took the winch elevator up to Das Kehlsteinhaus, which some believe Great War veterans renamed it 'The Eagle's Nest'. The SS had the house built in 1938 as a gift to Hitler for his fiftieth birthday. Situated on an outcropping, the panorama around the mountain range and into the valley was glorious.

At the Eagle's Nest, Hitler had Schmid face southwest. "You can't see it from here, Schmid, but over the former border with Austria…I mean *Ostmark*. Damn, even *I* forgot I renamed it. Anyway, there is a castle over there. It will be a perfect hideaway for your scientists. No one will bother you there. The SS liquidated some wealthy Austrian nobody for subversive activity and then decided they didn't need the place. It's called Stone Curtain Castle."

"A curious name, Sir."

"From what I've been told, you'll understand the name when you see it. Now then, list what else you need. Equipment you have in Himmler's Westphalia castle and your scientists will be moved in. What can't be moved, the SS will commandeer as needed. I suspect you will grow out of that place too and then I will put your group in with our rocket program at Kummersdorf or Mittelwerk because it goes hand in hand. At the beginning of September, I placed the total fusion project under the command of the Army Ordnance Office and they will supply anything more you require. So, now you'll have no excuses, will you?"

"No, my Führer, I will not, and I will succeed. May I ask one further thing? The Gestapo once supplied information to track the killer of my son, is there any news?"

"I've more to concern myself with than one son. He's dead, forget him. Concentrate on your Fatherland and your duty!"

* * *

David Royce had to be sure and appear depressed when he spoke to people about England and it's declaration of war on

Germany. Inside however, he was elated. It had all come together. Eventually and without question, his debts would be paid and he'd become wealthy, quite wealthy, with the power that his money would bring. He felt nothing about the extent of Germany's strength and worse, never gave a thought to the possibility that England could lose.

"Well, James, a long time ago I predicted this would happen and now, unfortunately, it's come to pass."

"Unfortunately? I can't believe you're upset about it, David."

Mary Royce had only now left the room with three Austrian children to join the other five they had taken in, but she overheard Royce's remark. "That's a terrible statement, James. Shame, don't say something like that."

She didn't wait for an answer.

David was amused, glib. "Yes, James, why would you say something like that and upset my poor wife?"

"I'd tell her why and other things, too. But if I did, it would break her heart."

"And we wouldn't want to tell her anything that would break her little heart, would we?"

"What did you want me for, David?"

"I heard you made a miscalculation yesterday on a gear ratio. Don't tell me I'll have to find someone to check your work."

"It might have been the eighty hours I put in last week."

"Or perhaps something else? She's left you, hasn't she?"

"Watch yourself, David. You might not like the answer."

"Oh, and what might that be?"

"I'd bet you're upset because she didn't run to you, right?"

David was cautious. "What do you mean? What did she say about me?"

"She didn't have to say anything. The look on your face says it all. I'll bet Mary sees it too. You want Daphne, but she knows you're an adulterous bore and wants nothing to do with you. And that just kills your ego, doesn't it? She's not like that tart you were with at the Dorchester."

David was angry, yet kept himself under control. He went and closed the study door, then came up to Royce. "Keep a civil tongue in your head or you'll wish you had."

"My word, a threat, David? I believe that's the first time

you've had the nerve to threaten me physically, Why? Is it because I've now a bad hand and you think you can take me on?"

David didn't flinch. "I always thought I could take you and with little trouble, James."

"But you never dared the gamble, did you? Even when we were younger and you treated me like dirt, you never had the courage."

Royce was sure his brother wouldn't come at him and David did debate that for a moment. "That would be too childish. Besides, I can't afford to have one of my employees do some other stupid thing and injure himself again."

"Oh, I'm just one of your employees, am I? You know, perhaps I should take General Arnold up on his offer for a position in America, wire my money over there and be gone."

David was apprehensive. If James learned his bank account was shy over one hundred thousand pounds there could be hell to pay. If Royce had a mind to, he could reveal David for the thief he was. David stared at his brother, then strode from the room.

Royce eyes followed him. It seemed he had stumbled onto something. It wasn't the potential of a fight, however unlikely. But something else stopped him. Was it the possibility he might leave for the States? David might not know it, but there was no chance of that.

His thoughts shifted to Daphne. God, how he missed her. He had made an elementary rectilinear miscalculation because she interrupted his thought process. Should he call her, ask her to come back? Not right now. There was too much work ahead of him. He'd wait. Yes, he'd get her back. When he had the time.

* * *

September, 1939

On the day England declared war on Germany, the Cunard liner *Athenia*, carrying evacuees from Liverpool to Canada, was sunk by a German U-Boat. There was a loss of 112 persons, 28 of those, Americans. On 17 September, the first Royal Navy loss in WWII, the old former battlecruiser, now RN aircraft carrier, *HMS Courageous*, returning from action in Norway, sank in the western approaches from two torpedoes. She took with her 576 sailors and her Captain.

And on that very same day, the 17th, Soviet forces, in accordance with the secret protocol pact with Germany, attacked Poland from the east. Poland was torn, beaten and dismembered. Around the same time, Elements of the British Expeditionary Force, the BEF landed in France and RAF Hurricanes flew onto French airfields. Both branches of the military were uncontested. Conscription and petrol rationing began in England. Thousands of children were evacuated from London. Once again, as in WWI, Winston S. Churchill was named First Lord of the Admiralty.

The United States proclaimed neutrality, it was considered a European war. With the exception of raging conflicts at sea, there was little fighting in Western Europe, other than minor aerial and land skirmishers. There were no land hostilities throughout the month in the no man's land between the French Maginot Line and the German Westwall Line. The bitter winter of 1939/1940 became known as the 'Phony War' or 'Sitzkreig', in England, and the 'Twilight War' by Churchill.

11 November, 1939

Lady Jane rose to greet her friend. "Welcome, Daphne, I'm so glad you're back."

"Don't get up, Jane, it's good to be back. It was wonderful of Chauncey Fellows to post me for ferry service for some of the aircraft manufacturers. I've been busy ferrying aircraft around to the different Groups over here, but darn it, nothing to France."

"I think that Chauncey chap has taken a shine to you."

"No question, and I'm going to do all I can—within reason mind you—to see that he continues that way."

"Does it bother you when you have to use your feminine wiles with these Chauvinistic men?"

"Good Lord, no. It's a man's world. But if all it takes is a little flirting to do all this flying, I've no trouble with it."

"I was that way a little, once in my life. I enjoyed it."

"No reason you shouldn't, Jane. Oh, one other thing of interest. I flew shuttle service for a General Miles Alcott. He remembered me from David Royce's New Year's party, although I didn't speak with him at that time."

"I knew Miles when he was a Colonel in the last war. He was a friend of my husband's. I spoke with him at David's New Year's affair. Where did you take him?"

"He was in charge of that Chain Home RF whatever, but now he's been transferred to MI6, or MI5, I forget which. All very hush, hush, you know. Anyway, I flew him from Dover over to London."

"Well, that's of interest. Did you know Sir Hugh Sinclair, head of MI6 died on the fourth? Perhaps Miles is going to head that up. But he told you that's where he's headed?"

"Feminine wiles at work, Jane. I'd make a wonderful spy. In fact, he asked if I would be interested in being his personal pilot. I told him no, said I want to fly Spitfires."

"Have you flown yet, Spitfires I mean?"

"Not since I qualified at Southampton, they're still ferried by male pilots."

"I was wondering one thing. How do you get back when you deliver your aircraft?"

"I take a train, bus or shanks mare. Sometimes I thumb, you know, hop a ride."

"Isn't that dangerous, Dear?"

"Not at all. I leave my flight suit on. People think I've just crashed or parachuted down. They're glad to stop. I give them a story to tell and they love it."

"How do they seem, what with another war and all?"

"Oh, you know. British stiff upper lip. But then again, there's a war and then again there isn't. Is there?"

"It's better this way, Daphne, believe me."

At that moment the telephone rang, both women jumped. Albert answered and pointed to them. "Kenneth wishes to speak with both of you. Although not at the same time he said."

Lady Jane spoke. "I'll take it first, Daphne. I'm the oldest and I'll be quicker than you."

She heard his voice. "Hello, Mother, how are you?"

"I'm fine, dear. But more importantly, how are you and where are you?"

"I feel good, and as far as where I am, I'm not in England. I'll speak to Daphne, she can work it out. How is she?"

"She looks wonderful to me and I think she'll sound

437

wonderful to you. Now, don't try to dupe me, I know you called to talk to her, so here she is."

Daphne eagerly took the phone. "Hi, Ken, tell me how things are, at least as much as you can."

"I'm good. I've longed to hear your voice. So please, don't make me wait, what's new with you and up in Coventry?"

"Well, I guess you could say it's all you wished."

"How about you, is it what you wanted?"

"I'll be honest. It's never pleasant to have something die, no matter which side one is on. I've never let things go this far. It hurt, although I suppose that's better than taking it out to a spiteful end. Anyway, I won't burden you with it. I look forward to seeing you. When do you think?"

"It's not a burden to me, Daph. It gives an insight into you. I look forward to seeing you, too. Don't know when. When you ferry aircraft, you must have heard where the RAF Advanced Strike Force is at present. Don't say it, but that's where I am. So, until this boiling kettle goes back to simmer, we're up in the air, if you'll excuse the pun."

"Can't you use your contacts to have me ferry something to your Wing?"

"Doubtful. Female pilots aren't allowed in combat zones."

"God, doesn't the RAF understand we're not helpless, sweet little things anymore?"

"I'm laughing, Daphne. I should have you speak to them. That would surely start a row. But I really want to tell you how much I...blast it, hang on a minute, Wing's on another line."

Minutes passed before he came back on the line. "Damn sorry, Daph, got to run. I'll call back in an hour or two."

"Okay, Ken, I'll..." The contact was gone.

"What happened, Daphne?"

"He got a call from his Wing Commander, he had to run. Said he'd call back later."

"Too bad, dear, I knew you looked forward to a pleasant chat together."

They went back to planning the entertainment when the phone rang again, the women hoping it was Ken, calling back.

Albert looked in to Daphne. "It's a Mrs. Mary Royce, do you wish to speak with her."

Surprised, Daphne nodded yes. She had given few people The Mount's number, Mary being one. "Hello, Mary, what is it, are you all right?"

"Daphne, it's James, he collapsed. He's a bit better, but in the Warwickshire Hospital."

With few words, Mary gave a quick report and Daphne said she'd be up early the next day and for Mary to call her.

As best she could, worried over Royce and embarrassed, Daphne explained the situation to Lady Jane.

"Daphne, I'm a trifle more worldly than you give me credit for, so dispense with your discomfit, there's no need. I've a, um, story in my own life, which could perhaps exceed your circumstances. So now, with that never to be mentioned again, I'm sure you realize you have no choice. You must go. If you feel otherwise, you would not be the woman I thought you were."

"I must and want to go, Jane, he meant so much to me at one time. It's just...I don't know what to say. And Ken said he'd call back, what will he think?"

"Kenneth will understand. He won't like it, but he wouldn't want it any other way either. He would never try to stop you. Now it's almost eleven, if you feel all right to drive and want to leave now I understand. I'll explain to Kenneth when he calls."

"That would be so good of you, Jane. I'll head out now. That would get me to Jim's cottage by two AM. I'll try to nap. Mary Royce will pick me up and I'll go with her to the hospital."

"Fine, Daphne. And don't doubt that Ken and I wish this Royce chap the best."

Before she left, Daphne called Mary back and they planned to meet at Blackbird Cottage early the next morning.

Daphne worried her way along the lengthy drive north to the cottage. There she slept fitfully until six.

Awaiting Mary's call the following morning, the doorbell rang. Daphne simply thought Mary forgot to phone and opened the door.

"Hi, Mary, how..."

David Royce pushed the door open the rest of the way. "Hello, Daphne, I hope you're pleasantly surprised to see me."

She was stunned, although not speechless. "What the devil

are you doing here?"

He walked in, pushing the door behind him. "Now Daphne, stop playing coy with me, I know you've only made believe you didn't want to see me."

"Made believe! You are a true idiot! I can't stand the sight of you, you God damn cheat!"

David's ego wouldn't believe that and he grabbed her by the shoulders, pressing her against the wall. She'd been taught how to react in this situation and didn't hesitate. She cupped her hand, moved it inside his arms and drove it up into his chin. David's head snapped back. Momentarily confused, he lost control. His hand came back to hit her, but he was too slow. Daphne's other lesson came without thought. She moved into him and rammed her knee into his groin. Crippling pain burst through his head. His face contorted, he dropped to his knees, gasping, close to vomiting. She had no pity for him and grabbed a poker from the fireplace.

"Get out! Get out you pig! You ever try this again and I'll tell Mary about your London bitch. Now get out!"

Only then did she see a devastated and shamed Mary standing in the doorway.

Chapter 28

"GOD, MARY, I'M SORRY you saw this."

Mary glared after her husband as he painfully struggled to his feet. Pain continued to sear through his groin as he hobbled past her toward his car, sit agonizingly at the wheel and drive off.

"Don't apologize, Daphne. I more or less knew. When David started to drive himself down to London and stay overnight more and more often, and have less and less to do with me it was becoming clear. But this morning, I wasn't quite dressed when I saw him leave. It was hard to believe he might be up to something with you, yet I had to be sure. So I didn't call and came directly here. I apologize for that and for him, Daphne, I'm sorry."

Daphne had managed to calm down. "Apologize for him? Don't bother, he's not worth it. After this, what will you do now?"

"Do? Nothing. I've thought about it, yes. Yet although I have nothing but distain for him, I won't divorce him. It would disgrace my family's name and my children. And David won't divorce me. It would mean the end of his dream to become Prime Minister someday. So you see, we'll have a mutual arrangement."

"That seems so callous to me."

"I know, it is. Yet I've been schooled in this. My mother and father lived this way, and if I accept it, I'll be able to take care of my children, and the others that come in. Now I won't belabor this or I'll break down. Let's put it aside and go see James."

At the hospital lobby, Clive Henderson was about to leave.

"Daphne, how are you? Thank goodness you've come."

"I'm all right, Clive, how's Jim?"

"Better than he was. I should have expected what occurred. Still, it came as a shock."

"So tell us what happened, we don't know the whole story."

"We'd gone down to Hertfordshire, at Salisbury Hall. De Havilland has a design group there for a new twin engine aircraft."

Daphne knew about the plane under development. "Isn't that the prototype 4050 Jim worked on the Merlin engines and motor mounts?"

"My word, Daphne, he told you about the DH Mosquito?"

"If that's what they call her. I just knew the code name. And that's all he told me."

Henderson appeared bothered she knew, then saw there was no need to keep it secret, so he continued. "As you said, James designed the welded steel tube frame for the engine mounts and the DH engineers fabricated and mounted two of them onto the wings of a prototype fuselage then fitted the engines. Over in Hatfield, we stabilized the fuselage and the run ups went well."

Mary couldn't wait. "Then what went wrong?"

Clive was startled at her intensity. "Not a thing went wrong, Mary. She's a wooden aircraft, completely against the best minds for a fighter bomber, and I felt that was why James wouldn't stop his vibration tests. One engine held on high RPMs, then alternate, then both at peak. He went on for hours in the sun with no hat.

"Why didn't you say something, or at least get him a hat?"

"A hat would have blown off, but he should have at least used a helmet. Still, you know him, when he gets this way. No one does anything to break his concentration. But let me finish. After he had the engines shut down, he used a magnifier on the frame right next to hot engines. For some reason he seemed possessed. If it was one of the final stress tests, I might have understood, but not a basic visual inspection. Anyway, the engineers were quite relieved when he seemed satisfied and we walked off. James lagged behind, still looking at the engines. When I paused for him to catch up, he was on the ground. His eyes were glazed, and when we sat him up, he was incoherent and couldn't say a word."

Clive stopped, his mind on the incident., Daphne interposed. "So you got him to a hospital?"

"No, there was a clinic nearby and we took him there. After we explained what transpired, they said it was heat prostration and he should be hospitalized for observation. I ordered an ambulance and brought him back here. Right now, he seems sound. Just remember when you see him he's under moderate sedation."

When they entered the room, he was listless, although Mary told him he looked chipper as she fluffed his pillow. "Jimmy, Daphne's come to see you."

Daphne could see he was on drugs as his eyes barely came to focus on her. "Hello, Jim, How do you feel? Push the old body too far again?"

"I suppose…Like you said, should…pace myself."

"Oh, I'm sure you'll do that. Think you might turn over a new leaf this time?"

Mary broke in. "I'll see that he does, that is if you're not going to be here, Daphne."

Royce appeared unresponsive. Perhaps it was the drugs, Daphne thought. Yet she was uneasy with Mary's comment, felt out of place with the two of them.

They chatted a while longer, until Royce fell asleep. Mary held his crippled hand and kissed his forehead as his eyes closed. "Sleep tight, Jimmy."

The women sat on the couch in his room. "I was a bit taken aback when I saw the scar has showed up again, Mary."

"Sorry, Daphne, I should have mentioned it. Clive thinks it's because James was in the sun so long the color blanched."

"Makes sense. That woman in Canada gave him some vials to re-stain it. Maybe we can find them. But I'd like to move on to something else."

"Oh? There's something more important than this?"

"Yes. How long have you loved him, Mary?"

Startled, she didn't deny the truth. Tears formed. "It's that obvious to you?"

"I've wondered a couple of times in the past, but didn't think it further. It was just now, when you called him Jimmy and kissed his forehead that it became quite apparent."

"That was a slip. But to answer your question, I don't know how long I've loved him. When I met David, and he took me home to meet his father and James, he told me that James was ugly. I admit I was shaken, and he was very withdrawn. When we married and lived here, you wouldn't know he was in the house.

Then, one day when no one was about, I decided to go and talk to him. I found him on the third floor, drawing. He tried to avoid me, wouldn't let me see his artwork. It was so strange. I think that no one had ever tried to hold a simple tête-à-tête with him. He simply had no conversational skills. I remember it was only when I asked him what he did when he went off to Cumbria that suddenly he glowed. He came out of a shell. He told me about his climbing, the Scot's heather, how the purple tips waved to him in the breeze. And the shadows, how they turned the mountains darker, brooding, from storm clouds. He made a dream of it, said the heather bowed down and then the sky would blaze as the clouds passed and the heather would wave to him again. It wasn't only the climbing. You see, Jimmy had freedom there. No one was there to wince or bother him. That meant a lot to him. I wished I had been there. I wish he were there now, with me."

Daphne said nothing until Mary came out of her dream.

"Anyway, Daphne, I missed him terribly when his father died and he left to live in Austria. I put him in a special place of my memories as best I could, even when he returned. But when he was injured, it just flowed out again. I accepted I loved him."

"What do you intend to do about it?"

"What can I do about it? There are times I don't care who learns of it. Other times I'm afraid what David might do if he found out. He's vindictive. He knows how to hurt Jimmy."

"Just do what I did to him."

"I wish it was that easy. You have nerve, I don't. And, you haven't said what you mean to do. If you come back to him, I would accept that."

Daphne closed her eyes and put her hands over her mouth. Mary strained to hear her next words. "I can't come back to the way things were, and I don't think Jim will change. Worse, when I see him now, I'm ashamed to say all I feel is sadness and pity. That's all I have left. There's no future if that's all to hold us. And I have to be honest, Mary, there's someone else."

They promised to stay in touch. Daphne went back to Royce's cottage and this time knew it would be for good. There was little there of him, half empty bottle of scotch, plates in the sink, rumpled bed sheets. She smiled. He never did like to make the bed. She made it, hung up his clothes and cleared the sink.

She wanted a clean break from the memories and drove her

Christmas present from Royce, the Riley Sport Saloon, to Jaguar of Coventry. She bought a 1938 Jaguar Super Swallow 100 Coupe and told the salesman to have the Riley delivered to Blackbird Cottage. She knew that would say it all.

She felt ashamed and saw how, with their first difficulty, she couldn't work through it. Yet she couldn't help recall something she had once read. Hate wasn't the opposite of love, indifference was. And that killed her love, his indifference.

Chapter 29

IT WAS A STRANGE BEGINNING to a conflict that would become the most devastating known to humankind. On the ground in Western Europe, there were few contacts between the combatants. In the air, British Lancaster bombers dropped leaflets with anti-Nazi catchphrases on German territories. Churchill said all the leaflets were good for was toilet paper.

At sea, German U-boats crept through the deep, then surfaced, told the crews of merchant vessels to abandon, then destroyed the vessels. The German pocket battleship Graf Spee prowled the South Atlantic, sank ships and, if they could, saved and interned their crews.

It started, after all, as a very gentlemanly war. In the west that is. In the east, the unbounded slaughter went on unabated.

14 December, 1939
RAF Advanced Air Strike Force airbase south of Rheims, France.
Wing Commander Keith Park finished his overview to five Squadron Leaders. "To summarize all this gentlemen, the circumstances here in Europe are in flux. You see Messerschmitt 109s, the enemy sees Spitfires and Hurricanes. Little contact. Same on the ground, Troops of both sides huddle in their fortified bunkers and everyone waits. The politicians fiddle with peace while Europe smolders. England's position is the Germans must leave Poland and pay reparations to the Poles. Of course, it's an absurdity to think that will happen. The military's belief is the Germans don't want to start a war in this damnable cold, but we must stay alert. We have four hundred plus fighters here and more bombers fly in every day while we wait for the powers that be to decide. So, questions?"

"Sir, it's different at sea. From what we hear from Coastal Command, quite a number of merchant ships are being sunk by U- boats and the battleship Graf Spee."

"That's true about the U-boats, no longer true about the Graf Spee. After quite a mauling, the Royal Navy brought her to bay in Uruguay's Platte River and the Admiral scuttled her."

There were cheers all around, yet confusion.

"But Wing Commander, Sir, I'm still baffled. At sea, we're killing each other. Here and in the air, we don't. Why doesn't the Government see there actually is a war going on?"

"My personal thought is, it's because our leaders choose to ignore the deaths at sea while trying to find if there's a chance of peace. That's the difference. Let me give you an example. It was suggested to Sir Kingsley Wood, our Secretary for Air, that we should bomb a munitions dump in the Black Forrest. Do you know his response? 'Are you aware that is private property?'"

He looked at each bewildered aviator. "I'll leave you with that thought, gentlemen. Squadron Leader Sommers, a private word with you."

As the pilots left, Wing Commander Park glanced to Sommers. "Get me a whiskey, will you, Ken? And make yourself one as well—a stiff one."

They sat by the Squadron's pot-belly stove and touched glasses. Kenneth respectfully silent.

"Ken, I know all this waiting is tough on the pilots and Squadron Leaders, but they look to you as their point man with Wing. I've done the best possible to explain the state of affairs in England, and I thank you for helping maintain morale here."

"Sir, it's the apprehension. The German's aren't about to tell us when they're going to strike and here we are, all these aircraft assembled in the open with no camouflage or RDF. We should be dispersed into smaller fields as we did in England. Then again, I'm not telling you anything you don't know, Sir."

"Yes, I do know. Yet until there's confirmation from the French on our position, we stay put. I know you have flights in the air for an early warning…"

"Excuse me, Sir, that's only in daylight. A night attack and…."

Kenneth didn't have to finish. The Wing Commander knew it all. Even British General Gort, leader of the BEF was angry with the difficulties he kept finding when he attempted to make the French comprehend his army was not under their command.

"Ken, that's the way it is. Although I have an additional assignment for you."

"Sir?"

"I've decided to split your command duties."

Kenneth was leery. "Exactly what does that entail, Sir?"

"Hear me out, Ken. This is for your ears only. We're certain the German's won't start a war until spring from a number of factors. One is the weather. This is quickly becoming a tough winter. Tough on tanks and tough on troops. The other, more important factor is their front line, battle experienced troops are only now being withdrawn from Poland, and they're being given leave. To top it off, our agents inform us there's disagreement on their Yellow Plan. That's their attack on France."

"We know all this? Sounds like a long cold winter here for the Squadrons then."

"Fighter Command will soon begin rotating Squadrons in and out until early spring, a little before the weather breaks."

"The men will be happy to hear that, Sir."

"Yes, the men will be, but not you, I've a special job for you, so you may not feel the same."

"Anything within reason to relieve the boredom, Sir."

"I thought that would be your attitude. So, firstly, when we're alone call me Keith. Understand?"

"Yes, Sir…Keith."

"Good. Now the good news is you're to have two weeks leave, and no argument. That's an order. Lieutenant MacHalpen will act as Squadron Leader until you return. At that time, he will get his own Squadron. Is that acceptable to you?"

"Yes, Sir…Keith. As long as I get my Squadron back."

"Good. Now, we're still in the plan stage for the program, this is why you have two weeks leave. We'll want your input on the program of course, but this is what it's about. Escaped pilots from Poland and Czechoslovakia are filtering into France and England. The French don't see the need for them, so most continue to England. We've sorted them. You know Jesus Peron?"

"Yes, quite well…Keith."

"All right. Peron has reported a number of them are good pilots, quite aggressive and sure of themselves, which is good, up to a point. He warns us they are individuals, like the French. They're not given to teamwork, which leads us to this discussion. I want you to train them to fly Spitfires and Hurricanes, but mainly to teach them as you've done your Squadron. Teamwork."

"Thank you for the compliment, Sir, and as much as I wish to stay with my Squadron, there will definitely be a need to add more pilots. I'll be pleased to assume the assignment."

"Kenneth, this is a request, although tempered by the thought you would say yes."

"Then I will accept your request, Keith."

"Excellent. I'll detail MacHalpen for Acting SQL and you for responsibilities at Wing. Your leave starts now. Talk over duties with Mackie, then look up Peron at the training school to get his input. So unless you hear otherwise, enjoy yourself for two weeks. You'll be damn busy after that."

"Two items, Keith, do these pilots speak English?"

"I'll be damned—don't believe so. That's another thing you can look into while you're resting. Find interpreters who understand Polish, Czech and airplane technology. See, that's solved. What's your other query?"

"If an air war breaks out, I get my Squadron back. Correct, Keith?"

"You've my promise on that. And Mackie will get his own."

* * *

"For God's sake, Ken, why do you want to know if I speak Polish or Czech? You plan on my being a spy over there?"

"No, nothing like that. Just tell me, Daphne."

If he wants to play games, she thought, two could play.

"Well, my Major in college was Languages and patois. I learned Polski was quite a complex West Slavic Indo-European language with a number of dialects. However, it's mainly standard Polish taken from the Latin with umpteen variations.

Now, Czech, is another combination of Czech and Slovak and forms a language continuum, but that too has variations as well as added diphthongs and consonants. The dialects can be confusing and there are definite grammatical differences, but there is an *intermediate* or transitional dialect between Polish and Czech. So, in other words, the languages are close…and not…to a degree."

"Good, Lord, Daphne, all I asked was do you speak those languages."

She couldn't help laugh. "Didn't I just answer that?"

"God, do I feel foolish."

"Well, you deserve it for all those language classes you skipped. Now, why do you want to know?"

"How would you like to work with me?"

"Excuse my silence. What on earth are you talking about?"

"Wing wants me to instruct Polish and Czech pilots after Jesus Peron clears them for RAF training. So I've been told to get an interpreter to translate and a flyer. That simple. What do you say, interested?"

"Will I be able to fly Spitfires?"

"Spitfires and Hurricanes. I'll teach you."

"I already know how to fly Spitfires."

"Daphne, excuse me, but now you're being foolish. You know how to take one off, turn her around, and land her. I'll show you how to *fly* her. You've got the talent. If you can survive my training, there won't be a pilot who will question your ability, or what you teach them in Pole-Czech, Indo-European diphthongs or whatever the devil it's called."

"I'm excited! This sounds fantastic. And you actually have approval for this?"

"More or less, although you'll have to help."

"What does that mean?"

"Daph, you'll have to look beautiful."

"To get the job, no problem."

* * *

RAF Station, Biggin Hill. Air Chief Marshal, Hugh Dowding and now Air Vice Marshal, Keith Park, commanding 11 Group, looked across the table to Squadron Leader Kenneth Sommers and Daphne Elliot. Kenneth had laid out Daphne's qualifications point by point regarding her ability to act as his interpreter.

450

Dowding and Park's moods cycled through rejection, to doubt, on to maybe, and then admiration.

On the table in front of them were Daphne's flight log, certifications for single, twin engine, night and instrument licenses. Added to these were written firm recommendations from Jesus Peron and Chauncey Fellows. Included was Fellows' flight and written test score of 96 out of 100 for Daphne in Spitfires. Dowding and Park shook their heads as they also noted she qualified as copilot for Lancaster four engine bombers and, the capper, she had logged more flight hours than most of the Advanced Air Strike Force RAF pilots. A final decision was made when a Polish pilot was brought in and Daphne, though a little rusty, quickly began to speak fluently to the pilot in his language.

"Dzien Dobry." Good day to you, she started, and the pilot's eyes lit up. He was the only one there who knew what else she said. Which really was just as well—the pilot said the Poles weren't too keen on what they thought to be British dithering.

After the pilot left, the Air Chief Marshal asked her to wait in the outer office, and then gravely contemplated Kenneth. "First of all, Kenneth, she is a striking woman. She has looks, talent and obviously brains. Which begs the question—why on earth is she entangled with you?"

Daphne heard the laughter in the next office and wondered why the hilarity. If it was over her, she'd give them a dressing down they warranted.

"Now, Kenneth," Dowding continued, "I guess we would be terribly Chauvinistic if we turned her down. Yes, she could become a distraction, yet perhaps that might be a good thing. So, we're agreed, she's a go. That brings us to her classification. She's an alien. We'll have to find a way to get her Top Secret clearance. I don't think that will be difficult. As far as a pay grade…"

"Excuse me, Sir. She's already said she would donate any income to the military fund. She's quite wealthy in her own right."

"Good Lord, wealthy along with everything else? You should stop your wandering , Sommers, and marry that girl."

"I'd like to, Sir, but she's a long way from that."

"Resisting all your charms? Even more brains than I gave her credit for."

They still joshed him as they opened the door and went out to

451

her. "Miss Elliot, you are now the official interpreter between 11 Group, RAF and the Polish and Czech pilots."

Her mood turn around. "Thank you, Air Marshal. I'm most pleased," She was lighthearted, "and if you need any help with Russian, German, or even American English, I hope you'll call."

"We may find we need a lot of that help, Daphne, especially with the Americans and the way they're mucking up the King's English."

They shook hands. Impulsively, Daphne kissed the cheeks of the Air Chief Marshal and the Vice-Air Marshal.

Dowding pulled back, appearing embarrassed. "Here, here. From this point forth, there will be no further fraternization with the RAF. One Squadron Leader exempt."

Surprising herself, Daphne blushed as Dowding continued. "Kenneth, you take care of this young woman. She has all the credentials and at some time I feel we're going to need every pilot we can get, whatever language they speak."

Chapter 30

JAMES ROYCE SLUMPED in his chair in front of the fireplace. He had worked until late that evening and on his way home stopped in to see Mary and the children at Ravensmoor. David was away once more, and Royce, after a short visit, drove on to Blackbird Cottage and started a fire.

Work was a struggle. He mentioned to the doctor that when he collapsed on the runway, he had struck the back of his head and was having sporadic headaches and at times a visual aberration of color that fluttered in a band across his right eye. Although not painful, the color distortion was annoying and made it difficult to concentrate on his work.

After examinations, the doctors believed the aberration to be visual migraines, and wanted to do more research. Royce declined, and was given a small quantity of Diluadid, a drug similar to Morphine, and cautioned to restrict its use because of the possibility of addiction. This night, he split a pill and used half to ease the headaches and for sedation, along of course, with his scotch.

He had started his second drink when he saw headlights turn into the drive. Mary came to the door. He helped her in out of the cold as she handed over Scotty in his woolen coat.

"You look concerned, Mary. Why? You just saw me, I'm all right, don't worry over me."

"I know I do so worry, but David's away and nanny was putting the children to bed. So I thought it would be nice to stop by for a drink and simply to talk, if you didn't mind."

"Of course not. Sit beside the fire while I get you a drink. Put Scotty in my chair, he can sit on my lap."

They settled into their chairs, touched glasses, quiet, mesmerized by the fire, while Scotty settled in.

"This is like old times, remember, Mary? No one around, we'd get together and talk."

"Of course I remember. They were good times. Except we're together now, and not talking."

"What is it, Mary? You've something on your mind."

"I'm concerned about you. You aren't yourself. I can see it in your actions. Clive said you're having trouble with concentration at work. You don't work to flex your fingers. And I might as well sound like Daphne I guess, and add you've let your scar blanch."

"Mary, please let it go. The doctor gave me some pills. I'll get by."

"Jimmy, there's more to life than just getting by. My, listen to me, of all people to say that."

Royce nodded, not really picking up on her meaning.

Mary resumed. "There's something else, Jimmy, isn't there?"

He took a sip of his drink, absentmindedly scratching the dog's ears. "If you mean her, yes. I think of her quite often."

"You know you treated her shabbily, don't you?"

"I'm afraid you're right. Work consumed me, probably still does. I often think to call her, get back together for a drink."

Mary hesitated, at a loss what to say. She could tell Royce was, in an offhanded way, asking her advice. Did he think that was all he had to do? Ring her up and she'd come back? How could he?

"Jimmy, I hate to say this, but I think there may be someone else in her life now."

"That RAF chap?"

"RAF chap? She hadn't mentioned an RAF chap to me. You seem to know more than I."

"Yes, perhaps. He took her for a flight, helped her get an instructor to become a pilot. She's probably grateful to him for helping. That's all. Grateful...grateful, nothing more."

"I simply don't know anything about him. But, there is something else I want to speak to you about. I know you're aware that David has...how does one say it nicely? Been unfaithful to me in no uncertain terms."

"Daphne told you?"

Mary had to be careful. She knew if Royce ever learned of David's attempt to force himself on Daphne, there would be a terrible row between the brothers.

"No, I learned from another source. Daphne only accidently confirmed it one time."

"What are you going to do?"

"Nothing, Jimmy. It doesn't matter any longer, I'm reconciled to that. However, I would like to ask you one thing. David's away quite often and I don't wish to converse with him even when he's here. Do you, when you have time, think we could get together now and then, you know, simply to talk? I would like that, especially now that I'm at odds with David, and you're without Daphne."

"Of course, Mary, whenever I have time around work. Still, I intend to get back together with Daphne, when I eventually get the time."

"I understand, so let's change the subject. Did you know Daphne's brother Robert is coming over here? At least to London, I mean."

"No, I didn't. When? I would think he'd never return here."

"Why would you say that?"

"Please, forget it. My mind wandered."

"If you say so. I really don't know when he's coming. David mentioned her brother would be over with a group of US senators, military officers and industrialists. I'm surprised Robert hasn't mentioned it to you. I assume you'll see him when he's over here. And you know, it's odd, I don't even think Daphne knew about him coming over."

"I don't know whether Daphne knows or not, but I won't be seeing him. We had a disagreement, actually quite a falling out, in the States."

* * *

Hitler was impatient; that was his posture when he didn't comprehend a problem.

"So, Schmid, you're telling me that Paul Harteck, the Army Ordnance advisor went to you after he alerted the Reich Ministry about the possible military application of a nuclear reaction."

"A nuclear chain reaction, my Führer."

"Don't correct me! Don't *ever* correct me!"

"I apologize, my Führer. There are just so many groups

involved, The REM, RKM , HWA and now Army Ordnance and the Reich Research Council. All of them constantly interfere with our research at the Castle. We cannot turn around without another big Mercedes or Horsch pulling into our castle and..."

"Stop! I've enough of this! I will issue a Führerprotokoll. No one is to enter your jurisdiction without my specific permission, and anything you require is to be supplied immediately. I assure you, Schmid, there will be hell to pay for anyone who disobeys."

Hitler calmed. His enemies, England and the US, were interested in an indistinct, perhaps unattainable goal, so he had to do the same, whether necessary or not. It was time consuming and costly. Every damn thing, he thought, was costly.

"As I told you, Schmid, an Uranmaschine, a nuclear reactor, is under construction at Haigerloch. And once again I'm told it will take time. Every damn thing is costly and takes time! But be sure your physicists oversee the work. As far as the heavy water needed, we will have all you require by the time you need it."

"You mean the Norsk Hydro plant in Norway?"

"Do not ask questions. I will get what you need. Now, how are all your little brains up at the castle? Acting properly?"

"Yes, my Führer. I did as you said. Any complaints and we will send them to a camp in Poland. That quieted them, although I do allow their wives and children a Sunday visit every week. They sit outside in the warm weather to have a midmorning meal and music. That helps keep them in line."

"Is that wise? Do you fully inspect the wives, and have a background check?"

"Yes, Sir. I have Wehrmacht women check them each time."

"Very well, it is your responsibility. But no one goes anywhere inside the castle without a Waffen SS guard, remember that. How many people do you have there now?

"Twelve physicists and twenty researchers, and, of course, my liaison officers with Peenemunde, Haigerloch and the Army Ordnance Office scientists. I don't know how many Wehrmacht guards are around the grounds and we have about twenty town folk serving us."

"Be sure to concern yourself only with those involved with the weapon. The Wehrmacht or SS take care of everyone else."

Chapter 31

ROBERT ELLIOT WAS IMPRESSED with himself. Yet concerned as well. He was headed back to England, handpicked by President Roosevelt's staff, to represent the industrialist factor of a fact-finding commission to evaluate the strength and resolve of the British Government in their state of war with Germany. The group consisted of three senators, Clapper of Kansas, Barkley of Kentucky, and McNary of Oregon. Added to the senators were three Military officers, Bradley for the Army, Stark for the Navy, and Vandenberg for the Army Air Corp. Their main goals were to find if England, and her Commonwealth Nations, could withstand a war with the Axis powers or, would she seek a peaceful solution. Their other goal was to privately delve into the American Ambassador to England, Joseph Kennedy's damaging assessment of England's inability to withstand Germany's onslaught. Was his report based on fact, or resultant from his Irish ancestry and unusual friendship with Nazi Germany's Foreign Minister, von Ribbentrop?

Robert looked forward to surprising Daphne once he was settled. Nonetheless, his primary disquiet in returning to England was apparent. He had knowingly given secret information to a German spy. This was a traitorous act, certainly not to be forgiven if discovered. Conjoined with that, he had murdered two people. Robert, however, felt he was safe. Yes, he had stupidly told Jim Royce of his transgressions, yet luckily, Jim's love for Daphne precluded any chance he would ever bring those facts to light.

The conference with the US Commission's English counterparts proceeded as planned until General, Sir Miles Alcott, now with MI6, made the request to have Robert Elliot attend a private luncheon. Robert readily agreed. He knew the General wanted to get together as old friends and present the British views and requirements for war material. As the two men sat, Robert thought it strange there were no place settings. Shortly after his arrival, four other men appeared, stared openly at his mask, and took assigned places around the table.

General Alcott was formal, as he made the introductions.

"Robert Elliot, the gentlemen here are, Mr. Maxwell Knight from MI5, Counter-Subversive, Trevor Crow, from His Majesty's Diplomatic Service and the American attaché, whom I believe you know. I will introduce the gentleman on my right in a moment. This meeting is being held in camera."

Robert's mind raced. He was in trouble. These people knew more of this encounter than he. What…Counter-subversive? Moreover, who was that young, Spanish looking man who Alcott didn't name to his right?

General Alcott glared hard at Robert. "Mr. Elliot, herewith, you are charged with the crimes of treason and murder."

Robert was staggered into silence. His mouth gaped, no sound escaped. They knew, but how? No one alive but he and Jim Royce knew. The only word he could utter was, "Who…?"

General Alcott tried to control his anger. "Who? I'll introduce you to who."

With that, he asked the man on his right to speak.

"You don't know me, Elliot, and I don't know you. I do however, know *of* you. I was informed of your treasonous acts by Donnatta Maria Aenar y Mira."

"Donnatta…?" Robert struggled for breath.

"You probably know her better as Madame Tosca, a Spanish spy for Germany. She worked for the Nazis, and don't say you didn't know that."

"Who are you? Who are you to accuse me of any…"

"Shut up! I shall accuse you of any blasted thing I want. I was Donnatta's lover. My name is Jesus Peron."

General Alcott could see Peron grow angrier by the second and, whereas the General wanted the mood tense, he didn't want Peron to explode.

"Stand down a minute, Jesus. Mr. Elliot, Jesus Peron is a counteragent for British MI5, home security. He was ordered to become friends with Madame Tosca and unfortunately, he became too good a friend. To his credit, he continued to report her activities."

The General hesitated, peering over his glasses at Peron.

"Although I believe he would have found some way to spirit her away if a war started. You, Elliot, saved that from happening, and, I might add, undoubtedly protected Jesus's reputation. Nevertheless, for some reason, you decided to kill her and her lackey. Why, because you didn't want witnesses?"

Robert was stunned by it all, knew all was lost. "No, it…it wasn't that. She tried to have that Irish bastard, Sean, kill Jim Royce, and I knew she would try again…so I killed them."

"We had begun to think that from the clues. Thanks to Peron, we intercepted some—actually most—of Tosca's missives. Most were harmless, even the information that concerned the Chain Home system and the info you supplied her on the Merlin's petrol starvation shortcoming in a dive were already known by the Germans. However, our interceptions were intermittent at best due to weather and we weren't able to catch and decipher the information the Germans wanted about Royce until after she tried to kill him. The other problem was Jesus didn't know of Tosca's other hideaway. You obviously did, our reason unknown. We weren't informed of her death until after she and the IRA blighter were dead a month. You were very accurate, shooting her in the back of the neck when she tried to escape."

Peron finished up for the General. "It took next to no sleuthing to track you down. Donnatta told me about a 'Robert' who was hopelessly in love with her and fed her information. He had half a face, and had Top Secret clearance at Royce…"

General Alcott stopped Peron. "As I was, at that time, in charge of Chain Home and when we received this information, I was thunderstruck. You, Robert, whom I knew as a friend, an angel helping the wounded at Lancaster, you were a traitor to your adopted country. I was shamefaced and admitted I gave you Secret clearance. Yet, it was done, and you were gone, so how were we to get you to return, to get you back on English soil? I know you'd like to continue, Jesus."

"Very much so, General, thank you. You were easily fooled, Elliot. When we learned of a fact-finding commission forming in the States, we spoke with our contacts at the FBI and Edgar Hoover had a word with your Secretary of State, Cordell Hull. He had you attached to the Commission and so here you are, trapped like the rat you are. You thought you were an important person, but in our midst you're nothing but a traitor and I espero que se qumarà en el infierno!"

"That's enough, Peron. Most of us wish he would burn in hell. Elliot, do you have anything to say in your defense?"
Robert shook, buried his head in his hands. "No."

"Very well. In a time of war, the penalty for treason is death. That is what you should pay for your manipulation of our trust and jeopardizing the security of our country. However, we have a unique state of affairs here and you can be more valuable to us alive."

General Alcott looked questioningly at the other men present. Each nodded yes—with the exception of Jesus Peron.

"Mr. Elliot, we offer you a chance to redeem yourself in some small way. The American ambassador to our country, Joseph Kennedy, recommends the United States remain neutral in this war. It has reached a point where he is so obsessed, so anti-English, he avowed to your president that we do not stand a chance. Why on earth the Americans named an Irishman, Ambassador to the Court of Saint James, is beyond me other than some political payoff. Of course, his being a lovely chum of Ribbentrop, the Nazi Ambassador, doesn't bode well for us either. However, he's here and we're stuck with him. What we need is a counter-voice in your country. A person who will speak out firmly against Kennedy on your side of the pond. From the moment you meet him, you're to state you'd been sworn to secrecy at a crucial conference with key players in the British Government and military, and what you've been shown makes you believe we can beat the Germans. This will irritate the ambassador to no end. If people think you know more than he does, he'll lose credibility. Another thing we propose you do for us is war material. War supplies at a reasonable fee. You get us the armaments, Elliot, we'll carry the fight. Do you understand?"

Robert would grasp at the barest straw. This allowed him a road out. He understood. "I will do as you say."

"*And*, it would be best if they were sent at your true cost."

Robert nodded, beaten.

"We will see you keep your word. It will be a simple matter to issue an extradition request for murder. The US may, or may not honor it, but doubtless your reputation in America will be ruined."

When the General asked if Jesus Peron had anything further to say, Jesus was brief. "You know what I think of this murderer and this whole damn blackmail thing, General."

"Yes, I do and I agree wholeheartedly. However, expediency wins out once again. Elliot, the rest of your committee is at Hampton Court. You will be driven there. One more thing, don't ever return to England."

"May I ask that my sister, Daphne, not find out about this?"

"Everyone here is sworn to secrecy and that includes Mr. Peron who, bizarrely enough, at one time was your sister's flying instructor. Now leave, not another word. We may supply more requests later."

Robert left, crushed. The General mumbled out loud for everyone to hear. "This thing we do for expediency is distasteful, although I believe it will work to our advantage. There are two less spies, and now a very successful industrialist works for us. Sorry, Peron, but that's how it is. Thank you for all you've done on this, you're dismissed. On your way out, send in the two chaps waiting in the foyer."

As left. The General spoke to the others around the table. "I liked that Elliot, a good chap once. Yet I was at fault mentioning Chain Home to him at Ravensmoor. He did such wonderful things for the old wounded up in Lancaster that it's difficult to believe he became such a traitorous bastard."

A Royal Marine Colonel entered along with another man not in uniform. Both, nevertheless, saluted General Alcott.

"Have a seat. Gentlemen, this is Colonel Charles Wentworth the third. CW to those who know him. Now, to the subject. CW runs a series of agents throughout Germany, Switzerland and Austria and has only now returned from Germany via the Baltic and Finland despite their continuing war with Soviet Russia."

The men turned and nodded in admiration. They knew the person was gambling with his life.

The General continued. "With him is an American from the

US Military Intelligence, whom I shall not name. He is here as an observer and will report to the office of the US President.

"Now, with that said, CW came out because of a potentially serious situation arising in Germany. As we've discussed in the recent past, there is a significant possibility of a dangerous expansion of German interest in developing an atomic device of some sort. That increased interest is why CW took the chance of coming out. CW, the floor is yours."

"Gentlemen, what I have to report is fact, conjecture, and lastly, instinct. What I know as *fact* is the Germans have fusion and physics experts Strassmann and Hahn under surveillance by the Gestapo. They've been demoted, and all their papers and assistant physicists have been removed from the Kaiser Wilhelm Institute in Berlin. I've also found—through binoculars that is—a heavily guarded site at what is called a nuclear pile being created for fissionable research in Haigerloch. Staff cars with civilians go to and from the site and we assume they're physicists working there. Who they are, where they went when they left? That we didn't know. This is where facts end. I think I know where they go now, but the rest is conjecture and…luck."

General Alcott interrupted. "I want to say that I've found CW, and his sleuthing's always turn out to be right on the money, and this is the frightening part."

"Thank you, General. Now, in discussing this 'where' with my agents, one of them in southern Germany had the same situation in his area. A small town in Austria had staff cars moving back and forth up an unpaved road. He followed the road through the woods until he spied a roadblock with Wehrmacht guards, not Gestapo or SS. That is strange. My man hid most of the week until two cars came up. He took photos of the plates and eventually we found a match with mine from Haigerloch. So, now we knew where the vehicles at Haigerlock came from, but not exactly where they went. To shorten this, we learned there is a castle up that road, hidden from view unless a person is quite a distance away. That's where the scientists or physicists, whatever you want to call them, live and work."

One of the men present spoke up. "You're certain these are the people working on the nuclear program? Not others in the Uranium Club like Schumann, Diebner, Heisenberg or others?"

"Nothing is certain. No one you mentioned has been recognized as being at the Haigerloch site, at least not while we watched, but of course that isn't a hundred percent. We do know Himmler has most of those chaps under surveillance. It's odd, as I said, because as far as we can see, neither the Gestapo nor SS have been shadowing those vehicles."

"So now, as to the castle. Fifteen to twenty townspeople are trucked there each day to clean and cook. They are never alone, or stay overnight and are thoroughly searched. Once every week on Sunday, wives and children of the scientists are allowed to visit for a late breakfast. But again, they are searched and never left alone, even the children. The townspeople secretly told me that in good weather, the visitors and scientists are kept together on a terrace at the rear of the castle until noon to eat and have a concert or reading. No one's excused, the commandant is a stickler. A few other sticklers. Wehrmacht troops are to be seen everywhere, in the castle and the forests surrounding it. That it's the Wehrmacht is something I can't explain, there should be SS with an operation like this. My guess is that Himmler is keeping himself hidden. Again, why? I can't figure, but it seems Hitler is letting some Colonel run the show. At least for now.

That sums up my report, except for these photos of the castle we took with a telephoto lens from across the valley. One other separate item. Abwehr agents are everywhere there and even more severe. They're breathing down my agent's necks."

Wentworth passed the photos around while General Alcott took charge once again.

"You all know of Albert Einstein and the weight his words have. Well, it seems he has written a personal letter to President Roosevelt that in essence states a fusion bomb is feasible and the US should develop one before the Germans do."

Alcott studied the pictures of the castle again. "Another important point, CW's report is the most devastating and serious information we've had so far out from there."

The General considered the thoughtful faces around him. "We must be of one mind on this, so let's put our heads together and come up with a plan to *eliminate those physicists*!"

Chapter 32

The two Spitfires circled the field once in a lazy arc, then touched down side by side on the twin runways. The aircraft taxied off and stopped on the frozen field alongside five other Spitfires and three Hurricanes. The engines expelled their breath, ground crew in winter uniforms ran out to chock the wheels and help the pilots out of their harnesses. The pilots thanked them, and in fleece boots, gloves and flying jackets, hurried off to the Operations shed to get out of the swirling, cruel wind.

"Nice bit of flying, Daph. You slipped perfectly into that wingover and held the dive quite well."

"Thanks, but before that you sure fooled me once again, damn it. I had you lined up in my Giro one moment, and the next thing I knew you were above and behind me."

"What I did was the same as a fool's mate in chess. I'll show you on the chalk board what you should have done to counter. Then you can impress your Polish friends when training starts."

"Fine, but hot tea and shortbread first."

They warmed their hands with the mugs.

"Am I improving though? Come on, compliment me."

"I'll compliment you when you've learned to master the Hurricane as well as the Spitfire. I know the 'Cane's a different handling ship, but she's a stable gun platform and you're rough feeling the adjustment running up from 5,000 feet to 25,000 feet. You must get the feel quicker and also when pulling out of a dive give her more power and get that yoke back. I know the G's are harsh, but you've got to take it."

"God, is there anything I'm doing right?"

"Of course there is. You've learned more in the time we've been here than most pilots learn in two months of this training."

"Ah, ha! I knew I could get a compliment if I kept at it."

"So, the sly fox in you comes out. Still, Daph, don't get too cocky, don't rush. Learn something every time, don't just fly. You're gaining experience from every flight. I fooled you on that last tactic simply because you didn't keep looking about, check the sky. You must be aware of your surroundings every second. We wear silk scarfs so we don't get a rash from turning our heads, so stay alert. You already know enough and you'll have to pound all this into the Poles here and then you'll have to do the same with the Czechs at Biggin Hill."

"I understand, Ken. It's just I feel your intensity. I want to be as good as you. I know I can't, but I want to try. I'm reaching too far, yet I want it so much."

"Daphne, it's in you, but you're tired. There is an old saw about fliers, there are old pilots and there are bold pilots. But there are no old, bold pilots. The same goes for dog-tired pilots. Tell you what. I'll take you away from that cold water hut you're staying in. We'll head for Edinburgh. We can tour the castle there."

"In this weather?"

"It's either that, or stay here."

"I'll dress warm."

At present, RAF Grangemouth was a small satellite airbase being set up in expectation of a war. Should there be an attack, the base was strategically placed to protect the Firth of Forth Bridge and the Royal Naval Docks at Rosyh. Its secondary use was its designation as the future base of the 58th Operational Training Unit, being formed for Polish pilots to hone their skills in British aircraft. This was the reason for Kenneth and Daphne's presence at the base.

Ken marveled at her fortitude. She made no complaints about weather conditions, the endless hours of mock aerial combat, developing her agenda. Her only respite was her woodstove heated hut. Yet he acknowledged she'd refuse to stop as long as he kept at it. Perhaps he could slow her down for a while.

The roads to Edinburgh were icy in spots, although Ken handled them as well as one could hope.

"You should have been a race car driver like Jesus Peron, the way you handle these curves."

"Thanks. I handle curves quite well you know. And about Peron, any further questions about your brother?"

"No, about Peron. Hasn't asked of Robert or you at all. And no, I *don't* know if you can handle *some* curves at all well."

Smiling at each other as they drove the south side of the Forth River, he teased her, asking its name in Gaelic.

"Linne Foirthe." She replied. "And what the Scot's call a forth, in Norsk is known as a fjord. In the US, it's simply a long or large inlet. There, see, I'm a fountain of useless trivia."

"May be, but you make me smile, Daph."

He looked over to the southeast. "You don't know this, but over in Lothian a German HE 111 bomber was shot down the end of November."

"First kill for a Spitfire?"

He hesitated. "No."

"What was the first kill?"

"I shouldn't have said anything. Forget I said it."

That was Royce's manner, she thought, yet Ken could see she was hurt. "Well...believe it or not, the first kill for a Spitfire was a Hurricane. That's right, one of ours. Over North Weald, three days after the war started in September. It was a RDF mistake. The Hurricane pilot was killed."

"Gosh, what a shame. Sorry, did you know him?"

"I trained him, then he transferred to Hurricanes down at Hornchurch. Didn't know him well. You don't want to know your men too well."

"I'm sorry I asked. Tragic though, isn't it? Starting a war by shooting down one of your own."

"Whatever way it starts is tragic, Daph, and it will come all too soon for us."

"Why do you say that? I thought you were ready for it."

"That was before you."

"I'm glad you feel that way. It means a lot. But there'll be times you've got to forget me. Not now, however. So let's put war from our minds on this trip. Tell me, have you given any thought to where we'll stay?"

"A little. There are a few small hotels along Whiskey Row we could stay in."

"Whiskey Row?"

"It's an area where all the old whiskey barons have, or once had, their in-town estates. Some of the homes have been converted to hotels or hospices."

"I see, and what are you thinking about for rooms—now that we're on our own at last?"

He looked mortified. "Well, that's something I'd like to discuss."

"Then—go ahead, discuss."

"Ah…let's have a drink or two first."

"Coward."

The sitting room of the hotel where they ordered dinner was warm and mostly empty. Ken ordered lightly cooled Moet Brut.

"This is good to get away, Daph. A person could burn out doing the same thing over and over without a break."

She smiled ruefully, how different from Royce. "Yes it is. Although I enjoy what we've been doing. It's a feeling of accomplishment and well, to know I'm helping you makes me happy too."

She gave him a sideways glance. "Before we discuss what you want to talk about, I'd like to say something."

He waited.

"Ken, have you ever heard of the expression 'on the rebound'?"

"On the rebound? No."

"It's an American expression. It means if someone breaks up with you, you go and fall in love with the next person you meet. You know, sort of rebound to the next person."

He was bothered by the implication. "But you liked me when you were going with your Jim, didn't you? You think you've rebounded from him to me?"

"No, I truly don't, but I want to be sure. Please, Ken, don't get upset. I more than like you. To be frank, there's a more than good probability I love you. Still, Jim was my error. Give me time. My recent past makes it's obvious I'm no wide-eyed innocent, but I want to be right this time, for both of us."

"Daphne, I love you. That's no secret. If you say you want two rooms, then so be it."

He left the table, she couldn't tell if he was angry or not. He must have thought they'd have only one room. Gad! Why was she behaving this way? Well, she was, so why gnaw it to death.

A key dropped on the table. She glanced over, as he sat down seemingly cheerful. "I thought there was no sense letting awkwardness wreck our weekend. That's the key to *your* room."

"Damn it, Ken, thanks. You're doing that means a lot to me Now, with that more or less settled, at least for the present, tell me, when do you expect Polish pilots to reach Grangemouth?"

"From my information, the Air Vice-Marshal has already posted Wing Commander Hallings-Pott, as Commander of two squadrons, 602 for Spits, and 263 for 'Canes. However, I've also been informed it won't be before Christmas. So, after we leave here, I suggest we go back to Grangemouth for a few days. I can bring you up to speed in Hurricanes, and you finish up your classroom curricula. I saw on the cockpit mockup that you had already relabeled all the controls from English to Polish."

"That's right. Still, when I'm finished, they'll know the English words as well. And, one of my side programs is to teach you the pronunciation of the Polish words so you don't make an arse of yourself in front of the pilots."

"We don't have that much time, you know you can't teach an old dog new tricks."

"Be careful what you say about old dogs. I suggest you remember I'm four years older than you."

"Perhaps, but you look four years younger."

"Come off it, Ken. Like I really look twenty-one. Anyway, what do we do after the programs are ready?"

"I'll report to Wing that we're available to begin training. I hope we'll have Christmas and New Year's together."

"I should hope so. However, I'll have to go to Ravensmoor Christmas afternoon. I can't say I want to, yet I think it's only right and I do want to see Mary and the children."

"And see David, and your friend?"

"David, I can do without, as you're well aware. And if Jim's at Ravensmoor, yes. Otherwise, I won't go to his cottage."

The Moet and the fire warmed them, lulled them. The hectic schedule they'd been on found them ready to relax and when it was time to go into the dining room, both were stress free. Roast Beef with Yorkshire pudding and another bottle of Champagne mellowed them out. Their work and the Moet caught up with them and the early darkness made it feel even later than it was.

It was a warm kiss at her door and a few steps to the room that adjoined hers. On a wish, Ken made sure his side of their interconnecting door was unlocked. He washed, fell into bed and snapped off the light. In the blackness, he thought of her with no doubts she was all he wanted. He could wait. He started to doze, then—a click. Fully awake, he tensed—someone was in the room. The covers moved, a smooth, warm body slipped in.

His smiled in the dark. "If you're the chambermaid, I want to caution you. The woman I love will be here shortly."

Unable to hide her giggle, Daphne whispered lovingly in her low whisper, "You conceited, egotistical bastard…"

Chapter 33

17 DECEMBER, 1939
MI6.

"GENERAL ALCOTT, a Mr. Otis Kinsley on three, Sir."

Jesus Peron, ordered in for a new assignment, looked up. "I know Otis, Sir."

"Do you now? He's the man I have on Robert Elliot's trail until he leaves the country."

"Why, Sir? I felt you took care of Elliot rather well."

"You never know. I thought he'd take the first available Clipper out of here, but we followed him to that place he had at Windermere. He's gone there for some unknown reason."

The General left Peron at the chart table and picked up the phone. "Kinsley? Alcott here, what do you have?"

Alcott listened, his mouth went slack, then a booming, "*God damn it!* You can't be serious, man! *When?*"

He turned to Peron. "That traitorous bastard Elliot shot himself! He's dead. Suicide!"

Peron fell back in his chair. "Christ!" Then, thinking quickly. "Is there a suicide note?"

Alcott asked, nodded at the answer. "Kinsley got it, a workman found Elliot. The workman ran out of the cottage and Kinsley went inside. Found Elliot dead and a sealed envelope. Addressed to his sister. Kinsley didn't open it."

"Shouldn't you order him not to, General? There might be something incriminating."

Alcott ordered Kinsley not to open or mention the envelope, and let the workman notify the authorities. Then he was to slip away unnoticed and return to London immediately.

Peron had a half smile. "The old adage the best laid plans of mice and men, oft times go astray, certainly fits here, Sir."

"Yes, damn blast him! Well, what's done is done. We'll have to find a way to stay clear of it. Another God damn thing!"

"What now, Sir?"

"You know Elliot's sister is working as a ferry pilot. She flew me here from the coast and spoke of him on the flight, they seemed close. Christ! What a mess. Peron, find someone who can tell her what happened, or you'll have to do it yourself."

"What should we tell her, Sir? You know, *why* he committed suicide."

"We'll read the note first. If we don't like his reason, we'll decide the *why*."

* * *

Agent Kinsley arrived with the envelope late the same evening. General Alcott sequestered it and ordered counteragent Peron back to his office. After Alcott read the single page, he shook his head and without comment handed it to Peron.

Dear Sister,

By your reading this you will know I have taken my life. The cross I bear has been too much to carry any longer. The Government found I had unknowingly mentioned a minor military secret to a Spanish woman I was in love with. It turned out she was a spy for Germany. I felt it was a small matter as we were not at war with Germany at the time. However, the military said I had disgraced my family by being a traitor, giving England's military secrets to a German spy. What I had done was inadvertent. I asked Jim for help, but he didn't understand and will no longer contact me. This was despite her being killed by an IRA agent while she tried to save Jim's life.

I'm lost without her love. You know General Alcott, it was he and another man who threatened me with prison if I didn't go along with their plans. I would have done that without their threats but now, they have made me feel even dirtier. They've convinced me I'm guilty and are hounding me, saying I don't deserve to have a decent life.

They are liars. My woman, Donnatta, loved only me-that I know.

We planned to run away together but the military caught her and helped the IRA kill her. I escaped to the States but came back to help England and instead they tricked me and tried to make me do things against my ethics or they'll say I killed her. It isn't true. Daphne, always believe that no matter what you hear.

Don't try to dig deeper, you'll never find the truth, they're all liars, hiding behind military secrecy. And they will hound you to if you look too deeply.

Everything I own is yours. It's in my will at the office and with Attorney Anthony Butler in Boston, I don't have his number here. Please stay with Jim Royce, even though he turned from me. He's a good person no matter how he thinks of me. God bless you, and please think kindly of me. Your brother, Robert

"Well Peron, what do you think of that epic?"

"Me, Sir? I'm only a young, lowly agent. I don't think at your altitude."

"Come now, man, I'm sure you can tell me. Speak your mind, get it out."

"I'm afraid there'd be a lot of curse words if I did, Sir."

"Well, do your best. You were Madame Tosca's lover, give me your thoughts on what the letter says of her."

"It's a jumbled letter from a chaotic mind. This is made out of whole cloth, a pack of bloody damn lies…Sir. She told me everything. The bastard was obsessed, thinking he could run off with her. That letter is the delusion of what he dreamed and why it didn't happen. I am astounded that he was so bad off as to commit suicide, but this is an attempt to get off Scot-free for being a traitor."

"Get off Scot-free? Think, man. He killed himself. That's getting off Scot-free?"

"It was to him, he must have been totally irrational. As long as his sister believed him, that was what mattered."

"Interesting observation, not shallow at all, Peron. Still, that was the last thing I thought he would do."

"True. He may have had a touch of integrity after all, Sir."

"Perhaps. Yet consider this, Peron. If you had only half a face, wouldn't you be easy prey for a pretty woman who paid attention to you? Well, wouldn't you? Yet, doesn't matter I suppose, what's done is done. Who do you know who can tell his sister the news?"

"The only person she's close to now, Sir. Squadron Leader Kenneth Sommers."

After Jesus Peron left, General Alcott had two thoughts on the letter. He would need a calligraphy forger for the changes. That wouldn't be a problem. The other thought, more troubling, was the letter mentioned James Royce knew of the traitorous conduct, yet Royce had not reported it. And, Royce had Top Secret clearance. What to do about him? Yes, what to do?

* * *

The service in Saint Martin's Church, Bowness-on-Windermere was short and lightly attended. Present were Franklyn, the cottage caretaker, two representatives from the Soldier's Home, Mary Royce and of course Daphne, Kenneth and Lady Jane. David Royce said he couldn't fit it into his schedule, and James Royce made no excuse for his absence.

Daphne was devastated for her loss, hunched over in the cold of the church, wordless, her eyes fixated on the urn at the altar. The minister intoned, those attending said how sorry, then hurried away into the squally weather.

When Mary came up, Daphne had to ask. "I hope Jim didn't stay away because of me. He and Rob were friends."

"Something happened between them, Daphne. Jimmy said they had a falling out in the States. Wouldn't say what over."

"That shocks me, everything's so bizarre. Jim and my brother had a falling out? Why? Rob came to England with some committee and doesn't even call me? Then, I'm told later he had cancer and he went up to the cottage and… What is going on?

I'm terribly muddled."

"I can't help you. It is strange, but I simply don't know what to tell you. If I find out anything from Jimmy, I'll call you."

Mary hugged her, nodded to Kenneth, then she too was gone. The minister brought the urn to Daphne, started to say a few words of sympathy then trailed off. She wasn't listening.

She asked to be left alone. Kenneth understood she wanted to have a few last words with her brother in the church. Kenneth and his mother went out to his staff car and started the engine to warm the interior. They didn't know Daphne's brother, their concern was solely for her.

As an RAF Officer, Kenneth's mind was still absorbed with the shocking news from two days previous. Bomber Command decided on a bombing of German warships at Wilhelmshaven. Unfortunately, the British Wellington bombers were detected by experimental enemy radar stations and been decimated by ME109 fighters. Out of twenty-four bombers, unescorted by British fighters, twelve were shot down, with the loss of their crews. The debacle caused Bomber Command to rethink their strategy. Kenneth, and other Squadron Leaders and Fighter Wing Commanders, were ordered by Fighter Command's Dowding and Bomber Command's Hewitt, to appear at High Wycombe, Bomber Command's headquarters. There were new concepts to work out. They had never formulated plans of how to *protect* bombers.

Daphne sat by the altar. Reaching into her pocket, she took out the single sheet of paper and again read the letter she received from government authorities.

Dear Sister,

By reading this you will know I have taken my own life. The cross I bear, & the pain I endure has proven too much. The doctors I met with secretly in Boston confirmed I have inoperable intestinal cancer. I have hidden it as much as possible, but now it is too rapidly metastasizing & too painful to hide or go on. And, I wanted to die here, where we were all together, here at our cottage, thinking of you, Mother & Father.

Everything I own is yours. It is in my Will at the office & with Attorney Anthony Butler in Boston. I've loved you & all you have done for me throughout my life. You, & only you, made my living worthwhile.

I wish to be cremated & my ashes spread here along the mere. God bless you. Please forgive for what I have done.

As Dickens wrote, 'tis a far, far better rest that I go to, than I have ever known.

Your loving brother, Robert

Her voice trembled. "Thank you, Rob, for thinking of us, of me. I hope it really is a far better place you go to."

She neatly refolded the letter and placed it in her purse. She felt warmed by Robert's thoughts that she made his life worthwhile.

Had General Alcott known how she felt, he would have been even more pleased with his creative writing.

Kenneth drove to the cottage on the mere. He stayed in the vehicle with Lady Jane, and watched as Daphne walked along the bank of Windermere. She scattered Robert's ashes to the wind and stared as they blew across the water. The urn slipped from her hand and sank into the mere. Then she turned and came toward his car. Kenneth stepped out and went to her. He said nothing as he opened his arms and enfolded her in his greatcoat.

* * *

22 December, 1939

While Squadron Leader Sommers was at the Command conference at High Wycombe, Daphne decided it was time to settle her brother's estate. She telephoned Anthony Butler; formerly their father's Attorney and then Robert's.

"Mr. Butler, I contacted you by Telex in regards to the loss of my brother."

"Yes, Miss Elliot. I'm sure you received my condolences,

and let me now say it verbally. Robert's loss is most distressing to me personally and to the corporate officers and employees."

"Thank you. I've received quite a number of sympathy wires. Please forgive me for not responding and thank them all."

"I will. Might I also add, it was an absolute shock to us. Robert never gave the slightest indication. In fact, he seemed in high spirits and so pleased he was going to England to help. There was not the slightest inkling he was ill. We haven't any idea who the doctors were."

"Mr. Butler, Rob was stoic and that was his way since the war. He kept his feelings private. If only I knew, perhaps I could have helped, although the last line in his letter stated he felt it would be a far better place he would go to. Our mother died of cancer as well. I suppose it's in our genes. I've begun to tear up, Mr. Butler, please forgive me. I'll get to the point of my call."

"No need to be forgiven, Miss Elliot. How can I be of service to you?"

"Am I correct to believe you are…were, my brother's private Attorney? That you are not affiliated with the corporation in any way other than through my brother?"

"That is correct. It would be unethical to be both."

"Thank you, it's good that you feel that way. So with that understood, I would like you to represent me in my relations with Robert's Corporation."

"Consider it done. I'd be honored."

"Thank you again. You drew up my brother's will, which left his assets to me. Please give me the main sections so I know what I have to deal with."

"Certainly. Robert retained fifty one percent of the Corporation after the stock offering to his key employees and other investors. As you know, you owned seven percent and, off the top of my head, I believe you have another three million dollars due over the next three years. I was the attorney of record and responsible for all the papers drawn for him and you. So, obviously this means you now own fifty eight percent of Elliot Corporation, along with the house on Beacon Hill, his vehicles and miscellaneous other assets."

"I wish to retain the home on Beacon Hill, although I wish it closed. Secondly, I would like you to research the company and determine an estimated market value."

"Surely you've not thought to put up the company for sale, Miss Elliot? It's poised to be far more valuable when the US enters the war, as I believe will happen eventually."

"You're more than likely right, Mr. Butler. Although I certainly hope it's soon. However, I do not wish to make money out of war. Please do as I ask."

"Miss Elliot, as Robert had in mind a hostile takeover of an exceptionally significant corporation, he asked me for an estimated value of his holdings. I've just taken that figure out of my file if you would accept a fairly accurate number."

"Of course."

"I'll omit the home and the other minor items. Your total stock ownership now has an inexact value of fifty million dollars."

Daphne's hand went to her mouth. "Good Lord, Mr. Butler, I had no idea."

"As I'm sure you know, Miss Elliot, Robert was an amazing businessman, an artist and person. Others would have buried themselves in the woods away from people and the world."

She found herself crying. That was exactly what he had done.

"Mr. Butler, thank you for your thoughts. Now, I would like you to offer my brother's entire business assets to whom you feel is the right group to carry on the business and his memory. My one proviso being that the name of the Company cannot be changed."

"You're sure of this, Miss Elliot? This company could easily double in a few years, especially if war comes."

"I'm sure it could, nevertheless, that is my decision. And in all our future discussions over this, please call me Daphne, and I will call you Anthony. I'll have my Barrister, Stephan Chalmers, contact you with further instructions when we have an agreement. You will inform my Barrister of the fee for your services, and add a bonus of one million dollars out of my share. I know of your friendship with my brother. Now, I find that once again I've become saddened so that will be all for now. Thank you, Anthony."

After he hung up, Attorney Butler tapped his pen on his desk blotter. What a concise, resolute personality, he thought. One could tell she and Robert had the same parents.

"Too bad," he spoke aloud, "too bad she didn't want to take over the reins."

* * *

The Attorney over with, Daphne decided she would travel to Ravensmoor before Christmas to see Mary and the children. That way, she felt, her obligations in Coventry would be covered and she would be able to spend the holidays between her home at Belgravia, and The Mount.

She rang up Ravensmoor to let Mary Royce know she would be up early the next morning, the 23rd.

"Hello, Mary, how are you feeling?"

"I'm all right, and you, how are you, Daphne?"

"I'm fairly well. It takes time to heal. It's not been the best of years as I'm sure you're aware."

"Yes, you're right, for all of us."

"You don't sound too good yourself. Anything you can talk about on the phone?"

"Not really. Things have gone from poor to worse. We'll talk when you get here."

"All right then. Do you have other children there? Other than Beth and Victor, I mean?"

"No, the war scare seems to have receded and the children we had were returned to London or Bristol. That's why there weren't any at Windermere either when…well, when Robert …"

"I understand. I did wonder about that, but other things were more pressing."

"Oh, Daphne, what can I say? The world goes round and plays dreadful tricks on us all at times. We're rich, but poor, sad people. Anyway, do you want me to tell James you're coming?"

"What do you think? I don't want to sneak in and out like a thief in the night. He deserves more than that. Still, I don't want to make him feel any worse."

"It's only fair to tell him, Daphne. I'll mention it and he can decide on his own whether to come here."

"That's fine, thanks. Now with that resolved, what can I bring the children?"

"Not a thing, please. I've overdone this holiday in my stress.

478

I'll simply change a few tags. And, Daphne, I'll mention to David you'll be up. I'm sure he'll find reasons to absent himself."

"You're a dear. I'll see you then."

The servants made her feel welcome, the children chatting, the dogs slobbering around her. It wasn't until an hour passed, that she and Mary found time to talk alone.

"It's been nice to see you and the children, although I noticed there's a dog missing. Nothing's happened to Scotty, I hope."

"Mary laughed. "Not at all, he's found a new master. He and James are now bosom buddies. Whenever James was here, Scotty was in his lap. When he was let out, the old boy always managed to trot down to Blackbird cottage and wait for James to come home. James asked the children if he could keep him there for a while and they said yes. They've been inseparable since. They go to work together and if James stays over at the office he keeps a pillow and dog food on hand."

"I'll be damned." Daphne looked around. "I notice you're back to calling him James again."

"When I'm here, of course. Too many servants and children around. The walls have ears you know, I don't want to slip up. When I'm down to his cottage, I call him Jimmy."

"Oh? Are you at the cottage often?"

"Not often enough. As you're aware he works so darn much. Still, we get to talk," She was quick to continue, "and only talk, Daphne, dear."

"I wasn't thinking anything improper, Mary."

"Well, see that you don't—at least for the present."

They went into fits of laughter. The more they tried to suppress it, they'd look at each other and the worse it got. At last, red faced, they managed to continue their conversations.

"And now, Mary, after the laughter, tell me about your husband."

"There's certainly no laughter there. He's away more and longer. And when he's here, I want to be somewhere else. The servant's see it, thank goodness the children are too young."

"Why don't you pack up and leave?"

"Think, Daphne. I've the children. And where would I go? To my parents? No life for me there, listening to their opinion that I should have stayed with him, no matter what, as they've done."

"You could start over. Away from him, with the kids, alone."

'Daphne, I have no money of my own. Every cent comes from David. Besides, it's not that poor a life. Now that I'm adjusted to it, I live well, I have my children."

"That's what it is, isn't it? You're afraid if you left, David would take Beth and Victor away from you because of his power. Am I right?"

"That's one of the reasons, yes. The others are crass, if you must know. I'm going to have James someday, even though David thinks I'm going to be the silent wife of a future Prime Minister. Before then, the children will be legally old enough to decide who they want to be with. And, that's when I'll expose David for the cad he is. And I'll shame him, shame him like he's shames me now. Can you imagine what's being said behind my back?"

"Yes, I'm afraid I can. Still, how can you get even?"

"I've planned it all out. Just before the vote for Prime Minister, I'll file for divorce, claiming adultery. That will forever destroy his chances."

"Mary! How delightfully wicked! I didn't think you had it in you, I really didn't."

"I didn't think so either, but I've set my mind to it. I was going to wait until he became Prime Minister, but I'm weak and afraid I might like being the PM's wife. Then, I thought, if he lost the vote, didn't become the PM, then I wouldn't have my revenge. So it has to be just before the vote comes up when he'll get his comeuppances, what's due him."

"My word. Good for you! You've really given this thought."

"Yes. Away from him and this monstrosity of a house. How do you think I'll do as the gay divorcee, Daphne? Gay, but poor."

"Mary, don't ever concern yourself on that score. Even if you weren't with Jim, I'll see to it you're never poor. David will never get that satisfaction. Anyway, by now it seems Jim isn't coming so I'll run along. You stay here, I'll say goodbye to all." The goodbyes were sad for the children and servants, even the dogs had their stub tails down. Daphne asked Alfred for an envelope, and then wrote a check for the children's jackets…and one other check.

While Mary walked her to the door, Daphne handed her the

check for the jackets and the sealed envelope. "I don't want you to worry, Mary. Open this if things don't work out."

She recognized Royce's Bentley parked halfway up to the road and stopped behind it. Royce got out holding Scotty, walked back and slid in beside her. The dog jumped over and licked her gloved hand, wagging his tail nonstop as she patted it.

"I wasn't sure it was you in this Jaguar, Daphne."

"How are you, Jim? You still look weary."

"Yes, I suppose I do. Quite a bit going on."

Daphne couldn't help show her concern. "So, that's the reason you haven't re-stained your scar? And the metal brace is still on your fingers. Jim, tell me, why won't you take care of yourself?"

"Jesus, Daphne, don't start on me again! Why didn't you understand? I've got to work, I can't help it!"

The dog, startled. Daphne was shocked by his intensity.

"You can't help it? What the devil does that mean? Jim, you've got to help it, no one else can. Why do you think so little of yourself?"

Royce shrugged, withdrew into himself, not speaking. She saw it happen and changed the subject. "I hear my brother and you had a falling out. You were good friends. What happened over in the States?"

"Nothing."

"See, now we're back to the way you were when we met."

"You won't stay?"

"No." She was amazed he even asked.

He didn't respond, only stared through the windshield.

"There's someone else, isn't there?"

"Yes."

He reached into his pocket. "I want you to take this back."

The black star sapphire ring she had given him shone in the dashboard lights.

"I don't want it back, it's yours."

"You returned the car I gave you."

"That's different, this was personal. If you don't keep it, I swear I'll throw it out the window on the way back to London."

He looked so forlorn she wanted to hold him, comfort him,

but didn't dare. He slipped the ring onto his finger, picked up the dog and got out, bending down to see her. "I love you, but you don't know what real love is. If your RAF lover doesn't work out, don't come back to me."

He closed the door, protected Scotty from the swirling snowflakes and walked back to the Bentley. She watched his vehicle drive away, feeling as if she'd been slapped.

He blames me. He blames me for this. What the matter with him? What's happened to you, Jim? You make me want to cry.

* * *

Christmas Day, 1939

At The Mount, there was happiness tempered by the loss of Daphne's brother. However, the gifts and drinks passing back and forth lightened the atmosphere. That was especially true when Lady Jane and Kenneth presented their presents to Daphne.

"My, God! What have you two done? What is all this?"

"It's your new uniform, Daphne. The RAF can't have you training pilots in your old climbing pants and boots. Not proper at all, you know."

"You tell her what it all is, Kenneth. I don't have the foggiest what it's all about, Daphne."

Ken started. "This is a standard blue gray serge RAF Service Dress uniform with Battle Dress blouse and tie. Without rank, of course, but on the shoulders are Fighter Command Interpreter patches, Training Corp Badge with Crown and 11 Group with Squadron patch. All that's to make you look important. Over on the chair, there are two cotton jump suits, canvas, fleece lined flying boots, flying gauntlets and fur lined flying trousers. Oh, and I spoke with Fighter Command. They've allowed you to wear the Spitfire Pilot pin I gave you over the right…ah, pocket."

Daphne rolled her eyes. "Isn't he ever the shy one, Jane. Didn't want to say to pin over my right breast."

"He always appears that way, Daphne, but never doubt it's all a sham."

"I've come to grasp you've been only too right, Jane."

Seeing Ken turning scarlet, Daphne felt bad for him and let

the subject slide. "Is all of this RAF issue?"

"Everything but the uniform. We had that made in Leeds. Can't have standard issue make you look shabby. And one more thing from Mother. A whistle, to get your pilot's attention. Then again, as I think of it, perhaps it's to get my attention."

"God, I thank you both so much, I can't put it into words. And I'm embarrassed. My mind wasn't on Christmas, I'm afraid. I only managed to get you a few small things."

Lady Jane opened her gift, an Opal necklace with matching bracelet, which she loved, more so, as it was from Daphne.

"And this is for you, Ken, you better like them."

"I wouldn't dare not."

He jumped as the package, under pressure from being sealed tightly, burst open with six multicolored polka dot scarves. They laughed aloud.

"Daphne, I love them dearly. I'll never fly again without one. That is if I can get away with it."

"And I've one more for you, Ken."

He unwrapped a layered gold cigarette lighter, emblazoned with the 11 Group Spitfire graphic, tooled and glazed on one side. On the other, the RAF roundel. Below it, three words in script:

Kenneth, Your Daphne.

He was speechless. After a kiss, he handed her another giftwrapped package. As she opened it she smiled. "Ah, a silk scarf to stop from chafing my neck craning around for aircraft. Thanks for the not so subtle reminder. Oh, and a hat to complete my uniform."

"It's called a side cap, Daph. Two brass buttons on the front you'll have to keep polished."

"What's this pin with wings on the side? Whose initials are RFC?"

"It stands for the Royal Flying Corp. They predated the RAF. They were my Father's in the Great War."

"Your Father's? My, God, I can't have these. These are yours, or Jane's."

"Daphne," Lady Jane spoke up. "Those were the wings my husband wore throughout the War. They brought him luck. He never got a scratch. Kenneth and I want you to have them."

"But what of Ken's luck?"

"I don't believe in luck, I don't need it."

A fashion show followed. Everyone, Daphne included, agreed she should be on a poster for the Woman's Auxiliary Air Force.

* * *

"Daphne, can you hear me?"

The static between their aircraft was fading. "Yes, where the devil are you?"

"Coming up on your port. Wing contacted me and I drifted speaking with them."

"What's up at Wing?"

"You're going to love this. All fighter aircraft on the east, southeast coasts and Scotland are now considered to be in a battle zone and must be combat ready."

"Which means?"

"We'll land at Grangemouth and have the armorer load us."

"You mean I'm going to fly around with charged guns?"

"Eight .303 caliber Browning's to be exact. And believe me, you with live weaponry is not my idea. Still, it does give me a chance to complete your education."

"What do you mean?"

"We're on Grangemouth approach, I'll tell you there."

At Grangemouth, while they waited for the armourer, Ken explained further. "I called RAF Aberdeen. There's a target range off the coast. The fighters have cleared the area, so it's ours for the rest of the day."

"You mean I'm going to live fire this, don't you? I've wanted to do that all along!"

"My word, I'd *never* have guessed. Let's go over what you've been taught. Remember, each machinegun has only three hundred rounds and they fire seven-hundred rounds per minute, so in three seconds, eight guns can put three hundred rounds on a target. If one of my pilots couldn't blow an ME109 out of the air with that, I'd get them a cannon."

"I think I need more guns. I forgot everything you just said."

They orbited over the North Sea off Aberdeen while he reminded her. "All right, here we go. There's two targets side by side I estimate fifty yards apart. So now get the glare shield down on the Giro* and follow down beside me, sight in, and fire when you see my flashes out of the corner of your eye. Run the shell splashes right up into the target, hit it two or three seconds then get your thumb off the button and break left."

"You ready."

"We'll find out."

Dropping down toward the targets. Lined up the aircraft as best she could. Then, firing for the first time the noise and vibration from the eight machine guns of startled her, yet she kept on line, her thumb frozen on the firing button for an additional two seconds. Over the earphones, she heard Ken's laughter.

"Damn, Daph, you really believe in overkill!"

"Sorry, my thumb froze for a moment. How'd I do?"

'Oh, I don't know, you might have put an extra two or three holes through the canvas."

"Don't tell me that. Really?"

"Just kidding. Go around again. Drop lower. Estimate less than four hundred yards, use very short bursts to run , align and then, no more than three seconds on target. I'll watch."

She didn't hesitate. Her aircraft looped down close to waves with the airspeed at 170 MPH. She found the distance by quick bursts, then blasted the wooden target. Her Spitfire flew through splinters and windblown canvas, then broke sharp left.

"Jesus, Daph! You're lucky your wheels were up! You've a killer instinct."

"If that's a compliment, thanks. But really, I was shocked by how she shook and the racket."

"Well, when eight machine guns fire and recoil, something's got to give."

---

*Giro gun sight. Used in the Spitfire and Hurricane. Later in the war called 'The Ace Maker' for its success.

"God that was one of the most incredible experiences I've ever had in all my life!"

"Even more than with me under the sheets?"

"Of course. That couldn't come close to this."

"Damn, Daph, you sure know how to put a guy in his place."

"I have to. I don't want your head to get any bigger than it is, you might leave me."

"Be careful what you say, Ops may hear."

"God, Ken! Don't tell me that."

Their chatter was interrupted by Grangemouth giving them clearance to land.

Ken continued part of their conversation in the empty officer's mess. "You know there's no chance I'd leave and you know it, so let's change the subject. I want to know what happened up at Coventry before Christmas. You never said a word and I wasn't going to ask, but my curiosity's got the better of me."

"Gosh, Ken, I didn't mean not to tell you. I wanted to shut it out of my mind, I guess. Briefly, Jim has serious problems and Mary showed me a side of her I didn't know existed."

"Good or bad? About Mary I mean."

"Alarming. She intends to eventually get even with her husband over his disgracing her. It will take years, but she says she'll do it. At least that's what she says."

"Years? That's a long time to waste on anger and revenge. I think that could change one's personality, and not for the better."

"That's observant of you."

Another part of him, she thought, very aware of how actions could change people. "And, I suppose you would like to know about the other man?"

"Not really, unless you feel the need to talk about him."

"You phony. Despite your feigned indifference I'll tell you. Yet to be honest, that's the part I wanted to shut out of my mind. Jim's worn, on edge, not taking care of himself, blames me for our breakup and of all things, he's replaced me with a dog."

Ken sat back in thought. "Well, let's think about that, Daphne. A dog causes far fewer problems, they're loyal, warm, loving, don't talk back. You know, what every chap looks for."

"You mentioned something like that before. May I suggest

you remember there are still a few rounds left in my guns out there?"

"Sorry, dearest. Please continue about a man and his dog."

"It will be about a man in a doghouse, you keep this up. Anyway, there's not much left to tell. I met him in the drive, he asked if there were someone one else, I said yes—which, at the moment, I'm beginning to regret—and he wanted to give back a ring I gave him. I said no, and he left. End of story."

"I feel bad for him, in the past you made him sound a decent sort of chap."

"He is. It's something just drives him. I honestly don't know what. But I loved him, found you and left him. Still, I worry something unfortunate will happen to him, and I'm sorry."

"Well, Daph, there's not much you can do about that now. We've got nineteen Czech pilots to train at Brooklands. And on that subject, you've met Vice Air Marshal Park, but Vice Air Marshal Leigh-Mallory, Wing Commander of 12 Group may show up if he hears about our programs. If he does show, just do your job. Don't get into any deep conversation."

"What the devil does that mean? No deep conversation. Should I act retarded?"

"No. I simply mean that Leigh-Mallory and Keith Park don't see eye to eye on battle tactics and I don't want Mallory getting any unnecessary 11 Group information from you."

"And if he asks me a direct question and expects a direct answer, I do…what?"

Ken winced. "Suggestion. Bat your eyelashes, then faint."

"You know, Ken, there are times when you're an ass."

"You only say that to try and keep me in my place."

"No, I say that because there are times you act like an ass."

Chapter 34

30 January, 1940

HOW MUCH FURTHER to the cottage, Casey?"

"If this chap Royce gave you the correct address, a mile west of Ravensmoor, then we should be there in five minutes, Sir."

General Miles Alcott turned to Brigadier Tomlinson. "So, we're agreed, we'll play this low-key, see his reaction, then take it from there."

"It's the 'take it from there' element that still bothers me, Miles. To me, I think Royce is a decent chap, but I also think he has a short fuse. Remember that New Year's party? Look at his reaction when CW said he'd been in touch with Royce's friend Becker in Austria. Royce was ready to for a go at CW until you intervened. It could be the same here when you question him on being in violation of the Military Secrets Act when he didn't report Robert Elliot as a spy."

"I don't think we'll have a problem. You were with the SAS Commando and Sergeant Casey here has his beloved persuader handy. Right, Sergeant?"

Casey patted a blackjack in his side pocket. "At your beck and call, Sir."

"Fine. Remember, Sergeant, try to ignore the scar. After that, if he's not forthcoming, we arrest him one way or the other, and get him out of there without bothering David."

"Still, from what we've learned," Tomlinson added, " there's no love lost between the two brothers, so it shouldn't be a bother to Sir David when he finds out."

"No, except David needs him in the company and we don't want to interfere with that unless we must. Still, we do have to cover our hind quarters should someone learn about Royce's knowledge on Elliot and we let it slide."

Royce met them at the door, and whereas not rude, it was obvious he could do without the interruption to his workday. He asked them to sit and, not ready for small talk, impatiently forced the issue by inquiring. "General, you wanted this meeting kept secret and away from David and the Company. So, what is it now that you find a bother?"

"Mr. Royce, you're aware Robert Elliot committed suicide?"

It was not a subject Royce expected. He became cautious. "Yes, I'm aware of that. He had cancer."

"You read the note?"

"No, I heard about it from Mary Royce, my brother's wife."

"Had she read the note?"

"How the hell do I know? What's all this about? I've better things to do."

"No, Mr. Royce, you don't have better things to do at the present. So, it's best for you shut up and listen."

Brigadier Tomlinson cringed. So much for a low key approach. Yet he knew all along the General wouldn't put up with Royce's irritation for long.

General Alcott resumed. "What you've heard about the note is false. This is a copy of the actual note Elliot wrote."

Royce took the page and moved to a better light. Alcott's eyes followed him, momentarily distracted by the painting over the fireplace, then looked again to Royce who was hard to read. There was no telling his thoughts.

Royce handed the note back. "You've confounded me. He didn't have cancer?"

"No. That was a ruse we devised to eliminate all the foolishness that letter would cause if it became public. I should think that would be obvious to you."

"It is quite obvious. Am I correct to assume you'd like my comments on this?"

"As many as you'd care to make."

"There's a lot of self-pity and delusion in it. I imagine you're the *them* he writes about being out to get him?"

"In his delusion, yes."

"So, what you're really after is, did I know he was a traitor?"

"You're quick to pick that up. Yes, that is what we're after."

"I did know, after the fact. In the States."

"Thank you for being frank. Saves a lot of talk. Now, his being a friend or no friend, why didn't you report this? This puts us in a difficult position as you can well expect."

"I didn't report it because I'm in love with his sister and, at the time, she was in love with me. It would have meant the end of our relationship. Also, he couldn't do additional harm over there and he would have done some good. Yet that's all water over the dam now, isn't it?"

Brigadier Tomlinson took up the questioning. "From what you've said, I gather you're no longer with his sister. Why didn't you report him after you two separated?"

"Because it would have destroyed her, she loved her brother."

"Do you know what secrets Elliot gave to this spy?"

"He mentioned information on the Chain Home, the lack of petrol injection on the Merlin engine, and something on vacuum tubes. I sent that information to MI5, I might add."

The Generals looked at each other. They weren't aware of MI5, but well aware it was General Alcott who carelessly gave this information to Elliot at Ravensmoor. It was time to gloss over the affair and bury their blunders along with Robert Elliot.

"So, Mr. Royce, if I follow this correctly, you failed to report a breach of the Secrets Act because of a woman, and Elliot breached that Act because of a woman."

"With Robert, I think his hatred of war warped his thoughts. The woman only played off that, reinforced it."

"Very well then," Alcott added, "we'll let it go at that, Mr. Royce. You can continue with your efforts at your brother's Company and we will assume you will keep this little get together a private affair between us."

"Yes, if Daphne doesn't learn the truth."

"Fair enough, agreed."

"Then we're done here, Mr. Royce."

As the men were leaving, Tomlinson mentioned the painting. "That's an attractive oil painting over your fireplace."

Royce smiled roguishly. "Yes, isn't it? It's from a photo I took in Austria. Read the signature."

The Tomlinson squinted. "I'll be damned! Look, Miles, of all things, it's signed Robert Elliot."

* * *

21 February, 1940

"Schmid, you seem smug. That's a change from the last few weeks. Do you think you are finally on the right track?"

"Yes, my Führer, we're now convinced the possibilities are real for a fusion bomb. Of course, it's a long way down the road, but it looks positive."

"Very good. Reichsführer Himmler stays away?"

"It is as you ordered. He bothers none of my people. In fact, he offered to send me some prisoners from Ohrdruf, as servants."

"Ohrdruf? That's our Racial Hygiene camp. No one comes out of there. What does Himmler think he's up to? Spying? You keep the local people, as long as you watch them. I'll tell Himmler to mind his own business."

"Thank you my Führer. The local people will keep quiet. No one learns a thing from my castle."

"Good. And another detail, Schmid. I assure you the heavy water problem you complain about will soon be resolved to your satisfaction."

"You mean, Norway…?"

"Be closemouthed and patient two more months."

Chapter 35

15 March, 1940
THEY WALKED ALONG the landing strip at Grangemouth. "Daphne, you were outstanding the whole six painful weeks. That took some doing."

"Why thank you, Squadron Leader. I couldn't have done it without your able assistance. I'll see if I can put in good word about you to Wing."

"So nice of you. Wing, however, has already contacted me about you. They're extremely pleased with our program and the language tutelage you did with the Polish pilots."

Kenneth hesitated, smiled over at her and then continued. "I probably shouldn't tell you this, but from what I hear, there was a bit of a kerfuffle when Air Marshal Dowding heard that besides translating and ground school, you also taught aerial combat in your own personal Spitfire. Name of Tiger, he believes."

"They found out about Tiger? The pilots painted that name on my aircraft, not me! What do you think Wing will do about it?"

"Not sure, but you better brush up on your other Indo-European dialect. Wing has given us two days leave, then we're to be down at Biggin Hill to begin instructions on the Hawker Hurricane with the Czech pilots."

"Isn't that wonderful, Ken? We make a great team. Still, we had something to work with didn't we? Those men were good pilots to begin with. And they accepted me as an equal without question."

"Accepted you? Why on earth shouldn't they? You could fly circles around most of them and keep up with the rest."

"If I could out fly most of them, it was because of your pushing me to reach. You've worked me damn harder than I ever thought I could put up with."

"All I did was make you begin to find your potential. Still, you've a way to go."

"Really? I can get better?"

"Of course, don't for a moment think you can't always improve. Yet you may get better in a different way, some different course. Look at Beryl Markham, first person, man or female, to fly alone from here to Canada, or look at the records your Emilia Earhart set before she was lost."

"Is that what you have in mind for me?"

"God, not the lost part, Daph. I'm simply saying that there's more to flying than what we've done. When this war is over, open your horizons."

"I will if you will."

"Then you've a deal."

"Ken, there's one thing you didn't enlighten me about. What happened between you and those two pilots who thought they were cock of the walks?"

"What do you think? You saw us fly off in three planes and you saw us come back, didn't you?"

"I just told you I don't know. All I know is they came back thoroughly chastised."

"I took them where they couldn't be humiliated in front of the rest of the pilots and played a game I call chase and be chased. It can get close at times. Two against one—they lost."

"I thought it was something like that. The rest of the pilots could see the anxiety in them when they returned."

"It's unpleasant to do, but at least the lesson came from me, not some enemy pilot."

"Teach me how to be that way."

"I can't. I showed you some of the most advanced tactics you're able to handle at present. The rest comes from experience, brains and instinct. It will come together for you whether you're conscious of it or not. When it does, then all at once you'll find your aircraft will do what you're *thinking*. I don't kid you. When that happens, you'll be one of the best. After that, just add deceit. Do everything possible to make sure your enemy isn't in a fair fight. If you're in a fair fight, get out and recalculate."

"You're serious, aren't you?"

"Never more so. I told you I wasn't in it for the glory."

"Anyway, our birds are back from Biggin Hill. They've learned the Chain Home Command sequence, and this is their Squadron base under Air vice-Marshal Brand. We've had a party, said good luck and I know you'll miss them, but we're finished here. So let's go down to London, see Mother, then have a couple of days to ourselves."

* * *

18 March, 1940

"Blast it! Stone the damn Crows!" Kenneth slammed the phone into its cradle.

"Ken, what the devil is wrong?"

"Damn! I can't think straight! Daphne, the Germans bombed our base at Scapa Flow."

"The naval base up north?"

"Yes, Scapa Flow's the Royal Navy base up in the Orkneys. The Germans bombed it yesterday! Our Polish pilot's did an incredible job, shot down three Heinkel 111s. We had no losses."

"That's fantastic, proves we did our job with them. So why are you upset?"

"I wasn't there!"

"My, God. Now I see why you're so bothered. One day's difference, one damn day. We could have shown them."

"We? What do you mean we? You're not going to get anywhere near a dogfight."

"You're crazy, Ken! If I got the chance, you'll have to shoot me down to stop me from getting at them."

"Please, Daphne, don't make me worry about you. Don't do that to me."

She saw he meant it. This was a one-way deal. She was to worry about him. "I'm kidding, don't be worried about me."

Leaving Ken to his deliberations, she began packing for Brooklands and the Czech pilots. Given the slightest chance, she'd attack any enemy, whether he worried about her or not. When she returned, Kenneth still seemed troubled.

"What I said still bothers you?"

"It does, but…. The call was also about you, Daph."

"What? Tell me!"

"Well, the good news is you've now received Top Secret

clearance. The not so good news is I'm to report to RAF Biggin Hill in two days. Then go back to my Squadron in France."

"Why isn't that good? You live for your Squadron."

"Yes, getting my Squadron back is excellent, but it means I'll be away from you for a long time."

She came and sat beside him. "I guess we couldn't expect to be together all the time, yet why so sudden? We did a great job with the Polish pilots, why did they stop it?"

"They haven't stopped it, they're sending an RAF pilot from the Central Flying School to assist you."

"So I'll ask you again then, why not keep you here with me?"

"Daph, do you remember last February when the RN destroyer Cossack went into a Norwegian fjord and recovered three hundred British prisoners from the Altmark? She was the German supply ship for the Graf Spee, that was before the German's scuttled the Spee."

"Vaguely. I was in training at that time, remember? Not much else was on my mind, I'm afraid."

"Doesn't matter, the point is our intelligence network thinks that because of that skirmish, the German Kriegsmarine recognize their warships are vulnerable when they try to get into the North Sea and on out into the Atlantic. If we get serious about deploying troops to defend Norway we could also interrupt their iron ore flow from Scandinavia. Intelligence thinks the Germans will make a dash for Norway and Denmark in the near future."

"What will the Brit's do?"

"As I say, we'll send troops. If we get our butts in gear."

"How does that involve you, the RAF?"

"It doesn't directly. It will be a Navy, Army effort, with the Fleet Air Arm as cover."

"So, as you're RAF, why are you being sent back to France?"

"It's a precautionary step. Bring all Squadron's up to full complement."

"I see. Makes sense. Still, I see something else bothers you."

"Yes, there is, Daph. I don't know how long it will be before I see you again."

"I know, we're going to have to…"

"Please, Daphne, let me finish." He took her hand. "I want to ask you to marry me."

She was puzzled, yet remained composed. "You *want* to ask me to marry you. Does that mean you *are* asking me, or you only *want* to ask me?"

"God, I've messed this up. What I'm trying to say is I want to marry you, but with the war outlook, I don't know the future. Is it right to get married? What if something should happen to me?"

She interrupted, infuriated. "What do you mean *if* something should happen to you? Nothing will happen to you! *Nothing!* Damn it—you're the best! You've convinced me of that. The best! I don't ever want to hear you ever say 'something might happen' again! *Do you hear me!* I'm not going to think that, and you better not either!"

"Daphne, please. Calm down. I only said you never know…"

"Well, *I* know, and you're to stop those thoughts this minute. End of subject! Now, I don't know if you've asked me to marry you or not—but if you have, the answer is *yes*!"

Kenneth was elated and laughing. "God damn, Daph! When you get your dander up you're going to be difficult to live with."

"We'll discuss that when we're old and gray. Right now, get over to your Squadron," she was astonished at her next words—all her past independence—gone, "and find time for us to get married!"

* * *

1 April, 1940

OPERATIONAL CENTER, MI6, LONDON.

"Gentlemen!" General Alcott demanded, "You've now read Charles Wentworth's full report. Can I emphasize more the gravity of what we're up against? The PM has ordered us to find a solution to neutralize these fusion physicists and what I get from all of you is negatives. We can't find the site to bomb it, and if we found it and missed, they'd be warned and move. Then you say it's a suicide mission for commandos because it's too well guarded. Well damn it, suicide or not, come up with something! CW stated the servants felt the physicists were all excited. About…about what? He's out there busting *his* arse taking chance after chance and telling us there's no time to sit here on *our* arses not doing a damn thing! For Christ's sake put your heads together and come up with schemes or I'll knock your heads together! Get out of here! Get me a solution—whatever the cost!"

Alcott sipped on a whiskey, frowning at Brigadier Tomlinson who appeared detached.

"What's your problem, Tommy?"

"Something's started bothering me, Miles. Do you have that photo CW took of the castle?"

The general reached into his briefcase. "Yes, it's in here and if I can find the bloody thing. Ah, here it is. Why do you want it?"

"Just a wild thought, Miles. Before I say anything more, let me look at it again."

Tomlinson stared at the photo until Alcott got impatient.

"Why the interest? You see something I don't?"

"Perhaps. You remember the painting of that castle Royce had over his fireplace? Is it possible this photo and that painting are the same castle? Remember, Royce said it was in Austria."

The General did his best to recollect the painting. "You're really desperate, Tommy. I don't see it. Nice try though. That could have made things interesting."

"Think, Miles, of course the perspective is different. Still, I'm guessing it's the same castle. It's the single offset tower that convinces me. Royce's painting is from a different perspective of course. I think above and off to the right. Yet again, there's that single tower that's the odd detail. And look there at the wall and the low gun port in the tower. It could match. You can see part of it in CW's photo and I remember it there in Royce's painting."

"Don't agree, Tommy. Possible? Doubtful. Don't hang your hat on it. Besides, look at the height of that wall in the photo, how could anyone get that perspective?"

Tomlinson grimaced. "There you have me. But there's that wall in the photo and in the painting. Miles, with your permission, I'd like to follow up on this. Is CW trying to get out again?"

"We've no word. He signaled things are tight. The Abwehr caught another of his agents. If they make him talk that would roll up our last cell there. We have to assume our codes for this mission are compromised. My belief is CW's on the run, so when he'll surface again is anyone's guess. "

"Damn, then that puts a blasted damper in it. Did he give you the name of the castle or any other information on it?"

"No, the last message was short and succinct. Only to say they could be on to him and he's going to ground."

"Let's hope he's safe. Still, about the photo, if CW can't help, could I speak with Royce again?"

"I'll clear it through Director Menzies, but I don't see anything wrong with that. As I recollect, you climbed in the past. Use that approach. That you were curious where the castle was and how he got that angle. Do *not* say more. We've allowed him to retain Top Secret designation, but still, I don't want him to know a thing about this operation."

* * *

9 April 1940

German troops opened a massive assault by sea and air into Norway and Denmark. King Christian of Denmark, realizing the futility of resistance, ordered his people to surrender. Norway fought. German Alpine troops, loaded on fast Kriegsmarine destroyers, landed in bitter weather at multiple points along the Norwegian coast. The British fleet struck back ferociously on German warships in battles costly to both sides. The British could absorb the losses, but the German High Command was staggered to learn one third of their naval power was sunk, including the loss of fifty percent of their total destroyer fleet at the Skagerrak and along the Norwegian coast.

Yet, despite their losses, German land objectives were realized and, aided by the treachery of a coup d'état of Vidkun Quisling,* the self-appointed Prime Minister of Norway, they soon occupied their main objectives. British, French and Polish forces landed at a few ports, including the retaking of Narvik, but it was a case of too little too late, as events of the month that followed caused them to be withdrawn.

* * *

*Executed by firing squad for High Treason 10.4.1945

12 April, 1940

Brigadier General Tomlinson's meeting with Royce went better than the Brigadier expected, at first. Royce felt the painting and photograph were of the same castle. This was exciting news. But now, Royce questioned Tomlinson's interest and wouldn't accept the offhanded remark that he was curious about the castle simply as a recreational climber.

"For Christ's sake, Brigadier, don't feed me rubbish. You expect me to believe you drove over ninety miles to find out if it's the same castle? With that solid wall behind it, what you want to know is how I got a photo from that angle. Right?"

"Well, yes, I'm curious how you did that."

"Tell you what. You tell me why, and I'll tell you how."

"Sorry, I can't do that."

Royce was inquisitive, although he wouldn't let on and headed for the door. "If that's all, I've got work to do."

"Mr. Royce, please wait, trust me, it's important we know."

"Who is *we*?

"General Alcott, and...a few others."

"Ah, the plot thickens. Still, it comes down to you tell, I tell."

"Before I make a phone call, Mr. Royce, might I ask if you have the original snap?"

"Yes, it's taped on the back of the painting."

Tomlinson studied the photo. "What lens was on your camera?"

"I have a 50 mm Leica, it's in the other room."

"So, you weren't too far away when you took it."

Royce simply smiled.

"May I use your phone, Mr. Royce, in private?"

"Certainly, it's in the kitchen. I'll go to that room there, and call me Royce from now on. Most everyone else does."

Tomlinson went to the kitchen, taken aback by the knife stuck through a piece of paper and into the wall. He kept his composure, struggled not to read the note and kept his voice low when General Alcott got on the line. "Miles, Royce has confirmed that it's the same castle."

"My word, Tommy. That's brilliant, good show. How did he get that shot?"

"That he won't say. He knows I'm interested far more than a

mere climber would be and wants to know why I'm so curious."

"I'm sure he knew that from the start. Anything else?"

"Only that I saw the original snap, and he said he took it with a 50 mm lens. I said he couldn't have been too far away and he just smiled."

"Of course, that would be him. Nevertheless, we have to know how the hell he got that photo. Any ideas?"

"Tell him the truth?"

"Jesus H Christ, no, Tommy! Just tell him we're interested in something or other."

"That won't fly, Miles, he's too smart to let it go at that. I'd bet he's already figured out we're after someone there."

"Blast it! I'm not mad at you, Tommy. Your finding out about the castle is of uppermost importance. Yet now we've got this damn cuss to contend with. Give me your number there, I'll ring up the Chief, get his counsel and be back to you as soon as possible. Sorry to have to leave you with him."

"I'll be all right, Miles. I don't think he's such a bad sort if we reason with him."

Tomlinson went to find Royce, and found him about to walk out the door. "Stay here, General, I'll be back in ten minutes."

Tomlinson had no choice other than to wait, irritated at Royce's abrupt departure, although grateful for the brief respite.

Royce returned minutes later. He turned to a dog-eared page in a book and handed it to Tomlinson. "This the place you're interested in, General?"

Tomlinson saw it was a clearer picture of the Castle from the front, although not closer.

He read the caption. "Steinvorhangburg, (Stone Curtain Castle.) 14th Century, NW Austria. Private, no tours." He looked over to Royce. "Not much information."

"That's what my brother thought. So, now you know the name, but you're still not enlightened, are you?"

"Not really. Even if you won't tell me how you got that snap, could you at least tell me how close you got to the castle?"

"Best as I recall, I would say less than a hundred yards."

"Less than a hundred! I'm shocked, Mr. Royce, this is important. Do you…"

The phone rang. "That's probably for you, General, not many

call me here anymore."

Royce waited as the call went on. Something important was happening at the castle and he wanted to know what. There must be someone there they wanted, or wanted to get out. Then he remembered the SS vehicles, how they alarmed him and caused him to slip. He shuddered. The SS must be there, that's got to be it. The SS were there, they have a prisoner that...

"Mr. Royce, General Alcott would like to speak with you."

Royce took the phone. Tomlinson knew of the scar, but the crippled hand was new.

"Mr. Royce" The General began, "I must be careful what I say on the phone, but the activity at that location may have a devastating effect on England's ability to survive. Please don't doubt me. We must know how to get close to that area. We would like you to come to London where we can speak privately."

"I will, General, but I have ten management assemblies set up for Sunday, Monday and Tuesday. These are imperative. I will be available to you on Wednesday, the 17th. That's the best I can do at present."

Alcott was furious, yet contained himself. He needed Royce's cooperation. He could have Royce arrested. Yet that wouldn't help. He'd wait. "I'll have a vehicle at your house at 0700 hours on the 17th. Put Tomlinson back on the phone."

Royce handed off the phone. "Treat him with kid gloves, Tommy. He's going to come down on the 17th. I couldn't get the bastard any sooner. However, listen. I've got two important developments in the works, so come back on the quick."

Royce seemed cool when Tomlinson hung up the phone.

"They'll pick me up on the 17th, so you'll be seeing more of me, I expect."

"Mr. Royce, let me say something here, you may not like us, and, frankly, you don't present much of a likable chap either. Still, there's one thing you *must* keep in mind—we labor for England. We never forget that, and if you remember that as well, it would certainly be helpful for us...and England."

Brigadier Tomlinson was happy to be away from Royce and back at MI6. He was also ready to hear some good news after he learned German forces had forced their way into Denmark

501

and Norway and wasted no time in consolidating their positions. Most of the inadequate British and French forces were driven away with little trouble. Despite that setback, the General had the look of a Cheshire Cat.

"Okay, Miles, please, something to pick me up."

"I'll give you two things, Tommy. First, Charley, CW, is alive and well."

"Alive? That's damnably good news."

"Yes. And guess where he turned up?"

"I can't imagine."

"Someone CW's cultivated since he heard the name from James Royce."

"Still not enlightened."

"Put on your damn thinking cap, man. Ernst Becker's spa, BergFalke!"

"CW is hiding at BergFalke? My, God. That's great. But my word, once Royce hears this it will certainly put his nose out of joint. You know, he really isn't a bad sort once you get past his defensive front. But I wouldn't tell him where CW is."

"Whatever, who cares about him. With CW confirmed we now have the upper hand."

"Before we discuss Royce, Miles, how did CW contact you? You're sure he's safe?"

"Yes, he's all right, and how we contacted him is my second piece of great news. I couldn't mention this on the phone because this is ULTRA, Top Secret. The new American Office of Strategic Services, the OSS, has developed the most marvelous piece of equipment for contacting agents in the field. It's called the J-E System* and their testing was done here in Bovington."

---

*The Joan-Eleanor (J-E) System was a high frequency system developed for agents to relay information while in enemy territory. Developed by DeWitt Goddard and Lt. Cmdr. Stephen Simpson, with contributions from mobile radio pioneer, Mr. Alfred J. Gross, it eventually superseded the previous, and greatly inferior, S-System.

German intelligence never looked for it, because they never knew it existed. The J-E System remained classified Top Secret until 1976.

The General continued. "The PM heard something about it, knew of our atom weapon operation, and worked it out with the OSS. They've a prototype, small hand-held transceiver for the agent, another transceiver in a plane. They dropped one to CW."

"Can't the enemy overhear with their listening devices and trace it like all the others?"

"That's the beauty of it. You know the Americans, if something can't be done they simply ignore that fact and do it. They explained it by speaking some foreign language about dual triodes, super-regenerative detectors and toss in some super heterodyne mishmash or other, and expect you to fathom it."

Tomlinson laughed. "And of course you nodded sagely."

"Damn right I did, for all the good it did. Saw right through me. Blast them."

* * *

17 April, 1940
General Alcott was ready, impatient for Royce's arrival. He had listened to Tomlinson describe Royce as more intense than difficult, so Alcott had decided to be pragmatic. He would start as being reasonable. Still, he was ready to pounce if, as he expected, the conversation became challenging. He had the card to play.

It was the J-E System that gave Alcott the card. By being able to contact his agent and most importantly, CW, Alcott had all the information needed to confront Royce.

An extended-range bomber had left on its nine-hundred mile round trip from an airfield south of Lyon, France, flew at thirty-thousand feet over Switzerland and deep into Austria. There, at night, the aircraft reduced altitude and began great concentric sweeps, passing over areas of Salzburg, Kufstein and Ernst Becker's BergFalke Spa. The crew of the aircraft included a J-E operator utilizing the UHF bands, which could not be effectively monitored by the enemy. The second key to the System was the low output power and its limited range, making the transmissions virtually undetectable. The effect was similar to a vertical tube with no extraneous sound emanating from it.

As there were no longer German Officers at the spa due to the war, the J-E operator in the aircraft and Charles Wentworth, at BergFalke, spoke directly to each other with no interference or code. General Alcott knew everything that happened at the spa and that included the information that Royce had stayed there during the time he found the castle.

The pieces were in place. Now, all Alcott had to do was guide an inflexible James Royce.

Chapter 36

ROYCE HAD NOT MET three of the men present at his meeting with General Alcott and Brigadier Tomlinson. The introductions were cordial as was the conversation, at first.

"Mr. James Royce, let me introduce, Colonel Donovan, US OSS Intelligence, Mr. Samuel Hoare, from the War Cabinet, and Mr. William Stephenson, OB, MC, DFC."

Royce was attentive. He had not expected these upper-echelon men. General Alcott had made the impression he desired. Brigadier Tomlinson showed everyone to their seats, where they managed to ignore Royce's scar and hand.

General Alcott strode to the front. "Gentlemen, with the exception of Mr. Royce, all of you have received my memo, which concerned the present dilemma and its possible solution. To refresh your memories, not that it is required, but to also introduce Mr. Royce to the crisis we are facing, let me reiterate and add to the facts, as we received them. The Germans are presently attempting to develop a super weapon, an atomic bomb. A bomb, which could make all England's weapons worthless."

Royce leaned forward. Alcott's statement had the desired effect. "That a weapon of this magnitude is possible is confirmed by Dr. Albert Einstein's letter to President Roosevelt, warning of such a possibility and stating outright that he would recommend the United States begin development of such a bomb."

The men stared raptly at the General. This was indeed Top Secret intelligence. They wondered why an outsider should learn of this, all of this.

"That is correct, gentlemen. This is the seriousness of the situation. Our agents in Germany and Austria, the few we have left, found the Germans have over forty fusion physicists and their assistants, hidden away. They are working secretly and feverishly on this bomb's development. The main group, some twenty of them, we've found tucked away in an isolated castle in Austria."

Alcott watched Royce's eyes narrow, yet before he could focus his thoughts, the General continued. "The castle is called Steinvorhangburg, Stone Curtain Mountain. Mr. Royce, I believe you're familiar with it, aren't you?"

Royce fell back in his chair breathing deeply. Tightness compressed his chest. At this point, the General went from being conversational to combative and staggered Royce with his next remarks.

"And of all people, Mr. Royce, can you guess who is in charge of these physicists? You can't? You're speechless? Then I'll tell you. None other than your old *friend*, Dieter Schmid, Colonel Dieter Schmid. That's right, the father of Fritz Schmid, whom you killed, or caused to kill himself, whichever you choose. Because…really only you know the truth."

Royce tensed. The four youths, the contest, tragedies, and Schmid tore through his brain. Sheer reaction, devoid of thought, utterly overcame him. He rushed at his accuser. The fifty-five year old General was thrown backward into the chalkboard as Royce's fist caught his temple. The blow split Alcott's eyebrow and blood spattered his face. One of the men grabbed Royce's arm as he was about to swing again, another gripped and twisted his crippled hand. Gasping from pain, he dropped to his knees, his arm locked behind him. The sergeant rushed in, blackjack at the ready.

General Alcott held a handkerchief to his eye. "We won't need that, Sergeant, but thank you for the thought. Take this man to detention and don't do more than you need to make him go there and stay. That's an order."

General Alcott expressed his gratitude to those who came to his aid and ignored the suggestion he seek assistance and have the eye tended. "Nonsense, gentlemen. I took worse than this at Verdun. Of course, I'm considerably older now, that's why I was so slow to react. That and I didn't expect such a violent response when I goaded him. Yet as I think now, his past would indicate it.

Now, what I did was intentional and I want you all to know this. Royce is the key to eliminating the physicists at that castle. My agent hiding in spa said he learned Royce left on a climb from there and did not return for around three days. We believe that on that climb, Royce found the castle and a way to get close to it. All we have to do is get close, gentlemen. Royce, however, is an obstinate person, things have to be his way or he won't play the game. Many geniuses are that way and have to be put in their place. What I started with him, and will continue to do, is to find the way to get close to the castle."

Even the American, Colonel Donovan, known as 'Wild Bill' was puzzled. "In this case, don't you think a slightly softer approach might have been better, at least at first, General?"

Donovan saw Brigadier Tomlinson, who stood behind General Alcott, nod. Yet the General was adamant, "No, *Colonel*, I don't. I know how to bring misfits around. So, now you know the situation and what we're up against. Gentlemen, I'll keep you informed and I expect you to keep those few with 'need to know' updated. Good day."

Only then did the General, holding the handkerchief to his eye, go down to the dispensary. There, the medic saw him remove the cloth. "General, you've got quite a gash there, let me see to it."

"Yes. Walked into a door. Stupid of me. No need for you to bother. A bottle of Hydrogen Peroxide and one-inch tape will do for my needs."

Alcott took the supplies and went to a sink. He rinsed the inch long wound and dried it, then closed it with his fingers. He had the orderly cut four one inch long, quarter inch wide strips and, while holding the sides of the gash together to stop the bleeding, Alcott pulled each strip tightly over the wound.

The orderly winced. "I've never seen it done that way, Sir. We would have sutured it."

"It wasn't that deep, Corporal. We did it this way in France. Suturing leaves more of a scar."

"I'll certainly keep that in mind, Sir."

As the General left, the Corporal snapped him a salute, knowing the General was a tough old son of a bitch. Never so much as flinched all the while.

General Alcott walked with pain. When he fell back from the blow, his back struck the chalk holder fastened to the board. His lumbar throbbed, yet he'd be damned if he was going to let on. He hoped three or four aspirins with equal shots of whiskey would help tremendously with the ache.

The General was blind to the fact it would have been a simple matter to learn how Royce got close to the castle. All he had to do was ask David Royce, his wife, or Daphne Elliot—who ferried him to London and was Robert Elliot's sister. Royce had told all of them how he found the ledge. Miles Alcott, however, was so used to ordering people, it never occurred to him to ask.

With the Sergeant nearby, General Alcott stood in front of Royce once more.

"Well, Royce?"

"Alcott, if you expect me to apologize, you're mistaken. In front of those people you falsely accused me of killing someone. How would you have reacted? You intentionally got me angry. Why, I don't know. I reacted and you got what you deserved. What did you want to know? How to get near the castle? When I heard you say its importance, I would have you told right out. You're as phony as your dramatics."

The General was seething. "Then tell me, God damn it!"

Royce showed his disgust. "Perhaps I should wait until the others are brought back so you don't say you forced it out of me, but here's the answer. There's a ledge. Runs almost to the castle."

Alcott sat down, his back pained him. He was angry and felt stupid. He had mishandled Royce. Still, one way or the other, he had the key. "You know how to get there, don't you?"

"Not really."

"Now what's your game—'not really'?"

"General, in the mountains a person doesn't go anywhere in a straight line. Can you at least follow that? I was walking west by north, not going anywhere special. I stumbled on it. When I left the ledge I was totally unnerved because I had slipped off it and barely got back on. So by then I wasn't quite right in the head."

"Still, you started from BergFalke Spa, isn't that right?"

"How did you know that?"

"Charley Wentworth found out from your friend Becker. You had told us about him before and CW's there now. Think we can't figure it out from there?"

Anger welled again. "General, if you and that Wentworth guy think you're going to involve Beck in this, then I'll…"

"You'll nothing! And we'll involve anyone we want, you horse's arse. Hasn't the seriousness of this sunk in? "

"Serious or not, that's your business and your problem. I'm not going anywhere near that damned castle even if I knew how. Besides, what the hell could I do if I got there?"

Chapter 37

30 April 1940
KENNETH SOMMERS' sat impatiently at 11 Group's Headquarters in Middlesex and waited for Wing Commander Keith Park. Kenneth was of two minds. One, he looked forward to returning to his squadron. The other? He missed Daphne and must invent a way to obey her order—Find some time to get married.

Ushered into Park's office, he came to attention and saluted. The Wing Commander returned the salute and pointed to the person on the couch behind him, Air Marshal Hugh Dowding. Surprised, Kenneth turned on his heel and saluted the Air Marshal.

Formalities concluded, the three men took seats around a map table designating RAF airfields in France.

Air Marshal Dowding spoke first. "Kenneth, while you were away in Scotland training the Poles, we kept you in the dark about your Squadron activities. This was deliberate because your duties up there were of considerable value and we did not want you to worry over your squadron. Although there has been little ground activity, there has been some action over northern France. Your squadron has lost two pilots."

Keith Park handed the Air Marshal a folder. "Flight Sergeant Harry 'Nobby' Harvey and Pilot Officer Edward George."

Kenneth was restrained, inscrutable knowing nothing of the battles. He blinked twice. "Total losses, both sides, Sir?"

Keith Park cleared his throat. "Your squadron lost two aircraft, with another written off. Flight Sergeant Winslow is all right, but broke both legs landing after he bailed out."

Kenneth remained passive. He'd been kept in the dark. At least his wing man, Mackie was all right. "Enemy losses, Sir?"

Both men were disturbed by his reserve. "Four ME109s

destroyed, one probable and two Heinkel 111s. Better than other squadrons, but not good enough. Yet you must recognize we're up against seasoned enemy pilots from the battles in Poland and some from combat with pretty good Russian fighters in Spain."

'Yes Sir. Nevertheless, My pilots should be better."

Air Marshal Dowding was pensive. "See here, Sommers, while you were away, I've had all the Squadron Leaders, Group Captains and Wing Leaders here for a briefing about revising our strategy in France for the future. As you may not know, last month Prime Minister Daladier of France resigned over their Finnish-Russian war, mess. That leaves France in a muddle. We know the individual French pilots are brave. It's not for lack of verve, or élan, as they call it, but their individual fighting techniques in an inferior fighter will be the death of them. With us, and correct team tactics and experience, the Spitfire more than matches the ME109. We are now sure the Spitfire turns tighter at low altitudes and is faster in level flight—as you thought. The Hurricanes also turn tighter and are giving a good account of themselves."

Ken felt guilty enjoying life with Daphne while all this was going on. "Then what can we do, Sir, if our outfighting them isn't good enough?"

"Quite simply, it's the structure that isn't good enough. The French have no early warning system worthy of the name. That makes us scramble too late, lose the advantage of altitude. Add to that the estimated strength of the enemy, all aircraft, is well above ours and they have the advantage of surprise and experience. The RAF has only a total of twenty-five Spitfire Squadrons in all of England. And to judge by the few bomber sorties we've flown, without fighter escort, our Fairly Battles and Blenheim bombers will be nothing short of flying coffins against the ME109s."

Kenneth was perplexed. "What's wrong with fighter escort for the bombers, Air Marshal? Don't we have air coordination with the French?"

"The answer to that is no, Squadron Leader. And now, I'll preface my next remark with a caution that this is all under strictest secrecy. With that understood, my personal belief, and I believe Keith Park's also, is the French lost the war before it got truly started."

Kenneth leaned forward, eyes narrowing. "If that's true, then why are we there, Sir?"

"Mainly aiding an ally, Sommers. Although by the way it appears I believe it could cost us an army and an unacceptable percentage of our aircraft."

Wing Commander Park spoke. "The French have asked for ten squadrons of Spitfires. The Air Marshall, backed by Chief of the Air Staff Newall, is against sending additional Spitfires. It would strip England of her defenses should France falter, as we privately believe she will. We will send a further four or five squadrons of Hurricanes and that will be our air commitment."

Kenneth could not make sense of their comments. "Again, Sir, if I may be so bold, or perhaps ignorant of the decisions from on high, what is the reason for us fighting in France then?"

Hugh Dowding spoke up. "I know you don't think too much of the French Air Command, and justly so, but our reasons are twofold, Kenneth. One, politics. It wouldn't be cricket to bail out on an ally, at the start of a war, now would it? Two, of more importance, what we destroy of the enemy there we won't have striking us here. A man of your intellect should be able to see that without being told."

Kenneth was chastised. "I didn't think it forward, Sir. Sorry."

"Even you should eat a slice of humble pie at times, my lad."

Known for being serious, Hugh Dowding nevertheless smiled at his Squadron leader. "I've heard you speak at the RAF College, Sommers. You know what you're talking about and you keep the cadets paying attention and make sure they absorb it. You're really quite a good scholar, you know. And, as I think of it, I've also heard about a few of your other flying antics."

"Sir?"

"I've heard of a pilot having some sweet young thing in a Gladiator, flitting around the RAF College and over to see Wing Commander Gibson in Lincolnshire."

Kenneth was caught. "Yes, Sir."

He then remained mute. The Gladiator biplane. The Spitfire tour with Daphne hadn't reached Dowding—at least yet.

"Sommers, I knew your father in France during the other war, so all I can think is that his flying and wilder genes are in your blood, although you couldn't possibly match him. Despite that, I know something of the sort won't happen again. Understood?"

"It will not happen again, Sir. At least from *this* point forward. Yet, in my defense, it wasn't just any sweet young thing, and you know her. She's 11 Group's interpreter, Daphne Elliot. She's also the woman I want to marry as soon as possible."

"Of course. The beautiful woman with as unruly flying habits in a Spitfire as you do. So now we know you're the reason. You must have hidden talents, most certainly good taste. Did you know about this, Keith?"

"No, Sir. Although I must say, knowing how much they trained together, I'm not surprised and also pleased."

"Yes, Sommers, we're both pleased. Still, I must say it's a bloody chancy time to get married."

"Yes, Sir. I feel the same way. Although to be frank, she ordered me to find the time and I don't want to miss the chance."

Both men laughed. Air Marshal Dowding became serious.

"Yes, bloody chancy. However, back to the subject. All Hurricane squadrons have lost aircraft, but at least they've held their own or more. Your squadron of Spitfires is doing better. It's the French pilots who are being punished the hardest. Their problem is their aircraft are inferior to the German ME 109Bf, and worse, as I said, they fight individually. No sense of teamwork. French ground personnel and communication between the services is little to none. And we're paying for their failure as well. Yours is the only Spitfire squadron in France. We're not going to send more, that's certain. I'm going to be frank with you, Kenneth. We will not replace your losses in aircraft or pilots. My goal is for you, along with others, to prove our aerial tactics are better than the Germans' and will prove better than Wing Commander Leigh-Mallory's as yet untested Big Wing concept. But remember, we *will not* send more Spitfire Squadrons or replace your aircraft."

"Sir. I'll do my best."

"I know you will. Go over as soon as you can. Prove the fundamentals of how to get at their bombers. Their fighters are one thing, yet despite them, it's the bombers we must get through to and learn how to kill. When it's feasible I'll pull your squadron back. Bye the bye, one last item. Your wingman, MacHalpen has requested we hold his promotion. He wants to stay with the Squadron. Loyalty to you, I assume. Oh, and I'll see to it the latest model Spitfire II is waiting for you at Biggin Hill. It has the

Merlin XII engine, 110 more HP, domed canopy, three-blade airscrew, and other touches you'll like. Call it a pre-wedding gift from 11 Group."

After Kenneth left for the drive to Biggin Hill, Air Marshal Hugh Dowding stayed a while longer with his 11 Group Wing Commander. "Well, Keith, you know him, what's your take?"

"Well, for one thing, Hugh, Sommers is hard to read. He hardly blinked when you told him two of his pilots were lost. Never even asked about his wingman. It's not that he doesn't care, he's simply a sphinx at times, or hides behind that persona."

"Yes, could be, yet that was an eye-opener. Still, his next questions were to assess the pro-cons of the combat. He doesn't miss a trick. However, I am concerned over his plan to get married. Not a good combination, combat and marriage. However, we want a fair evaluation of our tactics, Spitfire versus ME109 and their bombers. I believe he'll supply it."

"I think he *and* his pilots will supply it, Hugh. We expect this Squadron Leader to win against top Luftwaffe pilots and I don't doubt that. But what we have to know is if the pilot's he's training will win out."

"Yes, I suppose that's true. Still, one never can be sure of Sommers' actual backbone until pressure is applied."

"Sadly all too true, Sir. Yet I'm damn sure we'll soon learn about Sommers' backbone."

On his way to Biggin Hill, Kenneth's mind wasn't on his squadron. Daphne engulfed his thoughts as he followed the turns and roundabouts. He felt the word love left too much out. What could he add to it? Deep within his brain, there was magnetism impossible to define. An ache to be with her he couldn't describe. He was always an analytical person, able to rationalize every action he made, and yet his feelings for her were beyond any rationalization.

He laughed to himself and saw he wasn't clever enough by half to explain her or how he felt. He would simply have to accept the all-encompassing word, love. Well enough of that, back to work. Anger began to bubble to the surface. Anger and hurt and shame. His squadron had been in battle while he was in England.

Some of his pilots were dead and wounded while he gave them little thought. And his superiors never mentioned what was going on while he was in Scotland. Yet he should have taken it upon himself to find out. Let that be a painful—no, *shameful*—lesson for him.

Chapter 38

May, 1940 11 Group, France

"Ho, Mackie!" Kenneth Sommers slid off the wing of his Spitfire and into the arms of his wingman.

"How ye be, and your nice, sparkly, new bird, Kenny? We missed you dearly, we did."

"Been better than you, from what I've heard. And let me first tell you I'm ashamed I didn't know what was happening."

"Hell, Kenny, it was only three days past. Our wireless was down, so even Wing didn't know for a day."

"Still, I should have been on top of it."

"That's best dismissed over a shot or two, Laddy."

They retired to the squadron mess where the rest of his pilots gathered around, glad to have him back. After a couple of shots of scotch, Mackie still refused to accept that any apology was necessary. They heard an aircraft approaching and tensed until the recognized the crackling pops of a Spitfire engine backing down, followed by another.

"Evening patrol, Kenny. Two ships home again safe, thank Christ. That will be all for the night. Now we can rest comfortably behind our blackout curtains."

The two patrol pilots wandered in, bone weary. They hung their helmets on their hooks, then saw their Squadron Leader and stopped to welcome him. After a while, the pilots reluctantly drifted off, they knew their Leader and his wingman wanted to talk privately. Ken and Mackie moved out of earshot. Slouching on a worn davenport, Kenneth kicked off his boots.

"Well, Mackie, what have you got?"

"We're getting the bloody crap kicked out of us. They pay dearly, but, Christ, they've got more than we have up there and it's taken a toll on us."

"Doesn't take much to see that, Mackie. Give me a report."

"So far the Squadron's lost Nobby Harris, Eddy George, Paddy O'Brien…"

"Paddy? Damn, I didn't know that. When?"

"Yesterday. The two of us bounced three ME 109s. I put one down. I was on the tail of another bandit when I saw one of their pilots was really good. He snapped off a half roll and got the angle right on Paddy while he finished off the other 109. I shouted, but I was too late. One of those God damned 20mm shells caught his forward tank. The ship just blew apart, Kenny. I was so bloody shocked I lost my concentration and my second bandit escaped. The Hun who got Paddy and the one I missed flew toward their lines and that would sucker me by going into that—wicked heavy concentrations of antiaircraft over there. While we haven't even one bloody Bofor's AA to defend us."

"I know and blast it—Paddy was a good pilot. Fun chap to have around. Wild Irishman. Odd how some of them fight with us and some against us."

"I think he simply thought we were the lesser of the two evils, Kenny. Then again, he was an Orangeman."

"Northern or southern Ireland, he was a damn good man. Damn, Mackie. And I know Winslow's out with broken legs. So where are we with planes and pilots?"

"On line, six tired aircraft left, yours makes it seven. Pilots? Ten now, with you. They're worn, Kenny. Not worn out, but worn. Three, four, five scrambles a day, always combat, seven days a week."

"Can't do very much about that for now, Mackie. Other problems?"

"What you'd expect. No new aircraft, not enough replacement parts, not enough heavy equipment to replace them if we had them. No Bofors, too big a sector to cover, no help from the French Commanders or their Air Armee. The individual French pilots are brave, no doubt of that. They don't shy away from a fight. But that D500 is a mediocre fighter at best and they have even less support than we have. I feel damn bad for them."

"I can't apologize enough for not being here Mackie. You've done what you could with a bad operation. All right, enough for now. I understand. Let's hit the bunks. You and I will take dawn patrol and go hunting tomorrow. After I get the feel here, I'll speak to the men. Other than air patrol, have them stand down tomorrow unless there's an alarm. Then I'll review everything. That make sense to you, Mackie?"

"It does and it will be good to be on your wing again. Like old times in Egypt."

"Oh, one other thought, Mackie, I'm getting married. You're my best man so don't get hurt. That's an order."

* * *

Hans-Georg von Bauer, was proud of all he had accomplished in a few years. Glider expert, aeronautical engineer at twenty-three, and in 1935—when Hitler ignored the Versailles Treaty—von Bauer became a Luftwaffe pilot. Now, he had also become one of the youngest Oberstleutants, Lieutenant Colonels, in the German air force, the Jagfliegerverband, the Air Fighter Command.

He had the credentials. During the vicious Spanish Civil War, four swift Soviet Union Tupolev fighter-bombers fell to his Messerschmitt 109Bf. In Poland, he destroyed three PZL P.11 fighters. He wasn't proud of those kills. The Polish planes were outdated, high gull-winged aircraft, poorly armed with only two Vickers Machineguns. However, though helpless in the air, they could fire on German troops on the ground, so that left von Bauer no choice.

Now, on the western front, his sorties over French lines had brought down five French Dewoitine D500 fighter planes. Although better than the previous Polish planes and with good pilots, they were shattered with little effort by his ME 109s 20 mm nose cannon.

The aircraft he was gratified with defeating were two British Hawker Hurricanes. They required him to be focused, although he was confident he would win out. Von Bauer's last Hurricane kill managed to put twelve holes in his aircraft. At that time, as the Hurricane headed into a smoldering, black, death glide, von Bauer maneuvered next to it as the Hurricane pilot started to bail out. Von Bauer gave a thumb up to the shocked pilot, who in return tossed a hurried salute, before disappearing from sight.

4 May, 1940. 0600 hours
Von Bauer decided to broaden the intent of his orders. His Staffel, his hunting wing, was only recently posted at the German-French border across from the only known Spitfire Squadron in France. A successful squadron, he was reminded. Still, his orders were to be strictly defensive. Combat only if the English intrude on German airspace. He was to repair, re-equip and prepare. New fighter planes would arrive soon. No need to tell him the reason.

He shaved and glanced at his new Lt. Colonel's collar tabs. He thought how his Father, the Baron Ulrich Wilhelm von Bauer, a hero in the Great War, was wondrously proud of his only son. He will be prouder, Hans-Georg mused, when he got his fifteenth kill. Only one more and his Führer would put the Ritterkreuz, the Knight's Cross, around his neck and pin gold pilot's wings on his lapel. He would be what the British called a triple ace. After that would come the commendation from Reichsmarschall Hermann Göring, head of the Luftwaffe. Hans-Georg von Bauer did not like the porky, inane Göring, or Hitler for that matter. Still, no one dare disparage the Fatherland now. At least Hitler did that for the country. It compensated for his leader's other transgressions against people he didn't find suitable for the Third Reich. Hans-Georg, indifferent, decided he'd ignore that element.

Hans-Georg wanted his fifteenth victory to be a Spitfire. Then he would have bested all that Germany's enemies could put in the sky from Spain, to Poland to France.

After he washed, he wrestled into his flight suit and lounged into a tattered chair outside his billet until his wingman,

Hugo Brandt strolled up with his dog. "Hey, Hugo, you ready for us to get carelessly lost over the English side?"

* * *

5 May, 1940, 0630 hours
"All right Mackie, we've been flying patrol at ten thousand for twenty minutes. You said things begin to hot up before now. What's going on?"

"I'm surprised Kenny. They're late this morning. Strange, not complaining mind you. Anyway, how do you like that new bubble canopy?"

519

"Love it. Great visibility. I can see...hold on! Tally Ho, two bandits, Eleven o'clock. I'll break right, one will come after me. You know the drill."

"Ken! You don't want more altitude?"

"No, I've worked out something different."

"Hell of a time for practice."

Kenneth didn't answer. He threw the Spitfire into a half-roll and slid into a routine dive.

Von Bauer smiled. 'Wrong move my friend. I have the height and my 109 dives faster. You must be new. But so what? A Spitfire is a Spitfire'. He pushed the nose of his ME109 down, leaving Hugo to confront the other aircraft.

Von Bauer was gaining, then saw the Spitfire turn sharply right and questioned why—what the pilot was up to? He was either canny or stupid. Stay alert, he decided, don't be fooled, ease the dive; slip in behind him like a cat after a mouse.

His quarry kept in a tight right turn. The ME 109 tried to stay with him yet was slipping out of the rotation. Von Bauer promptly realized his opponent wasn't stupid. The 109 couldn't match the Spitfire at low altitude. Becoming perturbed, Von Bauer decided to veer off, climb and readjust. Knowing his 109 has a modest climb velocity compared to his prey, von Bauer decided to gain as much altitude he could while the Englishman was still turning. Then he would wait for his next gambit.

At full power, he held the Messerschmitt in a rising arc. For a few moments, von Bauer thought about his Father, and Göring and a gold Knight's Cross. Not in one of those moments, did he think the English fighter was no longer turning away to the right.

Once the German pilot turned up and off to the left, Kenneth knew his Spitfire couldn't be detected for a few precious seconds. He hauled the yoke over into the tightest left turn he could hold. Rivets strained and the thrust of the superchargers spooled to their peak made the G forces painful.

Still unseen, he came up under the ME109's unarmored pale blue belly at two hundred yards. His mind thought of nothing else. Kill it, kill it. He fired a one second burst, followed the incendiary tracers past their target and then thumbed the button again for a three second deflection shot. Oberstleutant Hans-Georg von Bauer saw the tracer too late and unwittingly flew his climbing fighter directly into the unseen torrent and couldn't, for an instant, understand the plane's shuddering. Scores of Browning machine gun projectiles ripped through the lower cowling, shredded the radiator, ruptured the oil pan, then hammered the engine, injectors and petrol lines and shattered the undercarriage. The instant Bauer knew what happened, his plane was dead. Devastated, without thought, he released his harness, struggling to open his canopy. It jammed. He couldn't roll the 109 over so he could drop out. Now, he saw his enemy, but the enemy wasn't finished. Transfixed, von Bauer watched the cowl in front of him blown into ragged pieces. The shells stalked him. Mouth open, the windscreen exploded, petrol burst, flames engulfed the cockpit.

"Dear Father help..."

Fifty-seven seconds had passed since Squadron Leader Sommers started his dive. As he banked away, the Messerschmitt became a fiery torch, tumbled and struck the ground.

Ken felt no elation, he had destroyed a machine. "Mackie, Mackie, where are you?"

No response. "Mackie! You all right?"

"More or less, Kenny. Can you see a trail of black smoke?" Kenneth cranked his head around, on the lookout for enemy fighters. Nothing, then saw the trail of smoke off to the south. "I see smoke, Mackie."

"I'm at the front of it, Laddy."

"Christ! Are you all right?"

"Aye, ships not though. Catch me up. I'm not too far from base. Don't think my wheels will lower."

"Bloody hell, Mackie, your port wing is a sieve. Is he around somewhere?" Kenneth scanned the sky again.

"Righto, he's around, scattered all around the ground, he is. Had a lucky shot with that damned 20 mm. My wheels down?"

"No, you'll have to belly in. Done that much?"

"Don't make me laugh, Kenny me lad."

"Just trying to lighten things up, mate. Sure you can do it?"

"Sure, top of the world. Like that Cagney chap in the movie."

"Sure, as he sat on that petrol tank while it blew up."

"Base coming up, Kenny, I'm ready."

"I'll call. We have a fire brigade?"

"Bit late to ask."

"Don't try to be funny, Mackie."

"Of course we have one, but I won't need it."

True to his word, Mackie glided, cut his power, petrol and ignition as the plane juddered, impacted, and slithered sideway to a stop. Kenneth breathed again as Mackie squeezed out of the ruined aircraft while a four door French Renault—the squadron's fire brigade—raced up. Two RAF pilots jumped out spraying the aircraft with extinguishers. Mackie was only slightly shaken up. Nevertheless, another Spitfire lost. The odds had grown worse, another aircraft turned into scrap.

They sat in the officer's mess with the ubiquitous scotches, "What happened, Mackie?"

"I'm not sure, Ken. We got in a tussle, he was good but he rolled the wrong way and I caught him inside his turn. The only thing I can think of is on the pass that finished him off, his plane must have jibbed as I flew by and he let loose with his cannon. For a moment, I thought there was another plane."

"Bad luck."

"I came up a cropper on that one, Kenny."

"Not totally, you put him down first."

"Aye, but we dinna can afford one for one. How did you do?"

"Too easy. Your man must have been the leader, because mine seemed a rank beginner. Went for the bait like he had something else on his mind."

"He dead?"

Kenneth nodded his head. "Made sure. I didn't know if we were over German territory and he didn't bail out. Couldn't risk his getting another chance to kill someone in my squadron."

Mackie stared at him oddly. "Did you plan to do that? Kill him I mean?"

"Mackie, he had ten or more kills plastered on his fuselage. That got my blood up. He didn't bail out, so I kept after him."

"Would you do that if he was in a parachute?"

"No. I did it because he was still in a machine that could kill me, exactly like the chap you just shot down almost did to you. They're not dead until they're dead, Mackie. My father taught me that and that's what I teach the pilots, you know that."

Mackie said no more. Kenneth was uncomfortable and didn't

like it. "Look, Mackie, you've learned this is a real bloody war. Somewhere along the way it isn't going to be gallant. Get used to that. If a person doesn't quit and bail, put him down."

* * *

May, 1940

"Ken! It's not a clear connection, speak slower." She was frustrated trying to hear.

"I said it's nice to hear your voice."

"Same here, Ken. You in the same place?"

"Yes. What've you been up to?"

"Ferrying planes, mostly your type, over to Croydon, High Wycombe. Other types to..."

"Don't say where, Daphne."

"Damn me. I'm stupid, sorry."

"Anyway, I hope they're keeping you busy, very busy."

"They are, believe me. How about you?"

"Bit busy, two encounters, things went my way. Other than that, quiet, too quiet if you know what I mean."

"I don't."

"You know, calm before the storm sort of thing."

"Is that how you feel, Ken, or other people?"

"Yes, those types. Don't ask too much."

"Damn, what are we going to do then?"

"Don't misunderstand what I'm saying, Daph, but we don't matter right now."

"This isn't much of a romance you're showing me."

"It will get better, trust me."

"It has to, can't get worse. I'm just ribbing you, Ken. I know what you mean about *we* right now. Understand I love you, and I'll wait, no matter how long. But you better take care over there. You get yourself hurt, you'll make me angry, and you know what I'm like when I get angry."

"I sure as hell do! I'll take care for you...for us."

Chapter 39

May 1940, Fall Gelb, Plan Yellow.
The attack on the western front.
The night of 9 May. German units invaded and occupied the quaint Grand Duchy of Luxembourg. From there the might of Germany's ground and air forces would rush west and engulf the neutral countries of Belgium and the Netherlands.

10 May
Prime Minister of England, Neville Chamberlain resigned after losing a vote of confidence in the House of Commons. Winston Spencer Churchill became Prime Minister of Great Britain.

The German invasion gathered an unstoppable momentum, paratroopers, the Luftwaffe and tanks paved the way. Capturing key strongholds, the spearhead forced an entry for German Army Group B to pour into the Low Countries and capture positions in eastern France. Although certain units of the allied armies fought bravely, German Panzer corps easily outflanked them and then neutralized the vaunted and highly costly line of underground Maginot forts. After that, the enemy raced, virtually unhindered, into France. Blitzkrieg entered the English lexis.

From the beginning, the Luftwaffe enjoyed air superiority. Hundreds of ME Bf109 fighters, Stuka dive bombers, Heinkel 111 and Dornier 17 twin engine bombers owned the skies. Half of Holland's one hundred-fifty combat plane air force was caught on the ground, the rest scattered. Front line squadrons of British Hurricanes bore the brunt of the seasoned German fighter pilots and though disrupted at first, and severely punished, the Hurricanes fought back and more than held their own. French Bombers were seldom committed, and the English Bristol

Blenheim and Fairly Battle bombers were decimated by the score. RAF Command in England sent seven additional squadrons of Hurricanes to France, yet the battle raged on. Stuka dive bombers blazed a path ahead of the panzers and infantry. The allied armies began to collapse in on themselves.

* * *

12 May, 1940

17 sorties in the past three days and it was their fifth sortie of this day. All that was left of Kenneth's squadron had degraded to four Spitfires. On this sortie, Ken and Mackie flew cover against a swarm of ME109s while his other two pilots shot down fleeing Stukas. Those fixed wheel aircraft, without fighter cover, were easy prey as they came out of a dive, despite a rear gunner.

Mackie and Ken had a good hunt through the day. In the five sorties, they destroyed three ME109 fighters with two damaged.

Ken sent off the two Spitfires assailing the Stukas, ordering them to base for refuel and rearmament. He and Mackie started clearing the battle zone when Kenneth caught sight of eight Kampfgeschwaders, flights, of nine Heinkel 111 bombers each, heading in the direction of Rotterdam.

"Ho, Mackie! Heinkels, queued up for us! Christ! I can't count how many. No fighters. Let's take them head on. Hit the gate, Mackie. Yank her up after your run, then hightail it out of here for home."

"Got you, Kenny. Tally Ho!"

Kenneth pushed the throttle to the gate; the superchargers screamed their songs at full boost as he brought the Spitfire ahead of the enemy aircraft. Until too late, the formation of Heinkels bore on their course oblivious of the two Spitfires coming straight at them. German front gunners were not prepared, relaxing, then abruptly shocked to see tracers hurtling directly at them, into their turrets and slash on and up into the pilot's raised cockpits. Kenneth's target shuddered and broke formation, sliding into a neighboring aircraft, before spinning out of control.

He continued straight along the trailing Heinkels and struck three more until his guns emptied. Then, he held full power and could hear his ship struck by shells that hounded him. He zigzagged, racing from the fray.

While the rest of German formation re-queued and resumed on their mission, Ken backed down from full throttle, turned from side to side and checked his rearview mirror. No other aircraft were in sight.

"Mackie, check in."

No response.

"Mackie, where in blazes are you? Respond."

Backing his speed down to 150 to save fuel, he bent the Spitfire into a one hundred-eighty degree turn, all the while trying to raise his wingman. The sky was empty. He saw two fires; one blew into a massive explosion. Bombs on one of the Heinkels, he guessed. He dropped lower. There were the crumpled remains of another Heinkel. Mackie got one too, yet there was no sight of his aircraft or parachute. Desperately low on fuel, Ken's only hope was that Mackie's transmitter had failed and he had headed for their base. Fragile hopes, he knew his wingman would never leave him.

While Ken's four aircraft were absent, enemy fighters and bombers devastated his airbase from the east and departed as quickly as they arrived. Ominous, grimy smoke partly obscured the landing area. No one responded to his transmitter. A quick scan showed Kenneth the disaster. Craters littered the grassy field, no Nissan huts were spared. The smoldering wreck of a Spitfire lay off by the trees. He was low on petrol, no choice other than land. There was hardly a line through the craters and, for once glad the Spitfire had a narrow landing carriage, he slipped through the cavities just as the Merlin exhaled its last breath.

Mackie wasn't there.

Kenneth dropped off the wing as Flight Officer Hastings and an armourer ran up. "Give it to me quick, Hastings."

He turned to the armourer. "Get my munitions loaded now. Where's the refueling tender?"

"Blown up, Sir, Corporal Archer with it."

Kenneth turned back to Flight Officer Hastings. "Get some petrol at the French base."

"They've only 87 Octane, Sir. Your new Spitfire takes 100. Not tuned for 87."

They could see their Squadron Leader was angry. "If you've a lorry left, God damn bloody it, send someone to get me petrol from one of the Hurricane bases!"

A driver rushed off in the remaining Squadron lorry while Kenneth again asked for the FO's report.

"Squadron Leader, our patrol plane, Flight Sergeant Perkins, never returned and we knew that your four aircraft were due so we were ready to refuel and rearm. We heard aircraft and when I looked up, there was combat at 12 to 15,000 feet. There were two spitfires and six Messerschmitt's. Our aircraft were shot down, Sir."

"Of course they were. Low on fuel, probably not any ammunition left. Get on with it."

Hasting's unraveled. "We were all outside, Sir! We had no warning! While we watched above, other ME's came across the field, strafing the hell out of us! We were being hit everywhere. Sandy Waters and Murph went down and our two reserve pilots were strafed as they tried to get that damaged fighter airborne."

Hastings wilted. "And then the bloody damned Stuka's came with their God damned…screaming bombs…screaming…"

Ken's time in the Spanish Civil War rushed back—the Legion Kondor's Heinkels bombing without interference. Yet, it was the Stuka's that instilled fear, a wrenching, mind shredding fear. Attached to their fixed landing gear, sirens screamed in their dives, shattering nerves and followed up by explosions. Trumpets of Jericho, they called the sirens, and if you were still alive, you trembled and waited for the next scream, the next bomb. Ken had been through it all. Hastings brought the memory back. It unnerved for an instant…then back to reality.

"All right, Hastings, let's get our wits together. There's things to be done. Where are the rest of the men?"

"They're in what's left of the Signals shack. They're rather shaken, Sir."

"They should be. Get them out here and we'll give them work. It's almost dark. We've got to get my ship into a revetment in the woods, checked out and loaded."

It took some goading, but once the ground crew began to move they fell back on their training, they aligned and pushed the Spitfire far into the dirt barricade. After this, he put them to work finding the missing men, some of whom, wounded, had run into the forest to escape the enemy aircraft, and died there. Three others of the crew were found dead in the bomb trenches. The British had no antiaircraft weapons. On this day alone, the Squadron lost seven ground crew and five pilots. Kenneth refused to include Mackie.

With all his men occupied, Kenneth had to relieve himself and seeing the latrine shattered, walked unsteady into the wood. Devastated, he leaned against a tree and lit a cigarette. His eyes watered. The facts engulfed him. This meant he had lost his entire squadron. Overall, fourteen Spitfires, seventeen pilots, and seven ground crew. True, Mackie's losses were in those numbers. Still, it was Kenneth's squadron and ultimately, his responsibility. He was filled with remorse...and guilt. Where had he gone wrong? His training, his tactics? They had failed. In less than thirty days, he had lost his squadron. Wing would be infuriated. And worse, twenty-four men were dead.

Forget Wing—*He* was infuriated. Nothing mattered now but *revenge*. The scene was identical to World War I movies he thrilled to as a child. Time to settle with the enemy. Kenneth planned that at the crack of dawn, with a full ship he would find the nearest German airfield and wreak havoc. His Father would do it! Honor demanded it! What would happen to him would happen. Daphne no longer mattered. Revenge for his men was obligatory. There was no other recourse, it had to be done.

He straightened up, his men expected it; then went back into the wreckage of his base. The men were grim. He mistook it for anger directed at him.

He called them to him. "Men, this is a disaster, I can think of no other word but they're going to pay and pay dearly..."

The feeble glow from blacked out headlights bore through the dusk. The crewmen barely made out the snap of a staff officer's standard on the front fender.

"Good God," one of his men stammered, "it's Air Vice-Marshal Playfair! He heads up the whole bloody Air Strike Force he does."

Kenneth quieted the man and brought everyone to attention.

Getting out of the car, The Vice-Marshal returned a salute.

"So, Squadron Leader, one of your men showed up at 73 Squadron while I was there. Told us what happened, wanted some 100 Octane petrol. For you, he said."

"Yes, Sir. I've one of the newer Spitfires and…"

"I know, I know all about it. German bombers, fighters, everything blown up. Can't help that, what's done is done. What's left of your Squadron?"

"Excepting the one you see burnt out over there, Sir, and mine in a revetment in the wood, I've lost every plane."

One of Kenneth's men couldn't be still. "And the Squadron Leader's is pretty well shot up too, it is…Sir."

Playfair glanced at the man, but said nothing. Seeing Flight Officer Hastings he asked. "You have the Squadron totals from this blasted wreckage?"

"Yes, Sir. First thing we recovered, Sir."

"Then get it and bring it to me, now."

As Hastings hurried off, Playfair dismissed the men. In the dim lights of the staff car, he contemplated his Squadron Leader. "Jesus, Sommers, what in bloody hell happened? Every aircraft except yours? Anyone mess up here?"

"No, Sir. No one here's to blame. I was with what was left of my squadron, out hunting. We have no early warning, no Bofors, and no fighter control station. We were ripe to be picked. I informed Wing of that previously. As far as losing the Squadron, Sir, that is my responsibility."

Playfair deliberated, then spoke. "Course it comes down to that. But, Ken, you're not the only Squadron Leader who's had to face up to this. You do, however, hold the distinction of being the only British squadron that's been bombed. As yet that is. The Germans already hate the Spitfire so much that may have played into their effort here. Keith Park told me he would not replace the aircraft you lost to attrition and that, in retrospect, sort of left you naked. To be frank, Kenneth, we're being overwhelmed…"

FO Hastings hurried up. "I've totaled the enemy losses, Sir. "Stuka 87b- 8 destroyed, Heinkel 111- 6, Dornier 17- 2, Messerschmitt 109- 8, Storch- 2. Total of twenty-seven, Sir."

"I can add, Hastings. That's twenty-*six*. These are definite, not probable, correct?"

"Yes, Sir. The squadron Leader is a stickler for that."

Playfair smiled at the word stickler. True, the Squadron Leader was a stickler.

"What's the score for today, Sommers?"

"Dailey and Gillis, shot down three Stuka's. Mackie had a 109 and a Heinkel. I two 109s and one Heinkel, Sir. Not adding a couple of probables."

The Vice-Marshal mulled over the numbers. "Thirty-four enemy aircraft. Except for the two Storch, all combat aircraft. That looks close to two and a half of the enemy for every Spitfire. That's pretty damn good, Squadron Leader. Better when you consider the conditions as well as some of your probables might be added as well. And better than the other Squadrons."

Kenneth was not mollified. "Sir, that's not just fourteen planes, that's seventeen pilots lost."

Playfair looked over to the Flight Officer. "Hastings, look to the men. Tell them to pack it up, I'm pulling them off the line. They're being ordered to Kenley."

With Hastings gone, Playfair addressed his officer. "Kenneth, the loss of your trained pilots is tragic, yet at the risk of sounding coldhearted, for the present the RAF has enough good men and pilots to train them. It's aircraft we can't get fast enough. Your odds, the number of our aircraft shot down versus the enemies' losses is what we need and more. I can see you're disheartened and you've probably planned to refit and get even tomorrow—don't bother to deny it, I would—but *you're* not. No dead heroes, you preach that, remember? It's not going to happen. You'll come with me to RAF Rouvres Headquarters and then over to 11 Group tomorrow for an Intelligence Summary."

Kenneth was tense. "Sir, what's left of this is my squadron. I'm responsible for it until relieved."

Playfair could see the tension rising. "Then consider yourself relieved. I'll see your men are well taken care of during the transfer. Your Father once told me about your family's fierce Viking ancestors, so don't think for one second I'll leave you here with that Spitfire. I'll have someone I trust fly it back. Now get your gear and say cheerio to your men. A lorry will come for them. And a second with petrol—and collect the...others."

"Sir, while I think of it, three of my pilots were American.

They damn well proved themselves."

"That's the kind of reports coming in on them. Same as the last war. We'll contact their next of kin and find where they want them buried. That's all I can promise."

Kenneth rummaged through the wreckage of the officer's hut, there was really nothing to take, nothing to show he'd ever been there. A sad observation, he thought.

He had to speak to his men. As he approached, they came to attention. Before he could say a word, Flight Officer Hastings stepped forward. "Sir, the crew knows what you're thinking and before you say anything we simply want to have you understand that we all would be proud to serve under you again...we truly would and with pride...Sir..."

Hastings voice broke, "and that you'll prove the best damn— sorry, Sir—the best Squadron Leader we'll ever serve under."

Kenneth fought his emotions. "Thank you, Hastings...and all of you. If there comes a time to be your leader again, I would consider it an honor."

He was humbled, not deserving. He came to attention and saluted them.

There was one final deed. "Sir, I believe this is yours."

Hastings handed him an officer's badge. Kenneth recognized it instantly; his father's Royal Flying Corp wings. "How on earth...?"

"I'm not sure I know, Sir. From what Mackie, Lieutenant MacHalpen told me, that is, he said a woman you are fond of mailed them to him and asked that he hide them somewhere in your aircraft. For luck, I believe, Sir. Only last night Mackie hid them in your cockpit and told me about them in case something happened...to him, Sir."

Closing his hand over the wings, Kenneth struggled with words. "Thank you, they were my father's in the Great War. Men, you more than did your duty to your country. And remember, Mackie's only missing, he'll show up in England someday. You just wait and see."

Chapter 40

May, 1940
THE DISASTER, which became known as the Battle of France erupted and raged on unabated. On paper, in men and equipment, the combatants were nominally equal. Yet in fact, it was superior equipment, training and tactics that ruled the battleground.

The three combat 'Os', Outmaneuvered, Outwitted and Outfought by two German Army Groups, soon threw the Allies back in total disarray.

13 May
Prime Minister Churchill of Great Britain delivered his famous speech: 'I have nothing to offer but blood, toil, tears and sweat...'

14 May
Preceded by area bombing from the Luftwaffe, three Panzer Corps of Group 'A' broke the Meuse River Line at Sedan. Breakthrough into the French interior was near. The consequence of an incomprehensible defense plan will lead to the eventual doom of free France.

15 May
Holland surrendered. Belgium fights tragically on. After five days of fierce aerial combat, the RAF had lost 205 bombers and fighters. The next day, only a pitiful six days after the German invasion, French Prime Minister Paul Reynaud, informed Churchill, "We have been defeated, we have lost the battle."

French General Gamelin, when responding to a question from Churchill said, 'We have inferiority of numbers, inferiority of equipment, inferiority of methods'. He, and France, had given up.

19 May
The RAF withdraws from Belgium, ahead of the Wehrmacht. British Hurricanes and Spitfires fly sorties into France and Belgium from southeastern England.

25 May
The seaports of Calais and Boulogne fall to the German onslaught. Four-hundred thousand Allied troops are encircled and squeezed into a small seaside port in the Nord-Pas-de-Calais Region of France. Reichsmarshall Herman Göring, Commander in Chief of the Luftwaffe—and, in the Great War, credited with twenty-two enemy aircraft destroyed—convinces Hitler that his Luftwaffe would obliterate the Allied army on the beaches. The German Panzers ground to a halt in front of Dunkerque.

* * *

26 May to 4 June, 1940. Operation **Dynamo**.
England is in haste. A sense of urgency permeates the people. The news from the continent is grave, yet there was one singular, one imperative course that must be undertaken above all else. Rescue the British Expeditionary Force from Dunkerque.

The Royal Navy organizes an armada of over two hundred light warships to rescue the surrounded allied troops. RN Reservists pilot a myriad of ships—small, citizen owned powerboats and commercial fishing boats with shallow drafts— to shuttle thousands of men from the Dunkerque beaches onto RN destroyers. Other RN ships fought through Stukas to reach breakwaters and board thousands more.

Air Vice-Marshal Keith Park, 11 Group, assigned sixteen squadrons for the task of protecting the beaches where the trapped men waited for deliverance by the strangest armada ever seen.

A main element of Operation Dynamo's plan called for 11 Group to intercept the Luftwaffe before its aircraft reached the beaches and Hurricane fighters were assigned to attack the German twin engine Heinkel and Dornier bombers and Stuka dive bombers, while Spitfires fought off the ME 109bf.

It was impossible for the British fighters to cordon off all enemy planes from the beachhead and many Stuka's and ME109s got through and ravage the men in the surf and small wooden boats. Yet the cockleshell craft and the Royal Navy, kept coming to pick up men wading out to them. Loaded to gunwales, the fragile boats ran the gauntlet to the warships waiting in deeper water. The soldier's cursed and asked where in hell was the RAF.

Squadron Leader Kenneth Sommers, now credited with twelve kills, and his rebuilt squadron were in the thick of it. With seventeen hours of daylight, the squadron flew five and six, two hour sorties a day from RAF Gravesend. Exhausted, the pilots had no time to think and fought purely on instinct, concerned only with their mission. Protect Dunkerque. Land from one sortie, petrol, munitions, starter trolley out of the way, takeoff, gain altitude to twenty thousand feet in the sixty mile flight past the beaches of Dunkerque.

The RAF tried to form a cordon to the landward of the village to protect the shore line, yet at times, the cordon was a sieve. It was impossible to bottle up the Luftwaffe completely.

With eight Spitfires left and his Squadron's fifth sortie of the day, once again the adrenalin escalated.

"There's the bombers! Now, where are the fighters? There! To the right, above them." Kenneth's voice calm. "Red Sector break left, get the bombers. Blue, Yellow, follow me. You know the drill. I'll take the red spinner. Tally Ho!"

The pilot in the ME109 with the red spinner sees Kenneth's Spitfire and breaks left. Kenneth, with the advantage of height, turns tighter inside to cut the 109 off. Two hundred yards, thumb the button. The enemy pilot jibes. Missed. Damn, get closer! Make him turn. Turn with him. Hold the turn, hold it, hold it, hold it! Stay with him. Christ! Watch your air speed. Guess his next move. Yes! That's it, Now! Thumb the button, three seconds. Got the bastard at the wing root with a full burst. He's spinning out of control. Break away, break away from him. Back down the power.

"Leader, Bandit on your tail!"

Quick look to the mirror. "See him Bertie!" Full power again. "I'll break left towards you. Sandwich him."

The trailing Spitfire slides into an oblique angle behind the bandit and shreds his rudder. Now, quick check of the sky. Increase altitude to angels 14. Now circle. Another 109.

"I got one Leader! I got one...he's bailing out!"

534

"Good, stay alert, there's plenty more!"

Another voice. "Leader, Leader, I'm hit! I'm hit! Petrol's igniting."

Who's shouting? There! "You can't make the beach. Bail out! Pitch out *now*!"

"No! I'll be captured!"

"That's better than..." The Spitfire explodes.

"Christ! God damn it! I can never get over it. Damn it! Damn, Damn!"

Another Bandit coming in, no five. Flick the transmitter. "Five gatecrashers, Angels 13!"

"I've got the angle, Leader! I got him, I've—shit, I've overshot! The SOB's slipped me! Someone get the blighter off...!"

Sound through the earphones like stones on a steel roof. A scream. Nothing more.

Another one gone. Kenneth checked his timer. Twenty minutes over target, feels like two hours. Another 109 crosses right in front of him, only a hundred yards. He must be blind, kick the rudder, push the yoke, increase the power, press the button...got the bastard...right across the cockpit!

The enemy plane stalls, hangs for a moment, then gyrates down...pilot is already dead. There's no time for pity, even if...

"Okay Eleven Group. Get the devil out of here."

Below him, a squadron of Hurricanes has broken off its attack on the bombers. Two of the enemy had spun out of control, another fleeing, engine spewing acrid plumes.

English and German parachutes blossom in a charmingly cloudless sky. Wispy, white fighter contrails entwine to the north. Sun sparkling off pilots canopies. A delightful late spring day.

Wipe the sweat off. Have I breathed yet? Headed home again. I'm heading home, Daphne...heading home...

He checked the area. A lone bandit below him and ahead, slipping behind one of his squadron's aircraft. The ME109 pilot must be new, should know he can't catch a Spitfire at low level. After a quick check of the sky, Kenneth pushes into a shallow dive. The young pilot doesn't see him, he only notices he's foolishly flown over the channel and banks around to the east. Both Brit and German pilots fear the cold of the channel.

Couldn't be a better angle of attack. Never give anyone an

even break. He thrust the throttle forward. The German pilot sees him a moment later and pushes the nose over. Kenneth recognizes the pilot doesn't have enough altitude to outrun him in a dive and follows him down in a shallow dive. Wait, watch, he's got to break, but which way? Wait...wait...

Running out of air space the 109 finally breaks left and zigzags, fighting for elevation.

"Not the thing to do in a 109." Kenneth mutters. He eased the throttle, aligned his Giro and, with a deflection shot at one hundred-fifty yards, his incendiary tracers slashed the 109s cowl and on into the fuselage. A fuel tank ruptures despite the self-sealing coats. Flames erupt. Frantic, the pilot rolls the aircraft and drops out. Kenneth circles, watches the parachute burst open and drift toward the sea. He knows that it's a tossup whether a Kriegmarine E boat or the Brit Coastal Watch will pick him up. Or maybe no one. God...the channel's cold.

"But that's our channel," he asserts grimly, "you son of bitch's are going to find that out!"

Find the base, last one to land. Eight planes back. Four missing. He knows two went down, perhaps the others landed at Manston or Hawkinge.

More petrol, rearm. A bite on a sandwich. The open cockpit allows fresh air to dilute the petrol fumes. A minute to think. Daphne. He had seen her for only one hour since his return from France with the Air Vice-Marshal. She loves him, worries for him. She'd wait to get married until they found out about Mackie. Two days ago he watched her climb into a Hurricane for delivery to 12 Group. They tossed off salutes to each other...he could have cried. He worried...ached so much for her...God, protect her...

"Sir? You awake...Sir? I hear you got three 109s!"

Abruptly to the present. "Three? I doubt it...someone making up stories. How many I have, Sergeant?"

"Five airworthy. Includes yours, Sir. No reserves left."

Swallowing petrol and air, the Merlin III snarls to life. He signals to the remainder of his squadron. Five Spitfires turn into the wind. By midday...only three will turn into the wind.

* * *

The attack by the two German Army Groups had gone according to plan. So much so, that Hitler feared an impending reversal. So, when Air Commander Göring assured Hitler that the Luftwaffe could wipe out the Dunkerque pocket, Hitler ordered the ground attack there to halt. His army commanders were furious. The unplanned pause then became a blunder of epic proportions. The British commanders hoped 20,000 to 30,000 troops might be rescued. Instead—ultimately due to Göring's arrogance—the courage of civilians, the Royal Navy and Royal Air Force, and the heroic last stand of rearguard French Army units, 338,000 British, French and Belgian soldiers were rescued.

England celebrated. Prime Minister Churchill called it a 'miracle of deliverance'. Yet tempered the remark by gruffly reminding the people that, 'Wars are not won by evacuations'.

At the end of 4 June, 1940 the British costs of Dunkerque was summed. The BEF lost all their heavy artillery, tanks, armor and mobile transport in France. The Royal Navy lost two hundred and thirty-five ships of all types. The RAF lost one hundred and six aircraft. There were five thousand British dead. This total was for Dunkerque alone.

RAF losses in the Battle of France, excluding Dunkerque, totaled eight hundred and ninety-four aircraft.

Britain would soon stand alone. Churchill was defiant.

"We shall defend our island (It was rumored he whispered, 'God knows with what') whatever the cost may be...We shall never give up."

The Battle of France was over.

The Battle for Britain was soon to begin.

Chapter 41

7 June, 1940

WAITING FOR JAMES ROYCE to arrive, General Sir Miles Alcott relaxed, undisturbed. Finally, he held all the cards. In addition, with the information his agent Charles Wentworth had brought out of Austria, Alcott was sure on how to use those cards.

Royce tensed as he entered the room and saw Wentworth. Two SAS soldiers were ready to come forth, but the General waved them back and smiled at Royce.

"Welcome, Mr. Royce, nice to see you again. Come in, sit down over there."

The General was too cheery for Royce. Something's going on. Especially with that SOB Wentworth present. Be careful, Royce thought, as he nodded to the General.

Alcott continued. "You know Tomlinson, here, and I'm sure you remember CW."

Royce promptly ran out of patience. "Get on with it, General. Why am I down here again? I thought you'd seen enough of me the last time."

"I thought I did, too. Still, now that you've somewhat solved our problem of the castle, I felt we should let you in on it."

"You brought me down here to tell me that? And I'm supposed to be interested enough to ask how you've solved it?"

"Oh, I think you will be. Because with, or without you, CW here is going to find your ledge."

Royce couldn't help but smile. "Well, it's not going to be with me, so—have a death wish do you, Wentworth?"

CW leaned back. "I think whatever you can do, I can do."

Irritated with the smirk on CW's face, Royce was tempted to lunge at him. Yet something in their faces said there was more to the story.

"How much climbing have you done, Wentworth?"

"I did some when I was with Beck in Austria."

Royce frowned. "I've found when an engineer says he's done 'some' engineering, it means he doesn't have the foggiest about how to put two things together. It will be the same with you. Is it true you left Austria with your tail between your legs?"

Now CW was angry. General Alcott nodded for the two guards to stay alert. Yet before CW could get out his response, the General imposed. "Mr. Royce, it doesn't matter whether CW can climb or not, he'll have company."

"Who?" Royce was mystified. Who could possibly help?"

The General stood behind his desk. "Ernst Becker."

Royce started to rise, the guards came closer. Unexpectedly, he fell back into his chair and after a moment began to laugh. Slowly at first, then, the more he thought of the General's words and Ernst Becker, the louder he became.

Alcott's face turned color. He was being mocked. Royce was laughing at him. "What do you think is so blasted amusing, you son of a bitch?"

Royce ignored him and turned to Wentworth. "How much do you think Ernst Becker weighs, close to three hundred pounds?"

"He's a large man, could be, why?"

"Why, you cocky, stupid man? I'll tell you why. The ledge is barely eight inches wide! That's why I'm laughing. You're both bloody mad, and fools to boot."

General Alcott and CW grasped the picture. They never gave a thought to the width on the ledge. A three hundred pound man on an eight inch shelf, two hundred feet in the air, made their jaws go slack. Shocked, they fumbled for a retort. The General wouldn't believe him. "You're lying! You couldn't have made it along there yourself."

"Think whatever you want, General. But I'd bet that even with this crippled hand I could out climb anyone you or your secret agent here could come up with."

General Alcott took a gamble, and threw down his next card. "What you say doesn't mean a tinker's dam, Mr. Royce.

Becker is the only person who has a vague idea of where you went and he said he'd give it a go. We're not gambling with his life, it's you and your pigheadedness who's gambling."

Royce rose carefully, as not to cause the guards concern. He went to a window. The summer day was crisp, clean. His mood, melancholy. Deep inside he knew this would happen. It was destined, his fate. He knew Becker could try, but never make the castle. For some obscure, fey reason, its shadow fell across his life again. He had named that ledge after himself and now had no one else to blame. He hated the thought. That tiny fraction of his lifetime he wanted forever over, was not to be.

They had skillfully put the onus on him. Becker's life was in his hands. Once Ernst was named, Royce never questioned that he would try for the castle. Becker had saved him, now Royce felt obligated, to return his gratitude. His friend wouldn't have wished that. In fact, Royce would bet Ernst knew nothing of the scheme hatched by Wentworth. But he couldn't prove it.

General Alcott watched Royce at the window. He knew he had won. Royce would do it to avoid endangering his friend. No other reason. Still, that was good enough. Alcott was reflective. He would quite possibly send this man to his death, but that was nothing new for him. During the Great War, at Verdun, he had sent thousands of men to their deaths. All in vain. Royce's loss really mattered little, as long as it wasn't in vain.

Back at the table, Royce stared at the General. "What's your plan—or do you even have one?"

"We do. CW will explain it."

"It's not complicated, Royce. We get you in there, we go along the ledge with a weapon, shoot it a few times and get out. Piece of cake."

Royce became incensed again over Wentworth's flippant response. The General was quick to see it. "CW, I think you had better be more forthcoming. And I mean *now*."

CW wasn't repentant; still he was quick to obey.

"Yes, Sir. We have a low profile airbase south of Epinal, in France. From there we have an aircraft that few people know about called the Mosquito. It's a high speed..."

"I know all about it, worked on the motor and mounts."

CW was impressed. "Quite tidy, four nuts and bolts and off comes an engine, quite tidy indeed. But you probably don't know is she's faster than any fighter today, and agile. There are only a few prototypes built so far, but we've managed to secure two. Wish we had one when I managed to escape Austria."

Royce wanted to ask how he did, but felt it would all come out, so he waited. Though CW had sounded friendly and informative for a moment, Royce wasn't interested in his stories.

CW ignored the silence. "As I stated, we have a base at Epinal, we'll use it if the German's haven't overrun the region by the time it's a go for us. If they have, there's a small airfield at Ambri, in Switzerland that the Swiss will let us use, with a wink, that is. Whichever field, we'll go to twenty thousand feet, straight over Switzerland and into Austria. If we use the French field, the Swiss probably won't even know we flew over them, and from what my agents had seen, so far there's no radar in Austria and few people or military around to report us. By that I mean nearly all the German military is in France grinding us down."

"Where do you land? Or do you plan that I'm going to parachute in? If you do, you've another think coming."

"No, we land, and that's the beauty of it. The Armistice after the Great War restricted the Germans from having an air force. To get around this they had the Flieger Hitler Jugand. That means Flyer, Hitler Youth, to teach glider flying as a sport. Those clubs and glider pilots, I might add, formed the basis of what we know today as the Luftwaffe. Anyway, a mile below BergFalke is one of those old, abandoned glider fields. The fields were made longer as it took a greater length for a plane to get a glider off the ground, and that's exactly what we need. It was overgrown, but no real problem. Becker mows it now, makes it look as though it's always hayed. And, if you remember, other than BergFalke, there are no houses until far down the valley."

"All right, we get in there, then what?"

"We get up to BergFalke, you see Becker, then we pack and head for the castle…"

"*We* go nowhere, Wentworth. From the spa, I go alone."

General Alcott interrupted. "Look, Royce, that can be decided some other time. Right now, listen to the plan. Minor matters can come later."

"This isn't minor, General, but I'll let it pass, for now." Wentworth seemed strangely detached. "Royce, I don't give a sweet fig if I go. The point is someone has to carry the gear required for the climb plus the rifle, ammunition and grenades."

"What is this rifle and grenades, and what do I do with them?"

Wentworth was in his element. "To answer the first part of your question, the rifle is a standard Lee-Enfield, Number 4, Mark 1. I won't get into the specifics because we're not far enough into this operation to decide whether we'll use a number 36 Mills Bomb or a Mark 1 Rifle Grenade. I considered using a basic two inch mortar, but now, if that ledge is as narrow as you say, then it can't be mounted firmly."

Royce mulled over what he knew so far of the plan.

"So tell me, what am I to do with this rifle? Bomb the castle into rubble?"

Wentworth expected the question. "No, all you have to do is drop two or three grenades into an open semicircle about forty-five by thirty feet. It will be approximately seventy to one hundred yards away."

"How do you know all this?"

"When I trailed German vehicles to the castle, I took photos of it with a 500 mm Zeiss lens from across the valley. Then, after you said there was a ledge, we enlarged the negative umpteen times into a positive with high contrast film. By doing this, we were able to see the faintest trace of your ledge. Barely a hairline, but enough. It also appears that the wall goes off in a concave curve behind the castle but the ledge ends at the bend. Once we judged the scale, we could estimate how high above and away you were from the rear terrace. That's all we had to know."

"How could you see the terrace?"

"We saw most of it from your photo and scaled up the area."

Royce saw that Wentworth, or someone, had done their sums. "Why is the terrace so damn important?"

"The terrace is the key to the operation. Sundays, in good weather, all the physicists and their assistants have breakfast out there along with minor entertainment. I might add, your friend, Colonel Schmid is usually there."

Royce tensed. It all unfolded. So, that was it. Liquidate the physicists. Physicists developing this bomb. British grenades drop on them, end of program. The plan was elegant in its simplicity. He would stand on the ledge—he knew he would have to tie himself very tightly to those pitons again—and lob grenades onto the terrace. And fate's joke? Colonel Schmid. It had come full circle. All else was superfluous. There was really no need to question or give it further thought.

"When?"

General Alcott was pleased. Royce had been curbed.

"It's now 7 June. We have to carry it off no later than the end of July, beginning of August. We can't trust the weather after that. So, my timetable is for you to have two weeks to do what you must in Coventry, settle your affairs…"

Royce was amused "Not a subtle way to put it."

"Only a precaution, Mr. Royce. We do that with all our agents. CW's been through it more than once. Now, after that, we'll have you get back in shape at the STS, the Special Training School up near Lochaber in Scotland…"

Royce interjected again. "I can do that myself."

The General was irritated by the interruption. "Damn it, let me finish. You'll need some help with that hand, you've apparently not done so yourself and you'll need the use of two of hands. Then, you'll train on the grenade rifle. After that, we should be ready. When our friends in the RAF and your Ernst Becker can coordinate, we insert you and CW."

The General paused a moment, Royce could see he was mulling something over. When he spoke again, he was cautious.

"Mr. Royce, I want to impress upon you the fact that it's not simply Becker you owe. You have a debt to several thousand others."

"Now what the hell are you on about?"

Alcott eyed the two guards, assuring they were alert.

"After the debacle of your hiking contest with those boys in Austria, and your ensuing struggle to escape from Colonel Schmid, your pursuers caught scores, no hundreds of Jews, Masons, homosexuals and priests—people who, up until then, had successfully hidden from the Nazis."

Royce rose. Every person's nerves on edge. "General, don't

say another word. If you do, you'll see me again someday."

The General shook off the undercurrent of the words, and nodded his head to the guards to let Royce leave.

Wentworth glared after him. "I'd take him quite seriously, General, if it were me."

"Yes, but that's all well and good isn't it? Then again, CW, I noticed you carefully omitted mentioning that wives and children will along the terrace. So might do well to take him seriously yourself. Although, perhaps he won't come back, don't you think? So why should we be concerned?"

Wentworth was left to deliberate…was that a recommendation?

* * *

The furious sea war continued unabated. For the month of May alone, 90 British, Allied and neutral ships were lost, mainly to the U-boats. The evacuation at Dunkerque had also cost the Royal Navy severe losses.

British fighter planes sustained a persistent battle in the air over France. In England, other than German bombers analytical probes to test the British air defenses and secure coordinates for the Luftwaffe, there was a respite. A needed breather—to prepare for the onslaught to follow.

14 June, 1940
German troops entered a marginally bombed Paris.

22 June, 1940
Defeated, France signs a devastating Armistice with Germany. Their war lasted a few days. Britain's war would last years.

Chapter 42

7 July, Sunday, 1940

THE WEDDING was private. The civil marriage was held at The Mount. Daphne and Kenneth decided it was improper, during wartime, to have a lavish affair. Another reason was that although no word of Flight Lieutenant John "Mackie" MacHalpen had been received, they both hoped he would somehow return. When that happened, and the war was won, there would be still another wedding, truly celebrated with extravagance.

For the service, Lady Jane and Mary Royce stood beside Daphne. An old friend, Flight Officer Bertram 'Bertie' Goodman, Kenneth's new wingman, stood in for Mackie. Minister and Lord Mitchell C. Conover performed the ceremony. Also present were Air Vice-Marshal Keith Park, two members of Kenneth's squadron who were briefly off duty, Chauncy Fellows from Supermarine, and members of The Mount's staff.

After the formalities and toasts the newlyweds mingled and Daphne had a chance to take Mary aside. "How are you, Mary? Come, sit with me, what's the latest at Ravensmoor?"

Mary lowered her head, appearing on the verge of tears.

"He's gone, Daphne, I don't know where. Something terrible is going to happen."

"What on earth are you saying? You mean *Jim's* gone? Where? What are you talking about?"

"I don't know where! Jimmy wouldn't tell me. He just said he had to help the country."

"That could mean anything, Mary, Jim's an engineer. Tell me exactly what transpired."

"He came back from London totally changed. Said he had to

go off and help the military. But he was so secretive, so vague. I don't know quite how to put it. He wasn't the same person. Then he kissed me and said not to worry, he'd be back. Yet it seemed so final. Then he handed me Scotty, said goodbye and a military vehicle picked him up at his cottage. I was so worried I even had the nerve to ask David if he could find out what was going on.

David knew nothing about it and thought Jimmy's leaving bizarre too. He needed him at the plant. All he learned was that Jimmy had talked with people at MI5 or MI6 and someone told David—in no uncertain terms mind you—that he was to cease asking questions. Can you imagine? David was furious! A person of his prominence, he said, told to shove off. But he obeyed, so it must have been someone well up in command who didn't give a tinker's dam what David thought."

"This is strange, Mary. If David couldn't…"

"Daphne, there's worse. My barrister, Brewster Hall called, asked what was going on. Said Jimmy sent him a letter leaving his entire estate to me! Mr. Hall wasn't right in telling me, but he's my barrister and friend. Jimmy didn't know that."

Daphne sunk back on the divan. "I'm dumbfounded, Mary. What in the devil is Jim up to? He wouldn't do that to be dramatic, he simply wouldn't. And if David can't find out, then it must be serious—possibly dangerous. I know how you feel about him, I'm afraid for you both."

Mary's hands covered her face, her next words came unexpectedly. "Jimmy and I are having an affair, Daphne. I don't know how it happened, it just did. We were both shocked, but we didn't regret it. We're in love. We were trying to think of what to do, to plan our future…it's the children we worry about. David would take them from me. And now this, whatever *this* is, has come between us. I'm at a loss at which way to turn."

"We're both at a loss. I'm as bewildered as you. I certainly don't know what to tell you. It sounds like all you can do is wait for Jim to come back. I can't think of anything else to do."

"That's what I thought also, but I wondered if he contacted you—said something."

"Me? No, I haven't spoken to him since the day before Christmas, outside Ravensmoor."

"Oh? I didn't know you spoke to him then."

"It was nothing, Mary. He was parked halfway up the drive. We talked, He asked if there was someone else. I said yes, at least I think I did. He blamed me for what went wrong and that was that. Off he went with Scotty."

Mary was obviously desperate. Dreams she harbored of a new life with Royce were dashed. "I'm sorry to have bothered you like this on your wedding day, Daphne. It was thoughtless of me, I'm just so upset…lost…"

"It's not a bother. My God, don't ever think that. Why don't you stay overnight and…"

"No, no, Daphne, don't be silly, I really must get back to Coventry. But again, I wish you the happiest of times and hope we'll always be friends, and forever."

"Thank you so much, and if I find anything, I'll be in touch."

For her own reasons, Mary omitted mentioning that Brewster Hall had also alluded to David's removing funds—amounting to three hundred thousand pounds—from James' account. After that information, Mary allowed Hall to privately hire a clerk to track those withdrawals. Jimmy had never mentioned he loaned David money. And if he didn't come back…?

After the guests left, Daphne apprised Kenneth and Lady Jane of what Mary had told her about Royce. Jane offered to contact people she knew in Government, but Kenneth advised against it.

"If there were some plot underway, poking at a hornet's nest wouldn't help."

"Then what should we do, Ken?"

"I hate to sound heartless but there's nothing we can do. And I've only two days leave. So, now we're off to the Cotswold's, there's a wonderful little village there called Castle Combe."

* * *

10 July, 1940

James Royce, ensconced at the Special Air Service training school for three weeks, had been too out of shape and too old for his instructors and it showed. Even the first day a two mile trot was a chore. Add was the agony of forcing his damaged fingers to squeeze a tennis ball found him incessantly gritting his teeth.

Regimental Captain Clyde Adams orders were to whip this civilian into shape in the shortest possible time and he took his orders seriously. The Captain wasn't brutal, yet there's a fine line between being a taskmaster, and cruelty.

At the end of the first two weeks, Royce had progressed to five miles at a steady jog while he gripped and re-gripped the tennis ball until there was little flexibility left in it. Still, his fingers did begin to bend, so Captain Adams supplied another ball.

Royce put up with it all. He knew it would come to an end only too soon. Unexpectedly, it seemed time was running short. The Captain's orders noted that his charge was once an excellent climber. As that would be required in the unspecified operation, the Captain was directed to find if Royce was still able to climb. Royce's fingers had been judged adequate for what Adams had in mind.

"Mr. Royce. A change for you. See that wee bit of a hill there? Go climb it."

"Wee bit you say, Captain?" Royce laughed. "More a fairly vertical pitch, don't you think?"

"Come now man. Here's a cute little alpenstock if you need help. I was told you could climb. It can't be more than three hundred feet. Want me to go to the top and drop down a line to help you up. Would that do? The Captain caught Royce's sly smile. "Why the smile, Mr. Royce?"

"Just a thought, Captain, but ah, forget it."

"Forget what? Don't be shy."

Royce sank the hook. "Really, forget it. I don't want you to look foolish in front of your men."

"Me look foolish? Oh now I see. You want a contest. Cocky are we? I gracefully accept your offer. And how about a tiny wager. What do you say?"

"I'll go along with that. I'll bet a hundred pounds to your shilling. But no gear."

Captain Adams was leery, yet he had to accept, the wager was too good. "Done, and the hundred goes into the Brigade Fund."

"You almost want to make me lose, Captain."

Royce walked to the base of their climb and stared at the cliff's challenging face. Time to end the chatter. A few of Captain Adams men kept a discrete distance. Wagers would have passed between them, but no one would take Royce, even with odds. Royce tossed aside the alpenstock.

Their ascent began. Despite the pained fingers his skills flowed back. He saw the line he wanted and methodically, effortlessly, glided along the seams and fissures that scarred the damp wall. The game was over in the first quarter hour. After half an hour, there wasn't even a pretense of a contest. The Captain had been outfoxed, although he took it well.

"In my life, I've never seen anyone put on a show like you just did, Mr. Royce. With that hand, how on earth do you do it?"

"I really don't know. Basically, my vision forms a path for my mind, and with years of experience I've learned to trust the image and developed a technique to follow it."

"Well, from my point, if your operation involves climbing—which I'm lead to believe it does—you'll have no problem. Still, I think there's more to it than that."

Royce was cryptic. "Yes, it's not the climb so much as the reason behind it."

At the Brigade Mess that night, Royce, by himself for a few minutes, watched Captain Adams mingle easily with his men. Off duty, he was first among equals. Royce had noticed it before. In return, his men idolized the Captain. Even now, when he'd been beaten in the climb, they listened quietly to every word he spoke. It was obvious they would never question his orders. Royce listened to their banter. "…how we stood at Sedan, Sir." Another spoke. "And the Kraut surrounded us yet you got us through…and then at Dunkirk…"

The Captain responded. "Yes, I guided you, but always remember, men, it was your spirit that carried us. They gave us a bloody nose. Never forget that. Next time our Brigade will crack their heads so hard their noses will be out of joint forever."

A raucous shout followed the Captain's words. Bunkum, Royce thought and shook his head. How do men, any men, he wondered, possess or earn such undying, blind faith…or is it love, from other men? Royce couldn't fathom how it occurred, yet he grasped one thing. He didn't envy the Captain, or want his burden.

Adams fell into a chair across from Royce and stretched across to touch his glass. "Once again, I applaud you, Mr. Royce."

He reached into his pocket and slid the shilling he'd lost

over the table. Royce pocketed it with an immodest thank you.

"It must be hard on you, Captain, I mean keeping these men together in high spirits, especially after Dunkirk."

"Hard, Mr. Royce? I suppose that's true in a way. Of course I would rather have peace in the world and be at Glen Eagles taking some whacks at that silly little ball. But I have my duty now. We all do, don't we? Just as you."

"Yes, yet there's a difference between us. I doubt you were conscripted into this—as I basically was—you're doing this voluntarily."

"Many feel the call without conscription, Mr. Royce, and quite a few do answer. Still, it's those few who can make the difference. Now to change the subject. It's obvious we can't teach you a thing in climbing and you're probably in shape enough to hike for a time. So, I've now been told to teach you the imprecise art of the grenade rifle. That will start tomorrow."

Tomorrow came all too soon for Royce. Still, in the classroom he paid close attention to the Captain.

"Before MI6 informed me about the confines of your operational theater, that is the location, a narrow ledge and the target, I thought to go with a two inch mortar. However, that's out now. It can't be hand held and fired, and the ledge doesn't sound wide enough to support it. So, I've had cobbled together what you see here. This is a standard Lee-Enfield, Number 4 Rifle and this foolish looking thing is a Number 68/HEAT or High Explosive Anti-Tank grenade. This combination is meant to be fired with a ground buttress, yet after consideration of the position you'll be in we've modified the setup. Because the 68 grenade must impact at close to five degrees center or it won't fire, we've changed the head to a convex dome so that at any frontward angle it hits, the grenade will explode."

Royce intruded into the presentation. "What is it packed with, high explosives?"

"Yes,the ones you'll use have high explosives and three hundred ball bearings."

Royce closed his eyes, confounded. For all his work with bearings, he never expected this use.

"If you're through with your rest, Mr. Royce, I'll continue. Usually we affix a cup to the rifle for the grenade but that can be a problem. Instead, we've fitted shafts to the grenades and this shaft obviously slides down the rifle barrel. Unfortunately, we can't fit a flash suppressor with this configuration. That means your foe may see the flash if you fire it at night. Sorry about that. However, we've lessened the powder charge in the blank cartridges to reduce recoil since you'll be firing from your shoulder and we don't want to cripple you."

"Thoughtful of you, Captain."

"Yes, isn't it. We've also mounted two small hydraulic pistons in a rubber cushioned butt on the stock to help absorb the kickback. Still, you must remember, keep the stock firm to your shoulder. We've tested it, Royce; we've done what we can."

Royce recognized the Captain was not the cause of the circumstance and was only trying to help.

"Yes, I can see that. What else?"

"These fins here give the grenade some stability in trajectory. But to be frank, not a hell of a lot. And the fixed shaft worsens the aerodynamics. You'll find that out when we go into the hills and recreate the distance and downward angle you'll face. The grenade has, what I facetiously call, a consistently erratic flight. Oh, and one more tiny point. This pin holds the striker. Remove it and the grenade is armed. So, with that, grab this satchel and we're off to the country."

Two days of trial and seemingly endless errors with dummy grenades finally paid off. Royce understood that between the questionable value of the sight, and the irregular flight of the grenade, deeming where the missile would land was subjective to guesswork. Adapting to that knowledge, his ranging skill improved to the point where Captain Adams felt there was nothing more to accomplish. He then passed that information on to GHQ.

At Mess, both men were strangely relaxed, Captain Adams particularly. "You know, Royce, when I received the order you would arrive and the type of training required, I sensed something amiss. Then you showed up with two 'escorts'. It was all too evident you were a special bloke, and your scar added to my interest. Still, after these few weeks, I find you became quite easy to read."

"Not to be rude, Captain, but I'm really not interested in the subject or your observations."

"Ah, but you see, you don't have a choice. I'm in charge."

"In that case, I'll go get another scotch. You?"

"Please. And be a good fellow will you? Don't wander off."

The comment amused Royce and he still smiled as he brought the drinks.

"So, Captain, my Captain, if you feel the necessity of all this, have at it."

"You're a loner."

Royce waited, nothing further was said. "That's it? No long, tedious insight? I'm quite upset with you."

Royce stood to leave.

"Sit back down, Royce. Mock if you like, but it is rather simple. I submit you're an unyielding outcast. Also definitely an angry outcast and perhaps even a lonely outcast. Still, one word encompasses it all— outcast. In addition, I'll tell you something even more enlightening. Once I saw there wasn't the slightest chance that I could beat you in our climb, I watched you. You didn't give a damn about the race or whether you won. It was written on your face. You were where you wanted to be— climbing alone. Why? The scar? Who knows? But that's you. My advice, for what's it's worth? Get back to where you want to be, outcast's don't survive in the real world."

Royce tried to give as good as he got. "And you, Captain? With that trace of Eton in your speech pattern, you want to be at that golf place. When do you think you'll see it again? Puts us in the same boat, don't you think?"

"No, because I'm not angry about it like you. I accept where I am and must be for the time being. You don't and that's the flaw in you. I truly hope it's not a fatal one."

Royce started to leave. Again the Captain stopped him. "I called London, told them you're a go. A plane will pick up you, and all the gear you need tomorrow, 0700. It will take you to RAF Boscombe Down. After that, I don't know. I'll say goodbye now, I'm off this evening to Glasgow for Brigade reassignment. I do wish you luck and remember what I said."

"And you'll go someplace you don't want to be either."

The officer started off, then returned. "One other little thing, Royce. Put that ring away. You catch it on something and you'll tear your finger off."

Royce studied the black star sapphire. "This ring goes where I go, and on my finger."

"Suit yourself. No surprise, I'll bet you never do accept advice and truly, it is your finger, to do with it as you wish."

Royce left after handing the Mess orderly a sealed envelope containing a check for one hundred pounds to the Brigade Fund.

Chapter 43

COLONEL SCHMID was at first startled and then alarmed the moment he stepped into Hitler's office. There, lounging in a chair in front of Hitler's desk was Reichsführer SS Heinrich Luitpold Himmler, the second most powerful man in Nazi Germany.

After the Colonel saluted, Hitler glanced up with a cold smile. "Stay at attention, Schmid. We have much to talk about. Heinrich, why don't you start?"

Himmler stared, savoring the moment, looking at Schmid coldly through round, thick, black rimmed glasses. His thin mustache twitched over a receding chin. His stare froze Schmid.

"So, Colonel Schmid, what stories do you have to tell our Führer today?"

"Stories, Herr Reichsführer? I don't follow what you mean. I've always tried…"

Hitler intruded. "Come now, Heinrich, you're not being fair."

Turning to Schmid, Hitler prolonged his gaze, which Schmid had to endure in silence.

"You see, Schmid, I have read your reports for quite some time now. Reports that state how your group has progressed, always researching new processes, always improvements."

Hitler stood, leaned over his desk, hands flat on the blotter, his voice rose. "But now I discover all that *is…not…true*! You've invented the whole thing! I've had other physicists reading your reports on your progress and they say you've found practically nothing, nothing, *nothing*!"

Schmid was panicky. "My Führer, that's not true! We've created…"

"Silence! *I* decide what is true or not! You've created nothing! Did you think I would let you play in your own fiefdom without a watchdog? Do you think I am a fool? Do you? You are a fool! A worthless, stupid fool! Heinrich has two of your so called physicists in detention right now. They've both admitted practically nothing has been developed. Nothing that we haven't done already! *You Lie. Lie. Lie!*"

Schmid was terrified. There was no way out. It was true. "If I had more time…"

Hitler was screaming, spitting out. "NO. NO. NO! You've had your time! Get out of my sight! Heinrich will tell you what you're to do. You are scum! A sneaking Jew! Get out of my sight, NOW!"

Reichsführer Himmler, now in his element, led Schmid past Hitler's cringing staff into another office.

"Stand at attention, Colonel! Now, what are we to do with you? You know I'm quite offended with you and your attempt to come between me and our Führer…"

"I didn't mean to do…"

"Don't interrupt me! I don't like that anymore than Adolf. Let me explain something to you, Schmid. Fate has given me the mantle, after my Führer of course, to cleanse the Germanic race, to bring it back to pure Aryan blood. Back, even before the Teutonic knights. Back before the Vikings. Back to the grandeur of our race and the glory of war. And you? You are nothing. A subhuman, a blight on our history—to be used and discarded.

Our Aryan race has a destiny. But your race is an ugly stain on the memory of that race. Look at you. Look at your nose, that nose and your dark eyes. Do you think we did not know your grandmother on your father's side was a Bernstein, a Jew? Your lies prove you haven't been purified of your abominable Jewish blood. You are fortunate your weak Jew son committed suicide so that he didn't see your shame."

"Please, Sir. My son was killed by an Englishman."

"Don't lie to me, Schmid. I found out the truth. You covered it up, but I found it. Only your son's fingerprints were on the gun! You knew that. Your son was weak and shot himself! To think you were an officer in the SchutzStaffel, makes me want to vomit. I should strip that uniform off your body and send you to a death camp. I do, however, still have a little use for you."

"Whatever you ask, Herr Reichsführer."

Himmler leered at him. "No, not what I ask. Whatever I order. You will return to the castle and act as if nothing is wrong.

That nothing has changed except to tell them the Führer is going to visit there sometime and you must get all information in order for him to see, no exceptions."

"The Führer is going to visit?"

"Of course not, you dull-witted buffoon! I simply want any bit of information that *may* be of some value organized. I believe in organization. When that is done, my SS will come in to interrogate and decide who is to be sent to the camps. That includes all the townspeople. I believe one of them supplied information to a British agent that the stupid Abwehr let slip through their fingers. The amusing thing is, he doesn't know what he found is only your hoax!

Anyway, do not change your agendas or let on what we have planned. You think you can grasp that, is it too much to follow?"

"No, Reichsführer Himmler, I will follow it to the letter. And Sir, may I…may I ask, what will become of me?"

"Ah yes, Schmid the *Jew*. What about you? I've given you a lot of thought and I will be fair. Once this subterfuge is over, you're to be reduced in rank to Lieutenant and put in charge of one of our Jew hunting battalions in Poland and after that, when the time comes, the same in Russia. You were good at digging out scum like you, at least. You will no longer be a member of the SS Adolf Hitler. You will no longer have the honor to wear the Death's Head insignia. Should you somehow redeem yourself, you will be removed from our death list. Yet don't ever forget you are a Jew—because we will not."

* * *

9 July, 1940
Twenty-nine days after the start of hostilities with Germany, the French National Assembly voted itself out of existence. Germany, with its puppet French government installed at Vichy, had conquered all France.

10 July, 1940. The commencement of Operation Sea Lion. The Battle of Britain.

Phase 1. The Germans knew that to have an amphibious invasion of England, they must have air superiority over the English Channel. To this end, beginning 10 July, units of Luftwaffe Air Fleet's twin engine bombers, Stuka dive bombers and ME109s of Luftflotte II & III began offensive probing by attacks on British shipping in the Channel. Other units of the Luftflotte were directed to destroy the British RDF masts and station houses as the German Command had finally deduced the RDF towers may have importance. The towers were a difficult target, yet constant bombing caused some to be severely damaged, although the system never stopped functioning.

From Norway down to the south coast of France, German air power accessed the landing zones in Britain. Reichsmarshall Göring pledged he would wipe out the Royal Air Force and secure air supremacy. The Germans goal was to relentlessly challenge the RAF's Air Defenses until they were devastated.

11 Group was the thorn in the enemy's path.

* * *

13 July 1940

"Kenneth-talk to me. Ken, are you okay? Ken, talk."

"I'm…okay, Bertie…hit…where are you?"

"On your port wing. Can you see me?

"Can't turn that way, shoulder…shrapnel, bleeding."

"Ken, I can see where the 20 mm hit just forward, below the cockpit. Ripper of a hole. How it didn't hit the forward petrol tank is beyond me. Shrapnel must have caught your shoulder. Do you have control?"

"Mostly…I think. I must have been…out a few seconds. That gatecrasher…sneaky bastard…jumped me when your guns jammed. My gauges…wrecked…my gauges…can't see well…canopy shattered… fragment hit me…where are we?"

"Just off the coast. West Malling. Think you can make it?

Ken's new wingman, and friend, Bertie Goodman, felt terrible. During the combat, there'd been little he could do, once his guns jammed. However, what he was able to do was protect his Leader's back by becoming a weaver, a lookout, and warn him of the additional German aircraft, known as gatecrashers. This he was late in doing.

He slipped his Spitfire under Kenneth's and came up on his starboard. "Ken, I'm sorry. I should have warned you…"

"Don't bother me with that…right now. My damage?"

"Your undercarriage is shot up. Do you think you can make it? Want to bail?"

"Don't have a choice…canopy won't open…flame?"

"No, nothing."

"Good…Damn it! Smell glycol…coolant jacket's been hit. What's my airspeed and altitude?"

"Airspeed, 150, altitude, 1,000. White smoke starting."

"I'll back her down to 110, bring me to…150 feet. Let me know…when…"

"Okay, Ken, we're past the towers, there's no balloon cables. You're two miles off the field. I've contacted them with our call sign so they won't mistake us. They say the strip is pretty bunged up with bomb craters. You're lucky to be landing on grass."

"Thanks for…good news."

"You're ordered to belly in, use the grass beside the strip so the rest of the squadron can dodge craters on their way in."

"I thought the same. While I think, Bertie…our guns…still harmonized too far out. Three hundred yards too much…no accuracy, get closer. Range them…one hundred…one fifty."

"For Christ's sake Leader, it's not the time to discuss this."

"It is…if something happens to me…you pass it along."

"Okay, I won't argue with you, but that might be too close for some of our boys. By the by, if you're interested, you got three of them."

"One of them…Stuka…sitting duck. Göring's…damn fool…to send them."

"He'll learn that someday, but right now they all count. Makes you a triple ace."

"What do you know…catching up to Father…I'm losing it, Bertie…line me up."

His Spitfire bellied in and slithered to a stop. Ken managed to force the canopy open and the harness undone as his rescuers arrived. They hosed down the aircraft, then unfastened his parachute. Helping him out, wads of gauze were pressed to his shoulder while they assisted him into an ambulance. Dodging craters, repair crews and landing aircraft, he was raced off to the field hospital.

After a shot of morphine and with the most serious wounds dressed by medical technicians, Kenneth was forwarded on to his base at Biggen Hill.

There, doctors evaluated the injuries. "Squadron Leader, you have lacerations of the major and transverse humeral ligaments."

"That's great, Doctor, I was afraid it was something serious and I'd have to stop flying."

A feeble attempt at humor by a drugged up patient left the doctor unimpressed. "If you think not flying for two months after we stitch you back together isn't serious, then well…knowing you, you'll be a bitch to live with."

After the doctors left, he lay back. The shock of being struck still bothered him. He should never have trusted Bertie. Mackie would have covered him, jammed guns or not.

A nurse intruded. "Mrs. Sommers is here to see you, Squadron Leader."

"Thank you, nurse, Have my Mother come in."

The nurse smiled when Kenneth out to the corridor. "Hello, Mother. I'm quite all right."

A female voice. "Don't call me mother, at least not yet."

A smile lit his face. "Oh, Christ, Daphne!" Tears welled. "Come here, it's so great to see you. I forgot for a moment there are two Mrs. Sommers now."

Daphne leaned over and kissed his lips. "See that you don't make that mistake again, I'm already mad at you as it is."

"What on earth…now what?"

"I told you I'd be angry if you got hurt. Look at yourself. All wrapped up, nicks all over your face. Looks like you had a really bad shaving day. Dear Squadron Leader, Sir."

She sat on the edge of the bed, held his hand. He closed his eyes. The drugs made him sleepy; he was fighting to stay awake.

"Thanks for coming, it means so much." His words started to become slurred.

"I had to come. It's for better or for worse now, remember?

559

"I don't have a choice any more. I could have been playing footsie with some suave American colonel in London, but... Hey, come on, Ken, I worked hard on these remarks. How about you stay awake for a few of them?"

He tried to sit up, fought off a haze in his mind and listened to her. He loved her voice—God, he loved to hear her tease him.

The cheeriness left her. "What happened, Ken? Don't tell me you've found a match for your talents up there."

He wrestled with his thoughts. "No, I got my man. There was other 109s...gate crasher...got me on my port..."

She thought there was more to the story, but he was fading and she didn't want to press him and went on to other subjects. She'd been busy ferrying planes, even co-piloted a four engine Lancaster bomber. His mother was coming tomorrow...

The same nurse escorted in another visitor, Air Vice-Marshal Keith Park. They chatted a bit about 11 Group, the increased enemy air assaults and quality of their aircraft. Intelligence estimated German air strength at twenty-five hundred aircraft. The British strength at six hundred.

Lastly and seemingly embarrassed, the Air Vice-Marshal asked Daphne if she could spare them a few minutes alone.

Park was direct. "All right, Ken, what happened? Your wingman, Bertie, asked to be reassigned."

Kenneth could feel his head start to nod. "I'm not...thinking too clearly, Keith, but...probably...the best."

"So, again, what happened?"

"His guns jammed...I ordered him to be...weaver...Um, he spent too much time...trying to clear guns...forgot us... needed...his eyes."

"One of them you?"

With the nod, Park confirmed his suspicions. Since he heard that Kenneth had, more or less, been shot down. His wingman's request for a transfer compounded those suspicions.

"So, Ken, where does he go? I can't palm him off on another front line squadron. What do you think of Training Command?"

"Good idea, Sir...Bertie's...good pilot. He'll make...good teacher."

"Then you definitely think it for the best? No regrets?"

The drugs began to fade. "Regrets? Yes, Keith…Though would have…more regrets if…if he stayed…other pilots must know…never trust him."

Ken took a painful breath. "Could happen again…one of my pilots could be injured…or worse. Germans give us…enough problems without…"

"Very well then. Now to you. Two weeks convalescence, no discussion. After that, back to Biggin Hill to be my advisor until you're bang on. Your squadron's depleted again. I'll rotate it to 14 Group, Inverness, for rest and re-equip. When you're cleared to fly, a day to loosen up, and you've your squadron back with full complement. Then once more into the breach, I fear."

"One thing, Sir. I must…talk to you about our…tactics."

"Right now?"

"No, Sir…I wouldn't make…enough sense."

The Air Vice-Marshal said goodbye and had a few words with Daphne in the corridor. When she returned, she was saddened at the news.

"I'm sorry about Bertie, Ken. I know you liked him."

She brightened for a moment. "I also knew you were too good to be shot down unless some freaky thing happened. The Air-Marshal also said you were brave to bring the ship back instead of bailing out like most pilots would."

Ken tried to laugh through the drugs. "Brave? I, I, I brought the ship back because…I was afraid…afraid to bail out. I even told Bertie my…canopy stuck…jammed."

"Ah, I see. To late I find the titanic ego has a flaw."

At last, they broke into smiles and then talked of their life together after the war was won. They'd travel, see the world, relax, get their own plane, maybe two. Perhaps start a small airline. Where? That didn't matter as long as they were together, pilot and copilot. Who would be pilot? They'd work that out.

"But remember," Daphne laughed, "I have the multiengine license. I'll have to have a ton of patience to train you."

"Speaking of wings, Daph…"

"Who was speaking of wings?"

"No one I guess…they came to mind."

He started to roll on his side, pain shot through his shoulder.

"Damn it, Ken! Typical man, doesn't think, won't ask. What is it you want? I'll get it."

"In the drawer...get them...please"

"What?" She pushed aside tissues, salve, bandages and found them. His father's wings.

"Thank you for having Mackie...hide them in my ship. I'm not ashamed to say I got...got choked up. It looks...I won't fly for...spell. You...you take them."

"All right, I will. But only while you're laid up, then you get them back."

"We'll talk about it...another time. I'm worn out, Daph. Hold my hand...will you?"

Without another word and shortly after, she felt his hold relax. She watched him sleep, listened to his breathing. Now he couldn't see her cry—yet again. Tears slipped down her cheeks. He was safe, thank God he was safe. For now at least. She spoke softly so he wouldn't waken. "I'm frightened, my dear husband. Please, don't...don't make me go on without you. Please, please...Oh, God...just the thought of..."

Chapter 44

27 July 1940.

TWO DE HAVILLAND .98 MOSQUITO AIRCRAFT stood poised at RAF Biggin Hill.

With difficulty, Kenneth Sommers, his left arm strapped to his chest, eased out of his vehicle and stood at a distance to admire the aircraft. Although he had heard of them, these 'Mossies' were the first he'd seen. The two Merlin engines packed 1290 horsepower each and made the aircraft— capable of over four hundred miles an hour in *level* flight—able to outrun any plane in the world. The fact she was essentially made of veneered plywood and completely unarmed, didn't bother the pilots. Her defenses were speed and maneuverability.

The two aircraft were cordoned off, so it didn't take much thought for anyone, Kenneth included, to recognize some unannounced intrigue was underway.

As he entered Wing Ops, he saw Air Vice-Marshal Keith Park and, angling his head toward the two aircraft, Kenneth couldn't help asking. "Some nefarious mischief afoot, Sir?"

"Imagine so, Ken. Haven't received information on her. Rumor has it the Guard's notorious Colonel Charley Wentworth is there with a new agent who'll be inserted in some enemy country. God knows where, the poor bastard."

Kenneth glanced out the window. "Well, all I can say is good luck…to that poor bastard."

The Air Vice-Marshal went over and stood beside Kenneth.

"Amen to that poor bastard. Still, they better get the hell out of here before some German pilot shows up and gets lucky."

"Sir, could we talk now?"

"Of course, come into my office and close the door."

Kenneth leaned over Park's desk and set down the RAF Manual of Air Tactics, 1938.

The Air Vice Marshal wasn't surprised. "I've heard some negative remarks regarding this from Mahan and Ungar, and now I have the feeling I'm about to get the full treatment."

Kenneth was disarmed. "Sir, Keith, the Air College is teaching our new pilots incorrect information on battle tactics."

"Specifics then. Give me specifics."

"One, they still teach that dogfighting is no longer practical because the modern plane is too fast. That is so outdated it is flat out wrong. We learned that quickly. Two, Air College tactics call for fighters to still fire at distances of three to four hundred yards and turn away from a bomber as they are too dangerous to close on. That's not true, Sir, and we've missed a lot of kills by not closing. It doesn't make sense. We've eight guns to a bomber who can bring only one gun to bear at any time. On top of that we're smaller and faster. And setting up fighter formations for attacks are useless, there's no time. The Manual should say use the sun if you can, otherwise attack at any angle and kill them!"

The Air Vice-Marshal nodded. He knew his Squadron Leader was right. *If* a pilot was good.

"Keith, the German fighters decimate our set formations, and these new kids can't keep to a battle plan even if it's simple. I have to correct their training every time I get new pilots."

"So? Other than complaining, what are you doing about it? As I recall, you, along with a few other top pilots, used to try teaching these tactics at the Air College."

"Yes, we did, Keith. But that was only now and then. We weren't on the college staff."

"Do you want to be on their staff ?"

Kenneth saw where his criticisms were leading him, and backtracked. "Not at all, Sir. I just wanted this information to be passed upstairs. That's all…"

Keith Park held up his hand for silence and leaned back.

"I've heard some of this, Ken and I'll make a deal with you. You get together with Ungar, Mahan, Boitel-Gill and a few of the other aces who gripe about this muddle—I know, in good faith—get it down on paper and I'll pass it on to Dowding. Then get packed. I'm going to get you to the Air College and don't worry, it will only be until that wing of yours is healed. Then you'll be back. We're going to need every ace we have when the eggs hit the pan. And worse, if you know what I mean."

* * *

Across the runway from Sommers and Keith Park, Charles Wentworth climbed through the fuselage hatch of the DH Mosquito and stowed the weapons Royce needed for the operation. After that, Royce handed in the gear he acquired for the climb. With their kit strapped down, the two men climbed back out and waited in silence for the four pilots to arrive.

"Royce," Wentworth began, to his remarkably benign accomplice, "these pilots don't know the operation, only their segment of it. For your benefit, I'll give you our flight plan."

Wentworth laid out a map on the hood of a lorry. "Because France has capitulated, we can't use the strip at Epinal, and the Swiss decided not to let us use Ambri. So it's roundabout we go. From here, our two aircraft will go to thirty thousand feet, south by southeast for just under a thousand miles. We'll have oxygen masks of course and fly straight across Normandy at over three hundred-seventy miles an hour. Then we'll throttle back to three hundred, go across the Bay of Biscay and northwest Spain into Portugal. Subject to headwinds, it will take us about three and a half hours. Portugal's neutral, but money gets us a strip to put down and petrol. We'll be safe as long as we stay away from the intrigues of Lisbon. From there—and this is the longest leg—it's thirteen hundred miles across Spain, over the Med, kiss the tip of Tunisia and reach Malta. That should take us four hours, give or take. Reports say there'll be moderate headwinds."

"Malta?" Royce was surprised. "You mean to tell me there's no shorter way?"

Wentworth shrugged his shoulders. "Sure, we could go directly and blindly across Germany into Austria and hope for the best or, we could set you ashore at Dunkirk and you could take a train across occupied France. Something like that could work. Yet somehow I don't think you'd make it, by your choice or not, I wouldn't be certain."

Royce walked away, fought his anger, taking deep breaths.

Wentworth smiled. The two flight crews, as they came up, were puzzled at the distance between the two men.

Royce returned, seemingly under control once more. He simply told Wentworth to get on with it and his tormentor ordered the pilots to prepare for takeoff. He then spoke quietly again to Royce. "We leave these crews at Malta and four new pilots and navigators who are familiar with where we're headed will take it from there."

Royce was doubtful. "I'm not the best in geography, but I know Malta is below Italy and Italy's not on our side, so, how do we get from Malta to Austria for Christ's sake?"

"Oh ye of little faith. If you'll stay calm this time, I'll explain it all to you slowly. Actually Malta is south of *Sicily* and with a new crew, we race—look here on the chart, where I'm pointing—we race across western Sicily, exit at Palermo, gain altitude north by west and head right up the middle of the Tyrrhenian sea to just west of Livorno, Italy. There we change course to the northeast, cross northern Italy and into Austria. With no known radar in Italy and a little luck, no one will even know we're there."

"Seems to me you depend on a lot of luck."

"Mr. Royce, I'm alive because of luck, probably you are too. I'm just hoping you don't ruin my run of it."

"All right, let's say it could work. What happens when we get to Austria?"

"That's too complicated to explain right now."

With that, Wentworth was about to give the signal to crank up the engines on both aircraft when a staff vehicle pulled to a stop. General Alcott stepped out, followed by two civilians.

Alcott was quick. "Colonel Wentworth, Mr. Royce. These two men have made this operation possible and wanted to meet you. Mr. Geoffrey de Havilland, owner of de Havilland Aircraft, and Mr. Eric Bishop, Chief Designer of the DH.98."

Royce and Colonel Wentworth nodded to the men as they shook hands.

"I simply want to say," Geoffrey de Havilland began in clipped English, "that when General Alcott asked us—on the quiet mind you—to supply two of the .98s on a rush, rush basis, even before we had acquired RAF approvals it was against my better judgment. However, when he vaguely described the circumstances, and his approval from 'On High', Eric and I relented. We have put into the plane revisions not yet fully tested, yet we believe them to be for the best. My only counsel is you might want to keep the airspeed a whisker under four hundred."

De Havilland continued. "Mr. Royce, I thank you for the work you did for us on these engines. I recall you got heat prostration working on them. Now I hear you are to embark on a mission that will take character, resolve and love of country. I'll say no more other than Godspeed. I pray you both return to receive the honors your country should bestow on you."

* * *

It all proceeded as Wentworth planned. The German army was yet to learn the value of air detection stations and none were in place along the French coastline. Aside from that failure, there were no German fighters that could catch the Mosquito, even if they knew about them.

The Mosquito aircraft, not designed for more than a pilot and navigator, had a carrying capacity of four thousand pounds, although little headroom. Because of this, both passengers were forced to sit or lie on jury-rigged cots. After landing at the hidden field in Portugal for petrol and a quick stretch, the two planes were soon airborne again.

During the long Portugal to Malta flight, the men came to an agreement. Far removed from camaraderie, there was at least the acknowledgement they needed each other if the operation was to succeed. Royce begrudgingly accepted Wentworth was a professional as he spoke of their last leg to Austria. He had a military expertise, yet couched to enable a civilian to understand.

"I lost contact with my last agent in central Austria a week ago. His report stated he knew of no German troop bases in the area west of Salzburg where we're to insert. Nonetheless, anything can happen in a week so essentially we're blind on the ground, except for Becker's immediate zone. With that said, we'll stay at Malta for a day and I want you to exercise and keep working those fingers. You're going to need them for the

Man on the Edge

climb and the weapons."

"I'll be ready; I know what's ahead of me."

"Good. Now, the area. Our pathfinder will take off an hour before us with a wireless operator copilot. They'll take the same course I showed you on the map, with the same airspeed that we'll hold. The pilots will check the zone for a fifty to sixty mile radius and if it's clear, he'll contact Becker through the JE unit and he'll..."

"JE...what? I thought the Germans could track wireless."

"I forgot you don't know about that. Trust me on this; we use a narrow beam radio transmission system the German's can't tap into because they don't know about it."

"Never heard of it, but you better be sure of that. If you're wrong, Beck is dead."

"Mr. Royce, if I'm wrong, we're all dead."

"I'm more concerned about Ernst Becker."

Wentworth shifted his position to give him time to rethink his accomplice. He wanted Royce concerned about Royce, no one else. A person who didn't care for his life was a liability. More so when it was your life at stake.

"You don't perchance have a death wish—do you?"

Royce had to laugh. "Why would you ask that?"

"When you think of someone else's life before your own, it makes me unsure of your worth."

"Then let me assure you, Wentworth, I have every reason for wanting to get home. If it wasn't for you and that blasted Alcott, I'd be with someone important to me this minute."

"Then good. Now let me finish. *If* Becker tells the pathfinder it's clear to land, they turn back and we should be in wireless contact with them somewhere north of Venezia, Italy. The pathfinder says go and returns to Malta. Now, Mr. Royce, this is where it gets critical. Our plan is to get in range of the sector at dusk, then line up and slip in. By that, I mean we have just enough power to glide in as noiselessly as possible with no lights."

"The pilot must be good, you think this will work?"

"The pilot's the best. Will it work? He flew in from Switzerland and got me out with a far worse aircraft than this one. That's how good he is. Regrettably, Switzerland's now out, so we do it this way. Now listen carefully, once we land we move like bats out of hell. I open the hatch, you jump out. And for Christ's sake don't twist an ankle! I'll throw out gear and the weapons then jump out behind them. We grab our gear and start running uphill to Becker's. You stay right on my heels. The pilot comes about and wind or no wind, takes off. That's when there's a hell of a racket from those engines and we've got to be gone."

Royce was overwhelmed. Great Jesus Christ, he thought, we're really about to do it! After all the fear I knew escaping from Austria, I'm headed back, back into the very hell I thought I'd fled forever. What in hell am I doing?

Wentworth saw the apprehension etched in Royce's face.

"Royce, remember it's on your shoulders now. The fate of your country. You've got to be strong…"

Royce brushed him off. "Don't feed me rubbish. Get me on the ground up there! That's all I need."

Malta, the rather small island in the Mediterranean Sea southwest of Sicily, had been coveted for its location and conquered by empires for centuries. Phoenicians, Greeks, Romans, the Knights of Malta and the French under Napoléon were among the dozen or more rulers until the British took overall control in 1814. Now, one hundred twenty-six years later, Malta was a bastion of the Royal Navy in the Med. And the Navy intended to hold it.

The two Mosquito aircraft landed. Crews and the two passengers managed jumped down to stretch cramped muscles in the sunlight. Wentworth gazed about while a Major came up to him and saluted. "Colonel Wentworth, on behalf of the Royal Navy, let me welcome to the Fortress Malta."

"Thank you, Major. Looks to me as though you've had a bit of commotion recently."

"Yes, Sir. The Ities fly out of Sicily most every day and drop a few expressions of their displeasure for our being here, then scurry back. Sometimes they drop their bombs in the ocean before they get here. They don't care for our reception committee."

Wentworth laughed. "Last I heard was you had only three Sea Gladiator biplanes."

"True, all too true. Although we did find four more crates with disassembled aircraft that we're rushing to assemble. The three we have airworthy are referred to as Faith, Hope and Charity. Although we do have good AA weaponry, Sir."

CW let out a belly laugh. "Good old F H and C, eh? Well, you've done a bang up job here, Major. And don't call me Sir every time. I'm in civvies. CW will do."

From some unexplained cause the Major laughed. "Okay, then CW. As you know, the Naval Air Arm is here. Malta's only one hundred-twenty square miles, omitting the smaller islands, but we're strategically placed on the Med's sea routes, so the enemy dislikes us. They're only toying with us at present, but I'm sure we'll get their full attention once they set their mind to it. Anyway, the wireless let us know you were on the way and you sure arrived in style. So, these must be the new plywood wonders we've heard rumors about."

"Rumors no more, Major. These are the first, and they're great. A little tail flutter at around 400 MPH, but I'm sure de Havilland will get it worked out on the quick."

"We certainly could use some here, CW."

"Well, straight out, at present they're designated for recon only so you won't get them. And England has first call when they come off the line. But, and you'll be glad to hear this, I'm told to tell you the first twelve Hurricanes of 261 Squadron will be in shortly on the carrier *Argus*. That should shake up the Ities when they come flying over one day."

"A carrier? Here? That makes my day, CW."

"Thought it might. Now, where's my new crew for the next leg of our trip?"

As they walked along, Royce felt the ultimate outsider. Wentworth hadn't bothered to introduce him to the Major, and, as he thought of it, the Major hadn't even said his own name or even glanced at him. Was it all part of this secret agent game? If it was, it was ridiculous on the face of it. So what? The only time he'd probably see this Major again was on their return. And that was a dicey issue to begin with.

Wentworth told Royce to go find some coffee or tea for himself in Ops while he and the Major talked.

The Major, as it turned out, was Branson Cole-Swindon, MI6 agent in charge of the Middle East Zone of agents. He had been detached from other duties for the duration of Operation

Harvest Time. General Alcott's latest sardonic code for the elimination of the physicists in Austria. Royce's castle came under Cole-Swindon's province.

Branson Cole-Swindon smiled. "Well, CW, I see you haven't lost a bit of your playacting since I saw you last."

"Comes natural to an old liar like me, Bran. Still, you matched me and didn't so much as blink. Although I saw your shifty-eyed look at my cohort's scar."

"That was difficult I'll admit. And this stuff about the pretense of not knowing who's who that the chief insists on when people are around is a bang-on pain in the arse."

"Granted, Bran, but if you didn't follow along you know I'd turn you in without a second thought."

"CW, every time we talk only confirms what I've always said of you, once a fatherless child, always a bastard."

CW smirked. "Thanks, keeps my reputation intact."

"So tell me, good friend, who's your unnamed partner?"

"Didn't General Alcott tell you?"

"Alcott? Of course! You've been flying and don't know. He's been given the sack."

"The General's gone? You can't be serious, mate."

"It's true. Churchill cashiered him last night. Had it in for the General since the Somme attack in '16. Winnie always blamed him for his part in costing England forty thousand dead. Named Brigadier Tomlinson for the interim."

"Well, Tomlinson's acceptable and the General was a loose cannon and damn vindictive. He was that way with the chap I have with me. As I think of it, I think Alcott's attitude rubbed off a bit on me."

"How so? You were always an independent SOB. Seldom right, but independent."

"May be, but as I recall, you were always ready to muck up alongside me."

Wentworth emptied a shot glass of whisky Bran offered and poured him a second. "Anyhow, this bloke I'm with is an odd duck. Name's Royce. Alcott had run-ins with him previously, before me, and indicated he was a genius of an engineer. Also that he was rich, selfish and indulged himself the last few years wandering around Austria, and did whatever he felt like while we worked our arses to the bone. In other words, Alcott said the bloke was worthless and I took it for gospel. He got in a jam over there in Austria and caused the death of a Nazi Major's son. It was this Becker fellow we're to meet, who got him out safe to Switzerland. Royce's escape caused the imprisonment of a lot of pour devils so, I admit, I played off Alcott's assessment of him. Shouldn't have done that, should've judged on my own. Although, as I say in my defense, he is an odd duck."

"Still, it does sound as if you've pretty much changed your mind though, CW."

"To some extent, yes. I had some words with him on the trip and watched him. He may be well off, yet he has no airs, and he's no coward, too much the opposite at times. And you know what they say about geniuses, there's only a fine line between that and insanity."

"You think he's over that line?"

"Definitely on it. Tipping over? Not sure. I do know there's darkness in his head, probably caused by that scar. Addled his brain along the way I should think. Where his demons will lead him, who the hell knows? But I kid you not, he's on the edge."

CW paused, puzzled. "Christ, odd I should use that word. Anyway, he's only doing this mission to stop Becker from giving it a try."

"Well, that's in his favor. Still, on the face of it, you don't give me a good feeling about this. Think he'll keep it together? You've got to be candid with me on this, CW. It's our necks."

"Let me put it to you this way, Bran. I can't tell you why we must get to that castle, but if I told you this could possibly be our best chance to save England, what would be your answer?"

"I'd say you were over the top. Well, tell me...aren't you?"

"You heard what I said. What would you say, go or no?"

"You're that serious?"

Wentworth nodded. Cole-Swindon turned away from the eyes that bore into him. CW was not given to hyperbole.

"First, tell me, CW, with all the confusion about Alcott given the sack. Do you think the Chief or even Tomlinson would continue the operation?"

"I do, but I won't take that chance and ask. Give me your answer, Bran. I need your nod on this."

Inside Cole-Swindon knew how he would respond. A deep breath. "Jesus Christ, CW...go."

The four pilots and navigators were well versed on the operation. Cole-Swindon wanted the aircraft off by dawn, before the Italian bombers morning visit as the planes were too valuable. That however, didn't fit the time frame CW needed for his dusk insert into Austria.

The Mosquitos were camouflaged. Cole-Swindon had complete charge of the base for the mission and ordered one Sea Gladiator into the air at first light, with the other two Gladiators at readiness on the tarmac. If it was heard Italian bombers approached, the two Gladiators were to scramble, the pilots to do whatever it took to stop the enemy aircraft. Bofor AA batteries ordered to throw everything into the air to drive off the intruders.

At 0930, Italy's Regia Aeronautica sent six Savoia-Marchetti bombers from Sicily. Malta's defenses sprang into action. Three bombs fell in the inner harbor, destroying seven fishing boats, more bombs fell outside the harbor and others dropped in the ocean. The Sea Gladiators shot down one bomber, another spewed smoke from an engine as all the bombers turned away.

Twice more, late morning and early afternoon, the activity was repeated. Bombers were spotted, British Gladiators and antiaircraft countered. Results of these attacks were two bombers damaged, one bomb hit directly on the fortress and other bombs damaged five houses along Grand Harbour. One Gladiator belly landed, the pilot survived and hours later, an enemy pilot and crew were fished from the water. The Med was warmer than the English channel, pilots could survive.

By midafternoon Wentworth laughingly told Cole-Swindon he had enough, it was too fearsome to stay longer. The Pathfinder Mosquito roared off for Austria.

An hour later Bran and CW embraced. "You're too old for running around behind enemy lines, CW. We're both too old."

"No doleful goodbyes, Bran. After three days, you just be sure a Mosquito's shows up there every day at 1700 to make contact. We'll be along, trust me."

"When haven't I, my friend?"

The two Merlin engines erupted, Royce was ordered through the hatch. CW was last in. He looked back, returned Cole-Swindon's salute, and slammed the hatch shut.

With air speed at three hundred, the Pathfinder, returning from its mission over Austria, was on time when it approached the other aircraft northeast of Venezia, Italy. The pathfinder signaled 'Go good luck', and the two aircraft passed and parted at a combined speed of seven hundred miles an hour.

Across the apex of the Italian boot, the twin engine Mosquito thundered into Austrian airspace at fifteen thousand feet before throttling back.

In the fading sunset, both the pilot and navigator became intense. There were the landmarks. Retard the throttles more, drop lower, slower, slower. Becker's excited words blurted out over the JE unit. "You coming over...right...*now*!"

The navigator, acting J-E operator, responded. "We see the spa and losing sunset. We clear?"

"Ja. Come, no wind. You see hay bales? They *start* runway."

"Goodo, mate. Our gear is down, we're nearly lined up."

Engines throttled to a low bark, the aircraft side slipped, aligned and glided onto the field. Little room for error. The plane braked, the two passengers felt the jounces from the uneven field as the aircraft lumbered to a stop.

The expected urgency began. CW threw the hatch open, Royce jumped, rolled and grabbed the weapons container as CW dropped the rest of the gear and followed.

CW shouted to the pilots. "Go, go, go! They're coming about, Royce. Look out for the tail swing!"

CW scrutinized up the plateau, then saw the signal, a faint glimmer up on the plateau. In a furious dash they crossed the field, the gear weighing heavily on them. The roar of the Merlin's ascent across the valley was deafening.

The uphill mile to the spa, most of it in the dark, exhausted them. Their lungs pained in the thinner mountain air when they fell through the doorway. Becker grabbed both the bags and pushed them aside. He picked Royce up bodily in a bear hug him. "Royce, my friend. You back. I knew I see you more."

Royce was breathless, and panted out an hello as best he could without retching. After a few moments, Becker let go of Royce and grabbed CW. "The other one, how you are?"

574

CW managed to gasp out he was a little the worse for wear before he fell into a chair.

Becker had drinks waiting, and when they had caught their breath, he asked CW. "I call now?"

CW nodded, Royce was confused. "Call who?"

Becker went to his old Telefunken wireless, threw two switches and started to speak in German. Royce heard the word Wehrmacht and looked alarmingly to CW, who in turn, started to laugh.

"Just hold your horses, Royce. Whisper. I guess it's not funny, I should have told you."

"Then tell me now before I shoot you both!"

CW continued to smile. "Look Royce, come in the other room and keep your voice down. This is a trick we worked up when I hid out here."

Becker could be faintly heard on the wireless, and he interspersed listening with: "Was sagen sie? Was?"

CW explained. "You see, Royce, when I was hiding here we were concerned that when the plane landed to pick me up, someone would report it. We figured Beck, as close as he is to the field, would be in trouble with the Nazis for not relaying the information. So, what we did one night was to have him call the Wehrmacht Headquarters at Salzburg and report he heard an airplane very close. Of course, there wasn't one. Well, I'll tell you, the Germans must have covered the distance in record time, and they checked the field and found nothing because there wasn't anything to be found. They thanked Beck for calling them, although he said they were irritated. Then, to add a little spice to the ruse, Beck had them believe he's a bit deaf. That's why, when he just called in, you hear him saying, 'Was sagen sie?' 'What are you saying, what?' In other words, he feigns he's deaf, so they start to wonder among themselves how in hell can he hear an airplane? He's hearing things."

Royce couldn't help smile. CW held up his hand. "Wait, hear the rest. The second time Beck called them, they didn't come until the next day and they didn't even check the field. The third and fourth times they didn't come at all. Now, follow this. When the plane *did* come in to pick me up, Beck called the

Wehrmacht and no one came then, either. And more importantly, they told him no one else down in the valley called in so he had to be hearing things."

Royce was fascinated. "In other words you took a page out of Aesop's, The Boy Who Cried Wolf'. He kept crying wolf so often, no one came when a wolf actually showed up."

"That's it in a nutshell, and as long as the Germans haven't read the same story, we're safe. Now, in the morning Beck will go down to the field, throw dirt over any oil from the engines and start to mow. If someone comes, it's just another day of Becker haying the field."

At this point, Becker shuffled in, appearing sad. "They not happy with old, deaf, Beck."

It broke the stress. There was laughter all around, laughter they all dearly needed.

Keeping an eye out for vehicle lights along the dirt road to the spa, they shared drinks and stories. Becker and CW listened to Royce's life after his escape from Austria, his engineering, the attempt on his life. He spoke haltingly of his decision to return to BergFalke because of the castle. Beck said the Nazis stayed at his spa in winter, but didn't bother him. Wentworth mentioned nothing of his life.

As Royce mentioned the ledge, it became obvious Becker didn't know the first thing about the plan. More clearly, Becker never said he would try to find and negotiate any ledge. Royce felt that was the story all along and remained silent.

CW closed the reunion. "Gentlemen, we're all tired, so this is the program. It's now 0200 Thursday, we must be in place at the castle by early Sunday morning. The problem is, with Royce so blasted vague about how long it will take him to find the damn ledge, we must leave no later than midmorning. In other words, time for some shut eye."

Becker had built a false wall in the shed behind the old Opel. Royce and CW stowed their gear and slipped into spare sleeping bags from the spa.

In the dark, CW spoke quietly. "You know I lied to you about Beck trying to reach the ledge."

"Yes."

"I did what I had to, to make you come."

"It doesn't matter. Fate dragged me here."

CW shrugged, he gave no truck to fate or the will of God.

"One more detail, Royce. Before we leave, you'll put on the battle uniform of a Sergeant in the 27th Royal Marines Commando. You'll have the device of the 27th, but no other identification on you. That way, if you're captured there's a chance you won't be shot as a spy. At least not immediately."

CW couldn't help but chuckle at his own humor.

"I'm comforted to hear that. And what about you? Will you be dressed as a Field Marshal?"

"No, no uniform for me."

"Why not?

Wentworth didn't answer. Royce insisted. "Tell me. Why no uniform?"

"If you must know, the bad guys know me."

Chapter 45

IT WASN'T GOODBYE. Becker insisted on that. See you both in a few days he said, as the men strode off across the escarpment. At ten in the morning, after mowing part of the field, Becker went to his telescope to watch them ascend. He smiled, pleased. No Nazis had arrived after his wireless call.

This Wentworth fellow is shrewd, Becker thought, to think of how to outfox them. Shrewd yes, but something threatened behind his eyes. It was apparent Royce felt the same.

Becker was no fool. It didn't take him long to perceive there was no love lost between the two men. What was it, he wondered. Clearly they were poles apart. From the moment Wentworth initially showed up at the spa weeks ago, he was unduly confident, despite his dire situation. Being hunted by the Abwehr should have been frightening. Yet Wentworth wasn't frightened. He was convincing when he used Royce's name as if they were friends. Because of that, Becker hid him.

Becker didn't regret his help. Still, when he observed Royce, his behavior towards Wentworth was reserved, conversations short. But they were together on this mission. Strange bedfellows. It definitely had to be a serious matter to put them together, although they never said what they were up to at the castle.

Becker, however, felt he knew Royce's intellect well enough to feel he would not go against his principles. They were going to try and rescue some poor soul from the SS, Becker presumed. Most likely a friend of Wentworth's or the English is a prisoner in that castle and Royce is the only one who knows how to find it and get the man out. That must be it. Becker was comfortable with the thought.

* * *

They traveled only a mile when Royce made his move. He did not want Wentworth with him and when Wentworth stopped to wipe off perspiration his attention lagged, Royce swung his rifle butt into the man's knee. Wentworth collapsed onto the stone ejecting a string of blasphemies. Royce was shocked at how quickly an automatic weapon was in his companion's hand.

"You son of a bitch, Royce! I should kill you right now."

After regaining his composure regarding the pistol still pointed at his chest, Royce bared a crooked smile.

"Ah, but you can't, can you? At least not yet. You need me to do my job and keep your repute intact, don't you?"

Wentworth heaved to his feet. The knee barely supported him. He knew he was beaten and put the Beretta away.

"Why, why'd you do that?"

"I told you from the start, I would go alone. You wouldn't agree and I decided not to argue."

"Think, you asinine bastard, how in hell are you going to carry all this stuff?"

Royce emptied the two packs. He repacked one with the five rifle grenades, and then placed in a clip of blank cartridges, a coil of line, sandwiches, water canteen and pitons.

"What's in this clip, Wentworth?"

"Armor piercing shells, six."

"Armor piercing? You expect tanks up here?"

"You never know, they'd be handy if we ran into one of those Mercedes staff cars you talked about before. Better safe than sorry. That's why I'm still alive. Take them."

Royce dropped the clip into the pack. "I'll humor you."

He tied on the sleeping bag, then settled the pack on his shoulders. "This Enfield can fire both grenades and these armor shells, right?"

"Yes. Just be sure you use the blank clip for the grenades or the barrel will explode."

"I'll try to remember that."

"You shouldn't have done this, Royce. I've got more experience than you...and more guts."

"I suspect you'll to be able to prove that before we get out

579

of here, but right now this is the way I want it. You don't fit. I assume you can limp and drag this stuff down from here?"

Wentworth grunted. "Your concern overwhelms me."

Royce grabbed the rifle and started off.

"I'll wish you luck, Royce. I want you to make it back so we can settle this when I've healed."

The clarity of the August day warmed him as he hiked on without a hint of indecision. Intuition took over. He moved unerringly over ground he had not travelled for years. Awareness came to him, the multicolored fissures in the stone, the scent of a gnarled pine, the splash of color on the early fall leaves, a shimmering rivulet struck by sunlight. "God, my God, I love it here."

By evening, he felt his first goal was close, and there it was—the overhanging shelf. The shelf where he spent the first night in the rain, trying to rid the demons that had haunted him. It seemed so long ago. The four Hitler Youth came back to mind, yet there was no lasting emotion left in him. Time had swept passion and guilt into the wastebasket of his past. They were gone, washed away in the rain that night he was here.

Royce dropped his pack, unrolled his sleeping bag and sat. He had pushed the four German's from his thoughts. Now he could only think of...who? Daphne and their time here in Austria flooded through him. He'd driven her away. He knew that. Still, he loved her. But what of Mary? He loved her in his own way as well, yet, yet what...

The affair they had started certainly was forbidden by the moralistic world they lived in. Royce couldn't have cared less. It was Mary and the children he worried about. He'd face down his brother, try to work it out. David wouldn't want a commotion, it would ruin his image of the future. Still, Mary wouldn't leave without the children. He could never blame her for that. Nevertheless, he intended to have her and the children. He startled himself by laughing aloud. "And the dog! I want Scotty, too. I won't leave Coventry without him."

They would migrate, that was the thing to do. He had money. America seemed great, or Canada. General Arnold offered him a position. Elsie McGill would give him a place too. But would Mary like it? His mind wandered on. Then there was Daphne.

And when he slept, it was dreams of her that enfolded him.

By well after noon Friday, Royce sensed he was close, he recalled the upward slope of the shelf.

Something was out of place. He stopped in his tracks. He stayed low, scanning with his monocular. There was movement, but what? An indistinct shape, not human. Yet it moved. After five minutes, he moved closer and could have kicked himself for his fear. A knapsack flap moved in the breeze. His knapsack, left there over two years ago, when he went to traverse the ledge and then forgotten when he walked away bewildered.

The pack had swept into a depression in the shelf, and rotted through the Alpine weather. The leather straps were chewed off by some animal, even the soap had teeth marks. But the tattered insides still held the relics of pitons, a climbing pick, rain slicker, disintegrated sleeping bag and other objects. Maybe a mountain goat gnawed it, he mused. Royce felt thankful. No one had found them. And that meant no one had been here.

The top of the castle's roof tiles came into view, but he did not go along the plateau above the ledge to look further. He spotted the rubble of rock at the start of the ledge. The ledge, his ledge. He remembered he had named it in his stupor after he slipped. Well no more of that, he convinced himself it held no fear. No more panicked memories or wandering about like a muddled idiot. He had beaten his fears here. He felt alive. He had never grasped how the past few years had stayed within him, preyed on him. Now erase them. Now he intended to live.

He had found the castle without problem, thus he was early and had time to plan. It was now Friday eve. He would rest up, eat and get a good night's sleep. Saturday he would check the pitons he had hammered home in the past.

He decided on three trips along the ledge. One to replace the old line with new, the second to carry the grenade sack and tie it off to a piton. The last trip would be to get in position with the rifle. When the time came, the dark of early Sunday morning, he'd tie himself to the pitons at the curve of the cliff, just out of sight from the castle. Then, with the physicists gathered, he would lean out and fire the grenades onto the terrace.

"I can do this, I can. It will work out."

Saturday at 0900 Royce coiled the new cord over his shoulder and worked down the rubble to the ledge. The old line was deteriorated between the pitons. After he checked that the first piton and carabiner were firm, the task to connect new cord to each carabiner began. His impaired hand was adequate and he was confident moving along the ledge to check each piton.

The last of the cord fastened off, he looked down to the heavily forested land below him. Then, impulsively, he peeked around the corner of the stone wall. A hasty glance took it all in. The terrace, workers milled about pushing a piano into a corner, servants bustled around tables, aligning chairs. All this for the next morning, he reasoned.

He worked his way carefully back across the ledge, then sat on the rubble for a snack. After that, two grenades were removed and set aside. The still heavy and awkward sack with three grenades was difficult, unbalancing him as he travelled the ledge once more and attached the sack to the last carabiner.

Soaked with sweat, he was finally done for the day. It was glaringly evident he was out of condition and he was glad to be back to his sleeping bag to rest and sleep. Tomorrow would take its toll for then would be the race to get away. Still, his mind was clear, he understood the challenge, yet remained remarkably calm. Don't probe the reason, he reflected. He simply decided to accept the aura surrounding him and leave it at that.

He found the castle was closer to BergFalke than he'd previously imagined. He was glad of that. His strength wasn't sufficient if he needed to sprint.

"Put it out of your mind," he warned. "Don't ruin your self-control. Stay calm, you can do it."

After doing what must be done on the ledge, he would move as quickly as the terrain allowed and reach the spa by early Monday morning—at the latest. They'd contact the plane and be gone. Up to this moment, Royce didn't want to think of a chase.

He woke and couldn't get back to sleep. His mind flowed with disconnected thoughts. Why? Through the day, he'd been methodical, every move laid out. Like a good engineer, he grinned. Even his escape planned. So why did he get up and pace, why? Don't start thinking.

His memory drew him back to the past. Feelings led to recollections. The last time he was here. It was more than the slip off the ledge. More than that fright. It was the aftermath he remembered. When he had looked into a pool, saw his reflection and wondered. Wondered if he was going insane. That troubled him then. Did it still?

"Damn it! Stop! I've proven I'm all right. It's them. They all think I'm unhinged. No, not everyone. Not Daphne, not Mary, not Clive. They know I'm not crazy. It's the others, David, General Alcott, Wentworth and the rest, they hope I'm not right in the head."

Royce laughed. "Then again, as I think of it, who in hell would do this if they had all their senses? This is a suicide mission. That's why they sent Wentworth with me, to make sure I followed through. And if I didn't come back, there'd be no tears shed by him or Alcott."

Royce continued to pace, talking aloud, his mind on Wentworth. "It was smart to take out his knee. If he were with me, I'd put money on my not seeing England again. I'll have to watch him when I get back to the spa. First thing, take his gun. Be sure of that. All right, that's enough. Put your mind to the mission. Act like an engineer—Zero error."

With luck, he thought, the enemy didn't know about the ledge and wouldn't know where the explosions came from. They might think it was a mortar from the forest below them. He'd lean out, sight the rifle, fire and duck back out of view. True, he'd have to glance around to see if he hit the target, then repeat the same action if he missed. Then it came to him. That could be the problem, someone could notice him.

What if they saw him and came after him? Could they? How long would it take them to get through the trees? Would they know where he would go? There was no road to follow. He recalled the hike to get here. True, no road to follow, but they could climb the rubble and chase him. He could be out of sight. But what if they had dogs? Also, his escape route was through a low swale between two heights, so in truth that would show a path of sorts. Added to that, he'd be above the tree line most of the way. That meant no cover. A plane could spot him.

The more Royce gave it thought, the more convinced he became that trouble lay ahead. It had been effortless to say he'd do it to save Beck, yet the further he delved into the problems, the more stressed he became.

There was only one way to solve his dilemma. Don't be seen when he fired the grenades. It was that simple. Simple to say, but damn difficult to do. He needed practice. He needed to find how slack the line had to be so that it allowed him to lean around the bend, yet not so loose as to let him fall. That damn fall! He tried to shake off the thought yet again. Even though it was dark, he had to go along the ledge. He had to practice getting back along the ledge.

"Be careful." The ledge was damp with night mist. He faced the stone wall, the rifle slung over his shoulder.

It was cumbersome. His weight unbalanced again. A wane moon crept from behind the haze to help him inch along. It was impossible to move easily with the rifle and he had to rely on the taut line far more than he had planned. He heard something.

Music, he became aware of music. A waltz, Strauss. Its name eluded him. That damn music erased the present. The sounds evoked Father. Yes, his Father entertaining business cronies at Ravensmoor.

Royce would hide in the corridor and listen to the music until he was seen, slapped and locked in his room. And David's laughter. Always David's damn laughter.

Royce moved in a trance, yet managed to reach the bend of the wall and tie himself off to the pitons. Anxiety arose. He couldn't go back along the ledge. He'd fall. He knew he'd fall! He tightened the line that secured him. His knees sagged. A curse of anger exploded aimlessly into the night. "Damn it! Why did I allow them to lure me here *again*?

His fingers rubbed across his black star sapphire ring. He quieted…remembering. In sorrow he whispered.

"You tried to help me, Daphne…yet I drove you away."

He grasped his surroundings and gazed into the night to face the terror of his undertaking. Bile came to his throat. He vomited.

Waning moonlight signaled the coming dawn. He glanced at the wall of stone that loomed above as it disappeared into the night sky. The wall continued down past him to fall away a hundred feet into the trees. The castle was below him, off to the right. Lights flickered within.

Shadows moved, phantoms behind the drapes. He thought it strange there were no blackout curtains, then remembered the castle was far from the cities, and the bombers. The waltz still emanated faintly from within the castle. It was all that disturbed the night. That…and his own harsh breathing.

He moved to ease the ache of his cramped position. His forehead caught the eyesight of his weapon. He gritted his teeth and wiped away the blood as it dripped down along the scar. The cold night air would soon ease. The east sun will bring some warmth. Yet with it, would come the beginning, and the end, of his undertaking.

Chapter 46

THERE WAS MOVEMENT in the castle. Servants scurried about at first light, guards awoke for their shift change and at 0800, transport from the town below began bringing the servants, wives and children of the physicists.

Colonel Schmid knew this was his last day. He would soon be reduced in rank and sent east...east to Poland. Once there, he'll have gone full circle and root out more Jews for the labor camps. Hitler and Himmler had caught him in a lie. His physicists were of no value in helping to develop a nuclear device. After this last day, he would pay for their failure. Poland. He'd be there as a lowly lieutenant, outside hunting Jews with winter on its way. Could anything be worse?

The transport arrived as scheduled. Family meetings took place and people began to filter onto the terrace.

Schmid watched with indifference. His physicists' were no value to him now. How, how on earth did he ever think he could get away with it?

He was about to go out and inform the group of their dismissal when the front door of the castle opened and six SS men entered, machine pistols drawn. They encircled him and he cowered. He knew they were about to drag him off.

Reichführer Himmler entered, ridiculing Schmid as he feared for his life. "Ha, Captain Schmid, frightened for your paltry little existence, are you? Perhaps I should make you a corporal in my new Angriffstaffel."

Schmid couldn't speak, simply stood there shaking.

Himmler was amused. "I knew you were a sham. I knew that trace of Jewish blood in you would surface. Your type blights the German nation. I'm taking over here. Go out there and get all the women, children and servants out front. Trucks are there.

My men will separate the Jews. The rest will be questioned."

Terrified women and children streamed past the scowl of the arrogant Reichführer. When Schmid returned, Himmler ordered his SS out onto the terrace.

"Now, Schmid, go order everyone to attention. I will go out there and demonstrate how to handle frauds."

The moment Himmler heard Schmid order the physicists to stand, the windows exploded inward, doors shattered, plaster blew in, swirling down onto the struck dumb SS Leader.

Royce had watched the people go on to the terrace. As they entered, he was unsure of just what was happening. There were the men who he assumed were the physicists. But women and children were out there as well. He waited. There was no way he would fire his grenades into them. If something didn't change he'd leave. He paused, observing a German officer come out the door and order the servants, women and children away. Royce acted quickly now, in case they might return. He inserted the grenade's shaft into the barrel, leaned out to aim and then remembered he had to remove the pin. He pulled back and took a slow breath. He was ready. As he sighted, SS soldiers entered. Royce was pleased. He'd take them down too. He yanked the trigger, the rifle recoiled.

His grenade arced off course and struck twenty feet up the rear wall of the castle. Yet the effects were devastating. The munitions detonated, tore off great chunks of the wall, shattered doors and windows and hurled hundreds of ball bearings into the people below.

Inside the room, Reichführer Himmler, his uniform coated with plaster dust and shards of glass, still stood, frozen, struck dumb. Then…he screamed.

Another explosion! He ran for the front door. Shouting to the remainder of his SS troopers that anarchists were there, they and to surround him and get away as fast as possible. Himmler beat them to his Mercedes, dove in and huddled on the floor.

Royce was astounded at the damage one grenade could do. The carnage staggered him. Yet as he stared, a few people crawled or stumbled around, trying to comprehend what had occurred.

Despite the apparent slaughter, many were still alive. Without thought, he loaded another grenade and removed the pin. He didn't question if he should shoot again, he sighted and fired. The missile struck dead center onto the terrace floor. Three hundred steel balls lashed out. No one survived.

Captain Dieter Schmid sat propped against the wall of the castle, stupefied. He watched his life's blood bleed away. He managed to cough out. "Mein traum ist über..." My dream is over.

At first Royce couldn't turn his gaze from the devastation. At last he slung the rifle over his shoulder and took one last look at the terrace while removing the cord tied to the pitons.

A Wehrmacht trooper on regular patrol in the forest, had rushed toward the rear of the castle when the grenades landed and looked up to see if there was a plane. Through the trees, he caught a brief sight of Royce on the ledge. The trooper couldn't get a clear shot, but his firing was near enough for a fragment of stone to catch Royce's pant leg.

Other troops, now alerted, saw the figure on the wall and begun to fire, rousing him. Escape! He needed to escape! There was one grenade left in the sack. He threw it down into the trees and was gratified to hear it explode. There was a lull and Royce made use of it.

The race was on. He had to reach the cascaded debris of stone, climb up and attain the plateau before his pursuers. Wehrmacht soldiers, although leery about another grenade, followed him through the trees firing, but failing for a clean shot.

Royce made it to the rubble field and then up on to the plateau without being sighted again. As he looked down, the soldiers had only now started to scale the rubble from ground level. He had the two grenades he'd left in his knapsack on the plateau. Pulling the pin on one, he threw it as far as he could, saw it explode on the stone below and slivers rip into some of the enemy. He continued to watch as he detached the blank grenade cartridge and locked in the magazine with six armor piercing shells.

He sat, exposed from below, rifle across his lap. Why, he wondered. Why didn't he run? Was it the challenge of those soldiers below? Did he expect to die here and this was his stand?

There was movement, a stray shot splintered stone off to his left.

"This is stupid! I'm as daft as people think. That's what they expect. Do something senseless. Get myself killed. I'd be much easier to explain away."

Royce stood in the open, defiant, and shouted to the world. "I'll show them, every damned one! I'll get back, that will infuriate them. And Alcott and Wentworth will be first."

He dropped out of sight behind the lip of the plateau. Removing the last grenade, he then grabbed the sack and threw it to the north. Perhaps the enemy would think he went that way. He checked the soldiers below, fired twice in their direction and lobbed the last grenade down on them. After that, he shouldered the rifle, heard the explosion and scurried south.

The Major in command of the castle's troops had a sterner backbone than the Reichführer. With pistol drawn, he had reached the terrace immediately after the second grenade exploded. He was unnerved, the ravage complete. Only two bloodied survivors attempted to crawl. Bodies in crimson shirts, shreds of ties and jackets tangled with red spattered black uniforms of the SS. The screams of children and wives as they rushed from the trucks to find their lifeless fathers and husbands added to the carnage.

The Major's mind was taken off the devastation when he saw his troops below firing upwards along the wall and realized there had to be someone there. How a person could be there, the Major didn't question. He shouted for the troops to chase and capture the sniper—kill only if they had to. He then called Wehrmacht Headquarters in Berlin. They in turn, called Hitler's adjutant at the Berghof.

Operguppenführer Reinhart Heydrich had been in deep discussion with Adolf Hitler. Heydrich, the foremost leader in the attack on the Jews during Kristallnacht, was more recently in charge of the Nacht und Nebel. Night and Fog. The cover name for the secret elimination of suspected resistance fighters in northern Europe.

Stolen away at night, it was never recorded what happened to them. Once again, Heydrich was executing his orders beyond expectations.

After Hitler read the messages from his adjutant and took

more calls, he returned to Heydrich.

"Well, Reinhart, that was incredible. It seems someone, probably a Britisher—they're always up to some mischief—assassinated our nuclear group at the castle."

"The whole group? How could one person do that much damage, my Führer?"

"It appears the assassin used a sort of aerial mortar. Some SS were killed also."

"The English are a decadent people, my Führer. They should be taught a severe lesson."

"Now, now, Reinhart, be charitable. I'm still sending peace overtures to the English."

"I hope the overtures are inside thousand pound bombs."

Hitler considered the remark and smiled. "That may very well come in time, Reinhart, in time."

"I thought you'd be more upset than you seem about the castle being bombed, my Führer."

"Ah, that is the joke my friend. I'd known for some time the SS Colonel I had put in charge was attempting to fool me into believing his physicists were on the cusp of great things on this super bomb research. This is a prime lesson, Heydrich, always have spies everywhere, never forget that. In this example one of my spies told me differently. *Nothing* had been achieved. In fact, I had sent Himmler to the castle only this morning. He was on the verge of shutting them down when the explosions went off. Poor Himmler, he must have got the shock of his life. The commandant at the castle said our Reichsführer—and here I only quote—'left in a hurry'. I don't doubt that. He must have taken his nerve from the chickens on that farm he once owned."

Heydrich laughed as expected.

"So what happens next, Sir?"

"That is what bothers me, Reinhart. How did the British know what was going on there? It could only have been the servants from the town nearby. Have the town eradicated and the people sent to any camp you chose. No, wait. I'll have Goebbels take his propaganda apparatus there and make a newsreel of the town burning and the peasants being executed or dragged away. That is the sternest way to show everyone what happens when they don't report subversives or act against the security of Reich."

"I will order that. There is something else on your mind about the castle, my Führer?"

"Of course there is. I'm sure it was a British agent. The information is unclear right now, but soldiers from the castle are hunting a man. It appears he is well armed and heading who knows where, although there's really nowhere to run except south. Our nearest military base is at Salzburg and that is more than fifty miles southeast of the castle, so trucks are heading west to cut him off. There are two Storch aircraft searching and all this should box him in. I want him alive. Yet, it becomes too obvious there must be some sort of escape plan. The British don't do suicide missions, at least intentionally.

"And one other little detail about this is vexing. When the Colonel at Salzburg discussed the possibility of a British plane he also mentioned they'd been bothered by that very thing from calls by the owner of a spa over to his west. This owner keeps reporting he hears airplanes very close. They've checked three or four times, found nothing, other than to learn the owner is deaf."

Heydrich, amused for only a moment, frowned. "A deaf man who hears phantom airplanes? Quite extraordinary."

"Yes, too extraordinary. I ordered the Gestapo to get to that spa and find me the reason. However, let's get back to a more important subject. You will be Deputy Reich Protector of Bohemia and Moravia. Their old world mawkishness must be crushed. Be unsparing. We will Germanize the vermin…"

* * *

Royce was exhausted. Yet he had made it to the overhang before darkness hid the way. He hadn't seen any pursuers. Other than hearing a plane once or twice, he knew neither plane nor soldiers could track in the dark. Now spent from tension and physical effort, he laid back soaked with sweat.

He slept the sleep of the dead. Awake, he now cursed. It was past daybreak. The sun was well up as he rolled from under the overhang, groggy from a deep sleep.

He thoughtlessly stood in the open, aching, as he got his wits together. His senses finally stirred, hearing a plane. It came straight towards him. He dove under the overhang. Did the pilot see him? God, no, no. He waited. Held his breath. The sound faded. He breathed again.

The drone returned, the plane circled over his shelter, slower this time. He'd been spotted. The plane was relaying his location for his pursuers. Trapped. No cover other than this overhang. Nowhere to run.

The plane flew over again, imprisoning him. He felt the pilot mocking him. Then he remembered. Wentworth said the shells in the second clip were armor piercing. A few were still in the rifle. They were his only chance.

He readied himself. He could see the Storch as it came up along the shelf. It held a straight line this time and that would take it directly above his overhang. As it came, Royce rolled out onto his back. The plane passed straight over him. Two quick shots were all he could fire off as it went past unswerving.

He rose, stared after it for seconds, not knowing one of his shells had ripped through the aluminum fuselage and pierced the light armor plate under the cockpit's seat. The missile penetrated seat springs and fabric, tore vertically into pilot's groin to finally explode in his rib cage.

Mesmerized, Royce stood, watching the plane ascend steeply. It hung for an instant, then fell tail first, impact and break apart, pirouetting across the stone.

There was no time to celebrate. He left everything except his rifle and ran. Confident his ability in the mountains was such that no one could catch him, he assumed the pilot had reported him and that left the dread of the unknown. What would he running toward?

At the escarpment, he looked down toward the spa in the distance, below a copse of trees. No movement. He looked back, no one in sight. Nerves on edge he wondered, was it too quiet? Then, coming out of the trees towards him, a limping man waving and frantically shouting.

Royce ran down as Wentworth hobbled up on a cane he'd found at the spa. "You did it, Royce! You did it…right?"

Royce was gasping. "Yes! How'd you know?"

"Becker's wireless. German communications are going bonkers! No code, they want your blood. Come, get into the trees, we've got to get the devil out of here! I saw you coming through Beck's telescope and told him to call in the plane."

No sooner were they hidden among the trees than Royce turned his rifle on Wentworth.

"What in hell are you doing, Royce?"

"Give me your gun."

"Are you crazy? What are you up to?"

"Making sure I get back to England without getting shot in the back."

"You're crazy. We don't have time for this. Right now Beck's using the J-E to get the plane in. We've got to get down to the field. I'm telling you we don't have time for this!"

Royce said nothing; Wentworth reached into his jacket and handed the automatic to Royce.

"There, that satisfy you?"

"Now reach inside your boot and remove the knife."

"Christ. Damn you."

Yet he complied. "Now, can we get the hell out of here?"

They moved as hurriedly as Wentworth's leg would allow until they came to the verge of the trees. They stopped short. In the distance, beside the spa there was a Mercedes, people in front.

"What do you make of it, Royce?"

Royce squinted through the rifle's scope. "It's a Mercedes staff car, but I'm not sure what's happening. Wait, There's two Germans…they've got Beck kneeling on the ground!"

Royce sighted in on one of the Germans. Wentworth grabbed his arm. "Don't shoot, Royce! It will give us away!"

Royce shoved him away and turned the rifle on him. "Say one more word and I'll kill you!"

Wentworth moved back. "Royce, you're signing our death warrant."

Royce struggled to sight through the scope. His mind screamed as his eyes transmitted the tabloid that unfolded. The kickback of the pistol from the back of Ernst Becker's neck. The sound of the pistol's report as Becker pitched forward.

With blind rage, Royce squeezed the trigger. The bullet ripped through the chest of the German. Thrown into the grill of the Mercedes, he then slid off the fender, his coat caught on the bumper, the murder weapon slipping from his hand.

Royce tried to sight Becker's other attacker, but the person instantly grasped what happened and scurried behind the vehicle's trunk and stayed there, hunched down.

Wentworth grappled with their problem. "We can't stay here, Royce. We've no time. How many shells do you have left?"

"One—I think."

"Well you better think right—because we've got to flush this bastard out fast! He probably only has a Luger. Not a lot of range. For Christ's sake give me my automatic."

Royce nodded.

Wentworth grabbed it, thinking fast. "The auto is head on. I'm going to go to the right first and take some shots at him from that side and get his attention. You go to the left. You've the range with the rifle. I'll try to drive him to the rear on your side. You leave after me. If you can see any part of him, shoot right through the car and hope it isn't armor plated."

Before Royce could say a word, Wentworth lurched off, cane in one hand, his gun in the other. He shouted back to Royce.

"Remember, he's scared! He'll see there's two of us and he doesn't know how many weapons we have. Get going!"

Wentworth fired off two rounds while Royce eased to the left. He watched Wentworth in the open, exposed, limp off further to the right, holding his weapon on target and fire again. The rear side window fragmented. The German moved farther to the left rear of the vehicle.

Royce saw his chance. A small section of the man's leather coat was visible. Royce aimed just to the right and triggered. The round tore into the body of the Mercedes, exited the trunk and ripped through the man's shoulder. The German collapsed backward, the gun flying from his hand. Royce ran for Becker. Wentworth heaved up to the wounded SS officer and put a bullet in his head.

Royce knelt over his friend. Wentworth could read his mind.

"Royce, don't even think about it! He's dead. If you want to get back to England, get it through your thick skull we're not burying him. So make your peace on the quick, I'll be right back and you'd better be ready to run."

Wentworth labored up to the spa. He knew there was a good chance they might not make it out, and he had a duty. He pulled the small cover off the J-E transmitter/receiver and set the unit in the stone fireplace. Taking a grenade, his Sten gun and two magazines from his sack, he placed the grenade in the J-E's chassis, pulled the pin and stood along the wall.

The building shook, fireplace stones loosened and soot filled the room. After a quick check of the destroyed J-E, Wentworth found his way to the door. The Germans would never know what he'd blown up. It also dawned on him it was too late to wonder if Becker had got through to the aircraft.

That question was answered as he exited the spa. The shriek of twin Merlin's blasted his ears and he looked up to see the Mosquito roar past.

"Yes, yes!" He shouted. "Yes! By Christ, we can make it!"

The explosion in the building ended Royce's stupor. "What in hell happened in there?"

"I got rid of something. Come on, we've a long run to the field. You go ahead, get the hatch open and help me in when I get there."

"What's that in your hand?"

"A cane."

"Trying to be funny at a time like this? For Christ's sake, CW, don't be a horse's arse."

"Oh, you mean this hand? It's a submachine gun. Get going or I'll use it on you."

Royce started running downhill, and shouted back over his shoulder. "I'm surprised you haven't already!"

The Mosquito touched down, rolled out to the end of the runway and spun about, engines growling. The pilot slid his side cockpit window open and pointed past the two running men. They saw a swirl of dust welling up along the dirt road.

CW was calm. "I expected this might happen, Royce! Ignore what I do next. Just get to the God damn plane!"

Royce obeyed. CW took a few steps toward the lead vehicle racing at him. He stopped, placed his 9mm Sten machinegun behind the back of his leg, holding up his hands up in surrender.

The German 108 Horch, its top down, slowed. An officer stood, holding a machine pistol as he looked toward the plane and then to Wentworth. No one seemed armed. This man was yielding and the officer had been told to capture, not kill. The vehicle crept forward. In the rear, a gunner sighted down a post-mounted heavy caliber machinegun aimed directly at the airplane's cockpit. The officer ordered him to fire if the plane moved one inch.

Wentworth willed the Horch forward, muttering under his breath. "Come on, come on...I don't have all day God...damn you...come to me...give me a chance said the spider to the fly...come in under ninety meters, come on..."

Royce stood by plane, spellbound. The Horch edged along. The officer held his pistol leveled on Wentworth, who kept his hands high. The Horsh came within range of Wentworth's weapon. The officer turned to the Mosquito, motioning for the pilot to cut the engines. Those three seconds were all CW needed. In one fluid motion he snatched up the Sten gun, whirled and scarcely pointing, emptied the thirty-two round magazine into the vehicle. Metal shredded, glass shattered, the officer fired off two wild shots before the fusillade threw him into the rear seat.

The machine gunner, with not a chance to rotate his weapon to Wentworth in time was knocked off the side of the vehicle. The driver sagged over the wheel.

CW dropped the submachine gun and started hobbling for the aircraft. Royce ran to help him.

"Change of heart, Royce?"

"Just shut up! I saw you get hit in the shoulder. Can you make it to the plane?"

"You can be bloody well sure I will! That bit of heroics wasn't for you."

At the plane, Royce lifted Wentworth by the knees, pushed him through the hatch, climbed in and tripped over him.

"You clumsy lout Royce! You're stepping all over a wounded hero. Gorblimey! Get me a rag for my shoulder!"

He shouted forward. "Get this damn wooden box moving! What the hell's the matter with you?"

The pilot yelled back. "There's two more vehicles *on* the field, CW coming straight at us—what do you want us to do?"

"You're the blasted pilot! What in hell do you have to lose? I say go! They'll blink, trust me."

He turned, stared at Royce. "You in the game?"

When Royce tripped over CW, he had fallen and struck the back of his head on a bulkhead. He winced from a splitting pain across his eyes. He had lain silent, in an attempt to fight off the agony and could barely answer. But he reached across, grabbing his cohort's hand.

"I'm with you, CW whatever…!"

The engines increased their roar. The Mosquito sprinted forward. Wentworth was fanatical. "Hang on, Royce. We're in for the ride of our lives!"

The aircraft roared down the strip at the two automobiles. They slowed. The plane rushed on. One vehicle swerved out of the way as the driver of the other vehicle floored the gas pedal…the engine bucked and stalled. The driver leapt clear.

The Mosquito's navigator went into shock.

"We're not going to make it, Captain!"

The pilot nodded. "I know."

The Mosquito rose. The landing gear tore off the Horch's bumper, fenders and windscreen. The plane pitched over, plunging her nose deep into the field. Tumbling, the impact tore off the wings and engines. One after the other petrol tanks burst and detonated. Four immense spheres of flame exploded, hurling blazing debris from the wooden fuselage and a Merlin engine far into the forest.

EPILOGUE

August, 1940

THE BATTLE OF BRITAIN witnessed the confrontation of two great air forces.

1st. Directive 17. The plan for the German invasion of England, Operation Sea Lion, is postponed to early or mid-September. (Eventually Sea Lion will be cancelled).

2nd. Hitler orders the elimination of the RAF and Britain's aircraft industry.

8th. Göring orders directive 'Alderangriff'. The Luftwaffe is to destroy the RAF's air defense system in four days. Massive surges of German bombers assault England.

12th. ME109s, ME110s and Stuka's attempt to devastate the RDF towers and command structure in southeast England. Though crippled, the system never breaks.

13th. 'Adlertag.' The main aerial offensive. Luftwaffe sorties against airfields, radar systems, shipping ports and factories, pass a thousand per day. RAF Fighter Command responds with Spitfires and Hurricanes, directing them to the bombers with radar and ground observers. The RAF learned Squadron Leader 'Sailor' Malan's, *Tenth Rule of Air Fighting:*

Go in quickly—Punch hard—Get out!

Both sides suffer severe losses. The Luftwaffe high command mistakenly believes there is little left of the British air defense.

RAF Fighter Command stays with Air Marshal Dowding's prewar strategy of cycling squadron after squadron in and out of the conflict. There is no sign of Britain's collapse.

23/24th. Night. A single German bomber, off course, bombed London.

25/26th. Night. The RAF bombed Berlin in retaliation.

The London Blitz. German bombers turn from the RAF airfields to bombing cities. From 7 September, through 2 November, London is bombed 57 times. All told, 41,000 civilians were killed in the Blitz. But the German blunder of turning away from the airfields sealed the Luftwaffe's fate.

Thanks to the sacrifice of the RAF pilots, England was never to be invaded by German ground forces. In his growly, intense and flowing manner, Prime Minister Winston S. Churchill spoke sincerely and truthfully.

"Never in the field of human conflict was so much owed by so many to so few."

* * *

18 August, 1940.
11 Group, the sorely worn tip of the spear, bore the brunt of the storm with critical losses.

The strain of combat took its toll on all the Squadrons and their leaders. Kenneth Sommers being no exception. He tried not to let on, but he was tired and ached from the shoulder wound that hadn't completely healed. Each time the remainder of his pilots and Spitfires wore out, they were rotated to 13 Group and Fighter Command replaced 11 Group with new aircraft and pilots. Yet Kenneth, now billeted at Biggin Hill, moved between there, Hornchurch and Tangmere fields, never leaving the rotation. New junior pilots who entered 'Hellfire Corner' were mainly inexperienced and rushed into action. Of the British, American, French, Czech and Polish pilots posted to his squadron, most had only five or ten hour's flight time in Spitfires and some of those hours still embraced outdated combat tactics. Even as the battle raged around them every day, Kenneth knew it was his obligation to train as many pilots as he could in the newer Quick, Punch, Out tactics the battle line RAF employed against the Luftwaffe. 18 August proved appalling for pilots of both air forces—and changed Kenneth Sommers' future.

Despite German losses, this day had seen an intensification of their constant day and night Blitz of London and other cities. In addition, the inception of new Luftwaffe tactics for their fighters to escort above their bombers proved difficult to counteract.

The RAF sent squadrons up sequentially to offset those tactics. The plan was a simple one—Attrition. Give up planes and pilots to wear away the German air fleet by persistent attack. 11 Group fighters, guided by ground control, ripped through the German escort cover and slashed into the bombers and other pilots, the veterans, challenged the ME109s. The unrelenting toll on aircraft and aviators was incredibly devastating.

In aerial losses alone, seventy enemy aircraft went down this single day. Thirty-one British aircraft were lost in battle with further losses caught on the ground. More importantly, Luftwaffe losses were set at one hundred veteran pilots and aircrew over England. The RAF lost ten pilots.

Air Marshal Dowding's persistence in staying with his overall strategy, and Air Vice Marshal Keith Park's combat tactics, were to save England. Although not known on 18 August, this was the beginning of the RAF's triumph.

The remnants of Kenneth's squadron lost four fighters during this day's battle, while tallying five ME109 fighters, two Dornier 17s and three Stuka's. Kenneth had been responsible for downing two of the fighters and damaging a Henkel 111. During the sixth and final scramble of the day, Kenneth's guns emptied. He stayed in the battle as a weaver, warning his pilots and diving at attacking fighters to force them away from imperiled Spitfires.

At last, he risked too much. ME109s doubled up on him. Habit had made Ken lower his seat at the start of the latest melee and that saved his life. Another ME109 gatecrasher waited for a chance and caught him, striking the armor plate at the rear of his seat with a 20mm round. It shattered his canopy and tore off his mirror. While Kenneth zigzagged trying to look back and find the assailant, another 20mm shell struck his fuselage, sending shrapnel into the cockpit. A fragment caught his eye. Half blinded, he fought his own wound and his wounded ship into a series of rolls and evasive maneuvers. Seconds later, the sky around him was empty of all but feathery white clouds.

Struggling through the pain and failing vision, he found Tangmere airfield and, with the polka dot scarf held on his eye, made the worst landing in his career, driving the landing gear up through the wings. Kenneth's final kill, a ME109, would prove the last of his combat career in WWII.

Between France and England, this was his seventy-eighth combat sortie. He was credited with twenty-eight enemy aircraft downed, eight probable, four damaged and three shared. Although the war was to go on for five more years, he was gratified yet humbled. He was his Father's son. He had done his duty and, when war was gone, stood with those justly honored.

* * *

Air Vice-Marshal Park was pleased to order Kenneth off the combat available roll. Air Marshal Dowding first thought to offer Kenneth the position of Group Captain over five squadrons, then changed his mind. He remembered when Kenneth's shoulder was healing, his stint at the RAF College had proved his worth as an instructor. His loss of an eye was all the excuse Fighter Command needed to ground him and offer Kenneth a posting to the College.

Although the Group Captain position held more prestige, to no one's surprise, Kenneth agreed to the college post. He had enjoyed instructing and came to understand he could save more lives by teaching neophyte pilots how to survive combat. They were his students, his pilots and he became protective of them. His training took a toll, yet when they left, they were ready.

He missed his old squadron, yet he could still fly and was intelligent enough to grasp he had been like many other men on the edge, stretched to the point where he had always grounded pilots with his warning signs.

Daphne was heartbroken by her husband's loss of an eye. Still, her emotions became tempered. He was alive, she knew he would never see combat again and, importantly, he readily accepted his new role in the RAF. She had noticed his deterioration as the battle had progressed. His constant rubbing his shoulder, tapping fingers, equally intense and distracted, his temples now quite gray.

With his transfer to the college, she smiled whenever she saw him, handsome, with a blue eye patch to match his uniform.

In every way, he was coming back to his prewar personality. The rogue she met at Ravensmoor that New Year's Eve, seemingly so long ago. The only difference now? He was *her* rogue.

Whenever Daphne found time between ferrying aircraft, she would fly into the Air College to stay with Kenneth. Many evenings, the two would mingle with the cadets. The former Squadron Leader and his wife idolized, each for obvious reasons. Camaraderie arose, and plans to meet with pilots after the war formulated. Kenneth, opposed to this in the past, now found it agreeable. He had changed. Openly admitting he loved his boys.

In their quiet hours, they, along with Jesus Peron, made sketchy plans to start an elite airline after the hell ended. It would service the major cities in Britain and along the coast of Europe.

They learned Mackie was a prisoner of war, so another plan took shape. When the war ended, they would be married again and send invitations to all his pilots. Mackie would be best man and general manager of their embryonic airline.

Daphne never mentioned one event until well after the war. That was the time she was ferrying a fully armoured Spitfire Mk II and crossed paths with a German ME109bf. What happened? Well, *she* was around to tell the tale—if, it was ever told.

* * *

During the night of 14 November, 1941 Coventry suffered a devastating Blitz. 512 German bombers destroyed the industrial infrastructure and the center of the city, killing 568 people.

A memorial to that night is the one remaining great wall of the destroyed St. Michael's Cathedral. It still stands to this day.

David Royce's unprotected factories were gutted and the great house of Ravensmoor burnt out to a shell.

Only days before the Coventry Blitz, Mary, with her two children, left David to live in Daphne's cottage at Windermere. Mary's investigators had found such a trail of infidelities and theft that David had no recourse but to let her and the children go.

Another destruction of that terrible night was David's dream of becoming a major player in English politics and the world stage. With his factories in ashes, he found how few true friends he had—and the fewer still who wished him well.

Daphne and Kenneth, despite the chaos around them, found time, in their private hours, to start a family of three children, exactly the number Lady Jane wanted to spoil.

* * *

21 July 1950.

Two women eased out of their vehicle and stopped for a moment to gaze at the gray limestone mass of Ravensmoor. No longer the fine manor house from before the war, the two wings David Royce had added were gone, along with Blackbird cottage, destroyed by indiscriminate bombing during the Blitz.

Daphne Elliot-Sommers purchased the scorched main building from David Royce and had it restored. She bequeathed it to the Parish Sisters of Czechoslovakia and Poland, in remembrance of the foreign pilots she'd taught, and fallen, during the war.

Daphne looked to Mary as they started down a brick pathway.

"This is never easy for you, is it?"

"No. It's been seven years since we put the markers here. Yet it's still so vivid…how he said he loved me and then…he was gone."

Daphne remained silent, she had heard this many times. She was sorry for Mary. Sorry for both her and Jim.

The young groundskeeper was startled and shy as he saw the two beautiful women approach. He doffed his cap when they smiled. The boy was captivated each time he saw them. The green eyes of the tall woman, the blue eyes of the other, warmed him. He watched them continue until they stopped by a secluded pine. Deer looked up, indifferent to them and went on grazing. The boy was ashamed for staring and returned to his work. Still, he couldn't help but peek through the trees as they sat on a meditation bench.

The boy knelt to pull some weeds and trim a shrub, losing track of time. An auto started. Glancing down to the bench, the boy saw the women were gone.

He found his steps drawn to the site and first noticed a modest marker. He read the script across the stone.

Scotty

He moved across to the granite stone, gently pushing two roses aside and read the memorial plate.

JAMES ANDREWS ROYCE
Born, July 21, 1905 Died, August, 1940

The boy thought it strange; the day of this person's death was not engraved. He continued to read:

Bestowed the GEORGE CROSS for Gallantry
Great Britain's Highest Civilian Award
He rests not here, but in our hearts

The boy replaced the roses and meant to walk away. Then, looking up the path, he recalled the two beautiful women and turned back to the memorial, thought for a moment and smiled.

"Mr. Royce, you must have been quite the chap."

*"The air Battle of Britain never really ended.
It sort of, you know, just sputtered out."*
Anonymous

Bibliography

Pictorial History of the Second World War Wise & Co., 1944

Spitfire Mark I / II Aces Dr. Alfred Price Osprey Pub., 1979

Forgotten Voices of the Blitz Joshua Levine, In Association with the Imperial War Museum. Ebury Press, 1979

The Hardest Day, Battle of Britain, 18 August *1940* Alfred Price, Cassell, 1979

Voices in the Air 1939-1945 Wing Commander Laddie Lucas, CBE, DSO, DCF,. Arrow Books, 2003

Airplane Power General Motors, Published by GM, 1943

Information on the Spitfire, Hurricane, DH Mosquito. Battle of France and *Battle of Britain* RAF Official Website

Life in England before 1940 and miscellaneous information Google

Central Europe Lonnie Johnson, Oxford Univ. Press 1996

Robert D. Colburn, Research Coordinator, IEEE History Center, Rutgers University.

Lost Voices of the Royal Navy Max Arthur, Holder & Stoughton Books 1997

Guerrilla Leader T E Lawrence and the Arab Revolt James J. Schneider, Bantam Books 2011

Also by Barry Wood

MURDERS in a SMALL TOWN
The HOUSE of GRAVES
The HOUSE of GRAVES Book II
Book III is coming

Also by Barry Wood

MURDERS in a SMALL TOWN
The HOUSE of GRAVES
The HOUSE of GRAVES Book II
Book III is coming

CPSIA information can be obtained at www.ICGtesting.com
Printed in the USA
LVOW04s0229060615

441454LV00002B/8/P